The Hod King

The guard ripped the card and the banknote, turned them, and tore again. He dropped the scraps at Senlin's feet. Even as Senlin looked down at his destroyed offering, the guard gripped one sleeve of his coat and ripped it half from his shoulder. He repeated the treatment on the other sleeve.

Before he could speak, Senlin was brusquely elbowed aside by the arrival of several men in suits that were as black and sleek as hot tar. The guards saluted, and one said, "Good afternoon, Sir Wilhelm." Ignoring them, the nobleman continued a cheerful conversation with his companions, all of whom seemed oblivious to the man in a torn gray coat.

This was not Senlin's first glimpse of the handsome duke, but it was the closest he'd come to the man who'd made off with Marya. Senlin pictured himself stealing the guard's sidearm. Pictured the shot striking the duke, pictured him crying out in surprise, clutching the mortal wound as he fell at Senlin's feet in a lifeless knot. Doubtlessly, he would be dead a moment after the duke, leaving Marya twice-widowed and half-rescued. And that assumed she wished to be saved. It was a question only she could answer, and he could not ask.

Senlin had the Sphinx to thank for this absurd state of affairs.

Praise for
The Books of Babel

"*Senlin Ascends* is one of the best reads I've had in ages...I was dragged in and didn't escape until I'd finished two or three days later"
Mark Lawrence, author of *Prince of Thorns*

"*Senlin Ascends* crosses the everyday strangeness and lyrical prose of Borges and Gogol with all the action and adventure of high fantasy. I loved it, and grabbed the next one as soon as I turned the last page"
Django Wexler, author of *The Thousand Names*

"Senlin is a man worth rooting for, and his strengthening resolve and character is as marvelous and sprawling as the tower he climbs"
Washington Post on *Senlin Ascends*

"What is remarkable about this novel, quite apart from its rich, allusive prose, is Bancroft's portrayal of Senlin, a good man in a desperate situation, and the way he changes in response to his experiences in his ascent"
Guardian on *Senlin Ascends*

"*Senlin Ascends* is an adventure rife with character, voice, and beauty—a well-polished knife drawn out slowly"
Sam Sykes, author of *The City Stained Red*

"Brilliant debut fantasy.... This novel goes off like a firework and suggests even greater things in the author's future"
Publishers Weekly on *Senlin Ascends* (starred review)

"*Senlin Ascends* is a unique masterpiece. A brilliant debut. Highly recommended!"
Michael R. Fletcher, author of *Beyond Redemption*

The Books of Babel
Book III:
The Hod King

Josiah Bancroft

www.orbitbooks.net

ORBIT

First published in Great Britain in 2019 by Orbit

1 3 5 7 9 10 8 6 4 2

A CIP catalogue record for this book
is available from the British Library.

ISBN 978-0-356-51084-2

Printed and bound in Great Britain by
Clays Ltd, Elcograf S.p.A.

Papers used by Orbit are from well-managed forests
and other responsible sources.

MIX
Paper from
responsible sources
FSC® C104740

Orbit
An imprint of
Little, Brown Book Group
Carmelite House
50 Victoria Embankment
London EC4Y 0DZ

An Hachette UK Company
www.hachette.co.uk

www.orbitbooks.net

For Barber,
who left us with too many stories untold.

SILK GARDENS

PELPHIA

NEW BABEL

THE BATHS

THE PARLOR

THE BASEMENT

THE SKIRTS

THE MARKET

THE TOWER of BABEL
a Map of the Lower Ringdoms

Truth does not erode, nor forgive any debt.
A child may recall what her father would forget.

—*I Sip a Cup of Wind* by Jumet

Part I
The Mermaid

Chapter One

Some men seem to think that temperance is preservative, that moderation somehow pickles the soul. They would place their beating hearts inside jam jars if they could. Which does beg the question, what on earth are they saving themselves for?

—Oren Robinson of the *Daily Reverie*

The sun clacked along an iron track among the gaslight stars high above the white city of Pelphia. The domed ceiling was a perfect shade of sky blue, except where the paint had flaked away, leaving behind jagged clouds of naked mortar. Gas flames ringed the smiling face of the mechanical sun, which left a trail of soot in its slow circuit over the city. In the evening, the sun set inside a ballroom, built to evoke a great nimbus cloud, called Horizon Hall. In addition to acting as the sun's stable, Horizon Hall was the site of frequent and often wild galas. It wasn't uncommon for the sun to rise late, delayed by gears that were clogged with confetti, vomit, and undergarments. And every so often, when repairs to the sun were particularly slow, Pelphia would experience an eclipse that might last two or three days. In more sophisticated ringdoms, such a span of unanticipated darkness could easily have triggered riots, if not a revolution, but in Pelphia, these protracted periods of dark were hardly remarked upon because no one wished to be the yawning party pooper who said, "It seems to have gotten terribly late, hasn't it? Perhaps we should call it a night?"

The ringdom's king behaved more like a court jester than a regent, and was beloved for it, much in the same way a permissive father is adored by his unruly brats. The ringdom attracted the occasional tourists from the far-flung coasts and hills of Ur, but Pelphia's only reliable industry was the production of fabric and its transformation into high fashion. The upper ringdoms of the Tower were loath to admit that they took any cues from such an ancient and ironically juvenile ringdom, but for all their irritating histrionics, Pelphians had a knack for buttons, thread, and taffeta. It was for this reason the fifth ringdom was sometimes called the Closet.

But while the rest of the Tower only recognized the customary four seasons of fashion, the obsessed natives of Pelphia somehow managed to squeeze fifteen or sixteen seasons into a single year. The dressmakers, cobblers, haberdashers, and tailors were in constant competition, hoping to spark the next craze even as they indulged the present one. Wars were waged from the shopwindows of the most famous clothiers, until one neckline or hem or hue rose above the rest, and a new fad overwhelmed the last. Then the population would change color as quickly and uniformly as a forest in fall.

But the natives' obsession with appearances did not extend to their streets. Pelphians were terrible litterers. The white cobbles of Pelphia were often obscured by trash. Playhouse programs, handkerchiefs, dance cards, love notes, the feeble heels of ambitious shoes, and a thousand tokens of unwanted affection overwhelmed the gutters. Early each morning, while half the city groaned through hangovers and dawning regrets, hundreds of hods emerged from alley shacks with brooms, brushes, and pots of whitewash to paint over the graffiti and lamp soot. The army of indentured cleaners blanched the ringdom from port to piazza, where the spine of the Tower rose from the city's center like a pole in a circus tent.

Pelphia's three most ancient institutions stood in the shadow of the ringdom's spine: the Circuit of Court, a sprawling, winding hedge of silk and wire; the Vivant Music Hall, a cathedral that seemed as frail as a bleached reef; and the Colosseum. Once, the Colosseum had been a university, and its fat columns and carved gables still bore the

4

evidence of that former use. Scenes of laureled philosophers and robed poets still decorated its high lintels, though the bottom halves of those women and men had been chiseled away. The remaining legless figures looked like bathers wading into deep water. The colonnade entrance, once as wide as a town square, had been shrunk by the addition of iron bars and a cage door that was never unguarded.

Inside the Colosseum, a cheering crowd watched two half-naked men fight like dogs.

The battling hods shoved each other about the red clay ring. Their iron collars clanged together as they grappled and strained. In the surrounding bleachers, where students had once sat absorbing the day's lecture, men now shook their betting slips and shouted themselves crimson.

A lavish balcony haloed the common bleachers. Its railing, sparsely attended a moment before, now grew crowded with noblemen attracted by the uproar. They peered down at the brawl, sipping leaf-green liqueur from crystal glasses and smoking black cigarillos that stank like wet bedclothes. Magpies and doves swooped about the great dome overhead, driven from their nests by the mounting noise.

Trembling from the effort, the old hod lifted the youth over his head and held him on his shoulders like the yoke of an ox. He turned in a slow circle, showing every seat his defeated rival, who had not ten minutes before strutted out of the tunnel, thumping his chest. The mob bayed. The old hod drove the youth to the ground, where he bounced once and settled in a prostrate sprawl.

Every spectator in the arena—save one—made thunder with his hands. The victorious hod paraded with his arms up, his expression as inscrutable as an executioner's hood.

A team of groomers emerged from the tunnels that ran under the stands. Some raked the clay; others dragged the moaning youth underground. The victor was gathered last, his iron collar hooked to a pair of poles, by which he was escorted from the floor amid a shower of losing betting slips.

In the arena's lower tier, the man who refused to clap scanned the balcony railing, studying the faces of the noblemen in military and dining jackets. They did not pay him the compliment of acknowledgment.

As a wanted man, Thomas Senlin found the snub amusing. But the same realities that had frustrated his own search for Marya now befuddled the ringdom's search for him. The Tower overwrote the obsessions and longings of men and women with an indifference so intense it almost seemed purposeful. One did not have to hide long nor change much to disappear inside the churning mass. Thomas Senlin had slipped again into the camouflage of the crowd. It didn't hurt his anonymity that the published bounty for the pirate Tom Mudd included a sketch of a much fiercer-looking man, with an anvil chin, cannonball cheeks, and a gaze like a crucible full of slag. Perhaps Commissioner Pound had been too embarrassed to describe the man who'd robbed and eluded him honestly as a thin man with kindly eyes and a nose like a rudder.

The crowd funneled from the bleachers to the lobby, a great vaulted room that didn't so much echo as boom with voices and commotion. A rowdy queue formed at the concessionary, where cloudy beer was being poured and splashed upon the floor. Another line grew about the betting cages, where guards in severe black-and-gold uniforms watched the room for men who were overly drunk or overly distraught. Finding any such show of excess, the guards offered a first warning by rifle butt and a second warning by bayonet.

Caught for the moment in the human vortex, Senlin engaged in some idle eavesdropping. Most of what he heard just concerned the last fight or the next, but one conversation distinguished itself from the rest.

"I heard they're recalling Commissioner Pound," a man in a plum-colored vest said.

"It wasn't in the *Reverie* this morning," his companion complained.

"It will be tomorrow, I'd wager. Commissioner Pound: outwitted by a pirate named Mudd!"

"How quick the wind turns!"

Senlin resisted the urge to pull up his collar.

Wedging through, he splashed across a growing lagoon of beer and made his way to the balcony entrance.

A pair of sharp-eyed guards stood at the base of the balcony stairs. They shared a common uniform, which included a gold sash, a saber, a pistol, and, apparently, a mustache. Senlin tried not to look at the swords that hung on their hips as he smiled and said, "Hello!"

One of the guards shifted his forward gaze just long enough to size Senlin up. And seeing nothing deserving further conversation, he looked away.

Senlin reached into his coat pocket, a movement that inspired both men to show him several inches of their swords. With the slow care of a surgeon navigating a wound, Senlin drew out his billfold. He extracted a stiff white card and a five-mina banknote, an amount that once upon a time would've been enough to feed his crew for six months. "Perhaps you could give my calling card to the club manager." The nearest guard, whose mustache had been waxed into two perfect loops, took the money and card. "With my warmest regards," Senlin said with a wink.

The guard ripped the card and the banknote, turned them, and tore again. He dropped the scraps at Senlin's feet. Even as Senlin looked down at his destroyed offering, the guard gripped one sleeve of his coat and ripped it half from his shoulder. He repeated the treatment on the other sleeve.

Before he could speak, Senlin was brusquely elbowed aside by the arrival of several men in suits that were as black and sleek as hot tar. The guards saluted, and one said, "Good afternoon, Sir Wilhelm." Ignoring them, the nobleman continued a cheerful conversation with his companions, all of whom seemed oblivious to the man in a torn gray coat.

This was not Senlin's first glimpse of the handsome duke, but it was the closest he'd come to the man who'd made off with Marya. Senlin pictured himself stealing the guard's sidearm. Pictured the shot striking the duke, pictured him crying out in surprise, clutching the mortal wound as he fell at Senlin's feet in a lifeless knot. Doubtlessly, he would be dead a moment after the duke, leaving Marya twice-widowed and half-rescued. And that assumed she wished to be saved. It was a question only she could answer, and he could not ask.

Senlin had the Sphinx to thank for this absurd state of affairs.

Three days prior, the Sphinx had wasted no time introducing Senlin to his role as contracted spy.

Mere hours after the Sphinx had unveiled Edith's astonishing new command, the *State of Art*, he led Senlin down the rose-colored canyon of his home, through one of a hundred indistinguishable doors, and into a queer and cramped dressing room.

Sizing charts hung upon the walls. A seamstress's dummy stood in one corner, wire ribs rusting through cotton skin. Much of the room was dominated by an immense wardrobe. It quivered and rumbled like a boiling pot. Brass tumblers and dials consumed one of the wardrobe's doors. Byron, the Sphinx's stag-headed footman, attended these controls, making minute adjustments and muttering to himself. The Sphinx loomed in one corner, his black robes long and tapering. He looked like a leech with a mirror in its mouth.

Senlin hardly glanced at the Sphinx or his curious wardrobe, which seemed part closet and part engine. His sense of wonder had been depleted by his time in the Bottomless Library, where he had been forcibly nursed off the Crumb with the assistance of nightmares, booby traps, and a feline librarian. He hadn't yet had time to fully absorb the mysterious vault the Sphinx had shown him, the so-called "Bridge," which the Brick Layer had built to hold an untold something and sealed for reasons also unspoken. And that was to say nothing of the loss of Senlin's former command, nor his ill-advised visit to Edith's room and the kiss they'd shared with the sort of starved passion one expects of the young. It all left him feeling out of sorts.

And then Byron told him to strip to his underclothes.

He reluctantly did, and Byron assaulted him—throat, shoulder, waist, and inseam—with a tailor's tape he pulled from his pocket. Every new measurement sent Byron back to the wardrobe to turn one tumbler or another.

Senlin was so distracted by the process that he was slow to absorb the Sphinx's announcement that he would not be traveling with his old crewmates aboard the *State of Art* and would instead go on ahead to Pelphia, early and alone.

Senlin's voice rose with his alarm: "But why? We're all going to the same place, aren't we? What possible reason could you have for dividing us?"

"Will you stop fidgeting!" Byron said, cinching his tape about Senlin's chest.

"You mean breathing? Am I being fitted for a casket?"

"Not yet!" Byron said.

"Stop it, both of you." The Sphinx's voice buzzed and crackled over the humming of the wardrobe. "Senlin, please reassure me that you're not an absolute fool. Tell me, why would it be a mistake for all of you to march, arm in arm, into Pelphia together?"

Ignoring Byron's probing as best he could, Senlin said, "I suppose it might make us easier to recognize. We are a rather...memorable troop."

"Ah! It's good to see the Crumb didn't cook your brains entirely."

The stag bleated in frustration. "You'd think your ears were on your hips, the way you twist about!"

Senlin was too distracted to return Byron's quip. "So I'm to go alone?"

"Don't be so dramatic, Tom! We'll exchange messages every day," the Sphinx said, and when Senlin asked how such a thing would be done, the Sphinx described his mechanical moths, which were predecessors to the clockwork butterflies Senlin had already seen. "The moths are more rudimentary; they record sound but not sight. But for the purpose of correspondence, they're more than sufficient. Byron will intercept your missives from the *State of Art*, pass on any pertinent information to the crew, then send them on to me. You'll only be alone in body. In spirit, we'll be as close as moth and flame."

"Splendid," Senlin murmured.

"Now, I know you will be tempted to look for your wife, especially once the inevitable lonesomeness sets in. But listen to me: You will make no effort to contact your wife when you—"

"If!" Senlin gripped the carpet with his bare toes. "*If* she is there." He had been poisoned by hope once already and was determined not to let it happen again.

"Byron, do you have the paper I gave you?" the Sphinx asked.

The stag threw the tape measure over his shoulder with a snort and began to rummage through his leather satchel. After a moment, he produced a folded newspaper and handed it to Senlin before retreating to the panel of the wheezing wardrobe.

Senlin read the headline aloud in a dwindling voice: "'Duke Wilhelm Horace Pell to Wed the Mermaid, Marya of Isaugh.'" He looked to the date at the top. The paper was almost seven months old. He wished to read on, but his arms failed him, taken by a sudden weakness. The paper fell like a stage curtain.

It was a fact now, and yet his mind was slow to accept it. The feeling reminded him of that nauseating confusion he had felt when, as a boy, he had been told that his grandfather had died in the night. He *believed* it was true at once because his mother had told him, and she would never lie about such a thing. But that evening, when he was shown his grandfather's body, washed, and dressed, and laid out for the wake, it had become true in a different way. Believing was not the same as knowing.

"She married the count," he murmured, his throat closing about the words.

"Duke, actually," the Sphinx said.

A cry like a swooping bird interrupted them, the sound rising from a murmur into a muffled shriek. It seemed to come from the wardrobe, which rattled more and more frantically, its hinges chattering like teeth.

Neither the Sphinx nor Byron seemed overly concerned. When the shaking abruptly stopped, Byron pulled the latch on the wardrobe and opened the doors.

Inside, Voleta Boreas hung from a wooden coat hanger as if it were a trapeze. Pink-cheeked and with scarves and stockings tangled about her neck, she leapt into the dressing room. Despite her relatively small stature, Voleta had a way of filling up every room she walked into. With her dark hair cut short, her wide mouth and bright violet eyes seemed to have grown more prominent. "That was absolutely terrifying!" she joyfully exclaimed. "It goes so blasted fast! I've never ridden anything so fast in my life! It was like falling in double time. I have to go again!"

"I told you, Voleta, it's not a ride. It's the Fardrobe," Byron said.

"And you're supposed to be waiting your turn to be fitted, not running amok in my storehouse."

Voleta, apparently oblivious to Senlin's state of half dress, began speaking to him in an exhilarated rush: "It goes to a vault full of gowns and suits and socks, all hanging like bats from the ceiling. There's hardly any light, and there are these mechanical arms that reach out and snatch the hangers, and then whiz all around through the walls!" As she spoke, she passed the loose garments she'd collected along the way to an unhappy Byron. "I promise you, Captain, one go-around and that frown will be blown right off your face." Voleta reached into the back of her blouse and pulled a black velvet disc from the collar. She flipped it about, rapped it with a knuckle, and the disc popped open. Voleta put the top hat on. It sank over her ears at once.

Still in a fog, Senlin handed her the newspaper and said, "I found her."

Voleta took the paper, her expression blooming with excitement and then wilting as she read. Sheepish now, she pulled the hat from her head. "A duke? She married a duke? I don't understand. She's your wife. She can't . . . I thought she . . . I'm so sorry, Captain."

"Not *captain* anymore," the Sphinx said, as if searching for a bottom to Senlin's humiliation.

Senlin turned back to the Sphinx and said, "Did she *want* to marry him or was she coerced?"

"Eavesdroppers and newspapers can only tell so much, I'm afraid. I don't know whether Marya said, 'I do,' or if the duke said, 'You will.' What was whispered, what lies in the heart—those are things that require a closer ear." The Sphinx shrank as he spoke, his black robes pooling upon the floor. He put his face, large as a silver platter, level with Senlin's.

"Then I must ask her," Senlin said, resolute in his undershirt.

"Is your memory really so short? I just told you, you are not to speak to your wife. You won't write her letters. You won't spy on her from the bushes. You won't go near her, her husband, or their home."

What had begun as cold, numb sorrow now warmed Senlin from core to extremity. "How can you be so heartless? Is there no humanity in you at all? You act as if she's a fancy, an errand. She is not! She is a woman whose life I ruined! Ruined with my pride, my inability, my selfishness. I *will* find her. I *will* offer my help if she needs it, my heart if she wants it, my head, even if she would see it on a stake! And you, with your plots and contracts, you with your cowardly mask and tick-tock heart, you will not stop me!"

Voleta and Byron stood frozen in the silence that followed. They waited to see whether Tom would survive his outburst, or if the Sphinx would spark the life from him.

At last, the Sphinx sighed, the sound like coins rattling down a drain. Reaching up, the Sphinx twisted the mirror. It fell away even as the black shroud piled upon the floor. Senlin gasped. Her face was a quilt of metal and flesh that was as tan and creased as a walnut. Plates of precious alloys crowded about an eyepiece that would've been better suited to a microscope than the face of an ancient woman. Perhaps strangest of all, she did not stand, but sat cross-legged upon a floating platter. Senlin passed a hand near the red glow that emanated from the bottom of the floating platform. The air there was vaguely warm and unsettled, as if possessed by static, but it did not burn him.

He looked to Voleta to share his amazement. When she caught him looking, she blurted out a not particularly convincing "Oh my god! It's a flying crone!"

"Really, Voleta," the Sphinx said, moving the brass horn that distorted her speech away from her mouth. Her unfiltered voice was creaking and reedy but remarkably ordinary. "The only living persons who have seen my face are standing in this room. You see, Thomas, a business contract is just a sort of artificial trust. But we four are beyond that now."

"But I don't . . . Why me?" he asked. "And why Voleta?"

The Sphinx pulled thoughtfully at the thick lobe of one ear. "Perhaps because you are capable of remorse. There is nothing in the world so inspiring of trust as regret. And I trust Voleta because she reminds me so much of myself—"

"We're virtually twins," Voleta piped up.

"—right down to that pert mouth of hers."

"But if you have such faith in me," Senlin said, his confusion verging upon ire, "if you understand me so well, why would you forbid me to speak to Marya? Surely, you must know remorse is not enough. If amends can be made, they must be."

"Just because I trust you, Thomas, doesn't mean you're not sometimes a fool." Before Senlin could balk, the unveiled Sphinx pressed on, her tray pacing the carpet before him. "Let's think this through; let's think how your attempt to see your wife would probably go. Let's say that you defy my counsel, my orders, your contract, and our friendship, and go in search of Marya. Let's say you actually manage to meet her, which is no small feat because she is married to a popular and very powerful duke. How do you think she will react when her husband of old materializes?" The Sphinx stopped shifting about, as if to give Senlin a chance to reply, though as soon as he drew a breath, she carried on for him. "Perhaps she'll be happy! Perhaps she'll say, 'Oh, Tom! My love has returned! I am saved! Carry me home!'" The Sphinx clapped her still-gloved hands together in a mockery of joy. "But perhaps she'll be angry. Perhaps she'll say, 'You! You ruined my life, you miserable worm!'" The Sphinx shook a fist at him.

"Whichever it is, whatever her feelings are, one thing is certain: She will be surprised to see you. And what do people do when they are *actually* surprised?" The Sphinx cut her gaze toward Voleta. "What if she blurts out your name or gasps or faints or screams? It won't really matter whether it's done out of delight or fright if the duke overhears it. Do you really think he will be pleased to see you, his rival? If you are lucky, he will take his displeasure out on you. But if he is an unreasonable or jealous man, if he is cruel, might he not take that displeasure out on her as well?"

Senlin scowled at the Sphinx's logic because he could not think of how to argue against it. At least, not yet. "What do you propose?"

"Voleta will speak to Marya on your behalf." The Sphinx swept an arm toward the young woman. "Voleta can wear a dress. She can curtsy her way into court. She can, I think, get invited to the sort of parties the duke and duchess go to. She can wait for the right moment, and when it arrives, she can make a discreet inquiry."

"I don't want Voleta doing my dirty—" Senlin began, but Voleta interrupted him.

"I'll do it."

"Wait a minute. You don't know what you're volunteering for. Is it dangerous?" Senlin asked.

"Of course it's dangerous!" The Sphinx laughed. "Most things worth doing are. But she won't be alone. I'm sending the amazon with her."

Senlin had no doubt that Iren would protect Voleta with her life, but she was still only one person. What could she do if the duke or the navy or the whole ringdom turned against them? "I can't put their necks on the block for my mistakes. We'll have to think of something—"

"You aren't captain anymore," Voleta said. She did not say it meanly, yet even so, the words stung. "You can't give orders any longer, Mr. Tom. So. I want to go to Pelphia."

"The parties are glorious!" Byron said, with a happy shake of his antlers. He helped Senlin slide his arms into a new white-collared shirt. "The people are dreadful, but the parties are sublime. I've read a hundred stories: the waltzes, the music, the hors d'oeuvres, the wits—"

"I'm not going for any of that!" Voleta said. "I don't care about waltzes and minces and how-do-you-dos! I'm going because this man saved my life. He saved my brother's life. So it's my turn to be . . . good, or whatever it is we are." She turned to Senlin. "I promise, I'll bring her home."

"That's incredibly brave and selfless and . . . thank you." Senlin knew her too well to think she would be dissuaded once she had decided on a course. "But, Voleta, please, you must be honest with her. Tell her everything. Tell her about the thievery, the piracy, and the bloodshed. Tell her about the starving, and the Crumb addiction, and . . . all of it."

"*All* of it?" Voleta said, squeezing the hat flat again. "What am I supposed to say, 'Hullo! You don't know me, but your old husband sent me to tell you what an awful person he is now. A real stinker! But he wants you back. Oh, yes, he does! Wait, madam, where are you going?'" She popped the hat out with her fist. "That's a hard sale, Mr. Tom."

Senlin pushed his arms into the jacket Byron held out for him. It fit perfectly. It felt strange to wear a new, tailored suit again. He looked at his scarred and weathered hands, protruding from the pristine cuffs. He felt like two different people stitched together.

"Marya has to know what she's signing up for." He tried to put his hands in his pockets but found them sewn shut. "I won't trick her. I won't pretend I am the man she married. I don't think I'm completely ruined, or at least not beyond redemption, and perhaps there will be a homecoming for us, but if she is happy in her new life, I would not pluck her from it."

Not knowing what to say to this sincere declaration, Voleta attempted a curtsy. She bent both knees, threw her head downward, and popped up again like a spring.

Byron brayed in horror and said, "What on earth was that? Are you bobbing for apples?"

"There'll be enough time for practicing curtsies later," the Sphinx intervened before Voleta could retort. "Now that your business has been settled for the moment, I'd like to discuss mine."

"I imagine it has something to do with Luc Marat," Senlin said.

"I suspect it does. Someone is destroying my spies, my butterflies. Specifically, someone inside the Colosseum. That's where the locals watch hods bleed for their amusement."

"They sound like lovely people," Voleta said.

"It's just the sort of injustice that rallies hods to Marat's cause. It's not that Marat is truly against bloodshed; he just prefers it to be spilled on his own account. Whether he's involved or not, one thing seems certain: Someone doesn't want me to know what's going on inside the Colosseum."

"But if it isn't Marat, if it's the locals who're blinding you, what do they have to hide?"

"Ah! Now you're asking the right questions. I knew you'd make a fine spy, Tom. There is one other thing you should probably know. The Colosseum is run by the Coterie, which you may recall Duke Wilhelm is a member of. So your investigation will probably put you right in his way. But you will do your best to avoid him."

"For such a large place, the Tower seems awfully small sometimes," Senlin said with a sour smile.

"'Small,' he says. *Small*." The wand she gripped began to spit and spark like green wood on a fire. "If you'd prefer I can dispatch you to the ringdom of Thane, where a hundred rifles have vanished from a locked armory. Or I can ship you to the ringdom of Japhet, where a street recently collapsed, apparently the result of some errant tunneling. Or I could send you to Banner-Wick, where two libraries have burned down in the past month. The shipyards in Morick have suffered from repeated sabotage. Perhaps I should send you there!" Her voice had risen to a shout. "I choose to dispatch you to Pelphia because we share a common interest there. But do not confuse my charity with fate. Only a small man believes the Tower is small."

Feeling sufficiently chastised, Senlin raised his hands in surrender. "I'm sorry. It was a facile thing to say."

The apology seemed to appease the Sphinx. The bright spark dwindled from the tip of her wand. She pulled what appeared to be a little ball bearing from the sleeve of one glove. She presented the copper pellet to Senlin, who was horrified to see it sprout eight legs and run a circle about her open palm. The Sphinx tut-tutted and tapped the mechanical arachnid with her finger. The spider balled up again. "Swallow this."

"You can't be serious," Senlin said.

The Sphinx pointed at Voleta, whose mouth was already open. "Young lady, if you say one word, you'll be eating this instead. Now look, Thomas, it's perfectly harmless. It will only help us find you if you get lost. Consider it a safety line, like the airmen wear." The Sphinx again presented him with the balled-up spider. "Or if you'd rather, I can have Ferdinand assist you with the insertion?"

Senlin took the pill, placed it on his tongue, and swallowed with a small shudder.

"There we are. That wasn't so bad, was it?" She plucked a leather billfold from her tray and handed it to him. Opening it, Senlin found a thick stack of twenty-mina banknotes. "You will be posing as a Boskop tourist; an accountant by the name of Cyril Pinfield."

"Cyril!" Voleta laughed.

"We'll have to work on that laugh of yours, too," Byron said.

"Is it genuine?" Senlin asked.

"Of course it's genuine. You'll need it for lodging, meals, and bribes. If you find that you're running low, let Byron know. We can always print more."

"Genuine!" Senlin scoffed.

"There are a lot of people looking for you, but very few who can recognize you on sight. Don't roam about. Stick to the Colosseum and your room."

Senlin nodded and slid the billfold into the inner pocket of his jacket. "And what will Captain Winters be doing while I'm off on assignment?"

"Once she's delivered Voleta and Iren, she'll reclaim the ringdom's copy of *The Brick Layer's Granddaughter*. I want it back before Luc Marat gets his hands on it. Assuming he hasn't already. Now, as soon as you're packed, Byron will take you to the stables, and you can be on your way."

"Stables? Wait, I'm to leave tonight?"

"As soon as possible."

Senlin smoothed his graying temples. "I suppose I'll say my goodbyes, then."

"There's no time. I promise you Marat will not let sentiment slow the pace of his advance. Besides, you will all see each other again soon enough."

"But what possible harm could it do to say goodbye to—"

The Sphinx cut in, showing the jewelry of her smile. "I think you've seen enough of Edith Winters, don't you, Tom?"

Feeling suddenly transparent, Senlin shut his mouth.

Chapter Two

Wallflowers are harmless. They are pretty things that stand in corners with a pleasant look on their face. It's the wall-weeds I can't stand. They moan about the mantles, mope upon the sofas, and pout about the punch bowls, waiting to be asked, "Are you all right? You look so sad." Wall-weeds will linger for hours if you let them. And the only thing that seems to drive them away is other people's happiness.

—Oren Robinson of the *Daily Reverie*

The staff of the Bon Royal Hotel of Pelphia thought the guest in Room 356 distinctly odd.

Since his arrival three days prior, the guest had requested dozens of copies of newspapers, *old* newspapers, which had to be retrieved from the archives of the *Daily Reverie* at some expense, though the guest had no qualms about paying the archivist's fee or tipping the porter who had to jog the half mile to the newspaper's offices.

Stranger still, the guest in Room 356 hadn't gone anywhere except to the noonday fights at the Colosseum, for which he departed wearing the same sort of grim expression the maids wore to unclog a drain. The guest returned to the hotel as soon as the early fights were through, nodded to the concierge, and vanished up the stairs. He never took an aperitif at the bar, or participated in the evening singalong, or played a hand of cards in the parlor with the other tourists. He fled to his room and didn't reemerge until the next morning. The staff couldn't help but wonder what the lanky recluse did all day and night. The cleaning girls, who were usually quite good at dispelling mysteries, reported that other than stacks of newspapers, his room was free of obvious intrigue. There were no empty bottles of gin in the waste bin, no bawdy manuscripts under the mattress, no pinned-up treasure maps, or bloodstains on the carpet. The most shocking thing about the guest in Room 356 was that he apparently owned only three coats, all of them the same doleful shade of gray.

All the ladies agreed he wasn't attractive. No, his features were too severe and his limbs too long for him to be considered handsome. But he possessed a certain bearing that was alluring, though perhaps only because it was so uncommon in the Pelphian male. He never fussed with his hair or publicly preened, never posed in a doorway or at the foot of a stair, blocking traffic just for the attention. No, the tall guest was polite to everyone, expressed interest in no one, and tipped like a man on his way to the gallows.

The staff couldn't help but feel a little offended that he never sampled any of the city's many culinary offerings. Pelphia was renowned for its bakeries and cafés, a fact that the doormen and elevator attendants brought to his attention, unprompted, more than once. Nor did he take advantage of the ringdom's bountiful culture. As far as anyone could tell, he had not attended a single gala, concert, play, or burlesque. The guest took his meals in his room, read his outdated newspapers, and went to the noonday fights.

The concierge, Mr. Aloysius Stull, was finally forced to shush his gossiping staff, saying, "Leave Mr. Pinfield alone. He is a Boskop," which was both an unsatisfactory answer and also a very complete one.

Boskops inhabited the seventeenth ringdom of Boskopeia. Amid the colorful flora of the Tower, the Boskops were a dull little species of mushroom. A Boskop's ideal party was one that no one attended and that ended early, with the host going to bed with his own wife, of all people.

Indeed, that was why the Sphinx had chosen the disguise for Senlin. No Pelphian would see a Boskop and think pirate, or burglar, or spy.

In his room, on the third evening since his arrival, Senlin opened the cigar box the Sphinx had packed for him and plucked out a cigar. He removed the thin tobacco-leaf wrapper to reveal a metal tube, perforated like a saltshaker at the head. He twisted the body until it clicked and then began to speak into the device in a low, clear voice.

"July ninth, six thirty-five in the evening. Today, I made my third visit to the Colosseum." Senlin paced his room as he spoke. The Sphinx had insisted his lodging be modest for the sake of appearances—it would not do for a Boskop accountant to sleep in a suite. Still, his "single" was neither small nor modest. Every room in the Bon Royal was larger than his quarters aboard the *Stone Cloud* had been, though the luxury was wasted on him. The gorgeous four-post bed deserved honeymooners, not an insomniac who napped on top of the covers in his clothes.

"I tried to get access to the balcony again, but was...soundly rejected. For the record, the guard who tore up my banknote did not give me a receipt. I've never had a bribe turned down before. I'm not sure whether that's inspiring or terrifying. One thing's for certain, the Coterie Club's security is as tight as a tick."

He lingered over the newspaper that lay open on the bureau. "I think I've seen all I'm going to see from the bleachers." Picking up the paper that was dated December 3, he scanned the headline that he had read many times in recent days: DUCHESS M. PELL CANCELS WINTER RECITALS, UNDISCLOSED ILLNESS CITED. He squinted at the accompanying image: an engraving of a woman sitting at a piano, a large black whale of an instrument. Her head was thrown back. Her arms were held straight as a sleepwalker. Her expression was one of ecstasy.

Senlin dropped the paper and cleared his throat.

"I'm beginning to suspect that the fights are rigged, or perhaps choreographed. There's just something about the way the men grapple that doesn't quite sit with me. The blows are too regular, the fighting too flamboyant." Senlin thought of his own experience with brief, brutal, and chaotic violence, which had been many things, but never graceful, never so coherent. "If the fights *are* fixed, the public doesn't seem to know. I've never seen so many wagers being thrown about. But I think we can rule out your thought that the Colosseum is being used to train the hods. That is, assuming Marat isn't plotting a war of charades. I think the whole enterprise probably exists to line the pockets of the men upstairs. Perhaps they just don't want you to know they're getting rich at the expense of your workforce.

"I'll try a larger bribe with the club guards tomorrow." After a pause, he decided not to mention his sighting of Duke Wilhelm H. Pell. "If that fails, I might try leaping into the ring. Unless you have a better idea. End of report."

Senlin twisted the head a second time, and the cylinder began to wriggle in his palm. It unfurled a pair of thin, painted wings. Six fine, brass legs curled out from the thorax, and the domed head of the clockwork moth began to rotate, taking in its surroundings.

Opening first the curtains, then the glass doors to his small balcony, Senlin was met by a blat of noise. The third-floor gallery opposite his hotel room was crowded with the overflow of a party. Many of the attendees wore masks and brandished champagne coupes so wildly they sloshed onto the street below. Pedestrians shouted up at them: some in derision, others in solidarity.

A woman in a sunset dress noticed him. She pushed her black mask onto her forehead to get a better look at him, or perhaps to show herself off. She was beautiful but aging and caked in makeup. She blew him a kiss. He did not catch it.

He said, "I found a moth in my room." And to prove it, he let the Sphinx's recorder flutter from his hands into the gulf between them. Clapping with delight, the woman watched the moth bounce up toward a sky that guttered with gaslight stars. Then pitching forward, she retched over the balcony rail.

At night and from above, it was easier to see one of the city's more curious features. The regular cobbles of the streets were interrupted by discs of quartz, each as large as a barrelhead. The dials glowed faintly, like candles behind wax paper. About a dozen or so of the dials dappled each block, though without any discernable pattern. He thought they were perhaps manhole covers or windows into some sub-terranean space, but when he'd tried during the day to peer past the sallow glow into what lurked below, he'd been unable to discern anything beyond the foggy light.

Surrendering his momentary curiosity, Senlin shut the glass doors and returned to his newspapers.

Early on in his research, Senlin had read several accounts of Commissioner Pound's increasingly embarrassing attempts to apprehend the man who had stolen a painting from the Baths, which was a Pelphian protectorate. The paper described the criminal as "a tourist with a murky past named Tomas Sinlend, whose ready transformation into the dread pirate Mudd evidences a singular and wicked genius." Senlin was amused to read one account that referred to him as a "criminal mastermind," and another that said he was an "infamous pugilist." Numerous editorials described Commissioner Pound as a man haunted by his own failure, a fixation with which Senlin could sadly sympathize.

But it wasn't his own infamy or Pound's pursuit of him that sparked Senlin's obsession with the local rag. It was the fact that Marya's story unfolded in the society pages. Much of the account came from a single source, a reporter for the *Daily Reverie* named Oren Robinson. Over the course of months, he had written nearly two dozen articles about Marya. Robinson was also responsible for coining what would become her stage name, "the Mermaid." The fact that she was once married to the criminal "Tomas Sinlend" was never mentioned.

Robinson was a shameless gossip and a bloviating prig, but he wrote well enough, and Senlin thought his account was not without at least some kernel of truth. According to Robinson, Marya's history began when the Duke Wilhelm H. Pell discovered her in the Baths and saved her from a life of destitution and ruin.

Marya's introduction to Pelphian society occurred at Duchess Dostler's End of Summer Soiree.

The Daily Reverie

THE DUCHESS D'S LATEST CATASTROPHE

AUGUST 19

...Duke Wilhelm Horace Pell was in attendance this evening, having returned from his summer holiday in the Baths. He brought with him a companion who appeared to have never passed before a looking glass in her life. Despite the duke's assurances that she was a rare and worthy lady he'd found bubbling about the Baths, her frock was a shade of terminal gangrene that appeared to have been clipped from an onion sack. If she hadn't such a pretty face, I would've thought the duke had engaged us all in some tasteless prank.

Modest as her fashion was, the rustic lady was elsewise bold. She introduced herself as "Marya, Just Marya" while the duke was still drawing his breath. Then she shook my hand like a pump handle.

I don't think I've ever met a more unnecessarily opinionated woman in my life. Seeking an inoffensive subject of conversation, I asked her what she thought of the hired quartet. She went on to evaluate each player, one by one, and in some detail. (I won't defame the poor musicians by reporting her amateur assessment here, but neither can I find it in my heart to defend the trumpet work of Mr. Molyneux, who tips the bottle more often than a fop tips his hat.) When the duke's companion concluded by remarking that our ringdom's sacred anthem sounded a bit like a "dog startling a flock of geese," the duke nearly choked on a fig.

I cannot imagine we will see Madam "Marya, Just Marya" again.

Senlin smiled at the thought of Marya deflating the puffed-up reporter. (She had, after all, plenty of practice deflating a certain puffed-up headmaster.) While she had been off scandalizing reporters, he had been trying to disappear inside the Baths, trying to blend in with the mode and make himself inoffensive. He had sought salvation through anonymity. She had sought it through distinction. He couldn't help but wonder if hers hadn't been the wiser course.

And it hadn't taken long for her to bring the press around.

The Daily Reverie

DUCHESS ROCKFORD'S WEEKLY FLOGGING

AUGUST 22

. . . now, it is with unanticipated awe that I must report the reappearance of Duke Wilhelm Pell's unvarnished escort, Marya (no-longer-Just). Not only did she return—she distinguished herself admirably. I daresay I like her. I daresay you might like her, too.

As previously implied (the snails smelled like feet, I tell you) Duchess Rockford's party had not begun well, and by the stroke of nine, her guests had begun to curdle about the exits. Even her most fawning friends began to make their excuses, all as transparent as a fart. No doubt they were hoping to catch the late fight or an early burlesque but didn't want to hurt the grand old dame's feelings, what she has left of them floating in that punch-bowl heart of hers. Not even Rockford's artisanal gin could forestall the exodus.

It was amid this run for the exits that Marya sat down, uninvited, at the duchess's piano and began to play.

I should not refer to it as *play* because the word conjures up a levity, a frivolity, which was absent in her performance. She engaged the piano in a lover's quarrel, an argument she was clearly determined to win. And then, after she had hooked us all on the strings of her instrument, she opened up her throat and began to sing.

I weep for you who were not present, because you must depend upon the faint notes of my fair words to hear the epiphany that resounded in those rooms. If her playing was a quarrel, her voice was a perfect reconciliation. She sang like a mermaid.

Her voice enticed the deserters back from the cloakroom. It made men recant their excuses and women cancel their good-night kisses. They flocked to this mermaid like doomed sailors, and the ship of our evening was dashed upon her song.

Though Senlin wasn't surprised to find that people adored her playing so much, it was strange to hear another man articulate the experience with such poetic excitement. It wasn't long after her performance at Rockford's party that Marya was invited to play at the Marquess Jean Clamond's birthday celebration. In review of this formal debut, Oren Robinson wrote, "Mark my words, if the Mermaid played the Vivant tomorrow, they would have to build a fifth balcony to accommodate her admirers." Senlin understood this to be no small compliment: The Vivant was the supreme venue in a city of venues.

The right people took notice of Marya's talent, and in a matter of days, she was transformed from a dowdy nobody into a fashion plate. According to Robinson, she single-handedly popularized the empire waist. "She looks," Robinson remarked of her third performance, "like a red-headed wraith in a white nightgown. Rather than make any effort to strangle her hair in one of the intricate architectures now popular with the aged and the ugly, she allows her locks to hang, tangle, and toss as they please, a choice that only dramatizes her feverish attitude." Her fame was so great, in fact, that it became the subject of a stage play called *The Mermaid's Tale*, which purported to be an authentic and authorized history of her life.

Then, in December, the tone of the headlines changed again. The bolded words were no longer *Rapturous*, *Genius*, and *Miracle* but were now *Confusion*, *Mystery*, and *Disaster*. Overnight, the Mermaid vanished from the public eye.

She became the subject of endless speculation, which ranged from the innocuous to the insane. Some suggested she had sung her voice right out of her throat and had been left a mad and violent mute. Others claimed she was a victim of poisoning, likely perpetrated by some jealous rival whose fame Marya had eclipsed. None of these fictions were ever corroborated, least of all by Duke Wilhelm. He sequestered

Marya in his home, shut all the curtains, removed most of his staff, and stationed guards at all the windows and doors. Then, without further explanation, he embarked upon a big-game hunting expedition in the southern plains of Ur, where he remained for nearly four months.

Only upon his return did the duke confess to the press that in December Marya had been stricken by a horrible and contagious withering disease. The royal physician, Dr. Edmond Rawlins, who had been charged with her care in the duke's absence, corroborated the fact and added that he suspected she suffered from an illness she had imported from her former life. The duke, it was then revealed, had been hunting not for game but for a cure, which he found at last on a mountaintop at the edge of everything, where an ancient hermit lived upon the very cusp of night itself.

The hermit was so moved by the duke's tale, he gave him a purse of dust he had gathered from the crater of a fallen star. The hermit promised the dust would cure anything short of death. And, miraculously, the royal physician proclaimed it had done just that. Marya soon recovered and then returned to public life at the end of spring. According to the accounts of the *Daily Reverie*, she was every bit her former self.

Senlin found the story of the duke's search for a cure far-fetched. But then, he supposed, it was possible that Marya had really fallen ill, and the duke had found a cure somewhere and only exaggerated the details. It was possible.

But it was also possible, if one took a more cynical view, that Marya had refused to play. It was possible she had tried to escape, possible she had angered the duke in some way. He might have imprisoned her in his home to punish her and then left to shoot elephants for all Senlin knew.

He wanted nothing so badly as to read her story, told in her own words, or at least to have a direct quote from her declaring that she was safe, happy, and free.

The only lengthy interview he could find among all his stacks of newspapers was from the first night she sold out the Vivant, months before her seclusion.

It was on that night, Oren Robinson would later claim, that the Mermaid cemented her fame.

The Daily Reverie

AN INTERVIEW WITH THE MERMAID

SEPTEMBER 29

The following is an exclusive interview with Madam Marya (MM), conducted after her debut performance at the Vivant. It was conducted in her dressing room and in the company of Duke Wilhelm H. Pell (WHP). All quotes are as accurate as I can make them.

OR: Congratulations on your performance, Madam Mermaid. It was one of the most stirring unveilings I've seen at the Vivant in years.

MM: Thank you. It was an absolute delight.

OR: Tell me, what was it like to play in front of five thousand of Pelphia's most esteemed and cultured persons?

MM: Well, of course, I couldn't think about that while I was performing. Music is like romance; nothing ruins the mood so well as self-consciousness.

WHP: Oh, darling.

MM: I mean to say, I tried to play as naturally as I would to my friends back home.

OR: Which was where, remind us?

MM: A seaside town called Isaugh.

OR: Then my moniker for you was more apropos than I knew! And you were the starlet of this humble fishtown, I imagine?

MM: I wouldn't have called myself a star.

WHP: You are being too modest, my dear.

MM: I suppose I was as famous as anyone can be among friends.

OR: I daresay we are able to appreciate your talents more fully here. Could you tell me a bit about your musical philosophy?

MM: Well, I have observed a trend here that presses composers and musicians, particularly, toward a sort of holy boredom.

I mean, who said music had to be such a serious thing? I find musicians who just plink through the notes like a music box to be horribly dull. Songs are emotional. It's better to play sincere mistakes than lifeless perfection.

OR: So you are a sentimentalist?

MM: I play with sentiment, if that's what you mean. I don't just sprawl upon the bench like a washed-up fish.

WHP: Steady on, darling.

OR: Would you care to talk a little about how you and the duke met?

MM: It was at a party in the Baths.

OR: Yes? Could you elaborate? Indulge us all with a small anecdote, perhaps?

WHP: It's an impertinent question, Oren, really, but since that seems to be the spirit of the evening, I'll answer it with an impertinent announcement. I have asked the Mermaid to marry me, and she has accepted.

MM: Marya.

OR: Well, this is a banner day! Have you arranged a date? What will the theme be? Have you selected your flower? Your color? Your—

WHP: No, no, that will all be in the formal announcement next week. I just couldn't wait. The news has been puffing me up all night.

OR: I can't imagine the pressure you've been under, keeping something like that under your hat! Madam Marya, tell me, how did you say yes?

MM: In the usual way, I suppose.

WHP: We really must conclude it there, Oren. It's been an absolute joy talking to you. Come to the club sometime. I'll give you the royal treatment.

OR: Oh, thank you, Your Grace. I will take you up on that. And thank you, Madam Mermaid, for your time and your wonderful performance. You stirred my very soul.

MM: I am your humble spoon.

THE HOD KING

Needless to say, my faithful readers, this is the news of the week, brought to you by Oren Robinson, who found the Mermaid, named her, and made you love her.

Though he had read it before, the announcement made Senlin's heart feel as tight and beaten as a drumhead. He again skimmed the subsequent articles that described their elaborate wedding plans, which included a specially commissioned orchestral piece, abysmally entitled "The Twain Become the Twixt." He read all about the spectacle of the marriage ceremony, including the parade, which spanned the ringdom, and the release of one hundred floating luminaries, which caught fire when they bumped against the ringdom's stars and fell in flaming ruins about the city, much to everyone's alarm. Their honeymoon was no less opulent. The duke chartered a pleasure cruiser, called the *Astra Titanica*, which was emptied so the newlyweds could indulge in a moment of privacy, a moment that reporters frankly begrudged them. The honeymoon ship circled the Tower for ten days, a voyage that Robinson cheekily described as "a hundred laps spent upon one."

Through the balcony glass, Senlin heard the city laugh.

Chapter Three

The Tower is a pestle grinding upon the mortar of the earth. It pulverizes bones, fortunes, kings, love, youth, and beauty. That is its purpose—to crush.

So, no, I will not retract my one-star review of Café Sotto's shortbread. I'm sorry the baker is despondent to the point of suicide, but at least he knows now how I felt after eating his wretched biscuits.

—Oren Robinson of the *Daily Reverie*

Reading about Marya's new life had an uncomfortable way of bringing Edith to mind. The fact that those two emotional threads were now braided together in his heart was a source of extreme guilt. He still couldn't say if it was hope or hopelessness that had driven him to Edith's room that night. Marya had become such a confused specter—a cause, an ideal that was easy to adore but difficult to love. Edith was, at the very least, a real and devoted friend.

As he lay atop the brocaded duvet, staring at his three gray coats hanging vigil on the wall, the sleeves of one now torn and dangling, he recalled his final hour in the Sphinx's home. He had spent it tying knots.

After his fitting, he and Byron had carried his new luggage to what the stag referred to as "the stables," despite a conspicuous lack of horses. There were, however, piles of straw on the floor and leather reins on the rough lumber walls. Senlin dragged his portmanteau past stall after stall, all of them empty, and found himself wondering, not for the first time, if the Brick Layer hadn't been a little mad. What in the world did a man atop a Tower need with horses?

But when they arrived at the end of the long aisle, breathless and a little wheezy from the stirred-up straw, he saw that the stables had been built for a different sort of beast. Inside the pen, a machine that was as large as a wagon hunkered upon six legs. The legs curled at the end like the claws of a sloth. The machine's headlamps, presumably mounted on the front, glowed palely.

"Our noble steed!" Byron said with an enthusiasm Senlin did not share. "Why fly when you can crawl?"

"You can't be serious." The means of passage dawned upon him with a shiver. "You'll kill us both."

"I assure you, it's perfectly safe." Byron reached into the footwell and switched the engine on. The walker began to hum, roughly at first. Its joints seethed a little steam. "This," Byron said a bit too grandly, "is the last wall-walker."

"What happened to the rest of them?" Senlin asked, looking back at all the empty stalls. "Don't tell me they fell off?"

"Not all of them," Byron said, patting the engine's fender. "Some of them exploded."

"Wonderful," Senlin said drolly.

"You've already tried flying into Pelphia. Perhaps it's time you tried a different tack."

Before leaving, Byron gave Senlin the chore of lashing his luggage to the wall-walker. The stag suggested he do his best to preserve the machine's equilibrium. "The ride can get a little dodgy if she's too front heavy. Or rear heavy. Or heavy in general. Do your best. Fingers crossed!" Byron said.

Senlin was completely absorbed with the work of tying down his luggage and considering his chances of seeing another day when someone touched him lightly on the shoulder. He turned to find Edith standing alone in the aisle. She was smiling but not happily. Her dark hair had been recently brushed but not vanquished and was tucked behind her ears. Seeing her standing with the barn wood behind her made Senlin think of her former life. She was not so far removed from riding a horse about the countryside. Though he was not so distant from his blackboards and books. It was strange to think how they never would've met if the Tower had not driven them together.

"What are you doing here?" Senlin said, pulling a knot tight.

"I came to say goodbye."

"I'm glad you did. I would've come, but the Sphinx . . . forbade it."

"He does like forbidding things, doesn't he? He didn't want me to see you either. Byron came and found me and told me where you were."

"That's surprising."

Edith laughed softly. "I think we're friends now."

"Very surprising. Well, we could always use more friends." Senlin rubbed his rope-sore hands together. He was trying to decide whether he should shake her hand, or embrace her, or stand away and salute. He couldn't think of what to say, so he said, "How are you?"

She laughed again, perhaps at the awkwardness. "I'm fine. Good. Fine. It is a lot to take in all at once. A big new ship, a new arm, a new command. You, leaving . . ."

"Yes," he said, looking down. "That is an awful lot. And there's a little more. It appears my wife has gotten remarried."

"She has?"

"Yes, to the count, who's in fact a duke."

"Did she want to marry him?"

Senlin's mouth opened and shut twice before he could force an answer out. "I don't know. The Sphinx has *forbidden* me from looking for her. But I . . ." he began without knowing how to finish. They stood in the heavy silence for longer than either would've liked.

At last, he cleared his throat and said with all the dignity he had left: "I don't know what to wish for anymore, Edith. I don't know what I want or what I should want or if I have the right to want anything anymore. I blame myself for all of this and expect she will, too. All I know is before I can wish or want again, I have to be certain she is happy. I have to know what she wants of me, if she wants anything at all."

"I understand. And I think—we all think it's the right thing to do."

"I don't want you to suffer on my account, or wait, or worry. If I don't come back, don't waste a minute looking for me. We both know where that road leads."

"Do we? I don't have any idea what will happen. Every time I've felt sure about what the morning will be like, I've been wrong. There aren't any seasons here; there isn't an almanac to tell us what to plant or when to sow it, when to expect rain, when to brace for drought. Some days I wake up with a different arm at my side. Some days I wake up and feel like a different person."

She took his hands in hers, the one soft and warm, the other hard and cool. "All I know is that, at the end of the day, dreams don't matter, but neither does regret. We aren't what we want or wish for. We are only what we do."

Because he smiled at the thought, and because every farewell in the Tower could be forever, she leaned in and kissed him goodbye.

They crawled backward down the Tower. Byron piloted the wallwalker across the treacherous expanse of stone and crumbling mortar with the aid of a silver hand mirror pointed over his shoulder. They could've descended nose first, but only with the addition of many straps and belts, and Byron assured Senlin the experience was both uncomfortable and unnerving. It was more pleasant to back away from the heavens than to walk toward the grave.

Their journey, which had begun at sunset, was necessarily meandering. They had to circumvent jutting statues, friezes, air vents, skyports, pirate dens, solariums, and observatories. If anyone spotted one of the Sphinx's ancient grappling machines being driven by a stagheaded footman, it certainly would've elicited further investigation. Byron delayed turning on the wagon's lamps for as long as he could, but when clouds passed over the moon, he had no choice but to light the way.

They were awkward traveling companions. Senlin's impressions of Byron were both vague and conflicting. On the one hand, the stag had a barbarous wit, little patience, and could be aloof to an almost farcical degree. And yet on the other hand, Byron had defied the Sphinx's orders just so he and Edith could have a moment alone to say goodbye. Still, what do you say to someone who's scolded you about eating cat food, typed up your damning contract, and measured your inseam?

Luckily, they had a topic to discuss: Senlin's new persona, the Boskop Cyril Pinfield. Over the rattle of machinery and the scrape of grapnels, Byron educated Senlin on the race he would be impersonating. The natives of Boskopeia were the Tower's accountants. They kept the books for merchants and ringdoms alike. Boskops were considered honest, if not tedious. Renowned for their dislike of comfort and luxury, Boskops loathed flavor, fashion, laughter, rounded numbers, hot drinks, cold drinks, cocktails, and hats, for reasons that were not entirely clear even to Byron.

Senlin couldn't imagine a gloomier sort of person. He wondered aloud whether the Sphinx had selected the disguise to punish him, but Byron offered an explanation for the choice: "Most Pelphians would sooner converse with an unhappy goose than a Boskop. And that's precisely the point. You want to be left alone. You'll be safer if you are."

The rest of the journey, which took most of the night, was occupied by Byron's detailed account of the Boskop diet (which was painfully bland), their quirks (which were generally antisocial), and their fancies (which were very few and included things like button collecting, the breeding of mealworms, and poetry). "When in doubt," Byron concluded, "just blurt out the most disagreeable, unnecessary, and incongruous thing you can think of. Here, why don't we give it a try." He cleared his throat and said in a more formal tone, "Would you care for a ham sandwich, sir?"

"I don't like ham," Senlin said.

Byron shook his antlers. "Oh, come on! That's just garden-variety grousing. You can do better than that. You're trying to drive me away, not start an argument on the virtues of ham. The Pelphians are a contrarian race; if you give them something to disagree about, they will flock to you like gnats to a nostril. Now, once more." Byron held the hand mirror out as if it were a tray. "Would you care for a ham sandwich, sir?"

Senlin recalled an unlikable proctor from college, a man named Blester, who seemed to always have a handkerchief in his hand and who had the loathsome habit of sharing the details of his health, always unprompted. Inspired by the memory, Senlin said in a nasally falsetto, "No ham for me, thank you. I have a roaring case of gout."

Returning the mirror to its original angle, Byron made a small adjustment to the tiller to avoid a divot in the masonry. "All right. That's better. But really dig deep. *Repulse* me."

Their iron chariot rumbled and rocked. Its sallow lamps made little ponds of light upon the barren stone. The darkness seemed immense and their vehicle quite small.

"I've read that people taste like ham," Senlin said.

"There you are!" Byron's laughter reminded Senlin of a whickering horse. "See, now I don't want to talk to you at all."

The wall-walker's engine began to chug and seemed about to stall. Byron, suddenly very serious, plied the throttle and played with a pull valve on the dashboard. Senlin gripped the arm rail to stave off the wave of vertigo that the shuddering engine inspired in him. After a moment, the shaking subsided and the motor began running smoothly again. The scare reminded Senlin of his first brush with one of the Sphinx's engines. It had occurred while he was locked up with Edith in a wire coop outside the Parlor. He described the encounter to Byron, who smiled wistfully.

"That was a brick nymph," Byron said. "They used to be such a fixture of the Tower. They crawled all about, hunting after cracks and signs of deeper faults, patching and plastering and painting. Oh, so much color! The Tower was once as vibrant as a maypole. But that was years and years ago. And the brick nymphs are quite rare now." His curiosity aroused, Senlin asked what had happened to the mending machines. "A clever vandal discovered that he could turn the red medium that fired the Sphinx's engines into a powerful narcotic."

"You're talking about Crumb?"

"Yes, indeed. White Chrom is the Sphinx's medium, processed and diluted," Byron said. "Once people figured out that every brick nymph contained a small fortune of raw Crumb, the machines started to vanish in droves. Somewhere, there must be quite a mechanical graveyard."

Senlin found it strange to think that he had been addicted to essentially the same substance that fired Edith's arm. "I suppose that goes a long way toward explaining the Red Hand's demeanor. He's constantly smashed."

Byron snorted. "The effect of the medium is a little different before it's processed, but even so, you're not wrong." The wall-walker trundled by an enormous sandstone goat head jutting from the Tower wall like a hunter's trophy. They were close enough to pass under its great curling horns. The scrape of the walker's feet seemed to startle a colony of bats, which flew from the goat's open mouth in a noisy stream.

"But why not take the serum straight? Why cut it at all?" Senlin asked.

"Some adventuresome souls did just that: They injected the medium straight into their veins. The ones that weren't killed by the shock, or driven mad by hallucinations, soon discovered that the withdrawal is quite fatal. And before you ask, Edith is perfectly safe; the medium powers her arm but never enters her bloodstream."

It was nearly dawn when the wall-walker halted alongside an uninhabited pier. The joists that sank into the Tower had been sistered and repaired many times over the years. The decking was sun-bleached and full of gaps, though the wood had not rotted through quite yet. A crooked, doorless shed and a rusting crane were all that remained of the former outpost. Byron said the station had once been manned by machinists from Pelphia, whose job it was to help repair and refuel the brick nymphs. "That was back when the ringdoms still cared to do their part," the stag said sourly. "And before a crate of batteries was worth its weight in gold."

Byron pointed to a wooden walkway that ran out from the pier, curved along the face of the Tower, and vanished into shadow. The rickety path, which looked primed for collapse, led to Port Virtue, Pelphia's northern port. When Senlin arrived, he would hide outside the port and wait for the arrival of the airship *Half Carter*, a gray tub of a boat that would be flying the flag of Boskopeia.

"What's the Boskopeian flag look like?" Senlin asked.

"The crest is meant to resemble a gold seal on white stationery, I believe, but it looks remarkably like a urine stain on a bedsheet," the stag said. "When the *Half Carter*'s passengers disembark, you will join them and present to the customs officers the papers of Mr. Cyril Pinfield, an unremarkable tourist from Boskopeia."

"And you're a good forger, aren't you?" Senlin said.

"Not at all! This is just part of our elaborate plan to kill you in the most roundabout way."

Senlin was not enthusiastic about the prospect of dragging his luggage over such a flimsy pier, and yet, it seemed fitting that his final path to Pelphia would be such a forbidding one.

Byron helped him untie and unload his suitcase and trunk, plastered in the colorful travel seals of other ringdoms and bearing a dummy Boskop address.

His luggage unloaded, the two fell into that momentary quiet regard that passes for a farewell between some men. Senlin turned to go, then stopped and came around once more.

"Byron, the Sphinx said you'll be intercepting and reviewing my daily reports. I'm sorry you'll have to listen to me drone on." The stag's ears twitched, but he offered no quip. Senlin continued, "If there's an occasion that calls for the passing of a private message to a certain…captain, do you think you might be able to deliver it to her and not forward it to our employer?"

"Oh, so the former headmaster wishes to pass notes in class now, does he?" Byron said with a merry snort, but then seeing Senlin's open, almost mournful expression, the stag turned away. The light of dawn bled over the distant mountains. The dark specks of airships threw whisker-like shadows across the hazy sky. Byron cleared his throat. "Well, of course I can't sabotage my master's work, but sometimes a moth does get lost on its way home. Birds can be quite a nuisance."

"Well, crowned hornbills are abundant in the valley and they are especially fond of…" Senlin trailed off with a shake of his head and a chuckle. "Sorry, I'm a bit nervous, apparently. I meant to say, 'thank you.'"

The stag accepted Senlin's gratitude with a curt nod, then said, "May I offer you a parting word of advice? The Sphinx is not often agreeable, but she is very rarely wrong. Avoid your wife if you can. You'll both be safer if you do."

Not knowing what to say, Senlin gave a stilted bow, took up the handles of his trunk and suitcase, and set out across the narrow path of old wood and open air.

Chapter Four

Originally, the parrots of Pelphia served as town criers. They raised the alarm when fires, rogues, or raiders threatened the peace. But more recently, a neurosis has gripped the flock: The birds have become insatiable gossips. Do not be surprised if a parrot divulges a neighbor's secret or your own.

—*Everyman's Guide to the Tower of Babel*, VII. III

Even from the safety of his hotel room days later, Senlin still shuddered when he thought about his walk to the Pelphian port. Twice, a bird had sprung out of an unseen cleft in the rock face, nearly driving him over the brink with surprise. He'd lost count of all the planks that had cracked and fallen away when he tested them with his toe. One long section of the decking was slick with an oozing flow from the Tower, which he could not identify and did not investigate. By the time he reached the edge of the port, shrouded behind a line of potted palms, Senlin was certain he'd sooner exit via the black trail than return the way he'd come.

Despite the Sphinx's direction to mind his own business, Senlin had only lasted a day before he gave in to his instincts and mailed a letter to the duke. He wrote under his pseudonym, of course, but included his real address at the hotel. He fabricated a pretense for why the two of them should meet, a plot that he would later admit was not his finest. Then, before he could lose his nerve (or perhaps return to his senses),

Senlin handed the letter over to the concierge to address and deliver. Since parting with the letter, Senlin had alternated between cursing himself for being so rash and then resisting the temptation to send a second inquiry. He couldn't say, moment to moment, whether the idea of receiving a response from the duke was a source of excitement or alarm.

But he was certain of one thing: He could not spend another evening waiting and worrying alone in his hotel room. He needed to have his thoughts interrupted; he needed a distraction: a lecture or a play, perhaps. The odds of him bumping into Marya or the duke were slim. It was a big city, after all! Meanwhile, the odds of him pacing himself into an early grave only grew by the hour.

The decision made, he thrust his arms into his second coat and dashed out the door.

The corridor of the Bon Royal Hotel roared. Tourists in coattails and long-trained gowns coursed down the hall like an outgoing tide. Top hats, turbans, and parasols bobbed above the flow like the flotsam of a shipwreck. A wave of gentlemen lit cigars, adding a heavy fog to the surge. Senlin slipped into the current and let it carry him down the stairs that were as wild as a waterfall, out to the lobby, and finally onto the street.

The stars were out, or rather the city manager had turned the twinkling pilot lights up to full blast. The constellations all shone a uniform yellow, forming shapes that called to mind a mobile over a crib more readily than the cosmos. The outlines of a tiger, and a schooner, and a wine bottle filled the ceiling above his wedge of the noisy plaza. Wealthy men and women rode above the crowd on golden chairs, their litters carried on the shoulders of footmen. Boys on stilts strode between them, selling cigars and fresh flowers. Music poured from the Vivant. The crowds inside the Colosseum howled.

Senlin's prior expeditions to the Colosseum had taught him that it was impossible to travel anywhere quickly. If the crowd didn't detain you, a spectacle surely would. On his first foray across the soap-white plaza, Senlin had been waylaid by a crowd who'd gathered to observe a duel. The two men stood frozen in the fencing position, exchanging heated (if not creative) quips, until it became apparent they intended to shed more spit than blood, and the crowd dispersed. The following day, he had come across an unconscious woman, splayed upon the arms of a small crowd, all dutifully fanning her toward revival. Concerned for the woman's well-being, Senlin joined the effort just in time to see a bottle, clearly marked with skull and crossbones, pried from her hand. A physician tried to take the woman's pulse at her neck, at which point she began to giggle and writhe. His suspicion pricked, the doctor smelled the "poison" and pronounced it gin.

The spectacle this evening turned out to be a young woman wearing a flocky white dress. It appeared as if she'd somehow gotten her head stuck in a birdcage. The wicker cage, lanced here and there with freshly cut flowers, enclosed her face and her golden curls entirely. She gamboled through the crowded piazza like a waltzer without a partner. Senlin saw her coming from some distance and tried to avoid her, but she locked eyes with him through the wicker bars and would not let him elude her no matter how he sidestepped. She bounced upon his chest theatrically, clearing a little space around them, and then clutching her caged head, she cried, "Oh, the dark! I can't stand it! I repent! I repent! Have mercy!"

A pair of passing port guards laughed, comprehending the joke that Senlin did not. She pulled a white carnation from the bars and tucked it into Senlin's breast pocket.

"Thank you," he said. "Are you supposed to be someone in particular?"

"Aren't we all?" she said, already twirling back into the collapsing mob, crying as she went, "Oh, the dark! Oh, the wretched dark!"

Senlin pulled the flower from his pocket and smelled it. The scent conjured up a flock of unwanted memories. He saw the flash of the sun on the ocean outside his cottage window, inhaled the hazy smell of his flowering hedge, and heard Marya humming in another room.

He dropped the bud underfoot and hurried on.

The plaza was too much for him. Having no destination in mind, he followed the gaps in the crowd back to the spokes and rungs of the city streets, all spotted like a leopard with illuminated plates. When the lane was obstructed by ladies boarding a line of rickshaws he moved to the sidewalk, and when that was blocked by a gang of yapping dandies, he fled into an alley.

Party streamers hung like cobwebs between the buildings. Three parrots observed him from the rail of a balconet. One of the red-pinioned birds squawked, "You burned the roast, you stupid cow!" The crimson fellows on either side of him whistled and repeated, "Burned the roast! Burned the roast!" Senlin buried his hands in his pockets and hurried on, kicking a path through the newspaper and confetti. He told himself: He must listen to the Sphinx. He must be patient. He must keep his distance.

A clapboard shed stood against one wall of the alley. When he passed it, he glimpsed through the cracks in the door a bald hod inside, squatting upon heels with his eyes closed. In the next alley, he encountered another shed, then another, none larger than a casket, each humble as an outhouse. Senlin wondered how many of those poor wretches had begun as tourists, how many had abandoned happy if unremarkable lives, how many had lost their husbands, their children, their wives?

Again, he told himself he must be patient. He must keep his distance. He certainly mustn't, for example, go see the musical inspired by Marya's life and history, which the *Daily Reverie*'s theater critic had called "a revelation on the order of birth, death, and chocolate ganache."

A smaller parrot on a windowsill overhead fixed him with a doll-like gaze and screeched, "You stupid cow!"

"All right! All right!" Senlin shouted back, at last admitting to himself that perhaps his walk had not been entirely without pretext or destination from the beginning. "I'll go see the play."

The front of the Gasper Theater reminded him of a young woman's boudoir: all voluptuous cornices and plaster garlands. He stood in line, bought a ticket for the best remaining seat, and went inside. There was no lobby, only a dimly lit tunnel into the auditorium, where playbills crowded and overlapped in a competitive jumble, like initials carved on a schoolyard tree. Senlin did not recognize any of the titles. He accepted a program from an usher and found his seat in the fourth row.

He'd first learned of the play's existence when he'd happened upon a review in the *Daily Reverie*. The play had debuted three months earlier in April and was widely considered a triumph, though some complained about the casting, particularly the woman who played Marya. In his lengthy write-up, Oren Robinson described the actress as "a mockingbird singing a nightingale's song."

Despite the program's claim that the play was "a true history of Duchess Marya Pell, as approved by the duchess herself," Senlin didn't expect the play to be perfectly factual. If guides and histories took creative license, why wouldn't a play? Still, he hoped the show might give him a glimpse into Marya's experience since their parting.

The play commenced with a drone of tubas and bassoons. The curtain rose on a shoreside scene—a canvas beach, heaps of fishing nets, and a backdrop of blue sky and green sea. A ship's prow protruded from offstage. Stuffed seagulls were wired to its rails. Fishermen in waxy overalls pretended to chop papier-mâché fish on a wood block. Women in aprons held dolls on their hips and hung fake fish on racks to dry.

The starlet entered in a rush, and the audience applauded furiously.

The Mermaid's dress was a little tattered at the hem but, in stark contrast to the other fishwives, was white and unstained. Her hair, obviously a wig of scarlet yarn, stood out in a wild thicket. Senlin cringed at the embellished imitation of Marya, but he could not look away. Barefoot, she ran back and forth across the stage, chasing after seagulls that swung through the air on wires.

Her first lines were "The sea runs deep, and the mountains stand tall, but where they meet, mud buries all!" She slapped the back of a man chopping a paper fish. The actor laughed. She spun on her toe, animating her skirt enough to show her thighs. Senlin sank lower in his seat.

Then he walked onto the stage. Or rather, the actor playing Senlin's part in the Mermaid's history arrived. He announced himself by blowing his nose into a handkerchief. He wore an ill-fitting brown suit and a crooked stovepipe hat. A prosthetic nose, large as a beak, had been glued to the actor's face. While shaking out his handkerchief, he stumbled on a limb of driftwood. He paused to apologize to the log.

The audience roared with laughter. The Mermaid said, "Oh, no! Headmaster Fishbelly!"

Approaching the Mermaid, the headmaster said, "Little miss, shouldn't you be home packing for our field trip? Have you forgotten we leave first thing in the morning?" Fishbelly had a heady, congested sort of voice that made him sound old and sickly.

"But it's such a glorious day!"

"It's a gray day," Fishbelly said. "I'm sure it'll rain."

"A glorious day!" the girl in the crimson wig insisted. The band began to play a lively tune full of sawing violins and piping flutes. The Mermaid strode about the stage, her arms swinging. She climbed upon the ship rails and hooked arms with the working women. All the fishermen beamed, their scowls broken by her playful antics. Their chores turned into choreography. Everyone danced, save Fishbelly, who blew his nose into his handkerchief and examined the results as if he were trying to read his tea leaves.

The song mocked the boring, scrounging life of the sea. The wives clapped; the fishermen swung their catch by their tails; and the Mermaid led them in a chorus line at the front of the stage. Fishbelly chased after her: grasping, falling short, becoming tangled in the nets. When the song ended, Fishbelly scolded her, shaking his finger while she shook her head. He wanted her to be careful, to be staid, to be quiet, because she was his favorite student, a distinction the Mermaid clearly did not want.

The villagers drifted from the stage. A painted moon lowered from above. A cello began a gloomy drone.

"You won't be a girl much longer, little miss," Fishbelly said. "Soon, you will be old enough to marry." He touched her cheek and she recoiled from his veiny hand. He didn't seem discouraged by her revulsion. "You will need a guide in this life. And who better to guide you than your trusted, beloved headmaster?"

In the audience, Senlin's stomach churned. He watched the beach disappear and a room take its place: a bed and a tattered afghan, an ancient vanity with a tarnished mirror. A faded bouquet of flowers hung among a string of paper dolls on the wall. It was unmistakably a young girl's bedroom. Inside, the Mermaid packed for the trip, happy and blithe and unaware that Fishbelly lurked in the shadows outside her window.

While he spied on her, he sang a sinister song about his plans for tricking her into marrying him. The audience booed his strategy, but applauded the actor's rich baritone, which was nothing like his character's phlegmy speech.

As nauseating as this version of him was, Senlin took comfort in the fact that it was also patently false. Was it any surprise that the duke would want to see Marya's previous marriage written out of her history? Was it any surprise that he would take the opportunity to skewer her first husband? But what did Senlin care what the duke thought of him? Let the man have his petty revenge! It revealed nothing of Marya's feelings. So far, the details of this supposed "true history" were the sort of thing one would divulge to even a casual acquaintance. The rest was just lies!

A paper sun rose, and the stage changed again, this time becoming two boxcars in a train, cut in half so the audience could see their interiors. The backdrop moved. The painted hills and hamlets seemed to flow by.

Fishbelly's class was introduced as they boarded the passenger car, six children in all, who, when posed in a line, formed a perfect little stair of age and height. Fishbelly alternated between scolding and swatting at his students, who were all rosy cheeked and dressed in pinafores. Quickly tiring of the effort, Fishbelly sank into an empty seat by the window, took out a book, and began to read aloud. "It says here in the *Everyman's Guide*, which is the most reliable book ever written on the subject, that in the Tower, all we will need are handkerchiefs!" The man at Senlin's elbow laughed so hard he began to cough.

"What about maps and tickets and reservations and a plan?" the Mermaid asked as she attempted to corral the children onto the bench seats.

"Two handkerchiefs apiece!" Fishbelly declared. Setting down his book, he stood and passed out the white pocket squares to the confused children, then returned to his reading, apparently satisfied that his duty had been done.

The Mermaid, who seemed to be growing more mature by the moment to compensate for Fishbelly's disregard, gathered the wilding children to the dining car, leaving the headmaster with his beak in his book.

In the dining car, a porter told them they couldn't have any tea because all the teacups were being used. The Mermaid said that it was quite all right and asked him to bring a big pot of tea anyway. Then she opened the colorful carpetbag she carried with her and unpacked seven teacups onto the table. The youngest child pointed out that the cups had all been broken and glued back together. When another asked why she kept broken cups, the Mermaid stroked their cheeks and touched their noses and sang a ballad while they listened attentively. The chorus of her sentimental lullaby went: "It's perfectly all right not to be perfect. A chip or a crack can be precious, too."

The words pierced Senlin like a stake. He shut his eyes and wished he could plug his ears. Marya had told the duke about her beloved heirlooms, and about his inane obsession with handkerchiefs, and about his idiotic faith in the *Everyman's Guide*. Why would she share such intimate details if not to inspire intimacy? And if she was being so frank with the duke, why had she then authorized this grotesque vision of him: a big-nosed, lecherous boor?

Unless she thought it fair. Unless she found it true.

The play continued through scenes in the Basement, where the Mermaid narrowly survived swindlers and thieves, and on to the Parlor, where dozens of identically dressed Mr. and Mrs. Mayfairs argued and reconciled, danced and canoodled, while the Mermaid weaved through them, singing an ironic verse about the joys of marriage. In the Baths, she was immediately approached by a hunchbacked painter in beret and smock, who lured her to his studio apartment with promises of a warm meal and a sympathetic ear. Once there, his vile intentions were quickly revealed. When she refused to undress for him and lie upon his wretched mattress, piled with stained rags, the deformed artist began to chase her about. He sang a feverish song about what an honor it was that he should invite her to "thrive upon my canvas, then writhe upon my bed."

Just when the grotesque, wild-eyed artist tore the Mermaid's sleeve from her dress and trapped her against his bed, the trumpets in the orchestra blew a fanfare. A troop of men rushed onto stage. Their leader, a handsome blond with a beard shaped like a spade, drew his sword. Behind him, a man in white pajamas with red-painted hands was followed by soldiers in black jackets.

"Get off of her, you villain!" the handsome lead cried. The audience cheered. "I am a duke of the ringdom of Pelphia, and this woman is under my protection."

The painter whirled about, drawing a pistol from under his oily smock. He fired, and the flash of powder felled one of the duke's men.

The duke dashed forward and plunged his sword under the painter's arm.

"Mercy, sir! Have mercy! I am but a cripple!" the painter cried.

"If you're hale enough to torment this woman, then you're well enough to suffer my sword."

The Red Hand dragged the blubbering artist offstage, singing a nursery rhyme about the hods and the hollow ground as he went. The two uninjured soldiers removed their fallen comrade, leaving the duke and the Mermaid alone.

A spotlight swaddled them. The tragic scene all but vanished. She stood, her face turned down, looking as vulnerable as a scolded child.

"Are you all right?" the duke asked.

The Mermaid threw her arms around his neck, kissed his cheek, and between sobs, blessed and thanked him. The music swelled with the intro of their now-famous duet: "The Heart Is Lost When Love Is Found."

Senlin could bear no more. Amid the huffs and muttered objections of the audience, he squeezed down the row and out to the aisle. He fled the theater as if it were on fire.

Chapter Five

Oh, how airmen love to say our stars are wrong! They call Nature the supreme artist, apparently forgetting that Nature also paints our deck chairs with bird droppings and our backs with hairy moles. Pelphia's constellations were designed by a panel of famous artists and installed by master plumbers, not plopped willy-nilly about the sky by drunken Nature. Really, who's to say it's our stars that are wrong?

—Oren Robinson of the *Daily Reverie*

What sort of man was the duke? The *Reverie* had painted him as eloquent, charming, and beloved. The playwright behind *The Mermaid's Tale* seemed to agree. But how could Senlin reconcile that heroic ideal with Ogier's brutish vision of the man? Though, admittedly, Ogier wasn't exactly a paragon of morality: Ogier the thief, the forger, the fraud who had no qualms about talking desperate women into disrobing for him. Perhaps the painter was the real villain. After all, the Sphinx had not claimed Ogier as one of her agents, which could very well mean Ogier was loyal to Marat.

For all the newspapers Senlin had read, he still had no idea whether the duke actually *cared* for Marya. For all he knew, Duke Wilhelm might be a perfect cad. He might begrudge Marya her beloved books or cluck his tongue at her tomfoolery. He might hate how she attacked the piano like a stubborn drawer. The duke was probably the sort of man who never took pleasure in a difficult poem, never stood before a painting so long that he fell into it. He was probably the sort who—

Senlin stopped short, realizing what he was doing. He was dressing the duke in the rags of his own insecurity. Hadn't he been the one to fail Marya first? Hadn't he dallied in the Baths when he should have hurried? Hadn't he been unfaithful to her?

Senlin rushed out of the theater's entrance tunnel, feeling almost eager to see the city again. But he found it erased. Beyond the lights of the marquee, the white city was drowned in gray rain.

Puzzled by the indoor monsoon, Senlin stuck out a cupped hand, catching water as it spouted from the theater's awning. The rain was warm and, when he brought it to his nose, smelled antiseptic. The luminous quartz dials set into the street made some puddles glow.

"If you're looking to poison yourself, I'd recommend gin. It takes a little longer but tastes a lot better."

Following the reedy voice, Senlin turned to find a man smoking a cigarette from an ivory stem. He wore his long, white hair in a braid so tight it made the already pronounced bones of his skull stand out further. The black feather collar of his coat lent him a vulture-like appearance.

"Why does it smell like a public house?" Senlin shook the water from his hand.

"It's the ethanol. The city gets a drink every month whether she needs it or not. She always needs it."

"But why?"

"To discourage the pox, of course. And to clean the streets."

"But where does it all go—"

"Are you mocking me?" The vulture squinted at him sharply. Surprised by the accusation, Senlin couldn't respond before he rattled on. "Do you think I didn't get a sufficient ribbing in there? I wrote poetry! Odes for the ages, I wrote. No one talks about them. Oh no!"

"I beg your pardon, but I don't know who you are," Senlin said.

"Anton Gavelle." When Senlin shook his head dumbly, Gavelle repeated his name twice, and with mounting suspicion. "*The Everyman's Guide*—you've heard of that, haven't you?"

"Yes, of course." Now it was Senlin's turn to squint. "You're the author?"

Gavelle scoffed. "Oh, yes, I ran up and down the Tower ten times. I went down every alley, looked around every corner, and knocked on every door. No, of course I'm not the author! There wasn't any author. I was one of hundreds of writers, *poorly paid* writers. Oh, don't give me that look! I know what people say. What you forget is that we were all very young and aspiring and I'm sure a little doe-eyed. But there was no conspiracy to mislead our readers, at least not on my part. Little did I know that the errors of my peers and the liberties taken by future editors—who deleted or declawed every word of caution, every warning, because they were invariably unpopular with someone, somewhere—that all of that corruption, deception, and incompetence would be credited to me. And god knows, you can't remove a public stain once it sets." Gavelle drew upon his ivory stem, his lips tightening into a pale rosette.

In recent months, Senlin had more than once fantasized about tearing the pages from the *Everyman's Guide* and feeding them one by one to its author. Now that he stood before this man who'd had a hand in beguiling him, in calling him to this awful place, all he felt was pity.

Senlin stared out at the rain-lathered road. If he ignored the acrid smell and the cloudiness of the water, the scene was almost familiar—the shrunken world of a passing storm.

"You didn't like the play either?" Gavelle asked.

"No, I didn't care for it." Senlin drew a deep breath and spoke in a long exhalation. "All the characters were flat as a penny."

The writer plucked the burnt cigarette stub from his stem and threw it onto the sodden street. "I almost feel sorry for that country girl who married the duke." Gavelle opened a black umbrella—a vulture spreading his wings. "Apart from the dinner table, Pelphians only know two appetites: one calls for a bed, the other a stage. And often the two aren't far apart." Gavelle disappeared into the downpour.

The rain accomplished what the late hour could not: It drove the crowds indoors. Green copper spouts spat water onto the empty streets. The culverts gulped and gasped like drowning men. With the stars snuffed out, the constellations Senlin had hoped to use to navigate his way back to the hotel were now invisible. Rainwater funneled down his collar and pooled in his boots. His brief nostalgia at the storm's appearance quickly turned to revulsion. This was not rain. He detected the stink of oil, offal, and rubbish under the ethanol. He covered his mouth and nose with his handkerchief and tilted his head down to keep the water from his eyes.

He darted into an alley and took shelter under a balcony, deciding it was better to wait the storm out than ruin another coat. But no sooner had he escaped the foul pelting than he heard a muffled argument and then the sounds of wet, rhythmic slaps.

Midway down the alley, lit by the foggy light of a burlesque theater window, three figures grappled against the wall.

Fearing he had stumbled upon some terrible crime, Senlin stole along the deeper shadows until he was near enough to observe the commotion without being seen himself.

Two of the men were dressed in soggy dinner jackets. Undone bow ties hung under their collars. The larger of the pair wore gold wire spectacles, which did little to improve the intelligence of his expression. The other gentleman, who had a beard that nearly hid his shapeless jaw, pinned a much shorter hod to the alley wall. The hod was dark skinned; the stubble on his skull was as sparse as the hair of a boar. White paint streamed down his face and flowed over his iron collar. The hod clutched something squarish against his deflated chest. The spectacled bully dunked a paintbrush into a pot of whitewash and slapped it across the hod's face. He drew the brush back and forth in deliberate strokes. His bearded companion laughed and resisted the hod's efforts to free himself.

"I think I'm getting the hang of this, Humphrey!" the bully with the paintbrush said. "Even strokes leave the best coat. Even strokes!"

The hod fought to catch his breath between the rain and paint.

"Excuse me," Senlin said. The two men twisted about, their dumb smirks stiffened by shock.

"What do you want?" the bespectacled bully demanded.

"A fair fight," Senlin said, and punched him between the eyes.

The blow broke the man's glasses and his nose. He dropped the paint pot, and it burst upon the ground, throwing a sash of white across Senlin's front.

His bearded friend let go of the hod, and after fishing through his pockets, drew out a penknife. He held it out as if it were a fencing foil, but his "en garde" position only exposed his knee. Senlin stamped on the top of the offered joint, and the man fell, dropping his penknife into the growing pool of white beneath them.

The two bullies grasped each other, attempting to regain both their footing and their composure. Forgotten for the moment, the hod slid down the wall onto his heels.

"You call that fair?" the taller of the two said, his voice muddled by a broken nose.

"Well, there are two of you," Senlin said.

"Then you won't complain if we don't take turns!"

Iren had taught Senlin to spot the markers of experienced brawlers— their form, stance, and gaze, and yet even without her considered help, he would've likely suspected these bullies had never been in a brawl. The bloody one cocked his balled-up hand back behind his ear. His bearded companion held his soft fists so far out from his body it looked as if he'd already thrown his punches and was hoping Senlin would do him the service of running into them.

"Gentlemen, we are getting wet," Senlin said. "Why don't we all just go home and wring ourselves out?"

"Look, Humphrey! See how quickly his courage melts!" the taller one crowed. The two shuffled about in ponding water until one stood on either side of Senlin, who held out his hands, still pleading for peace. The bullies pedaled their fists and kicked the milky water. Both seemed to be waiting for the other one to throw the first punch.

The taller brute sneered and said, "Here we go, Humphrey! Here we g—" The corner of a cobblestone struck him on the temple. The man fell without bracing himself and landed on his side.

Still clutching the brick, the white-faced hod turned toward Senlin.

"Now, wait a—" Senlin began. He didn't have time to duck before the hod hurled the brick at him. Though the shock of the moment seemed to slow the brick's passage, it did nothing to quicken Senlin's reaction. All he could do was watch the missile come.

The stone sailed over his shoulder. Senlin turned in time to see Humphrey, his face a crater of blood and splinted bone, fall to his back amid a great splash.

The water at Senlin's feet began to blush with blood.

He gaped at the hod, and his voice shook with anger when he demanded, "Why on earth did you do that?"

The hod squatted over the man he'd struck first, and finding he was still breathing, the hod pressed his knee into the side of the man's neck and gave it a violent jerk. The sound of snapping bone made Senlin shudder.

Standing again, the hod gave Senlin a conspiratorial nod. "Come the Hod King," he said, then turned on his heel and ran.

Without much hope, Senlin knelt to check the fallen men for breath and found none. The diamond-paned windows of the dance hall cast an argyle light upon the morbid scene. Inside, the band concluded a wild mazurka, and the dancers applauded and cheered.

Senlin still wasn't accustomed to seeing the shocked expressions of the dead. There had been a time in his life when he had not known that peaceful repose was often a mortician's trick. Perhaps his ignorance had been a gift.

He turned away, and his eye fell upon the corner of something jutting up from the water. He retrieved it from the puddle, recognizing it as the object the hod had chosen to clasp rather than defend himself. The rectangular article was wrapped in oil cloth. By its weight, Senlin guessed it was likely a book, probably a ruined one.

Without the murderer to point a finger at, it didn't seem wise for him to dally over the bodies. He tucked the wrapped book under his coat and left the alley with his head down and his collar up.

Chapter Six

There really is no point to teasing a Boskop. They are insensible to wit. One might as well whistle for a footstool or attempt to romance a mop.

—Oren Robinson of the *Daily Reverie*

From behind his lectern in the hotel lobby, Mr. Aloysius Stull dispatched porters to fetch luggage, deliver dishes, freshen vases, remove spots, change linens, uncork bottles, and fulfill every wish of the temporary kings and queens of the Bon Royal. He looked like a conductor directing a symphony through a difficult musical passage. He waved his arms and smoothed his hair, which seemed to grow grayer by the minute. He managed to seem at once passionate and absolutely constrained.

Yet, when he looked up and saw the Boskop, Mr. Pinfield, drenched to his socks and splashed with whitewash, Mr. Stull flinched like a man discovering a toothache. He marked the milky puddle spreading across his wool carpet with particular concern.

Stull snapped at two porters, who discerned the urgent need at once. They swaddled the guest, coat and all, in an immense, luxuriant bathrobe. They provided a towel for him to stand on, and wrapped another around his head, which, despite the guest's half-hearted protests, they twisted into a turban. When they were finished, little more than the Boskop's face was left uncovered.

"There! Isn't that better?" Mr. Stull said, his poise tested but not broken.

"Yes...no," the guest said, lifting his chin. "I'm afraid I've been involved in an accident."

"Oh, I see!" Stull said as if it were a revelation. "Shall I summon a doctor, or perhaps a tailor?"

The Boskop shrugged off the porter who'd begun dabbing at his face with a hand towel. "Given the circumstances, I think your constabulary might be more appropriate."

"Oh, my goodness! Of course I'll send for them at once. What shall I say is the crime?"

The guest began one answer, then fumbled into a second, and while struggling to keep the turban out of his eyes, seemed to decide to spare them all the embarrassment of a third attempt. "Please just say it's urgent. I'll wait for them in my room."

The porters who'd brought the bathrobe and towels had returned with a bellman's cart, the base of which was covered with yet more towels. "I can walk," the guest insisted.

"Ah, but think how majestic you will look riding through the halls and in the elevator aboard such a gleaming steed. How regal! How mysterious! How much better for the carpets."

With a defeated sigh, the Boskop boarded the cart and gripped the brass bar at his ear as if he were riding a tram.

As the porters wheeled Mr. Pinfield off to the freight elevator, Mr. Stull called after them, "Magnificent! A sultan glides among us! Bon voyage, sir! Pleasant dreams!"

The moment Senlin was delivered to his room, he shucked off his coat and soaked clothes, and drew a hot bath. He was not tempted to linger in the tub. Not only was the water quick to discolor, but he was also sick of being damp. Besides, he wanted to have a look at what the hod had left behind before the law arrived. He scrubbed himself off as quickly as he could and emerged while the water still steamed.

He donned a fresh robe—what a luxury it was to be dry!—and

opened the hod's parcel. The unwrapped oilcloth was nearly as large as his bed. He was right about it containing a book. The attractive leather-bound volume was cold and a little clammy, but the pages hadn't warped from the damp. Whoever had wrapped it had done an excellent job. He read the title aloud: "*Trilobites and Other Ancient Arthropods.*" It was a comprehensive study of fossilized shellfish, exactly the sort of book that would languish in a library for decades before anyone called for it. But then, the content hardly mattered. He knew what hods did to books. He thumbed to the back, expecting to find the words obliterated by blots of ink. To his surprise, the text was untouched and intact.

He felt a pang of shame. He shouldn't assume that every hod was one of Luc Marat's mystics. Perhaps the hod who'd bashed in the brains of those alleyway bullies was a paleontologist or an oceanographer or . . . Though, he had yelled the phrase "Come the Hod King," which certainly sounded like the sort of thing Marat would ask his followers to call him. Still . . .

The front board bore the brassy traces of binder's glue. When Senlin shook the leaves, a brittle bookplate fell out, bearing the name Ostraka University. On the plate, three stately pillars were laced in ivy and underscored with the motto: "Out of ignorance: inquiry. Out of inquiry: proof."

Senlin examined the seams for signs of hidden pockets but found none. There were some numbers scrawled in the margins here and there. It was as if a student had used the book as scratch paper for their mathematics homework. Otherwise, the volume was unremarkable.

Without a murderer to hand over to the authorities, Senlin knew he was more likely to be treated as a suspect than a witness. He had considered not reporting the murders, but then, he couldn't be sure he hadn't been seen in the alley or during his suspicious dash back through the empty, rain-flooded streets. His whitewashed jacket, which certainly had made an impression on Mr. Stull and his staff, tied him neatly to the crime, as did the spectacle glass lodged in his knuckles.

It had occurred to him that he could just run away. He could flee to the skyport, board the next departing flight, and send a messenger to the Sphinx with his new address.

But he just couldn't stomach the idea of leaving, not after everything it had taken to get here. Not while Marya's fate was still uncertain.

Senlin knew it was possible a local officer might recognize him as the burglar of the Baths or dread Captain Mudd, but Commissioner Pound and his crew's homecoming hadn't happened yet, and the published warrant for Captain Mudd was laughably inaccurate.

No, at the end of the day, his best option was to remain calm, to lean on his alias, and to hope the constables would think a Boskop too boring to be involved in something as salacious as murder.

While he waited, he delivered his evening report to one of the Sphinx's mechanical messengers. Except for his attendance at the play, which he omitted to save himself a scolding, he gave a full account of events. He repeated the hod's salute to the Hod King, shared his suspicion of Luc Marat's involvement, and concluded with the title of the disappointing book he'd recovered from the alley. He could only hope the Sphinx would be so taken with these details that she would not think to ask why he'd been out roving the city at night.

The moth released, Senlin fell heavily upon the bed in his terry cloth robe. The constabulary could be at his door at any moment. He needed to gather his thoughts. He closed his eyes and tried to think of what he would say.

Even for a dream, the scene seemed gauzy and golden. Senlin stared down a long banquet table that gleamed with the light of candelabras. Empty plates and bowls awaited the arrival of the first course. Servants poured wine over the shoulders of the seated guests, men with waxed mustaches and ladies with coiffures that bared their necks. They radiated prosperity and joy. A string quartet played sweetly in a corner of the vaulted dining room. Senlin's view swung gently, as if he were floating, as if he were riding along with one of the Sphinx's butterflies.

The guests of honor were seated at the head of the table: a golden-haired man with a beard like a spear, and a woman whose face Senlin could not quite see through the forest of centerpieces. But even by glimpses—a twist of her hair, the curl of one ear—he recognized her. He would always recognize her.

The duke raised his glass, rang it with a carving knife, hushing the music and laughter, drawing every eye to himself. He opened his mouth to deliver a magnificent toast, but then closed it again. He bowed to his new bride as if to say, *After you*. The guests all applauded until she stood. Her dress was as white as a mountain peak. She peered down the table, through the steam of bloody roasts that had suddenly materialized on the plates and the tall candle flames and the growing sprays of flowers—she peered through it all, directly at him, spying upon her happiness.

If he could've fled, Senlin would have. But the dream would not let him go nor look away. She squinted at him as one would squint at a fingerprint on a looking glass. "Why, Headmaster Fishbelly, is that you? Where are your children? What has happened to them?"

Senlin bolted upright and tumbled from his bed. He landed on his stomach and the heels of his hands. Something like a gunshot had startled him awake. He rolled onto his back and looked at the granddaughter clock on his bedside. It was nearly eight thirty. He'd slept through the night.

The door to his room rattled again, the sound suggesting more a battering ram than a human hand.

Recovering his wits, he called out that he was coming. He saw in the mirror that he was still wearing his robe. Briefly, he wondered if he had time to dress, then the gunshot knock came again, and he hurried to open the door.

Expecting a constable or two, he was surprised to find himself confronted by a troop of six soldiers, all of them armed and dressed in the crisp black uniforms of the House of Pell.

The men were led by two quite remarkable persons. The foremost gentleman, whom Senlin judged to be in his sixties, was excessively tall and militarily dressed. He wore his unnaturally dark hair oiled up into a sort of shark fin. A short black cape was tossed over one shoulder and a striking pin adorned his lapel: three white horizontal lines in a square of honey gold. He was clean-shaven yet gray-cheeked, and his heavily lidded eyes suggested a lethargy that his gaze did not. From his belt hung a pistol that was so long it ended past his knees. It seemed more a hip cannon than a sidearm.

Striking as he was, he was nearly eclipsed by the woman at his side. She wore a suit of golden armor, or at least the top half of one. But her cuirass and gauntlets didn't possess the common bulk of armor. They were as finely fitted as a blouse and gloves. Her hair was red as a flame with twists of smoky white at her temples. She wore a concerted scowl. Senlin had the distinct impression that she was furious with him. She still held up her gold fist, as if she had not yet decided whether or not to continue knocking now that the door was open, and he was standing in it.

"Morning, Mr. Pinfield," the tall man said. "I'm General Andreas Eigengrau. This is Wakeman Georgine Haste. We've come to see you about some murders."

Chapter Seven

Approach an officer of the law as you might a stray
dog in the street: Use dulcet tones; keep your hands
out of your pockets; and don't look them too long in
the eye.

—*Everyman's Guide to the Tower of Babel*, IV. II

No, no! Please, don't shuffle those," Senlin said to the constable rifling through one of the stacks of newspapers that consumed the room's dresser. "They're on loan, and there's a fee
if I return them out of order," he explained when the officer frowned
at him.

General Eigengrau did not seem the sort of man to move about a
room unnecessarily, perhaps preferring that a room move around him,
but he gave his man a small, conciliatory signal. The black-booted
officer quit scrambling the newspapers and began ripping the drawers from the bureau. Senlin's shirts and underclothes fell into heaps,
which the officer probed with his polished toe.

The first thing Eigengrau did when he planted his feet in the middle
of the room was ask for Senlin's credentials. Senlin produced his, or
rather Cyril Pinfield's, proof of citizenry to the ringdom of Boskopeia,
his business card, his accountant's license, and a letter from his bank.
Senlin could only hope Byron was the talented forger he believed himself to be.

Continuing his scrutiny of Pinfield's papers, Eigengrau said, "You were saying, sir: You felt unwell, so you left the play early, ran out into the rain. Whereupon you observed Mr. Cavendish and Mr. Brown with a hod in an alley." Senlin was doing his best to pay attention to the general while still keeping an eye on Wakeman Haste, who was making a thorough and more thoughtful sweep of the room. Senlin made an effort to avoid glancing at the cigar box full of the Sphinx's messengers. They were wrapped in a thin layer of tobacco to deflect a casual inspection. He could only hope she didn't smoke.

The general continued his summary. "You observed a scuffle between the three men. Then you approached and struck Cavendish—"

"It wasn't a scuffle," Senlin said. "They were torturing that man, the hod."

"Not an uncommon sport," Eigengrau said. "Though it's not usually a prelude to murder."

Wakeman Haste's angry expression seemed to soften when she spotted the cigar box tucked under an errant copy of the *Daily Reverie*. Her mechanical fingers were lithe enough to catch the subtle lip of the lid and flip it open. She peered in at the tobacco-wrapped moths and smiled.

Ah, Senlin thought, *of course she smokes.*

Shortly before his departure, Senlin had asked the Sphinx why she couldn't dispatch her Wakemen if she was so certain Marat and his hods posed a danger to the Tower. Surely the Wakemen were better equipped for such an enterprise, and wasn't that the entire purpose for their existence? The Sphinx had replied, "Need I remind you that Marat was once a Wakeman, too? The fact is, my employees are not as reliable as they were. I still hold out hope that some of them remain loyal. But some have aged and softened beyond usefulness; some have been corrupted by vice or luxury; some have had their sanity eroded by age and activity." Senlin thought that a very charitable way of describing the Red Hand, but he decided against correcting the Sphinx. "Some Wakemen are now more loyal to their hosts than to me. I admit, I neglected them. But there's no way to know now who I can trust. I suggest you continue to choose your confidants very, very carefully."

Wakeman Haste plucked out a cigar and rolled it between her thumb and forefinger admiringly.

Snatching up the cut-crystal lighter from his bedside table, Senlin smiled as he approached Haste. "Those are quite remarkable. They're hand rolled by gibbons in Algez. Gorgeous creatures." He flicked the flint wheel ineptly, drawing no flame. "They're diligent workers, though they do like to lick the cigars." The Wakeman, who'd nearly gotten the cigar to her lips, now scowled at it. "It gives them a musty flavor, but it's all part of the experience."

"A monkey licked this?" she asked.

"Technically, gibbons are apes."

She dropped the cigar back into the box and ignored Senlin's expression of mock hurt as he clicked the lighter shut. "Can you describe the hod?" Haste asked.

"Oh, come now, Haste," Eigengrau interjected. "Bald, underfed, lame, bad teeth, and an iron collar. They all look the same. You might as well ask him to describe a pigeon." The general folded Pinfield's credentials and tucked them under his arm. That seemed a bad sign to Senlin.

"He was not very tall," Senlin said. Hoping to appease Haste by answering her question. "About yea high." He held out his hand to mid-chest level. "He had very narrow shoulders. Was perhaps fifty years old. He was covered in whitewash at the time, but I think I could identify him if you found him. I'm very observant."

"That's very convenient," Haste said, crossing her beautiful arms. They chimed softly where they rubbed together. Wisps of steam rose from the engraved joints of her elbows. What Senlin had initially mistaken for a suit of armor was undeniably one of the Sphinx's engines. He saw her artistry in the etchings that swirled across the muscular plates. Those patterns were as complex as burl wood. "You admit to fighting with Cavendish and Brown, but you insist you didn't kill them. No, a short, narrow-shouldered, fifty-year-old hod killed them. He picked up a stone and struck first one, and then the other, *dead*, while you stood there being—how did you put it? *Very observant*."

"Yes," Senlin said, seeing he had not won any ground with her.

"No." She shook her head. "I think there was no hod. There was only Cavendish, Brown, and you in that alley. Perhaps they insulted you earlier in the evening. That's usually how these things go. They insulted your terrible fashion or your clumsy dancing or your inability to satisfy a woman. You took offense. You followed them into the alley, picked up a convenient cobblestone, and took them by surprise. Once they were dead, you splashed some paint about to make it look like a hod had been involved."

"'That's usually how these things go'?" Senlin said, his calm cracking. He knew she was baiting him, hoping that he might say something rash or revelatory. "Is presumption as good as proof here? That must make your job so much easier. Why even have an investigation, or courts, or a king for that matter when we have you to tell us how these things usually go?"

She strode straight at him, raising a gold finger as she came. The floor still trembled even after she stopped. "Why did you intervene on the hod's account? You expect me to believe that, in the middle of a storm, you saw a hod getting bumped about in an alley by a couple of drunks, and rather than go inside where it was dry or call someone of authority, you decided to mount a personal crusade for a hod? What am I supposed to make of that? You're either a madman or a liar!"

Haste fairly panted with anger. The air in the room felt thin and overused.

If they took him to their offices, he was sure he would be exposed. The moment they checked his ticket against the ship's passenger list, they would see it was a fake, and the rest would unravel. No, he could not afford to be taken in. He decided to try a different tack, something to remind them what he was: an awkward Boskop.

"I'll tell you what I am. I am a misfit!" Senlin's voice cracked as he shouted. Senlin heard the familiar yet no less electrifying sound of swords being drawn from their scabbards. There was no going back now, so he thundered on. "I am an oddity! Even among my countrymen, I am the subject of ridicule. They mock me because I am not ashamed of my passions. I am proud of my snail farm, my lace collection, my poetry. All my life, they've called me *namby-pamby* and *milksop*, because there's nothing that threatens a bully's delicate virility so much as the honest passions of other men. This world is full of tyrants, full of men who can't raise themselves up by their own pursuits, and so they spend their lives pulling others down to their low and loathsome level.

"When I saw those men tormenting that hod—that human being— I ran to his defense. If I had known the hod would take advantage of my help and kill them, I might not have intervened. I do not love bloodshed." Senlin closed his eyes, his voice shaking with delved emotion and genuine fear. "But I did what I wish others would have done for me. I stood up to the bullies."

When he opened his eyes, Senlin found Georgine Haste staring at him. She seemed to be trying to read something printed in very small letters on the inside of his skull. At last, she broke off, making a shooing motion at the other officers. The sound of swords sliding back into their sheaths filled Senlin with relief.

"Did this hod say anything to you?" Eigengrau asked.

The question caught Senlin off guard, and when he hesitated, he felt he had no choice but to confess the truth and hope it helped his case. "He did. He said something I didn't understand. He said, 'Come the Hod King.'"

Eigengrau and Haste exchanged a look that suggested they'd heard the phrase before.

"Perhaps we should move this conversation to a more formal setting," Eigengrau said, nodding at an officer who produced a set of shackles. "Don't look so forlorn, Mr. Pinfield. It's just a little public theater. Half of Pelphia has been arrested. No one minds it. It's just one more way to see your name in print. Now, if you'd like to make a scene, I'd suggest you wait until we're on the street. No point shouting yourself hoarse where there's no one to hear it. The officers will be happy to thrash you to heighten the drama if you like."

Feeling a sudden and radiating numbness in his chest, Senlin held out his wrists. He watched as the irons were placed on them. They felt heavy and cold. As he observed the tightening of the screws, his hands seemed to grow more distant. His vision began to retreat. He saw the top of his head as if he were standing upon his own shoulders, looking down. The hotel room shrank to the size of a desk drawer. His bed was like a sheet of stationery. The soldiers were as small as nibs and paper clips and coins. The drawer of the room began to close, and the darkness clutched at him.

"Excuse me," a young, unsteady voice said.

Senlin caught himself just as his trembling knees were about to buckle. He inhaled, and the breath brought the room into relief again.

The young porter in the doorway looked a little terrified but also thrilled to have happened upon such an extravagant scene. He stood at full attention in his crimson livery, holding a lidded serving dish. "I have Mr. Pinfield's breakfast. And a letter."

"Come here, lad," the general said. The porter stepped around the officers, who made no effort to spare his inconvenience. Hunting about for some clear space to put his tray down amid the general mess of clothes and newsprint, the porter had no choice but to balance the tray on an unsteady stack of papers. He lifted the dome cover on two pieces of pale, naked toast, a teacup full of tepid water, and a wedge of lemon. A stately letter lay on a second saucer.

As the general took the letter, he observed the man's bland breakfast. "Hoping to punish a tapeworm, Mr. Pinfield?" he asked with a chuckle. He gave the youth a few coins, then turned to face the shackled guest. "Since you're indisposed at the moment, perhaps you'll allow me to..." Eigengrau had already broken the seal and begun to read the letter when his voice trailed off.

When he looked up again, there was a different sort of light behind his eyes. "Yes, we can take those off, now," he said to the same officer who'd screwed down the locks. The relief that filled Senlin's chest was only slighted diluted by his confusion.

As the irons were removed, Eigengrau said, "It seems you have some business to attend to this afternoon, Mr. Pinfield. I wouldn't want to keep you from it. We appreciate your time this morning." He returned Senlin's credentials along with the opened letter and gave what seemed a knowing smile. "We'll let you know if we need anything further. I don't imagine we will."

And with that, the general and his officers filed from the room, departing as abruptly as they'd arrived.

Georgine Haste was last out and nearly through the door when Senlin said, "Excuse me!" She hesitated, turning her head just enough to show she was listening but would not listen long. The shield of her back was etched with a great tree whose leaves, canopy, limbs, and roots seemed to curl in, embracing her. A golden tree of life. "Do you know who the Hod King is?"

For a scant second, it seemed she might answer, then she swallowed hard and said: "It's none of your concern." She slammed the door so sharply the gust sent papers fluttering to the floor.

Senlin looked at the letter in his hand. The stock was made of fine, crisp linen. He opened it and read:

Dear Mr. Pinfield,

Thank you for your letter. I'd like to hear more of your proposal. Why don't we discuss the business later this morning? I have a regular table at the Coterie Club above the Colosseum. I trust you're familiar with it. I've enclosed my card. Show it to the man at the door, and he'll see you in.

Cordially Yours,
Duke Wilhelm Horace Pell

Senlin removed the duke's calling card. The front was embossed with his name and title. On the back, was a square of gold leaf that contained three white lines, hovering one atop the other. General Eigengrau's lapel pin had borne the same symbol. Beneath the white bars, in a tombstone script, were the words THE COTERIE OF TALENTS.

Chapter Eight

In the span of just a few years, the Coterie have gone from being a drunken fraternity to the most influential society in the realm. I've had an easier time getting an audience with the king than an open seat at the Coterie Club.

—Oren Robinson of the *Daily Reverie*

Senlin choked down the dry toast and tepid water that had been his daily breakfast since arriving at the Bon Royal. Blast the Boskops and their bland palates! He longed for a piece of fruit, a link of fatty sausage, or even a cup of weak tea. Then he recalled the days of hunger they'd suffered aboard the *Stone Cloud*, and he felt ashamed of his ingratitude. The hooks of entitlement were so quick to set!

It took him more than an hour to clean up the mess the general's men had made of his room, then he scrubbed the lingering flecks of whitewash from his wrists, shaved his cheeks pink, oiled down his hair, and put on his only remaining untattered coat. As Senlin packed his billfold with every last mina the Sphinx had given him, he reassured himself that he was not making a mistake. The fact that the duke had responded to the letter was promising in itself. It was not a bad plan. Probably.

When he stepped from the warm, glowing foyer of the Bon Royal, he was surprised by the heavy bank of fog that engulfed the city. The fog reduced the blazing coin of the Pelphian sun to an orange smudge. The city, he'd been informed by Mr. Stull, was always slow to dry after its regular baths. The fog would linger most of the day.

Hearing a now familiar rustle overhead, Senlin looked up to find a macaw perched upon an iron sconce. "You burned the roast!" the bird squawked. Senlin called back, "You stupid cow!"

An arguing couple erupted from the hotel doors. The pursuing gentleman had one arm in his coat. The lady was still buttoning up her tailored jacket when her companion caught her by the arm and tried to pull her back toward the lobby.

"I meant it affectionately, darling. Even the breath of a kitten reeks sometimes," he said.

She jerked free of his grip, and he stumbled backward up a few steps. "Well, since we're being so *affectionate* in our criticisms, Mr. Morris, I've pulled bigger worms out of apples!"

"I've pulled bigger worms out of apples, Mr. Morris! I've pulled bigger worms!" the big parrot said. It spread its wings and glided out over the hazy plaza, repeating the phrase as it went.

"Oh my god!" The gentleman cupped his forehead in horror. "Stop that bird! Someone shoot it! Shoot it!" he screamed as he charged after the vanishing parrot.

Trusting that the Colosseum had not moved in the night, Senlin set out into the fog. Though the white city was blindfolded, it was not gagged. The haze rang with a thousand voices that crashed, overlapped, and blended into babble. The singsong call of a newsboy rose above the chatter: "*Reverie! Reverie!* Read it in the *Reverie*! Sphinx's warship prowls the sky again! The Sphinx is back! What's his game? *Reverie! Reverie!* Read it in the *Reverie*!"

Senlin smiled. Edith was under way. The news refreshed his courage. He wouldn't be friendless in the city for much longer.

This happy thought was interrupted by the sudden realization that his toe had caught on something unforgiving. He had to trot several steps and swing his arms to keep himself from falling. When he looked back to see what had tripped him, he found one of the crystal manhole lids had popped a few inches up from its bed. He noted that, unlike the other quartz dials in the plaza, this disc was unlit. He was wondering what that could possibly portend, and then the plate began to rise from the cobblestones. It pulled along a bronze column like a nail from the ground. No, not like a nail, he thought—like a screw. The pillar twisted as it rose past Senlin's knees, his waist, his shoulders, and finally past the top of his head. There, the screw stopped turning, and Senlin found himself facing an ornate column that was as wide as a drum of wine. In between the threads of the screw, black grease clung to scrollwork that evoked the veins of a leaf.

An embedded plaque in the side of the column caught Senlin's eye. The bolded herald declared: WILL-O'-THE-WISP, and in a smaller typeface beneath that appeared the lines: DO NOT FEAR THE SHADOWS CAST BY MY LIGHT. THOUGH THEY MAY HOLD THE SHAPE OF TRUTH, THESE VISIONS ARE NOT REAL. A GIFT FROM THE SPHINX.

As Senlin read, a crack appeared down the length of the column, and a seamless door swung open toward him. He glimpsed a gloomy closet within, and he leaned in to investigate. Senlin was just starting to wonder why the Sphinx had built a device to spring unbidden from the Pelphian floor when he was pushed to one side. A buxom woman in an overlarge hat pressed past him into the cavity, crying as she went, "It's mine! It's mine! I saw it first!"

Before Senlin could argue, the curved door clamped shut behind her, and the column began to twist slowly back into the floor.

He wondered where the pillar led, and why the woman had been so keen to ride it down, but these were questions that would have to wait for another occasion. For now, he had an appointment to keep and the more pressing mystery of the duke's character to unravel.

When the Colosseum emerged from the mist, it seemed as abrupt and menacing as an iceberg. Senlin nodded to the guards stationed about the barred entryway and crossed the portico to the echo of his own heels. He could still detect snatches of the building's former glory: He saw it in the pillars, stout as oak trees, and in the pale red-veined marble floor, which seemed to have been sliced from a mountainside and delivered in one piece. The noble figures in the lintels stood half-obliterated, the result, Senlin had learned from an old article in the *Reverie*, of insufficient ladders and indifferent demolitionists. The plinths between betting counters held ashtrays that overflowed with cigarette butts. Doves and magpies roosted in the ruined remains of friezes. Their calls diverged and harmonized like a tuning orchestra. He had arrived in the lull between fights. A few men wearing slept-in suits studied betting sheets, reviewing past mistakes and laying the groundwork for future ones.

Approaching the stairs to the Coterie Club, he saw the way was guarded by the same mustached doormen who had torn his money and ripped his coat. Senlin couldn't quite suppress a triumphant smirk.

"Good day, gentlemen!" he said. The doorman with the hooped mustache raised his hand, preparing to strike. He halted when he saw the flash of the duke's gilded calling card. "Please tell the duke that Mr. Cyril Pinfield is here for our appointment."

The doorman directed Senlin to put his palms on the wall, which he did, his smile dwindling. The doorman frisked him so violently, Senlin thought his ribs might crack. He'd seen carpets beaten more gently. The doorman rummaged through his pockets, removing a set of hotel keys, a pad and pencil, and a plump billfold. Even when it was apparent Senlin had come invited and unarmed, they did not let him pass. The second doorman marched upstairs, presumably to consult with the duke, while the other stayed behind to glare at Senlin with his hand on his sword.

Bruised and annoyed that his moment of petty triumph had been spoiled, Senlin decided to torment the guard with some Boskopeian small talk. He said, "I had a dream last night in which I'd been turned into a sandwich." One of the doorman's eyebrows rose. "I had the distinct impression that I was delicious, but I don't know what sort of sandwich I was. Perhaps pickle?"

The guard gave a long and shuddering sigh.

A handsome young man with a jutting blond beard trotted down the stairs. He wore a long frock coat that flattered his broad shoulders and trimmed his waist and contained more buttons than could ever be practical. His complexion radiated vitality. He showed a flash of immaculate teeth and stuck out his hand. "So you're Cyril? Wilhelm Pell. But, please, call me Wil."

After the doorman's frosty reception, Senlin was surprised by the duke's warmth. He looked into the man's sage-green eyes and understood why Marya had trusted him. He projected a sort of friendly sincerity. Senlin bowed and said, "It's a pleasure to meet you, Your Grace."

"Let's not stand on ceremony, Cyril. In my experience, the men that lean hardest on their titles are the ones who did nothing to earn them. I loathe men whose greatest accomplishment was being born."

"Indeed, Your Grace!" Senlin said, and deciding there was no time like the present to introduce his Boskopeian awkwardness, he added, "And speaking of loathsome, I seem to have developed a hole in my sock. Isn't that just the worst sensation: moist leather on bare skin? It's like stepping on a toad." Senlin gave a snickering, unsettling laugh but laughed alone.

"Yes," the duke said in the slow, vague way of a man reconsidering his first impression. "Well, let's get you out of the hall." He clapped Senlin on the arm. "I'll show you the club."

During Senlin's time at university, a distinguished don of letters had once invited him for a drink at the Fox and Chase Gentleman's Club. The club, an old, converted manor, stood on a hill overlooking the campus, a spot chosen to give underclassmen something to look up to and admire. The don had extended the honor because he wished to discuss Senlin's essay on the influence of maritime ballads upon the poetic canon. The gray-maned don wanted to edit the essay for publication. Senlin had felt more than a little flattered by the don's attention and by the gin punch he was handed at the door. But the superior feeling was short-lived as it soon became apparent the don intended to assume complete authorship of the essay while Senlin would be compensated via that great nontransferable, nonrefundable currency of academia—*gratitude*.

Yet, for all its leather upholstery and gin punch, the Fox and Chase Gentleman's Club had been little better than a glorified reading room. The Coterie Club, by comparison, was a shrine to leisure. The bar, which encircled the entirety of the club, was fortified with exotic bottles and voluptuous glassware. Tucked among the rare port wines and brandies stood the stone busts of noble gentlemen and ladies, all of whom had been amusingly decorated with eyepatches, fussy hats, scarves, grease makeup, and wigs. The high tables that hugged the rail over the arena were set with bone china and tented napkins. Overhead, a system of belts turned a bank of fans, creating a leisurely, pleasing breeze. The hour still being relatively early, the club was empty save for the staff and a few gentlemen reading the *Daily Reverie* at the bar.

But it was what lay underfoot that first captured Senlin's attention. The floor was tiled in capital letters, turned this way and that, forming an unintelligible jumble that frustrated his habit of reading whatever was set before him.

"I see you've noticed the floors."

"There seem to be an awful lot of misspellings," Senlin said with affected earnestness.

The duke laughed. "It's only decorative." The duke went on to explain that the letters had once been part of the building's masonry that had been removed during the renovation and repurposed as floor tiling. Senlin wondered what lofty maxims had been lost in the tile-layer's shuffle.

"What was this building before? A courthouse?"

"No, it was Ostraka University, College of Arts and Sciences." The duke noticed his guest's fleeting expression of surprise, though he misunderstood its cause. Senlin was thinking about the murderous hod and the book on trilobites that had once belonged to this now defunct university. It seemed a funny coincidence. "I know. It's quite a mouthful, isn't it? But you know academics: Why spend one word when you can waste three?" the duke said.

"And those old stone heads wearing lipstick and wigs behind the bar—the former faculty?"

"And deans, department heads, a laureled alumnus or two. I like bringing a little humor to the humorless." The duke gave another winning smile. Though he smiled back, Senlin took the duke's disrespect for academia as something of a personal slight. Surely this was proof that the duke was a scoundrel of the first degree! But then, knowing what he knew of the Tower's institutions, publications, and so-called scholars, Senlin wondered if it was so unwise to assume that Ostraka University had been a bastion of enlightenment. For all he knew, the duke was scorning the men behind the *Everyman's Guide*.

The duke said, "I have a regular table, but I prefer the bar, if you don't mind." Senlin said he didn't mind and followed the duke to a spot at the bar where an open newspaper and empty cup awaited his return. The bartender was a lean man with a short ponytail and a protruding Adam's apple. The duke called him Joachim, and after asking for more coffee, invited his guest to order something.

"May I have a cup of warm water, please?" Senlin said.

"Warm wa—" The bartender looked to the duke, who seemed just as surprised. Senlin pretended not to notice their confusion, and the bartender recovered his professional air. "One cup of warm water coming up."

Senlin withdrew and opened his billfold. The fat edge of his banknotes, packed as tight as the gills of a fish, drew the duke's eye, which of course had been the point.

The duke waved off the offer. "Please, you are my guest. And I think I can afford a cup of warm water." He smiled, perhaps hoping for some further explanation. Senlin only thanked him and promised to buy the next round. "So, Cyril, tell me, what business are you in?"

"Accounting. Most of my clients are importers: sugar, coffee, tea, lard, rum, that sort of thing." Their drinks arrived and Senlin sipped his warm water while the two other men watched with thinly veiled disgust. He rolled the water about in his mouth, swallowed, and made a sound of great satisfaction. "Tongue temperature: Perfect!"

The duke's smile was beginning to lose its luster. "Your office is here, in Pelphia?"

"No, in Boskopeia."

The duke slapped the polished bar and belted out a laugh. "Oh, you're a Boskop! That explains it! Here I've been wondering if you weren't mad after all that business about the hole in your sock and drinking spit water. Now it all makes sense!"

"Do you really have such a prejudice against my countrymen?"

"Don't take it so hard, Cyril! We Pelphians just like our cakes sweet, our spirits strong, and our parties wicked. But honestly, we have too many idiots running about." The duke opened his frock coat and reached into the breast pocket. Senlin recognized the letter he pulled out. "I'd rather talk business with a Boskop accountant than a Pelphian fop. Which brings me to your letter." The duke tapped the corner of the folded sheet on the bar. "I get dozens of these every day— men asking for loans or investments or the use of my name, which is a sort of currency itself. But you . . ." He clucked his tongue, his smile tinged with disbelief. "You want to turn my wife into stock?"

"Yes. Yes, I do." Senlin laced his hands upon the magnificent bar.

The idea had developed over the hours Senlin had spent studying Pelphia's obsession with Marya. It was obvious to him that the ring-dom had turned her into an ideal. It was an urge he understood all too well. Perhaps it was only human to heap perfection upon another person and then worship the figment that resulted. And surely many of her devoted fans adored her without expectation. But so many had a stake in her fame—newspapers, venues, to say nothing of the social-ites who wanted her at their parties—that at some point Marya had transformed from the subject of affection to an object of value. Senlin felt he had a fair notion of how Pelphia conceived of the Mermaid, but what he didn't know, what he *needed* to know, was how the duke thought of Marya. Had he married her out of real affection or some base ambition? Senlin's plan was to tempt the man with riches and fame and see if his love had a bottom line. So in his letter he proposed that the duke allow him to manage the sale of shares in his wife's musi-cal career. If the duke agreed to the transaction, Senlin would know for sure the man was a cad and Marya was in trouble. If the duke refused . . . well, the jury regarding his character would still be out.

"I'm just not clear on exactly what you're suggesting," the duke said. For the first time, and to his credit, the duke's smile vanished and was replaced by a frown. "Marya is a person. She is my wife. I'm not selling my wife."

Senlin glimpsed in the man's passion what seemed to be sincere adoration. But he wouldn't be so readily convinced. He pressed on.

"No, you'd be selling stock in her name, in her likeness, her performance, her songs, her fashion, her brand of scent, and so on. She's more than a person at this point, isn't she? She's a concept, an enviable ideal. And an ideal you can sell."

The duke drew a long breath, his beautiful brow beetled with thought. "I like your perfume idea. There's something to that, I think. But as for the rest of it, you're just describing her accomplishments. She's already wealthy and renowned. Why does she need to be turned into stock?"

And here it occurred to Senlin that his efforts to test the duke might incidentally corrupt him. But Senlin knew the duke was a savvy communicator, a man accustomed to dealing with the press and presenting himself in a positive light. Senlin had to tempt thoroughly without pressuring him into doing something beyond his moral inclination. It seemed a tightrope in the dark: He had to feel his way forward.

Senlin said, "The Tower is a big place. There are many, many ringdoms, many venues, many opportunities. What if your wife's play was popular in the ringdom of Thane, or Japhet, or Banner-Wick, or Morick? What if she could tour the Tower, sell out shows in all the great playhouses? What if her perfume was on the neck of every fashionable lady in Andara Nur?" Senlin saw in the duke's roving gaze that he was imagining the future as he painted it for him. "I think all of this is possible, but you will need help sowing the seeds of her success. You'll need local partners, men who know how to promote and peddle and curry favor with local trendsetters: the journalists, dandies, and young ladies. You could try to research and finance all of that on your own, or you could sell stock in her; give many people a small sliver of her potential. Those shareholders could prepare the way for her, so that when she arrived on each stop of her tour of the Tower, the crowds would be ready, waiting, and immense. She could be the Tower's first real star."

The duke squinted with thought. "It's ambitious, I'll give you that." He examined the last sip of coffee rolling about the bottom of his cup. "But you're forgetting something."

"What's that?" Senlin said with a hopeful eagerness that had nothing to do with money.

"The lady has a mind of her own. She's not a pork belly or a sugar beet. She would have to agree to it. Because, after all, she'll have to live it."

Senlin tried to hide the sudden lurch of disappointment he felt. The duke had refused the lure. "Of course," he said meekly.

"And what's your place in all this? It seems to me you may have already given me your greatest contribution—the idea."

"I have spent the past twenty years handling the books of some of the most wealthy and influential businessmen in the Tower. I know who's solvent, who's good with money, who's looking to expand into new markets. I have the contacts. I would be your business manager."

"And take a salary, I imagine?"

"I'd prefer stock. A three percent stake."

Wil twirled a finger in Joachim's direction, making the buttons on his sleeve ring. "Tell me, Cyril, have you ever tasted peridot? It's a liqueur. Some people say it tastes like medicine. I think it tastes like candied springtime." The bartender poured the brilliant green liqueur into two small flutes. The duke took up his glass. "Now, I know most Boskops don't drink, but most don't try to chop my wife into parcels either. So take that up, and here's to you."

Senlin feigned reluctance but picked up his glass. "And to you."

Realizing that a show was in order, Senlin downed the sweet liqueur and made a face like a man attempting to suppress a sneeze. He coughed and lifted his hands over his head.

The duke laughed and twirled his finger a second time. Joachim, who'd been hovering nearby, set a clamshell box on the bar. Inside, a pin glistened upon a velvet pillow. "Consider this a provisional loan," the duke said, plucking the pin from the case. It was just like General Eigengrau's pin and the one on the duke's lapel: three white horizontal bars in a gold square. "It's the club's herald. We call ourselves the Coterie. You'll have a much easier time getting past the doormen with that on."

Senlin took the pin, his expression of surprise genuine, though something in the duke's smile made him suspect he had not yet begun to pay for this privilege. "I feel remiss," Senlin said, affixing the pin to his coat. "I didn't bring any jewelry for you."

"Ah, but you've given me an idea. And if my lady likes it, perhaps we'll both be rich."

Senlin felt a sudden urge to grab the duke by the neck and choke him upon the bar. As if his murder might convince Marya that Senlin were the more deserving man. As if she would ever leave this life and return home with him and pretend that none of this had ever happened. Though how could they pretend? What would it be like to live such a charade? Would she pick at him with rueful laughter and bitter looks? Would he make her the widow of his daydreams? Would they become the old couple in the corner of the pub who never spoke, never smiled, never sang with the round?

Senlin realized Wilhelm was staring at him and that he had not said anything for a long moment. "To you and your wife, Wil."

The duke grabbed Senlin by the back of the neck and shook him merrily. "You aren't so bad, Cyril. You aren't so bad at all. Don't let anyone tease you about being a Boskop! Now bring your vase water and let's find a spot at the rail. The brawlers are about to come out."

The club had filled up while they had been talking. Still, the duke had no trouble elbowing a little space on the wide stone rail. The general admission benches below were nearly full.

Adolescent boys raked the clay as the bookmaker, a stout elder in suspenders with a tobacco-stained mustache, climbed the podium above the caged entrances to the ring. He cupped his hand to his mouth and began to bellow with impressive volume: "Third fight! Third fight! The Iron Bear and the Ritzy Pup!" Senlin had seen the Ritzy Pup fight several times—he was a young man with large red lips who never fared very well, but who was exceedingly good at getting tossed about. He hadn't heard of the Iron Bear before. "Final odds, the Iron Bear by five to one. All bets are in. No more bets! No more bets!" The groomers raked their way out of the ring.

"We haven't seen the Iron Bear in a few weeks. He broke a toe last time, I think," the duke said.

"Who's going to win?"

"Odds say the Iron Bear."

"But don't you know? Aren't the fights fixed?"

"No! What are you talking about? It's not fixed! Where's the fun in that?"

Senlin frowned but said no more. Perhaps he didn't understand the rules of the sport as well as he thought. Senlin noticed that the gentlemen at the rail beside him gripped betting sheets.

"I'll tell you what, Cyril: There's a little soiree this evening. My wife will be there. If you'd like to come along, perhaps you could tell her all about your idea. I assume you have something else to wear?"

Senlin knew it was a terrible idea to accept and yet did not hesitate to do so. "Yes, yes, of course."

"Have you met my wife?" Wil asked, and Senlin could manage little more than a shake of his head. "The papers don't do her justice. As incredible as her performances are, she's even more spectacular in person. You've never seen a more arresting vision of beauty. She is imperfect, but absolutely peerless."

Senlin wanted nothing so much as to scream.

"I think I have an extra invitation around here somewhere. Just a moment." The duke began to pat his pockets distractedly, and as he did, his hips pressed against the low railing, festooned with ropes of silk flowers. Senlin watched as his hand rose over the center of the duke's back. He couldn't stop what was happening. A moment before, he had thought himself in control, but now his heart thundered inside him like an apocalyptic beast charging upon myriad legs, crowned with gory horns, a mount too large and wild for the small jockey of his rational mind to steer. One good shove would send the duke over. One good shove would see him broken upon the bleachers like a skiff on a reef. The Tower did not care if a man was righteous or vile. The Tower ruined the just and the unjust with equal appetite. The Tower—

A shriek of hinges sent a shudder up Senlin's spine. His hand dropped from the duke's back.

Far below on the arena floor, the brawlers emerged from their tunnels to a gust of cheers. The young Ritzy Pup strutted out first, his lips curled back, his teeth as prominent as a baboon's. He dragged his toe, striking up theatrical sheets of dust, and thumped his chest triumphantly.

The Iron Bear slunk, head downcast, out of his unlit cave. He rubbed his face as if he'd just been awakened by the arrival of spring. He was immense, nearly half again as large as his rival and twice his age. His shoulders and arms were rolled with muscles. He shook his great head as if to clear the fog of his slumber. Then the two points of his dark beard jabbed toward the crowd as he threw back his head and roared.

Senlin recognized the voice at once. He had listened to that bark over wine and snails for many an evening at Café Risso in the Baths.

John Tarrou ducked and caught the Ritzy Pup by his ankles, then shook him out like a sandy towel.

Chapter Nine

Don't saw off your arm to feed a dog. You only have two arms, and the world is full of dogs.

—Oren Robinson of the *Daily Reverie*

enlin gave the duke a rushed excuse about the liqueur not sitting right with him, though he promised he'd make a full recovery before the evening. Wil laughed and said something about the delicate constitution of Boskops before giving Senlin the invitation for the gala. Then Senlin fled the crowded clubhouse, shouldering through the noblemen ascending the stairs, past the guards brooding in the lobby, and out to the plaza. The haze had lifted, but the crowds were just as thick.

Tarrou's grim fate and abrupt reappearance were shocking, but Senlin couldn't think clearly enough at the moment to empathize with his friend. No, what whipped him out the door was the realization that if he stayed one minute longer, he would kill the duke or die trying. The fact surprised him. He'd defied the Sphinx's orders and Byron's advice because he was certain that if he armed himself with a plan, sufficient research, and a healthy dose of introspection, he would be able to control himself, control the base impulses that ruled lesser men. But the moment the duke paid Marya a frank and discerning compliment, Senlin had lost all sense of reason.

Wil's words echoed in him still: "She is imperfect, but absolutely peerless."

He had lost her, had lost her one final time, not to the crowd, but to a man who appreciated her fully, baldly, boldly—a man who knew her blemishes and thought them beauty marks. It seemed the duke had already learned what it had taken Senlin too long to discover: Intimacy was not about maintaining the idealistic charade of courtship; it was about embracing and adoring the flaws, the very things that the headmaster of Isaugh had never been quite able to admit in himself. The Mermaid's train song to the children rang again in his ears: "It's perfectly all right not to be perfect. A chip or a crack can be precious, too."

Even when he was safely back in his suite, Senlin could not repress the nervous urge to pace. He crisscrossed the rug in a fury, rubbing his face as if he would shed it. He couldn't hold on to a single sensible thought. *Of course, she loved the duke! How could she not love him?* Wilhelm was handsome, amiable, wealthy, and he had been present when she had needed him most, been present when Senlin was loafing in the Baths.

Senlin snatched up the edition of the *Reverie* that recounted their wedding day and glared at the etching of Wil and Marya, arm in arm, on the prow of a rose-strewn yacht. The joyous couple waved to him from the past. He had been too late for a very long time.

He tore the paper and hurled it across the room. Before the tatters had time to settle, he took up another edition and tore it to ragged shreds. He ripped into another paper, then another, blackening his hands with ink, filling the room with the noise of ripping paper, a sound that had once upon a time grated his nerves, but which now harmonized with the roar inside him. He shoved the stacks from his bureau and kicked the pages as they fell. He wanted to tear each sentence separately, tear them down to the word, the letter. He tore as if he could rend history with his hands.

The last copy ruined, Senlin stood panting in a shin-deep marsh of newspaper. He felt relieved and spent and ashamed of himself.

A jaunty knock upon his door made him catch his breath. Had someone complained about the noise? How long had he raved?

He half-expected to find the concierge, Mr. Stull, behind the door, but it wasn't someone he recognized. The smiling dandy wore a burgundy suit, a matching top hat, and a white daisy in his buttonhole. He held a clipboard with gloved hands.

"Are you Mr. Pinfield?" The dandy's voice was musical, his pronunciation exact.

"Yes," Senlin said, trying his best to block the devastation behind him.

"Mr. Cyril Pinfield?"

"Yes. What is this in regard to?"

"I have a message for you, sir, from Mr. S. Finks." The dandy pulled a cream-colored envelope from the clipboard and presented it to Senlin with a perfunctory bow. Senlin looked down at the envelope and back up just in time to see the dandy's arm swinging at him.

The slap caught him on the jaw hard enough to turn his head.

Senlin was about to lunge at the man when his outrage was foiled by the presentation of the clipboard and a fountain pen. "Could you please sign here confirming that you received the letter, and also here, confirming you received the blow?" the dandy said.

Stunned, Senlin took the board and pen. The inventory sheet bore the herald of the company: BIERMAN BROTHERS—ANNOUNCEMENTS & TELEGRAPHIC SLAPS. In smaller print beneath the letterhead was the company motto: DO NOT SHOOT THE MESSENGER. OUR MESSENGERS SHOOT BACK.

Sensing Senlin's puzzlement, the dandy pointed to the lines that required his signature. Under the paragraph entitled BLOWS, ETC., the description read, "One open-palm slap delivered enthusiastically to the cheek, temple, or ear." Senlin was so confused, he nearly signed his real name. He returned the clipboard and was about to shut the door when the dandy cleared his throat and held out his hand.

"You must be joking."

"Sir, I'm just doing my job. I have mouths to feed."

Grumbling, Senlin fished a few coins out of his pocket and slapped them into the man's palm.

Alone again, he opened the letter and read:

Dear Mr. Pinfield,

You seem to forget, my eyes are widely set.

I know I was clear in my instruction that you not expose yourself unnecessarily. Going to plays, fighting in alleys, and becoming a person of interest in a murder investigation are all primary examples of unnecessary exposure.

I know what you're up to, young man. And I will tell you again: You are the wrong tool for that job. You are a hammer attempting to do the work of a wrench. If you continue to bang away, you'll only make it harder for the young lady to do her job. Don't be a fool.

Warmest Regards,

S. Finks

Senlin felt suddenly aware of the high walls of his suite, the scribbling pattern of the wallpaper, the great volume of drapes, and the fringed skirt of his bed. There were so many places for the Sphinx's spies to hide.

"Right," he said to the audience of an empty room.

Senlin would be the first to admit he had been shirking his duty to the Sphinx. In his defense, the Sphinx's suspicion that *something* sinister was transpiring in the Colosseum did not seem as pressing as Senlin's certainty that Marya was present and within reach. Even so, he could hardly resent the Sphinx's reminder that he had a job to do.

Senlin didn't think it wise to report that he had wheedled his way into the Coterie Club. Doing so might raise the question of whether he'd bumped into the duke. If he had discovered that the clubhouse was a secret torture chamber or contained a hidden munition factory or a ceremonial altar surrounded by men in black cowls, of course he would've confessed the intelligence at once. But the Coterie Club had turned out to be nothing more than a pretty bar with a nice view.

To placate the Sphinx, Senlin filed a report on some information he'd at first considered too trivial to mention, though that was before he'd had a visit from the slap fairy.

A day earlier, he'd overheard a gambler in the betting queue complain about the ousting of the Coattails: "Those little scamps were always good for a laugh. Too bad Eigengrau doesn't have a sense of humor. Bring the Coattails back, I say!" His curiosity piqued, Senlin made some inquiries and learned that the Coattails were young boys who were allowed to sell papers, tobacco, and matches inside the Colosseum lobby. The inspiration for the nickname was just a poor pun on the word *Coterie*, but the boys embraced it and soon appeared wearing long, colorful tails sewn onto the back hems of their coats. Their coattails were so long, they often dragged upon the ground.

When they weren't selling their papers and tobacco, the Coattails found other ways to entertain themselves. They stuck matchheads into cigarettes, so they'd flare up when lit. They cut coattails out of newspaper and took turns trying to pin them onto unsuspecting victims. Their favorite game was something called Bump and Basket. First, one of the Coattails had to procure a "lure" by stealing a shiny button from the cuff or lapel of an inattentive costumer. A strip of colorful cloth was sewn to the button, and then the boy would toss his finished lure in the air. The goal was to attract the attention of one of the magpies that nested in the lobby or arena. If a magpie swooped down and hit the lure but dropped it, this was called a *bump* and was worth one point. If the magpie caught the lure and took it back to its nest in the high, inaccessible friezes of the lobby, this was called a *basket*, which was worth three points. Over the course of many months, the nests had filled with buttons, until the magpies sat like dragons upon glittering hoards.

The Coattails were as much a fixture of the Colosseum as the beer vendors or betting counters. Even the men who went home missing a button did not wish to see the imps driven out.

But then one morning one of the Coattails was found inside the dormitory where the brawlers ate and slept. The boy had gotten in despite the fact that the dormitory lay in a separate section of the Colosseum behind a series of barriers and a constant guard. Finding the boy inside the dorm was like discovering a child in a bank vault. General Eigengrau, who oversaw the Colosseum's guard, interrogated the boy, who confessed that the Coattails were playing a new game, a game where they saw how far they could explore beyond the public areas. Incredibly, the boy had managed to squeeze through a barred door, slip past the guards, and pick a lock. Eigengrau did not like the idea of his security being tested (and bested) by a bunch of paperboys, so he barred them all from the premises.

Senlin noted that though the players had been banished, the birds had not lost their appetite for the game: No shiny thing was safe in the arena. The magpie hoards continued to grow.

Out on the balcony, Senlin released the Sphinx's spy over the city streets. Below, a brass band seemed to be terrorizing the diners of a café with an excessively merry polka. His eye fell upon the gallery opposite his room. Someone had tried to push a sofa onto it, but the piece of furniture had gotten stuck halfway out the door and at an angle. He recalled the masked woman who'd laughed at his moth from that balcony. He wondered why she had shown him her face just before becoming violently ill. If he had been in her place and on the brink of such an embarrassment, he would've kept the mask on.

No sooner did the thought form in his head than he knew just what he would do.

Mr. Stull made a point of never forming an opinion about any of his guests. Developing an opinion on them was as futile and juvenile as pointing out the shapes of passing clouds. The guests came, they cast a little shadow, and they flew on.

And yet increasingly, Mr. Stull was finding it difficult not to develop an opinion about the Boskop, Mr. Pinfield, who for all his blandness, was proving to be an inventive nuisance. First, there were all the trips to the newspaper archives, which had tied up his porters for hours. Then there was the whitewash on his carpets, which would probably have to be cut out and replaced, and finally the summoning of the law, whose arrival had all but paralyzed his staff with gossip.

So when Mr. Stull looked up from his lectern and the timetable he was drafting to see the Boskop standing before him, he nearly blurted out, *Oh no, what have you done now?*

The Boskop asked if there were a more secluded place where they might discuss "a matter of some delicacy." Ever-obliging, Mr. Stull escorted the Boskop to a corner of the grand lobby that was empty except for a silk-leafed plant in an urn. The Boskop eyed the plant as if it were a snake, then asked if there weren't somewhere "perhaps a bit more out of the way." With a whisper of a sigh, Mr. Stull took the guest to the kitchen, which was, admittedly, quite crowded with cooks and porters and scullery maids, but the clamor of crockery, the chatter of knives, and the incessant barking of an ill-tempered chef afforded them a deafening sort of privacy that Mr. Stull hoped would satisfy his irksome guest.

But it did not. The Boskop looked over both shoulders before half shouting into Mr. Stull's ear that he was not trying to be difficult, but wasn't there somewhere still a little more remote?

Though not quick to feel abused, Mr. Stull had arrived at the terminus of his patience. He was about to invite the guest to sit on a fork when he saw the glint of the Coterie's insignia on the Boskop's lapel. He would've been less surprised if the Boskop had sprouted a third eye.

His patience refreshed a little, Mr. Stull ushered the guest into the storeroom where jowly hams hung from the ceiling and cakes of cheese soured the air. He shut the door, plunging them into an intimate darkness that he quickly dispelled by the lighting of a match. Stull braced himself for the worst—a bloody body in one of his tubs or some fire-eaten drapes.

Looking very grave, the Boskop said, "I have been invited to a party."

"I'm sorry?" Mr. Stull said.

"It's all right. These things happen."

"Yes," Mr. Stull said and briefly considered strangling the man. "What can I do for you, sir?"

The Boskop presented a folded scrap of paper. "My measurements. I need a suit."

"I see. Perhaps you should visit a tailor, sir."

"No, I'm afraid that's impossible. I also need a mask. Something bland and unremarkable. The same goes for the suit. I don't wish to stand out."

"Yes, of course," Mr. Stull said, pausing to light another match. "I understand completely."

"No, wait. On second thought, find me a plain suit and a grotesque mask. I want it to be ridiculous. Laughable. Here's a ten-mina note. If more is needed, I'll compensate you of course, and here's another mina for your absolute discretion in this matter. I'll need the items wrapped and delivered directly to the Coterie Club before the evening."

Relieved that there were no bodies to dispose of nor drapes to replace, Mr. Stull pocketed the money and said, "Your parcel will be there in an hour, sir."

"Oh, and I don't want to alarm you, but there's something of a mess in my room. I had a bit of an accident with my borrowed papers." The Boskop presented another mina note. "If you would salvage as much as possible, I'd be very appreciative."

"Of course," Mr. Stull said through a smiling dam of teeth.

When Senlin returned to the Coterie Club, he received a very different welcome from the doormen. They bowed when he approached and waved him up the stairs at once. The club was still more or less full. Most of the members were giddy with drink and still reveling in the afternoon fights. After a fruitless search for the duke, Senlin approached a man seated at the bar whose head was as bare and beaming as a thumbnail. Senlin asked him how the Iron Bear fight had ended.

To Senlin's surprise, the man leapt from his sturdy stool to his less steady feet and shouted, "The Ritzy Pup was due! He was due! It was an unjust match. The Iron Bear is not a man! He's not a hod! He's a devil!" With that, the man slapped a curly, white wig onto his head and stumbled toward the stairs.

Senlin took his place at the bar. The duke's bartender, Joachim, greeted him, his empty cheeks rising in a hollow smile. "Don't mind the baron, sir. He's just mad that his champion couldn't win a fight with a curtain. Warm water for you?"

"Yes," Senlin said, looking down at the polished bar before him, marred by fingerprints, balled tissues, and torn betting sheets. Joachim cleaned away these ghosts of the baron's grief, and soon Senlin could see himself staring back from the inky mahogany.

When Joachim came back with a nearly steaming teacup of water, Senlin held a mina note on the bar. "I have a parcel coming, if you wouldn't mind keeping an eye out for it." Joachim took the bill with an acknowledging wink. Senlin found the exchange somewhat amusing. He'd been harassed and scrutinized for so long that this trend of silent agreement and acknowledgment felt almost magical. The joy of privilege resided in the unspoken.

Senlin had just begun to pretend to savor his cup of bathwater when a familiar fin of jet-black hair rose over the horizon of the stairs. The general was so tall, he made the ceiling fans that tilled the air seem uncomfortably low. He unbuckled the long-nosed pistol at his hip and handed the belt, holster, and all to one of the half dozen guards who followed him in a pack.

The genial atmosphere of the club did nothing to soften his severity. Eigengrau cast his gaze about the room as deliberately as the beam from a lighthouse. When his hooded gaze landed on Senlin, it stopped, as did Senlin's heart.

He was certain the general had checked his name against the ship's passenger list and had now come to arrest him for the fraud that he was. Senlin turned back around on his stool, his thoughts veering toward escape. He would vault over the bar, grab one of the bottles of liquor, and wield it like a club until it broke, then slash with the jagged remnant. He'd fight his way down the guarded stairs, to the guarded lobby, out through the guarded doors. By that point, he would've likely accrued a few wounds, but he would fight on through the pain and across the plaza, to the port...And there, his imagination perished.

There would be no escape, no rescue, no miraculous twist of fate this time. He would die here, and die alone.

He had just raised a finger to order a glass of rum when he felt the general's presence on the stool beside him. He listened to the settling creak of Eigengrau's boots and the rustle of his cape as he threw it off his arm. Senlin tried to force himself to affect some casual moment of discovery, to turn and say, "Oh, hello! I didn't see you there." But his neck seemed to have fused with his spine. Out of the corner of his eye, he watched the bartender produce a glass that was as tall as a vase. Joachim filled the immense flute with the vibrant peridot liqueur.

"To monstrous lobsters," Eigengrau said, lifting the glass to his hawkish nose. He inhaled deeply, then drank.

Feeling he had no choice, Senlin turned to face the general. "I'm sorry?"

"I was just thinking about your book. Trilobites and arthropods is quite a mouthful, though. I rather like monstrous lobsters." Eigengrau's voice was deep, his delivery ponderous. "Unusual reading for a Boskop accountant, isn't it?"

"Is it?" Senlin wished he'd just told the general where the book had come from in the beginning, but he'd wondered if perhaps the Sphinx would want to inspect it. Perhaps she could discern a significance he could not. "I've always found the idea of ancient sea life compelling."

"Why?"

"The mystery, I suppose. I can't help but wonder what else lives down there in the dark."

"Well, I don't go looking for mysteries. Enough mystery finds me as it is. Speaking of which, we've located your hod."

"You did?" Senlin said, his voice brightened with relief. "That was quick work!"

"There aren't many places for the hods to hide in the city, and they're not the cleverest of beasts."

"You'll need me to identify him, of course."

"No, no, that won't be necessary. He already confessed and implicated his coconspirators."

"Conspirators? But, surely, he acted alone? There were only the four of us in the alley."

"Hods never act alone."

Senlin scowled at this, and before he had time to think better of it, he voiced his disagreement to the man who'd just delivered his salvation: "I always thought of the hods as just unfortunate men and women."

"That's like believing a jackal is just an uncombed lapdog, or a flood is an overdrawn bath. The hod's misfortune is an expression of their nature. A hod is born a hod, even if he poses as a man for a time." The general put the flute of the syrupy liqueur to his lips and drank. When he set the glass down again, it was half empty. "I didn't know Boskops were such a tenderhearted tribe."

"We aren't, but we are practical. It seems a waste of resources to squander so much human potential and talent on carrying sacks up a slope—work a crane could do or an airship."

"There are more and more like you every day. See, this is the trouble with society: It lulls the individual into believing that security, sanity, and order are natural states. You think that humanity is an ennobling force. I assure you, it is not. It's not cruel to say the hods are dangerous, unfinished, incapable souls. It would be cruel to give them opportunity and responsibility and then expect them to succeed. We do the hods a great service by giving them a simple, practical occupation. You've seen firsthand what happens when their hands are idle."

"Call me overcautious, but I've seen firsthand what happens when a couple of Pelphians don't take a hod seriously. Underestimating subordinates is how revolutions begin."

"Well, I wouldn't say—" Eigengrau's protest was interrupted by the arrival of Senlin's parcels. Joachim presented the three brown boxes, bound in white string.

Before he excused himself, Senlin thanked the general for locating the real murderer and insisted on buying the general's drink. In parting, Eigengrau said, "You know, sometimes I wonder if we wouldn't all be better off if we just bricked up the Old Vein and let the hods rule the walls."

Senlin recognized *Old Vein* as polite society's preferred appellation for the black trail. It was a phrase Tarrou had used, though that was before he was banished to it.

Senlin took his parcels to one of the club's water closets, which could scarcely be called a closet at all. The darkly paneled room held a vanity, a settee, a bar cart with a full decanter of port, and a large painting of a buxom nude on a tree swing.

He locked the door and savored the moment away from the boastful nobles and the Sphinx's spies. He poured a glass of port and drained it. The relief he felt at the murderer's capture was tainted by the thought that innocent hods, those unnamed "conspirators," may have been caught up in the general's net. The Pelphian sense of justice prized swiftness and certainty over all else, even accuracy. The Baths had taught him that much.

The first parcel held a black suit that seemed half tuxedo, half military uniform. The shirt was a vivid shade of orange and, combined with the suit, made him look a little like an oriole. The second package held a pair of shoes with a mirror polish that were as comfortable as bear traps.

The final parcel contained the mask. Even though he'd asked Mr. Stull to find him something grotesque and laughable, he'd not expected something quite so repulsive. The mask, which covered only the top half of the face, was maned with purple fur and topped with curling orange horns. It had the snub muzzle of a pug and deeply set eyes that were lensed with yellow glass. It looked like something conjured from a child's drawing. When he put the ghoulish thing on and smiled, he looked like an absolute lunatic.

But at least he did not look like himself. He hoped it would be enough to fool the spying butterflies, hoped the duke would find it such an amusing gaff he'd let the foolish Boskop parade before his noble friends. And when at last he was reintroduced to Marya, Senlin hoped she would see the garish disguise and not the man beneath it.

Something inside the mask poked his cheek, and he took it off to search for the culprit. A small paper tag fell out, and he caught it from the air. On one side of the tag was the price, twenty-five shekels; on the reverse side, in bold block letters, was the description: MASK OF THE SPHINX.

Senlin laughed until he wasn't sure what he was laughing at anymore.

Chapter Ten

Why do we call a dishonest person *two-faced*? Is it really so honest to wear the same face day in, day out, regardless of our mood, our condition, or the event? We are not clocks! Have a face for every occasion, I say! Be honest: Wear a mask."

—Oren Robinson of the *Daily Reverie*

By the time he left the Colosseum, the Pelphian sun was glowing over the roof of its stable at the ringdom's western edge. The curious acoustics of the domed ceiling and narrow city blocks made the clockworks rumble like an approaching train. The chatter became a clamor, and the clamor became a roar until the shopwindows rattled and the mannequins trembled, and no one could hear over the racket of the setting sun.

The quiet came as suddenly as a door slammed upon a storm. The sun went out, the gaslight stars grew more pronounced, and the hieroglyphic constellations emerged.

What Wilhelm had earlier called "a little soiree," the invitation declared THE LIGHTING OF JULY. The festivities would take place in the Circuit of Court, which lay behind a hedge that cordoned off nearly a quarter of the plaza. Senlin's daily track had taken him past the barrier, which appeared to be made of boxwoods. He had wondered how the hedge survived with only gaslight and alcoholic rain to sustain it.

Now on nearer inspection, he discovered the hedge was made of green silk leaves and wire vines that were anchored to a stone wall.

The entrance to the Circuit of Court stood open. Previously, he'd only seen the iron gates shut and locked. They bore the pattern of a great, convoluted spiral like the whorl of a fingerprint. He could hardly see the design now through the elevated crowd. Even the lowest lord and lady came to the court by sedan chair, carried on the shoulders of footmen. Some of the sedans were scarcely better than a dining room chair balanced upon a pair of broomsticks. The more opulent sedans were encased in rice paper and gold foil screens.

The sedans bumped together like logs in a river, and Senlin felt as if he'd fallen into some sort of maelstrom. He tried to get closer to the gate but was drawn into a hopeless vortex of nobles, servants, poles, and chairs. A lord toppled from his throne into the crowd. An elbow punched through the paper window of a sedan, exposing the shocked face of the lady within. There were screams of pain and cries for mercy. Senlin looked down and saw a man with a bloody ear crawl past his leg. Something slapped his neck, and Senlin turned to see a footman menacing him with a slipper. Senlin snatched the shoe away and struck the footman on the nose, surprising them both. He looked about, hoping for some person of authority to materialize and call for order or peace. Instead, he saw that most of the footmen wielded slippers. They beat upon the hopelessly frozen throng, receiving as many blows as they gave.

In the end, Senlin wasn't sure if he had escaped the mob by his own power or if it had merely ejected him. Either way, he was relieved to discover he had reached the front of the line.

A page in a gold tabard asked for Senlin's invitation, then held the card up to a lamp and inspected its watermark. Satisfied, the page nodded to the sentries who stood with rifles crossed before the entrance.

Senlin was about to pass through when the page caught him by the elbow and presented him with a six-inch glass tube with copper caps on either end.

"Don't forget your candle, sir," the page said.

"What is this for?" Senlin asked, thinking how the object didn't resemble any candle he had ever seen, but the page had already begun attending to the next in line. Senlin slid the curious cylinder into his coat pocket and strode past the guards.

Perhaps it was a side effect of his mask, which had a way of tunneling his vision and turning everything a uniform shade of yellow, but his first impression of the Circuit of Court was that it seemed a little desolate. The few attendees clumped together like scum on the surface of a pond. The orchestra, having been goaded by the maître d' to *Play something! Anything, for heaven's sake!* stumbled through the opening passage of a popular waltz. The conductor quickly decapitated the effort with a swat of his baton, and the ensuing silence was enriched by the rattling crash of a platter dropped by a waiter. Senlin felt the particular mixture of glumness and regret that only people who've arrived early to a party know. After having fought so hard to get in, his impulse now was to leave.

But he was quick to remind himself that he had not come to revel, and it didn't matter what sort of party it was so long as Marya came. The hour was still early. He had to be patient.

And the Circuit of Court was not without charm. Planters bloomed with fresh-cut flowers. Fountains bubbled over the schools of koi and goldfish that swam in their basins. The orchestra recovered and began to play a medley of romantic preludes. And because the attendees were still arriving, the servers outnumbered the guests. Senlin could hardly take six steps without being offered a sweet morsel or a full glass. No one seemed the least bit put off by his disguise. He was relieved to find that he was not the only one wearing a mask, though plain dominos were the more popular choice.

The dance floor of the Circuit of Court was made of polished sandstone, and at the center of that yellow-grained expanse rose a pyramid, some twenty feet in height and plated in white marble. A glass-paned star capped a pole that jutted from the peak. The star housed a filament that held an orange spark. The front of the pyramid was distinguished by an entrance, the lintel of which bore the gilded inscription THE UNFINISHED BIRTH. It was a phrase that Senlin would discover over the course of the evening no one could explain, except to say that the words and the structure seemed to reference something that predated the Tower itself. An iron track encircled the pyramid, and a caravan of mechanical beasts bobbed upon it at a leisurely pace. The beasts of the carousel, which were bronze cast and obviously very old, were all missing one piece or another: The camel lacked a head, the vulture had clipped wings, and the long-snouted hound had a bobbed tail and only three paws. The animals bore the remnants of ancient paint, much of which had flaked away, eroded by generations of riders. Even at that early hour, all the saddles were occupied.

Senlin was careful to keep off the dance floor, which consumed much of the court. The few couples who braved the floor were either very old or very young. Both seemed to enjoy the opportunity to dance without an audience. Observing an elderly couple sway in each other's arms, Senlin felt a pang of loss so sharp his thoughts fled it without further investigation.

It was only when he reached the opposite end of the court beyond the pyramid, where the stout central column of the ringdom met the floor that he noticed the two tunnels blistering up from the ground, and the curious train track that ran between them, and the small railcars that sat idle upon the track. The railcars were no bigger than a country buggy and were brightly painted. The track was separated from the general admission area by brass stanchions and velvet ropes, which were attended by a couple of jolly-looking old men in blue coats and gold kepis. Senlin nodded to them. They nodded back. He decided this was not the time to go in search of new mysteries.

As he walked, his hand was drawn again and again to his jacket pocket and the tobacco-wrapped messenger concealed there. He recognized the irony of skirting the Sphinx's gaze while carrying one of her spies around with him. But that moth was more than a courier; it was also a tether to his friends. At the very least, it could carry his final words to them should the evening go horribly awry.

He found a high table from which he could watch for the duke and Marya's arrival. After months of thinking of what he might say to Marya, it was finally time to decide what he *would* say to her. And yet faced with that question, his thoughts dove after every opportunity for distraction. Suddenly, everything was fascinating: a sweat ring on the table, the constellation overhead of a lion that looked markedly dog-faced, the congested laughter of a passing lord, a pair of young ladies dancing with their skirts held out like the wings of a bird.

For months, he had fought to be here, and now he wished to be anywhere else. Because the closer he came to the moment of their reunion, the more certain he felt that it would mark the end: the end of their marriage, the end of their shared history, and the end of a pursuit that had sustained him for many months, giving him purpose and strength.

Then he heard a voice that transported him as readily as a bookmark to another place and time. He was standing in the Market again with sand in his eyes and the sun on his neck, and that same sweet voice filling his ears, saying, "We'll meet again at the top of the Tower!"

He turned around, following the sound of her voice.

Marya held Wilhelm's arm as the two of them passed through a hidden door in the hedge. She thanked the doorman and laughed with relief at having skirted the mob at the gates.

At first sight, Senlin did not notice her auburn hair, twisted up like a conch shell and held in place by diamond-tipped pins, nor her fiery gown, which faded from smoke gray at the collar to flame orange at the hem, nor her bare white shoulders that he'd only seen behind closed doors before, nor the pearls around her neck. He saw nothing but her familiar face and her foreign gaze that flitted over him—a stranger in a frightful mask—and passed on.

But the glance was enough to stoke his determination. It was cowardly to pretend he had any right to reject himself. It was cowardly to fall before the blow landed. He could not beat himself for her, nor blame himself enough to steal her right to blame him if she wished. He had to face her, be truthful, and accept her choice.

He approached the handsome couple, bowed, and said, "Good evening, Sir Wil!" The duke looked at him with guarded perplexity, obviously not recognizing the man under the mask. "I'm so sorry. My name is Cyril Pinfield. We met earlier this after—"

The duke slapped Senlin affably on the chest, laughing as he did so. "Cyril! I didn't forget you, you idiot. You're wearing a mask!"

"Oh, of course! I am, aren't I. What do you think? Do you like it?"

"No, it's awful! Where did you get it? Those were popular, what—six months ago?"

"Really? The man at the shop said it was very popular. That's why he only had one left. Though, now that I think of it, it was rather dusty. Should I take it off?"

"No, no, no. Keep it on. It suits you. And who knows, perhaps you'll reinvigorate the fashion!" Struggling to contain his laughter, the duke said to Marya, "Darling, this is the gentleman I was telling you about. Now, don't let his looks fool you; he's really quite sensible."

"How do you do," Marya said, presenting her hand. It was difficult for Senlin to see the subtleties of her expression through the mask's warping and colored lenses, but the tone of her voice was discernably cool. He wondered if Wil had already told her about his proposal, wondered what she must think of a man who wished to sell her off in parcels.

When Senlin touched her hand, he could feel the quiver of her pulse, or perhaps it was only the shaking of his own hand. He bowed. "It's a pleasure to meet you, madam."

She withdrew her hand quickly, and before Senlin had straightened, she'd already gripped the duke's arm again. He couldn't help but feel rebuked by their intimacy.

The duke insisted they have drinks before the first word of business was uttered. Wil declared his intention to get Cyril "well and truly drunk," a campaign that began with a glass of champagne in one hand and a gin and tonic in the other. Feeling nervous and exposed, Senlin had little trouble maintaining the Boskop's awkward character. The mask made it difficult to drink anything, requiring him to turn his head to one side and pour the drinks into the corner of his mouth. Wilhelm found Senlin's frequent dribbling and sputtering highly amusing, and so proposed a toast whenever a new arrival joined their circle.

Senlin spoke little, though no one seemed to mind it. The court continued to fill, and as it did, more nobles were drawn to the duke and duchess. The famous couple managed the attention with practiced grace. They knew each earl and baron by name. Wil joked with the lords about their expanding middles, their graying temples, or their dwindling fortunes. He turned what might've been an insult in the mouth of a lesser man into a gibe so affectionate it seemed a compliment. Marya, meanwhile, listened to the ladies, each of whom were eager to impress her with the victories they'd won over a lazy maid, or a gossiping shopkeeper, or a spendthrift husband. Senlin observed the banalities from the margins, all but forgotten except when the duke raised a toast.

In an effort to keep himself from gawking at Marya, Senlin devised a sort of internal timer: He recited a ballad in his head, one that she had been quite fond of, which took about a minute to get through, and then he would permit himself a slow, passing glance. It seemed entirely likely that she wouldn't be able to see his eyes through the lenses of his mask, but it wasn't the fear of being obvious that made him ration his gazes. When he looked at her, he had a sudden urge to rip the mask from his face and declare himself, to be seen by her, to share in this awkward thrilling reunion, even if that meant his immediate execution. He was feeling impulsive, reckless. The dousing of alcohol wasn't helping matters. How foolish he had been to assume that an opportunity for a private moment with the Mermaid would present itself! He felt like a man who wakes in the dead of night to jot down some epiphany in the dark, only to rise the next morning to discover he'd written an unintelligible scrawl. He had no plan! There would be no revelation! He would go back to his hotel room having only tormented himself with the duke and duchess's apparent wedded bliss.

"Cyril, I heard you had a spot of trouble recently."

"What?" Senlin said, stirring from his thoughts. He looked about to see who had spoken and found Wil was smiling at him. "Trouble? You mean the hole in my socks?"

Wil's laughter was like a rallying cry that brought the encircling nobles to join him. "No, the hod in the alley, and those two idiots—what were their names?"

"Brown and...the lanky one. Uh, Cavendish," an earl with a red beard and corn-yellow teeth said.

"Yes, those two idiots. Killed by a hod. And apparently a little one. I'm glad I don't have to give that eulogy." The circle of men snorted their agreement. Senlin took from the duke's tone that the murdered men had not been members of the Coterie. When he looked around, he saw most of the nobles in orbit about the duke and duchess were wearing the club emblem. "Eigengrau said they were already down when you dashed in and scared the mudder off."

"Yes," Senlin said, though without much conviction. He wondered why Eigengrau had changed the details of his story. To ease the course of the investigation? As a personal favor? Now did not seem the time to delve into it. "I heard they caught the man."

"Yes, well, we can't have mad hods running around killing people, can we?" The duke sipped his champagne, and Marya, who'd been nodding along to a conversation with the red-bearded earl's wife a moment before, now pulled the duke's arm and said something only he could hear. The duke frowned as he listened, perhaps annoyed by the interruption, but as she spoke, his expression brightened and finally broke into a grin, which he directed at Senlin. "Oh, that is an idea! Cyril, are you prone to motion sickness?"

"No," he said, then sensing the duke's disappointment, he quickly added, "Well, except for on airships. I spent my trip down hanging over the rail. And on horses—I always get sick on horses. And I don't care for rocking chairs. Chairs should not have a sense of wanderlust. We don't have rocking tables. Why have rocking chairs? It's obscene! Otherwise, my constitution is hardy."

"Yes, you sound like quite a rock, Cyril. To the rock!" the duke said, raising another toast. Senlin gamely knocked his glass against his plaster nose and spilled champagne on his jacket. "I asked because my wife had a thought. She'd like to hear more about your notion of a Tower-wide tour but would also like to show you one of our more novel diversions. We call it the Merry Loop. It's sort of like a sleigh ride, but it goes all through the underground. You can tell her all about your grand vision and—"

"And all this madness about cutting up my name and selling off the letters," Marya interjected. "Oh, here's an *M* for you and an *A* for you and an *R* for you—" she said, miming the act of handing out the letters to the noble ladies of the group. "And here's your *Y*, Mr. Pinfield." She made as if to throw it at him. He flinched, and the ladies sniggered. But he had not flinched at the pantomimed throw; he had cringed because of the passionate, almost trembling disdain with which she glared at him. "What in the world makes you think I'd trust a stranger with my name? You seem to have done a very good job of stuffing my husband's head full of imaginary riches, but I promise you: I'm not so easily stuffed. So"—she tugged her gloves off as she spoke—"I'll give you one go-round on the Merry Loop to convince me that you're not a scoundrel. And if you bring your dinner up in the process, then the deal's off."

The duke laughed. "I did warn you, Cyril: She is a spirited woman!"

Senlin let himself be pulled along by the party toward the short, roped-off train track. The duke's merry troop bypassed the line of nobles who waited outside the ropes, though Wil shook hands with half the gentlemen waiting in line, exchanging salutations, compliments, and promises as if the queue were his own reception line. The two elder porters in blue greeted the duke with salutes and quickly unclipped the rope so his party could approach the tracks where a single cart waited to be filled. Wil tipped them both handsomely.

One of the noblemen grabbed Senlin's shoulders and shook him, though Senlin didn't know whether it was meant to stir his nerves or spark some enthusiasm in him. Someone took his wineglass. The porter asked him if he had his candle, and he mumbled that he did. The party cheered, and someone pushed him onto the hard bench of the cart. Ahead, just inside the mouth of the mineshaft, the track dove into darkness. He felt someone take the seat beside him. A metal bar was lowered over their laps. He watched her hands grip the front lip of the cart. He marked the gold glint of her wedding band.

Then the cart lurched toward the darkness. A mechanical rumble traveled through the seat and up his spine, and the cheers of the party turned to howls of laughter, which he knew was for him: the terror-stiffened Boskop, off to lose his supper on some twisting ride. And when the floor seemed to fall out from under them, and the cart plunged into the dark, Senlin yelled, not out of horror, but anguish.

The track leveled out a moment later, and the darkness was subdued by the appearance of soft electric lights along the roof of the tunnel, which ran nearly within arm's reach. The stone around them was so roughly cut it seemed almost natural, like the eroded tunnels of a subterranean stream. The music and the chatter were replaced by the dreamy regularity of the clacking wheels.

"You can take that ridiculous thing off now," Marya said. "What are you doing here, Tom?"

Chapter Eleven

Eventually, the certainty of a noose is preferable to the agony of an appeal.

—Oren Robinson of the *Daily Reverie*

The Sphinx's mask sat in his lap. It seemed to gaze up at him with keen, catlike eyes.

They stared straight ahead, breathed hard, and said nothing. The walls of the tunnel changed. It was a moment before he understood what he was seeing—a re-creation of the Tower's construction in miniature. It began with square-edged blocks jutting from the rough-hewn rock as if from a mountainside. The blocks were surrounded and climbed upon by hundreds of figurines, none larger than a thimble, wielding hammers, pulleys, and ropes. The workers were frozen in the act of cutting the stones and pulling them free of the mountain.

The tunnel opened around them, and the scene that had begun in the walls now continued on a passing ledge, sculpted to resemble a desert floor. The ceiling was painted sky blue, blotched with white clouds. Teams of miniature men hauled blocks over a path of logs down to a model train. A black locomotive pulled a line of flat-bedded cars, each loaded with a single block.

Ahead of their jangling cart, the tunnel contracted about an archway. The passage beyond was unlit, presenting a yawning inky black. The scene on the tunnel ledge ran up and around the archway, crowding about the unlit hole as if gravity had turned a corner. The figures worked bucket cranes, as if excavating the dark. Senlin felt a little thrill of revelation when he realized what the scene was meant to re-create: the digging of the well beneath the Tower. For a second, he had the queasy feeling that they were falling into that well as their cart passed into darkness.

And the sensation was made much worse when the cart plummeted sharply down.

The mask flew up from his lap and into the gloom. It seemed to chase after his stomach. The sense of free-falling into nothing blew away the awkward silence that had gripped them a moment before. Marya threw her arms around his neck even as he embraced her. Her full cheek pressed into the hollow of his neck as snuggly as a dovetail joint. Amid his terror, Senlin felt a great pitch of emotion at the contact. The cart around them rattled so violently he was sure it would fly from the rails. In the deathly dark, he turned his lips to hers, and they kissed as if it were the end of everything.

Then the track leveled out and the wrenching sense of doom faded.

As the weight of gravity returned to their limbs, their embrace weakened. A glow appeared before them and lit them well enough to see each other again. They came apart as if stunned by what they'd done. The railcar slowed to a stop. Ahead of them, the track angled upward, supported by a trestle that made the rails seem to hang free in the air. The track proceeded upward about a central column, spiraling out of sight.

The column held a frieze that depicted the building of the Tower, level by level: the fitting of blocks, the laying of foundations, the carving of the edifice. The air was lit by pale electric lights that tinted everything orange. The base of their cart caught on some unseen gears in the tracks, which began to carry them up the curling spire at a crawling pace.

She stared at him. He couldn't interpret her gaze, and she didn't give him long to consider it. That vulnerable, uncertain expression was as short-lived as a wink. Quickly, her lips straightened and thinned into a formal line. The kiss they'd shared suddenly seemed long ago. "I thought you'd gone home," she said.

He twisted to face her in the cart, one arm on the rail before her, one on the back of the seat. The spread of his arms was open and pleading. "No, I couldn't. Of course I couldn't. I've spent the past year looking for you."

She studied his face, perhaps searching for honesty at first, but then he watched as she discovered each new crease, the scar like pink yarn that cut his chin, the dappling damage of the sun. Powder and tint flattered the contours of her face, though the effort seemed entirely unnecessary: her beauty radiated through the paint.

"You look very . . . well. How are you?" he asked. His heart urged him to say more, but he was afraid compliments would only chip away at her happiness. If she was happy.

"I am well. I've been very busy. I've been . . . preparing for the new concert season."

She had never spoken to him so formally before, not even in the classroom. The tone made him pull in his arms and look away. The column their cart coiled about was inlaid with glowing rods placed at regular intervals.

"Why are you here, Tom?" she asked. "Why come now, after all this time?"

The fact that she asked the question seemed all the answer he needed. Yet, he had come this far, and he had to speak his heart. "I've come to rescue you. That is, if you need rescuing."

Her laughter seemed to surprise her. She stifled her mouth with a cupped hand and shook her head apologetically. When she spoke, she was a little more her former self. "Where have you been? How did you survive? How are you here, dressed like that, convincing everyone you're a Boskop? You're going to parties and wearing a tuxedo, and that ridiculous mask!"

Her words left him at a loss. There wasn't time enough to explain a year, to account for it all. The teeth that carried their railcar up began to grind and their cart wobbled like a top losing momentum. "I've made a lot of mistakes," he said.

"What?" she all but screamed over the noise.

"Mistakes! I've made a lot of mistakes! I've robbed. I've pirated. I've killed men. Never carelessly. I was addicted to Crumb, though I'm off it now. I completely lost my mind. I still feel like I've only got a part of it back," he shouted. Abruptly, the cart passed over the noisome patch, though he hadn't time to correct his volume before he cried, "I kissed a woman!"

He saw the disappointment crimp her brow. If he could've picked between a gunshot and witnessing that flash of pain on her face, he would've chosen the pistol. She sighed and said, "Well, I did remarry, so I suppose . . . in the grand scheme of things, I . . ." She couldn't finish the thought.

"Tell me, are you happy?" When she deliberated, he quickly added, "If you are, it's perfectly all right. I'll be happy for you. But if you're unhappy, please tell me."

She had pressed her hip into the corner of the seat, retreating as far from him as she could. She turned her chin up, studying the ascent of the rail, gauging, perhaps, how long they had left.

When she didn't answer, he blundered on, "I know this might be hard to believe after listening to me crow about my failures, but I have some resources and some powerful friends. If you want to leave this life, I can help you. And if you love it here, or are happy enough, I will go, and I won't bother you again."

She made a sound, a gentle scoff, as if complaining in her sleep. "What does happiness have to do with anything? I haven't let happiness make a decision since . . . I'm resigned, Tom. That's what I am. I am resolute." He heard the formal tone creep back into her voice. "And once you decide to just accept things, there may not be much happiness in it, but there is . . . certainty. And that's comforting. Or at least bearable."

The urge to argue made him twitch. It seemed one thing to surrender her to a happy life, but quite another to give her over to the meager pleasures of *certainty*. "I know I have no right to judge, but that doesn't seem good enough. Not for you. I can't offer you a life like the one you have here—the fame, the wealth, the certainty—but I would try, I would strive with everything I have, to make you happy."

"There are some lovely things about this life," she said, as if reading from a script. "I get to play the piano and sing my heart out, and there's always some event to attend. You can't be bored. It's not allowed. And I've grown accustomed, I suppose, to having someone do the wash and cook the meals and make the beds and—"

Their cart halted, jerking them forward against the bar that held them. The unexpected stop made Senlin look down, and he saw how high they'd climbed already. Somehow not moving made the height insufferable, and despite his months aboard an airship, he felt a pang of vertigo.

"Do you have the candle?" Marya asked. Senlin looked at her, his confusion apparent. "The glass tube they gave you at the door. Do you have it?"

Remembering at last, he felt his pocket and pulled out the cylinder. As he did, he saw that their cart had stopped on a gloomy patch of the track. He looked and found the culprit: One of the lights in the modeled Tower had burned out. He opened the glass plate over the fixture. A darkened cylinder, much like the one he held, stretched between two copper clasps. He removed the depleted cylinder and replaced it with the new candle. The whisker of wire at the heart of the glass tube began to glow at once. As soon as he closed the glass hatch again, their cart resumed its ascent.

He pocketed the spent candle, deciding that this was the real purpose of the ride: to replace dead links in some larger circuit. The Brick Layer or the Sphinx had here again attempted to hide some necessary function behind an amusement.

"Do you love her?" Marya asked, shocking Senlin from his thoughts.

He looked at her, his stranger-wife, and wished he had an entire answer, one that would fit inside a yes or no. "She has been a good friend and has put up with an awful lot of my nonsense."

She laughed at that. "The basis of any good relationship!"

"But I can't give her my heart, Marya, because that still belongs to you. I am so, so sorry for—"

"Oh, Tom, we can't do that. We haven't time. If we had days, weeks, maybe. But the ride is almost done."

And sure enough, when he looked up, he saw their spiral upward was drawing to an end. The tiny figures raising the Tower began to disappear, their forms not carved so deeply, their edges indistinct as if rubbed down or covered by a cloud. At its peak, the wild facade of the Tower eroded into a featureless blank, though Senlin couldn't say whether it had been left unfinished or if that represented the real peak of this world—an eraser at the end of a pencil.

"Are you sure you want to stay? If you want to leave, it doesn't mean you have to return to me or Isaugh. You can choose another life. Any life you want. I will do all I can to deliver you to it. Just say the word."

She touched his cheek. What might've seemed an intimate gesture in another context, here felt like a dismissal. "Go home, Tom. Or go to her, whoever she is, the one who puts up with your nonsense. I give you back your heart. Make her happy. Make a home. If you came for absolution, you are absolved."

The track crested upon an uncarved, undecorated tunnel. The light at the end of the line grew brighter. She seemed to grow calmer, even as everything inside Senlin tilted toward war. Had he squandered his only opportunity? Had he spoken too much or said too little? Would he in twenty years look back on this moment as the defining blunder of his life?

"I love you," he said.

"I know you do. You wouldn't have come here, risked so much, if you didn't. And I love you, too. With all my heart. But this isn't about us, Tom. This is about the lives and hearts of others. For their sake—for mine, too—I want you to get as far away from here as you can. Please."

The distant purr of the court became a roar as their cart broke from the tunnel. As soon as the duke and his party saw them, they raised a cheer. The railcar stopped, and Wil offered Marya his hand. She stepped out lightly, wearing an expression of perfect poise, even as Senlin was more roughly removed by the duke's friends, who shook his hand, rocked his shoulders, and jostled his elbows. They remarked how pale he looked. They declared him damp and shaky as a new-born, which delighted everyone in the group. Senlin swayed on his feet when they released him.

"Well?" Wilhelm asked Marya, drawing her to his side. "What do you say, dear? Did Cyril make a convincing case?"

Marya glanced at the unmasked, unsteady Boskop who looked on the verge of being ill. "I wouldn't let that man manage a cart full of socks," she said, and everyone howled with delight.

Senlin excused himself soon after, citing again his delicate constitution, which the Merry Loop had upset. He offered a few unsavory details, which no one cared to hear, and the duke ushered him to the exit amid a wash of ambiguous hurrahs.

Before depositing him outside the gate, the duke offered Senlin some apparently sincere but misplaced consolation: "Oh, don't fret, Cyril. We've not heard her final word on this. She'll change her mind. Come by the club tomorrow. I'll have better news."

Senlin returned to the Bon Royal. Upon unlocking the door, he briefly believed he was in the wrong room: All evidence of his tantrum and all the stacks of newspapers were missing. But then he saw his two ruined coats hanging upon the wall and found the bill on his dresser for the destroyed archival copies of the *Daily Reverie*, which came to thirteen minas.

Thirteen minas. The amount renewed his shame. He had come to the Tower with less in his pocket. The same amount would've fed his crew for months and months and fed them well. And he had ripped it apart in a fit of indulgence.

Loosening his tie, he flopped upon the bed. Marya's parting words echoed in his ears: *This is about the lives and hearts of others*. Again, he saw her take Wil's hand as he helped her from the cart. He watched the handsome duke's arm wind about her waist, saw the smile they shared in that intimate space amid public scrutiny where couples refreshed their bond.

He shivered. He was no rescuer. He was a voyeur, or worse. He was a despoiler.

Leaping up, he snapped open the lid of the cigar box and unwrapped one of the Sphinx's messengers. He twisted the moth's head, and said, "All right, Byron. I hope you remember my request. I promise this is the one and only time I will impose upon your discretion, but please,

please: I'd like to say a few words to Edith alone. Thank you, Byron. You are a good friend." Senlin paused and pressed the recorder against his shirtfront.

Opening the curtains over the balcony doors, he peered through the light-streaked glass at the bank of balconies across from his own. Each seemed a discrete little stage, complete with actors, a story, a dramatic question, a crisis. Whether anyone was watching or not, whether it meant anything or not, those players poured out their hearts to keep them from bursting in their chests.

Senlin shut his eyes, drew a deep breath, then spoke into the recorder: "Dear Edith..."

Chapter Twelve

To whiten the complexion, one may drain a little blood. And the same is true of our pale city.
—Oren Robinson of the *Daily Reverie*

For the first time in many days, Senlin slept through the night. He was spared the torment of bad dreams and racing thoughts, and when he woke, he awoke refreshed to a room that was free of all the paper ghosts of the past.

He understood why Marya had chosen a stable, if imperfect, life over the ordeal of escape, the realities of his changed character, and the question of whether their former home could ever be home again. He did not blame her for choosing the duke. Yes, Wilhelm was a bit overbearing and perhaps too ambitious, but he was nice enough and obviously keen on her. And more importantly, Senlin had her answer; he knew her heart. After a year of wretched ambiguity, even the certainty of rejection felt like a gift. He was filled with a buoyant sense of relief.

The pickled light of the mechanical sun seemed to shine more brightly that morning. As he struck out across the crowded plaza, he was not thinking of Marya, the duke, the Sphinx, Marat, or even Tarrou, who was still, for the moment, forgotten. He thought only of Edith. He imagined their reunion aboard the *State of Art*. He imagined what they would say. He romanced the moment until it was larger than either of them, perhaps even larger than their feelings. He knew, coming so quick on the heels of Marya's rejection, that this longing was a shameful indulgence, like drinking wine in the morning or spending all day in the bath. But he didn't care. It felt as if the old headmaster of Isaugh were dead, and he was finally free.

He set out for the Colosseum out of habit more than purpose. Of course, the new day brought a new spectacle to clog the way, and soon he found himself caught in a gauntlet of newsboys who flapped papers and cried headlines in such heated competition with one another he couldn't distinguish a single sensible phrase. Girls in white stockings with bows in their hair sold sachets of raisins and almonds. Men on stilts strode over the crowd like water striders on a pond. They sold cheap wooden periscopes to people wishing to peep over the heads of their neighbors.

Feeling in no mood to spend his morning in such a human bog, Senlin was firm with his advances. Whenever someone turned to give him a sour stare for shoving against them or stepping on their heel, he tugged at his lapel, brandishing the Coterie's pin like some sort of official badge. More often than not, the ploy worked, and the citizenry parted before him.

When he broke upon the front edge of the crowd, Senlin was surprised to find General Eigengrau standing at the center of the spectacle. Not far behind the general, a rubble wall patched with gobs of mortar protruded from the white cobble floor like a wart. Sixteen soldiers in full dress stood about with rifles held at rest. Their black caps were decorated with a gold medallion, a black pom-pom, and a yellow plume. They looked more like painted dolls than men of war.

"Mr. Pinfield!" General Eigengrau said, spotting him before Senlin had time to decide whether he wished to be seen. His high, broad shoulders and narrow waist made him look like a splitting wedge. He did not so much seem to stand upon the ground as pierce it. "I heard you took a turn on our Merry Loop last night. How did you find it?"

Senlin was surprised to discover that word had traveled so fast, or that it had traveled at all, really. What did one tourist's queasy evening matter to a general? But he understood the implication quickly enough: Wilhelm and Eigengrau had recently discussed him. "It was dreadful!" Senlin said and dashed his handkerchief out in the air. "I don't understand the appeal at all. It's like being sealed in a barrel and kicked down the stairs." He blew his nose and inspected the result. The general's lips curled with revulsion. "Wil said you had apprehended the murderer."

"Yes. And you're just in time to see the closing of the case."

"Is this some sort of public courtroom?"

"We've already been through all that. This is what we call the Wall of Recompense. This is where sentences are carried out."

"Sentences?" Senlin asked, fearing he already knew the answer.

"Executions." Eigengrau spoke the word with a sort of formal sincerity. Senlin recognized that tone of voice. It was one he had often used with parents who came to complain about their child's poor marks. It was a tone of mutual regret and personal absolution, a tone that said, *I am as disappointed as you are.*

The revelation brought a slew of questions to mind: Who had identified the murderer if not him? Who had defended the accused in his trial? Was justice always doled out so quickly in Pelphia, or was this alacrity reserved for the hods?

Before Senlin could decide where to begin his inquiry, they were interrupted by a man carrying a leather satchel and a peculiar three-legged box. One side of the box had an accordion snout that ended in a brass-capped nostril. The opposite side of the box was draped with a black cape. The young man wore a brown suit that seemed too short at the sleeves and cuffs, and he had brown hair that draped and swung like the ears of a cocker spaniel. He asked the general where he should set up his equipment. In answer, Eigengrau organized his troop with a few curt words. The men's training was immediately evident. They formed a pencil-straight line parallel to the rubble wall. The young man set his tripod down so close to the end of the rank he almost seemed a part of it.

"It's called a camera," the general said to Senlin with a confiding sort of admiration. "It captures light and shadows and shapes. It creates a physical record of a moment in time. Isn't that incredible?" The general rested his hand on the pommel of his long-nosed pistol. "Soon,

I'll be able to bottle an entire fleet, a fortress, even a battle inside one pho-to-graph," he said, carefully pronouncing each syllable of the unfamiliar word. "I'll be able to count the guns on an enemy warship from the comfort of my own home. Imagine that! This little squeeze box is going to change the way we fight wars forever."

"Wonderful." Senlin spoke the word without any enthusiasm. The photographer removed the cover from the camera lens and tucked his head under the cape. Something about that hunched posture reminded him of the White Chrom den where men and women sat with their heads under cloth napkins to collect the intoxicating vapors and to hide their shame.

"For the moment, the technology is still unreliable, and the quality of the picture is inconsistent. But it's good enough for the papers, and they're leading the charge to build a better phu-ta-graph." Senlin noticed the general had pronounced the word differently but thought better than to offer a correction. "Right now, the *Daily Reverie* uses engravings for all of their publications, but in the near future, the news will be filled with pages and pages of pictures: the whole world sliced up and delivered to your door." They both watched the photographer carefully extract a square panel from his satchel and fit it into the camera. "You know, they used to send a sketch artist to draw the executions. They'd ask us to leave the bodies of the condemned so that they could prop them up and finish their drawings. Gruesome stuff, really."

"Sir, could you please have the subjects line up? I need to get them in focus."

"Certainly!" Eigengrau called to the sergeant standing beside the rubble barrier to bring out the condemned. The shackled hods were waiting behind the Wall of Recompense. The hods' appearance accomplished what few spectacles in Pelphia could—it unified and focused the crowd. The explosion of boos was so intense and sudden it made Senlin jump.

The heads of the hods had been freshly shaved. Otherwise, they looked very little alike. Their skin was of every color. One was lame with age. Another seemed to have not yet grown to her full height:

Her limbs rattled inside the iron cuffs that held them. Some of the hods looked out at the roaring crowd—the hawkers on stilts, the glinting lenses of periscopes—with expressions that ranged from panic to anger to confusion. Some hods stared at the ground before them as if they were toeing the edge of a cliff. One stood gagged, with his hands chained so tightly behind him, his breastbone stood out like a plowshare. Some cursed. Some wept. There were eleven of them in all, and not one among them was the murderer Senlin had seen in the alley.

"General, I think there's been some mistake. None of these are the murderer."

"Really? Are you sure? Look, that hod matches your description perfectly." Eigengrau pointed to the eldest of the hods. His skeleton seemed swollen under his cinder-dark skin.

"No, that's not him at all. It's obviously not him. Call the judge. I'll testify to it this instant." Senlin was having trouble maintaining his awkward, ineffectual persona. His passions only grew stronger when the photographer walked out from behind his camera and began to direct the condemned hods to move a little this way or that, to change their posture, to lift or lower their chins. The hods complied in numb disbelief.

"Well, the man confessed to it, so there really isn't anything to be done about it now."

"But who are all these other people?"

"Mr. Pinfield, are you really so unversed with the basic tenets of the law as it pertains to the hods?" Eigengrau tossed his short cape aside so he could access a waist pocket. He drew out a small notebook, which he consulted as he continued to talk. "Mr. Cavendish and Mr. Brown's total fortunes, including all their assets and subtracting their not inconsiderable obligations, came to 219 minas, 8 shekels, and 11 pence. The total debt of these conspirators comes to exactly 219 minas, 8 shekels, and 11 pence. Their death will balance the books."

"That doesn't make any sense! Surely someone holds the debts of these hods. Aren't you stealing from their pockets?"

"Sir! Everyone understands the risk of holding a hod's bill. Hods perish all the time. The Old Vein is full of bones. Is there anything rarer in the Tower than a hod who lives long enough to pay his debt down entirely? Every law-abiding citizen shares the burden of the hods. It is our civic duty."

"But look at her!" Senlin said, pointing a finger at the young woman against the wall. Her narrow chest was wrapped with fabric so dingy and rough it wouldn't serve for sackcloth. "What is she? Fourteen, perhaps fifteen years old? What possible justice could have brought her here, to this?"

Eigengrau looked down at Senlin with a pitying smile. When he spoke, his tone was so full of condescension Senlin considered throwing his life away just to strike the smug look from the man's face. "Mr. Pinfield, I did not impoverish that girl. I did not give her parents license to bear a child they could not support. I did not direct them to run up debts they could not repay. And I did not sell their child, like a sow at the market, into hoddery." Seeing that his explanation had not softened Senlin's expression of perplexed distress, the general put his arm around the Boskop's shoulder and said, "Perhaps it might help to think of justice as a sort of moral accounting. Like accounting, justice doesn't deform to accommodate excuses or bad luck or good intentions. Justice draws a bottom line: a line that is straight, clear, and unequivocal. It is my duty to balance the accounts upon that line. I must be accountable for the people who are not accountable for themselves. I've accepted this fact. I do not expect to be adored for the work I do, the sacrifices I make. Righteousness is its own reward."

"How much?"

"Pardon?"

"How much does the young lady owe? What is her debt?"

With a great show of tolerance, Eigengrau consulted his notebook. "Eleven pence."

"Elev..." Emotion constricted his throat before he could finish. It dawned upon him that she had been chosen only because she fit the bill. In the eyes of the law, she was loose change. He pulled out his billfold. "Well, I'll pay it. In fact, I'll pay for all of them. It may take me a day or two to get the funds together, but I'm sure you know I'm good for it."

"Mr. Pinfield... *Cyril*," Eigengrau said and laid a very long, almost slender hand upon Senlin's arm. "It isn't your fault. I think you are a little traumatized by what happened. I'm so accustomed to seeing death that I sometimes forget that not all men are unaffected by the sight of violence. Even if you paid the debts of these hods, I would still have to fetch more to pay the blood debt that is owed. This is hard, manly work. Perhaps you should leave before—"

"All good! I'm ready!" the photographer said.

The sergeant called for the squad to ready their aim. Sixteen barrels swung up to point at the hods. The photographer raised a small trough on a stick. Gunpowder lined the flash pan. "Perhaps we could count to three? That would be very helpful. They should fire with the flash."

"Wait! Stop!" Senlin pulled his arm free of the general's grasp and moved to restrain the photographer, to put a hand over his mouth if he had to.

But before the count began, the black powder in the flash pan ignited with a percussive poof. Sparks leapt onto the sleeve of Senlin's coat. The sergeant shouted his command a split second later. The *whump* of lead balls into flesh and bone was nearly drowned out by the crack of gunshots. Some of the hods went rigid as if pinned by their wounds. Others slumped down, pulling upon the chains that linked them. The young woman had been struck in the lung. Though the weight of the other bodies and her shackles pulled hard upon her, she fought to stay on her feet.

But the shock that stanched her wound did not last. A red streamer ran from the hole in her chest, crimped by the fading beats of her heart. She coughed up dark blood. Her legs failed her, and she fell in line with the dead.

Senlin swatted at the flames that ran up his sleeve. Seeing he had no choice but to take the burning garment off, he threw it to the ground and stamped the fire out. He stood over the smoking coat, panting with fright and rage.

The thunder of gunshots still rolled around the bowl of the sky. The crowd stood silent.

The photographer, who'd been examining his camera, looked up with a scowl and said, "I'm sorry. I didn't get the shot. Could we prop them up and try again?"

Chapter Thirteen

I never respond to invitations. It just smacks of desperation. The only event I am certain to attend is my funeral, and I hope to arrive very, very late.

— Oren Robinson of the *Daily Reverie*

The usual, sir?" Joachim asked.

"No. No," Senlin said, feeling almost nauseated by the thought of having to choke down another glass of blood-warm water. "Rum. A tall rum. A pail full of rum, please."

If the club bartender felt any surprise at this departure in the Boskop's character, he didn't show any sign of it. He produced a large tumbler that was half filled with a fine, oaky rum, the complexities of which were entirely wasted upon Senlin. He finished the glass off in three gulps.

After the execution, Senlin had gone back to his room to change out of his burned coat. He'd had no other option but to put on the tuxedo he'd worn the night before, which seemed a little flamboyant for such an early hour. Though what did it matter? What did any of this nonsense about fashion matter?

The Sphinx hunted for a dangerous conspiracy while so much evil stood out in the open. Of course a revolution was coming! How could it not be? Senlin disagreed vehemently with Marat's means and egotistical motives, but he could not argue with the manifest need for change. The need was so great, in fact, it had a stupefying effect upon the spirit. How could one hope to change a culture, save an entire class? And why even try when he could adopt Eigengrau's exonerating pragmatism? Why bother saving one young woman when another would only take her place? Why save anyone if not everyone could be saved? The tree of history rotted faster than it grew. The Tower crumbled more quickly than it could be repaired. Any effort to forestall the inevitable collapse was not only futile, it was naive.

No. Senlin could not allow cynicism to pardon his conscience. He might not be able to save all the hods, but he could save one. He must save one.

"Joachim, which Coterie member owns the Iron Bear?"

"The Marquis de Clarke," Joachim said, refilling his glass without having been asked.

Senlin sipped from the pour he had not objected to. He had been hoping for a man of some lower rank: an earl or a baron. "And what sort of man is the marquis?"

"He's famous for his parties. He has a doting daughter who he'd like to see married, and he has the largest bar tab of anyone here."

"Aha!" Senlin said, raising his glass to this ray of hope. Perhaps the marquis was in need of some liquidity.

"He's very attached to his champion," Joachim continued. "The Bear makes him a lot of money. He's only lost one match, and that was a few months ago. The marquis was livid when it happened. He had a large wager riding on the Bear that night and was in no mood to pay it out. The marquis had snuck a pistol into the club—which is completely against the rules, of course—and he would've shot his champion dead in the ring if he hadn't been restrained." Joachim gave a laconic laugh, though Senlin wasn't sure a joke had been told. "The Iron Bear hasn't lost since."

"How much does a brawler usually cost?"

"Well, I've seen champions sold for as little as a shekel in a fit of pique, and for as much as a thousand minas."

"You could buy a yacht with that sort of money!"

"You could, indeed. But there really isn't any way to know how much a champion is worth until money changes hands."

Senlin pondered all of this as he sipped his rum. After all the bills and bribes, he had 194 minas left of what the Sphinx had sent him with, which didn't seem enough to purchase the marquis's beloved champion outright.

"When is the Iron Bear's next bout?" Senlin asked.

Joachim consulted a program he had tucked behind the bar, squinting like a man in denial of the onset of middle age. "He fights this evening. Seven o'clock. He's facing the Djinn. Should be quite a bruiser."

"Do you have pencil and paper I can borrow? I need to write a quick note."

To Senlin's amusement, the bartender produced an entire tabletop writing desk. He opened the lacquered box to reveal an inkpot, two colors of stationery, envelopes, a selection of nibs, and sticks of red melting wax for the production of a seal. Forgoing all the peripherals, Senlin selected a single sheet and a pencil to compose his note.

Dear John,

I want to buy your freedom, but your habit of winning puts you out of my financial reach. If your record were to be tarnished by your performance this evening, I believe I can convince your master to part with you. I hope you still trust me, at least enough to allow me to repay my debt to you.

Look for me on the club rail.

Faithfully Yours,
The Great Grim Scowler of Café
Risso

Senlin folded the note and promised Joachim he would return with his pencil in a moment.

He descended to the lobby floor and joined the noisy stream of men arriving for the early fights. The stands had only begun to fill, so Senlin hadn't any trouble approaching the worn wood rail that separated the bleachers from the arena floor. Leaning down, he showed a five-shekel coin to a young lad raking the ruddy clay. The groomer edged his way near enough for Senlin to make his proposal: If he delivered

119

the note to the Iron Bear and returned with a reply, the coin would be waiting for him. The lad glanced about and, deciding it was safe, took the card and pencil and vanished into one of the service tunnels.

While he waited for the young man's return, Senlin watched the birds swoop down from the dome into the footwells of the stands and peck about for scraps. A magpie hopped onto the neighboring bench with a penny clenched in its beak. For a moment, Senlin thought the tuxedoed bird was offering him the coin as a tip, then the magpie spread its wings and flapped away.

The wait was a nervous one. Senlin wondered if he had just penned what would become the first exhibit in his trial. Even if the young messenger didn't turn his note over to the Colosseum guard, it wasn't inconceivable that Tarrou's loyalties had been turned by his time on the black trail. Perhaps he had fallen in with Marat's zealots and had pledged his allegiance to the Hod King. Perhaps he'd learned to babble in their inscrutable tongue. Senlin's former café companion might expose him with a word. Senlin shuddered at the thought as a white-aproned bookmaker stepped onto a bench and announced the day's fights through a battered bullhorn.

The groomers raked up their footprints as they retreated to the tunnels. The heavy portcullises shut behind them with a finality that seemed an answer in itself: Tarrou would not be joining him in a new conspiracy.

It had been foolish to try to get a note to John. The best Senlin could hope for now was to escape before the messenger identified him to the guards. He fled to the lobby, half expecting to find the kettle-chested Wakeman waiting for him. But the lobby was deserted except for the bookies, the tapsters, and one or two drunks. Cheers from the arena bounced about the vestibule like a taunt.

Senlin was preparing to bolt for the exit when the young groomer emerged from a door behind the betting booths. The youth trotted over, presenting the folded notecard and pencil. He collected his payment and retreated the way he'd come without ever uttering a word.

Feeling obvious standing in the middle of the unpopulated lobby, Senlin moved to the periphery to lean upon the trunk of a fat column. He unfolded the card and read:

Dear Scowler,

I can't believe you're not dead. Well done and congratulations on your continued good luck! Still, I have not forgotten what happened the last time I threw my lot in with yours. Part of me is quite sure that one adventure with you is enough for a lifetime. Then again...

I don't know, Headmaster. I just don't know.

I suppose my decision will be plain enough. If you see me getting the spit knocked out of me, you'll know I've thrown my lot in with yours. Heaven help me. Heaven help us both.

J. T.

Senlin had prepared himself for a yes or a no, but he wasn't prepared for a maybe. Perhaps he should cut his losses and make for the port. The *State of Art* would arrive soon enough. He could admit defeat, return empty-handed, and hope the Sphinx would be satisfied with his marginal efforts at espionage. Or he could hold out hope that Tarrou would take his offer, throw the fight, and let himself be won away from the marquis. Surely the Sphinx would not complain of the opportunity to interview a hod who'd spent so much time inside the Colosseum. If he could get John out, everyone might be happy, most of all Tarrou.

He stared at the floor as he pondered the question. The red lines in the marble were as fine as the veins of a bloodshot eye. Sprinkled all around the base of the column were dozens of what seemed to be large chips of plaster in varying shades of pink, gray, and white. Curious, he bent and retrieved a chip. Even before he had straightened, he saw what it really was—the paper wing of a butterfly, painted to resemble stone. He was standing amid a graveyard of the Sphinx's spies.

He circled that pillar, then another, and though he found many more wings, he didn't find a single clockwork thorax. All the recorders were missing.

The implication was clear enough. Someone was catching the Sphinx's butterflies, stripping the wings off here, and pocketing the recording devices. The fact that he'd found the wings in the lobby seemed to exonerate the hods, who weren't allowed to roam about. That left the Coterie and their staff as the more likely suspects. Senlin wondered how they caught the butterflies. He tried to imagine the guards charging about the lobby, swinging butterfly nets. Regardless of the *how*, the evidence did nothing to answer the more pressing question of *why*. Why would the Coterie go to such lengths to destroy the butterflies? Senlin hadn't seen any evidence that the duke or his compatriots gave the Sphinx the slightest consideration. The Sphinx was little more than an oddity.

The discovery of the stripped wings drove off any thought of a premature escape. Not only did he owe Tarrou the chance to make up his mind, but Senlin felt he owed the Sphinx answers to at least some of these questions.

The matter settled, Senlin returned to the Coterie Club and reclaimed his stool. He asked Joachim if he would point out the Marquis de Clarke when he arrived, but the bartender assured him that wouldn't be necessary because the marquis pointed himself out well enough.

And Joachim was right. An hour later, a footman wearing a pillowy cap mounted the club stairs and announced in a theatrical timbre, "The most honorable, enviable, unimpeachable, and amicable Marquis de Clarke!"

Senlin turned on his stool to mark the man's arrival. The marquis wore a swallowtailed coat and white hose, which accentuated his bulbous knees. His robust middle was scarcely contained by an orange vest, and a small, white wig sat atop his considerable bald head like the lid of a teapot.

The marquis warmed every corner of the club with his breath and presence. He visited table after table, overwhelming every conversation with his own endless sentence, which seemed to have begun that morning when he awoke and which would only conclude that evening when sleep applied a full stop. Senlin gathered that no one in the room particularly liked the marquis half so much as he liked himself.

Senlin asked Joachim what the marquis drank and was not surprised to learn the marquis only drank from a particularly rare and expensive bottle of peridot. Senlin ordered two flutes of the refulgent syrup, then intercepted de Clarke just when he seemed to be running short of members to harass with his wit.

Handing the marquis his drink, Senlin said, "Oh, your lordship, it's such an honor to finally meet you." On nearer inspection, Senlin saw the marquis wore a conspicuous amount of makeup. His complexion looked like a porcelain mask that had been shattered, then glued back together numerous times.

A moment before the marquis had been describing the mulish kick of his newest rifle, but switched midsentence to say, "Is this the Peridot Deluxe Reserve: Rosa Absentia?" He stuck his piggish nose into the glass and piped up the air. "Oh, it is! I like you, sir! What is your name?"

Senlin introduced himself and observed the marquis take note of the pin on his lapel. The minute de Clarke learned that Mr. Pinfield was a new member, he undertook a sort of rambling education on the virtues of the club, many of which concerned his own contributions to it. After several minutes of smiling and nodding and making modest noises of astonishment, Senlin managed to insert a question about the marquis's champion.

"I'm not sure you'd ever entertain a peripheral wager, but I—"

"Cyril!" the marquis exclaimed, dispensing with formalities. "Side bets are the best bets. The rest is just paying the bookmaker's salary. What do you fancy? Ten? Twenty minas?" The marquis punctuated the words by sipping from his flute with the rapidity of a hummingbird.

"Certainly, if that's more in line with your budget," Senlin said.

The marquis pursed his reddened lips. "Budget! What a filthy word. You had a different figure in mind?"

"I was thinking one hundred and ninety minas."

"At fourteen to one odds? Are you mad? That would make my pay out, um..." The marquis snapped his fingers at his footman, who extracted a small abacus from his satchel, spent a moment slapping beads back and forth, and then whispered into the marquis's ear. "Two thousand eight hundred and fifty minas!" the marquis exclaimed.

"I was thinking of a different sort of wager, your lordship. If the

Iron Bear wins tonight, you take my purse. But if he loses, I take the Iron Bear."

For the first time since entering the club, the Marquis de Clarke was at a loss for words. He consoled himself with nursing his drink and with presenting Senlin with a carousel of expressions that ranged from suspicion, to admiration, to amusement, to disgust.

At last the marquis declared, "All right, I'll take that bet, but we must let Joachim hold the money. I don't want to have to chase you across the plaza when you lose."

Senlin agreed. He surrendered his wager to the bartender, who placed the banknotes in a heavy iron lockbox, apparently reserved just for that purpose. Joachim set the box upon a shelf under the watchful eye of a marble bust who wore a feather boa about its noble neck.

The size of the wager and the marquis's habit of drawing attention to himself made the passing of Senlin's fortune to Joachim something of a club event. Members flocked to the bar, and when the marquis toasted his own inevitable victory and thanked the Boskop for his donation, all the club cheered and saluted and gave the servers plenty of work pouring out and mopping up drinks.

When Wil emerged from the festive scrum, Senlin was almost relieved to see him. The duke removed the more inebriated revelers with straight-armed handshakes and hellos that somehow communicated *goodbye*. Having cleared a space, the duke took up residence on the stool beside Senlin.

The duke looked like a man struggling to contain a secret; his cheeks were plump with a suppressed smile, and his eyes shone with light. "Hullo, Cyril! You're wearing the same clothes you were last night! Don't tell me you never went home? Are we corrupting you?"

"Perhaps. I just made a wager, a very large wager, which is odd. I've seen the accounts of enough men to know better than to gamble. The only people who gamble are the ones with either too much money or too little. My wife will be furious!"

"And how does the wife of a Boskop show her fury?"

"Well, last time I displeased her, she left my terrarium open, and all my snails crawled out. It took me weeks to find them all."

"Monstrous!" the duke declared, obviously amused. He ordered an elaborate cocktail called a Conspicuous Melon, which required the preparation of a variety of fruit muddled with dark rum. Joachim set a cutting board and paring knife on the bar and began preparing watermelon, lime, strawberries, and mint with all the attention and care of a surgeon. "Speaking of wives," the duke continued, "as promised, mine has had a change of heart."

Senlin frowned as he tried to process this unexpected news. "But her refusal last night seemed rather...adamant."

"Oh, you know how women are!" The duke swatted the air and shared a wink with Joachim, who returned it with a swiftness befitting his profession.

"Meaning what?" Senlin's former sense of clarity about Marya began to fog over. The snap of the bartender's knife upon the board nipped at his nerves.

"Sometimes you have to help them think a thing through. Women are very good at seeing the details of life: the seconds and minutes. They immediately perceive a crooked necktie or a drowsy footman or a cinder on the rug. But they can't stand back and see the months and the years. They haven't that sort of vision. They can plan a dinner perfectly well, but not a war." The duke paused to observe Joachim tamping fruit into a tall glass. When he looked back at Senlin, he gave a playful scowl. "But why are you making that face? I thought you'd be happy! This is excellent news."

"Yes, yes, it is. Wonderful news," Senlin said, his expression of confusion broken by the flicker of a smile. "It's just so surprising. How did you convince her?"

"Your concern for my wife is touching, but really, what does it matter? You're not having second thoughts, are you?" the duke asked, and Senlin saw the change in his attitude—a darkening of his gaze and a rounding of his back, like a cat pressed into a corner.

"I suppose I just don't want to think I've had a hand in coercing her into something—"

The duke gripped Senlin's forearm where it lay on the bar. Instinctively, Senlin tried to pull away, but the duke jerked him back and drew him closer still. "Some of my friends are calling me a fool for conducting business with a Boskop. They say you don't have the backbone to see a thing through. There's a difference, they say, between counting money and making it. But I told them—" The duke pressed his face nearer Senlin's until they seemed to share a common breath. "'No, no, no. Cyril is different,' I said. 'Cyril has real ambition. He has the vision of a magnate, of a regent, of a Pelphian. He's not one of those stupid fops who hides behind scruples because he's too afraid to do what has to be done, too afraid to take what he wants.'" The duke squeezed Senlin's arm until the muscle pinched painfully upon the bone. "Well, you've got what you want, Cyril. Now be happy."

The revelation came on like a guillotine: Senlin felt a sudden shock of pain, the disorientation of his severed thoughts, and the dwindling of all light and sense.

He had made a terrible mistake.

In his eagerness to defer to Marya's wishes, in his determination to admit and account for his own faults, he had failed to see the duke for what he truly was. There had been plenty of signs that the man's character was driven by antipathy, entitlement, and the sort of insecurity that praise alone cannot sate, an insecurity that requires the suffering of others to be assuaged. Wilhelm's contempt for institutions of learning and educated persons; his tolerance of violence and indifference toward injustice; his habit of mocking and tormenting everyone, even his friends—were all the hallmarks of a bully.

Senlin had thought Marya rejected him to protect the life she had built for herself, but no, she had commanded him to get as far away as possible to protect him from the duke. Because she knew what Wilhelm was: He was a brute. And Senlin had let himself be charmed. His heart ached to think what the duke had done to her to change her mind.

The duke released Senlin's arm and sat back with a contented sigh. He straightened the flower on his lapel. His charming smile bloomed again. "I have a surprise for you."

Senlin hardly heard him, nor did he pay much mind to the voices around him as they pitched higher, nor the commotion behind him as chairs and tables were moved. He was too busy planning how he would help Marya escape. He would wait until after the *State of Art* had docked, then he would concoct an excuse to get Marya out to the port unaccompanied. He would tell the duke that the fresh air was good for conditioning the voice, that sunlight improved one's range, that the birds in the sky were the best voice coaches of all, and—

The sudden thump of drums interrupted his plotting. Finger cymbals tinked and rang. A clay horn buzzed like a wasp. Senlin turned toward the music. The club members parted around a band of musicians. The men sat cross-legged on an old rug, playing their instruments with a sort of delirious fervor. Three women, voluptuous as vases, posed in the clearing. They wore simple domino masks and very little else. Gold slings cupped their breasts; split skirts framed their thighs. Their facelessness made them seem disrobed in a different, more unsettling way. With Marya so near the fore of his mind, the parading of these masked women filled Senlin with a revulsion so intense it made him cringe. He tried to swivel around on his stool again, but the duke gripped him under his arm and faced him forward. "No, no, Cyril. Don't look away. Here is your surprise. A burlesque in your honor!"

At some indistinguishable musical cue, the frozen women thawed and began to dance. Their skirts flicked and whipped, animated by the motion of their hips. Their arms wove through the air. The tempo quickened, spurred on by the whistles of the gazing mob. The horn player's cheeks swelled; his eyelids looked bee-stung. The music drove the magpies from the nests, and the birds wound about in the air overhead, shedding feathers, black and white, amid squawks of alarm. The faceless dancers undulated like sails in a squall.

The music grew more frantic, and the dancers advanced upon Senlin. The duke laughed in his ear, pulling Senlin to his feet. He shoved him roughly forward. Senlin staggered a step, then halted, his throat hardening about a lump. The middle dancer, her eyes gleaming inside the holes of her mask, stared at him. Her movement slowed, as if her limbs were falling asleep, and then she stopped dancing altogether, though the other two continued to writhe.

She approached Senlin, tentatively at first, then with violent speed.

She struck him across his face before anyone could stop her, then struck him again even as two club members moved to restrain her. She ripped off her mask before the men got a firm grip upon her arms. Even as they held her, she kicked at Senlin, her bare feet catching him on the ribs.

The music stuttered, then failed, and her voice resonated in the sudden quiet: "You monster! You killed him!"

"Cyril, do you have any idea who this woman is?" the duke asked, apparently amused by the outburst.

Senlin looked at the woman. He knew her face, but it took him a moment to retrieve the memory. Then he recalled the flying cottage, the books he'd stolen, and the idealistic doctor who'd come with his daughter in search of a Tower, a beacon of civilization, that did not exist. The young woman's name echoed up from the recesses of remembrance. Her name was Nancy.

"How do you know Mr. Pinfield?" the duke asked the irate woman.

"He's no mister! He's a pirate!" Nancy cried. "He's the coward who robbed my father and broke his heart! He stole his books, his faith, his hope! You murdered him, Thomas Senlin! You killed him with despair!"

When Senlin turned to look at his host, he found him wearing a curious smile. He seemed to have just woken from the most wonderful dream.

"Ah, there you are," the duke said.

Chapter Fourteen

Ecstasy lies in that brief silence at the end of a play,
when the performance is over but the applause has
not yet begun.

—Oren Robinson of the *Daily Reverie*

Everyone in the club seemed caught in a moment of confused uncertainty. They did not understand the significance of the name the burlesque dancer had spat like a curse, nor could they tell from the duke's macabre smile what he thought of the revelation.

Seeing at once that this was all the head start he was going to get, Senlin bolted.

There really was only one direction open to him. The club members who'd crowded in to watch the burlesque dancers blocked the stairs and formed a sort of tunnel stretching from the bar to the balustrade, beyond which there was only open air and fluttering birds.

Snatching the paring knife from Joachim's cutting board, Senlin ran for the rail. The masked dancers shrieked as he passed narrowly between them. The musicians dove out of his way, clutching their instruments. He stuck the knife between his teeth, dug out his handkerchief, and wrapped it around his hand as he went. When he reached the railing where he'd once contemplated ending the duke's life—a missed opportunity he now sorely regretted—he gripped the garland of silk flowers and pulled. The garland, which was regularly lashed to the spindles with twine, came away just enough for him to get the knife under it. He clipped the festoon and, taking the loose end of the rope in his handkerchief-wrapped hand, stepped onto the flat top of the balustrade.

He turned to see the club members had closed upon him, the duke at the fore of an intimidating wall of suit coats and oiled hair. Wil looked delighted. He held out his arms, restraining the men nearest him from attempting to catch the interloper. He seemed curious to see whether Senlin really would try to leap from the balcony.

Senlin looked down at the clay of the arena floor far below. The height made his head swim, and in that moment of dizziness, he dropped the paring knife. He watched the blade flash as it tumbled end over end, landing amid a little puff of red dust.

Deciding that deliberation was the enemy of courage, he took a deep breath and stepped off the rail.

His descent was a halting, jerking one, as each bit of twine that held the garland in place snapped free. With each break, he was yanked to the side along the curvature of the balcony. Soon, he was swinging as much as falling. As the garland grew longer, and his spiraling descent quickened, he sailed farther and farther over the crowded stands, carried by centrifugal force. Then his grip failed him, and he plunged into the crowd.

Rather than suffer the injury of his fall by himself, Senlin spread the pain across a row of men, none of whom were grateful for their share of it. His landing caused an explosion of beer and oaths. He scrambled over the bowled-flat bodies of the men who'd caught him and leapt to a clear seat on the row below.

As he stepped from one open seat to another, descending the bleachers in hops and strides, the crowd about him began to pelt him with trash. He leapt into the main aisle at the base of the stands and ran for the exit tunnel. A man slung a full beer at him, dousing his hair. A hail of peanuts drummed upon his back just as he reached the shelter of the tunnel.

Thus far, he seemed to be fleeing more quickly than the news of his discovery. So when the guards in the tunnel accosted him for running so recklessly through the turnstiles and upsetting the queue of incoming men, Senlin pulled his soggy lapel at them, showing them the Coterie pin, and they let him go at once.

When he broke from the tunnel into the airy lobby, he was dismayed to find it now stuffed to the walls. He tried to make a path for himself, but not even the flaunting of his pin could clear a way. He turned when he heard shouts and saw the duke leading a gang of club members down the stairs. Senlin ducked behind a column, hoping he'd not been spotted.

He pulled the Sphinx's recorder from his pocket and peeled off the tobacco leaf with trembling fingers. He switched the device on and spoke into it in a rush. "I've been discovered. I'm probably done for. It doesn't matter. You have to get Marya out of here. Don't be fooled by the duke. He is not what he seems. Tell Marya I love her. Tell her I'm sorry I failed her once again."

He turned the moth's head, and the brass thorax sprouted legs. Its wings, painted the same blue as the Pelphian sky, unfolded and beat the air with tentative, rousing strokes. Senlin lifted the messenger, even as the shouts of his pursuers drew near.

The moth lifted from his palm, bounding upward, unsteadily at first, then finding its stroke. Senlin observed it rise as hands clamped his arms, his neck, his shoulders, pulling him downward. He resisted the weight, the inevitable descent, watching the moth's flight.

A streak of black swooped down and snatched the moth from the air.

Senlin watched the magpie return to its nest with the Sphinx's messenger pinched in its beak. The bird tore the painted wings free and dropped the brass body into its nest, where it clinked and rolled down a little trove of buttons and trinkets.

Senlin shouted in despair. The force of many hands drove him to his knees. He tried to fight back, tried to worm his way free. Someone drew a sack over his head.

In the dark, he heard Wilhelm say, "The ether! Douse him. Douse him!"

A single thought resonated in Senlin's head: Wilhelm would blame her for this. He drew a hard breath and yelled through the sackcloth, "She wanted nothing to do with me! She laughed at me! She rejected—"

An arm pinched his neck like a nutcracker, pulling his head back as a knee dug into his spine. The cloth about his nose and mouth took on a tingling, piercing scent. The fumes made the gloom inside the hood bubble with light. The light filled his head, flowed out to his limbs, and down to his fingertips, erasing all sensation as it spread. Pupil-black stars swam into view, spreading across a whitewashed cosmos. The swimming constellations grew larger and nearer, strangling out the light. The closer the black stars came, the farther away everything seemed, until he could see nothing beyond the empty, gawking dark.

His senses returned one at a time and gradually, like guests arriving to a party. And like a nervous host, Senlin discovered his anxiety did nothing to quicken their arrival.

His hearing returned first. He distinguished a man's voice, though he had difficulty following his speech, then the wet splash of something dripping onto stone and the patter of distant footfalls. The feeling in his hands came back. At first, he thought all strength had been sapped from them, but then he perceived the cold edge of the irons and realized his wrists were shackled together. When he could see again, he found the Colosseum had vanished. He lay on his shoulder upon a bare flagstone floor. A puddle reflected the orange glow of a lantern, which seemed the only light in the room. The bricks in the walls were rounded with age and the flow of water. Everything was damp. The smell reminded him of the odor of a well: the cold scent of mosses and minerals.

At last, Senlin recognized the voice as Wilhelm's, and when he sat up—awkwardly, painfully—he saw the duke pacing between two soldiers, both of whom had their swords drawn. The duke held a pistol in one hand and a lantern in the other. He swung the lamp about, dramatizing a speech Senlin had not heard the start of: ". . . the baying hounds, and the fevered chase, when the grass and trees whip me as hard as I crop my horse. Then a stillness comes over my very soul and my hands are as steady as stone, and my eyes are clear as spring water, and the flash of the muzzle is like a sunrise. And it's always the same: Before the beast submits, it first must buck and kick at death. It makes no difference, of course. Deer, bison, wildebeest, elk, I have bled them all, skinned them, gutted them. Transforming a beast into a trophy is not so different."

"Not so different from what?" Senlin asked. His throat was as dry as straw.

The duke stopped and examined Senlin's face in the swinging lamplight. "Turning a man into a hod."

Wil knelt, set the lamp down, and pointed the barrel of the pistol at Senlin's nose with an indifference his expression did not reflect. His eyes gleamed with sadistic delight. He was savoring every facet of this moment. "I've bled you of all your strength, hope, and wealth. I've skinned you." He wagged the barrel, directing Senlin's eye down. Senlin discovered he was undressed to the waist and wearing nothing but a rough loincloth. His boots were gone as well. "And now I'm going to gut you."

Without relinquishing Senlin's gaze, the duke said over his shoulder, "Get out. Close the door. I'll knock when I need you." The soldiers saluted and shut the iron hatch behind them. It closed with a resounding clang that echoed for quite some time. Senlin turned to look, realizing that what he had taken for a room was in fact a passage, and one that ran beyond the lantern's reach.

Senlin tested the limit of his chains and found his shackles were latched to the floor. The rattle made the duke smirk. "I knew you were too old for her, but I thought you would be handsome at least. How did you ever snare a creature like her? I suppose that's the benefit of being a bachelor in a small village. There's not a lot of competition. You would've done well, Tom, to have gone back and settled for someone closer to your caliber. An old widow or a willing sow." The duke stood again, shaking his head and clucking his tongue. "The fact that you're here can only mean one thing: You are stupidly, hopelessly, dangerously in love with my wife." He backed across the chamber, his arms crossed, the pistol dangling.

"Do you have any idea how many people would like to be in my place right now? If I were Commissioner Pound, I would've sawed off your head and used it for a pisspot an hour ago. You have spent the past year running about kicking every hornet's nest you could set your foot to. I bet if I auctioned you off to your enemies, I could make a small fortune."

"Marya had nothing to do with——"

With two quick steps, the duke covered the gap and caught Senlin on the chin with his boot. The kick threw Senlin to his side, where he again found the limit of his chains. "Don't say her name again."

Senlin spat blood onto the hard flagstone, his ears ringing. He scowled at the duke but said nothing.

"I still owe you a gutting, don't I?" Wil said, a familiar note of irony returning to his voice. "You seem to be under the impression that I am somehow Marya's jailer, or that she is here unwillingly. But that is not the case at all. You see, very early on, she and I developed an understanding, a mutually beneficial agreement, which gave both of us what we wanted most. I got a talented, beautiful, obedient wife who is beloved by all, and who, very soon, will bear me enough sons and daughters to start a dynasty. And she got to keep your little runt."

Senlin choked. "What?"

"You didn't know?" the duke said with contrived surprise. "Honestly, I didn't know either at first. If I had suspected she was pregnant, I doubt I would've let myself develop such warm feelings for her. But the heart is a cat; it does what it pleases." Wil shook a fist at the round roof of the passage, a wistful gesture that was lost on Senlin, who was too busy recalling the last night he had shared with Marya aboard the train to the Tower. Never would he have thought that such a tender memory could fill him with such despair.

"She came to me in a most shameful and frankly dangerous condition for an abandoned woman. It's tempting to say that it ruined her, but I think the unborn millstone put one or two things into perspective for her. I admit, she was not keen to marry me at first, not even after I brought her here, showed her my home, introduced her to my friends and my easy lifestyle. I think she refused me out of stubbornness— you know how willful she can be—rather than out of any lingering feelings for you. I was growing a little frustrated with her, in fact. But then, your little whelp announced itself, and the prospect of her being penniless and friendless in the Tower with an infant child made my proposal seem just what it was: a gift.

"Because she is quite intelligent, she understood why I could not publicly welcome a bastard and a spoiled woman into my home, and so she agreed to conceal her pregnancy and hide the child once it was born. I can hardly express how much trouble I've gone to, to keep that little bitch of yours out of the papers. But I am not without understanding of a woman's irrational attachments, and so I promised her that as soon as she bears me a son, we can pretend to discover your child abandoned on our doorstep, and Marya can live as the adoptive mother to the girl, who I will treat as my own. Well, nearly my own."

Senlin had never felt such anger in his life. But amid the immediate urge to murder this man, there was a flutter of pride and love. "What is her name?" he asked.

"I will tell you, but only because I know it will torment you more. But I do want to stress something first, Tom: If by some miracle you escape the black trail and worm your way to freedom, if I or anyone I know ever sees your face again, I will slit the child's throat."

"What is her name?"

"Olivet," Wil said, raising his knuckle to the iron door. "Now, remember, mum's the word. If you want to keep them safe, you'll keep your mouth shut." The duke knocked, and the clang of a heavy latch releasing reverberated through the iron. The hatch opened, and the soldiers returned with a third man between them. Tarrou's expression was so slack it could've passed as a death mask. Though Senlin hunted for it, his former friend would not meet his gaze.

"We found this in your pocket," the duke said, holding up the folded note he and Tarrou had passed. "So I thought why not send you to the black trail with a friend to guide you. I'm sure he won't blame you for robbing him of regular meals and a warm bed."

"John—" Senlin began but stopped when the duke holstered his pistol and took something from one of his men. The object was about as large as an urn, made of brass, and bullet shaped. There was a clasped enclosure at the open base and a few peephole-sized openings drilled near the middle. The duke bounced the urn in his hands, testing the weight. "Oh, it's heavy!" He raised it over his head and pulled it down as if it were a helmet, though it had no slits nor visor for the eyes and mouth. "How do I look?" he asked, holding his arms out wide, his voice muffled. He pulled the contraption off again. "Oh, that was horrible. It's like putting your head in a casket. You know, they use these in the Parlor to aid in the removal of eyes. They call it a *blinder*, I believe. It seems a little unnecessary. I mean, why go to the trouble of removing a man's eyes when you can just pickle his whole head?"

The duke held the cylinder over Senlin, who was making a conscious effort to resist the overwhelming urge to struggle. "My suggestion is that you look for a good straw because you won't get anything larger into that air hole. I hope you like broth." Wil sighed deeply, luxuriantly, savoring the moment. "I want my face to be the last face you ever see. Now, if you'll excuse me, I have a date with my wife. Goodbye."

The duke pressed the blinder down, eclipsing the amber light. The weight settled upon Senlin's shoulders. As he felt the clasp tightening about his neck, the voices in the room were overwhelmed by the sudden resounding rasp of his own breath and the roar of blood in his ears. He could hear nothing else, and the panic was so intense, it petrified him. Dimly, he was aware that his shackles were unbolted from the floor and then removed from his wrists. Dimly, he felt himself gripped under the arms and hoisted to his feet. Dimly, he felt the gust of air from the closing hatch upon the drumhead of his chest.

Senlin screamed until his ears ached and his breath was gone. Tears burned his eyes, and he reached up to wipe them, only to knock his knuckles against the brass shell about his head. Every instinct told him to run. He groped the air and staggered forward until he jammed his fingers against cold masonry. He couldn't breathe. He was suffocating. His stomach seemed to press upon his throat. He screamed again and began to choke.

Large, heavy hands grasped him by the shoulders. Senlin bucked wildly at the unexpected contact, but the hands held him more firmly and pressed his back flat against the wall. Underneath the booming of his own breath, Senlin heard shouting.

"Calm down, Tom! Calm down! If you don't calm down, you're going to make yourself sick, and believe me, you'll regret that for a long, long time. Breathe in through your nose. In through your nose!" Tarrou's familiar baritone, though muted by the walls of the kettle, was enough to temper his panic. Senlin focused on his breathing. "That's it. Slow. Deep and slow."

In the utter dark, Senlin closed his eyes and pictured the dazzling blue sky as he'd observed it from his old cottage door—boundless and untroubled. He saw the cerulean horizon of the sea, the paper-white sails of ships. He smelled the wind, briny and crisp. And when he opened his eyes again, the darkness was not so deep, not so entire.

"That's it, Headmaster. That's it. Nice and slow." Tarrou patted him on the chest. Then sensing the moment of panic had passed, he added, "That was quite a rescue, Tom."

His voice trembling, his cheeks hot with tears, Senlin said, "It's all part of the plan, John. All part of the plan."

Through the blinder, he heard Tarrou's rumbling laugh.

The Black Trail

The Old Vein is like the scullery of a fine
restaurant: We know it is there; we are glad it
exists; but seeing the mountains of dirty dishes
with our own eyes only spoils the appetite.
—*Everyman's Guide to the Tower of Babel*, IV. Appendix

Though dank and charmless as a bilge, the tunnel the duke had locked them in was not exactly the violent netherworld Senlin had imagined. The floor appeared to be level and the walls smooth. The air was ghastly. There was no denying that. It smelled like an outhouse behind an abattoir. But there was no human wailing nor churn of bodies. In fact, as far as he could tell with his head in a can, the black trail was deserted. He wondered whether the wretchedness of the tunnels had been exaggerated by the soft-handed tourists who'd been cast upon it.

Admittedly, his impressions were probably being skewed by the blinder. The duke was right: It was heavy. Senlin had been wearing it only a few moments and already the crown of his head, which bore most of the weight, ached. The clasp about his neck was tight enough to make him conscious of every swallow, and if he focused too long upon the sensation, his panic began to return. The ear holes, neither larger than a pea, made it hard to hear anything clearly, and despite the presence of a third hole over his mouth, Tarrou had trouble understanding him unless he spoke slowly and distinctly, and then, the tinny boom of his voice inside the bucket made Senlin feel horribly claustrophobic. It felt as if he were shut inside a coffin and shouting at the lid.

The thought made his breath quicken again. He had to resist the impulse to pant because the faster he breathed, the more his thoughts churned. He could not afford to dwell on certain questions, such as how would he eat and drink? How would he sleep? How would he scratch his nose or trim his beard? What if a fly got inside the blinder? What if it laid eggs?

No, if he wished to live long enough to have the privilege of starving to death, he'd first have to survive the next minute and, if he were lucky, the minute after that. His sense of the future shrank to the span of breaths, swallows, and small, tentative steps.

There was no question in his mind that he had to survive. He had to find Marya again and beg her forgiveness for having been so easily fooled by the smirking duke. Senlin wondered how he could've learned so much and still know so little about the world and human nature!

What could he possibly be worth as a father? And yet, that's what he was: The father of a little girl named Olivet.

He tried to picture her face. He knew it could not really belong to her, and yet, he could not resist the urge to conjure up a little cameo. In his imagination, Olivet had Marya's eyes and her perfect slope of a nose, but had his mouth and ears, in gentler proportions, of course, because she was not some little sturgeon. No. She was beautiful. She was perfect. He could almost feel her in his arms.

Then he took a foul breath and swallowed around the collar, and the vision of his infant daughter vanished.

Yet that small and probably delusional glimpse was enough to carry him through another moment. And that was all he needed to do: survive the next moment.

At least the black trail was well paved, a helpful feature for a blind man. Trying to build upon this hopeful thought, Senlin shared with Tarrou his opinion that perhaps the Old Vein wasn't so bad after all. Ignoring that comment altogether, Tarrou warned Senlin that he should brace himself: They were nearly at the gatehouse. "Don't speak to the gatekeepers," John said without a hint of his usual levity. "Keep your head down and, if you can help it, don't let go of my arm. When they open the gate, there are always a few idiots who'll try to rush in. If you fall, you will be trampled, and I'll be trampled trying to save you. Don't be afraid to swing your arms. Just try not to hit me."

A militant voice ordered them to halt and show their hands, which they did, though it meant Senlin had to give up his grip on Tarrou. He could only listen and try to guess at the scene: Heavy footfalls surrounded them. He thought he counted at least eight men, but he wasn't sure. He heard the creak of leather armor and the rattle of arms. Someone shouted, "Look at the teapot!" Then there was laughter, followed by a hard knock on the side of his head. He winced and shrank, though without any sense of which direction safety might lie.

A more commanding voice said, "Cut that out! Open the inner door!"

The rattle of chains and clank of gears shivered through the blinder and into Senlin's skull. He began to breathe more heavily and so missed the next command when it came. The butt of a rifle jabbed him in the back. He stumbled forward, bumping against a broad wall of muscle, which he could only hope belonged to Tarrou.

A heavy thump reverberated behind them. Feeling around, Senlin discovered they had been closed inside some sort of chute. Just ahead, Tarrou called out, "They're opening the gate. Hold on, Tom! Hold on!" Senlin had just enough time and sense to grope about and find his friend's arm. He latched upon it. Then the outer portcullis opened, and they were hurled back against the shut gate by a wave of frenzied bodies. He felt Tarrou's muscles strain and shake. Tarrou seemed to be managing to throw some of the hods back, but when he did, others squeezed under his arms and pinned Senlin against the rough timber of the latticed gate.

Senlin lost his grip on Tarrou but, recalling his large friend's suggestion, he struck blindly at the riot of arms and fists and knees that assailed him. He heard, with a glimmer of satisfaction, knuckles crack upon his blinder. Some hands pulled at him, attempting to pry him from the door; others beat him back, as if they meant to use him as a battering ram. Ragged nails raked his bare chest; an elbow drummed against his ribs. He began to slip downward, and he knew in another moment he would fall underfoot.

Something staff-like bumped the side of his blinder, and amid the chaos, he heard a hoarse voice squawk, "Rifles!" Then there was a burst of heat, a lungful of smoke, and the ringing of a bell that pitched higher and higher and did not fade.

The press of bodies that had pinned him to the door a moment before broke. He stumbled forward, tripping over thin and lifeless limbs. The smooth flagstone path broke beneath him, giving way to loose, unstable rubble. He threw his arms out but felt nothing and no one. It occurred to him that he might be standing on the edge of some great precipice, and the mere thought gave him such vertigo, he fell to his hands and knees.

He coughed the gun smoke from his lungs, but the air that replaced it was so foul it made him gag. The stench reminded him of the storm tides that struck Isaugh, when high water stranded mounds of fish and seaweed far up the beach to fester in the sun.

If Tarrou had been shot and killed inside the gatehouse tunnel, Senlin knew exactly what he would do. He would find a rock and attack the clasp at his throat. He would remove the blinder by any means, even if he had to hack himself off at the neck.

A moment after that self-destructive urge flitted through his head, he rebuked himself for it. No, he would not do the duke's dirty work for him. Wil had been foolish enough to let him live. Senlin believed the duke's threat, believed he would kill Olivet just to spite him and terrorize Marya. But much as Senlin had underestimated his enemy, the duke had underestimated him: his resourcefulness, his determination, and the strength of his friends. He was not some sniveling Fishbelly! He was a survivor, a schemer, a man of the clouds! He would not die here in this stink with a jar on his head. No! He was at the bottom of the bottom, in the gutter of the gutter. He could sink no lower. It could only be death or resurrection from here, so let the resurrection begin!

He scrambled to his feet, raised his arms, and shook his fists at the darkness around him.

It was a theatrical indulgence, but he didn't care. He roared into his prison, roared for the lives he was determined to save, until the ringing in his ears faded and the sound of his voice was no longer so distant.

He felt a large hand settle upon his shoulder, and through the peephole near his ear, he heard Tarrou shout, "Yes, yes, we're alive. We survived. Congratulations. But you do realize, you've lost your loincloth? People are staring. Perhaps you should stop shaking about?"

In a panic, Senlin reached down to cover himself. But he found his sarong hanging just as it should. The sound of Tarrou's rumbling laughter made Senlin's temper flare. "How can you joke at a time like this?"

Tarrou's laughter was pinched off by an ugly moan. "Well, if you'd rather spend your last days weeping, Headmaster, I'll oblige you. I'm sure I can recall a sad ballad or two." Tarrou surprised Senlin by staggering against him. Senlin narrowly managed to catch his heavy friend. "But you've got a bucket on your head, and I've been shot. I'd say this is as good a time as any for jokes."

Every step of the black trail was uniquely crooked. The path seemed to have been engineered for stumbling, for twisting ankles and piercing heels. Senlin would've preferred to stoop and crawl along on all fours, to feel the pitfalls he could not see, but Tarrou could not walk unassisted. So Senlin acted as his crutch, and Tarrou acted as their eyes, guiding their progress with a stream of directions: "A little to the left, Headmaster. Duck a bit. That's good. Another hole here. And then a big step up. Easy does it, easy! To the right . . . a little more. There."

When they fell, they fell together, landing in a sprawl on the uneven rock. They took each tumble as an occasion to catch their breath, and as they wheezed and huffed, Senlin asked where they were going, and what did the trail look like, and who was muttering in the dark around them? Senlin found he preferred even the grim picture Tarrou painted of the black trail to what was forming in his imagination.

Tarrou admitted he had no destination in mind. For the moment, he was only eager to put some ground between them and the gatehouse. Gatehouses, he said, were notorious, dangerous places. The desperate and dishonest congregated there, waiting to take advantage of new arrivals to the trail.

Every hod's collar included an iron pendant called a *bondlet*, which contained the history of the hod's debts. Bondlets were sealed with wax and stamped with the insignia of whichever ringdom had inspected them last. Hods without a bondlet, or those whose bondlet showed signs of tampering, were not allowed to take on new loads, which essentially left them stranded on the black trail with little honest hope of escape.

Tarrou told Senlin tales of hods who came to the black trail with minor debts, only to be befriended by desperate hods, men who owed fortunes. Those hopeless debtors would convince the newcomers that they alone, of any soul on the trail, were worthy of trust. Then they would kill the novice hod just to get at their bondlets. "If anyone asks," Tarrou said, "you owe a king's ransom."

"Probably not far from the truth," Senlin said, remembering who had pinned the bondlet on him. He had no doubt the duke had chosen some extreme figure and would have little difficulty fabricating the paperwork to support the history of the debt. "But is everyone on the trail really so ruthless?"

"Not at all. It's mostly fine and ordinary folk. If I had to pick between sharing a bottle of port with a man plucked from the upper ringdoms or the black trail at random, I'd pick the trail every time. But since there are no laws, no judges, and no constables here, the wicked hold a lot of sway."

Tarrou had been shot in the thigh. Mercifully, the ball had missed the bone and major arteries and passed cleanly through. John had bound the wounds as best he could with a strip he tore from the hem of his sarong, but the effort did not stanch the flow completely. Even as they walked, hip to hip, Senlin could feel the growing slick of blood. They did not remark on it because, Tarrou continued to insist, this was a time for jokes. Though at the moment, neither of them could think of any.

The black trail was like an old, poorly maintained mine, Tarrou said. The tunnels rambled and crossed and ended abruptly upon cave-ins or shrank into impassably narrow chutes. "I have seen hods try to wriggle their way into the smallest gaps, hoping to find a shortcut up or down or out. There are always rumors of shortcuts and new means for divining them. And I've seen hods stuck in holes they couldn't wriggle out of. They died with nothing but the soles of their feet showing. They lie entombed like a nail in a plank."

Because the grade of the trail was so slight, and often ranged alternately up and down, it was not uncommon for hods to get turned around and then waste hours or even days traveling downward when they meant to go up. Some hods were lost and didn't suspect it; others were going the right way but doubted themselves. Disorientation was just part of the natural order on the black trail.

"But what *is* that incessant barking? Are people barking?" Senlin asked.

Tarrou's laughter was tinged with pain. "That is the tattle post, Headmaster. They're not barking. They're saying *hark*."

The tattle post, as Tarrou described it, was essentially gossip that was passed from hod to hod like a germ. The majority of messages that traveled by tattle post were brief statements that communicated danger, or opportunity, or some other tidbit of news. There were a few conventions for using the tattle post. Each broadcast was preceded by the word "Hark!" and concluded with "Relay!" No requests for information regarding missing persons were allowed because everyone had lost someone. You could not use the tattle post to plead for help because everyone needed it. And obituaries were barred because everyone was dying, more or less at the same plodding pace. These rules were meant to keep the tattle post clear for important announcements, or at least salacious gossip. Because each message relied upon the participation of every hod in the chain, frivolous messages never traveled far. Generally, posts dwindled after a few hours or days, but the more urgent warnings or sensational rumors could linger for weeks, bouncing about the black trail like a ripple in a dishpan.

Senlin asked Tarrou what news was passing by at the moment, and Tarrou said he would have to listen awhile. They eased their backs against a rough wall that seemed to be coated in a fine dandelion-like fur. When Tarrou repeated what he'd heard, he did so at a shout for the benefit of farther-off ears. "Hark! The watering trough at the Kiver Gatehouse is dry. Relay. Hark! The trading station at Andara Sur is closed. Relay. Hark! Eight hods were lined up and shot in Pelphia. Relay."

"I was there. I saw that," Senlin said, the memory returning with unwanted clarity. "They executed old men, women, children. It was senseless."

"People who pretend that executions are sensible forms of communication are the same sort of people who believe in articulate bombs and swords that sing. Violence is always incoherent; it only babbles. Speaking of which—there's a lot more hoddish being spoken on the tattle post than the last time I was on the trail, though that was a few months ago."

"Really?" Senlin said, wondering again about Luc Marat's increasing sway, and whether that influence reached as far as his old friend. Hoping to get some sense of Tarrou's fidelities, Senlin asked, "Do you speak hoddish?"

"I understand it some, but I don't speak it."

"Why not?"

Tarrou shouted a laugh, though it seemed to wind him. "Because they don't have a word for *rapturous* or *effervescent* or *sublime*. It's a stupid language that's only good for articulating a primitive sort of life. It's only slightly more sophisticated than pointing and grunting."

Encouraging as Tarrou's dislike for hoddish was, Senlin noticed he'd begun to slur his words. Suspecting that Tarrou was nodding off, Senlin found his shoulder and shook it.

"We can't sit here, John. You can't fall asleep. Not until we figure out what we're going to do about your leg and my head. We need help." Under Senlin's prodding, the two got to their feet, knees shaking, unsteady, and gripping each other like men attempting to stand up in a rowboat.

Once his arm was hooked over Senlin's neck again and the two had resumed their stagger onward, Tarrou said, "Help is not easy to come by here, Headmaster. Honestly, sometimes the help is worse than the need."

"What do you mean?" Senlin said, trying to not let the strain of supporting Tarrou's weight affect the pitch of his voice.

"If you want a collar removed or a wound cleaned, there's really only one option on the black trail, at least for men of our meager means, and that's the zealots."

"Marat, you mean," Senlin said.

Tarrou expressed his surprise that Senlin knew the name. Though there didn't seem time enough for a full explanation, Senlin provided a brief account of his ill-advised search for Luc Marat and their disastrous meeting in the Golden Zoo. He concluded that they had parted on poor terms.

"What do you mean poor...Left a bit. More. No, don't step on that. That's someone's lunch. How poor of terms?"

Correcting their course, Senlin replied, "My crew and I killed a dozen or so of his men, and we blew up some of his supplies and helped ourselves to some others."

Even through the blinder, Senlin could hear the amazement in Tarrou's voice. "How can one little tourist make so many mighty enemies? Commissioner Pound, Luc Marat, Duke Wilhelm...Is there anyone left in the Tower you haven't burgled or irked?"

"I have been on a bit of a spree." Senlin knew he would eventually have to offer a complete explanation of what he had done to anger the duke, which would also require a confession of how he'd failed his wife a second time. It was only fair that Tarrou know the whole reason he had been expelled. But that wound was still too fresh and their circumstance too dire to go into that now. "I don't suppose we have any other options?"

"We could try to find you another head and me another leg."

Senlin chuckled. He just happened to know someone who might be able to help with that. He wondered what his friend would think if he confessed to having met the mythical Sphinx. Probably John would just assume the blinder had driven him mad. "It works in our favor that I was traveling under an assumed name when I met Marat. To him, I am Captain Mudd. As long as we don't run into him or any of the—let me see—probably three dozen hods that saw my face, we should be all right."

"Only you would break into a man's house, then think to sneak around to the kitchen to beg for scraps," Tarrou said, just as his wounded leg gave way and shoved the both of them hard against the ragged tunnel wall.

The coral-sharp stone abraded Senlin's shoulder, but when Tarrou asked if he was all right, rather than answer, Senlin resumed the conversation: "Well, it seems that our options are either the zealots or a slow death. I find the older I get, the less patient I am."

Without a better option, the only question that remained was where to seek the zealots out. Tarrou had encountered a zealot camp during his hateful trek up from the Baths to New Babel. He estimated it was perhaps a day's walk. At least it was downhill.

They fell into a regular rhythm of direction and step. The process was oddly hypnotic, which was not a good thing. Senlin discovered how quick his imagination was to fill the void created by the blinder. He began to see specters in the darkness. At first the hallucinations were just sprites and jets of color. But soon the fireworks began to gather and organize. Faces emerged, some of them familiar, some of them strange, but none of them kind. And though he did not recognize them all, he knew who they all were. They were the people he'd wronged since coming to the Tower, people like Nancy, whom he could not blame for hating him or exposing him to his enemies. She had every right. He saw the faces of men he'd killed, saw the faces of the widows he'd made and the children he'd orphaned.

It was curious to think there had been a time in his life when he could lie awake at night, stare into a dark corner, and ponder the world without dread or loathing. Back then, he might dream up a new lesson plan, or contemplate the latest chapter he'd read in a novel, or puzzle out a new design for a kite. Now he wondered if the dark would ever be so friendly again, or if for the rest of his life, the witching hours would only invite all of his lurking sins.

He couldn't bear it. He interrupted Tarrou's stream of directions to beg for a distraction.

"A distraction? I didn't wear my dancing shoes, Tom," Tarrou said.

"Well, tell me more about the black trail. I have so many questions!" Senlin wished to know what all the hordes ate and drank and where they slept. Did everyone just flop down on the rocky path and hope not to be stepped on? How did everyone see where they were going? Wasn't it as dark as a grave inside the walls of the Tower?

Tarrou answered as best he could, though the effort made him a little breathless. Senlin learned that the black trail was lit by the same lichen that illuminated the Silk Reef. The gloamine grew in stretches and patches, and was so plentiful in some spots, it could be harvested, jarred, and carried as lamps. Some tunnels were murkier than others. There were stretches where the lichen had withered from drought or been harvested to scarcity. Though even there in the stumbling gloom, an open flame was considered an option of last resort. In the course of its history, nearly as many hods had perished from fire and smoke as hunger and thirst.

A complex system of airshafts had been built to serve the trail, but not all of them produced air anymore. In addition to those vents, the engineers of the Old Vein had installed oxygen springs to sweeten the air. The springs were essentially little ponds of algae that were fed by well water, which was fresh enough to drink. The algae produced breathable air at a ponderous though reliable rate.

According to Tarrou, the trail had once been full of such springs. Clean water had streamed from fountainheads and pooled in troughs, some for drinking, others for the breath they made. Over the decades, lengths of plumbing had clogged and others cracked. Once upon a time, the ringdoms attempted to maintain and repair the pipes of the Old Vein, but what was called a duty by one generation was considered a charity by the next and, soon enough, a burden. Eventually, the ringdoms refused to be exploited by their poor any longer, and the neglected plumbing began to fail.

The springs that remained were either desolate or overtaxed. The same was true of the mushroom beds, which had been laid to provide a sustainable source of food for the hods. The beds had been decimated, first by faulty irrigation, then by desperate and starving souls who overharvested them. The hods had been forced to expand their diet to include beetles, bats, and the rancid goods that were rejected by the ringdoms. It wasn't unheard of for a hod to starve to death while toting a sack full of grain, a basket of potatoes, or a rack of cured meat. In desperation, some would murder to get at the load of another hod. In despair, it was said some had resorted to cannibalism.

But according to John, the most terrifying danger of all was not hunger nor fire, not robbers nor man-eaters. It was the chimney cat.

"What's a chimney cat?" Senlin asked.

"They're wriggling death, is what they are. Their original purpose, I'm told, was to keep the air vents clear. They snaked through the ducts, sweeping away cobwebs, bird's nests, soot, bones, and anything else obstructing the flow of air. They have fur that's as coarse as a wire brush. They're living, breathing pipe cleaners that also happen to be omnivorous beasts."

"But what are they? What do they look like?"

"They have broad heads, short legs, long bodies. They look a bit like weasels."

"Weasels aren't so bad," Senlin said, thinking of the gray stoats commonly found in the countryside around Isaugh. They had twinkling eyes and naturally smiling mouths.

"These weasels grow to be fifteen feet from snout to tail. They have jaws that can crack a skull as easily as an egg and teeth as long as your finger. And they stink like a dead skunk in summer. The only thing worse than their smell is their disposition. Chimney cats will maul a man and then carry his corpse around in his mouth like an old slipper. I believe the consensus is, they don't like eating men, but they do enjoy chewing us."

The description left little doubt in Senlin's mind that the creatures had been bred by the Sphinx, much as she had created the spider-eaters and the bull snails. Like those creatures, the chimney cats had been bred to serve a practical need, which had resulted in some undesirable qualities, such as gnawing on people.

Even through the blinder, Senlin could discern the change in the ambient noise. There were more people, and they spoke more animatedly. Their voices seemed as distant as geese flying overhead and just as comprehensible. He asked Tarrou where they were.

"The Pelphian trading station. It's basically a big cavern. It's where we deliver our goods and have our debts docked. This is where they shave your head and give you a new load to carry. Excuse us!" Tarrou shouted, and Senlin felt a collision of shoulders and hips that nearly upended them both. They just kept their feet and carried on. "This is also where hods with clean records and minor debts can sometimes find work off the trail. City managers come here to recruit street sweepers, or a housekeeper will come to put out a call for a scullery girl. They're always crowded. Wait! Feel a bit ahead with your left foot. Feel that? That's a watermelon. Don't step on it."

"Why is there a watermelon there?" Senlin asked.

"There are melons everywhere, Headmaster. Melons, sacks of cotton, bundles of leather, jars full of eggs, spools of wire, and on and on forever. You can't see it, but we are staggering our way through one of the Tower's pantries. Every imaginable good is waiting here to be delivered. It's like a bazaar, only no one's making any money. Well, at least no one on this side of the gate. There is also an uncomfortably large number of soldiers pointing their rifles at our heads as we speak, so try not to make a spectacle of yourself. Come on. To your left. Lightly now."

Senlin was still listening to the receding din of the trading station when he felt something wet spatter upon his shoulder. His imagination surged, and he saw the vision of a monstrous weasel, reared back, teeth bared and dripping saliva. He shouted and would've run had he not been fettered by Tarrou's arm. Tarrou hugged him and gentled him, then said it was only a dripping pipe, which made Senlin feel very foolish at first, but then quickly brought a question to mind. "Wait. If there's moving water, does that mean there's a working fountain nearby?"

"Yes," Tarrou said. "We just passed one. There was a line, which is a good sign. Means the water's probably sweet enough."

Senlin came to a halt. "Why didn't you stop? Surely you're thirsty."

"I don't like to drink alone," Tarrou said with an unconvincing snicker.

"Don't be stupid. I'll be fine for a while longer. Besides, I'm not the one who's losing blood. You need to drink."

Upon Senlin's insistence, Tarrou left him leaning against the roughly chiseled wall and went to stand in line for a drink from the sputtering fountain. After a few minutes, he returned, and once they had staggered some distance from the watering hole, he said, "They were talking about somebody I think you might know. A man named Thomas Mudd Senlin. Apparently, he's captain of a pirate crew."

"Sounds like a rotten fellow," Senlin said, his heart rising into his throat. He thought of Marat. Someone must've exposed him to the leader of the zealot clan. He wondered who. "What else did they say?"

"Only that Marat would give the hod who delivered old Tom Mudd to him one hundred minas, not in debt, but in coin. I'm afraid your warrant is blasting all over the tattle post."

"That's a lot of money," Senlin said. "I'm surprised the zealots have so much."

"Well, they may be nitwits, but they still know money motivates more reliably than ideology. Lucky for Mudd, Marat is asking for the pirate captain to be delivered alive."

"Well, I'm very glad my name is Cyril Pinfield."

"I don't think I'd be *very glad* if that were my name," Tarrou said.

On they went, lurching side to side like a couple of drunks carrying each other home from the pub. Senlin persisted in his inquires, asking questions to keep Tarrou talking and to keep himself from spiraling deeper into the dark of his blinder. What did the native insects look like? How wide were the tunnels? What was the difference between gatehouses where hods were ejected and the trading stations where goods were received? And what happened to the corpses, to the men and women who died on the trail from exhaustion, malnourishment, or old age? What was done with their bodies?

After many hours and many answers, Tarrou reached his limit at last and cried out, "Have mercy, Headmaster! I'm not as observant as you, and I don't want to die in the classroom!"

Understanding that it was better to save John's breath for directing their steps, Senlin gave himself up to the silence and the abyss and the devils within. The blinder was at least diverse in its torments. In addition to the swirling faces of the men and women he'd wronged, Senlin found the darkness a perfect theater for reenacting his bungled reunion with Marya.

The memory of her expressions, her mannerisms, and how she had looked at him inside that rattling mine cart were all crystalline. It took a little longer for him to recall exactly what she had said, but as her words came back to him, they seemed to ring with a different meaning now.

One of the first things she'd said was "I thought you'd gone home." He'd taken it as a vague gibe, her way of expressing surprise that he'd not been chased home by the overcrowded and treacherous Tower. But no, what she had meant was that she thought he had deserted her. She felt abandoned. When she had told him, "This isn't about us, Tom. This is about the lives and hearts of others," she had been alluding to Olivet, though at the time he'd thought she meant the duke and had taken it as an indication that she did not love him anymore.

But then, he had made so much of their reunion about himself. He had gone to her like a confessional, so she had absolved him. What else could she have done? In parting, when she had announced she wouldn't trust him to manage a cart full of socks, he'd been too self-absorbed to recognize the reference. He did now, and with crushing disappointment. Once upon a time, he'd told her he would wait for her beside a pushcart full of socks and stockings. She had not forgotten his promise, though he had.

Perhaps she had felt compelled to speak obliquely. Her fear of Wilhelm or her uncertainty about the intentions of her prodigal husband might have made it necessary for her to talk around the truth. Yes, she had spoken to him in code, and he had deciphered nothing.

Tarrou's loss of blood and exhaustion turned his skin as clammy as unbaked dough. Senlin's thirst left him so parched it hurt to speak. The hours were stretched by their silence and the incessant bark of the tattle post. Tarrou nudged them left and right, and Senlin let his toes search out the gaps and ridges that Tarrou no longer had the strength to describe.

Tarrou's cold sweat gave way to trembling. At last, he collapsed upon an outcropping of stone, dragging Senlin down with him. They lay panting upon the slab for some minutes until Tarrou had caught his breath enough to announce that they had arrived at the edge of the zealot camp.

"I'm sure they'll want some sort of appeasement," Senlin said at a volume he hoped only Tarrou could hear. "We should do whatever they ask of us. As soon as you're strong enough and I'm free of this tin can, we'll strike out on our own again. I think our best bet will be to work our way down, outside, and then through the market. I have friends with a ship. A big one. We'll need to devise some method for getting their attention. Maybe we can walk out into the desert a little way and light a signal fire or write a message in the sand. Then we can go back to Pelphia. We could be there in a week or two with a little luck."

"Tom—" Tarrou said, then cleared his throat, remembering the bounty on Senlin's head. "I mean, *Cyril*, that's not a plan; that's a fantasy. Taking for granted all the miracles that would have to line up to make such a trek possible, why on earth are you so eager to return to Pelphia?"

"I have my reasons."

"And I have my doubts!" Tarrou croaked. "Once we go inside, once we put it all on the line and ask the zealots for help, once we convert, there isn't any going back. You can't just cross your fingers with these fellows. Marat's clan are a lot of things, but forgiving is not one of them."

"Then we'll just do our best to be forgettable."

"All right then," Tarrou replied with a sarcastic lilt. "After you, Sir Bucket."

Upon entering the camp, Senlin hardly understood what was happening. There was a lot of commotion, and it lasted for several minutes. He heard snatches of conversation, some of which included Tarrou's voice and the rabbling of hoddish. He tried not to flinch when hands touched his bare back and hooked around his arm. He allowed himself to be led to a stool, where he was pushed down by leathery hands. At last a clear voice distinguished itself from the muddle. The voice was rough with age and seemed very near to his ear when it said, "Do you swear to never raise a hand against a fellow hod? Do you renounce all devotion to the lies of the old tongue, both as it is spoken and written down? Do you promise to do all that is in your power to throw the Tower at the feet of the Hod King? Do you swear this upon your blood, upon the blood of your mother and father, and the blood of your sons and daughters?"

The gory vow reminded Senlin of the oaths his students used to exchange in the schoolyard, where every promise came with a catalog of consequences, each increasingly dire. Whoever broke their word would have to eat a worm, and sit on a blackberry bramble, and leap into the sea with rocks in their pockets. His students would pile more and more horrors onto their oaths, then seal the bargain by spitting into their hands and shaking.

Senlin had told them more than once that an honest word did not require italics to be true, and that no amount of underlining could reform a lie. It was strange to think there had been a time when he had been honest as a matter of course, as a matter of honor. But if the Tower had taught him anything, it was that honor was a whipping post and honesty a flail. He could tell the truth and die with a bucket on his head, forsaking his wife and child in the name of honor, or he could lie.

Marshalling all the strength he had left, he shouted his answer: "Yes, I swear it!"

"Then welcome, hodder." Senlin felt the scrape of metal on metal as something probed the pin in his collar. "Now, this will be loud. You should prepare yourself for a little banging."

When at last Senlin was freed from the blinder, his head felt like the clapper of a bell. He cupped his hands over his ears, though it didn't help, and squinted at the blue glare that seemed to shine from everywhere at once. A bowl of cloudy water appeared under his nose, and he drank it down nearly as quickly as he vomited it back up. His second attempt fared better, and as he sipped, the glare of the gloamine that grew in patches upon the ceiling and walls dimmed. He wept and couldn't say whether it was from relief or acclimation to the light.

Despite Tarrou's best attempts to describe it all, his surroundings were still strange to him. The chamber didn't have the natural features of a cave. Though he wasn't sure why he'd pictured it that way, he was nonetheless a little surprised that there were no horns of minerals dripping from the ceiling nor jutting up from the ground. Tarrou had said that the trail resembled a mine, though that did not seem quite right either. The chamber they sat in possessed none of the straight lines or support beams of a mine. The black trail, or at least this branch of it, seemed to share more in common with an anthill or a warren. There was no wasted space, no architectural flourishes. The ceiling was low and the corners rounded. The stone floor here appeared to have been rubbed smooth by the passage of generations of bare feet.

The zealot camp was not especially large, though it was quite full: Perhaps a hundred hods were pressed together inside the chamber. Some slept on mats of ashen straw, some sat with legs akimbo upon the floor, many with books open in their laps. Sticks of charcoal blackened their fingers as they worked to erase profane words from impious pages. The sentries were distinguished by their rifles, which looked a little odd strapped to their bare chests. Though obviously antique, the guns appeared freshly oiled and well cared for. A fountain bubbled at the center of the camp, and the hods who congregated there all ate from a common pot full of some colorless, cold stew. The fug of human bodies was thicker here, but the smell of decay was not as oppressive.

Senlin noticed that many of the hods were free of their iron collars and bondlets. They had made themselves permanent residents of the trail. He didn't know whether that resolve was inspiring or frightening.

A few paces removed, Tarrou stood with his hands on his hips and his head down. He was enduring a sermon from a hod about half his size. His lecturer was dark skinned, and his jaw bristled with gray hairs that stood out as distinctly as his ribs. He still wore a band about his neck. A wax-dipped bondlet dangled from it like the tag of a dog collar. He might have seemed frail had it not been for his gaze, which looked sufficient to stall a charging bull. That stare certainly appeared to have been affective on the Iron Bear.

The diminutive hod was saying, "If you came here hoping for wine, you'll be disappointed, Hodder John. You held out when you could've been of real use to us. Now you're just another mouth to feed. Yes, we'll take you in, but I won't pretend you don't have something to prove. You can't say no a hundred times and then say yes once and expect us all to believe you."

John said, "I know, I know, Hodder Sodiq, and I am sorry. I came to you before as a hod in progress." Senlin was relieved to see Tarrou's wound had been cleaned and bandaged. His scalp and chin had both been shaved since the last time he'd seen him in the arena. He looked so different, Senlin might've taken him for a close relation of the man himself. "My head was turned by the whole spectacle. And you have to understand, I went straight from the lap of luxury in the Baths to the harsh reality of the trail, and when the Colosseum gave me a little taste of ease again—a warm cot, regular meals, and wine when I won—I was charmed, I was seduced. What can I say? I was weak! But I am in earnest now. Hail the Hod King!"

"*Come* the Hod King," Sodiq corrected. He sighed in such a way as to signal that their conversation was not nearly finished, but only deferred for the moment. He glanced at the man who'd recently been freed of his head-snare.

Senlin's chin dripped water over his empty bowl.

Sodiq twitched in surprise. "You!" he said.

Even without the whitewash, Senlin would never have forgotten that face. He blinked and saw again the hod standing in the alley over two corpses in the poisonous rain.

Sodiq raised his hand no higher than the peak of his skull. He looked like a shy student wishing to be called upon. Senlin almost gave the elder permission to speak before he realized the hand had not been lifted for him. The subtle gesture summoned the attention of the camp. Hods rose from their mats and set aside their bowls. They pressed in from the edges of the chamber, their faces and bare shoulders painted a ghostly blue by the gloamine. When all had gathered, Sodiq's low, rumbling voice filled the silence. He gestured at Senlin, and his listeners gasped. He beat upon his bony chest and jabbed the air with the horny knuckles of a weathered fist. His voice leapt and ebbed with passion. It seemed a rousing speech.

Unfortunately, Senlin did not understand a word of it.

To his ear, the hoddish language sounded like a gregarious infant.

Mercifully, Sodiq concluded his declaration in the common tongue, giving Senlin at least a sense of what he had missed. "*This* is the man who came to my defense," Sodiq cried. "*This* is the man who saved my life."

Senlin waved at the silently gaping crowd. "Hello."

"What is your name, hodder?" Sodiq asked.

"Cyril Pinfield," Senlin said.

"Wait a moment—you're the same man who tried to stop the execution." Sodiq squinted and shook his head in disbelief. "But why? Why come to my aid, why to theirs? You weren't a hod, at least not yet."

"I still had a conscience. I still recognized injustice when I saw it." Senlin saw the creases of suspicion tighten at the corners of Sodiq's eyes. Speaking almost without thinking, Senlin twisted General Eigengrau's scorn for the hods into praise. "And are we not all born hods, even if it takes us some years to discover it? Is not every man a hod at heart?" Senlin tried to project a confidence he did not necessarily feel. This was not a time for subtlety. Whether he liked it or not, wanted it or not, it was time for him to accept a new persona. He'd heard enough of Luc Marat's sermonizing to have a sense of the zealot's philosophy, and he used that knowledge now. "Yes, I saved your life. Yes, I tried to save the lives of eleven other hods. I set myself on fire trying to save them." He raised his arms, as if offering himself to the sky. His fingertips brushed the stone ceiling as he did. "But I am Cyril Pinfield no longer. That man is dead, if he ever was alive. I am Hodder Cyril."

Senlin turned to survey the effect his words were having. The crowd appeared uncertain. Tarrou seemed to be gauging how far away the exit lay.

"I am a slayer of engines!" Senlin boomed. "I am a bloody cog who refuses to turn anymore in service of this beastly Tower. I stand in defiance of its kings and nobles who'd like to see us all put against the wall and shot. Shot, not because of what we've done, but because of what has been done to us." At this, several of the hods cheered in agreement. "All I ask is that you free me to continue to fight on your behalf, on behalf of Luc Marat!" Senlin clasped his hands together and shook them, shouting, "Come the Hod King!"

A chorus echoed back his words, once, twice, then on the third volley, the cheer switched to hoddish. He quickly learned to parrot the phrase. To his ear, it sounded like the nonsense syllables of a song—so many *tra-la-las* and *hey-nonny-nonnies*. But he repeated the new words as best he could and raised his fist with each cry. And as he cheered the Hod King, a man who'd once tried to murder him and his friends, he pictured his return to Pelphia aboard the Sphinx's pearl-bright warship. He imagined the duke's face when he knocked upon his door and shot him in his dressing gown. He would see Marya again. He would hold Olivet in his arms. He would not let his failings curdle into self-loathing. He would redeem himself yet!

As the cheer dwindled and he turned to ask if Sodiq wouldn't be able to spare some provisions for their mission, Senlin heard a slow, methodical clap bounce about the chamber.

At first, he couldn't find the source. But as the clapping drew nearer and hods shuffled to make way, Senlin began to feel like a man crossing a frozen lake on a warm spring day. The unreasonable optimism he had felt a moment before now turned to dread.

When the last hod stepped aside and revealed the man behind the droll applause, Senlin felt as if he had been plunged into icy water.

"Pinfield. Mudd. Senlin. You have more names than the village mutt, don't you?" Finn Goll said, polishing one small palm upon the other. Senlin's former employer smiled like a sickle and said, "Ah, but you'll always be good old Tom to me."

Part II
The Leaping Lady

Chapter One

If you want to read her future, don't peer at a young lady's tea leaves or probe the lumps on her head. No, look to her table manners. I can observe a girl eat a fig, and afterward, tell you whether she will grow up to be a marchioness or a mudlark.

—*Lady Graverly's Table: Rare Graces and Common Shames*

The *State of Art* wed the luxury of a pleasure cruiser with the claustrophobia of a cattle car. For all its plush and polish, there wasn't enough fresh air or natural light to keep a plant alive, much less sustain a person—or such was Voleta's opinion. The Sphinx's home had been secluded and the air a little stale, but what it lacked in sunlight it more than made up for in immensity.

The *State of Art*, grand a vessel as it was, could still be exhaustively explored in less than an hour. The ship had three decks, sixteen cabins, four state rooms, a ballroom, a dining room, a conservatory, and one single porthole. This lonesome window to the outside world was inconveniently located in the passage across from the main hatch and placed at such a height that Voleta had to stand on her tiptoes to see through it. Her face filled that small aperture, the glass of which was so thick it shrank the sky and warped the horizon until the whole world looked like a painted plate. Whenever she had a moment to herself, Voleta dragged a stool from one of the empty cabins, unscrewed the latches, pushed her face as far through the porthole as she could, and let the wind whip some color back into her cheeks.

Invariably, Bryon found her, and when he did, he'd scold her for shirking her lessons and for sitting on a stool, which a lady absolutely *did not do*. When Voleta demanded an explanation for why a lady could not sit on a stool, Byron's answer was hardly satisfying: "According to *Lady Graverly's Table*, stools are inherently masculine seats. It is impossible for a lady to sit upon a stool without inferring a certain . . . flexibility of virtue."

"Oh, really? What else can't a lady sit on?" Voleta asked.

Byron ticked the forbidden furniture off on his velveteen fingers. "Banisters, swings, saddles, ottomans, and love seats, for obvious reasons."

There were a thousand rules for how she must conduct herself in "polite society." If something wasn't a rule, then it was a custom. And if it wasn't a custom, then it was *ladylike*, an adjective that was as expansive as it was loathsome. Voleta had begun to build a mental list of all the beloved activities that were not considered ladylike, including: climbing trees, carrying fruit in her pockets, eating without a plate, eating without a fork, eating in general, letting a squirrel live in her blouse, hiding in closets, crawling through vents, tying knots in her skirts, spying on people, laughing, slouching, joking, running, and sitting where and when she pleased.

She knew it was all for a good cause—to reunite Senlin with his wife—and perhaps she could've even forgiven Byron the indignity and the tedium if it weren't for the fact that while she was learning how to manage a hoopskirt on a bench seat, Edith and Iren were off having the time of their lives on the bridge of the ship! They were plotting courses and hunting currents and firing the cannons and swooping so close to the upper ringdoms their draft sucked the caps right off the heads of the port guards. They were testing the hull speed of the greatest airship the world had ever known while she was learning the appropriate honorific for an earl's second wife and how to curtsy in a manner that did not evoke a bucking horse.

Edith had expelled her from the bridge the moment the ship had left the Sphinx's hangar. Edith—*Captain Winters*—had made it clear that she had been banished because she could not be trusted to obey orders and because the bridge contained more buttons than an accordion. No one, not even the madman, was sure what all the doohickeys did, but they were all convinced that she could not be trusted to leave them alone. Voleta found the assumption insulting, and she had half a mind to run in there and mash some keys just to prove them right.

It seemed a pity that Adam wasn't there to explore the ship and her intricate consoles. Voleta had no doubt he would've been smitten with the titanic vessel. She wondered if he would've stayed had he known about the *State of Art*. Or had he been so eager to get free of them—of her—that not even a winged marvel could've enticed him to stay? She didn't like to dwell on the question.

Voleta suspected that her exile from the bridge wasn't actually to punish her rebelliousness. No, the captain and Iren were trying to keep her as far away from the madman as possible.

When Voleta learned that the Sphinx had named the Red Hand as the ship's pilot, she had been baffled. Yes, the Sphinx was always mysterious and often contrary, but she wasn't an imbecile or a saboteur. So why in the world would she dispatch a recently paralyzed and half-dead murderer to serve under the very woman who had tried to kill him? It made no sense! Voleta had many questions she wished to put to the Sphinx, but she had not been given the opportunity to ask them. In the final days before their departure, the Sphinx had not only refused to see her, but she had also locked her workroom door, sealed the airshafts to the conservatory (and the only climbing tree for miles), and commanded Ferdinand to chase Voleta out of the corridor if he ever saw her. Voleta had tried on a few occasions to charm the locomotive doorman with song and play, but the lumbering engine would only allow himself to be distracted until she tried to open one of the myriad doors in the Sphinx's home. Then Ferdinand would stomp his elephantine feet, pick her up by her nightgown, and carry her swinging and upside down back to the crew's apartment. And so, Voleta's brief friendship with the Tower's most enigmatic hermit seemed to have come to an unceremonious end.

Which was fine with Voleta—or so she tried to convince herself.

Still, for all the captain's efforts to keep them separated, Voleta had met the Red Hand, at least in passing.

She had been on her way to join Byron in the dining hall when she nearly bowled into the Red Hand on his way out. She bucked and gave a little shout of surprise, and he pressed himself against the doorway with his hands up. He palmed something that glinted in the light. She got a good look at him then, this man who she'd only seen once from a distance and through a snowstorm. His head looked like a boiled egg. His hair was as spare and coarse as the fur of a kiwi fruit. He had deeply set, almost piggish eyes and a wide mouth. He was no taller than her, yet she could feel the greater gravity of his presence.

The Red Hand said, "So sorry, my girl! I'm as thoughtless as a comet."

Perhaps it was because she'd spent the morning practicing small talk with Byron, but before she could stop herself, she found herself asking: "Did you have a nice lunch?"

The Red Hand tossed a pair of empty glass vials into the air, caught them, and exclaimed, "Oh, yes! It was delicious! Like sipping sunshine from a volcano."

Then Edith appeared behind him, scowling to have caught him talking to Voleta. She said, "Go on, airman. You've had your victuals. Leave the lady alone."

"Aye aye, Captain!" the Red Hand said. Before he turned away, Voleta could've sworn she saw a little wisp of steam rise off of his eyes.

On the sixth day into their promenade about the Tower, Byron summoned Voleta to the dining room to review the politics of seating charts, the subtleties of utensils, and general napkin etiquette. The room was all mahogany and brass, curlicues and cursive. The high-backed booths were intricately carved with vines that melded with the wild hair of women who seemed to float just beneath the surface of the wood grain. Electric sparks suspended inside voluminous glass bulbs lit the ornate room. It was a cozy enough space that would've benefitted from the presence of other diners, or servers, or food.

Voleta slouched before an empty plate that was fortified on three sides by no fewer than eleven utensils. The formal setting also included five glasses, two saucers, and a pair of folded napkins.

"Sit up straight," Byron commanded. His precise pronunciation seemed at odds with his strange, reedy voice. "No, not like that. Like this. Straight, but naturally so. No, like a tulip, not a yardstick. Better. Now, once more." Byron took a deep breath. "Pick up the fish knife and fish fork."

Voleta surveyed her options miserably. "I think humanity peaked at the spoon, don't you? A spoon can serve as a fork, a knife, a ladle . . . A good spoon is all you need, really."

"And I will tell you again, if you ever eat your fish with a spoon, I will appear out of thin air wherever you are in the world, snatch the spoon from your hand, and rap you on the head with it!" Byron arranged the silky black cravat upon his red vest. "Now, show me the fish knife and fish fork, please."

Voleta selected a fork and knife, scraped them together, and started to saw at the empty plate just to make the porcelain squeal.

Byron's antlers shivered, and his long ears drooped. "That is the bread knife and the cake fork. Try again."

Voleta stamped the utensils upon the tablecloth, making the glasses ring. "This doesn't make any sense!"

"You're absolutely right." Byron reached across the table and scooted the utensils back to their proper place. "The reason you have to be taught this is that none of it makes any natural sense. None of it is logical. You could sail across every ocean, summit every mountain, survive a thousand seasons, and never discover the proper time to drink out of a saucer. The answer is *never*. Never drink out of a saucer."

"What if I just refuse to eat? What if I just sit on my hands and nod and smile and say nothing at all? They can't find any fault if I don't do anything."

"Of course they can! They'll assume you're an imbecile or a snob or someone who can't tell a gravy boat from a teapot. Voleta, you have to understand, customs exist for two reasons: one, to identify insiders; and two, to exclude outsiders. That's why they're so tricky and picky and peculiar. Table manners are like...like a long secret handshake, a handshake that goes on for hours and hours until everyone is so full they can't do their pants up."

"That's revolting."

"So it is. But, my irritating ingenue, if you want to get invited to the sort of parties Marya gets invited to, you have to practice the secret handshake."

"All right! Fine! What about this? Is this the fish fork?"

"Good! And what about the fish kn—"

The hull of the ship rang about them. The light bulbs swung, and the china rattled. Voleta knew at once it was the cannons. By the sound of it, all the guns on the portside had been fired in a single volley.

Voleta began to scoot out of the bench seat, but Byron reached over and took her wrist before she could get to the end of the booth. "No. No, no. Stay right there. We haven't finished our lesson."

"But there's a war on!"

"Don't be so dramatic! You know they're just showing off. If it's anything more than that, then they'll sound the alarm." Voleta's arm went limp in his grip, and she slumped back down. "And this gives us a chance to practice another important skill. You have to learn to keep your composure even when a plate breaks, or a lady chokes on an olive, or a candle falls over, or the curtains catch fire, or—"

"Why?" Voleta demanded with arms crossed.

"Because that's the benefit of etiquette: It tells us what to do when no one knows what to do."

The echo of the cannons on the deck below rumbled on. Voleta watched the tilting water in her wineglass. The ship was rising and turning. "This is torture," she said.

"Just wait until the napkin drills," Byron said and, to demonstrate the form, took her napkin, shook it once, and then drew it across his lap.

"Can I ask you something?"

"You may, but I'm still going to point out the fish knife. It's this one here. You can remember it because the back edge looks a little like a fin."

"Why do you think she saved the Red Hand? Why did she bring him back? Why did she put him in here with us?" The questions came as quickly as cards being dealt. Byron's expression ossified, and his large eyes stood wide. "I mean, do you think she's trying to kill us? Do you think she's just trying to get rid of me?"

Byron sighed deeply, his long muzzle nearly dropping to his vest front. "It's not always about you." The stag looked up again and shook his head. "Look, the Sphinx is shrewd, and adaptive, and almost certainly the greatest mind the Tower has ever produced. But she also doesn't like to admit her mistakes."

"And all of us have to pay for it."

"Perhaps," Byron said, his gaze following his hand as it arched upon the table, a tentative gesture, a small plea for patience. "And I have told her more than once that she should admit her errors, fix them if they can be fixed or destroy them if they're beyond redemption, and move on to the next attempt."

"I'm not saying I want to see the Red Hand destroyed, I just don't understand why the Sphinx had to—"

"I wasn't talking about the Red Hand. I was talking about myself."

Voleta scowled. "Wait. You asked the Sphinx to destroy you?"

"Yes, I did."

The intimacy of the admission made her squirm in her seat. She huffed through a few false starts, not knowing where to look or what to say, then finally blurted, "Honestly, Byron, and I don't mean this to sound awful...I don't know where you came from or even what you are."

"I'm a muddy miracle, is what I am!" he said with a flash of his former hubris, though it quickly softened. He gave a long, unsteady exhalation. "And also, I am an experiment. You see, the Sphinx learned after years of breeding beasts for specific tasks that animals are unpredictable and limited in what they can reliably do. She could breed bull snails to grease the Basement plumbing easily enough, and parrots to make the beds and serve as town criers. But try as she might, she could not, for example, breed an animal to find and repair the cracks in the face of the Tower. So she built a machine for that and for other jobs, too. For a while, it seemed that any need could be answered with an engine. For a while.

"But the trouble with autonomous engines is that they're dumb and easily manipulated. All the Sphinx's engines are easy to hijack. Every time she would send a new machine into the world, it was only a matter of time before someone captured it and recast it as a war machine or a mule or a steed. You can't imagine how much it grieved her to see her wall-walkers transformed into crawling cannons. The ringdoms turned all her gifts into obscenities. And then she made me."

"But where did you . . . Where did the stag part of you come from?"

"I was a pet. I was brought back as a fawn from a hunt in the north plains. I suspect the people who brought me here probably also killed my mother. I was given as a present to a princess in the ringdom of Oyodin, or so I'm told. I don't remember it at all. Apparently, after a year or two in her care, I fell ill or perhaps I was just neglected. Whichever it was, I was delivered to the Sphinx in a hopeless state. I was dying, all but dead."

"I'm so sorry. How awful! If I ever find the princess of Oingodin who mistreated you, the two of us are going to have words. Then we're going to have fists and feet. And maybe a shovel!" Voleta boxed the air and mimicked the pleas of a frightened princess. But soon, she felt silly and strangely helpless, and the play lost its fun.

"I don't know how the Sphinx gave me the ability to think and speak as I do, or how I came to inhabit this body. I suspect it involved her medium, but she has never told the details of my rebirth."

Voleta gazed at him with fresher eyes. "I still don't understand why you'd say you were a mistake. I think you're actually rather marvelous, I mean other than your personality."

"It's possible, I think, to be so many things at once that you're practically nothing at all. If you crush a mountain and spread it across a continent, it doesn't make little mountains; it just vanishes into dust." Byron drew the napkin from his lap and began absentmindedly folding it into the shape of a boat. "I'm not as tireless or amiable as the animals she'd breed in the past. I'm not as strong and dexterous as her other engines. I haven't been embraced by the men and women who

I've met, which makes me useless as any ambassador to the ringdoms. I am not a beast, a machine, or a man. I have no place at all and no purpose but to serve the Sphinx as I can."

"So you went to the trouble of learning all of this," Voleta said, waving a hand over the table setting, "because you hoped they would accept you?"

Byron finished the napkin boat and set it on the open table before him. "It turns out that knowing my cake fork from my snail fork can't quite make up for these." He reached up and flicked the thorny tip of one of his antlers.

"I don't think . . . no, I *know* the Sphinx would never do anything to hurt you, Byron. She loves you. And I don't think you're even in the same category as the Red Hand. He's something else entirely. I think he *is* a mistake."

"Well," Byron said, delivering a practiced and almost convincing shrug, "time will tell."

Chapter Two

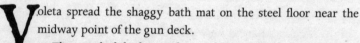

My grandfather, the royal magistrate, famously said: "Sometimes a prisoner would rather stare at a bare wall than a barred window."

Or, put another way, ladies: "Do not taste the cake your figure cannot afford."

—*Lady Graverly's Table: Rare Graces and Common Shames*

Voleta spread the shaggy bath mat on the steel floor near the midway point of the gun deck.

The gun deck had turned out to be a surprisingly good pitch. The floor was unriveted and as smooth as a watch crystal. The alley between cannons was wide enough to accommodate a field of nine or ten lanes, should she ever be able to assemble so many players, and that would still leave room for a verge on either side for the onlookers. Yes, when bath-mat sledding took off as a sport, the dimensions of the *State of Art's* gun deck would be cited as the standard.

Voleta still wore the big-skirted dress Byron had put her in for their evening dance lesson, though she had taken off the hard slippers that nipped her ankles and blistered her heels. For a few hours every afternoon, Byron sequestered himself inside the Communication Room, where he received and dispatched the Sphinx's winged spies and messengers, and in doing so, gave Voleta a much-needed break from the tyranny of polite society.

The cool floor felt good on her bare feet. On either side of her, two tiers of cannons pointed at the sealed gun ports. The barrels of the guns had been forged to resemble a variety of animals. They evoked the stretched and stylized bodies of tigers, dogs, elephants, lions, hawks, and wolves, and all of them with round mouths that seemed caught between a pucker and a roar. A mechanical figure stood by the breech of each of the sixty-four guns. The cannoneers looked like toy soldiers, with red jackets and black shakos and expressionless, perfectly round heads, but they were much cleverer than toys. Voleta had once managed to see the gunners in action, reloading the cannons between volleys. They twirled their sponge-rammers like batons and shifted cannonballs as if they weighed nothing at all. The cannons had been cleaned, reloaded, and reset before she could count to seven. Then they fired once more. It felt as if she were trapped inside a thunderclap.

But presently, the toy soldiers were still, the cannon zoo silent.

Bath-mat sledding was a dangerous sport. She had already bruised the underside of her chin during one tumble and cut her shin from another. The challenge was to carry as much velocity as possible from the run up to the leap, but not so much speed that she lost her balance and pitched forward onto her face. She used the cannons as a unit for measuring the distance of her sled rides. So far, her record was seven and a half gun bays.

Holding her skirt up over her knees, she charged and leapt onto the bath mat. She landed just right, her feet spread but not too far, and as the mat began to slide like a pat of butter across a hot plate, she knew it was going to be a record-breaking run.

She cleared the eighth cannon easily and felt a thrill when the ninth flashed by. The tenth cannon was a peripheral blur. Her momentary excitement was spoiled by the realization that she was picking up speed. She was hurtling toward the front of the ship, toward the vestibule where the stairs for the other floors branched to the left and right, and straight ahead, rushing at her very fast now, was a large steel door.

At last, she realized what was happening: The ship had veered downward, turning her playing field into a slope. Trying to slow herself, she fell backward off the bath mat, onto her skirts, which were nearly as slick. She attempted to use her feet as brakes, but even as the calluses on her heels heated with friction, she saw she wouldn't stop in time.

She struck the door feetfirst and so forcefully it stood her up. She bounced flat against the door with a tremendous thump and fell again onto her rear with a jolt. She lay back, hugging herself in pain. The bath mat slid to a stop against the top of her head. The ship leveled out again.

As she lay there, waiting for the sting of the collision to crest and subside, she stared up at the plaque on the door that read ENGINE ROOM, and beneath that in bold, NO ADMITTANCE.

"All right, all right, you don't have to rub it in." She knew the door was locked because she had tried it several times before. She was preparing to gather her mat and go find something soft to lie down on when she heard what sounded like a soft tap on the other side of the sealed door.

She pressed her ear against the cold steel. She heard the hum of the ship's engine or perhaps the drone of her blood. She raised a crooked finger, tapped her nail against the steel three times, then listened for a reply.

She didn't hear another tap, but if she strained, she could hear something else. Something high pitched and regular, like the crying of a mouse.

"Right. That's it," she said. She went to her room and rummaged through the luggage Byron had given her until she found a pair of bobby pins. She returned to the engine room door with the rather ambitious intention of picking the lock. It was ambitious because she had never picked a lock before, but she had heard one of the girls in the Steam Pipe describe the process once. How hard could it possibly be? She knelt before the door, straightened the pins, and began probing the keyhole.

As she worked, she heard the mouse squeak now and then and took it as encouragement.

"What are you doing?" Iren asked.

Voleta looked up from the lock to find her immense friend filling the stairwell to the third deck. She had no idea how long she'd been fiddling with the lock. She had completely lost track of time. She backed away from the door, pocketing the pins. She attempted to look nonchalant. "Oh, just cooling my ears. They get so hot, you know."

"What is that?" Iren pointed at the rectangle of chenille on the floor.

"That is a bath mat."

Iren squinted, began to ask another question, then thought better of it. Voleta noticed how exhausted her friend looked, and she felt a little guilty for adding another worry line to Iren's brow.

"What was that dive about?" Voleta asked.

"Nothing, just discouraging prowlers."

"But who was it? Where did they come from? Were they navy or—"

"It doesn't matter," Iren said with a dismissive wave. "The captain wants to see you."

"Oh, what've I done now?"

"Don't say that. You make me nervous when you say that." The amazon began to ascend the steel steps but paused halfway up. She bent down so she could look Voleta in the eyes. "Dress rehearsal tomorrow."

"I know."

"I'm going to serve you tea."

"I'll wear a helmet."

Iren stood and began climbing again, but her voice echoed down, "One lump or two, milady?"

Voleta laughed, collected her bath mat, and headed for the captain's quarters, wondering what sort of scolding she was in for.

The door of the captain's quarters was ajar and leaking light into the carpeted corridor. Voleta raised her fist to knock, then froze at the sound of a familiar voice.

Thoughtless in her excitement, she shoved the cabin door open and cried, "Hello, Senlin! You're back!"

Edith leapt in her chair, dropping the brass cylinder she'd been holding a moment before. It rolled across her dining table, then off the edge and onto the rug. Senlin's voice continued, and it took a moment for Voleta to realize it was emanating from the tube Edith had dropped. He said, "...I just feel grateful that there is someone in this madhouse who I know and can trust. Someone who is an endless source of encouragement and strength. I can hardly say how much I love—"

Edith, who'd been scrambling after the cylinder, finally got her hand around it. She cut off Senlin's voice with a wrench of the recorder's head.

"What is that?"

"Nothing. A message from Senlin. And what are you doing bursting into my room like that?" The captain righted the chair she had knocked over in her haste. She had yet to really put her mark on her cabin, Voleta noticed. The velvet settee, gold-leaf desk, and canopy bed all appeared untouched. The only surface that Edith seemed to have claimed was the square dining table, which held a couple days' worth of dishes, a few rolled-up maps, a silver model of the *State of Art*, a magnifying glass, a hairbrush, and a pistol. The tabletop seemed a little island of humanity amid the stately furniture and the walls full of decorative curios and the formal portraits of the ship's previous commanders. When Voleta had seen that stuffy gallery the first time, she had asked Edith when she was planning on growing out her whiskers.

Though to be fair, none of them had really settled in. So far, Voleta had slept in five different cabins, and none of them had felt right. There was just something impervious about the ship. It felt like she was trying to sleep in the lap of a monument.

"What was all that about happiness and love?" Voleta asked, tilting her head suspiciously. "He talked to Marya, didn't he? He wasn't supposed to do that. The Sphinx told him not to. Several times. Ha! Looks like I'm not the only one who can't follow orders!"

"We need to talk about those orders. There's been a change of plan."

"Is it about the wig? Because I agree: It's completely idiotic."

Edith collected her thick, dark tresses and bound them with a tie. "What? No, it's not about the wig. When we get to Pelphia, you are going to stay on the ship."

Voleta couldn't keep the disappointment from her face. The only thing that had kept her sane since being shut inside that flying casket was the thought of escape. Even if she had to wear a seven-layer dress and curtsy her knees off, it would be worth it so long as she could stretch her legs a little. The low-level claustrophobia that had been pestering her for days suddenly flared again. She tugged at the neckline of her dress. "But what about Marya?"

"You were right. Senlin did speak to her."

"What did she say?"

"That she is happy where she is and that she doesn't need rescuing."

"But how is that—" Voleta was cut off by a knock on the door behind her.

Byron's black nose pressed through the crack. "You wanted to see me, Captain?"

"Yes, come in. I was just telling Voleta that, as much as I and Senlin appreciate all the work you two have been doing getting Voleta ready for court, it won't be necessary."

"She's canceling my mission, Byron! Can you believe it?"

"You listened to the message," Byron surmised. "What did he say?"

"Just that he saw his wife, and asked her very plainly what she wanted, and she told him that she wanted to continue her life with the duke."

"And he believed her?" Voleta said, fists on her hips.

"Why wouldn't he believe her?" Edith shifted a scroll on the table, uncovering a pewter mug. She peered inside, deliberated a moment, then drank its contents. "I know you're disappointed, Voleta, but—"

"I'm not disappointed. I just don't believe it. I mean, think about it: The duke all but kidnapped her. What if he coerced her into marrying him? What if he's a tyrant, and she's just frightened of crossing him?"

"You think she is so afraid of him that she can't take the opportunity to escape?" Edith sounded skeptical.

"Yes, exactly! I saw it all the time when I was locked up in the Steam Pipe. If someone has absolute control over you, it's easy to believe they have absolute power over everything and everyone. They can't be defied or challenged or disobeyed, and every opportunity for escape just feels like a cruel test. Marya might even think she is protecting Senlin by turning him away. She might not be able to tell the truth until she's free."

"But by your logic, the only way to know if Marya wants to leave is to force her to leave. You want to kidnap her?"

"No! But I do want to speak to her. You don't offer a wounded person assistance once and then strut off, patting yourself on the back for the good deed you almost did. Believe me, desperation makes it hard sometimes to recognize help when it comes, to accept it when it's offered. If she's really happy, I think I'll be able to tell."

"Is that how you felt?" Byron asked Voleta. "Wounded?"

"This isn't about me," Voleta said with a scowl. She wondered if that were true. "We've already come this far; we've already suffered so much to be here. It seems silly to leave the good deed half done."

"The risk to Voleta *is* relatively minimal, Captain," Byron said. "She might embarrass herself and bring shame to us all—"

"Hey!"

"*But*," the stag continued, "the ringdom is lawful enough, and she'll have Iren to look after her."

"I don't think we understand the risk at all," Edith said, crossing her arms, flesh and iron, into an unhappy knot. "But I suppose you're right, Voleta. We've come this far."

"*And*," Byron said, raising a finger. "I just taught her how to spit gristle into a napkin."

"I can spit gristle like a lord!" Voleta declared happily.

"Like a lady," Byron corrected.

"Can we hear the rest of it?" Voleta asked.

"The rest of what?" Edith asked.

"What Senlin said."

The captain's expression seemed to suggest that she had forgotten the recorder entirely, though she still held it gripped in her flesh-and-blood hand. "I think seeing Marya again left Senlin a little...over-excited. It seemed to bring up a lot of feelings, and I think he'd be embarrassed to have all that blubbering and carrying on shared with everyone."

"He loves her very much, doesn't he?" Voleta sounded almost proud.

"Yes. Yes, he does," Edith said and slipped the recorder into her pocket.

On the gun deck, Byron blew a short, flat note on his bugle. "Wrong!" he shouted.

The teacup handle snapped free of Iren's thick finger, and the earless cup fell to the steel floor with a crash.

"Please be careful, Iren!" Byron hissed. "This set was a gift from the King of Bacheral. It's more than a century old."

On the card table that had been set up for tea service, Squit, Voleta's pet flying squirrel, ran twice about the sugar bowl, up the mound of crustless sandwiches, then pounced upon the bud vase, knocking it over. Ignoring the spilled flowers, Voleta concentrated on the mound of clotted cream balanced on the flat of her butter knife. She had managed to maneuver the knife halfway between the pot of cream and her piece of toast when the blob slid off and landed with a plop upon the tablecloth. Squit dashed over and began licking the mess at once.

The dress rehearsal had descended into absolute chaos, much to Byron's satisfaction. That was, after all, the point of the exercise and particularly the horn, which he said introduced a much-needed element of alarm to the proceedings. He blew another sour note on the bugle. Iren glared at him. Her governess's uniform was uncomfortable and constrictive. Already her stock tie and brocaded bib were stained with tea. She stepped on her skirts so often it seemed only a matter of time until she fell on her face. She returned to the tea cart to collect a new cup and to rattle out another pour.

Byron raised a book before his snout and read from it with the rolling cadence of a lecturer. The volume was called *The Ingenue's Primer*, and Voleta was certain it had been written by a sadist. "Scenario number five: You are attending a gala that includes hors d'oeuvres served from a buffet. You, and only you, observe another guest of equal rank insert his finger into the salmon pâté, remove it, and lick it clean. What do you do?"

Voleta pulled at the fallen sleeve of her puffy yellow gown. "Ask him if it's any good?"

"Stop fidgeting. Come on. What do you really think you would do?"

"I don't understand why I have to do anything!"

"Well, what if he licked his finger and put it back into the pâté a second time?"

"I don't know," Voleta said, picking Squit up and moving her away from the spill. "I'd offer him a spoon."

"No!"

"A fish fork?"

Today, Byron wore a pince-nez balanced on the end of his long snout. The spectacles, Voleta knew, were an affectation. The stag had bragged before about his perfect vision, and besides, the lenses didn't even cover his wide-set eyes. Voleta suspected he wore the pince-nez only because he liked removing them to punctuate his reproving stares, as he did now. "You're not even trying. No, what you *should* do is locate a maid or porter and discreetly request that they replace the dish."

"Why would I do that?"

"Because you don't want to embarrass the guest, and you don't want to eat after his finger. Will you please stop pulling at your dress!"

"I feel like I'm being swallowed by a boa constrictor!"

"It's called a corset, and it's meant to be snug." He blew into his bugle just as Iren turned with a brimming cup of tea balanced upon a saucer. The amazon jumped, and the cup popped upon the floor. Byron tut-tutted, then carried swiftly on. "Scenario number six—"

Voleta held up her hands. "Can't I just have a mo—"

"*Scenario number six*: You are a guest in a private parlor, listening to another guest play an impromptu recital upon a poorly tuned harpsichord—"

"Who writes this stuff?" Voleta all but barked. "When does any of this ever hap—"

Byron read on, speaking over her. "She is an amateur, and the performance is quite bad." Byron paused to toot upon his horn. "After a moment, the host begins to tease her with jeers and boos. What do you do? Now, think before you answer. How could you defuse the situation?"

"I could boo the host and see how he likes it," Voleta said.

"No! You're escalating again!"

"I'm tired of this game. Just tell me what I'm supposed to say, and I'll say it!"

"This isn't a game!" Byron shouted, shaking the open book. "The whole point of the exercise is to teach you to think of ways to avoid confrontation when it arises. I won't be there to tell you what to say."

"You say, 'avoiding confrontation.' I call it running from a fight."

"Voleta, my dear, all society will ever do is throw fights out in front of you. It exists to goad you and get your hackles up. But if you take a swing at every bully that steps into your path, you're going to end up with a lot of black eyes, and you're going to make a lot of enemies. You need friends where you're going. You need allies to shepherd you into Marya's privileged sphere. If you want to have any chance of seeing her, of saving her, you have to be cordial, pleasant, and contrite."

Voleta took a deep breath, closed her eyes, and after a moment's reflection said, "I suppose I might just applaud louder and try to pass the whole thing off as a good-natured joke."

"A fine and politic solution. Very good! And all it took was a second of earnest thought." Pulling his watch from his vest pocket, Byron marked the time with a smirk. "Now, for scenario number seven, I've asked the captain to help simulate what it's like to be in the middle of a roaring party at midnight. Iren, you should probably put down that teacup—"

All thirty-two of the starboard cannons fired. The roar of the blast and the scrape of the recoil sleds drew a scream from Voleta. Even though Byron knew the shot was coming, he still bleated like a lamb. When the stag looked at Iren through the haze of gun smoke, he found she was scowling at him, but still holding the saucer and cup steadily before her.

He gave an approving nod, and in response, Iren tilted the saucer and let the cup crash upon the floor.

"Oops," she said.

Byron sighed. "Yes, I suppose I deserved that. Now onto scenario eight..."

*   *   *

When Edith found them an hour later, Voleta was red-faced and shouting and Byron was blowing repeatedly on his horn. Iren sat straddled upon the barrel of a cannon with her fingers in her ears.

A spreading lagoon of tea on the floor crackled when Edith crossed it, pulverizing the swimming shards of porcelain.

Edith snatched the bugle from Byron's lips so abruptly he blew spit on her hand. The sight of the captain was enough to silence Voleta.

"You call this a lesson?" Edith said, glancing at Iren as she rejoined the group. "I'm on the bridge tracking the navies of a dozen different ringdoms, all of whom I'm sure are mustering up the courage to take a stab at us. Meanwhile, you're down here, throwing tea, blowing horns, and reaching for each other's throats. This doesn't give me a lot of confidence."

"I'm doing my level best, Captain," Byron said, wringing his hands, which moved as smoothly as cogs. "I'm not sure she has a single civil instinct in her."

"I got three scenarios right!" Voleta shouted.

"Out of twenty-eight! That's terrible. Iren could do better."

"Oy," Iren said.

"Shut up, all of you," Edith said, finding and holding each of their gazes. She looked angry and, Voleta thought, a little unnerved. "I don't think you understand our situation here. We are a castle without an army. If anyone suspected there were only five of us inhabiting this ship, they would break the hull open and pull us out like maggots from soft cheese."

"Oh my god!" Byron shuddered in revulsion.

"A buttload of anvils," Iren said. Everyone looked at her blankly, and she shrugged. "When I worked for Goll, part of my job was to spot the sluggards. If I caught a man loafing, or napping, or dragging his feet, I'd give him a boot." Iren's expression seemed almost sentimental. "But there was this one clever slug named Miter. He figured out he could fool me if he carried an empty crate or butt about and just acted like it was full. He was good at it, too. He'd go red in the face. His knees would tremble. His eyes would bulge out of his head. I'd ask him, 'What's so heavy?' And he'd always say, 'Anvils!' This went on for months. Then one day, just on a whim, I knocked on the butt he was lugging about and heard an empty thump."

"What became of Miter?" Voleta asked.

"What do you call a person who really comes to appreciate the taste of something?" Iren said, frowning with thought. "A *clowning sir*?"

"A *connoisseur*?" Byron suggested.

"That's it. I made him a connoisseur of my boot."

"Worse will happen to us if we're discovered," Edith said grimly. "But Iren is right: We don't want anyone knocking on our butt."

Voleta laughed at the phrase, and Edith swung about to face the girl. "Listen to me, Voleta." Edith spoke in a level voice that was more daunting for its lack of inflection. "I want to make one thing clear: Iren is in charge. If you disobey her, she is under strict orders to haul you back to the ship, in a sack if need be, and you will not leave here again so long as I'm captain. There'll be no discussion, no excuses, and no third or fourth chances. The Sphinx will not intervene on your behalf. I will install you in the galley and you will scrub dishes until you're old. You will do as Iren tells you. Is that clear?"

"Aye, sir," Voleta said and tried to swallow the lump that had risen in her throat.

"Good. The Sphinx has decided that we dock at Port Virtue in the morning. He's promised they'll be expecting us. The Sphinx has given us three days to conduct our business. Three days. That's as long as this little experiment will last. If anyone asks, we will tell them the ship has a crew of seventy-eight airmen. If anyone wants a tour, we will politely dissuade them. If anyone tries to board us, we will kill them at the door."

Chapter Three

At the round table of color, orange sits supreme. Orange is sublime. Orange is ablaze. And seated across from Lady Orange, we have Sir Purple. I ask you, is any color more vulgar? The word alone emerges like something from a lavatory. *Purple. Plopple.* It's all prunes, liver spots, and ink stains. If I ever utter a word of praise for that wretched hue, please snatch my pen away and gore me with it.

—Oren Robinson of the *Daily Reverie*

The Daily Reverie

THE STATE OF ART AND THE STATE OF US

JULY 14

After the sun and the moon, the *State of Art* must be the largest, brightest celestial body.

Yes, I too have stood out upon the viewing deck and watched that great silver scythe slink across the sky. I'm utterly certain it could slit the Tower's throat should it have a mind to. Binoculared oglers have informed me that the ship's envelope is decorated with the ancient herald of the Brick Layer. Because I was a poor student, but a better journalist, I researched the Brick Layer's emblem, so I could describe it to you here in reliable detail. It is a wheel of half-clad men and women, marching heel to toe, sharing burdens of bricks, jugs, and sheaves of wheat. In short, it is a dreadful little pantomime of perfect human harmony, which exists to remind us how noisy and thoughtless our upstairs neighbors are.

But it seems inarguable now—the Sphinx is back.

I have been warned by the authorities that we should not expect the Sphinx himself to emerge from the ship with tentacles flailing and mane ablaze. Purportedly, the Sphinx is sending one of his Wakefolk to speak at his behest. I've heard whispers that the Wakeman will come with an entourage of interesting persons for us to turn upon the slow spit of our attention. I can hardly wait. My pen waters with anticipation.

Is there anyone who inspires more overconfident and underinformed theorizing than the Sphinx? We are naturally suspicious of his intentions. I've heard learned persons suggest that he has come to stake a political claim. Other, equally wise men are sure his return portends the introduction of a new and dazzling technology. (Of course, the Colosseum bookmakers are taking bets on the nature of that invention. Presently, there are equal odds on it being drinkable lightning, a mechanical girdle, or a pork-beef hybrid called *moink*.) Still other scholars claim that this is all an elaborate humbug enacted by one of the upper ringdoms—a poor joke played upon us, the original cast of the Tower.

For my own part, I would like to know why the Sphinx vanished in the first place. Did we thin his patience with our squabbling? Or perhaps our independence made him resentful. I know the lower-ringdom jingoists like to believe he was exiled by our excellence, which forced him to admit that the Tower is only as high as its base is wide!

Personally, I suspect the truth is more banal: He is an immortal who retired too young, grew bored of his coin collection, and decided to un-retire.

I have observed some anxiety over why the Sphinx has chosen our port to be the first to welcome his warship. Is it a threat?

Is it an invasion, and, if so, should we expect a monstrous coronation? I do sometimes wonder why we are so quick to expect the worst of our guests. I prefer to believe the Sphinx has chosen us because he knows what we excel at. He wanted someone to make a fuss over him. And everyone knows we Pelphians have no peer in the fussing arts.

Ships bustled in and out of Port Virtue like bees through a rosebush. Of the Lower Ringdoms, no skyport saw more traffic in a day than Pelphia's north harbor.

Ferries full of tourists arrived almost hourly. Sow-bellied barges rolled in with the cool morning wind, weighted down with animal hides for the cobblers and bolts of wool and silk for the tailors, and left upon the afternoon thermals loaded with the freshest, already expiring fashions. The port, shaped like a four-pronged fork, jutted from a wide boardwalk. It boasted twelve slips that cradled enough open air to accommodate most vessels out to their midpoints. Gold-plated pollards studded each berth, and all were defended by eighteen turret guns called lead soldiers. The lead soldiers looked like kingly sarcophagi with arms stuck out in rigor mortis. They were eight feet tall and veined in gold. The soldiers could twist fully around on their bases and raise their arms from their hips to their ears, giving the gunners a range of motion with which no ship could compete. Between these daunting turrets, stout palm trees grew in pots like flowers on a windowsill.

In the *State of Art*'s vestibule, Voleta was looking forward to being ashore and in the fresh air. She was sick and tired of the heavy ship, which had a tendency to lurch and swing like a compass needle. She stood at the port hatch alongside Iren, Byron, and the captain, and tried her best to look as Byron said she ought: cordial, pleasant, and contrite.

Iren leaned upon the luggage cart, piled high with trunks and hatboxes, which she would be responsible for moving through the port. Byron pressed his snout to the steel door and peered through the peephole, watching for the port master's signal that the welcoming party was ready to receive them.

"This wig itches," Voleta said, scratching the part of her flowing locks. A charitable observer might have called the wig "blond," though she thought it was objectively yellow. "It feels like I'm wearing a mop."

"Don't scratch," Iren said, though without much feeling. Voleta could tell her friend was still getting used to her uniform. She almost didn't mind the long skirts and poufy shoulders, which did a fair job of concealing her bulk, but she found the frilly bonnet almost insufferable. Iren had told Voleta that morning that if the wharf rats of New Babel had ever caught her in a bonnet, they would have died of laughter—because when they laughed, she would have strangled them.

Voleta said, "I hardly recognize us."

"Good," Captain Winters said. She wore a military frock coat, one sleeve of which Byron had removed to make room for her iron arm. "Don't forget what happened the last time we tried to tie up here."

"What happened last time?" Byron asked.

"We covered the ship in rags, tried to pass ourselves off as wife-mongers, got pelted by the lead soldiers, and ran away with a hole in our sails." Voleta recounted the ordeal merrily enough.

"Yes, let's avoid a repeat of all of that." Edith peered at her warped reflection in the polished brass of the blowing horn that jutted from the wall. She shouted into the trumpet that connected to the bridge: "How does it look up there, pilot?"

The Red Hand, his voice muddied by its passage through the plumbing, replied, "The port is standing room only, but our airspace is clear enough."

"Good. Stand by with our salute," Edith said.

"Senlin got off easy: no wig, no dress, not even a false mustache," Voleta said.

"We're not using that name anymore, Voleta," the captain said. "It's Mr. Cyril Pinfield now. Though you shouldn't have any reason to mention him at all."

"Yes, right, sorry. I won't forget again." Voleta squeezed her eyes shut and shook her head so the curls slapped her cheeks. She knew better than that! A slip of the tongue was all it would take to send Senlin to the stocks—or worse! Much worse. She blamed the wig. It was just such an extravagant torment. She could hardly think through the pinch and the itch. Worse yet, she knew the moment she was introduced to the public as a golden-haired maiden, she would be forced to keep wearing it for the next three whole days. What if Iren made her sleep in it? It would be like sleeping with her head on an anthill!

Groaning with exasperation, Voleta marched to the porthole and undid the screws that sealed it.

"Excuse me, young lady, what are you doing?" Byron asked. "The port guard is standing at attention. It's almost time! The band is about to strike! For goodness' sake, stop that!"

But it was too late. Voleta had already opened the porthole, torn the golden tresses from her head, and stuffed the tangle through. The wind snatched the wig away at once.

"There." Voleta scrubbed her scalp happily. "Much better." Her dark hair was just long enough to lie down, at least in spots. She pulled at the neckline of her dress that was as purple as a plum, and in the process disturbed Squit's slumber inside one frilly shoulder. The fat-cheeked squirrel ran a lap about her waist and dove into the shelter of her other sleeve.

Edith inhaled sharply, and Voleta braced herself for the reprimand. But the captain seemed to change her mind. "All right. No wig."

"I'm still putting it in my report," the stag said, his long ears standing out.

Voleta beamed at her irritated tutor. "Your reports are going to be very boring with me gone."

"Not everyone finds peace and quiet boring, my dear." Byron peered through the spyhole once more. "There's the signal! It's time! Now, remember, smile with your eyes! No teeth! Teeth are the enemy of a demure smile." Byron stooped to fluff Voleta's skirts. "Bend your knees when you curtsy, and whatever you do, don't dance. Don't, because you can't. You dance like you have one foot stuck in a bucket."

"I was just following your lead," Voleta huffed.

"I'm a *wonderful* dancer," Byron said. Straightening, he turned the wheel lock to unseal the hatch.

"Let's keep our chins up. We don't want to look like we're skulking. Remember, we are emissaries of the Sphinx," Captain Winters said as she seated her tricorne upon her head.

Just before she passed into the daylight, Edith stooped and gripped the stag's shoulder with her iron hand. "If I'm not back by midnight, fire a volley over the port. If I'm not back by morning..." She took a deep breath. "Send the madman."

The moment their feet touched the gangplank, an orchestra struck up a lively concerto. The brass horns flashed in the sunlight. The guards that bordered the bandstand held their sabers at attention, black jackets spattered with the colorful ribbons of war. The bannered port was awash with gentlemen and ladies in coattails and dress trains. They spilled from the jetty, onto the floating docks between berths, and even swarmed onto the decks of the other anchored airships, all of which looked toy-like in the shadow of the *State of Art*.

Captain Winters paused at the foot of the gangplank. For a moment, she and her crew stood suspended above a rushing sea of wind. Voleta filled her lungs with the cool fresh air. Then the captain stepped ashore.

The *State of Art* fired her thirty-two starboard cannons in a synchronized volley. The crowd gasped at the concussive roar and waved their hands at the smoke that blew around the ship and across the port. A second volley followed very soon after the first. Voleta knew the Sphinx's cannoneers could reload the guns in less than seven seconds. Now the Pelphians knew that, too.

Recovering their enthusiasm even before the boom of the second salute had faded, the crowd began to cheer wildly. Young men dashed their handkerchiefs over their heads; young ladies shook bouquets of poppies and lilies like pom-poms. A line of noblemen in gold epaulets and fire-colored sashes applauded from the mouth of the city gates, which stood open and waiting to accept them.

The first thing Voleta noticed was that everyone in the port, save for the white-clad stevedores, wore the same colors: black and orange. They looked like a flock of orioles.

The crowd made just enough room for them to leave the gangplank, but no more. Voleta couldn't see over the perimeter of faces, and so relied upon Iren's hand on her shoulder to point her in the right direction. Everyone was leaning in and speaking at once. At first, they seemed to be competing for who could wish her the most health, wealth, and happiness. Then someone complimented her on the daring nature of her gown's color, and someone else expressed surprise that such a titanic vessel had produced only three visitors. Where were the dignitaries? Where were their wives? Where was the Sphinx? A lady asked Voleta if she were recovering from a bad case of lice or if there had been some sort of accident with her hair? Someone else asked whether she were really so brown or if it was only a bad tan?

Gathering all of her patience, Voleta answered in a long ramble, "Hello! Good morning! Thank you. Your dress is daring, too! Oh, no, I did it on purpose. Yes, it will grow back. No, I came out this color. Good morning! Excuse me."

She was beginning to wonder if she would be forced to traverse the whole city inside a scrum of gossiping nitwits when the crowd suddenly broke before her. A knight stood at the center of the little clearing. At least Voleta assumed she was a knight because the woman was shelled in golden armor from her waist to her neck. She wore a gilded cuirass and a matching pauldron and gauntlets. Then Voleta observed the knight's elbows cough a little steam, and she realized she was a Wakeman, like Edith. But unlike Edith's iron arm, this woman's engine was delicate and voluptuous. She looked more like a statue than a locomotive. Her red hair was stranded with silver at the temples. She stood with her wrists set upon her sculpted waist, looking heroic and a little out of place among the squawking throng.

Captain Winters was quick to offer her hand to the red-headed knight. "Wakeman Edith Winters, captain of the *State of Art*. Permission to come ashore."

"Georgine Haste. Welcome to Pelphia, Captain Winters." When Haste smiled, she showed her teeth, which endeared her to Voleta instantly. It was a smile that made room for intimacy amid the gaping crowd, a smile that seemed to apologize for the hubbub.

Still gripping her hand, Haste pulled Edith closer and Voleta scooted in to listen when she spoke. "Port Master Cullins is going to read a very dull speech. Don't worry, after five minutes, the orchestra will strike whether he's finished or not. Then there will be a short train ride and a parade. If you can stand it, smile and wave. It goes a long way. Then I'll present you to King Leonid, who, I promise, is not as silly as he seems."

With the last word out, Haste used her hold on Edith's hand to pivot them around to face the frenzied crowd. It seemed that everyone began to bow and introduce themselves in long-winded, self-important ways all at once. They talked over one another like turkeys gobbling in a pen. Haste pulled the captain through the commotion, and Voleta rode upon her wake.

At the head of the port, a man in military dress clutched a podium. His curled mustache looked as hard as a ram's horn. Voleta recognized him immediately as the port master who had once rebuffed them. To her relief, he showed no glimmer of recognition when he graced her with a toothless seasick smile. He stretched his neck, seemingly to soften the lump in his throat, and tamped the cards of his speech upon the lectern. When he spoke, his voice was small and unsteady.

Port Master Cullins underscored the honor of the occasion, using phrases like "annals of history" and "fraternity of ringdoms" and "honorable envoys of the Sphinx." The crowd, who did not care to spare Cullins's feelings, talked over his efforts. They reviewed the orchestra's boring performance of a tepid concerto and discussed how shabby the decorations seemed, despite being only hours old. And they returned again and again to their disappointment that so few guests had disembarked from so grand a vessel. Voleta overhead a man scoff, "The most interesting thing this week? Are you daft? This isn't even the most interesting thing to happen today!"

The port master was still mumbling through his remarks when the orchestra broke into a sudden and raucous march.

Released from the tedious proceedings, the crowd pressed back toward the city gates. The tunnel into the ringdom was tiled from floor to ceiling in squares as white as milk teeth. A glistening black locomotive steamed upon a sunken track. The engine towed a passenger car, a red caboose, and nothing more. Voleta discerned that the Pelphians were quite proud of their railroad, which seemed entirely unnecessary to her. Even so, when a matronly lady asked if she liked the city's "handsome iron stallion," Voleta managed to keep a straight face when she said, "It certainly is a train."

Iren didn't give the train a second glance, but she seemed pleased to see the porters. She handed the luggage off to them and watched as the customs agents in pillbox caps tagged each piece for inspection. Voleta knew they wouldn't find anything. Iren had petitioned the captain to let her bring her chains, or a pistol, or at least a sword, and Edith had explained why she couldn't allow it. A weapon, any weapon, would only raise suspicion when it was inevitably discovered and confiscated.

Wakeman Haste had just put her foot to the stairs of the passenger car when Port Master Cullins stepped into Voleta's path.

"I'm sorry, miss, but we can't have a loose animal on the streets. You'll have to cage it." The port master whispered something to one of the customs agents. He dashed off and returned presently with a birdcage.

Voleta scooped Squit off her shoulder and cupped her protectively. "She's quite harmless."

"I'm sure she is. But the law is consecrated by the Crown, and I don't have any discretion in how it's applied." Cullins opened the door of the cage, holding it up for her inspection. "As you can see, it's quite a pretty little cage. Your pet will be perfectly safe. I shall carry and protect it until after your court announcement."

Voleta turned to Iren, searching for support. But Iren's level gaze reminded her of what she already knew. This was it: the moment of capitulation, the moment of compromise. Byron had warned her the time would come when she would have to choose between society and herself. The challenge had come quicker than she'd expected and had struck a tender nerve. She knew Edith was watching to see what she would do.

The crowd began to murmur. The auburn sea of formal gowns pressed in around her. The port master's smile had soured into a nervous grimace. Voleta felt the sudden urge to reach up and rip off his mustache.

Instead, she lifted Squit and kissed her on her striped head. With soothing clucks, she placed the squirrel inside the cage, steeling her resolve when the squirrel's legs began to quiver with distress.

"There we are," Port Master Cullins said in a patronizing singsong. He closed the cage upon the cowering animal. "All the little beasties in their little cages."

"All aboard," Georgine Haste said from the top step of the train car. "It's time to meet the king."

Chapter Four

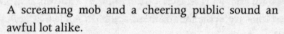

A screaming mob and a cheering public sound an awful lot alike.

—Oren Robinson of the *Daily Reverie*

Iren's first impulse was to throttle everyone who bumped into her.

She couldn't remember the last time she had felt so completely overlooked. Probably it was as a young girl, standing in a soup line and getting jostled by the larger children. But ever since she'd hit her growth spurt at the age of ten, people had just parted before her. At least they had until today. The moment she put on a bonnet and set her hands to a luggage cart, it was like she disappeared. The crowd didn't pay her the slightest attention, nor give her any space. She felt a powerful urge to rip off her cap and show them all exactly what sort of warrior they were dealing with. As she pushed the cart from gangplank to train steps, she glared at every lord and lady who dallied in her way or barked at her when she nudged them or made a point of not hearing her when she politely asked them to move. It would be so easy to wrench off the garment bar and beat them all to death with it. She could probably slay a dozen before breaking a sweat. And it wasn't until she was out of the crowd and sitting on a hard bench in the passenger car that she realized it wasn't true. She was letting her anger pull the wool over her eyes. It didn't matter how strong she was; she couldn't fight an entire ringdom.

The only ringdoms she'd ever known were dark and brooding

places. New Babel stank of sulfuric acid and guano. The Silk Reef was all cobwebs and pitfalls. But when she disembarked the train and emerged from the tunnel, she felt a scintillation of awe. Pelphia was as white as salt and clean as hanging laundry. The air smelled like freshly baked cakes and perfume and roses. The streets were narrow, and the buildings were faced with gleaming marble and glass. The city blocks were nearly sutured together by porches and galleries and terraces. Every window held a face, every inch of every rail was attended by a spectator. The city, which seemed to have been made for gawking, was leaning in and looking down.

Iren had never seen so much high ground. She felt as if she were walking along the bottom of a canyon. The confetti fell as heavily as a blizzard. The cheering sounded more and more like roaring. She felt a powerful urge to roar back. And perhaps she would've if Voleta had not at that moment reached up and taken her hand. Iren looked down at Voleta, her shoulder snowy with confetti.

"Did you see their tin-can sun? Isn't it hilarious?" Voleta asked. "It looks like someone smacked their sun in the face with a frying pan!" Iren was relieved to see that Voleta was taking it all in stride, though of course it made sense: She had experienced crowds and frenzy. Perhaps Voleta sensed her uneasiness because she patted Iren on the hand and shouted up into her downturned ear, "It's just theater, Iren. That's all it is. This show started long before we got here, and it'll continue long after we're gone. We're just actors walking across a stage." Voleta pointed down at the ground where a glowing glassy disc interrupted the cobblestones. "See, even the streets have footlights! It's all a play. Nothing but a play."

Iren found the thought consoling. She even managed to wave and grimace out something that could pass for a smile. But then confetti got in her mouth and a spray of champagne stung her eyes, at which point she decided it was best to leave the parading to professionals like Voleta, and she retreated behind the cover of her bonnet's brim.

Voleta was sorry to see that Iren was having such a miserable time because she was finding the whole spectacle quite entertaining. Yes, their reception was unnecessary and overdone, and she had no doubt the novelty of it would soon subside, but after days and days of being shut up inside the *State of Art*, it was nice to have such a thorough distraction.

Their procession carried them past chocolatiers, bakeries, and perfumeries. Shopgirls ran into the street to press candies into Voleta's hands and spray scent upon her neck. She was handed a teacup full of hot chocolate that was so sweet it made her teeth ache. The parade moved through an area the gold-breasted Haste called Cobblers' Ghetto. There, young models dangled their legs from balconies, showing off the season's most essential slippers and boots. Voleta followed in Edith's shadow as she marched under the jutting marquee of a theater, past posters of resident actors, who stared out with an intensity that almost passed for intelligence.

At last, they broke free of the high, white bluffs of the city blocks. The moment they stepped onto the open piazza, pinned here and there with lampposts and spotted with more of the luminous spots, the celebration ceased, or rather the revelers turned to other festivities. As the crowds dispersed, the hods emerged from little alleyway closets, armed with brooms and mops to clear away the drifts of confetti and lakes of champagne.

The ringdom's spine rose before them like the gigantic trunk of a barkless tree. Georgine Haste pointed out the Colosseum, an austere but disfigured landmark, and the willowy spires of the Vivant Music Hall. "And straight ahead," she said, "is the Circuit of Court." She gestured at the gated boxwood hedge. Here, the golden Wakeman stopped and, with an inclusive wave, brought their party into a huddle. Voleta liked the conspiratorial feeling of having her head sandwiched between Iren's and Edith's.

Haste said, "King Leonid likes to show off for his guests. I suggest you all prepare yourselves to be impressed."

"And respectful," Edith said, giving Voleta a meaningful glance.

"Yes, and also entertaining," Haste added.

"Entertaining?" Edith said. "They don't expect us to put on a show, do they?"

"No, nothing so extravagant." Haste swatted the notion away and scoffed reassuringly, then undid all her encouragement by admitting, "Not necessarily a show. But this is Pelphia. If you're boring, you'll just be dismissed. It's a good idea to distinguish yourself, especially while you have the attention of every noble in the ringdom."

"What would you recommend?" Voleta asked. "Juggling, tumbling, some light sparring, perhaps? I don't know any soliloquies by heart, but I'm sure I could make something up—something with plenty of *thees* and *thous.*"

"No, nothing so formal as that, I shouldn't think," Haste said. "When I was introduced nearly twenty years ago, I cracked a few jokes, talked a little about my travels, and let the king ring my chest like a gong." She tapped her gilded breastbone.

"Well, we're not doing that. It's a good thing we came with our very own comedian, isn't that right, Iren?" Voleta said, nudging her friend in the ribs. The amazon looked a little pale at the suggestion.

Ranks of pages in emerald smocks stood before the shut gates of the court. Something about the scene struck Voleta as odd, but it wasn't until they drew nearer that she could put her finger on what unsettled her. It wasn't the fact that the shrubs were obviously fake, or that some of the pages were boys and others were old men in bobbed wigs, nor was it the menacing black spiral formed by the ironwork of the closed gates. No, it was the silence of the court behind the silk bushes. In such a noisy town, it seemed like the sort of quiet that would precede a trap.

But when the pages blew upon their trumpets and opened the black gates, and their little party strode through a gauntlet of palm trees into the vast courtyard beyond, Voleta saw at once it wasn't a trap. It was something much worse than a trap: It was a dramatic tableau.

Dozens of costumed actors huddled before them, all caught in the grip of staged paralysis. Young girls wearing floral wreathes stood on their toes in a frozen frolic. Bakers, with loaves underarm, posed behind a table that was coated in flour and lumped with pallid balls of dough. Tailors held scissors to bolts of cloth; perfumers pinched the bulbs of spray bottles; chocolatiers staked whisks in mixing bowls;

and a clockmaker with a loupe to one eye studied the cogs of an open watch. A troop of soldiers knelt in formation, pointing rifles at some invisible foe. A flight of burlesque dancers, with legs hiked under shallow skirts, struggled to maintain their balance, while an ox with a heavy dewlap and gold-capped horns broke the perfect stillness with a swish of its tail.

Behind this bizarre display, a white pyramid held an ornamental star aloft. The moment Voleta laid eyes on it, she immediately imagined what it would be like to slide from its peak down to its base. She wished she had brought her bath mat.

Then she became aware that all around this staged scene, lords and ladies stared, not at the tableau, but at them, the honored guests, idling in the entryway.

Haste raised her hands suggestively. Catching her drift, Edith, Voleta, and Iren began to clap. The applause was contagious, and very soon the court pealed with the echoes of approval.

The frozen scene thawed. The children laughed; the dancers put down their legs; and the soldiers dusted their knees. They all assembled in a line and bowed in unison three times. Then the actors began to file toward an opening in the hedge, which Voleta did not think had been there the moment before. One of the bakers took the ox's rope and led the beast away.

While the troop retreated, the watchmaker advanced upon the visitors, who felt suddenly adrift amid the dwindling applause.

"What a magnificent tableau, Your Majesty," Haste said, bowing to the watchmaker as he pulled the loupe from his eye.

"You think so? I rather liked it, too. My own design, of course. I've had this costume for weeks. I've been spoiling for a chance to wear it." He lifted the lapels of his jacket admiringly, the undersides of which were as bright as a goldfinch. "And I have to say"—the king's voice rose so that it reached everyone in the court—"there really isn't anything more wondrous than the jungle of a clock! There's a tiger named Tick, and a bear named Tock. They roam the cogs and roar back and forth at each other. Tick, tock! Tick, tock! And only the watchmaker can tame them! Let us take a moment to appreciate the nimble-fingered watchmakers." The king paused to initiate a run of applause, which he ended with a flourish of his arm. "And what is the Sphinx, really, but the Tower's watchmaker in chief? Where is the Sphinx, by the way? I'm dying to meet him!"

"If it please Your Majesty, I would like to introduce Wakeman Edith Winters," Haste said with another formal bow. "Captain of the *State of Art* and emissary of the Sphinx."

Edith stepped forward and bowed with as much grace as she could manage. "Your Majesty, the Sphinx sends his warmest regards and his sincerest regrets that he could not come himself." She came up from her bow to see the disappointment plastered upon the king's face. He was an older man. His white hair stood out from his head like the wings of a dove. He had round, apple-red cheeks and lips as pronounced as a camel's. His eyes were wild and watery. "But I assure the court," Edith said with a sweep of her gaze, "I am authorized to speak on his behalf."

"The Sphinx hides in his cloud, where fun is not allowed," the king said in a singsong, apparently quoting a familiar rhyme. The reference drew titters from the court.

"But," Edith went on, "the Sphinx has sent his relative to entertain you in his stead. May I present to you Lady Voleta Pennatus Contumax, niece of the Sphinx."

Voleta stepped forward with her head raised and her chin out. While King Leonid watched and his court whispered, the Lady Contumax put one foot behind the other to begin her formal curtsy.

Byron had described Voleta's natural curtsy as resembling a theatrical sneeze. It was jarring and spasmodic. Worse, it came off as sarcastic. She was, Byron said, the first person he had ever met who could make a curtsy look like a curse. He had made her practice one hundred times a day for more than a week while they sailed about the Tower. She had rehearsed holding her skirts, bending her knees, and bowing her head until she was dizzy. Eventually, Voleta had declared that she knew how to curtsy. It wasn't that hard. She just hated the way it looked, so slithery and submissive. The old manner of curtsy just hadn't any personality. And hadn't Haste advised her to distinguish herself?

Voleta gave a quick, sneezy curtsy and popped up like a jack-in-the-box. If Byron had been there to see it, he probably would've fainted.

The court gasped.

"It is a pleasure to meet you, young lady," the king said, his delivery flattened by his surprise.

"The honor is all mine, Your Majesty," Voleta said with as much effusiveness as she could muster. "And may I say, you make a very convincing clockmaker!"

"Have you met many clockmakers?"

"Oh, many!" Voleta curtsied again, the motion like a man discovering a crick in his back. The court gasped a second time. "Your people seem out of breath, Your Majesty." This enticed a little laughter from the court. "Have you ever been to Miltonhead? It lies far, far to the west. Over the mountains and across the sea of grass. Miltonhead. It's an ugly place, but oh, the clocks they make. You wouldn't believe the roar of those little tigers and bears!" Voleta said, clapping her hands in delight.

Iren saw the strained look on her captain's face. Edith's jaw worked as if she were attempting to chew through a rubbery bit of gristle.

"Ah, yes, Miltonhead!" Something about the sluggishness of the king's reply convinced Voleta that he was not at all familiar with Miltonhead but was too proud to admit the gap in his knowledge. She would use that to her advantage. "But why travel so far?" Leonid asked.

"Well, as my uncle the Sphinx always says: Dear Voleta, go away. Go far, far away." This was met with another swell of laughter.

"I see you have a little wit, Lady Voleta. Come! Give us a story. Don't worry, I'll tell you if it goes too long." The king lifted his watch. The court laughed. Pages dashed from the gates with ice buckets and champagne.

Voleta smiled and held out her skirts in a quasi-curtsy, which made her look as if she were searching for her pockets. She said, "I have visited the mountain kingdom of Eos in the misty north. The ladies grow wool and the men grow beards and they have fat-faced children by the half dozen." Some of the courtesans, who had been withholding their approval, laughed and clapped at that. "I have met their chief. He drinks yak's blood for breakfast and keeps a condor for a pet. He was such a nice man, the chief. He gave me a tapestry that was so large I had to fly it home on its own ship."

"Very good, very good. Eos. Yes, quite remote and frigid, I think." The king affected a shiver, and again Voleta could see he was bluffing. "Condors are magnificent, though! Where else have you been?"

Using her scant knowledge of Ur's geography and a robust imagination, Voleta described the city of Cameer, where canals outnumbered the streets, and the poor lived in houses while the rich lived on yachts. The governor of Cameer had presented her with a teak rowboat with rose gold oarlocks. She spoke of the southern city of Nuxor, where the salons overflowed with talented playwrights, painters, and philosophers. The mayor of Nuxor had presented her with a poem that he'd commissioned, in her honor, which had required the invention of three new words.

"I see a theme to your stories, Lady Voleta," King Leonid interjected with a chiding shake of his finger. The court tittered without seeming to know exactly why. "Wherever you go, someone gives you a gift. If I didn't know better, I'd think you were angling for a present."

Voleta gave a more traditional curtsy, just to prove that she could, and said, "Oh, no, Your Majesty! After all my travels, I want for nothing. I have been heaped with jewelry, clothes, wine, and ships. In the Depot of Sumer, they even christened a bridge after me."

The king's smirk shriveled with displeasure, and the court murmured like a flock of starlings. "I must protest!" King Leonid blurted, his lips pursed in a formidable pout. "You mean to tell me there is nothing that my ringdom can offer you? Am I really such a pauper?"

"No, no, Your Majesty," Voleta said, appearing upset at the suggestion. "My sincere apologies! I didn't mean to insult—"

"Out with it! Out with it!" He rolled his hand impatiently. "There must be something you want."

"Well. There is one thing, which you and no one else in the Tower could bestow upon me," Voleta said, her voice suddenly meek.

King Leonid's indignation softened. "Ask, child, and you shall receive."

"Freedom, sir. I beg for freedom," she said, and when the crowd renewed their murmuring, she turned to them. "Is freedom not the greatest gift a king can bestow upon his subjects?" She faced the king with lowered eyes. "I can think of no nobler or more generous present."

"But you have your freedom, my dear."

"Not mine, Your Majesty. My pet's."

Behind her, Edith shielded her eyes.

"Your port master caged my squirrel. She is a perfectly tame creature, and it pains me to see her locked up. All I ask is that you grant her freedom."

The king made a brief show of deliberation, pacing and pulling upon the stays of his cape. The gathered nobles watched him intently until he abruptly stopped with a stamp of his heel, his decision made. He spoke with renewed volume: "What is your pet's name?"

"Squit, sir."

"Let it be known that Squit the Squirrel is hereby awarded honorary citizenship in all my lands and principalities. And as none of my subjects may be unjustly imprisoned, I hereby order the immediate release of citizen Squit."

Port Master Cullins, who had been quite invisible a moment before, now appeared with the gold cage. He looked sheepish if not nauseated as he opened the barred door. Squit dashed into Voleta's open hands.

"Oh, thank you, Your Majesty! Thank you!" Voleta said, nuzzling her pet.

"You are most welcome, Lady Contumax. Now, where are my volunteers?" Looking about, the king clapped twice. The noble crowd muttered and churned as young ladies shouldered their way to the fore. The ladies arranged themselves before the king, subtly elbowing each other for a better position in line. "Of course, we shall all endeavor to be perfect hosts to our guests during their stay, but I think that Lady Voleta would benefit from a dedicated guide, a companion who is keen, clever, and well versed in all the attractions and luxuries of our humble paradise."

King Leonid patted his lips as he examined the queue of courtiers, all of whom were doing their best to radiate cheer and charm. Iren thought they all looked remarkably similar. Their hair was piled in more or less the same way. Their dresses were all similar shades of orange, cut low across the bosom, and rimmed with freshwater pearls or silver sequins. The faces of the courtiers were so uniformly caked in powder and streaked with rouge they all seemed to be wearing the same mask.

"You," the king said, stopping before a blond, button-nosed beauty. "What is your name?"

"Xenia, Your Majesty, daughter of the Marquis de Clarke."

"Well, Lady Xenia de Clarke, do you believe it in your power to act as the Crown Escort and official friend to the Lady Voleta during her stay?"

"I shall treat her as my very own sister, Your Majesty." When Lady Xenia genuflected, her skirts bunched like a fallen cake.

King Leonid turned away before the lady had completed the bow, shifting his attention to Edith. "We have a few things to discuss, I think, Captain Winters," King Leonid said. "Clocks and tocks and ticks and such."

"As you say, Your Majesty," Edith said with a respectful dip of her head.

Edith gave Iren and Voleta each a little nod, then she, Georgine Haste, and a retinue of officious-looking men followed the king toward the court gates.

Xenia skipped up to Voleta, hair bouncing and eyes round. The courtier hooked her arm around Voleta's waist, and before she could argue, began to gush: "Oh, we are going to be such good friends, Voleta. What a pretty name! But my heavens, your nurse is ugly. Why is she so large? Have you ever played the Game of Oops? Oh, I am hopeless at it, but it's so much fun to see your friends look like dum-dums. But, no, first things first: You must try the sponge cake at the Vanilla Villa

Bean. I just love how that sounds. The Vanilla Villa Bean! Why did you cut your hair like that? Was there an accident? And my, you're as brown as an acorn, aren't you? That's all right. At least you're not fat!"

Voleta looked back at Iren, desperation tightening her brow as the babbling lady pulled her toward the court's gates.

For the first time that day, Iren smiled.

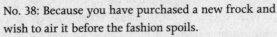

Chapter Five

No. 38: Because you have purchased a new frock and wish to air it before the fashion spoils.

No. 39: Because you are intoxicated and in need of an audience.

—101 Reasons to Attend My Party
by Lady Sandbom

ady Xenia de Clarke talked with the urgency of a burst pipe. She tugged Voleta by the arm through the crowded street, guiding her as if she were blind or dim-witted or both. The focus of the lady's monologue roved. She gushed about Amarillo's Bazar, where all the best dressmakers debuted their work and girls pulled each other's hair to be the first in line. She complained about how dreadful the theater had been all season long—nothing but historical dramas and military operettas, and she praised Café Castorea for serving the sweetest raspberry tarts in the whole wide world. She talked and talked, on and on in a breathless spurt.

Voleta stopped listening as soon as she was certain the lady wasn't saying anything important and let the city absorb her full attention. She had never seen anything quite so white or boisterous or beautiful as Pelphia before. All the shops, and there were so many of them, seemed locked in a battle for who could have the most overdone window display. There were wreaths of fresh flowers and live models posing as mannequins and trained doves clutching golden boughs and glass tanks full of live, darting fish, and all to sell a bobble or a boot or a square of caramel. No one seemed to find the excess the least bit strange. A big red-winged macaw sitting atop an awning cried, "Quick, out the window, before Father sees you! Out the window! Out the window!"

Squawking parrot notwithstanding, something about the place reminded Voleta of a dollhouse. It was so picturesque and tidy, and also a little false. It seemed an ideal stage for dramatic squabbles. In the time it took to walk the length of a single block, she observed no fewer than three spectacles. Outside an overflowing bakery, a man in a porter's uniform serenaded a disinterested woman with a poorly tuned lyre. Across the street, a woman in a hoopskirt swooned and fainted, though her timing seemed conspicuously good as she fell into the arms of a handsome shopkeeper. Officers in black-and-gold uniforms pulled a pair of brawling dandies apart, one of whom accused the other of having stolen his signature scent, thereby devaluing its appeal.

Even the brass sun in the sky seemed a toy, wound up and let go.

Ultimately, though, it was not the play but the playhouse that captured Voleta's imagination. She could not stop gaping at the white cliffs of buildings that loomed over the congested lanes. The city was as pinched and dense as a maze. Everywhere she looked, ledges, balconets, sills, and cornices called to her, suggesting footholds and perches. Yet, even as she imagined what exotic views she could glimpse from the rooftops, she recalled Byron's oft-repeated advice to her during their preparations for this day: *Don't let your mind wander, for your feet are sure to follow.*

Iren, meanwhile, was having to work very hard to keep up with Voleta and her young escort, neither of whom had any trouble cutting through the crowd. Iren was too broad to slip through the brief and narrow gaps, and so was forced to go around the queues that extended from shop fronts and surrender the right of way to the big-wheeled prams pushed by stony-faced governesses. She wondered how it was possible for traffic to be so bad. There weren't even any autowagons here, only litters and rickshaws. Iren was beginning to believe that everyone in the city was determined to ram into her with their elbows out. If she had encountered these fools on the sidewalks of New Babel, she would have shoved them into a wall. Well, not the infants in strollers, but certainly everyone else.

"If I may," a woman at Iren's elbow said, "it's easier to keep up if you walk in the middle of the street. The crowds clot around the shop-windows. Don't worry. We won't lose them. The lady dawdles, but she knows the way home."

Iren squinted down at the diminutive woman. She wore her brown hair in a neat bun, which was threaded here and there with silver hairs. Iren suspected her short stature and prim features made her seem younger than she was. "Who are you?"

"Ann Gaucher. I'm Lady Xenia's governess. And what's your name?"

"Iren."

"Is that a first or a last name?"

"Both, I guess."

"Well, it's a pleasure to meet you, Iren Iren." Ann paused long enough in the street to shake her hand. Her grip was firm and the up-down-up movement practiced. Good posture and a strong, clear voice further enlarged Ann's presence. Iren suspected that she liked her.

"We're going to your girl's house?"

"The lady's home, yes." Ann said it as politely as she could, but Iren heard the correction: She shouldn't call them girls. "Of course, she lives with her father, the Marquis de Clarke. Is this your first time visiting Pelphia?"

"Yes."

"What do you think so far?"

"It's . . . quaint."

Iren heard chuckling, though there was no sign of laughter on Ann's face when she looked up again. "I don't want to talk out of turn, but do you mind if I speak frankly for a moment?"

"I like frank," Iren said.

"Me too. I'm not sure what sort of society you're accustomed to, but this is a very political ringdom, *political* in the sense that very little happens here by chance. In fact, the more incidental a thing appears, the more likely it was rehearsed. So here's the tall and short of it: The

Marquis de Clarke paid the Crown a small fortune to have King Leonid pick my lady to host yours." They came upon a pair of sniping lovers, damming the street with their argument, and Ann parted them with a polite but resolute turn of her shoulders. Iren followed, widening the gap. "Since de Clarke has paid so much for the pleasure of her company, the marquis or his daughter will expect to accompany Lady Voleta to several parties. *Several*." Ann glanced up to see if Iren showed any sign of surprise or misgiving. The amazon's expression was as bland as custard. Ann forged ahead. "I'm afraid you're going to be subjected to some rather rigorous entertainment."

"My lady loves parties," Iren said.

"Oh, I'm sure she does. Everyone does . . . at first."

Though their route meandered, they eventually arrived at the Marquis de Clarke's abode, set a few blocks off of the piazza. Technically, the marquis's home was a third-floor apartment that shared a lobby and stairwell with two other lords, though to call it such was misleading. De Clarke's apartment consumed an entire city block. He employed a staff of three maids, two cooks, two porters, and a butler. Xenia rattled off the number of rooms, closets, and lavatories as if the figures added up to some meaningful sum. The ceilings of her home were high enough to echo and the stone floors were polished to a treacherous sheen. The home's main balcony could've accommodated a game of nine-pins, or so it seemed to Voleta. The air was bright with the tang of silver polish and the sweet must of tapestries. The home was undeniably fabulous.

Unfortunately, the Marquis de Clarke was the stupidest man Voleta had ever met. It didn't help that he was dressed like a harlequin. He wore a white girdle on top of an orange blouse. The toes of his boots curled up at the end, and the wig on his head was so small it didn't cover the top of his large, bald head. His facial features seemed to have been swept into a central pile, an impression that was not improved by his habit of pursing his lips so firmly it dimpled his chin. And, she would come to see, he almost always had a frilly white handkerchief in his hand, as he did now.

It was a good thing that Ann had whisked Iren away to view their room because Voleta hadn't any doubt the marquis would've made Iren laugh.

Xenia would later assure Voleta that her father was a trendsetter who was often paid by clothiers to sport their fashions, but Voleta didn't think the claim so much flattered her father as it insulted the tailors.

Still, it wasn't his appearance that outed the Marquis de Clarke as a first-class nitwit. Nor was it the fact that he met them in the great hall standing beneath his own portrait, which was twice life-size and very generous with its likeness. No, it was what flew out of his mouth that doomed him in Voleta's estimation.

Upon her introduction to the marquis, Voleta said, "Thank you, milord, for hosting me in your home. It's quite spectacular."

"It is! I like to think of it as my country château. You should've seen it while Pepper was still trotting all about the place. Such a beautiful creature! Pepper was my racehorse. He was as quick as a swallow. I was going to build a floating horse track for him. Isn't that a fantastic idea? A floating racetrack! But the backers pulled out before we even had the first fifty yards finished, and then there was a squall, and the whole thing blew away. Cost me a fortune. But Pepper was a real dear about it all, though I couldn't stop him from eating my bedding. He liked a good duvet better than a bucket of oats. Obviously, he had very good taste. In the end, though, I had to put him out to pasture, which cost me another fortune. The balloons were cheap enough, but I had a devil of a time finding a jockey who was willing to ride him through the mountain pass."

"Yes," Voleta said, smiling to hide her horror. *That poor horse!* "Well, I've just had the pleasure of touring your fair city, and I must say, I am quite charmed. I'm sure its history is as rich as it is deep." That was something Byron had coached her to say. The stag had assured her the phrase would spark a pleasant and productive dialogue.

"Oh, well, Pelly is a plum pie: saucy and full of fruit!" the marquis said, then shook his hips in a manner that he seemed to believe was charmingly playful, but which made Voleta want to knee him in the codpiece.

Not knowing what to do, Voleta tried another conversational volley. Xenia had referred to her father as the Czar of the Gatehouse, so Voleta inquired after the marquis's duties in that capacity. In answer, the marquis balled his lacy handkerchief against his mouth and began mewling like a kicked dog. He gripped the mantel and looked up at his own portrait, as if for moral support.

Xenia hissed at Voleta, "Papa doesn't like to talk about his work. They're very mean to him down there!"

"They are! They don't laugh at my jokes or rise to my quips. I used to go down to the gatehouse all the time. I'd talk through the bars to the dirty souls plodding up the Old Vein. I'd try to lift their spirits. That's all I wanted to do. But they're all just so stubbornly depressed! They were always crying, 'Help me! Help me!' No one ever asked if I could use some help with all the records and reports, all the hirings and firings. It's such thankless work!" The marquis sobbed into his handkerchief. "I am a slave to the hod!"

Voleta didn't know what to say to that. Concealing her exasperation as best she could, Voleta let Xenia step in with an account of her morning, a topic that helped her father to recover almost at once. The marquis interrupted his daughter's story frequently, asking who she had seen and what they had been wearing. They jabbered on and on while Voleta made small affirming noises with the regularity of a snore. Voleta had fallen into a trance of boredom when Xenia abruptly announced that they had to go prepare for the evening's festivities.

"Yes, of course!" the Marquis de Clarke said, stuffing his handkerchief into his sleeve and wiping his hands on his overtaxed girdle. "I am throwing myself a party in your honor, Lady Contumax. All my best guests are coming. There'll be music and champagne, dancing and champagne, chocolates and a spot of champagne." He stepped between them and draped a heavy arm around each of their thin necks. Voleta was glad that Iren was not around because she doubted the amazon would have stood mutely by while the marquis kissed her temple. He smelled like something sharp and medicinal, a scent Voleta could not quite place. "Most vitally of all, you and my dearest, darling daughter will be there having the most excellent, wonderful, glorious time that has ever been had in the history of history. I don't like people who don't know how to enjoy themselves. The pooping of my parties is simply not allowed."

"Milord," Voleta said and curtsied deeply so he could not see when she rolled her eyes.

The chandelier of the great hall blazed like a foundry, each pendant throwing out a thousand sparks of light across the feast upon the table. There were bowls of ripe berries, silver trays pyramided with pastries, and a bloody roast upon a carving board.

The marquis's guests flooded the hall. They sloshed from room to room, following someone else's spectacle or searching for space to make their own. They burbled with arguments, laughter, and heated flirtations while the rented band played waltzes for everyone to ignore.

Voleta surveyed the glorious disaster in amazement.

She still wore her purple dress, much to Lady Xenia's dismay, though there was nothing to be done since her luggage had not yet been released by customs. According to Xenia, it was shameful to attend court and an evening soiree in the same gown. Voleta, who was accustomed to wearing the same clothes for days on end, insisted the frock was fine and refused Xenia's repeated attempts to loan her a dress, or a shawl, or a stole, or at least a hat? Surely Voleta couldn't be opposed to a hat!

But Voleta steadfastly refused to alter her attire, though she had consented to Xenia's insistence that she apply some makeup. In retrospect, that had been a mistake.

A few hours before the party, the two ladies sat at twin vanities in Xenia's boudoir. Xenia presented her face to Ann, who applied layers of powder and tint with dainty precision, while Voleta sat for Iren, whose lack of experience with cosmetics was immediately apparent. Iren boxed Voleta's face with a powder puff, blanching her face and leaving her wheat-colored neck and ears untouched, and applied the lip reddener with what Ann charitably referred to as a "broad stroke." Attempting to save the charade, Voleta defended the efforts of her governess by assuring Xenia the slapdash style of makeup was all the rage in the ringdom of Japhet. It was of course a lie. Voleta only knew of Japhet because the Sphinx had mentioned the ringdom in passing, but the association was enough to ease Xenia's mounting fears that her guest was a hopeless dummy.

And so, Voleta was introduced to the Marquis de Clarke's bemused guests wearing clownish makeup and a gown that had been unpopular the first time she'd aired it. Lady Xenia, meanwhile, wore a dress in a blinding shade of persimmon that featured a prominent lace window for the advertisement of her bosom. The marquis wore a new wig that was even smaller than his first. Voleta wondered how it stayed on his head. Wallpaper paste? Roofing pitch? A thumbtack, perhaps? The marquis spent the early hours of the evening interrupting his guests' conversations with witticisms that ranged from scatological double entendres to odious puns.

Voleta wanted to stick his wig in his mouth whenever he spoke.

Though his abominable small talk was almost preferable to the inquisitions of his guests.

She had spent hours with Byron preparing for this moment, and still the questions came so quickly it made her head swim. What did the Sphinx look like? What was his ringdom like? Did he really sleep on a cloud? How many wives did he have? How many heirs? Did he wear a crown? A mask? Did he breathe lightning? Had he ever eaten a disobedient child? Where had all of his wonderful machines gone? Why had he withdrawn? What was he hiding from?

Voleta repeated Byron's prepared answers in fits and starts to a revolving audience half a dozen times over the course of the evening. Her story went something like this:

When she was seven years old, her parents took her along on a vacation to the Baths. She vividly recalled the sparkling reservoir, the girls selling oranges on the brick shoreline, the way their skirts bunched and swung. She remembered the wrinkled old men in fleecy bathrobes who hobbled across the pedestrian bridges to spend their day sitting in the steaming garden spire. She remembered the scene so clearly because it was where her parents had lost her. Or where she had lost them.

Whichever it was, the Sphinx found her with her feet in the water and her cheeks streaked with tears. After an exhaustive and fruitless search for her parents, the Sphinx had adopted her. He brought her home to his fortress in the clouds where he raised her as his own. Her childhood had been a happy one, if a little lonely.

As for the Sphinx, he looked like a man in the prime of his life. He attributed his longevity to an endless supply of work. He liked to say that he hadn't time to grow old. He had a kind face and the physique of a man who'd labored all his life. He was an inexhaustible, ageless force. He had not vanished. Not at all. He had just been attending to other business in recent decades. Yes, he was still building wonderful machines. No, she could not describe them. No, not even for ten minas. No, not even for a thousand.

Privately, Voleta found the details of the lie curious. After some pressing, Byron had admitted the story was entirely the Sphinx's invention. Something about the lost girl in the Baths rang truer than some of the other elements of her story. Perhaps it was the vivid details of the Baths; perhaps it was how readily the scene called to mind *The Brick Layer's Granddaughter*, the painting with which the Sphinx was clearly obsessed.

The more Voleta parroted the story to the marquis's half-invested guests, the more she wondered whether the girl in her tale and the girl in the paintings were one and the same, and both of them the Sphinx. If that were the case, then Voleta could only assume it had been the Brick Layer who had found the Sphinx after she was orphaned by the crowds, and the Brick Layer who'd given her a home and a purpose. It was strange to think of the wizened Sphinx as having ever been a lost child. But the more Voleta pondered the idea, the more certain she was: The Sphinx was the Brick Layer's adopted granddaughter.

But why would the Sphinx give her such an obvious clue about her past? Unless that had been the point. Perhaps she had wanted Voleta to know the truth. It seemed a roundabout way to communicate a history—wrapping the truth inside a lie. But it didn't feel out of character for the Sphinx. More importantly, it seemed to signal that the Sphinx hadn't cut Voleta entirely out of her life.

Voleta was surprised to discover how happy the prospect made her.

While Voleta was off mingling her vinegar with the room's oil, Iren lurked at the periphery of the great hall. Behind her, an immense tapestry covered the wall, depicting a dense forest scene of curling branches, contorted roots, and shafts of yellow sunlight. Ann stood beside her, watching her youthful charge flit about the room like a butterfly. The two governesses were doing their best to be invisible, an effect that was a little spoiled by the startled yips of guests when they spied Iren for the first time—as one did now. A red-nosed young man with gin-sharpened breath shook a caviar sandwich at the giantess and said, "Has anyone ever told you, you look like a shaved bear?" His starched dickey had come unpinned and protruded from his jacket like a fat, white tongue.

Looming over him, Iren plucked the sandwich from his hand and growled, "Would you like to see my cave?"

The nobleman swallowed hard, blinked unevenly, and bid a hasty retreat.

Ann hid a smile behind a cupped hand and said, "I think you've probably scarred the Earl of Enbridge for life."

"Oops," Iren said, and pressed the earl's sandwich into her mouth.

"Oh, it's all right. He's a horrid man. Though I can't say he's the worst either."

Iren smacked her lips and tried to decide whether she was tasting fish or some sort of brackish jelly. "Really? Who's the worst?"

Ann sobered and glanced about to see who was near enough to overhear. She located Xenia, bouncing circles about her father, who was holding a pair of grapefruits to his chest, his face already flush from wine. Apparently reassured by their distraction, Ann decided to speak. "King Leonid's nephew and third in line to the throne: Prince Francis Le Mesurier. He's the worst. It seems like he gets into trouble every season. Sometimes, the scandal makes the paper, and when it does, his father, the king's treasurer, ships him out on some scientific expedition until everyone pretends to forget what a cad he is. Prince Francis has been sent off to count birds so often, last year King Leonid appointed him the royal ornithologist. Personally, I doubt he could tell a bullfinch from a barn owl."

Ann paused to allow a guest, who was holding her dish of champagne under her nose because she "liked how the bubbles tickled," to grow tired of staring at Iren. When the guest wandered off, Ann continued: "Recently, though, Prince Francis found trouble even in exile. The latest is that he was indiscreet with one of the maids on his chartered ship. The next morning, she threw herself overboard in front of the captain and crew, half of whom were her relations."

"Why?" Iren asked.

"The poor maid left a note behind that said the prince had forced himself on her. The Le Mesurier family denied it of course. Since the editors of the *Daily Reverie* are in the treasurer's pocket, they tilted the headlines in his son's favor. One editor went so far as to suggest the maid had ended her life out of disappointment when she realized she could not keep the prince she had 'snared.' There was no evidence that was the case, but the paper echoed the conspiracy into fact. Her family promised to pursue a trial, but last I heard, they had failed to convince a single magistrate to consider the evidence. Then the usual social amnesia set in, and now the prince is back, and his dance card is full again."

"That's not right," Iren said, her scowl deepened by the shadow of her bonnet. She was thinking of Voleta, fearless and unsubtle, falling prey to such an unaccountable villain. The thought made her furious and fearful, and the feeling didn't abate even when she located Voleta amid the crowd, trying to smile while Xenia pumped her arms and shrieked with laughter.

"No, it isn't right," Ann said. "But it's why you and I will always have a job. The world is full of wolves and lambs, but precious few shepherds."

Chapter Six

No. 81: Because youth is fleeting and cannot be savored in retrospect.

No. 82: Because your enemy has RSVP'd, and you wish to make a scene.

—*101 Reasons to Attend My Party*
by Lady Sandbom

I f it had not been for the parrot, the evening might have ended as a reasonable success. Voleta and Iren might've retired to their room, crawled into bed, and slept like a couple of well-fed infants. The Marquis de Clarke might've grimaced through his champagne headache the next morning, content in the knowledge that his home had briefly been the pivot of Pelphian society. And Xenia's heart might've swelled with hope that her star was finally on the rise.

Were it not for the parrot.

The parrot—a large, yellow-breasted macaw—sat upon the highest ledge of the building across from the marquis's balcony. One of de Clarke's guests, a woman with dark ringlets of hair snaking from under a yellow turban, pointed out the bird and remarked how it seemed to be glaring at her—no, *leering* at her. It was probing her very soul with its bottomless eyes. She dramatized her horror until she had attracted a small pod of amused guests. They pressed against the balustrade alongside to observe the criminal, the villain, the lecherous cur. The parrot, after a long silence, gave a creaking cry and said, "Out the window! Out the window!"

"Oh, what a beast!" the traumatized guest said. She raised a wrist to her forehead and swayed as if she might faint.

The parrot lifted one wing and rifled through its feathers like a man searching for his wallet.

At that moment, the Marquis de Clarke was having what he believed was an immensely successful conversation with General Andreas Eigengrau. Their heady back-and-forth had attracted an audience of two earls, half a dozen viscounts, and a dozen young noblemen. He knew some of those lords were only angling for an opportunity to distinguish themselves in the eyes of two of the Coterie's foremost members. But de Clarke didn't care. Whether it was heartfelt or contrived, all applause rang the same.

Eigengrau was much taller than the marquis, more imposing, and had a head full of thick hair, but de Clarke was sure they were intellectual equals. In fact, at the moment, de Clarke believed he'd struck upon an idea that had not occurred to the venerated strategist. He said, "I'm telling you, Andreas, that ruddy great battleship sitting on our port isn't a threat, it's a treat. It's a new year's pudding. We should take it! We'd own the sky if we did." De Clarke's attention briefly flitted to a bowl of pickled quail eggs. He popped one into his mouth, then spooned several more into a napkin.

De Clarke did not notice the general sigh, nor the subtle deflation of his posture. "I don't think this is the venue for shouting out stratagems, milord. Think of your honored guest."

"The girl? She's off chitchatting somewhere. And if there's one thing I know for certain, it's that young ladies are as deaf as bats to the conversation of grown men."

The general seemed about to correct the marquis on the nature of bats but decided against the effort. "Regardless, milord, I believe you're misreading the situation. The Sphinx—"

"Don't give me that Sphinx stuff! It's just another ringdom with a funny name and a spooky mascot. There's no lighthouse keeper up there looking down on us. There's no boogeyman under the bed. I'm telling you, it's just a ship. And we could take her by surprise."

"*As I was saying,*" the general said more forcefully, "you forget, milord, the Sphinx forged our beloved Wakeman Haste. One of her is worth ten of my men. If that ship held a dozen more like her, I guarantee our advances would be rebuffed. We would lose the skirmish and lose it badly. And what would stop them from firing on our port then? That gunship could blow our city gates clear off the face of the Tower." The general rattled the ice in his empty tumbler. "It is not only an impolitic plan; it is an unwise one."

The marquis was about to argue his case further when he felt the attention shift in the room. Suddenly, there weren't as many men observing his conversation with the general. He looked about to discover his party was moving to the balcony. He could only chase after the shifting fascination, but to make it seem as if he were leading rather than following, he announced, "Excuse me, General. I am needed on the balcony!"

When de Clarke saw the turbaned woman, he knew he was in for a scene. Her name was Fortunée Wilk, the royal thespian, a woman of inarguable talent and unbearable personality. She wore her moods like an old woman wears scent—to grand excess. Everything she did was tinged with desperation. But she was still the Crown's leading lady and an actor in the royal troupe. Despite her tarnished beauty and diminished talent (an unlikable rasp had crept into her voice), she still had enough fans to make her presence at de Clarke's party an absolute necessity.

Lady Fortunée threw herself at him, and he was just sober enough to catch her. She clutched his arms and said, "There's a perverted parrot ogling me, milord. He's over there on that rainspout. Do you see him?"

The marquis did his best not to smile. She was hamming it up a bit, but he liked the gist of the scene. He decided to play the part of the gruff stoic. "Well, what do you expect me to do about it, Lady Fortunée? Throw a shoe at it?" He gave the joke room to breathe. "Or perhaps we shall chase it off with a little wit. Nothing discourages a Peeping Tom so well as laughter!"

"Your Grace!" Lady Fortunée said, flattering him with the elevated title, which he liked. "If you have any regard for my safety, you will not let that beast escape. Please, you cannot allow it to prowl the city. It is a beaked devil, a winged assassin! It would peck out my throat!"

The marquis looked into her eyes. They were red from the wine but not insensible or unlovely. He wondered if she might be talked into staying for an intimate after-party.

He threw out his arm and barked at the nearest porter, "You there! Put down that blasted champagne and fetch me my gun!"

The manner in which the porter paraded the long rifle through the penthouse was enough to bring a second wave of guests to the balcony.

Xenia, who had been trying to explain to Voleta why orange was the very best color in the history of history, broke off when she saw the bayonet flash above the crowd like a herald. "My goodness! Is there to be a duel? Oh, how I would love to see a duel!"

"You don't duel with one rifle. That's just an execution," Voleta said.

"Of course. How stupid of me. Stupid, stupid!"

Xenia seemed to expect an argument, but Voleta wasn't really listening. She was too busy wondering what sort of local parlor games could possibly include gunplay. "Come on. Let's go see who's getting shot," she said.

Voleta wound her way through the clumsy, drunk revelers and reached the balcony rail in time to see the marquis snatch the rifle from the porter. The marquis handled the firearm ably enough. He pulled the powder horn stopper out with his teeth and began to fill the barrel.

"You can't fire a gun in the city, milord," Eigengrau said.

"Can't I? That bird is terrorizing my guest." The marquis added the wadding and the shot and tamped it all down. "I'm defending her honor and my home."

"It's just a bird," the general said wearily.

"Sir! It is not just a bird!" the leading lady said. "I am absolutely certain when I go home that beast will be sitting outside my window, glaring at me in my underthings!" Fortunée struggled to hide her plea-sure at the growing crowd. She appeared to bite back a smile before voicing a single sharp sob. "Oh, it has the evil eye!"

The parrot opened his wings, refolded them, and began to preen.

The marquis drew the rifle to the shoulder of his flame-embroidered jacket. "If you must arrest me, General, then arrest me. But I shall defend my guest!"

Eigengrau finished off the watered-down gin at the bottom of his glass. "Just try not to miss, milord."

"Wait!" Voleta shouted. The crowd parted. Her purple dress stood out like a bruise against the wall of orange.

The marquis lowered his rifle in confusion. "I beg your pardon?"

"You can't shoot him. He's not hurting anyone." Voleta took advan-tage of the clearing to draw nearer to him.

"But he's disturbing my guest," de Clarke said with all the author-ity he could muster.

"Pettiness does not suit a man of your standing, milord," Voleta said, a diplomatic volley that Byron would've been proud of.

"I'd hardly call duty a petty thing!"

"But it's not for duty," Voleta said, her taste for diplomacy already exhausted. "You're just envious because the bird is better dressed."

The guests gasped. The marquis looked bewildered. "My dear girl, these clothes were made by Rolf de Witt, *the* de Witt. He is to cloth what the sun is to the sky. These girdle ribs are made of whalebone. My wig is made of garden silk. My stockings were imported from Berm, and my boots are sturgeon, sewn by the cobblers of Herriot and Son. I am the very spring from which all fashion flows!" His guests made supportive noises and smirked at Voleta.

"And yet, milord, you know how quickly even your finest fashion spoils!" Voleta said in a voice that rose over the burgeoning laughter. "I mean, what is fashion but the desire to clothe yourself with the herd?" She adopted the constrained posture of a lecturer, her hands behind her back, her brow knitted, a pose she had learned from Sen-lin. The guests who had murmured a moment before now listened. "We pretend fashion exists to express our inner character, but for something created to distinguish, it certainly does seem to encourage a lot of conformity, doesn't it? To be fashionable, we must pretend that what looks good on the mob looks good on ourselves. And we make-believe that we all look good because we are afraid of being judged ourselves. We are afraid of being singled out."

"I always stand out!" the marquis huffed. "My closet is the soul of avant-garde."

"But fashion doesn't change because we've discovered a better way to dress. No, it evolves to make us all feel anxious and old and out of touch. Fashion exists to exclude those who're too poor to afford it and to shame those who're indifferent to the whole fussy business. But why should we punish a parrot for our insecurities? I think he looks handsome in his blue sleeves and yellow vest. He didn't fly out and buy an orange cape just because everyone else did. He is perfectly himself, perfectly at home in his own feathers. I think he is better than fashionable. He is confident in his own beauty."

The marquis glared at her in the silence that followed. He seemed to have forgotten what the scene had originally been about. Handing the rifle to his footman, he reached into the gulf between city blocks and clapped his hands over the street three times sharply. The parrot tested his wings upon the air, then swooped away down the lane.

"There. The beast is gone," the marquis said mirthlessly. He announced that he was serving port and strawberries in the parlor and shouldered past Voleta without looking at her.

The attention Voleta had briefly commanded crumbled. As it did, she saw how many of the faces around her were wrinkled with offense and revulsion.

Lady Fortunée pierced the dwindling crowd and confronted her with a sneer so severe it cracked the makeup around her mouth. "You think you're clever, don't you? You're not clever; you're just rude!" The lady inhaled as if she meant to spit, then hissed, "And if you ever interrupt one of my scenes again, I'll cut off your nose!" She pulled up the train of her dress and strode away with her chin in the air.

As Voleta watched her go, her eye fell upon Xenia, standing by the porch doors with her fists balled at her sides and her lower lip jutting.

Voleta started to say something to her, but Xenia cut her off, shouting, "Why are you so stupid?" The young lady stamped her foot, then ran off with her face buried in her hands.

Voleta felt the creeping nausea of regret. Her success at bluffing her way into the king's good graces had given her an inflated sense of her own charm. But in one fell swoop, she had frittered the little goodwill she had accrued. She had insulted the pastime and industry of half the ringdom's nobility. She could've easily pleaded for the bird's life, asked the marquis to spare it as a favor to her. But instead she'd chosen to needle the marquis and his preoccupation with fashion because she found him fatuous and his passions silly. She had mocked him for conflating his inclination with his duty, but had she done any different?

Voleta looked for Iren over the heads of the guests inside. She found her friend standing before a gloomy forest scene. Voleta felt a pang of shame when she saw the expression on Iren's face. She could see at once that Iren had observed the whole ill-conceived scene. The amazon looked disappointed but not surprised.

If Voleta had wished for a reprieve from the other guests' interrogation, she got it. She was snubbed for the remainder of the party, which seemed to wind down more quickly than the marquis would've liked. As the guests began to collect their coats and stream toward the exit, de Clarke ran about with increasing agitation, assuring all that the party was far from finished. They could play charades, or cards, or a Game of Oops. He could bring out his collection of rare brandies. Xenia could give a recital, and they could dance on his furniture. None of his efforts delayed the exodus. It was still hours shy of midnight when his last guest squirmed from his embrace and ran out the door.

The mops and brooms came out, and the marquis's staff began to clean the spectacular mess the guests had left behind. The marquis announced he was going to bed but first stopped to urinate in the fireplace. Ann showed Voleta and Iren to their room where their luggage, finally released by the customs office, awaited them in a tidy pile. Xenia sent Ann to tell Voleta that she would not be coming by to say good night, a snub that Iren's continued silence seemed to punctuate. Voleta couldn't decide whether Iren was being quiet because she didn't know what to say, or if she knew exactly what she wanted to say but didn't wish to say it for fear of starting a fight. Though Voleta wouldn't have argued with her. She knew she deserved the scolding she had coming.

Their bedroom was large and well furnished, including a small bed in one corner where the governess traditionally slept. It was clear at once that Iren would never fit, and since the main bed was immense, Voleta insisted they share it. She hoped the gesture would spark some conversation, but to no avail. Voleta tucked Squit into a little nest of scarves on the bureau and Iren turned down the lamps. They changed into the nightgowns Byron had sent with them, both long and white and warm. They climbed under the ornate bedclothes amid the tall battlements of the bedposts, and Voleta peeped out a "good night." Rather than reply, Iren heaved a great sigh that shook the mattress.

It wasn't long before Iren's breath deepened and slowed, coursing like ocean surf. Soon, she was fast asleep, abandoning Voleta to her guilt.

She felt suffocated by the heavy blankets, gagged by the foreign stink of linen water, and smothered by the cosmetics that still clung to her skin. She bore the agony as long as she could, and when she thought she would scream, she slid from the warm sheets and set her bare feet down on the cool woolen rug. She breathed along with Iren for several minutes in the dark before tiptoeing to the curtained door to the balcony. Voleta cracked the door open, plugging the gap as best she could with her body, and slipped through.

Outside, the city seemed to shout at the stars, and the sky, being very near, shouted back.

Chapter Seven

Smiles are like candlelight. They can warm and cheer
the bleakest room. But we would be wise not to
forget: Even the brightest candle hides a blackened
wick.

—Oren Robinson of the *Daily Reverie*

In her white gown, Voleta vanished against the peaks of the city
like a snowflake into a drift.

Four stories down, the streets seemed even fuller than they'd
been during the day. It was nearly midnight, and the city appeared to
be just waking up.

The leaps between rooftops were tricky enough to be enjoyable. She
stumbled on patches of crumbling plaster, slipped on slick tiles, and
wobbled on loose bricks in the masonry. A ledge gave out when she
leapt upon it, and she narrowly managed to catch hold of a rainspout
after falling half a story. The thrill of it was so intense she couldn't help
but laugh as she looked down at the alley she'd very nearly bombed.
She scrambled up the peak of a decorative turret and looked up at the
constellations—a thorny rose, a wagon wheel, a crib, and a bear all
crowded together like stamps on a steamer trunk. A draft made the
stars twinkle. She thought of the wind and how much she missed it.
It felt as if she'd walked from one airless prison straight into another.

Every rooftop she came upon seemed to contain a celebration, but
the crowds were so drunk and full of themselves, it was easy enough

to skirt discovery. She hid under gables and crawled behind guard-rails. When the rooftops were too congested, she dangled from cornices and window ledges, inching along by her fingertips. Through the staging of well-lit windows and conspicuously undrawn curtains, she glimpsed trysts and spats and sobbing fits.

But she was invisible. It was such a luxury to be unseen and on her own.

Though it wasn't quite enough to eclipse the memory of the marquis's party, or her poorly conceived defense of the parrot, nor the disappointment in Iren's eyes. Voleta suspected she would have to climb over ten thousand more rooftops before she forgot that.

The real trouble was, most of the time she struggled to understand people's motives. Everyone was just so small-minded, so obsessed with observing and being observed, obsessed with popularity and reputation, with approval and romance, none of which meant much to her. It was exhausting to be constantly forced to validate so many people, all of whom held more sway in the world than she did. But it seemed to her, the more established the majority was, the more fearful the slightest divergence made them. It wasn't enough that they held all the power. No, they demanded adoration as well. It wasn't enough that he possessed you and lorded over every minute of your life; not enough that he watched you dress and stood at the foot of your bed and stared at you while you feigned sleep. No, you could never be small or apologetic enough. You had to thank him, and pretend to love him, and . . .

She didn't like where that train of thought had carried her and derailed it with a shake of her head. Her present distress wasn't about Rodion, her once captor and tormentor. No, she was irked by these Pelphians and all their blasted customs. The more these people banged on about politeness and popularity, the more she heard the underlying tremble of insecurity. She made them nervous because she did not take them as seriously as they took themselves.

"What are you doing down there?" a voice with a precise, cultivated accent asked from above. Voleta looked up to see a young man peering over the handrail at her. "Are you wearing a nightgown? Who are you?"

Seeing no reason to hide any longer, she stood and put her hands on the rail as if it were a fence in a yard and she were not standing on a ledge four stories above the street. "Oh, hello! My name's Voleta, and I'm ... I'm a gargoyle inspector." She patted the lion-headed grotesque on the corner of the rooftop. "Yes, yes, a fine specimen. Good shiny coat." She ran a finger over its exposed fangs. "Teeth are good, as well. This gargoyle is in perfect health."

"Why are you prowling about my roof?" Her discoverer was handsome and youthful. He looked as comfortable in his tuxedo as she was in her nightclothes. He had one hand tucked halfway in his pocket; the other cupped a coupe of champagne. His hair was tawny, almost blond, and his eyes were as blue as moonlight.

"Technically, only my toes are on your roof. Most of me is standing on public air."

"What if I told you I own the air, as well?" he said.

"What about the wind?"

"The wind, I only lease." He squinted and sipped his drink. He seemed to be deciding whether he was amused or annoyed. "Wait a moment, you're the young lady who came on the Sphinx's ship, aren't you?"

Voleta inhaled through her teeth as if she'd just grasped something hot. "Look, if you're going to interrogate me, the least you could do is invite me aboard."

"Of course. Permission to come ashore." The handsome young man offered her his hand.

Ignoring his hand, she climbed over the balustrade on her own. It was only when she had her bare feet on the marble floor of his terrace that she realized he was not alone. Perhaps a dozen men and women in jackets and gowns mingled about looking bored with the evening and weary of one another. It seemed a very exclusive party. The guests refused to acknowledge her presence, as if doing so would be paying her too great a compliment. Only the blue-eyed noble continued to watch her. "Do you usually run about the rooftops in your nightgown or is this a special occasion?"

"I like to think I'm just being a thorough tourist. Are you telling me that when you travel, you just crawl along the ground?" She walked past him, clasping her hands behind her back.

"Certainly not." He turned to watch her pass, his gaze lingering and low. "I like to see all angles."

She spun on the ball of her foot. The superior guests continued to reserve the compliment of their full attention, though she noticed some watched her from the corners of their eyes. "Then we're kindred spirits, milord."

"It's *Your Highness*, actually. I'm Prince Francis."

Voleta barked an unseemly laugh. She shook her head, disbelieving her awful luck. He would be a prince. He couldn't just be a lowly knight or an overdressed aristocrat. No, of course she had to barge in on a real noble. She couldn't even take a walk without stumbling into scandal. "Well, it's a pleasure to meet you, Your Highness. My name is Xenia. That's spelled Z-E-N—"

"You already told me your name, Voleta."

"Oh, that's right, I did. Well, I think I've eaten enough of my own feet for one evening." She sprinted at the balustrade, leapt upon the rail, and sprang across the gulf. Her nightgown fluttered, and when she landed on the adjoining roof, she tucked into a ball and rolled onto her feet.

She gave the prince a hasty, uneven curtsy and said, "Sorry to have interrupted your soiree, Your Highness. Please tell the other gargoyles I said good night."

Voleta woke to Iren in her bonnet looming over her. She held a breakfast tray, which in addition to eggs, ham, fruit, toast, and tea included a single pink carnation in a fine little vase. Voleta wondered what the hour was. After her jaunt across the rooftops, she had come back to bed and collapsed into a dreamless slumber.

"Ann sent this up." Iren set the tray over Voleta's lap roughly, making the dishes clatter.

Voleta stretched and rubbed her eyes. "I'm glad to see we're talking again. I'm sorry about that scene last night. It's sort of funny how upset everyone got, isn't it?"

Sitting on the edge of the bed, Iren picked up the entire slice of ham and fit it into her mouth. She spoke as she chewed. "After breakfast, I'm taking you back to the ship." She pointed at a wedge of toast. "Are you going to eat that?"

Fully awake now, Voleta squirmed under the tray, trying to sit up straight without upsetting it. "What? Why? Everyone will have forgotten the parrot by lunchtime. Let's not blow this out of proportion."

"Where did you go last night?" The amazon smeared all the butter onto a slice of bread and stuffed it into her mouth.

"Where did I—?"

"Look," Iren said, nodding toward the balcony. With the lamps in the room lit, Voleta saw what she had missed in the dark: a trail of dirty footprints emerged from behind the curtains and tracked across the rug to her side of the bed. "I thought we were going to be honest with each other."

"I went for a walk," Voleta said, snatching up the last piece of toast before Iren could get to it. "I just had a little look around, cleared my head, and came back to bed. Don't tell me that you're going to scuttle our mission because I stretched my legs."

"You can't stop, can you? You're just determined to be reckless. Determined to lie."

"I'm sorry, Iren."

"I'm sorry, too. I'm sorry I keep believing you."

"I never mean to upset you. That's the last thing I want to do, but sometimes it just feels like I'm choking to death. No, it feels like someone is choking me. The trouble is, it's just a feeling. I can't hit it, or yell at it, or drive it off. No one can help me because the thing that's choking me isn't real. It isn't here. The only thing that helps at all is running, climbing, moving about, getting my heart in my throat. I want to stop, Iren, I do."

"Is that why you picked a fight with the marquis?"

Voleta sighed heavily. "That was a mistake. I know it was a mistake. I was just feeling so—"

"Contrary?" Iren gave her a long and level look. Her bonnet had a curious way of trumpeting her gaze, and Voleta had to stop herself from looking away. "I don't think you mean to be bad, Voleta. I think you're—what's the word you used—*wounded*?"

"I wasn't talking about me. You know I wasn't talking about me."

"All right. Whatever you want to call it, I'm worried you're going to hurt yourself trying to get that feeling out of you. I'm not taking you back to the ship to punish you. I'm taking you back because I don't want you to run yourself to death."

"Oh, I don't want to die, Iren! I want to be cured. And maybe the only cure for it is walks and talks and a scare or two. Or maybe there isn't any cure for it at all, and I just have to be comfortable with surviving."

Iren drew her mouth into a thoughtful pucker. "Did anyone see you on your walk last night?"

Voleta cleared her throat, picked up her teacup and twirled her hand in the air. "I may have run into a nobleman."

"A nobleman?"

"Just some aristocrat in an expensive suit," Voleta said evasively. The fact that he had been a prince made the whole blunder seem worse. The king really seemed to have liked her, and she didn't want to spoil his opinion of her just yet.

Squit bounded across the bedclothes and leapt onto her chest. Voleta put down her tea to cuddle her. "Iren, please don't take me back to the ship. I really think this is better for me. I was going crazy in that cage. And I have to redeem myself anyway, don't I? After last night's terrible performance, I have a lot to make up for if I'm ever going to get invited to Marya's parties."

Iren squinted and said, "Next time you need to run, you take me with you. No more midnight walks on your own."

"That's absolutely fair." Voleta held out her hand. "Shake on it?"

As Iren shook her small hand, she added, "And tonight I'm going to tie you to the bedpost."

"You're going to tie me to the—?"

The bedroom door flew open under a hail of rapid, delinquent knocks. Xenia stomped into the room clutching a newspaper in one raised fist like a victory flag. Ann was two steps behind her, her prim bun bouncing from the jog. She shut the door as her lady ran to Voleta's bedside, speaking in a rush: "Look, look, look! You're on the back page of the *Reverie*. It's all about your little defense of the parrot, and everything you said to Papa, and oh, he's still furious at you, but a little less so now because everyone is talking about his party, and it's been a while since they did." Lady Xenia stuffed the paper in Voleta's face as Iren lifted away the breakfast tray. "Here, read it! Read it to us! Ooh, I'm so excited!"

Voleta smoothed and squared the paper. She scanned until she found her name and then began to read: "'After last night's party, it's safe to say that the Marquis de Clarke has reclaimed the mantle of Reveler in Chief. As always, he drowned us in wine, fattened us with confectionary, and stitched our ribs with laughter. But let it not be said that this was some rote affair. Not at all! The marquis's talent for inviting the most enthralling guests was again on display. Lady Voleta Contumax's unusual style seemed, at first, to be the product of some sort of hereditary defect. But what we learned from the young lady's apology for the polly is that her appearance and conduct, bizarre as they both are, are not senseless. She is a sincere eyesore, an unvarnished original! She stood tall in the court of the cabaret and left her voice ringing in our ears, crying out: "The prettier the mob, the prettier are we all!" How right the lady was! And her eyes are very, very purple.'"

"They are!" Xenia squeaked.

"What is this rubbish?" Voleta said, cracking the newspaper in half. "I didn't say that. If anything, I said the opposite of that!"

"*Milady*, you're missing the point," Xenia cooed. "They liked you. That's all that matters."

"What part of me did they like? All I see are insults!"

"Have you never read a paper before? That's a glowing review. Papa can't be mad at you now. You're a hit!" Xenia dug through the pockets of her day dress and produced a gold-foiled envelope that had obviously been opened by someone who was in a hurry. "And I saved the best for last. Look at this! It just came."

"What is it?"

"It's an invitation to Prince Francis's Summer Cotillion! He must've read about you in the paper this morning and said to himself, 'Now there's somebody I want to have at my party!'"

A flush ran up Voleta's throat at the mention of Prince Francis's name. "I suppose it's an important party?"

"You suppose it's a...Voleta, you really are the biggest dum-dum in the history of history. It's the prince's Summer Cotillion!" Xenia said each word more loudly and distinctly, apparently believing volume could cure Voleta's stupidity. "Everyone will be there. I've only been invited once before, and it was the most fantastic evening of my life!" She gasped. "We must start getting ready."

"Right now? But it's morning."

Xenia clasped Voleta's hands and pumped them excitedly. "Oh, you silly goose! If we start now, we just may be ready in time!"

Chapter Eight

Xenia insisted that they go through each and every article of
clothing in Voleta's luggage, which was no small undertaking.
Byron had filled an entire steamer trunk with frocks, another
with blouses and skirts, another with boots and shoes, and a fourth
with all the supporting accoutrements a young woman could wish
for: scarves, tights, girdles, vests, jewelry, and even a muff or two.
Since the stag wasn't sure what would be in vogue, he packed as if
for a theatrical troupe. Xenia found most of the garments so hilarious
she insisted she be allowed to try them on. Voleta wore a plastered-on
smile while Xenia modeled a pair of baggy bloomers, a bare wire bustle, and a feathered cape.

Every piece of baggage bore a tag that said PASS in big block letters,
evidence that customs had searched them for contraband. Their luggage had arrived with a short inventory of confiscated items, which
included the reason they had been seized:

2 six-inch hat pins (*potential for violence*)
1 unmarked bottle of scent (*general suspicion*)
1 tortoise-shell hair pick (*potential for violence*)

1 brocaded belt (*general suspicion*)
1 set of hair-curling tongs (*general suspicion*)

Iren found the phrase *general suspicion* galling. She had worked long enough in a port to know what that really meant. It meant one of the agents wanted to take a present for their wife, daughter, or mistress and had to make up some excuse for stealing it. And why in the world had Byron thought to pack a hair curler for two women who hadn't enough hair between them to make a single ringlet?

If only customs would have confiscated her bonnets.

In the end, there was really only one item in the luggage that concerned her, and that was the Sphinx's necklace.

While Xenia was absorbed with ransacking the dress trunk and Voleta was busy trying to keep her temper, Iren went in search of the jewelry box. She found the ornate rosewood box under a pile of silk scarves. She opened it and began to probe the collection of delicate chains and rings, her fingers moving clumsily between the small nooks.

When after her first pass she hadn't found the necklace, Iren suffered a flash of panic. What if an agent had pocketed it and just omitted the theft from the formal inventory? For all she knew, the Sphinx's necklace might already be hanging from some stranger's neck on the other side of the city. She could feel her heartbeat in her hands, and she shook them out to steady them before undertaking a second, more thorough search.

She found the necklace inside a small velvet pouch. The round moon that hung from the silver chain was no larger than a coin. Finely engraved craters decorated both faces of the piece, one side of which was white-gold; the other, dark pewter. The light and dark sides were meant to evoke the full and new moons. It was a simple but lovely piece. More importantly, it was their lifeline. The necklace was a beacon that called the Sphinx's messengers. As long as they had the necklace, they could communicate with Edith and Byron and, if need be, the Sphinx.

"What a pretty piece. Is it very valuable?" Ann said from her elbow. Iren turned and realized the small governess had been watching her.

Iren closed her hand around the moon. "Just to me."

"Well, it's only sentiment that's worth anything in the end, isn't it?" Ann said.

Iren smiled at her, returning the necklace to its sleeve and cubby. "I don't think your lady would agree with you."

"That's the first time I've seen you smile," Ann said with an appreciative cluck of her tongue. "I know it's not exactly part of the uniform, but it does look nice on you. I hope you aren't going to pack that away, too."

Their quiet conversation was interrupted by Xenia's pealing laughter. The young lady had begun to dance about the room using one of Voleta's gowns as a partner. Her romping knocked over a chair and swept the silver grooming set from the vanity. Ann's mouth tightened at the sight, but she maintained her good humor. "I'm so glad the papers were positive this morning. She hardly slept last night for sobbing."

"Voleta was up, too. Is the marquis still angry?"

"Probably, but he can't very well show it now. Everyone's dying to meet her."

"So. We're going to Prince Francis's ball." She spoke the name with a chilly inflection.

Ann looked up. Iren watched the smooth, almost translucent skin of her brow wrinkle like warm wax. She had large, kind eyes. "Don't fret. Balls are safe enough, even if there are wolves around. There will be too many people for anyone to get into too much trouble. Though perhaps your lady won't feel like debating tonight? I don't think she would want to ruffle the prince's feathers. He holds his grudges with two hands, if you know what I mean."

"She doesn't listen to me," Iren said, scowling.

"Sometimes it's enough to be heard. At least, that's what I tell myself," Ann said. "Can I ask you something? How old do you think Lady Xenia is?"

Iren considered it a moment. "Seven?"

Ann laughed. "No, really."

"I don't know. Sixteen, seventeen? It's hard to tell anymore."

"She's twenty-three."

"Really?" Iren looked at the silly golden-haired lady hopping about the room.

"The older she gets, the younger she acts. She's afraid her father will wake up one day and realize that his perfect little girl has become a perfect little spinster, and she'll go from being the feature of her father's parties to a millstone in his parlor. Pelphia isn't kind to ladies who don't marry. Honestly, it's not kind to ladies in general, but her juvenile behavior puts off a lot of good prospects. She has had a few proposals in recent months and years, some from perfectly fine young nobles, but she's determined to snare herself a higher place in court. She wants a duke, at least."

"So it's all just an act?"

"I don't know if it is at this point. If you pretend to be something long enough, you eventually become it, don't you?"

"Ann! Ann, tell Papa I need a squirrel. A squirrel like that one," Xenia said, pointing at Squit, who was sitting on top of Voleta's head and nibbling on her hair. "Tell him, if I don't get a squirrel, I'll propose to Count Orleans, and all our children will be fat, ugly dum-dums."

Ann smiled bravely. "I will communicate the urgency of milady's request." She laid her small hand upon the great shelf of Iren's arm, squeezed it, and whispered, "Let me know if you want to swap."

Hours later, the two meticulously scrubbed, dressed, and coiffed ladies left the marquis's home and undertook the promenade through the streets of Pelphia with their governesses in tow. And just as they had been during the reception parade the day before, nearly every lady within sight was dressed in one shade or another of orange. The auburn-colored river followed the trail of the sun, joining a growing surge of hopeful courtiers who carried bouquets, dance cards, their fathers' hopes, and their mothers' fears. Those young ladies who had not been so fortunate as to receive an invitation to Prince Francis's Summer Cotillion watched the parade from café patios and bedroom windows where they scowled and whispered about the shortcomings of their peers.

Voleta was blissfully unaware of all the glaring and gossiping. She had discovered that she could attain an almost trancelike state if she concentrated on her breathing, unfocused her eyes, and repeated the admonishing phrases Byron had spent recent days teaching her. *She would not raise a fuss. She would not make a scene. She would not speak her mind. When some numbskull nobleman said something horrible or foolish, she would smile and curtsy. She would be gracious, composed, and pliant.*

Though she had refused to let Xenia pick out her dress.

This "betrayal," as Xenia called it, had led to hours of argument and fountains of tears. But Voleta had stood her ground. She would wear one of her own gowns: a simple silver frock that was long and straight and without much shape. But it flashed like a blade, and she liked the way it fit.

Xenia said it was not silver. It was decidedly *gray.* And gray reminded her of pigeons and old men and ashes and grout. Orange was what everyone was wearing. Orange was the color of sunrises, passionate fires, and poppy flowers! Gray had never been popular; it never would be popular; and why did Voleta hate her so much? What had she done to deserve such a horrid guest?

Their spat had ended with Xenia declaring that she would never speak to Voleta again, a commitment she kept throughout their walk to the venue. Of course, Voleta hardly considered Xenia's silence a punishment, though she tried to look suitably forlorn whenever Xenia scowled at her because the sadder Voleta looked, the more determined Xenia was to punish her with peace and quiet.

The venue for the prince's cotillion was called Horizon Hall, which sounded grand enough. The hall stood at the city's edge, half-sunk into the Tower superstructure, where it served as the nightly stable for the mechanical sun. But when Voleta glimpsed the hall from a distance of several city blocks, she thought it bore a striking resemblance to a three-story blob of mashed potatoes. Gold light leaked like melted butter from a door at the top of a warped and bumpy stair. The clockwork sun jabbered down the blue bowl of sky toward the hall's irregular summit. To Voleta's surprise, the rattling star did not brake when it reached the rooftop. Instead, the flaming points guttered out as the gas was shut off, and the unlit disc disappeared through a slit in the hall's roof. Only then did Voleta understand what the hall's architect had wished to evoke: a fluffy cloud cradling the setting sun.

The flow of debutantes piled against the uneven steps of the hall, their advance temporarily dammed by the manner of admittance. Each debutante had to present her invitation to the doorman, who reviewed its authenticity before passing the title card to the herald, who in turn announced the lady. The process was necessarily slow as none of the young ladies wished to be hustled through her debut, and so everyone involved had no choice but to be patient.

Voleta looked back at Iren, nearly pinned against her by the crowd. She had never seen Iren look so miserable, though probably that was owed largely to the wig. It really shouldn't have been so blond.

The wig had been Ann's idea. While the young ladies were off taking baths, she and Iren had spent the better part of an hour folding and hanging up all the clothes Xenia had thrown about. Ann took the moment of privacy to tell Iren she might not want to wear her bonnet to the ball.

"It's completely unreasonable, but it will draw a lot of attention," Ann explained, shaking the wrinkles out of a scarf before she squared it and returned it to its rightful place in the trunk. "I don't think you would enjoy the scrutiny."

"I don't think it's the bonnet they'll be staring at," Iren said, impressed at how quickly Ann was able to chip away at the mess. Iren felt like she'd spent half an hour trying to hang the same silk blouse.

"Well, the thing is, the prince doesn't like women to wear hats. He holds the somewhat arcane impression that hats are masculine."

"You mean, they won't let me in if I'm wearing the bonnet?"

"No, I think they won't. And I know you want to be there for Voleta." Ann stopped folding for a moment and approached Iren with her hands held up as if she meant to offer to surrender. "So why don't

239

we just take a look at what we have under here." With the sort of care one might use to pet a stray dog, Ann reached up and pulled the bonnet from Iren's head.

Ann gasped. Iren's hair was silver, short, and standing out at every angle. It looked like she had cut it herself. Perhaps in the dark.

Iren frowned. "Is it bad?"

"Well," Ann said, shifting her pursed lips from one side of her mouth to the other. "We decided that we would be frank with each other, so I'll just tell you: I really think you might look nice in a run-of-the-mill, nothing too fancy, average sort of . . . wig."

Stuck in the crowd outside Horizon Hall, Iren was second-guessing the wisdom of that sentiment.

Ann had scoured the marquis's lost-and-found closet, where she kept all the garments and accoutrements that guests left behind. Iren had tried on several options, but the blond, layered wig had been the only one that she could squeeze onto her head. Ann sounded confident that Iren could carry the look off, but when Iren examined herself in a mirror, she thought it looked as if she were wearing a haystack.

Ann, who was pressed snugly against Iren's hip by the crowd outside the hall, smiled up at her encouragingly. Iren showed some teeth in the general shape of a smile and tried to ignore her throbbing, itching scalp.

Meanwhile, Voleta had come to the unfortunate conclusion that she needed Xenia to talk to her. Because as irritating as her host was, she was a source of useful information. Xenia would know if the "Mermaid" were attending the prince's cotillion and would be able to recognize her on sight. Voleta had only the briefly glimpsed painting of Marya and an etching in the *Daily Reverie* to go by, and neither were sufficient to give her a clear impression. She needed Xenia to point Marya out.

Voleta thought a moment about how she might bait the lady into talking to her again, then asked, "Xenia, would you like to marry Prince Francis?"

Xenia seemed to find the question irresistible. "One does not *like* to marry the Prince; one *dreams* of it. Oh, can you imagine what my life would be like? No more begging Papa for pets and dresses and money for the café. No more second-class seamstresses. No more grouchy Ann. I'd have three handmaids, my own penthouse, and a standing invitation to any party in town."

"That does sound grand. But what is the prince like?" Voleta asked the question innocently enough, though she had begun to wonder if the prince might be an ally in her effort to meet Marya.

"Well, he's exceedingly handsome and a very good dancer. He can talk with the smarties and still fight with the toughies. He's well traveled—he's off on a grand adventure at least once a year. He's always popping in and out of the papers. And he doesn't have to court anyone because everyone is so busy courting him."

From what Voleta had seen of the prince on the rooftop the night before, Xenia's version of Prince Francis was plausible. He was good looking, well spoken, and exceedingly impressed with himself.

"Wait a moment! Excuse me," the man at Voleta's elbow said. He pulled a folded newspaper from the inside pocket of his coat. "You're the girl in the paper, aren't you?"

"Yes," Voleta said with a tired sigh. "I was very rude at a party last night."

"No, no, you were on the rooftops."

Now the man had Iren's attention. He had begun to offer the newspaper when Iren snatched it away. "With my compliments," the man said, startled by Iren's appearance. He tipped his hat and shifted away through the crowd.

Iren opened the paper and let Ann pull her arm down so she could read along with her. Ann was a much faster reader, though Iren's attention had stalled on the etching, which took up a full quarter of the front page. It was of a slight woman in a white nightgown leaping between rooftops. The likeness wasn't perfect, but her short dark hair was unmistakable.

"It's the evening edition," Ann said, and began to read aloud: "'The Sphinx's niece was spotted last night running about the rooftops of our fair city in her nightgown. Lady Voleta Pennatus Contumax, who is rapidly making a name for herself, startled Prince Francis by pouncing on his terrace. The prince was in the midst of entertaining Duke and Duchess Kinneer, Duke Patrick...'" Ann stopped, glancing up at her attentive listeners. "It's just a lot of titles for a bit. Let me skip down. 'According to Prince Francis, Lady Voleta's acrobatics were quite entertaining. He said that he hopes she sparks a trend among young women to go skipping about the skyline in their negligees. The prince also remarked that "she was a pretty little thing," raising the specter of a possible romance, which we can only hope will blossom into the coupling of the summer.'"

"*Coupling? Pretty little thing?*" Voleta said, balling her fists. "Who does he think he—"

Xenia grabbed Voleta by the shoulders and began jumping up and down. "Oh, you're going to have his purple-eyed babies!"

"Stop that!" Voleta said sharply, then seeing the hurt in Xenia's eyes, quickly added in a kinder whisper: "I don't want to seem overeager."

A knowing look came over her host's powder-flattened face. Xenia smiled. "I see. Oh, aren't you clever. You want to play coy. I know coy. I'm the queen of coy. I've played coy loads of times."

Voleta wanted to tell Xenia to stop saying *coy*, but she resisted the urge. "Really? What's your technique?"

"Well, I stick my finger in my mouth like this, and I put my hand on my chest right here, and I open my eyes wide, just so, and the boys fall all over themselves and do all sorts of silly things trying to impress me."

It dawned upon Voleta that her host was an insatiable flirt. "You're obviously an expert, Xenia. And I still have much to learn." Voleta hooked her arm through Xenia's, trying her best to seem pleasant and friendly. The crowd shifted forward, and they made a little progress. The orchestra inside the hall rumbled and swelled. Voleta ginned up a little enthusiasm and said, "Oh, listen to that! Music! I adore music. It's my absolute favorite thing in the world."

"My favorite thing is a chocolate éclair dipped in pink champagne," Xenia said.

"Well, those are good, too. I've heard an awful lot about this pianist they call the Mermaid. Have you ever heard of her?"

"Have I heard of her?" Xenia scoffed. "She's only the most wonderful singer in the world! And she has the most perfect story. She was lost in the Baths and rescued by a duke. They had a whirlwind romance, right out in front of everybody. Her rise to fame has been meteoric!"

"Meteors go downward, my lady," Ann interjected.

"The other one then," Xenia snapped her fingers. "A stalactite!"

"Still no," Ann said, but hurried on before Xenia could try another word. "I'm sure that both of you can find more interesting and wholesome dance partners than Prince Francis. Isn't he a bit too infamous? He's a little rough around the edges, isn't he?"

"Oh, Ann, don't be stupid! If Prince Francis wants to be rough with my edges, he's welcome to them. No, he's not perfect, but I'm sure if he ever found the right woman to love and dote on him, he'd polish up perfectly well. Even a golden train makes a little soot!"

They reached the bottom stair, frilled like the lip of a clam shell. Above them, through the tiers of skirts, dress trains, and eager ladies, they saw the pages checking invitations, their gloved hands flashing from envelope to envelope. Inside, the warm baritone of the herald announced the newest arrival. Voleta felt an unexpected flutter of anticipation. "Will she be here tonight, the Mermaid? Can we meet her?"

"I shouldn't think so," Lady Xenia said. "She doesn't come to these sorts of parties anymore. She's too famous now; she'd just be mobbed. Since her return last month, she's been a bit of a ghost about town, really. She surprised everyone by making an appearance at the Lighting of July a few days ago, but that was unexpected. Your best chance to see her is onstage. I'm sure we could get tickets to see her perform. Papa never has trouble getting tickets to shows."

Voleta hid her disappointment with a smile. "I would like that. Please ask him. It's wonderful to have such well-connected friends."

"Yes, you *are* lucky!" Xenia beamed.

"It must be awful, though—to be so famous that you can't even go to balls anymore. I wonder if the Mermaid goes out at all," Voleta mused aloud.

"Oh, she probably still goes to teeny-weeny rooftop parties. Not the sort of thing I get invited to, unfortunately."

"But you're a lady!" Voleta said with an admirably straight face.

"Yes, but we're standing in a crowd of ladies!" Xenia exclaimed as she handed her invitation to the doorman. "Ladies are ten a penny. I'd have to be a duchess or a princess!" The herald took Xenia's card and announced her to the room.

While Xenia was making her entrance, Voleta pinched her chin and scowled with thought. Iren leaned down and whispered in her ear, "You're going to try to befriend the prince, aren't you?"

Voleta looked up, smiling at how transparent she was to Iren. "Well, you heard the lady. He's a golden train."

"He's full of soot," Iren said. "He's a cad."

"I'm sure he is, but we have two days to have a private chat with a ghost who only appears onstage in front of hundreds of people. If you have a better idea, I'm all ears."

Voleta presented her invitation to the doorman the same moment Iren said, for all to hear, "If he lays a hand on you, I'll kill him."

The doorman's eyes widened with fright. He looked down at the envelope held suspended between the lady and himself. His gloved knuckle was touching the tip of her finger.

Voleta patted him on the shoulder and said, "It's all right, she's talking about the herald."

Chapter Nine

I have seen men pierced by a wink and women gored by the cut of an eye. The gaze is a martial art.

—Oren Robinson of the *Daily Reverie*

Prince Francis Le Mesurier stood beside the set sun, which was much larger up close than it appeared in the glazed sky. From tip to tip, the wavy rays of the brass star stretched nearly twenty feet. It hung upon its iron rail, unlit and silent, wearing an expression that was meant to suggest delight, but which in shadow looked more like worry.

The prince reached out his wineglass and tapped the point of one ray, saying, "Cheers!"

Reggie Wycott, a fat, porridge-faced earl, and also the prince's most reliable friend, laughed at the jest. But then, the Earl of Enbridge laughed at everything. He seemed to believe that if he laughed hard and often enough, people would think he had a sense of humor. But Francis knew better: Reggie was an anti-wit, a comedic deficit, an ill-humorist. Francis liked having him around not for his contributions but for the flattering contrast: Reggie's flaws brightened the prince's virtues.

The party was off to a horrid start. Francis observed the full ballroom and all his mingling guests with a vague sense of revulsion. They squawked like a canyon full of geese. They had carried in with them a cloud of cologne and perfume that poorly masked the reek of their anxiety. None of them belonged here. None of them deserved this evening, and they all, deep down, knew it. Of course, it was not his fault the cotillion was terrible. He had filled the hall with wine, music, and a horde of hospitality girls who circulated with trays full of exquisite morsels and exotic cigarillos. He had hired professional dance partners to occupy the floor so that it never seemed empty, though the predictable fact was most of his guests were more interested in kibitzing than waltzing.

He could gin up almost any luxury, any treat, any wonder of the world except worthy company.

He suffered from what he called *the anguish of excellence*. He was cursed with an acute awareness of the idiots of the Tower, and he had a thorough understanding of their undeserved but pervasive influence upon the world. Because idiots outnumbered intelligent men, they had skewed all the folkways in their favor. The idiots wrote the laws and decided what constituted "decency," which was just a weakling concept to protect a weakling class. The fact was, most of the women of Pelphia were dumb and whorish, most of the men were toadying and impotent, and almost every one of them wanted to use him like a rung on their imaginary ladder to success. They all thirsted for distinction without understanding in the slightest what made a man worthy of notice, service, and devotion. That was the trouble with idiots: They believed their low birth and mental vacuity could be transcended with works—as if a house cat could become a lion by hunting a sufficient number of mice.

Francis's father, the influential treasurer of Pelphia, often accused him of going in search of trouble. But it wasn't trouble he was looking for—it was vigorous stimulation and an honest challenge, which were hard to come by in a place where all the men wanted to be your friend and all the women wanted to have you corrupt them in the cloakroom or debase them in the wine cellar. He was bored of the fox chase. He wanted to hunt something wild, something clever, something with claws and teeth.

"It's a real screamer of a party, Frank," Reggie said, raising his glass.

Reggie's hair was as black and thin as candle soot, and he touched the fringe of it obsessively.

Francis's eyes sparkled. "You think so? I think it's rather like feeding birds. I throw out a handful of crumbs, and they scramble like they've never been fed before."

"Only you could look at a room full of pretty girls and think of pigeons." Reggie shifted the black threads on his forehead. "The trouble is you're spoiled. You've eaten so many sweets you can't taste them anymore."

Francis nodded at his friend's paunch. Reggie's tuxedo shirt swelled like a full sail. "I think you have the two of us confused."

"You need to roughen up your palate. Eat a lemon. Drink some vinegar. Bed a homely girl. Then maybe you'll be able to savor this again."

"Look, just because you got caught with that horse-faced harlot, Beatrice, doesn't mean I—" The words faded on his lips when he caught sight of her: short haired, olive skinned, broad mouthed, her slight figure wrapped in silver. "There she is. That's the little foreign girl I was telling you about. The one who jumped onto my roof last night. She told me her name . . . what was it? Valet? Viola?"

"Lady Voleta Pennatus Contumax, niece of the Sphinx," the earl said, reminding the prince of the other reason he kept him around: He was good at remembering all the dreary details. "She came aboard that great brute of a warship that's stopping up our port."

"Yes, I know. The question is, why is she dressed like a penny whistle?"

"Where are you going?"

"To cleanse my palate," Prince Francis said, handing his friend his empty glass.

Ann nearly had to pry Iren from Voleta's side, a sight that wrung Voleta's heart a little. Though she never meant to, she had a knack for tormenting the people who cared for her the most: first Adam, now Iren.

Ever the diplomat, Ann promised Iren she would be able to keep an eye on Voleta from the servant's vestibule, which was separated from the ballroom by only a screen. Before following her counterpart into quarantine, Iren bent down and told Voleta, "If anyone lays a finger on you, I'll snap it off."

"And I'll feed it to them," she replied, and chucked her friend on the chin.

News of Voleta's nocturnal adventure seemed to blow in from the street with her. The crystal chandeliers, large as wedding cakes, shivered with whispers and laughter. *There she was! The girl who had leapt from roof to roof, right into the arms of a prince!* The next morning's edition of the *Daily Reverie* would declare it "an obvious romance, a natural fit: a wild woman for the reckless prince!"

Voleta felt the room's attention like a change in air pressure. The atmosphere felt thinner, the light less warm. The feeling surprised her. She was not one to suffer from nerves. But it wasn't nerves exactly. No, it was the same suffocating sensation that had chased her out of bed the night before. She felt a primitive impulse to run, to return to the ship, to fly away and not come back. For the life of her, she couldn't determine what had triggered that sense of dread. There was nothing very threatening in the hall, just champagne fountains, fancy dresses, and the same multitude of gazes that had followed her since she'd come ashore. The most unnerving element of the ballroom was the dopey-eyed sun monitoring the dance floor.

Voleta wondered if she wasn't suffering from too little sleep or too much rich food. Xenia had been stuffing her with cakes and chocolates since breakfast. She decided that must be the culprit.

Ignoring the alarms that were ringing inside her, she decided to charge straight at her goal.

Prince Francis, who was standing onstage beside the cradled sun, seemed to mark her the same moment she spotted him. Skirting the edge of the parquet dance floor, she strode toward him as he descended the stairs. Beside her, dancers swept about in one another's arms, their necks stretched, their heels hardly grazing the floor. Their expressions were as vague as sleepers.

Xenia was trying her best to be coquettish, but Voleta could tell she was having a hard time flirting at a full trot. The young lady was curtsying and greeting noblemen without waiting for a reply.

"Slow down!" Xenia hissed in Voleta's ear.

"But there's the prince," Voleta said, nodding at her target.

"I thought we were going to be coy!"

"We are being coy! I just want to get his attention first."

When Voleta refused to stop, Xenia slipped out in front of her at the last moment, reaching the prince a step before her guest. The golden-haired lady threw herself into a magnificent curtsy and cried, "Your Highness!"

Prince Francis greeted her with his hands in his coat pockets and a rakish smirk on his handsome face. "Ah, Lady Xenia! How are you? How is your father? What a wonderful man. Such solid parties. Please tell him I said hello."

Still winded from their sprint across the ballroom, Xenia straightened and said, "Ha-ha-ha, yes!"

The prince turned toward Voleta before Lady Xenia could think to say anything more. "And fancy seeing a gargoyle inspector skulking along the ground. I hardly recognize you out of your nightgown."

Voleta curtsied with all the grace of a hen pecking a tick, popped back up unsteadily, and said, "I'm sorry I barged in on your party last night. I was just so lost in my thoughts."

"I have a head on my shoulders, too, but I've never thought my way onto the rooftops."

"Well, what can I say? I suppose I'm an aerobic thinker." Voleta smiled with her cheeks, if not with her eyes.

"What a coincidence! I happen to be a philosophical dancer." The prince pulled his hands from his pockets, put his heels together, and gave a brisk, formal bow. "May I have this dance?"

At Voleta's elbow, Xenia gave a single, mournful peep.

Voleta was about to accept when she recalled Byron's parting advice to her the previous morning: *Whatever you do, don't dance.*

The stag had sincerely tried to teach her. Byron had given her several lessons during the week spent circling the Tower. As a pleasure-cruising warship, the *State of Art* was outfitted with all the essential amenities, including a conservatory, which featured a miniature harpsichord and a modest dance floor. There, she and the stag had practiced the basic steps for hours on end to the militant accompaniment of a music box. Even with two steel feet, the stag had been a dozen times more graceful than her. She bumped against him, stepped on his toes, and crossed in front of him, again and again. It took days for his patience to break, but Byron finally lost his composure when she tripped him, sending him down on one knee. He came up snorting and livid. "How is it you can climb a tree and swing on a trapeze, but you can't dance a waltz! A waltz! It's a step made for drunks!"

"I don't know! It's so rigid and plodding! It's *dun*-dun-dun, *dun*-dun-dun!" she said, chopping one hand into the other, mimicking the timing of a waltz. "It's just like marching in circles!"

"No! No, it's nothing like . . . All right, fine. Yes, it's like a march. It's certainly not a shimmy. It's not a stomp. It's like an elegant, gliding, silky march."

The moment the prince put his hand on her hip and the music began to play, Voleta knew the undertaking was a mistake. Her wild careening about would not fool or impress a man who'd spent the better part of his life dancing. He would see through the charade at once. Everyone would. She, a seasoned world traveler, who could not dance. It was beyond absurd; it was implausible.

"Although," she said, dropping her hands from his shoulders and stepping back again. "To be honest, I've never been *overly* fond of dancing. There's something about it that's . . . Well, it's just a bit tedious, don't you think?"

Francis made a scoffing sound, which didn't quite match his expression of surprise. Voleta imagined he was not accustomed to having his overtures deflected, and she watched him closely to see if he would take offense or find her challenge entertaining.

Prince Francis raised his hand to signal the conductor, who silenced the chamber orchestra with a similar gesture. Suddenly, Voleta could hear all the murmurs in the room. She glanced about for Iren, wishing for a friendly face, but found none. It occurred to her that she had just made the same exact error she had the night before. She had insulted one of the ringdom's most beloved pastimes.

Prince Francis tugged at his jeweled cufflinks. "You know, I have never once heard it said that dancing was anything but the epitome of beauty and culture." Someone in the crowd shouted out "Hear, hear!" The prince held up a finger to signal an addendum. "But, privately, I have often thought that dancing really is quite dull." Expressions of shock rippled through the dance hall. The hired dancers, in particular, looked horrified.

Voleta folded her arms, relieved to see the prince had recovered his wolfish smirk. He seemed to like shocking people. Well, if there was one thing she was good at, it was milking gasps from a crowd. "I'll tell you what, Your Highness, for every reason you can think of for why dancing is secretly an awful chore, I'll match it with one of my own. We'll see who runs out first."

"A parlor game! Splendid. I like games. All right. I'll start." The prince paced a moment, though this seemed to Voleta to be more of a theatrical performance than needed deliberation. "It's repetitive," he said, smacking his fist into his hand. "It's just counting to three forever and ever."

A woman in a flame-red wig seemed to choke upon a sob while her partner stifled a laugh.

"It aches your feet something awful! I'm all blisters and corns," Voleta said, pulling up the skirt of her silver dress a little to show off her silver slippers. Xenia looked positively green at the mention of corns, but the lady at her elbow applauded. "See, she knows it's true!"

"I nearly lost a toe last week to a lady with poor timing and an overfondness for Bundt cake," the prince said, turning to share his smirk with the crowd. Reggie applauded like a windup doll.

"The music's bad," Voleta fired right back.

"Now see here!" cried a young man in the crowd. His ire was quickly drowned out by a mixture of laughter and jeers.

"No, no, she's right. She's right! Our composers have been in a slump. Let's not pretend. Let's not spare the drunkard's feelings," the prince said. "Let's call it a draw, shall we?"

"Are you giving up already?" Voleta said, crossing her arms lightly.

"One last gripe, then." He extended his hand to invite hers. "A dance is all chase and no catch." The prince bowed his head and waited. Flecks of light churned through his thick hair and across his open palm. She puzzled a moment over where the light was coming from before she understood: She was the source. The glow of the chandeliers reflected off the silver threads in her gown, casting little white stars all about her.

Voleta drew a breath.

The mob leaned in.

She placed her hand in his, and he kissed it.

The moment she left Voleta's side, Iren had begun watching her through the daisy-patterned screen that ran the length of the servants' vestibule. The space was overcrowded, but the other footmen and governesses were very leery of the giantess wearing a haystack wig and were doing their best to stay out of her way. When out on the reception floor Voleta began to push through the crowd, Iren shadowed her down the length of the screen, sending porters and nursemaids diving from her path. She was too distracted, too anxious to notice the havoc she was causing. Ann, who ran along in her wake, was the first to realize who Voleta was making a beeline for, and said, "Oh, dear. That's Prince Francis."

Iren stopped and gripped the screen as if it were the bars of a cage. She glared at the prince, standing there with his hands in his pockets, and watched his mouth move. She hated him on sight. She couldn't shake the feeling that Voleta was being used as courageous bait in a cowardly trap. The whole plan stunk. She'd be sure to tell the Sphinx so the next time she saw him.

"Iren, not to be a pest, but didn't you warn her about Prince Francis?"

"I did. I tried to," Iren said, feeling the urge to defend herself. Ann didn't understand what Voleta was like. A warning was as good as an invitation.

"I know he seems charming at first, but—"

"We need him," Iren said. The music had stopped, and a crowd had circled around Voleta and the prince. Iren could hardly see the dark scrub of Voleta's hair bobbing in a sea of elaborate coiffures.

"You don't! No lady needs a lord as much as she needs her safety and happiness. There are worse things than being unmarried and untitled, believe me. It doesn't have to be so—"

"Not for that. We don't need him for that."

"I don't understand," Ann said.

"We need him to help a friend." The dance floor erupted in laughter and some applause. The crowd parted a little, allowing Iren a window into the scene. "That's all I can say," she said, watching the prince bow to Voleta. He seemed to ask for her hand. Voleta gave it to him, and he kissed it.

Something in Iren snapped. Ann, sensing the sudden change, said in a breath, "Wait, Iren dear, don't!" But Iren was already moving, knocking porters and governesses to the wall. She rounded the edge of the screen, brushed past the doormen, who scarcely offered a quibble, and thundered onto the main floor. Iren wasn't thinking, exactly. It was more like she was envisioning what she was about to do to the prince. She would pick him up by the foot and whip him about until he was just a bloody suit full of jellied bones. She would pop off his head and pour out his brains and stamp upon the puddle. And if anyone got in her way, she'd kill them, too. She'd kill all of them.

Iren parted the crowd like a crack in the earth. She knocked a blond lord on his heels, splashing his drink in his face. When a woman's waspish bustle blocked her, she bowled through it, spinning the woman like a top. She crushed toes, tread on skirts, and broke apart dance partners without acknowledgment or apology.

She startled Voleta and the prince so badly, they both leapt. Iren glowered down at them, breathing in great, angry heaves.

"I think your horse is ready, milady," the prince said, attempting to play off his fright with a joke.

Recovering her wits, Voleta clapped her hands and said, "Oh, you're right on time, Iren! Right on time! I need my calendar. Prince Francis has just invited me to join him in his box at the Vivant tomorrow night." Voleta paused to give the prince a half curtsy. "The Mermaid is debuting a new piece. I told him how keen I am to hear it. And His Highness also has invited me to the after-party. Isn't that wonderful of him?" When Voleta finished her explanation, she seemed to continue to communicate with Iren by the vehicle of her eyebrows, which said, *Calm down. It's all right. This is working out in our favor.*

Iren's posture softened a little as she absorbed Voleta's message. She couldn't bring herself to apologize, but she did bow her head.

"We can't have you telling the Sphinx we're a tuneless clan," Prince Francis said, studying the imposing governess as if he were preparing to guess her weight. "If the Mermaid can't redeem our music in your ladyship's ears, no one can."

"And I look forward to the redemption, Your Highness!" Voleta said brightly.

The moment Voleta shut their bedroom door on a still-babbling Xenia, she looked up at Iren and asked in exasperation, "What were you thinking? Charging at the prince in front of half the ringdom like that?"

"I don't know!" Iren tore the wig from her head and threw it at the vanity mirror. She couldn't very well say that she didn't really know what had come over her. She hadn't been thinking at all. She had just acted on sudden and insistent instinct. "He's attacked women!"

"What do you mean?" Voleta plopped down on the floor and began unbuckling the straps of her shoes.

Iren retold Ann's account of the chambermaid's tragic end aboard the prince's ship. Voleta listened as she hung up her dress and put her shoes in the trunk. "Well, how was I supposed to know all that?"

"I don't know!" Iren boomed.

"Then why are you shouting at me?"

Iren raised her arms and let them fall in one defeated flap. Her voice was quiet and contained when she spoke again. "Because you shouldn't go tomorrow."

"Of course I should go!" Voleta wriggled into her nightgown. "This is what we've been suffering for. This is why you're wearing a rag doll wig and I'm batting my eyes at a poisonous toad. If I can get one moment alone with Marya tomorrow, all of this will be over. We'll be back on the ship by morning and in the air by lunch, and Senlin and his wife will be together at last. And I tell you what, we're all going to deserve a honeymoon after this! I'm marrying Squit, and we're not doing any chores for a week. We're going to lie in bed all day and run around the ship all night."

Iren felt a sharp, peppery sensation in her throat, a feeling so unfamiliar, it took her a moment to realize what it was: the threat of tears. "You shouldn't get your hopes up."

"About what?"

"About Marya coming back with us."

Voleta began to shake her head in a small quiver, but the range of the motion grew as she spoke. "After just two days, I can hardly tolerate this stupid place. Imagine how she must feel after nearly a year! She will want to leave. She will jump at the chance. I know it. I know it!"

Iren sat on the edge of the bed. She suddenly felt drained and very old. She hated the feeling. "I've spent the past two days worrying about whether or not you could do this. Whether you could handle your temper and fit in at parties." She scoffed. "I should've been worried about myself."

Voleta sat down beside her. She had applied her own makeup that evening and had done a much better job. Even so, Iren didn't like it. She didn't understand why women's makeup was the color of bruises and blood, why the powder was as pale as a corpse.

She took up the edge of her apron and wiped away the rouge. "I don't like that prince," she said. "He's dangerous."

"He is," Voleta said, enduring Iren's scrubbing. "But don't you forget, Iren—we're dangerous, too."

Chapter Ten

A lady's figure is her ledger. Aging is forgivable. Fattening is not.

—Lady Graverly's Table: Rare Graces
and Common Shames

There was no breakfast in bed for Voleta the next morning. Instead, at the stroke of eight, a maid appeared to inform her that the marquis had requested the lady join him for breakfast in the dining hall in one hour's time.

Voleta had received the message herself because Iren had still been sitting on the bedside, misbuttoning her governess's dress.

"Didn't sleep well?" Voleta asked.

"No. Kept waking up to see if you'd snuck out again."

"Well, I didn't. I slept like a purring kitten all night long."

"I know. I saw," Iren said, scrunching her red eyes shut.

Voleta suggested that Iren get a few more hours sleep. When Iren balked, Voleta reminded her that she didn't need her for breakfast with the marquis and Xenia, but she would need her for their evening with the prince. Accepting this logic, Iren fell back on the bed still wearing her half-buttoned uniform and began snoring almost at once.

Voleta didn't know which she dreaded more that morning: being stuck at a table with the marquis or the arrival of the early post. She knew that their cause benefitted from the fuss the *Daily Reverie* made over her, but she did not understand it. She was not news; she was, at most, an aspiring star in a city full of amateur celebrities. Surely there were crimes and injustices that were more deserving of the public's attention.

But she was determined to maintain her composure and reputation long enough to accompany Prince Francis to the Mermaid's after-party.

All she had to do was get through one more day.

She didn't know what to wear to breakfast, but also knew that deliberation wouldn't deliver a better result. She selected a dress at random—a long, white, high-waisted affair—and spent the rest of the hour playing with Squit, who'd woken up in a frolicsome mood. She didn't look in the mirror once, applied no makeup, and tried not to think about all the things she would rather do than go to breakfast. The list was long.

When the appointed hour came, she left Iren sleeping soundly in bed and walked through the high corridors of the marquis's home alone. It seemed that every wall contained either an ornate and immaculate polished mirror or a piece of art that featured either Xenia, her father, or the two of them together. There was an oil painting of Xenia as a young girl with an oversized bow in her curled hair, and a tapestry of the marquis standing in front of a majestic-looking horse, and a mural of both of them lounging, foot to foot, on a red velvet couch. In all the family portraits, there was no sign of a wife or mother. Voleta's experience in the Tower had taught her not to inquire after absent family members because the answer was never happy and the memory seldom welcome.

It took her a little wandering to find the dining hall, but there was no mistaking it when she did. The immense table nearly filled the chamber. There must've been twenty or more chairs, and she was surprised to discover only one seat stood empty. The rest were filled with formally dressed men and women. The squeak of silverware on plates informed her that the meal had already begun.

The marquis, seated at the head of the table, saw Voleta lurking uncertainly in the doorway and waved her over to the only empty chair, which stood immediately to his right. The marquis was in high spirits. He spoke to Voleta in such warm, familiar tones she wondered for a moment if he had her confused with someone else, someone he liked. He insisted that she allow him to pour her tea himself, which he did, in a stream so weak and dribbling the tea was cold before it plinked into her cup. He spoke as he poured, telling her what a relief it was that she hadn't hurt herself on the rooftops, and what a wonderful influence she had been on his daughter, who, after just one or two ballroom seasons, still had not managed to provoke the interest of a duke, much less the son of the treasurer. Prince Francis! What a coup for them all!

Voleta did her best to listen as he flattered himself with her accomplishments, but her attention kept drifting to Xenia, seated across from her behind a centerpiece of holly sprigs and pheasant feathers. The lady seemed utterly changed. She stared mutely at her untouched eggcup and fiddled with her hair—what remained of it. Her long, flowing locks had been hacked down to a blond tuft. She looked like a dandelion. She seemed very uncertain of the choice.

The marquis was momentarily interrupted by his butler, who came with samples of several breakfast wines for him to taste and select for the table. Voleta leaned forward and asked Xenia, "Who are all these people?" She nodded down the line of chatting and chewing men and women in evening dress.

It was only then that Voleta realized Xenia was wearing a sparkling, silvery gown, reminiscent of the one she had worn the night before, though with a much deeper neckline. "They're just a bunch of gossips Father hired to fill out the table."

"They're what?"

"Well, somebody has to be here to watch," Xenia said.

"Watch what?"

Xenia took up one of her toasted soldiers and waved it about like a wand as she spoke. "Us of course. Well, mostly you. After last night, and everything with you and the prince, Papa didn't want to run the risk of something happening with no one around to see it. It was such short notice, he couldn't get his usual guests to come, so he hired some gossips. Don't worry. They're all perfect professionals."

Voleta regarded the gentleman in gold spectacles seated on her right. She realized he was sawing and shifting his food about on his china plate, and his mouth was moving in the mechanical process of chewing, but he was not in fact eating anything. He was observing her out of the corner of his eye.

"Why do you always pour such small samples, Billium?" the marquis shouted at his butler. "How can I taste anything if I can't even coat my tongue?"

"You haven't said anything about my hair," Xenia said in a stage whisper, pulling Voleta's attention back to her. Xenia petted her hair and rolled her eyes like a doll.

Voleta wondered if she wasn't still asleep. She looked at the lady beside Xenia, who slurped at an empty spoon, then to the impeccable settings and the steaming dishes full of food: kippers and olives, pork belly and cherries, homily and honey, none of which had been touched. She felt a sudden sense of dreamy vertigo, as if she were plummeting inside a nightmare. She sipped her cold tea to revive herself and said, "It's lovely, milady. But why did you cut it?"

Before Xenia could answer, the marquis inserted himself into the conversation. This morning he wore no wig at all but had a lacy handkerchief draped over his head. One corner hung down between his brows like a widow's peak. "Ah! Here's what we've been waiting for!" he crowed. A footman marched across the hall carrying a silver tray that held only a folded newspaper. "The morning wagging of the finger!" The marquis made a rude gesture, and the table erupted in a chorus of rehearsed laughter.

The Marquis de Clarke took the paper from the tray and opened it with a flourish of his flouncy cuffs. "Just as I expected! Front page. Look! Here you are, my dear girl, with the prince's lips pressed to your fingers. Isn't that a fine etching? I don't know how they do it."

He turned the paper so Voleta could see. She stared at the illustration of a waifish woman and a suited man standing in front of a stylized sun, and it was a moment before she realized it was supposed to be her and Prince Francis. He was kissing her hand, and she was touching her bare throat as if she swooned with desire.

Voleta's impulse was to rip the thing to shreds, though what good would that do? Thousands of other copies were being snapped open and read all across the ringdom at that very moment. She could hardly hope to destroy all of them.

"Here, I shall read the article to the table," the Marquis de Clarke declared. After a robust clearing of his pipes, he began to read. "'Lady Voleta and the prince came together like a pair of magnets. Oh, the electric sparks that filled the air of their conversation! The flirtations! The exchange of wits! It was like peering behind the horizon to that starless space where the sun and moon sometimes meet and fall into each other's arms like hungry lovers.'" The marquis paused to remark, "That's quite good! Wait, there's more. 'The Lady Voleta told a joke about dancing, which we should all expect to hear poorly reprised by the local wits for the next fortnight. Prince Francis kissed her hand, and the lady blushed with the ancient yearning of young loins. Then the band played Hobson's new waltz, which was well received by all.'"

"That is a lie, milord," the spectacled man at Voleta's elbow said. "Hobson's waltz plopped upon the floor like a dropped pie. No one applauded. Hobson got disconsolately drunk. He had to be carried home in a friend's sedan." The professional gossip, whose expression was avuncular and warm, had a voice that was as cold as high air.

"But the rest, Mr. Tut?" the marquis asked.

Mr. Tut wiped his clean mouth with his napkin. "The lady was a hit."

The table broke into constrained applause. The marquis folded the paper and presented it to Voleta. "For your collection, milady."

"If you don't mind me asking," Mr. Tut said, turning in his seat so he could better observe Voleta. "What is your opinion of the young woman who died?"

"The young woman who what?" Voleta said, looking about to see if she was the only one who was confused.

"It's not in the morning edition, but it will be all over the evening post, I'm quite sure."

"What are you talking about?" the marquis said, feeling under-mined by the change of mood of his celebratory breakfast. "I didn't invite you to eclipse our moment of triumph with your own filthy gossip!"

"It is related, milord." Tut held his hands up in a show of deference. "A young lady fell from the roof of her home late last night. She was wearing a white nightgown." He watched with undisguised interest as Voleta's amiable smile first cracked, then shattered.

"My goodness!" Xenia cried with a practiced quaver of grief. "Who was it?"

"Commissioner Pound's daughter, Genevieve."

"The poor man," the marquis said automatically, his thoughts already moving ahead to the more important implication. "His daughter was mimicking our guest, wasn't she?"

"I don't wish to speculate needlessly, milord," Mr. Tut said with false humility.

"Please." The marquis shifted the handkerchief, which had slipped farther back on his head. Voleta stared down the line of gossips, chewing air and watching her with unfriendly smiles. She had never wanted to scream so badly in all her life.

"No one knows what feelings reside within an unbeating heart, but among the living the consensus is that Lady Genevieve was paying homage to Lady Voleta." Mr. Tut adjusted his spectacles. "The *Reverie* editors are of the mind that your ladyship may be the next Mermaid. Actually, they've already coined a name for her. They're calling her the Leaping Lady."

Voleta watched as a maid set an eggcup before her, the soft-boiled egg already uncapped, the yolk inside shining like a wound. She thought of the young woman splayed upon the bleached cobblestones and wondered what her last thoughts had been. Had she time to grieve or regret as she fell? Had she thought of her life, her family, her loves, her hopes...or did she think only of the morning post? Her life was no more than a rumor now, spoken once by strangers over breakfast— a tragedy that would become a trifle before lunch, and by dinner, be forgotten.

Voleta stood up, surprising everyone, and walked from the table in a daze.

"You all witnessed that," the marquis said with a sweep of his finger. "That was the moment the Leaping Lady first heard her name!"

Voleta gazed down from her bedroom balcony at the people coursing through the streets. The dominance of the color orange had broken overnight, and no one seemed sure what should replace it. They wore every hue, every cut of dress, every accessory. The dispelled uniformity seemed a source of great anxiety. The citizenry dashed about with swiveling heads and darting eyes, searching shopwindows and one another for the new consensus.

Voleta felt a great welling up of pity for them; it was a cold and useless feeling.

She saw the evidence of her influence peeking through the waning orange. She saw women in simple silver dresses and white nightgowns, their hair shorn close to their head or slicked down to appear so.

She was distantly aware that Xenia had walked into her room without knocking. The marquis's daughter had spent a moment clucking and cooing at Squit, then she gave a surprised yip that made Voleta smile softly.

Xenia drew up beside her on the balcony, sucking her finger to soothe the spot Squit had just nipped. "Why would you have a pet that bites you? It's like having a maid who makes messes for you. Or a cook you have to feed. It doesn't make any sense."

"She's not a pet," Voleta said, closing her eyes. "And she doesn't like being picked up by strangers."

"Well, I suppose I wouldn't either. How stupid of me! Stupid, stupid, stupid!" Xenia said in a singsong as she slapped her cheek lightly. She waited for Voleta to argue with her dramatic self-recriminations. When Voleta offered none, she went on: "Oh no! Are you sad about the girl who fell?"

"Why did you cut your hair?"

Xenia felt along her newly uncovered neck and up the back of her head. "I just wanted to count the lumps. You know what they say: One lover for every lump. I have eight. Eight lumps."

"Stop that. Why really?"

"Because I have staked my name next to yours, silly goose. We are gossip sisters. Sisters in ink. I took a gamble on you, you know. I offered you my friendship. I stood by you when you made your mistakes. I think it's only fair that I share in your successes, too. I've not been a *bad* host after all." Xenia tried to arrange her pretty face into some expression of sincerity, though Voleta thought it looked more as if she had something in her eye.

"You're angling for an invitation, aren't you? You're trying to get into the prince's box at the Vivant."

Xenia huffed indignantly. "I'm sure I have no idea what you're talking about! I've never been so insulted in all my life! Here I am, having an innocent conversation with my friend, and, and . . ." Xenia blinked her cow-like eyes. "Yes, I suppose I am. I mean, there's *got* to be room for me."

"It's the last place you should be. That man is probably a fiend. You do realize that, don't you? You have to know what they say about him. Why would you ever want to be in the company of a man like that if you could help it?"

"Because he's a prince!" Xenia all but wailed. A trio of soldiers in black uniforms looked up to find the source of the outburst and tipped their caps as one. Xenia waved until she jiggled and then blew them a kiss.

Voleta slapped the rail top. "Why do you do that?"

"Do what?" Xenia said, still waving at the soldiers who had already lost interest and were vanishing again into the crowd.

"Why do you throw yourself at every man you see?"

"Because *I* have self-confidence." The lady's smile seemed to freeze upon her face.

Voleta blurted out a laugh. "Confidence! You are the most insecure person I've ever met. You're forever running yourself down, hoping someone will correct you. You need constant validation and approval and attention! I swear, if you ever do find a husband, you'll let him kick you around like a ball, just so long as he tells you you're pretty once in a while."

"What a horrible thing for a friend to say."

"We are not friends! I'm just a roll of the dice to you! I'm your gamble! Would I be a hit? Would I be a flop? Would I get you invited to better parties? You only cared about me because you thought I was a good bet. Well, let me tell you, my friends—my *real* friends—don't think of me as long odds or good odds or as any odds at all!"

"Why are you so angry?"

"Because somehow you've turned all this prosperity and opportunity into a prison! I don't know how you did it, but you did. This is a horrible way to live! And you could walk away from this nonsense tomorrow. You have the means to go as you please. If you could just squeeze that big head of yours through the bars of your parties and your princes and your morning posts, you could escape!"

"You don't know the first thing!" Xenia said, her voice snapping like a whip. "And if we're not friends, then I'll have to speak to Papa about your staying here any longer. Eating and drinking us out of house and home. Your little rat bit me!" Xenia held up her finger, showing off the invisible wound. "I don't like you. You're a dum-dum who didn't even smile when a prince kissed your hand! I saw you standing there like a corpse on a stick. I can't get anybody but fat old earls to look at me. But you! Prince Francis came to you like a called dog! And you wouldn't even dance with him. You are such a dummy. I wish you had been the one to fall off that roof!"

"Excuse me, ladies." Ann stood at the balcony door. She held up a stiff envelope like a white flag. "Prince Francis has sent his greetings to your father, Xenia, who was very pleased to receive them. The prince has also sent a ticket for you to join him and Lady Voleta in his box this evening."

Xenia gave Voleta a scorching look and said, "Please inform the prince that I humbly accept his offer." Voleta rolled her eyes. "And, Ann, please thank him for thinking of me. Tell him I expect to be in a rather lusty mood this evening. Sign it for me, please. Your signature is so much better."

"*Milady*," Ann said with strained patience.

"A lusty mood!" Xenia squawked back. She stormed from the balcony and made a great show of slamming the bedroom door.

Ann sighed and smiled at Voleta. "I hope the lady's . . . mood doesn't spoil your evening."

"Thank you, Ann. It's fine. I'm sure it'll be fine," Voleta said, her temper cooling quickly.

Crossing back through Voleta's bedroom, Ann's attention was drawn to the large, curiously patterned moth that was perched on the lid of the jewelry chest. The coloring on its wings appeared to be eerily similar to actual paisleys. "What a queer little thing," she murmured, picking up a folded copy of the *Daily Reverie*. She raised the newspaper over the insect. Its wings pressed together, as if in prayer.

Voleta swooped in and gathered the insect in her hands, startling Ann in the process. "Got him!" Voleta cried.

Catching her breath, Ann laughed at herself and said, "You do realize moths are a housekeeper's mortal enemy? Though we have lots of mortal enemies. Mice, crickets, dogs, or really anything else that likes to roll around in the street. We are friendly with cats, though."

"Well, they do eat mice," Voleta said gamely, raising her cupped hands. "I'll put the enemy outside."

Ann was still smiling when she turned and bumped into Iren, who was returning from her bath. She smelled like she had doused herself in rose water. Her uniform was wet about the collar and in patches across her hips. Her hair stood out in porcupine quills. "Don't you look nice!" Ann said.

Iren pulled at the excess fabric around her middle. "I think Byron thinks I'm fatter than I am."

"Who's Byron?"

"My . . . tailor."

Ann put her hands on her hips, holding her head at a contemplative angle. "Well, far be it from me to criticize another's work, but I'm reasonably deft with a needle. If we took in a few inches here and some more right here," she said, pinching the uniform elbow. "I'm sure it would fit much better."

"I don't know," Iren said, drawing out the phrase.

"You still haven't forgiven me for the wig, have you? Well, that's fair enough. I haven't forgiven myself. It was an awful idea. But the good news is that your young lady has blazed the public trail for short hair. So perhaps you can dispense with both the bonnet and the wig and just go as yourself. As you probably should've from the beginning. Anyway, if you'd like to test your luck with my needle, come by my room after tea, and we'll have a quick fitting."

"Oh, she'll be there! It's a wonderful idea," Voleta said, still clutching the moth that continued to flap and tickle her hands. "Now, Ann, if you wouldn't mind giving us a moment, we need to discuss my evening wear."

"Of course, of course. And I'll see you after tea." Without waiting for an answer, Ann pulled the door closed behind her with such practiced care it scarcely clicked.

"These people are insane," Voleta said in a very different tone. "Throwing themselves off roofs, blaming me. No, actually they *credit* me. I blame myself."

"Ann told me about the girl. She was Pound's daughter."

"I don't want to have to feel sorry for that man. Why is everyone here so determined to ruin themselves, just for a little attention? I've never met so many vain and desperate people in my life, and I lived in a brothel!"

"Everyone except, you think, for Marya?" Iren said.

"Marya is different. You'll see. Now let's hear what Byron has to say for himself."

Voleta twisted the moth's wings about its body, then turned its head. Byron's voice buzzed and pitched about like a fly in a jar. Iren made a bowl for the device with her hands, amplifying the recording. Byron spoke in veiled terms, so if the message were intercepted, its meaning would be unclear.

"To whom it may concern. The man in charge of the white city has agreed to return the master's picture. It would be wonderful if you two could wrap things up a little early, if possible. The captain thinks we should skip the long goodbye. She sends her regards. The master sends the usual assortment of reprimands and compliments." The recording seemed to end, but a moment later there was a shuttering sound, and Byron spoke again in a quieter voice. "Post script. The captain showed me the latest *Reverie*. I must admit, while I failed to turn you into *their* sort of lady, you somehow managed to turn them into *your* sort of crowd. Well done! Give my best to our imposing friend. And wear the moon, for goodness' sake. I might need to get a message to you in a hurry."

"There you have it," Voleta said, slapping the lid of the jewelry box open. She withdrew the velvet pouch and shook the silver chain and lunar pendant into her hand. Opening the clasp, she drew the Sphinx's necklace around her neck. "It's tonight or not at all."

"And what happens if Marya says yes? What if she wants to come?" Iren asked. "If we're caught with her—"

Voleta waved these details away, saying, "We'll put her in a wig or throw a coat over her. We'll be subtle."

"Not really our strength, though, is it?" Iren slid the dormant moth into her uniform's pocket. "And we are absolutely not going to kidnap her."

"No, I'm not going to kidnap her!" Voleta made a great show of looking insulted as she straightened the necklace in the mirror. She stopped mid-act, arrested by her own appearance. For a moment, she saw herself in the light of her new fame: the hair, the dress, the jewelry. She looked herself in the eye, stuck out her tongue, then turned to face Iren. She held up a finger to punctuate her declaration. "But I will persuade her."

Ann slowly circled around Iren's waist, pins clenched tightly between her lips. Ann's bedroom was small, tidy, and warmly lit by a single gas lamp that fluttered loudly enough to be heard.

It wasn't a particularly tricky job—all she needed to do was take in enough to trim the baggage without puckering the seam—and yet she worked with such deliberation and care, Iren couldn't help but feel a little flattered by it.

"I love this fabric. It's called bombazine. Isn't that a lovely word? I know some people think it's a little coarse to the touch, but I think it's the perfect texture. Some ladies like to wear nothing but silk and satin because it's so oily soft, but I don't care for that myself. It slips and slides and sticks to you. I'd take bombazine or a nice wool any day. Something firm enough to feel." Ann spoke in such an unguarded way, it almost seemed as if she were talking to herself. Iren didn't find the experience unpleasant. In fact, for the first time in a very long time, she found that she didn't feel the tug of vigilance. She wasn't thinking of Voleta or Senlin or the Sphinx's stupid plan. She wasn't really thinking about anything. She felt almost sleepy, though she wasn't tired. *This*, she thought, *must be what relaxation feels like.*

"My mother is a seamstress and a homebody who has never once in her life given a single fig about climbing the ranks or being seen and all that," Ann said, settling into a new topic. "She is a wonderful mother. She was a patient wife, too. My father was always so nervous about being liked at work and putting in enough hours. It was never enough hours." She sighed and shook her head, seeming to find the memory sad but familiar enough to no longer ache. "My mother still likes to sit at the kitchen table and snip out silhouettes after she gets home from work." Ann nodded at one of the walls where a pair of black profiles hung in oval frames. "She made those. That's my father and her."

Iren looked at the profiles, marking the man's sharp chin and the woman's high forehead. She saw a little of Ann in both.

"I was an only child, a good student all eight years," Ann continued. "When I finished school, I didn't want to sit at home. I had to work. I didn't want to wait to be called on by whatever suitor decided to settle for me. Marriage just seems like business and politics tucked into bed. It never appealed to me." Ann cut her eyes up. Iren looked down. Strangely, she felt as if she were staring down a mountainside rather than her own chest. "You're not married, are you?"

"No," Iren said.

"Don't hold your breath, dear. You'll pop all my pins out. There we go. That's better. I started working as a governess when I was seventeen. In the past thirty years, I've raised five children for three employers. Some turned out better than others, but so far, I've not raised any absolute ninnies. Not *absolute*." Ann pressed upon Iren's hip and she dutifully shuffled in a circle until Ann stopped her and began pinning again. "Xenia was a different person eight or nine years ago. You wouldn't recognize her. She was kind. Curious. Simple, but not fatuous. Just an honest, plainspoken girl. She had this way of twisting up her mouth whenever she came upon something that puzzled her. She was such a theatrical little thinker!" Ann laughed around the pins in the corner of her mouth. "She would rub her chin and scratch her head and pace back and forth until she solved the puzzle or gave up trying. She rarely gave up. But that was then. Now . . . she'll be married before the year is out. The marquis will shake my hand, perhaps give me a mina for my years of service, and shut the door. That's always a strange moment." Her voice dipped and slowed to something that sounded like a dreamy mutter. "It's odd to be so intimately involved and relied upon, and then after years and years of being essential, to suddenly become—" Ann stopped abruptly, shook her head, and patted the last pin she'd laid. "I'm sorry, how long have I been going on? What did you ask me?"

Iren's brow wrinkled with thought. "Did I ask anything?"

Ann put her stool away and stuck the leftover pins back into their cushion on her bureau beside a vase full of dried, colorless flowers. "I'm sorry. I don't know where all that came from. I suppose I—"

"I liked your story," Iren broke in. Now that she was free, she looked at herself in Ann's dressing mirror. The glass didn't show all of her, but what she could see, she liked. The chains she had worn about her waist for years and years had made her seem one shape. Now she was a different shape. She didn't know if she liked this shape better or worse, but it was interesting to look at. She turned until she could see her back. "Your family sounds nice."

"Thank you. But, um, but what about you?"

"What about me?"

"You know: Where were you born? Did you like your mother? Were they mean to you at school?" Ann gave Iren a pleasant but oddly pleading look. Iren had no idea what it meant, and the fact must've shown on her face because Ann explained. "I feel a little exposed, dear. Couldn't you tell me something about yourself, so I don't feel like such a—" Ann stopped, searched hopelessly for a better word, and finally said, "Fool."

All at once, Iren thought of a thousand things she could never confess. Not only because it might out her and her friends as frauds and pirates, but because Iren knew it would also make her very difficult to like. Ann's life had been all uniforms and silhouettes. Hers was all violence and thievery.

But looking at Ann, seeming so vulnerable and uncomfortable, she knew she had to tell her something. She racked her memory for some happy moment.

"There was a kitchen that gave soup out to whoever showed up before the pot was empty. They did it every, I think, Thursday night. I used to go there when I was a little girl, seven or eight years old, about this high." Iren put her hand at the bottom of her hip. "The cook who made the soup and doled it out refused to give me any the first time I went. I was so hungry and angry, I almost left, but then he said, 'Soup!'"—she wagged her finger, rehearsing a very clear memory— "'Soup's too thin for a growing boy.' He said, 'A growing boy needs a full belly!' And he gave me an enormous wedge of cornbread, bigger than my hand, and a big beer stein full of milk. He stood there and watched me eat it all to make sure no one tried to steal it."

Ann smiled, but her eyes glistened with a different emotion. "We've led very different lives, haven't we?"

Iren tried to keep from looking at the floor, but it seemed to draw her gaze. "I don't have a home. I've never had friends or a family. Well, not until a little while ago. This is all . . . very new to me." Iren spoke carefully, as if she were feeling her way along the edge of a cliff at night.

"You're here to protect Voleta, aren't you? Not just as a governess. You're more of a bodyguard, I think."

"Am I?"

"Yes. I'm sure you're very good at it, too. I certainly wouldn't want to cross you. And I don't think that you have to be like other governesses to take care of someone, especially someone like Voleta. Half of the governesses I know are so bitter they don't even pay attention anymore. Their girls are essentially on their own. Like so many of us are. And look, it's none of my business either way. I'm not judging you, and I'm not going to mention anything to anyone. I just wanted to tell you that I think Voleta is much better off for having you around."

Iren barked a laugh.

"No really. She respects you, as do I, regardless of what you've had to do. I'm sure your work comes with all sorts of hardships and . . . regrets." Ann carried the stool back out and set it down again beside Iren, where she stood, holding her breath, needled by the pins in her clothes.

Ann stepped up on the stool. "You must be very strong to withstand so much pressure. Yes, very strong and very brave." She held onto Iren's shoulder and stood on her tiptoes, raising herself to eyelevel. Iren wore a startled grimace, and her gray eyes were wide. "And quite pretty, too."

Ann leaned in and kissed her on her tightened lips.

"There," Ann said, wiping her lipstick from Iren's mouth. "Now all our cards are on the table."

Chapter Eleven

There is little less charming than a spurned woman. I'd rather be cornered by a house fire than a heartbroken girl.

—Oren Robinson of the *Daily Reverie*

If hubris had a temple, it would look like the Vivant.

The famous music hall was overbuilt and underthought and forever caged by scaffolding. It loomed over the piazza like a sickly patriarch: pale and gaunt and proud. The limestone that composed its bony spires, walls, and steps was as soft as chalk, and it rubbed off on all who touched it. A scuff of white on one's jacket was considered a mark of distinction, especially among the middling hordes that scrabbled desperately after fame and influence. In its history, the Vivant had witnessed the melding of fortunes, the drafting of wars, and the rise and fall of many kings. Its stage was reserved for only the very best players at the height of their careers. No one retired to the Vivant, though many a swan song had been sung there. It was said that from its high stage, a starlet could look out and see exactly how far she had to fall.

Lady Xenia and her guest shuffled with the well-dressed, perfumed, and coiffed masses across the piazza, inching toward the hallowed hall. Everyone was squeezed together like toes in a boot. With the narrow crags of the city blocks behind them, the sky seemed larger, the air more abundant.

The fact that Xenia was getting attention amid so much traffic and so many novel fashions filled her with a warm sense of worth. It had been the right choice, she was sure, to cut her hair, though her father had wept when he'd first seen her. (Her father could be so sentimental!) Her dum-dum guest was drawing a lot of attention, too, but of course she wasn't enjoying it at all. The sour little foreign girl had made her father send away the sedans he'd hired especially for the occasion. Lady Voleta had said it was undignified to be carried around on another man's back. "Undignified," said the girl who lived with a rat in her blouse and jumped from roof to roof in her nightgown. *Undignified!* Xenia was quite sure there was nothing more dignified than riding in a sedan, with one's ankles at eye level to all the world. Everywhere she looked, there were ladies riding upon rented chairs, their dresses as visible as flags, their expressions perfectly tranquil, as if they were just waking from some superior dream.

Xenia stamped her foot on the cobblestones and said, "Why can't you at least smile? This is the greatest night of our lives, and you look like a great sulking cow!"

The moment before, Voleta had been thinking very hard about what she would say to Marya when the time came. There seemed no good way to phrase what she had to say: *I'm here to take another crack at rescuing you since our last effort fell short. Assuming you want to be rescued, of course. Oh, you don't? All right. Is that because you're having the time of your life or is it because the duke has you over a barrel? Who am I? Just some girl your husband rescued from a brothel. But I'm sure Tom's already filled you in on all his errors and questionable friends...*

Then Xenia called her a *sulking cow*, and Voleta's head swiveled to find the lady's painted face pressed over her shoulder. Voleta's first instinct was to say something biting, but she knew there was no advantage to antagonizing her host, especially not now. She needed Xenia to distract the prince long enough for her to get in Marya's ear. Voleta couldn't afford to be petty. If there was ever a time for self-control, this was it.

But before Voleta could respond, their attention was stolen by a sharp shriek and then broad laughter. Just ahead of them, a young woman in a strapless gray gown began to spin and rise over the crowd. For a moment, it seemed as if she were being sucked up by a leisurely tornado, then the pedestal that lifted her became visible over the crowd. The curious column was threaded like a screw and engraved with beautiful arabesque whorls. Voleta spotted a plaque affixed to one side of the pillar. Her eyes were keen enough to just make out the words contained there: WILL-O'-THE-WISP: GIFT OF THE SPHINX.

The pillar stopped rising at last with a little bump that made the lady atop it give another a shriek, though this time it came between fits of laughter. No one seemed alarmed by the unscrewed monolith. Though when its edge cracked open, there was a mad dash to get into the chamber inside. After a tussle, the door into the pillar shut again, and the crowd sighed in shared disappointment.

"What is that thing?" Voleta asked, as the column began to twist back into the ground, lowering the young lady back to the arms of her escort and burying whoever was inside.

"It's a Will-o'-the-Wisp. Some folks call it a Wishing Box," Ann said from behind Voleta. "They're an old amusement." The governess, who was no taller than Voleta, wasn't shy about clearing space for herself. She dug her elbow into a drunk dandy who'd blundered too close before continuing. "You see them all over the city. They pop up now and then at random."

"It shows you things," Xenia added. "Some people say they see nice things inside them. They see their future or their dreams or dead loved ones. But I don't like them. I think they're nasty. I went in one once, and I saw a wrinkly old hag. She stuck out her tongue at me. I thought she was going to try to lick me. I screamed my head off. I couldn't sleep for a week. I don't know why people like them so much. You should try it, though. You'd probably rather kiss a hag than a prince."

Voleta wanted to know more about the Sphinx's "wishing box," and perhaps have a go in one herself, but there wasn't time for that now. She needed to prepare Xenia for her part in the evening's antics. "I'm sorry, Xenia. I know I've been in a foul mood." Voleta did her best to sound contrite. "The truth is, I'm just nervous. The prince is so handsome and cultured. I can't help but feel like I'm a little outclassed. What would a girl like me even do with a prince?" Voleta stole a glance back at Iren, stalking behind her. When she caught her eye, Iren tried to rally a smile of support, but Voleta could see her hackles were up. The amazon was on edge. *Good*, Voleta thought. "I just don't think I'm ready for such a big romance," Voleta concluded with a heavy sigh.

Xenia beamed at her. "Oh, it's not *entirely* your fault that you aren't ready." They reached the first of many stairs leading up to the hall. Xenia lifted her skirt and began to climb, talking at a near shout. "You've just not had enough experience in polite society. I mean, you were pretty much raised by airmen and mudbugs, weren't you? All that travel! And we all know why girls travel. It's because their families can't stand them. But foreigners make such terrible babysitters. It's a wonder you can hold a spoon the right way round, honestly. I've been preparing to marry a prince my whole life, and I only today feel truly ready." Xenia, who'd been smiling radiantly a moment before, suddenly scowled. "Is that really your best jewelry?"

Voleta's wrists and ears were bare. Her only adornment was the Sphinx's necklace. The modest moon pendant hung above the neckline of her simple black dress. Xenia had put on all of her best jewels; she spangled like a lump of jam. Her dress was swoop-necked and made of silver cambric. When she surmounted the last step to the Vivant, buffeted on all sides by the throng of ticket holders, Xenia stopped, turned, threw up her arms, and said in a gay shriek, "Your future princess has arrived!"

The gentry looked up briefly from the stairs below, squinted at her with a bland sort of irritation, then clambered on.

Ann gave the lady a little shove, and then they were inside.

When Voleta had been very young, nearly younger than her memory could reach, her father had taken them all on a trip to the seaside. She recalled only snatches of the day: a skittering red crab, a blue-green wave, and the castle they built by dribbling watery sand from their fingertips, making little spatters that grew into spires that stretched into palisades.

The lobby of the Vivant looked as if it had dribbled from the fingers of a giant. There was an undeniable whimsy and gracefulness to it, but Voleta no longer wondered why so much of the Vivant was pinned up with scaffolding. It was a frail sort of elegance.

An usher approached, bowed, and asked for their tickets, which Ann presented at once. Seeing they were bound for the prince's box, the usher gave a second, deeper bow and began to clear a path to the mezzanine stair. Xenia puffed up at this special treatment, though it seemed she couldn't help but stop to rub her shoulder upon a chalky pillar like a cat upon a leg.

After a few turns upon a coiling stair, their usher pulled back the black velvet curtain on the prince's box. Xenia nearly spun Voleta around in her bid to be the first one in.

The dim box looked more like a gentleman's den than a balcony. There were dark rugs on the floor, several worn settees, and a short bar near the rear of the room. An exotic flock of stuffed birds decorated the walls. Voleta thought the morbid decor an ominous choice for a man who'd been charged with studying the magnificent creatures.

Prince Francis Le Mesurier and Reggie Wycott, the Earl of Enbridge, leaned heavily upon the mahogany bar, their hands walled about tumblers of gin. Their black tuxedos were relatively staid, a symptom of the changing vogue. Behind them, a great barn owl hung with wings spread as if in blessing. When they saw the ladies and their governesses, Francis and Reggie both straightened and took to tugging their cuffs and smoothing their hair like a pair of guilty children. They were emphatically *not drunk*. They had merely been preparing for the evening. At worst, they could be accused of being a little overprepared.

The hellos were made a little awkward by Xenia's insistence that she speak for the Lady Contumax and Prince Le Mesurier, as well as for herself. She slipped breathlessly between the three roles, changing whenever Francis or Voleta opened their mouths: "My father sends his warmest regards, Your Highness, and I'm sure you wish to return them, and also we must express our undying gratitude for this honor, especially Lady Voleta, who has been a complete basket case all afternoon, worrying about what to say and do, but I told her Your Highness is famously gracious, and also she is lucky enough to have me here to demonstrate how a lady behaves while in the company of a prince."

This left out only Reggie, who stood awkwardly to one side of the trio, laughing like a winded dog for no apparent reason.

While Xenia blathered, Prince Francis's gaze darted back and forth between Voleta and Iren. Voleta could tell Iren made him nervous, though he seemed to be doing his best to appear unaffected.

Meanwhile, Xenia was still talking. "—but this is *so* fancy, Your Highness! Oh, look at that pretty thing. Is it a duck? I only know ducks. They all look like ducks to me. Are others coming, or am I to have you all to myself?"

"Others?" The prince smiled at her at last. "I know some poor devils have to resort to hiring gossips, but I've always found the practice pathetic. Isn't that what friends are for—to witness one's triumph? That's why I'm so glad you and Reggie could join the Lady Voleta and I this evening." Prince Francis didn't seem to notice the crestfallen expression that settled on Xenia's face.

Hoping to distract from Xenia's dejection, Voleta said, "What a view!" She waved an arm at the cavernous theater beyond the railing. The white aisles, dark orchestra pit, and black stage seemed very far away. Their box felt as private as a nest on a cliff.

"What would you care to drink, Lady Voleta?" Prince Francis asked.

"Do you have any rum?"

"Rum?" The prince laughed. "You really are full of surprises. A lady like yourself tipping back rum!"

"You don't have any?"

"Of course I have rum! I love rum."

"*I* love rum!" Xenia said.

"Well then. Rums all around. How do you take yours?"

"In a cup," Voleta said, much to the prince's amusement. He promised to use the joke in the future and, in a grand show of humility, went to make the drinks himself.

While they waited for his return, Reggie did his best to impress

Xenia with his wit. He remarked on the interesting fashion of her hair, saying how it reminded him of an infant, a comparison that Xenia did not like in the least, which sent Reggie spiraling into a series of apologetic revisions: her hair was fine, keen, beautiful, it was a golden dandelion! He brushed the fringe of his own thin hair up his forehead, his cheeks glowing with embarrassment.

Prince Francis returned carrying a tray. As he distributed the drinks, he said, "Don't blow so hard upon the embers, Reg. You'll put the fire out."

"I am ablaze already, Your Highness!" Xenia exclaimed. "Feel how my heart burns!" She took the prince's hand, still cold from the ice, and pressed it to her bosom. "Feel how it pounds!"

"Steady on," Reggie said, looking miserable.

A change in the murmur that filled the auditorium drew their attention to the balcony rail and the theater below. They gathered to the rail, though the glasses in their hands kept them from joining in the applause. The prince seemed content to let others do the clapping for him.

The Mermaid burst through the house curtain and ran across the stage at a tilt. She fell upon the black piano bench awkwardly and lay there panting like a castaway spat up upon a shore. Her long blue dress lay tangled about her feet. Her auburn hair was wild, and her cheeks were pale beneath the rouge.

There was a moment of terrible silence as everyone tried to decide whether this was part of the performance.

Then the Mermaid gasped deeply, and the orchestra bellowed from the pit. She struck the first chords before she was even upright on the bench. The exuberant roar from the boxes, mezzanine, and main floor drowned out the music momentarily, then the orchestra fought back, and the Mermaid began to sing.

The air swarmed with the reverberations of strings and horns and timpani, creating a thick fog of sound. Marya's voice cut through it like a pike of sunlight. She sang with helpless abandon. The timbre of her voice ran down Voleta's neck and along her spine.

It was strange to be peering down at the subject of so much striving.

Here was Senlin's miracle. His hope. His once-wife. Voleta gripped the balcony rail till her knuckles blanched.

She had no idea how long she had been listening to Marya play when the prince spoke so near to her ear she could feel his breath. "Do you like it?"

"Very much." Voleta forced herself to smile at him, though her gaze flitted back to the stage. "I've never heard anything like it. I can't wait to meet her."

"Then I have a treat for you." Something in his voice compelled her to look, and she saw that he held up a wooden chit, old and worn, with the word *Vivant* carved upon it. "A backstage pass. I only have one—they are quite coveted—but I will lend it to you."

As she took the token, Voleta wondered if this were some sort of trick. Most likely the prince was trying to impress her and make her feel indebted to him, though what did that matter? Voleta plotted it out in her head: She could go to the Mermaid's dressing room, meet Marya, plead her case, return to the prince's box, feign illness, skip the after-party, and retrieve Squit. She and Iren could be back on the ship before midnight. If Marya wanted to come with them, then they'd find some way to sneak her out of the duke's penthouse or palace or wherever it was they lived. Marya could climb out a window, slide down a drainpipe, and *voilà*. They could throw a scarf over her head and be safely aboard the *State of Art* before anyone was the wiser. Voleta wasn't delusional. She knew the plan was hazy in places, and the whole notion was audacious, but they hadn't time to deliberate.

She smiled at the prince and said, "Thank you, Your Highness."

Francis gave a treacherous little smirk in return. "You can catch her during intermission if you like. She usually spends all of it in her dressing room. You should start making your way down soon, though. It's a bit of a jog. I'll call an usher to guide you."

The prince excused himself. Reggie went to "enliven his drink," leaving Voleta alone with Xenia, who looked like she was about to scream in disgust. Voleta hurried to calm her in a voice that was too low for Reggie to overhear. "Xen, this is perfect. With me out of the way, the prince will naturally look to you. You'll have him wrapped around your finger before I get back. You'll be the one getting the special passes from here on out."

Xenia's expression brightened in a flash. She took Voleta by the arm and nuzzled her like a child. "You said we weren't friends, but I knew you adored me!"

Iren and Ann sat stiffly on the fat settee under the wings of the mounted owl. They watched the young people lean upon the rail and gabble over the music. It seemed such a harmless scene.

Then the prince left, and Voleta came to them after embracing a beaming Xenia. Voleta showed Iren the wooden chit and explained what it was.

"All right, let's go," Iren said at once, starting to rise.

Voleta gentled her mountainous friend back down. "No, no, no. The chit's only good for one. Besides, Francis will be here. I think you should keep an eye on him."

Iren grumbled but conceded the point. If they had to be separated, it seemed better to do it here rather than at a raucous after-party, and she really didn't want to let the prince out of her sight. The usher came, a harmless-looking runt, and Voleta left with him.

But no sooner was she gone than Iren's imagination began to torment her. So much could go wrong. Marya might decide that Voleta was a charlatan and call a constable, or the port guard, or worse, her husband. And what if the prince had hired a thug to ambush Voleta the moment she was out of the room? Where exactly was the entrance to the backstage? How could Iren find her if Voleta got into trouble? How would she know if she did?

Iren's fretting flared into anger, which having no better target, focused upon the pinch of her uniform. She could feel every button, every seam, every saw-edge of lace.

Iren barked, "I am not a doll! Why do you keep trying to tart me up?"

Ann leapt in her seat at the sudden outburst. The small governess looked terribly hurt by the accusation. "Iren! Dear, I never thought of you as a—"

"I am not pretty!" Iren said, thumping herself on the chest. "I'm better than that."

"I'm so sorry! I wasn't trying to insult you. That's the last thing I wanted to do. I think you're wonderful," Ann said, gripping her hands in a frustrated knot. "I was just trying to help you—*fit in*, not because you're deficient in any way, but because—well, because frankly, fitting in has served me well enough. There isn't any advantage to standing out, not for people like you and me. So I learned to be bland and meek and patient; I learned to hold my tongue and wear the uniform and play the part. And as a reward, I'm allowed to live. Not on the streets. Not with my parents or a husband I don't want. But on my own, under my own steam. And all I have to do is...look the part." Her final word seemed to be an admission she had not expected. Her gaze turned inward.

Beyond the rail, the music stopped. The applause cracked like thunder, swelled to a supreme din, then slowly rumbled toward silence. On the main floor, the opulent audience stood as one, pressed into the aisles, and hurried to the lobby where the wine flowed and the wits dueled. Some considered the intermission the main attraction of the night, and they were eager for it to begin.

An usher poked his head through the curtained door. The two governesses observed Prince Francis shake his glass at the earl as if to say, *Go see what the blighter wants*.

Reluctantly, Reggie broke off his failing effort to impress Lady Xenia with an amusing anecdote about the time he had killed three birds with one shot. The earl tugged his vest, tried to conjure a soberer expression, then went to see what the attendant wanted.

The usher, who was blond as a broom and nearly as thin, spoke to Reggie with his head ducked as if in embarrassment. Iren couldn't hear a word of what he said, but she observed Reggie's expression turn increasingly grave. After a moment, the earl pulled a few coins from his pocket and gave them to the usher, who vanished in relief.

Reggie turned to face them. When Iren saw the look in his eyes, she knew at once something had happened. She stood with such force that the settee nearly toppled. Ann had to grip the bucking bench to keep from falling off.

Reggie put up his hands as Iren charged at him, and shouted, "She's fine, she's fine, she's perfectly fine! She's only fainted!"

Iren halted just shy of his velvet loafers. Reggie's hands trembled in the air between them.

"The Leaping Lady? Fainted?" the prince asked, though without much concern. "I suppose we must credit either the excitement or the rum." He snaked an arm around Xenia's waist, who looked as if she had just won a prize. "For goodness' sake, Reggie, put your hands down. She's a nursemaid, not a bull!"

Reggie lowered his hands, swallowed noisily and said, "They put the lady in the fur cooler. They thought the cool air might revive her."

"Take me to her," Iren said, already striding for the curtained door.

Prince Francis shook the naked ice in his tumbler and cinched the Lady Xenia closer to his hip. "Yes, be a chap, Reggie."

Reggie raised himself up like a gallant knight who'd been given a noble charge. He bowed to Xenia and came up wearing a perfect simper. "Pardon me, milady, but duty calls. I shall return momentarily. Of that you may be—"

"Now!" Iren boomed from the corridor, and the gallant knight squealed.

Chapter Twelve

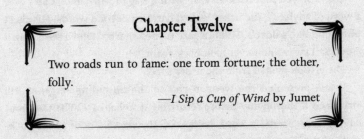

Two roads run to fame: one from fortune; the other, folly.

—*I Sip a Cup of Wind* by Jumet

Voleta followed the young usher, who had said twice already how honored he was to be guiding the Leaping Lady backstage. He stumbled upon a step while trying to keep her in sight over his shoulder, as if she were a hummingbird that might blur and disappear. He lavished her with praise: She was so much prettier than the etching in the *Reverie*, and graceful, and brave, and unique, and no wonder she had caught the prince's eye. And what a wretch he must seem to her, being only an usher without any hope of being anything better.

When the music stopped, and the audience began to pour from the auditorium, the usher cleared a path for her, calling "On your right, on your right! Make way for the Leaping Lady!" They descended to the mezzanine, then down to the lobby and around until the halls narrowed and the throng began to clear. Illustrious hanging tapestries gave way to solemn plaques that read, QUIET PLEASE and AUTHORIZED PERSONS ONLY and SNOOPS WILL BE EJECTED.

At last they came to a poorly lit and dingy dead end. A barricade of a man sat upon a stool reading a newspaper, both of which looked too small for him. He had the stripes of a sergeant on his arm and cotton wads in his ears. He folded the paper into quarters upon seeing their approach and came to his feet with an air of resentment.

The usher balked short of the guard. "Here I must leave you, milady. It has been an honor."

Voleta stayed him from leaving with a wag of her hand. "Can I give a word of advice?" The usher looked flattered beyond words. His chest puffed up like a dove's. Voleta's gaze turned sharp. "Find a port. Join a crew. Sail away and never look back again."

The elation melted from the usher's face.

Voleta presented the wooden chit to the unsmiling sergeant. He examined it thoroughly before returning it to her care. Then without having ever uttered a word, he opened the emerald door to the backstage of the Vivant.

Voleta was surprised by how familiar it all felt. The black painted hall was a tangle of ropes, props, and bodies, wedging one way or another. Musicians, flushed and perspiring from the first half of the evening's program, clung to their instruments and kept to their own. She passed a clique of violinists, a pod of cellists, and a herd of trumpeters, emptying their spit valves onto the floor. All of them were too preoccupied to notice her. The sudden sense of anonymity felt wonderful. She asked a group of flutists where the Mermaid's dressing room was. They rolled their eyes at the mention of the star's name but told her which turns to make and to look for the door that had a sequined star on it.

Digging through the crowd with her knees and elbows, Voleta soon found herself standing before a door emblazoned with a silver, spangling star.

She smoothed her dress, took a deep breath, then knocked.

The door flew open, and the Mermaid lunged at her with a joyful expression that seemed full of relief. Voleta yipped in surprise, dispelling Marya's excitement. Her face fell. Obviously, she had been expecting someone, and it hadn't been a shorn-headed stranger.

Marya let the door hang open and returned to the bench at her dressing table without another word.

Lamps bordered the immense mirror behind the vanity. The angle of the lights conspired to make whoever sat at the dressing table the brightest object in the cluttered room. Marya glowed like a full moon. A vase of ostrich feathers bloomed on one corner of her table. Among the many powder pots, brushes, and combs sat a headless bust, buried under strings of beads. Coat-trees lined two sides of the room, their branches swamped with robes, shawls, and capes. Framed portraits of past stars hung upon the wall behind the tree line. Those grinning idols seemed to stare at Voleta in judgment.

Marya's face was powdered to a skull-like paleness. Dark makeup made her eyes seem larger and brighter. Copper ribbons threaded her auburn hair, which was disheveled from her performance. Marya glanced at herself in the mirror, noted the disarray, but made no effort to correct it. She turned on her bench to face Voleta, her posture perfect, her gaze direct.

"You're that Leaping Lady, aren't you?"

"I don't like that name," Voleta said.

"No, of course not. I didn't care for the name they gave me either," Marya said, watching the young woman with undisguised curiosity. "You don't look much like your etching. But then, neither did I. They were done by the same man. Steeple, Stumple, Stimple, something like that. He has a terrible eye, or he's a complete hack, I'm not sure which. He gives us all the same face. He changes the hair, makes the bust a little bigger, a little smaller. Always the same face."

"I don't really like the papers either."

"Then there's some hope for you." Marya turned around on her bench, facing the voluminous mirror. She blotted away her lip rouge and then began to reapply it. "You came here on that enormous ship in the port everyone's talking about, the Sphinx's boat." It wasn't a question.

"I did."

"I'll give you this: You've made quite an entrance. I'm sure you'll do just fine. They like a big entrance."

"I'm not here for any of that. In fact, I'm looking forward to leaving.

I think all of this"—Voleta gestured at the parliament of hanging capes and smug stars, smiling in their gilded frames—"is a bit silly. You sing and play beautifully, but this place, these people, they're just awful."

Marya put down the lipstick and looked at Voleta's reflection. "You're rather young to be so disenchanted. Why come here if you're so above it all?"

"I came for you."

"For me?"

"Yes," Voleta said, and reached behind her to shut the door. "I've come to rescue you."

Marya's mouth dropped open as she turned to face Voleta again. A scoff turned into a laugh. "Rescue me? Whatever from?"

"From the duke. Senlin sent me."

Marya's mouth snapped shut with a click of her teeth. "If that were true, then you would know that I've already given him my answer. I can't go. I won't."

"Oh, they didn't want me to come. They said you'd already made up your mind, and—"

"They were right. You should've listened. What do you think you can say that he did not? And if he couldn't convince me, why do you expect to do any better?"

"What did he say?"

"He was very...frank." Marya began picking through the mess before her. She shuffled her brushes and powder puffs about distract-edly. She put on a bracelet, removed it, and put it on again. "He told me about all the desperate things he'd done, and how sorry he was for them. I forgave him, then asked him to leave me alone."

"Did he tell you that he saved my life, that he saved my brother's life? Because he did. More than once. He's made a lot of mistakes, but he's had a few victories, too. He has—"

Marya's arms came down heavily on her dressing table. "I am very glad to know he has such devoted friends. Really. It is inspiring. And I don't blame him for anything he did. I don't feel superior to him, or you, or anyone. We've all done desperate things to survive. But I'll tell you the same thing I told him: I'm not leaving my life."

"Why not?" Voleta shot back, crossing her arms.

Marya couldn't quite conceal her shock, or maybe she just didn't care to try. She shook her head, fluttered her eyes, and said, "It's really none of your business, young lady."

"Look, I understand you don't know me, but I have spent the past six months eating porridge, fleeing death, and looking for you. You say Senlin has made his peace with your answer. Well, help me make mine! Why won't you come? These people are horrid. This place is horrid! Your husband is—"

"Don't talk to me about my life!" Marya snapped, pounding the vanity hard enough to make her comb leap and clatter. "I know what my life is like!"

Realizing her lack of composure was not helping her case, Voleta took a deep breath and spoke again in a more constrained manner. "I've never had a dressing room like this, nor an audience as grand as the one you have. But not so long ago, there was a man who loomed over me and my life. His name was Rodion. He managed the venue... the *brothel* where I lived and worked, and which I could not leave. He berated me. He tormented me. He dominated me. He made me dance for my dinner and told me every day how lucky I was to be caught in his trap, to be lashed to his stage, to be under his thumb. Because the only thing standing between me and the most unspeakable fate was him. He was the devil holding back the darkness." Voleta found that her voice had begun to tremble. She cleared her throat and said more distinctly: "I had all but given up any hope of escape. And then Senlin—"

"I'm sorry!" Marya said so loudly and firmly it sounded more like a rebuke than an apology. "I'm sorry your life was so horrible. But please do not confuse your misery with mine. I love my husband. He is a sensible man, a keen business partner, and a fine fa... I have no wish to return to the scrabbling, silly life I lived before!" As she spoke, she began pulling off her jewelry—ring, earring, bangle, and choker—as if those glistening charms were the source or her unhappiness. "Now, you must excuse me, I have a performance to finish." Bared of her jewels, Marya rose stiffly and began to press Voleta back toward the door.

"I know it's frightening, but believe me, it gets easier when you're away from it, away from him. Believe me! You have to believe me!" Voleta pleaded in a desperate rush, retreating even as she begged.

Without answering, Marya opened the door, preparing to shove her unwanted guest into the hall. Both she and Voleta were surprised to find themselves confronted by a red-cheeked maid holding a swaddled infant in her arms.

The maid began speaking at once, "I'm so sorry, milady. I know I'm terribly late, but the duke kept us so long. He said I shouldn't even bother to come, but I knew you'd want to see her even if only for a moment." The maid passed the gently fussing infant into Marya's arms. "She had a long nap, and she ate well."

Marya's face glowed with an affection that dimmed the whole world for a moment. She kissed the infant, nuzzled her, and said, "It's all right. I know how he is. Thank you, Molly."

Voleta stared in amazement at the child. "Who is that? Wait, is that—"

"Be quiet," Marya said. She kissed the infant again and then slid her back into the maid's arms. "Take Olivet home, please. I hope not to be late, but don't keep her up on my account."

"Yes, milady," Molly said, wrapping the infant up again in the hall.

Marya shut the door, keeping Voleta inside with her. The whole attitude of her expression changed. Her former confidence and austerity were in shambles. She clutched Voleta's arm, her stare stretched by fear. "You must not speak of this."

"How have you kept this a secret?"

"You have no idea what he's capable of."

"Who? The duke? Wait, does Senlin know? Is that his child?"

Marya didn't answer, but she didn't have to. The truth was stamped upon her face. "Swear you'll never tell him."

"Why would I keep this from—"

"Because it's the only thing keeping us safe."

"From the duke?"

"Of course from the duke! He has agreed to raise Olivet as his daughter so long as I sing, and smile, and...give him a son next. As soon as I give him a son, he'll adopt my daughter publicly, formally. He'll say she's an orphan, but I'll get to have her." Marya looked away. "The doctors said we had to wait three months before trying for another child. Three months are nearly gone."

"That's all the more reason to flee! You have to come with me. Marya, we can protect you from the duke. My friends are very—"

"No, no, you can't. He's rich beyond understanding. He can move fleets and drum up armies. He has allies everywhere. Even if I could slip away, he would not stop until he hunted me down and dragged me back here. He would kill Olivet. He would kill me. He is a jealous, merciless man."

A sharp knock on the door startled them both. Someone shouted through the door, "Two minutes!"

"Please, please, I beg you for the sake of my child, for the sake of *his* child, do not tell Tom. Please. Just let us be."

Marya gathered up the train of her gown and opened the door of her dressing room. The hall was a flurry of commotion. Marya was about to step into the current of bodies, but hesitated long enough to say, "You should go. Go before they decide they want to keep you. Once they decide that...it's too late." And then she was gone.

Voleta stood in the Mermaid's dressing room, dazed and searching. In the corridor outside, the rush to the stage crested and then began to wane. A tardy violinist rushed past with one arm in the sleeve of his flapping tuxedo jacket. Then there was no one, and she was alone.

She realized her hand ached, and she opened it to discover she had been clenching the wooden backstage chit so hard she'd driven all the color from her hand. "Oh, fun," she said, remembering who had given her the token.

She looked up to find Prince Francis blocking the open door. An ugly leer curled his handsome mouth; his eyes looked black under his lowered brow. "Fun, indeed," he said.

"Oh. Hello. Come to walk me back, milord?" Voleta said, a thrill of fear rolling across her scalp. He shut the door before she could move to stop him. "Or are you trying to start a rumor?"

"Have you ever felt the torment of love?" the prince said, running his hand over the robes that hung from the coat-trees. There wasn't enough room for her to skirt him and get to the door. She thought, perhaps if she drew him in a little farther . . . "Back when I was a youth, I knew a young lady named Cordelia Tantalus." He spoke the name as if it were an exotic spice. "I was completely smitten with her. I pined for her for years and years. Her parents were friends of my parents, so we grew up in each other's company. She was beautiful, clever, quick-witted. She called me her confidant. She would sit on my lap as if I were her favorite chair and tell me all about her fascinations for other men." The prince took up the silk sleeve of a hanging blouse and pressed it to his cheek. Through the walls of the dressing room, they heard the rumble and trill of the orchestra. The performance had resumed. The framed stars rattled on the walls as if in excitement. Voleta took another step back. "She made me call her *Cory* as if she were my sister. She was an expert at finding ways to torment me with cold affection and warm flirtation. She could say she loved me, but in just such a way I knew it meant she never would."

Keeping her expression attentive, Voleta inched to one side, hoping to get a better angle at the door. She should've expected this. She had misread the trap in her eagerness to see Marya. She felt like a fool for allowing him to corner her. She could call for help, but no one would hear her through the closed door and over the blast of the orchestra.

Prince Francis made a sudden expansive gesture, and she jumped back, jarring the dressing table. "And yet I hoped, and I endured, and I suffered, believing that she would one day wake and realize that her presumptive brother wanted more than anything to be her lover." He reached over Voleta's shoulder and plucked a feather from the vase. "So it went for many years: I, without the courage to be frank; she, without the decency to love me.

"Then one day, not long after my seventeenth birthday, I found myself standing on the bowsprit of one of my father's airships, gripping a scarf that I had stolen from her neck while she napped." He stroked the feather under his chin. "I felt like such a worthless wretch! I was a man without birthright. My head was full of self-destruction. If I could not have her, then I would give myself to the void! Then, while I was imagining what sort of crater I would leave in the earth, a gust of wind blew up and snatched her scarf from my hand." The prince waved the ostrich feather about then touched the plump end to the tip of Voleta's nose. "The wind didn't ask if it could or should. It didn't say please or thank you. The wind just came and took what it wanted."

"We're missing the show, milord," Voleta said. He pretended not to hear her.

"The wind isn't hopeful or jealous or wicked. It is transparent. It is purely itself." He reached out and stroked the side of her head above her ear, pressing his body against hers. "I am the wind, Voleta, and you are my exotic little scarf. And I shall carry you off as I please."

She fixed him with an unwavering stare, and said, "Francis, I've blown stiffer winds out of my arse."

She brought her knee up with such force it stole his breath.

He doubled forward, lowering his head as he wheezed in agony. She snatched a powder pot from the table and smashed it upon the back of his head. A plume of talc billowed out as the prince grasped his head and staggered backward. The cloud of powder roiled across the floor and bunched upon the walls, vanishing the coatracks and the jealous stares of the dead stars. The stifled beat of a timpani rang in the distance as they coughed.

Pale as a statue, Voleta leapt atop the dressing table and kicked at the white-faced prince. She clipped his ear, knocking loose a puff of talc from his head. Though stunned by the blow, he was quick enough to catch her foot. He twisted it about, throwing her facedown upon the table. She crashed among the vats and brushes with a shout of frustration and pain. He grabbed at the skirt of her gown and pulled, trying to drag her from the high ground and get her onto the floor. She kicked with her free leg, catching him in the gut with her heel.

The prince staggered back among the coats, stirring up a thick cloud that enveloped him.

Voleta wiped at her floured face; her agitated eyes streamed with tears.

She hurled a ceramic vat of rouge into the fog, and heard it pop uselessly upon the wall. She threw another makeup pot and heard a splash of shattering glass. A picture frame clattered to the floor.

Realizing that the cloud gave him cover, the prince endeavored to stir up the powder even more. He shook the cloaks and fanned the fog until the air was as white and opaque as a bedsheet. Voleta attacked the smoke screen, pitching a pot of blue eyeshadow, a silver comb, a plated brush, and anything she laid her hands on, targeting the sound of flapping capes and rattling coatracks. She thought she struck the mark once or twice, though it was hard to tell amid the chaos. She picked up the heavy glass vase, dumping ostrich plumes everywhere, and raised it above her head.

The prince charged from the murk, catching her about the waist and driving her back against the mirror. She lost her grip upon the vase, and it rolled down his back and cracked upon the floor. Ignoring the flash of pain in her back, Voleta locked his head under her arm. She stretched and squeezed his neck against her ribs with all the strength she had. He tried to lift her, to raise his arms to get at her, but she hooked one leg over his back to give more leverage to her weight. She pinned one of his arms to his side. He grunted in frustration and heightening alarm. He seemed to have not anticipated such a fight. He had used the clumsy tactics of a bully who'd won more fights through surprise and intimidation than ability. She felt his panic, his gasping, the trembling of his hands, and knew she would squeeze his throat until he lost consciousness, squeeze until he turned purple then blue then white again. And only then would she think about letting go.

The twin-barreled pistol, no larger than his palm, seemed to appear out of nowhere, though he must've pulled it from his pocket. The prince waved the gun blindly over his trapped head, trying to point it at her as she craned out of the way. The first shot cracked the air, deafening them both. The boom of the orchestra shrank into a muted rumble.

The small caliber bullet punched a star into the mirror behind her head. The muzzle added a bitter whiff of smoke to the sweetly scented cloud that possessed the room.

As she wrenched his head like a stubborn weed, she wondered

what the morning post would make of this. LEAPING LADY CHOKES PRINCE UNTIL HE SOILS HIMSELF!

She could only hope the fashion would catch on.

Voleta did not hear the second shot, nor did she see it, nor did she feel the bullet when it pierced her head.

Then there was no room, and there was no light, and there was no her anymore.

Chapter Thirteen

Only people who go to bed early believe in happy endings. We night owls understand that happiness does not dwell in finales. It resides in anticipation, in revelry, and in worn-out welcomes. Endings are always sad.

—Oren Robinson of the *Daily Reverie*

Half an hour earlier, Ann Gaucher had been trying to decide whether she should say something to her charge about her shocking lack of self-respect. The lady was letting the prince pet her like the family dog. But then, the moment Iren and Reggie left to find and revive Voleta (the poor dear!) the prince seemed to lose all interest in Xenia. He dropped her hand as if it were a dead fish and went to the bar to make himself another drink. Ann noticed he did not pour from the same decanter he'd been tipping all night but pulled a dusty rarity from behind the bar. He splashed the honey-colored liquor into a snifter and inhaled it as if it were a rose.

Xenia pursued him, seeming confused by his sudden change of mood, but nevertheless determined to throw herself at him.

"Now that we're alone, Your Highness, you can tell me what you really think of that funny little foreign girl. She's an absolute shock, isn't she? Always dressing like she's going to her own funeral. She can hardly hold a fork, and she's a terrible flirt. I must've seen her kiss a dozen men since she arrived."

"You have not," Prince Francis said, smiling as he sipped and savored his brandy. "I understand why you don't like her, though. She's competition, and you aren't up for much competition, are you? The marquis has been squandering your inheritance for years. Oh, I'd like to see his books!"

The insult seemed to gore Xenia, and Ann watched as she flinched and paled.

"All those lavish parties just begin to smack of desperation after a while, don't they? And he still hasn't managed to scare up a willing spouse for his daughter. What are you now, Xenia, twenty-five, twenty-six years old? Thirty is just around the corner!" He leaned his elbows on the bar and addressed her casually, indifferently, as if she were his little sister. Xenia grimaced in despair. "Do you ever feel like your life is a balloon that has a hole in it somewhere? You can't find it, but you can hear it hissing, and you can feel the ship going down, down, down." He swirled the liquor up the walls of his snifter. "Really, you could do a lot worse than Reggie. In fact, I think you ought to be grateful for a chance at an earl."

Xenia's bottom lip trembled, and her eyes glazed with tears, but the prince gave her no mercy. Realizing the effort was wasted, Xenia moped back to the balcony rail, where she hung and writhed like an overtired child. The prince watched her with faint amusement.

A moment later, Reggie returned from the hall, out of breath, but composing himself quickly. He patted down his fringe of hair, thin as an eyelash, and tested his sour breath in the cup of his hand. He approached Xenia with what seemed renewed purpose. Xenia found a smile for the wretched earl, who at least was better than a count.

Reggie announced that Voleta was quite all right now—fully recovered, in fact. The chilly air of the fur cooler had worked its magic. The Lady Contumax had decided to go on to meet the Mermaid, and she had taken her monstrous governess along with her.

Xenia said, "Oh, I'm so glad," though she looked miserable.

The prince tossed back the last of his commemorative drink like a man steeling his nerves. He pulled a second wooden token from his waistcoat, flipped it with his thumb, and snatched the backstage pass from the air.

"All right, Reggie," he said. "Time to warm our hands on the fires we've built." The prince slapped his friend on the back, pulled the curtain over the door aside, and was gone.

"Alone at last, milady!" Reggie said, taking up Xenia's hand. He moistened it with a kiss, and she giggled dutifully.

Overlooked and all but forgotten, Ann observed the prince's abrupt exit from under the wing of the great owl. She frowned to herself. The whole situation made her terribly uneasy, though she didn't have long to ponder the cause of her apprehension because Xenia put her to work with a dozen petty requests. "Ann, can you freshen our drinks, please. And pour them the way Papa does. I like mine with a little more lime. And can you do anything about this light? I feel it's a little high, a little severe, isn't it? Can't we shade the lamps a little more so the earl doesn't have to squint? It's such a magnificent visage, milord! I could stare at you all day. Is there any candy? I would love a piece of candy. Could you have a look behind the bar, Ann? Yes, even a cherry would do. I love cherries in syrup, don't you, milord?"

While the earl and her ladyship flirted, Ann spent the intermission dashing about, feeling whipped by her worry. It wasn't until the earl stoppered Xenia's mouth with a flurry of noisy kisses that Ann had a moment to sit and think. The prince had always had two tokens, yet he had sent Voleta to meet the Mermaid alone. Why? To make the lady feel at ease? Surely not. To separate her from Iren? That would make sense, but then wasn't it convenient for the prince that Voleta had fallen ill, otherwise Iren would never have let him out of her sight, and he never would've had an opportunity to use the second pass. Unless Voleta hadn't fainted at all. Perhaps the original usher had been prompted to interrupt the evening with news of Voleta's sudden illness, a lie whose sole purpose was to draw Iren out. It had already been established the lady's governess could not accompany Voleta backstage. So why hadn't Iren returned? Where was she? Iren would never have allowed the prince to use his pass unless she—

Ann sprang from her seat at the realization. Working to keep the panic from her face, she marched over to Reggie and Xenia, canoodling upon the rail.

"Excuse me, Lady Xenia, shouldn't we go check on your guest?"

Xenia looked dazedly at Ann. "Don't be silly, Ann. Can't you see I'm talking to the earl?" The earl's mouth crawled along her neck like a snail upon a garden wall.

"Milady—" Ann began, but Lady Xenia cut her off.

"You're not my mother!"

Ann's patience snapped. "Look, you spoiled brat, either you come with me right this minute and drop this salivating hound, or I will go alone, and you will never see me again."

Reggie looked up with dampened cheeks, his irritation tempered by his lust. He seemed to elect to let the lady handle her staff.

Xenia coughed through her indignation and finally spat out, "You can't talk to me like that! You're just a *maid*! I'm going to tell Papa what you said. He'll put you out on your ear!"

Ann regarded her charge with pity, her affection finally exhausted. She said, "Lady Xenia, I hope you're still happy with your choice in a year's time. I think I shall be happy with mine."

Out in the corridor, Ann heard the thumping almost at once. She followed the drumming down the curving hall, lined on either side by eroded urns and chalky curtains to the other exclusive boxes. She came upon the same broom-thin usher who'd come to fetch Reggie, now stationed in front of a door plated in steel and trimmed in punched leather that led to the fur cooler. He was sweating and pop-eyed and could hardly look at Ann when she halted in front of him with her fists on her hips.

"I'm to say there's an ape loose in the fur room, ma'am, and you can't go in there," the usher said.

"Look, I'm going to open this door. That's not in question." The door bumped fiercely behind them, and the youth jumped. "The question is: Do you want to be here when I do?"

With hardly a moment's deliberation, the usher retreated down the hall at an undisguised sprint.

Ann tapped her fingernails upon the cooler door and spoke loudly into the seam. "Iren, dear! It's me, Ann. I'm going to open the door now. Please, don't crush me!"

Hearing nothing for a moment, Ann unlatched the door and swung it open, releasing a puff of frigid air. Iren stood panting in the middle of the dim fur closet amid a great chaos of coats, stoles, and racks, the evidence of her recent raging.

"Where is he?" Iren asked, her breath squalling from her mouth. "Where's that muddy earl?"

"There's no time for him now. Prince Francis has gone after Voleta. I don't know what he means to do, but I'm sure it isn't good."

"Where's the backstage?" Iren asked, stepping into the warmer hall.

"I haven't the faintest idea." Ann saw that the sleeves of Iren's uniform were split about the elbows.

"Where's the kid in the hat?"

"The usher? He ran away."

Groaning in fury, Iren ripped the sleeves from her dress, tearing them at the shoulder, and threw them upon the carpet. Meaning to rend the constricting skirt as well, her hands went to her hips, where she felt the lump of the Sphinx's mechanical moth.

A revelation pierced her fury: If the moth had been able to find the little moon inside a sprawling city, then wouldn't it be able to do the same inside the mazing halls of the Vivant?

Gingerly, Iren extracted the fragile cylinder from her pocket while Ann looked on, amazed by her friend's sudden composure. Iren turned the mechanism's head until it gave a small click, and its wings unfurled. The paisley wings moved slowly, as if testing the air.

"This is probably goodbye," Iren said, glancing away from the clockwork insect long enough to look at Ann. The small governess bent, took the hem of Iren's skirt in hand, and deftly split it along the seam up to the thigh.

"There, now you can run," Ann said, ducking Iren's gaze, apparently to keep her from seeing the emotion in her eyes. "How easy it is to undo a day's work!"

Still holding out her palm to hold up the waking moth, Iren stooped and pulled up Ann's chin with the side of one rough knuckle. Ann let her head be raised and forced a smile onto her face. "I think you enjoyed that," Iren said.

Ann coughed a teary laugh and threw her arms around Iren's neck.

The moth leapt from her hand and flew down the shapely corridor in a bouncing line.

The two women parted, and Iren began to run.

The doorman to the backstage shifted on his stool. His leg had fallen asleep yet again.

There had been a time when he enjoyed music, a time when he sought out performances in the evenings and saved the programs in a little box under his bed, a time when he held opinions on whether the waltz had killed the cadenza and whether an etude should be passed off as a melodic refrain, opinions which he had argued from the deep couches of the salons, long into the wee hours of the night.

But that was before he had sat down on the hard stool outside the backstage of the Vivant. He had discovered that listening to music through a wall was like kissing a woman through a pane of glass: It stripped away all the physical delight and left behind only the absurd shape of the thing, which was repulsive. Having to put up with the spoiled musicians and their entitled visitors only added insult to aesthetic injury.

The two things that kept him sane were the cotton wads that plugged his ears and the evening dispatch that occupied his eyes. The combination turned torment into monotony, which was at least endurable.

This particular evening had been slightly more tedious that usual. The writing in the *Reverie* was bad, and whoever was throttling the piano onstage was about to burst the dams in his ears. His thoughts were already drifting toward the bottle of tawny port waiting for him at home when the paisley moth landed on the top edge of his paper.

He regarded it curiously, and then realized a very large someone was charging directly at him. There wasn't time to react, though the music seemed to slow and thicken into a rumble. The doorman thought, *Ah, well! I've been wanting to retire*. Then a fist cleaved his newspaper and relieved him of the tedium of consciousness.

Iren did not linger over the flattened sentry and his toppled stool. She pushed open the door to the backstage, letting the moth continue its homing pursuit. The backstage, dark and all but empty save for a few furtive stagehands, reverberated with the music being played on the other side of the curtain. It was so loud it made her insides quiver. Though it was not only the music that made her tremble, but the familiarity of this place. It reminded her of the Steam Pipe's backstage. The association inflamed Iren, not just the memory of Rodion's belligerence, egotism, and abuse, but the memory of her own inaction, her own complicity in the exploitation of so many women. Guilt stabbed at her, and she raised no defense.

The moth fluttered onward like a fragment of a dream, leading her down a shrouded corridor that curved without apparent end. At last, the clockwork insect alighted on a dressing room door, distinguished by a glittering star.

Iren did not test the knob before opening the door with her heel.

The prince, covered from head to foot in talcum powder, stood smoking a cigarillo. He held one hand to his forehead like a man pondering a riddle. It looked as if someone had slung a bag of flour about the room. Everything from the floor to the coat-trees to the ceiling was swathed in white—all except for the red pool on the floor by the prince's feet. Voleta's head lay upon the crimson as if it were a cushion, and not her spilled life.

"Oh, blast," Prince Francis muttered.

Iren grabbed the nearest coat-tree, shaking the robes off in the doing, and charged the prince with the rack leveled like a lance. The point caught him squarely in the chest, the force lifting him from his feet, carrying him over the dressing bench and the table, awash with spilled pots and paste jewelry, to the wide mirror, framed in yellow light. Though the prince could retreat no further, the pole did not stop.

The mirror cracked under the stave. The shatter seemed to hold him like a spiderweb.

Pinned to the wall with his feet off the floor, the prince could neither speak nor move. His eyes roved the dressing chamber as it filled with a numbing light. He felt a tepid wind blow upon his face. A scarf flew by, vibrant and familiar. The blue sky filled the room. A flock of scarves soared past, their corners flapping like wings. He looked down and found no ship below him and no earth beneath that. Everything was a darkening blue, a starless sky.

He began to fall and fell forever.

Iren crouched over Voleta.

Suddenly, the girl who could never sit in a chair or stay in bed or walk past a tree without climbing it was lying very still. Her eyes were wide, but they did not look like her eyes any longer: They were dull and sapped of life. Blood brightened her lips.

Iren found the small, round wound under her jaw. She searched tenderly but could not find a second hole. Voleta's head rolled, unresisting, in her hands.

She was filled with a sudden urge to start a blaze, to burn the music hall to the ground with everyone still in it. She'd bar the doors and let them all cook inside their boxes.

That urge conjured up the memory of when she had caught Voleta and Adam conspiring in the stage curtains of the Steam Pipe. While the auditorium filled with smoke from a forgotten cigar, the siblings had been whispering so intently they had not noticed her discover them. When Iren yelled "Fire," Voleta had startled like a deer and run.

It had been the first word Iren had ever said to her. *Fire*.

She felt like screaming the word again now. This felt like a fire. Everything inside her was burning and turning black.

Then Voleta drew a whisper of a breath.

Frozen by hope, Iren watched as the young woman's chest rose, the movement small but definite. She was breathing. Where there was breath, there was life.

Though what could any physician do to treat a bullet to the head? This sort of injury required a miracle, and Iren knew of only one man who trafficked in miracles. If the Sphinx could save the Red Hand from a fatal fall, he could save Voleta.

Iren knew that as soon as the music stopped, the dead prince would be discovered. The constabulary would be summoned. When they caught her, she would be shot, and Voleta would perish. No, Iren's only hope was to get back to the ship and quickly.

She snatched a cloak from a coatrack that was buried well enough to have escaped being doused in talc. She swaddled Voleta in the hooded cape, cradling her in her arms. All she had to do was outrun the news of the prince's death. Considering the caliber of gossips that she was dealing with, Iren knew it was going to be a very close race.

The piazza was no less crowded now. The mob cackled and sang and argued with itself, an insensible herd that milled between the city and the landmarks about the ringdom's spine. Iren broke a path with her shoulder, glancing up at the stars to get her bearings. She had previously noticed that the wine bottle constellation pointed toward Port Virtue. She corrected her path before leaving the spacious mall and entering the tighter streets of the city.

It was more challenging to follow the gas stars from the bottom of the urban valleys, but her sense of direction was good enough to guide her through unfamiliar turns and around abrupt dead ends she encountered. She avoided the most congested blocks, where mobs clotted about theaters, parlors, and salons. She had a run of good luck, where it seemed each blockage funneled her to some clearer path, but then she found herself boxed in by a brass band, which paraded through the street ahead of her and wove around to cut off the next street as well. She turned down an alley that was scarcely wider than her shoulders. She pressed Voleta's head into her chest, afraid it might scrape against something in the gloom. Then, amid the compound shadows of that narrow passage, a rough voice rang out. It said, "Come the Hod King! Come the Hod King!" again and again like an inconsolable lunatic. Old bunting and rags tangled about her feet. She felt as if she were running in a dream. The alley seemed to grow longer, her feet heavier. She roared back at the madman shouting in the dark. The dry sound of flapping wings answered her.

Then all at once, the alley broke upon a more brightly lit lane. The storefronts on either side of the road were consumed with racks and racks of shoes. The shops were closed for the night, which thinned the traffic out. Realizing she had begun to wheeze, Iren paused to catch her breath. The street was dotted with glowing discs. A young boy crouched upon one of the plates like a frog on a lily pad. A large sack sat on the ground nearby, bulging with what seemed an assortment of sticks. He held his hand flat against the light and studied the orange glow of his fingers. She saw that he was missing an ear. The scar that ran out from the bare hole and down his jaw seemed too old for one so young.

Iren asked him, "Which way to the port?" It wasn't until the question was out that Iren realized the boy wore the simple wrap of a hod.

He looked up at her, towering and sleeveless, her immense arms clutching a bundle. "Her toes will get cold," he said, pointing at the pair of dangling bare feet that jutted from the bottom of the cloak. Iren gathered Voleta's feet back into her swaddle, wondering vaguely when her shoes had fallen off. Then the young hod pointed down the street and said, "The port's that way."

"Thank you," Iren said, already starting to move in that direction.

"Come the Hod King," the boy replied, and was smiling when Iren glanced back at him.

Two navy-coated constables appeared at the end of the lane ahead of her. They nodded, signaling that they had taken note of her, but they did not seem overly concerned, which she took as a good sign. It meant she was still outrunning word of the prince's murder. But then as she moved to one side of the street to pass them at a more comfortable distance, the uniformed pair seemed to reconsider. Perhaps they were curious to know why a woman in a torn uniform was running about with a person-shaped bundle in her arms. They moved to intercept her.

Iren entertained a violent impulse—she could take them by surprise, bowl them down, perhaps steal their pistols. But she decided against it. Once she outed herself, things would happen very quickly, and she didn't want to put the port guard on notice.

"What have got you there?" one of the constables asked. The black strap of his cap had come loose from his chin and bounced upon his lip. He stretched his neck, peering at the cloak.

Deciding it was better to tell the truth than show it, Iren said, "It's Lady Voleta. She is tired from the party, and I am taking her home."

"Lady Vo...It's the Leaping Lady, is it? I told you, Gaffo: Tonight had a lucky feel to it! Now we get to see if she's pretty as the papers say." The constable peered more curiously at the hood covering Voleta's face. Iren twisted to hold her a little farther away.

"The lady's not feeling well," she said. She forced a smile onto her face, though the result was a little more berserk than beguiling.

The constable looked disappointed, but in a professional sort of way. He seemed to understand the lady's governess was just doing her job. "Caught a touch of the champagne flu, I expect," the constable said. "I hear she's been having quite a—"

He was cut off by the sharp tweet of a whistle echoing down the street. "Another bulletin. That's our luck! Well, you get the lady home, and have a good night." The constables snapped their heels together and began to trot down the lane in the direction of the whistle. Iren could see blue-coated men gathering in the intersection. She had little doubt what the bulletin was about.

She turned the other way and broke into a run. She didn't care about being inconspicuous or jostling Voleta, much as she feared making the wound worse. They had to get to the ship. She could feel the ringdom closing upon them like a trap.

The city broke open and the crowd broke with it. The wall of the Tower, tiled in blue, rose darkly before her, curving overhead into the field of winking stars. The train station was near enough that she could see the steam rolling out of the tunnel. She reached it the same moment the night air came alive with the shriek of whistles.

Rather than risk the platform, she ran down the narrow path between the engine and the tunnel wall, then leapt onto the tracks and sprinted over the railroad ties, her footfalls growing louder with the receding chug of the engine. It was night, and the mouth of the tunnel opened upon an overcast sky. In a moment, they would be safe aboard the ship; in another moment they would be under way, flying back to the Sphinx and his miracles. By morning, Voleta would be up and running about...

Iren emerged from the tunnel, through city gates, and out into a deep and windy gloom. The port lights were out, a foreboding sign she did not immediately appreciate. She trotted down the steps that fanned out to the banks of lead soldiers.

Iren didn't notice that all the cannons of the lead soldiers were pointed at the tied-up *State of Art*, but she did observe that the ship's main hatch stood open and saw the light of the interior pouring out.

Three black moons filled the air behind the moored *State of Art*. The *Ararat*, which was lashed to the lip of the port, was almost indistinguishable from the starless sky. Iren had but a moment to marvel before the *Ararat* opened fire.

The dreadnaught did not attack the *State of Art*'s gleaming hull. It volleyed instead at the ship's envelope, that long regal pontoon of silk and hydrogen that held the vessel aloft. The arching missiles had fiery tails. Iren saw at once they were not cannonballs; they were burning lances.

The fiery darts struck the immense envelope in a dozen spots. Waves of orange flame bled across the silken skin.

Iren's legs shook and gave way beneath her.

The sun seemed to briefly rise over the beam of the Sphinx's ship. The explosion warmed her face.

From her knees and with Voleta pressed to her heart, Iren watched the *State of Art* fall from the sky.

The Black Trail

Hope is a dream. Despair,
a nightmare. Only the
nocturnal struggle is real.
—*I Sip a Cup of Wind* by Jumet

Though Senlin was ignorant of the exact manner of Finn Goll's fall from wealthy importer to beleaguered hod, he could only suppose that his devastating exit from his former employer's port had played a part in the man's downfall.

Senlin suspected it was more than foul luck that had carried him back into Finn Goll's orbit. No, Goll wasn't one to rely upon coincidence. He was a man who preferred hedged bets and fail-safes and byzantine snares. Of all the people Senlin had crossed since arriving in the Tower, it was Goll who seemed the most likely to be petty in his grudges and patient in his revenge. And Senlin had little doubt that if the former lord of port thought that he was owed a debt, he would demand it be repaid, though whether Finn would prefer to be compensated in gold or gore remained to be seen.

What was readily apparent was that the crimes of Captain Mudd were well known in the zealot camp. Mudd and his crew had invaded one of the movement's essential encampments, touched off a keg of powder, and taken the lives of eleven hods, injuring twice as many, during their escape.

Senlin briefly considered attempting to correct the record. The fact was, he had gone to the Golden Zoo in search of a fair and honest trade and had instead become the victim of Marat's false hospitality. It had been Marat who dispatched his men to sack the *Stone Cloud* and pick it down to the ribs. Senlin and his crew's only crimes were done in self-defense. They were otherwise innocent. Voleta's raiding of the larder notwithstanding.

But Senlin was not so foolish as to think he could reason with an angry mob. Seeing no better option, he continued to assert his reformation. He was a changed man. He was a hod now. Yes, he had been many despicable persons in the past, had led a number of lives under a variety of pseudonyms, but all of those personalities were dead. And had he not proven the earnestness of his conversion by his recent deeds in Pelphia?

Seeing that the main of the crowd was still unconvinced, Senlin professed his desire to learn the new tongue and (doing his best to not flinch at the lie) shouted at the pressing masses, "The written word only makes idle minds idler and the corrupt more dangerous!"

"You truly believe that?" Sodiq asked, seeming skeptical now of every word that came from Senlin's mouth. "Tell me, Captain Mudd, what do you think erasure adds to our world?"

Senlin's mind raced. What would a zealot say? Surely they would blame the knowledge rather than its application, much as a gambler blames the cards rather than his play. Quickly enough, he blurted out, "Imagine if our race could only lose the formula for gunpowder! Wouldn't that be spectacular? Imagine if we could forget the process for capturing hydrogen, storing it, wielding it. We have been bloodied by our own cleverness, have we not? We are bedeviled by books!"

The mob's baying was somewhat mollified by this, though the cooling of certain tempers seemed to fan the fires of others. Several hods called for the blinder to be put back on him, and Senlin shivered when someone suggested they introduce millipedes in the blinder before bolting it on his head.

But the more the mob squalled, the more placid Sodiq looked. Senlin saw he was clearly more perplexed than incensed. He appeared to be having a difficult time reconciling the fact that he had been saved by Captain Mudd, the hod slayer.

Abruptly, Sodiq barked at the frenzied hods to go back to their business. Didn't the camp have mushroom beds to tend, beetle traps to empty, and infants to nurse? The zealots dispersed at once and without a grumble, all except Finn Goll, who sat down on the stone bench before the burbling fountain. The former lord of port wiggled his rump to make it clear he wasn't going anywhere.

"What do you want, Hodder Finn?" The weariness in Sodiq's voice hinted at a strained history. Goll looked gaunt and older than the half year that had passed since Senlin had last seen him, though surely part of his aging was owed to his closely shaved head and the absence of his former tailored attire. Now he was as pale as a turnip and done up in rags. There was more silver than black in his stubble. Yet his expressions and gestures were as youthful and active as ever, and Senlin saw the specter of the man who'd interviewed him once upon a time on a beer-me-go-round.

"What do *I* want?" Goll said, pressing his short fingers into his puffed chest in a show of unconvincing innocence. "I just want to help my fellow hods. And of course, I want to see the Tower ground down to a stump no taller than a footstool. I want to prop my aching feet on this old pillar and—"

"Spit it out, Finn," Sodiq said with a roll of his wrist.

"Well, I suppose I want to collect the purse for turning this criminal in," Goll said.

"Now, wait just a minute," Tarrou said. Up until then, John had been silent and only making expressions of general shock, presumably for the camp's benefit. His act had been convincing enough that Senlin was left a little unsure that his large friend was still entirely on his side. "You didn't catch anyone! I dragged the scoundrel here. If anyone deserves that reward, it's me!"

"You? You didn't even know who you had!" Goll had to tilt his head back to a comical degree in order to look down his nose at John, though he managed it.

"I knew I had someone special. They don't put those blinders on just anybody."

"Well, I tell you what—you keep the bucket, and I'll take the man," Goll said.

Sodiq raised his hand. Previously, the gesture had made him look like a reticent student, but now Senlin thought he looked more like an old man in a café wearily attempting to attract the attention of a server. "Hodder John, Hodder Finn, I'm not sure you have an equal claim to the man, but I find your eagerness to pillage the cause equally disgusting. The bounty was meant to attract the assistance of outsiders.

It was not intended to encourage followers to drain our coffers. And believe me, a hundred minas is not enough to redeem either of you. You are hods. You will always be hods. If you want to escape the black trail, the only way is to destroy it." The old hod's sternum stood out as proudly as a breastplate. "But why am I wasting my breath on the two of you? Your greed has made you forgetful. Neither of you have yet to deliver this man to Hodder Luc, and those are the terms of the bounty."

"Then I'll finish what I started," Tarrou said, grasping Senlin by the arm.

Finn Goll hopped up onto the bench and seized Senlin's remaining arm. "Finish what *you* started? I found this rascal while he still had mud on his boots."

"Well, if you want to turn the beggar into a wishbone, I'm happy to oblige," Tarrou roared. "You pull that arm, I'll pull this one, and whoever comes away with the bigger piece wins!"

"Stop it, both of you!" Sodiq's voice was well suited to giving orders, and both the brawler and the little person dropped their hold on Senlin. "You'll deliver him to Hodder Luc in Mola Ambit together, and you'll share the shame of your reward. And just to make sure that neither of you get any wicked notions: If the both of you don't arrive, whatever the reason, the survivor will be charged with the murder of a fellow hod and hanged for the crime." The proclamation seemed to finally dampen John and Finn's passion. Sodiq smiled at their deflated spirits, adding, "Oh, don't worry: You can carry your reward with you to the gallows. A little extra weight never spoiled a hanging."

As the prisoner, it fell to Senlin to play the role of mule for the group. The pack he was given was an assemblage of sackcloth, twine, and stiff rawhide, which sawed blood from his bare shoulders almost immediately. The pack contained fresh bandages and herbs for Hodder John's poultice, three coarse blankets, six pounds of "beetle cakes" (which Senlin was disappointed to discover were exactly what they sounded like), two waterskins, and a hundred feet of hemp rope, broken into two lengths. It was clear to him that as humble as the provisions seemed, they were a great sacrifice to the camp.

For means of self-defense, Tarrou was entrusted with a knife. The bodkin was nicked and rust-licked but sharp enough. Finn Goll, who'd spent some months among the zealots, was entrusted with a short-barreled blunderbuss. The trumpeted mouth of the ancient gun was battered, and its stock appeared to be held together with a leather thong. But Sodiq assured him it would fire when called upon, though they only had enough powder for a single shot. The rest of the camp's black powder supply had recently been dispatched for another purpose.

They were each given a caged lantern that contained a thatch of gloamine inside a sphere of bubbly glass. A map that was as byzantine as a fingerprint and an inclinometer (which some called a *slope compass*) were assigned to Hodder Finn. The beetle-browed little person was quickly becoming the group's de facto leader, much to Senlin's discomfort.

Their destination, Mola Ambit, was marked on the map with a small black *X*. Mola Ambit lay in the walls near the fifteenth ringdom of Nineveh. They would climb there via the network of airshafts that delivered fresh air to the black trail and many of the Tower's ringdoms. The airshafts were generally untraveled because they were desolate, difficult to traverse, and confusing. Without maps, which were exceedingly rare and often out of date, entering the ventilation maze was considered just a roundabout sort of suicide. It was easy to get lost in the dark. And then there were the chimney cats to consider, as both Finn and John were quick to point out.

"Of course it's dangerous. Why do you think I've armed you?" Sodiq replied.

Tarrou held up the old dagger he'd been given, and said, "This isn't a weapon. This is cutlery."

Sodiq ignored John and addressed Senlin instead. "I realize, regardless of all the perils that lie ahead of you, you'll still be tempted to flee. I know I would be." Sodiq smiled at him like a wayward son. Senlin couldn't help but wonder what Sodiq had been before the black trail had cracked him and Marat had put him back together. "But you have fled before, Hodder Tom, haven't you? You have the haunted look of a man who has bolted in every direction, a man who has fought every adversary and somehow never run out of enemies, a man who has plotted himself nameless, friendless, and nearly lifeless. You already know what happens when you run. You know you cannot panic your way to freedom; you cannot worry yourself home. You must face your fears. The only way out is inward."

"Oh, yes, well, I agree," Senlin said, and wishing to make one last appeal to the man's emotions, he added with a little more feeling: "I believe I *have* faced my fears. I mean, didn't I stand up to those bullies in the alley with you? I'm only sorry I couldn't return your book."

"Its usefulness had passed. I took it for purely sentimental reasons. I wished to destroy it myself; savor its erasure like a cigar—when I partook of such indulgences. That volume contained such awful, beautiful knowledge. Perhaps future generations will be morally advanced enough to be entrusted with such a full and clear understanding of nature, the cosmos, and time. When we are gone, and all the books we penned have been destroyed, either by effort or indifference, those fossilized creatures will still lurk under the earth, waiting to be found. It's a comforting thought, isn't it?" Sodiq smiled wistfully, the expression sunken from absent teeth. Senlin realized, with some surprise, that not all of Marat's followers believed in his rationale, though they agreed with his conclusion: Man was too clever, and the Tower must fall.

The camp leader recovered his formal tone quickly enough. "I've informed Hodder Luc of your good deeds. Honestly, I'm glad I am not the one who has to decide whether your conversion is sincere. I will tell you this: You are not, in spite of what you might think, marching toward inevitable death. If Hodder Luc wanted you dead, he wouldn't have gone to all this trouble to say goodbye. He wants to speak to you, which means there is hope. Or at least an answer."

"I still don't understand why we can't just take the trail," Finn Goll interjected, seeming to have sat upon this complaint for some moments. "Yes, it's winding and slow, but it has to be safer."

Sodiq shook his head as he replied, "The moment word gets out that a giant and a little person are delivering Captain Mudd to collect the reward, you would become the target of every violent criminal on the trail. No, you are too obvious of a party to go publicly. You will take the vents because it is the safest way for the three of you to travel together."

The nearest entry to the airways lay just outside the camp at the summit of a warped stairwell that broke off from the main trail and spiraled around like a pig's tail. Before the three men began their climb, Sodiq offered them a word of parting advice, the tone of which sounded like a weary father who hadn't much hope for the children he addressed. "Listen to me: You will either survive together or suffer alone. Be good to each other. We're all hods here."

As the three men mounted the curling and uneven stairs with Goll leading the way, Tarrou hung back to speak to Senlin out of the corner of his mouth. "Don't worry, Tom, I've not turned on you. It was all an act. Not bad, eh? I had hoped I could convince them to let me take you off on my own. Oh, well. We'll figure something out. The mean little runt has to sleep eventually. When he does, we'll get that musketoon off him. See if he still feels bossy then."

At the top of the stairs there was a narrow landing. Already the commotion of the trail seemed far behind them. The airshaft entrance lay as low to the ground as a storm drain. The opening was no more than shoulder width and perhaps two feet high. What wind came from it was faint and warm. The air didn't seem particularly fresh; it smelled more like a desert corpse than an open window. Inside, the darkness seemed endless and entire.

The blue light of their moss lamps was far from beaming, but it was enough to thin the gloom. Tarrou, who still looked peaked from blood loss, volunteered to go first. He put his knife between his teeth, got onto his belly, and crawled into the chute like an infant on his elbows, pushing his lamp ahead of him.

When Tarrou's feet had vanished, Senlin turned to Finn Goll and said, "After you, sir."

Goll leveled the blunderbuss at Senlin's chest. "I'm glad to hear the two of you are such fast friends. Though obviously he's an idiot who doesn't know how well sound bounces around in here. I won't lie: A hundred minas would be nice. That's a drop in the bucket. A big drop. And yet..." Goll's curled finger tightened about the trigger. His balled chin began to tremble with scarcely bottled rage. "You ruined my life, Tom. You ruined the life I'd made for my family. I know on balance, you're worth more to me alive than dead. But, oh, it will not take much to tip those scales." Finn Goll bobbed the gun at the vent. "Now, keep your lips stitched and get in that hole."

It didn't seem the time to test Goll's temper. Pushing his heavy pack ahead of him, Senlin snaked his way into the shaft. The stone was coarse and warm beneath him. The slope was steep enough that he had to push against the sides of the shaft to keep from slipping backward. He began to sweat almost at once, and profusely.

Senlin suffered a moment of self-loathing so intense it felt almost carnal. He had been given so many opportunities. Over and over, ill fate had ruined the woman ahead of him or demolished the man behind him, and he had slipped by unscathed. And what had he done with all his good luck? Nothing. He'd somehow managed to defy the law of the Tower that said what was lost once was lost forever, only to bungle the miracle when it came. He'd made friends only to lose them. He deserved what he got. He deserved worse, and Marat would probably provide it. Just as well. Senlin would adjure his executioners to take their time.

Oh, but self-loathing was just so enticing, so holy, so unassailable! The cynic in him cried, *Take my hope! Take my life! Who cares?* As if surrender could make up for his failures or help the people he loved. What a lie to think he could whip himself to redemption. What a loathsome lie!

A sudden stream of cool air coursed around him. It chilled the sweat on his back and filled his nostrils with the scent of sky. He recalled that he had friends sailing upon that sky. And it was the same sky that stretched over the desert, the mountains, and the rolling hillsides, and reached all the way to his cottage by the sea.

The thought of home brought to mind an old sailor song about poor catches and bad weather that Marya had loved and that they had sung together in the Blue Tattoo—she with a voice like a nightingale; he with a caw like a crow. He began singing it to himself now, breathing in and savoring the honeyed air. He could not hate himself and love her at the same time. He had to choose to love. Not just once, but again and again for the rest of his life.

From behind him, Finn Goll told him to stop singing, or he'd shoot him in the brains he used for sitting.

Senlin interrupted his song just long enough to tell him *No*.

The steepest slopes Senlin had ever climbed were the grassy mountains outside of Isaugh. The locals called them "mountains," though they were objectively hills—a fact that Senlin had once liked to share nearly as much as everyone disliked hearing it. The highest peaks were given quaint monikers by the locals, names like Poppy Pike, Mount Goose, and the Two Picnics, so named because the climb was long enough to make the packing of a second meal advisable. Senlin had undertaken the exercise himself on many occasions. He liked hiking along with a walking stick; he liked feeling the sting in his lungs and the warmth in his thighs from the exertion of the ascent. Truth be told, he thought hills superior to mountains in almost every way. Hills did not require him to crawl along on all fours, nor did they test his faith in the power of ropes, nor scuff his hands on their unforgiving corners. The headmaster of old, who only ever attempted a summit that could be conquered in an afternoon, fancied himself something of an aspiring mountaineer.

The airshafts that snaked through the Tower walls quickly dispelled any pleasure Senlin had ever taken in climbing and any illusion he'd held about his abilities. Every inch of him ached. His hands could not produce calluses fast enough to compete with the sandpaper slopes. The constant act of looking up had knotted several painful kinks in his neck and back, and after the first day, his legs were left with all the elasticity of stovepipes.

The system of vents was like a maze set at an extreme angle. The inclines of the airways varied from uncomfortably steep to just shy of vertical, and they ranged in width from being as broad as a river ford to as narrow as a garden stream. Some stretches were so cramped, he was forced to crawl along on his belly, scouring his elbows and knees in the process. Other passages were so open they tested the limit of their gloamine lamps and forced them to ascend in a zigzag, back and forth like mountain goats.

At first, Senlin was surprised, though he probably shouldn't have been given the system's basic function, that the tunnels were so blustery. At times the drafts of cold air that bore down on them were so intense it made his teeth chatter and left him clinging to gaps in the masonry with numb and throbbing fingers. At other points, the desert-hot air coursing up from beneath them was so fierce he thought it might carry him off like a leaf. Oftentimes, the winds clashed violently where the shafts converged. Pocket tornados formed that were strong enough to polish the stone to a glass-like finish.

The wind was sufficient to discourage the growth of gloamine, which meant their lamps were all that stood between them and the madness of utter darkness. If they kept their glowing lichen damp, it would live for weeks before needing to be fertilized or replaced. The greater danger to their light source was accidental collision. If the glass shades that held the lichen ever broke, the wind would sweep away the last light they would ever see.

Beside their lamps, the company's most valuable assets were the map and the inclinometer. Senlin was in charge of the map. Its complexity was staggering, and its detail often murky. The builders of the ventilation system had not labeled the intersections, of which there were thousands. The only thing that distinguished one artery from another on the map were tiny numbers logging the angle of each slope. The inclinometer was most basically a level that measured the degree of an incline, which they could then use to discern one path from another.

Since Sodiq had given them a destination but not a route, it was left to them—or, more accurately, to Senlin, as bearer of the map—to find their way. It seemed like every time Senlin devised a path to Mola Ambit, Tarrou would return from a vent to report that he didn't like the smell of it. Sometimes the air was stale and thin, other times John detected the unique reek of chimney cats. Whatever blocked their way, it fell to Senlin to find an alternative. The new course often required backtracking, but they all understood that the penalty for haste was an unpleasant death. And so, none complained when many hours of climbing had to be retraced.

When on the fifth day of their trek they came upon a colony of bats roosting inside a vaulted junction, the stench of ammonia was so over-powering, the three men could hardly see for the tears in their eyes and could not speak for gagging. The discovery of the bat colony was particularly disappointing because they had journeyed there in hope of making camp. As it turned out, one of the rarest commodities in the maze of airways was level ground. A flat floor (denoted on the map with a zero) meant the possibility of real rest and a civil meal. The fact that a colony of bats had claimed the largest open floor they'd come upon only to use it for a toilet was dispiriting, to say the least.

But they had to rest. They could not afford the clumsiness that came with exhaustion. After poring over his map for a few minutes, Senlin found another level spot that was perhaps half an hour's crawl out of their way. The zero that marked the landing on the map was fol-lowed by an asterisk, which they all found intriguing. They crowded over the map, squinting at the speck that seemed to squirm in the sub-marine glow of their lamps.

"It could be a blot of ink," Senlin said, staring until the whiskery lines and minute figures began to swim about the tiny mark. "Or there could be something unusual there."

"Like a bed?" Goll said.

"Or a café," Tarrou suggested.

There was only one way to find out. When they arrived at the lip of the shaft that led down to the landing, they were surprised by its breadth. Their lamplight did not touch the other side of the gap, and they could not begin to see the bottom of the vent. The wind was chilly, and it poured down from above. When Senlin dropped a little stone into the abyss, he counted to four before hearing a distant and echoing click.

It was the first time that they had no choice but to use the ropes Sodiq had given them. They had two lengths, fifty feet apiece, both frayed at the ends and loose in the middle. The jute fibers were gray with age and creaked when pulled. But, surely, if Sodiq had meant to kill them, he could've thought of a quicker, surer method than sending them off with unsafe tethers.

Surely.

After some debate, they agreed to lash one of their lamps to a rope and lower it down first. If its light didn't find the hoped-for refuge in the rock face, then they'd give up the effort and camp where they were. The bubble of blue light sank thirty feet before revealing what they all agreed was the lip of a long shelf, though they could not see how deep it was from where they stood.

Senlin volunteered to lead the way, and Goll consented only after forcing Senlin to relinquish the map and his pack as insurance that he would not try to escape. Rather than reel the lamp back up, Senlin slid down after it, collecting some friction burns along the way.

When he swung onto the ledge, he was surprised to discover the floor was sodden and slick with some variety of jade-green algae. As soon as he was sure of his foothold on the slippery surface, Senlin untied the lamp, called up the all clear, and began to inspect the level ground.

The landing didn't appear to join any other vents. The back wall, which spanned some fifty paces, was dominated by a trough that was as deep as a bathtub. To his delight, Senlin saw that the long manger held water, fed by a dribbling spring. The sound of trickling water was almost musical. The green slime that swathed the basin appeared to have clogged the drain over time, causing an overflow that spilled across the outpost. The trough was home to a species of tiny glowing shrimp, which resembled a milky galaxy when they moved in a lazy school.

Three grout-spattered stone basins, which called to mind oversized birdbaths, stood near the precipice of the oasis. On either end of the outpost, piles of sand and cakey lime lay under racks of ancient wooden tools. After a moment's study, Senlin realized what the landing was: a long-abandoned mixing station for the preparation of mortar.

Once Goll and Tarrou were safely down, neither man made any effort to conceal his disappointment at the swampy floor, the scarcity of mattresses, and the absolute absence of a single café waiter. They were a little appeased by the fresh water, which seemed potable, and though the ground was smeared in a viscous goo that would not be very nice to sleep upon, there were at least wooden pails they could use as stools.

It had taken Senlin a couple of days before the crisis of his hunger overwhelmed his revulsion for their rations. The beetle cakes were grotesque in texture and foul in flavor, but surprisingly filling. Famished from the day's climb, they arranged their buckets in a circle and passed the sack of beetle cakes around.

Tarrou said, "You know, if you don't let yourself think about what you're eating while you're eating it, these are still nearly inedible." He made a show of inspecting the textured mauve-gray puck. "It's like an offal pâté with raisins, isn't it? No, not raisins. What do you suppose those are? Heads?"

"John, please. I just want to keep it down," Senlin said between sips from the waterskin.

They sat around a gloamine lamp as if it were a cold campfire. The remaining lanterns rested in the mixing basins, one on either end of the outpost.

Goll balanced his blunderbuss on his lap as he ate his insect cake and glared back and forth between Senlin and Tarrou, ever vigilant, ever suspicious. Before they had sat down, Goll insisted Senlin turn over the supply pack, which he now wore on his back as insurance against either man running off. Senlin wondered where exactly they could run off to. As clever as he was, he still couldn't fly. In his present state of exhaustion, he wasn't even sure he'd be able to shinny back up the rope they'd come down by. But Goll's paranoia appeared stronger than his sense.

In the five days since they'd commenced their climb, they'd had little chance for conversation. They had spoken enough for Tarrou to discern that Goll was well aware of his attempted conspiracy. Goll made no bones about his willingness to shoot Tarrou. Since there was no reason to keep up a pretense of civility, John took to needling Goll, and the two quickly developed a mutual animosity that only silence could pacify.

The mortar mixing post was the first time they'd been on level ground and in a position to talk since they'd left the zealot camp. Senlin wondered how long it would take the two men to begin sniping at each other. His answer came soon enough.

"So tell us, Mr. Gallstone, how exactly did you fall in with the zealots?" John asked. "Did you get caught in one of their rat traps? Or did they mistake you for an ugly orphan child and adopt you?"

"I was running from a pack of oversized goons like you who were under the mistaken impression that I owed them money." The shorn state of Goll's head and his noticeable thinness conspired to make his large, animated brows more conspicuous. Goll looked, Senlin thought, like a caricature of his former himself. "I knew the zealots were protective of their converts. And if it saves me a beating, I don't mind lying."

"Oh? Do you prefer to lie on your belly or on your back?"

"I suppose I'm like your mother: I let the gentleman decide, hodder."

Tarrou swatted at the air. "Oh, stop it with that hodder nonsense! You're the absolute worst actor I've ever seen, and I've sat through a thousand drunken dinner theaters."

"Or as your friends call it, 'Tea with John.'"

"Sodiq saw right through you. It was embarrassing watching you smirk and shrug as if you were fooling anyone. You seem to be under the misapprehension that sarcasm is a legitimate dramatic method."

"And yet somehow, I'm not the one who's been shot twice in a week," Goll said.

"I've only been shot once."

"Keep talking!" Goll shook the gun at him, eliciting a not very intimidating rattle.

"What happened to you to make you so sour?" Tarrou asked.

"What happened to me?" Finn Goll threw the remaining wedge of his beetle cake over his shoulder into the yawning gully at his back. "Thomas Senlin happened to me! I know he doesn't look like much. Oh, he had me fooled, too! But in the span of one evening, he murdered my business manager, made off with my starlet, destroyed my port, and kidnapped my personal bodyguard." Goll ticked each grievance off on a finger as he named them. "It took my enemies scarcely a week to carve up what was left of my assets, and another week for all my debts to be called in." He balled his hands into fists and shook them like an inconsolable infant. "I have a wife and six children! Six! Do you have any idea where they are now? They're living with cousins who hate them, washing soiled linens in the Baths. My youngest is four years old. A four-year-old girl wringing out pissy sheets for twelve hours a day. And she is waiting for her father to claw his way out of this inescapable hell and come rescue her!" Goll twisted the leather-wrapped stock of his weapon and glared at Senlin. "I gave you a job. I gave you a salary. And you ruined me for it!"

Senlin dusted his hands and shuddered as he swallowed the last of his wretched dinner, then said, "I'm sorry for your family. They really did seem lovely, and I don't enjoy hearing of any child's suffering. But do not pretend that I took advantage of you, or that I was ever a willing employee. The Steam Pipe was a human mill that turned women into shekels for your purse. And Rodion was nothing but a theatrical rapist who preyed upon his wards. You were not a businessman. You were a slave trader, a pimp, and a thief. The grudging part that I played in your despicable industry is a source of unending shame. If I could go back and burn your port down a second time, I would."

Goll swung the black mouth of the blunderbuss at Senlin's chest. Spit bubbled in the corners of his mouth. Making no effort to be subtle, Tarrou pulled the tarnished knife from his sarong and held it upon his knee. Goll spat when he spoke. "I enjoy seeing how well your decency has served you, Saint Thomas. I really do. I made hard decisions to feed my family. How fares your wife?"

"Not as well as I would like," Senlin said, patting his thighs and laughing softly at an understatement neither of his companions understood. "I have disappointed her several times over, but I'm still determined to account for those failures. And your loathing for me doesn't change the fact that John is right. You're not a very convincing zealot, Hodder Finn."

The change in topic seemed to dampen Goll's rage. The gun returned to his lap. "So what if I'm not? Who cares? I'm not in this for the cause." He rubbed his fingers together meaningfully.

"You do understand the moment you accept the bounty, Marat will have you executed," Senlin said. "It's a test. If you take the money, he'll kill you."

"You don't know that." Finn Goll spoke with a confidence his expression did not match.

"Sodiq all but said as much. Besides, I've met Marat. I've been to his camp. I've sat at his table and listened to him philosophize." Senlin shook his head at the memories of the gold-plated jail. "He has no compunction about killing hods. I doubt he even has the money, and if he does, I'm sure he's not going to give it to you."

"Oh, but you don't think he'll hang Captain Mudd, the hod slayer?" Goll asked.

"I'm certainly going to try to make a case against it." The stationary light of their lamp had drawn a cloud of small, colorless moths. They ticked upon the glass globe like rain upon a window.

"I bet when they cut off your head, you'll just keep right on wheedling and chattering for another fortnight." Goll rubbed his face with embellished exasperation. "Face it, Tom! You've run out of luck! You've had a fine run. You beat some long odds, but it's over."

"Perhaps. But I still have a plan."

"Do you?" Goll mugged an expression of delight and surprise. "Please, tell us how you plan to escape the black trail, that debt pinned to your neck, and the bounty on your head."

"I'm going to tell Marat whatever he wants to hear," Senlin said.

"Well, that should about do it!" Goll guffawed.

"We share an old friend in common. I think he'll at least want to hear an update about how she's doing." Senlin swatted at a moth that had begun to fly circles about his head. He drove the thing off for a moment, but it returned just as quickly. "And I'm going to come to him in the company of two true converts."

Tarrou, who had been listening with squinting skepticism, pointed back and forth between himself and Finn Goll. "You mean us?"

"Yes."

Tarrou rolled his head about as if dizzied by the idea. "Tom, I've mingled with the zealots, and I can tell you, they are very sincere. They're also quite good at spotting imposters. I can be convincing enough, but I doubt we have time to teach the mouse here how to act."

"No more name-calling, John," Senlin said quickly, surprising both men. "I know it helps lift your spirits, but we can't afford to bicker anymore."

Finn Goll interjected before Tarrou could defend himself. "I'm actually fine with the bickering. It's the cooperation I'm not so keen on, Tommy. You mistake me for a friend."

"No, I take you for someone with shared interests. We all want to get off the trail. Besides, we're not just going to put on an act for Marat. We're going to give evidence of your conviction as well. The two of you are going to turn down the reward."

Finn Goll snorted. "No, we're not."

"Yes, you are. You're going to insist upon it. No matter how he presses you, you're going to tell Marat you would never take a single penny from the cause." Finn Goll opened his mouth to argue further, but Senlin forged ahead. "The zealots have ways of getting in and out of the ringdoms undetected. I believe Sodiq used one of those back doors to avoid answering for the murders he committed in Pelphia. If we can convince the zealots that we are on their side, perhaps we can get into a ringdom. Then, we'll have options. If we can find the local Wakeman, I should be able to contact my friends."

"What sort of friends?" Goll asked.

"The kind with an airship and plenty of money."

"You're forgetting the brand, Tom," Tarrou said, and put a finger behind his right ear. When Senlin looked puzzled, Tarrou turned his head farther so he could show the button-sized scar behind his lobe.

"They brand you before they put you on the trail to discourage the exact sort of subterfuge you're suggesting. Any ringdom guard who sees one of these is going to ask for your papers. Unless you can produce documents that prove you're an emancipated hod who's paid off his debt, they'll shoot you on the spot."

Senlin rubbed the unmarred skin behind his own ear. He'd not noticed the brand on the hods he'd encountered, but it made sense why they would have it. The duke must've been so eager to box up his head, he'd forgotten to mark him. Senlin still had his hair for the same reason, which was long enough now to hang in his eyes and over his ears. "I suppose we'll have to figure out a disguise if we get that far. Perhaps we can just pose as what we are. The people of the ringdoms seem eager enough to overlook hods."

"I'm sorry, Headmaster, but this doesn't seem like much of a plan," Tarrou said. "Placate the zealots in the hope that we can parlay that access into a later escape? Seems a little thin, doesn't it?"

"Absolutely. But as I see it, our other option is to find a shaft that'll take us back to the trail, at which point every man would go his own way. Sodiq is right: We can't travel in the open together. So what I'm suggesting is absolutely risky. But Marat has influence, power, resources, and we could take advantage of those. Perhaps we could even volunteer for a mission. I know he's been infiltrating the ringdoms, probably for years. Or if you both prefer it, you could find the nearest trading post, pick up a load, and start walking off your debts."

"I just think it's a long shot that Marat will believe that you're truly a convert," John said.

"Perhaps. But a long shot is still more likely than a miracle. And that's what it takes to get off the black trail the legal way, isn't it?"

Finn Goll, who'd been stewing in silence for a moment, appeared to make a decision. "It's too bad. I would've liked to see you swing, Tom. But I think you're probably right. It's a trap. So we go back to the trail. Then it's every man for himself . . . as it always has been."

Senlin shook his head and sucked a breath in between his teeth. "I think you're making a mistake, Finn. You may not get another chance like this."

"Life never runs out of chances; a man just runs out of life. And this isn't a debate. You can tag along, or you can stay here, but I'm going back to the trail. And my god, gentlemen, if you're going to befoul the air with beetle farts, the least you could do is take a few paces off befo—"

Finn Goll rose with a jerk. The blunderbuss fell from his knees and clattered upon the slimy stone. He stood up on his tiptoes, and then kept right on rising until his feet kicked the air. He dangled from the straps of the pack, a round-mouthed expression of confused horror on his face.

The immense, inky chimney cat that had snuck up from the pit to lock its jaws upon Goll's rucksack began to shake its head in wide, violent strokes.

The sack of beetle cakes flew from the pack into the abyss along with two of their blankets and the second waterskin. Goll nearly followed after the gear himself. When the chimney cat whipped its head back the other way, Goll tried to slip out of the shoulder straps, but one of his arms tangled in the loop, and before he could free himself, he was flying over the brink again. He screamed as the strap tore free of the pack's shoulder, leaving him clinging to life by a leather strip and the strength of one hand. The fiend swung its head inland just as Goll's grip failed. He soared in an arc above the landing and splashed down in the trough among the slime. The school of krill fled to the other end of the trench with an angry flash of white.

Even before the plume of water slapped down upon the floor, the chimney cat dropped the deflated pack and settled his attention upon Senlin, frozen and crouching in its shadow.

It resembled a stoat only in its rough proportions. In all else, it looked like a monster cobbled from a nightmare. Its black hair was as coarse as quills. Its broom of whiskers seemed only to elongate a mouth full of beaming teeth. Bands of muscles writhed beneath its razor fur. John had said the beasts could grow as large as fifteen feet. This one seemed an overachiever. It stood on its hind legs, appearing to study Senlin, much as a diner might take a moment to admire the presentation of a plated meal. The butt of Goll's blunderbuss jutted from under one of its paws. Its curved talons called to mind a butcher's hook. But it was the creature's unblinking gaze that held Senlin's attention most. Its eyes were bulging, dark, and filmed with a spectral light. The curious sheen of the chimney cat's eyes swirled like an abalone pearl. Each time it seemed like those colors would fall into the black drain of its pupils, the rainbow revived, and the beautiful stirring began anew.

A dim and unimportant thought occurred to Senlin: The beast had mesmerized him. He was feeling abnormally tranquil for a man who was about to be eaten.

A wooden scoop bonked the chimney cat on the snout. Quick as a viper, the beast sprang at him. No, not at him, past him, though Senlin didn't quite evade all contact. The fiend clipped him with its shoulder. It felt as if someone had swatted him with a cactus. But the pain was enough to release him from his trance.

Knocked to his knees, Senlin began scuttling away. His only thought was to put something sturdy between himself and the monster. The broad foot of one of the stone mixing bowls was his nearest cover. Expecting any moment to be pounced on and chewed, he was almost surprised when he reached the pedestal. The base was wide enough to conceal him, though he didn't relish the idea of playing ring-around-the-maypole with a hungry chimney cat. It was only then that he stopped to consider what had allowed him to escape. The beast had turned its focus on Tarrou, who'd hurled the old measuring cup at it.

John dove into the narrow space under the spring's trough, and the chimney cat attempted to plunge in after him. It was foiled, at least somewhat, by the posts that supported the long receptacle and by John's scurrying. He crawled on his elbows through a thick bunting of cobwebs as the chimney cat chased along after him, with its head turned to one side. It snapped at John's hands and feet, missing him by a hairsbreadth again and again.

Whether he realized it or not, Tarrou was leading the beast straight toward Goll, still stunned and soaking in the bath he'd been thrown into. Senlin saw it was only a matter of seconds before the chimney cat came upon Finn, served up like a dumpling in a bowl.

Senlin made a dash for the blunderbuss, but in his haste, he lost his footing on the slimy ledge. He slid into the weapon, kicking it across the outpost. Finn Goll gave a terrified shout. The chimney cat had spotted him and had placed a sinewy arm on either side of the basin, pinning him in. Seeming to savor the catch, the fiend sawed its head back and forth, spattering the half-submerged Goll in gobs of slaver.

There was no time to retrieve the weapon, so Senlin picked up the only thing at hand and threw it with all his might. The gloamine lamp burst when it struck the beast on the back of its skull. The precious moss flitted away like the down of a dandelion. The empty cage clanked upon the floor.

The chimney cat dropped onto all fours and came at Senlin in a serpentine rush. It moved with startling speed. Senlin turned and ran along the lip of the shelf. He decided to make for the wall where the old equipment hung on pegs above the blunderbuss. He wondered if the gun would still fire after all the abuse, or if he'd be better off arming himself with one of the stirring paddles. They seemed hardly sufficient for fending off a wire-haired devil, but even an oar was preferable to bare-knuckling the beast if the gun failed to fire.

But when Senlin saw the rope they'd descended by, hanging just off of the edge not far from him, he changed his mind. The sound of claws striking the floor was so close behind him now, he doubted he'd ever reach the wall anyway. He focused only on the dangling cord as he swerved a few paces deeper into the outpost before driving out again at the brink with all the energy he could muster. He leapt at the rope, catching it with enough force to swing far out into the darkness. He half expected to strike a wall, but there was nothing at the limit of his flight except a second of suspension, a moment of absolute stillness. Then he began to fall back the way he'd come.

He twisted about to face his fate and found the beast had reared onto its haunches in anticipation of his return. It occurred to Senlin he had turned himself into a cat toy. He saw he would fly straight into the chimney cat's waiting maw if he did nothing, so he did the only thing he could: He let go.

His momentum still carried him into the beast, but his trajectory sank enough to fall out of the way of its fangs. Senlin struck the chimney cat feetfirst in the neck hard enough to rock it back on its tail.

Crashing down on his back and elbows at the cliff edge, Senlin suffered a shock of pain that stole his breath. But he hadn't time to wince. He rolled to one side, even as the beast attacked the ground he'd just occupied. Senlin scooted on his rump, pedaling his heels to propel himself away, though much, much too slowly. The chimney cat rose above him. Senlin turned away. He didn't want to watch the gory arrival of his end.

Dripping with water and battered in slime, Finn Goll pointed the blunderbuss over Senlin's head.

The gun boomed. In the near dark, the muzzle blast was almost volcanic, and for a split second Senlin thought it might be enough to kill the fiend or at least drive it away.

Then lead pellets bounced upon Senlin's head and shoulders like a handful of gravel thrown by a weak child. Finn Goll called Sodiq a "muddy gusset" and dashed the useless weapon upon the ground.

But the misfire was enough to startle the beast and perhaps blind it a little. It thrashed about, whipping its great length back and forth. The middle of its tail struck one of the mixing pedestals, budging it from its ancient spot and knocking the bowl loose. The basin split against the floor with a thunderous crack that seemed to shock the already unsettled beast. The gloamine lamp that had been resting inside it shattered, spilling its contents in a vanishing halo of light.

As the beast gyred about its own center, searching for some relief from the noise and light, Senlin got to his feet. Finding their second rope in a heap near the pack, he snatched it up and began knotting a wide noose at one end. While he worked, he saw that Tarrou had armed himself with an oar and was running at the blinded beast with an unsettling lack of deliberation. John bellowed as he chopped down with the edge of his paddle at one of the chimney cat's paws. The beast's cry was as sour as a yowl and as loud as a foghorn.

It swiveled about, snapping in John's direction, but the big man had already leapt away. Senlin took advantage of the brute's lowered head to get the lasso around it.

"Distract it, John! Distract it!" Senlin shouted as he ran backward with the other end of the line.

"Here, puss!" Tarrou shouted and batted the beast on its ear.

Its senses returning, the chimney cat lashed out at John a second time, this time catching his stirring oar cleanly in its mouth. The old wood splintered, leaving the big man holding little more than a stick, which he threw. By the time the broken handle had bounced off the top of the monster's skull, John had already turned to flee, though his injured leg turned his sprint into a lope.

Senlin scrambled to get the other end of the line wrapped and knotted about the decapitated column. He'd hardly had a chance to tie it off before the rope went rigid, and the pillar fell from its plinth, onto its side. At the other end of the leash, the chimney cat bucked, surprised to have been pulled short of John's head, even as it attempted to nip it from his shoulders.

"Goll, help me!" Senlin shouted, pressing upon the barrel of rock. "Push it off! Push it off!"

The two set their shoulders against the squat column, and together they rocked it until it began to roll toward the yawning precipice. With nowhere left to retreat, John was left pelting the beast with whatever he could lay a hand on—shovel, paddle, dipper, and trowel, none of which seemed to do much more than delay the beast with brief annoyance.

When the stone drum tumbled from the ledge and vanished into the gloom, Senlin wondered if the weight would be sufficient, wondered if the rope would hold. If it wasn't, or it didn't, then the only remaining uncertainty would be the order in which they were eaten.

But the line held, and the weight was enough to snatch the chimney cat onto its back. It slid along the slime-slicked stone, scratching at the air. In an attempt to get its claws under it again and reanchor itself, it wriggled onto its side. In another second, it might've caught the floor and saved itself from the fall, but it ran out of ground before it could get its footing and slipped over the edge with a grisly roar.

They listened, and after a moment, heard the hammer strike of the pedestal on the distant floor, then the softer impact of the animal a split second later.

The pitch of the chimney cat's fatal cry left Senlin with the uneasy feeling that he had not so much slayed a dragon as he had killed a rare creature who'd done nothing but obey its instinct. He felt no swell of pride, no sense of triumph, only the buzzing relief to find that he was still alive.

They took stock of their losses. The beetle cakes would be missed the least. They discussed the possibility of eating the tiny luminescent shrimp in the trough. But after some deliberation, and a lack of a volunteer to be the first to try the ghostly shellfish, they abandoned the idea. Better to go hungry than to be poisoned. All agreed they could last a few days without food, and that would be enough for them to reach Mola Ambit. They still had the rope they'd descended by, one blanket, one waterskin, and vitally, one lamp. The map, which had remained tucked in the pack, had not been lost, but the inclinometer was smashed beyond repair.

Even as Finn Goll bemoaned the overwhelming loss, Senlin began to cobble together a replacement. He didn't have the resources to build a spirit level, but he could fashion a plumb line, which could serve a similar purpose. He used the hollow handle of a scoop for a scope, the broken end of a paddle for a measuring board, threads pulled from his sarong for a line, and fashioned a plumb bob from a lump of mortar. He lashed the pieces together with wire from the broken lanterns and used Tarrou's knife to make regular notches in the board to create a crude scale. He explained that they didn't need to know the true angle of any shaft, only the relative angles of an intersection. So it didn't matter if a slope was in actuality 32 degrees or 51 degrees, so long as they could keep their place on the map, they could use his makeshift inclinometer to distinguish which slope was the steepest, which the most gradual, and compare those general readings to the map.

Even after Senlin explained the basic premise of how they'd use his crude replacement, Goll was unsure how it could possibly work. Senlin could only ask that Goll believe he did not wish to be lost in the walls any more than Goll did.

Tarrou, who had a better grasp of what Senlin was proposing, pointed out, "But if we make a wrong turn, we probably won't realize it until it's much too late."

"True. But it's better than picking a course blindly," Senlin said, testing the fasteners that held his instrument together. Satisfied it wouldn't break with the first use, he was in the process of wrapping the inclinometer in their remaining blanket when Tarrou noticed his wound. Senlin's chest was marred with livid strokes, like the lashes of a whip, from when the chimney cat had brushed him aside. Rivulets of drying blood seeped from the deepest gouges. John asked if perhaps they shouldn't clean the wound and use the blanket to bandage him, but Senlin insisted the inclinometer was more precious at the moment.

"I suppose you expect me to be grateful now that we've saved each other's lives, and just go along with your half-cocked plan," Goll said, working to scrape the coat of slime from his bare legs.

"Not at all," Senlin said. "We'll make for the trail, and anyone who wishes to get off can. I'll carry on to Mola Ambit on my own." He topped off the waterskin from the spring. "It's not that I can't use a willing ally, Goll. I just have no need for a hostile companion."

"You're acting as if I should be grateful for the chance to die with you in Marat's camp. Allies usually have something to offer each other, Tom." Finn washed his hands in the trough.

"Indeed," Senlin said, apparently unconcerned.

"All right! All right! I'll bite. Tell me more about these friends you have. You say they have a ship and money. Do they have a name as well?"

"Do you remember the woman with the engine arm who was in your port the night it was destroyed?" Senlin slid the bundled inclinometer into the pack.

"Didn't it start with an *E*? Eveline? Ermine? Ester? She was Billy Lee's first mate, wasn't she?" Finn Goll squinted at the memory. "As I remember, he called her a 'Wakeman in waiting,' whatever that means. God, that dolt liked to talk when he drank."

"She was my first mate aboard the *Stone Cloud*, which I borrowed from Lee. She's been promoted since then. She's captain of the *State of Art* now."

"You mean the Sphinx's flagship?" Tarrou said, pawing his jaw in wonderment. "Even in the dorms of the Colosseum, it was all anyone was talking about last week." When Goll continued to look puzzled, Tarrou relayed the news that the long-dormant Sphinx was flexing his muscles again, starting, apparently, with the relaunch of his most magnificent and imposing warship. "Tom, you're telling me you know the captain of the *State of Art*?"

"Very well," Senlin said.

"And the Sphinx? You haven't met the Sphinx, have you?" John pressed, smiling in ready disbelief.

"I've made his acquaintance."

Goll and Tarrou looked at each other with a mixture of amazement and incredulity. "No, Tom. That's too much." Tarrou waved at the air as if trying to disperse a puff of smoke.

"As may be. I'm happy to drop you off on the trail, too."

"Can you prove it?" Goll asked, setting his fists on his hips. "Do you have evidence of any of this?"

"No. I can't prove it to you. But I can to Marat. He was a Wakeman once, and I think he'll be very interested to hear how the Sphinx is doing at present."

"If it's true, these are some very big players you're talking about, Tom," John said. "Are you sure you're not in over your head?"

"I think the question you should both ask yourselves is, do you want to throw your lot in with a man who's willing to fight chimney cats with you, or do you want to face the black trail on your own?"

"Would the Sphinx be willing to open his purse for a useful man in need?" Goll asked.

"I think it's safe to say the Sphinx rewards his friends."

Goll laughed. "Are you sure you want to offer yourself up as proof of that?"

Goll's barbed question seemed to bring several things into relief at once for Senlin, and with a vividness that resembled an epiphany.

Senlin saw clearly that the Sphinx had put him in an impossible position quite on purpose. She had not believed he would follow orders in Pelphia. No, she had dispatched him to the city where his wife was imprisoned because she knew he would not do as he was told. He was too stubborn for that. He was the sort of man who climbed immeasurable towers and got to the bottom of bottomless libraries. Yet despite his obstinance, Senlin had proved time and time again to be adaptable and resourceful in a manner few were.

The pill-like spider the Sphinx had made him swallow, a thing that she claimed could be used to locate him should he get lost, was like a tether, a sort of fishing line. Which made him the lure. She had cast him into Pelphia not knowing exactly what she would catch but believing that he would thrash about like bait, as he indeed had. Senlin doubted the Sphinx would be surprised to learn that he had been thrown onto the black trail. In the past, he'd proven he could change skins easily enough: headmaster, thief, bookkeeper, pirate, and spy. Why not a hod? Why not a zealot? Now he was in a position to lead her to Marat's new camp, something that she would surely wish to know.

All of this suggested to him that there was a chance, albeit a small one, that things were not as desperate as they seemed. Perhaps he was not so lost.

Smirking at his own optimism, Senlin said, "You know, it's strange to say, but I think I may be exactly where the Sphinx wants me."

Part III
The Gold Watch

Chapter One

Sadly, the secret to longevity may very well be mediocrity. We see evidence of this in the history of the menu of Café Tertre. The dreadfully inventive specials—the slink pie and lemon soup—were seen once and never heard from again. The perfectly succulent ambrosia krill, which lit up its bisque with an ethereal light, was so popular we relished the crustacean into extinction. But the merely palatable, unremarkable pigeon pie will linger on the board forever.

—Oren Robinson of the *Daily Reverie*

Ferdinand thundered at Edith with all the restraint of a hound who'd broken free of his leash. At a sprint and with his head ducked, the Sphinx's doorman looked alarmingly like a train engine—chest like a cowcatcher; head like a tunnel lamp; jets of steam blooming from the pistons of his arms. The Sphinx's elevating corridor shuddered under the doorman's approach. His elbow clipped a sconce, and the brass gooseneck flattened against the wall like a poorly hammered nail.

Edith found the great empty plate of Ferdinand's face disconcerting. Yet even without eyes or a mouth, she sensed an undeniable awareness there, a presence that the lumbering engines in the Sphinx's dock lacked. Though Ferdinand's clumsy antics unnerved her, she was no longer afraid of him.

Ferdinand had spotted her exiting the stables, caught her while the warmth of Senlin's kiss still lingered on her lips. Tom's duty to his wife had brought to mind her own distant spouse, Mr. Franklin Winters. Franklin had had the irritating habit of interpreting her stoicism, her earnestness, and her unwillingness to defer to his authority as a sign of insensitivity. Because she was not emotionally demonstrative, at least not in the way he preferred, she was frigid. The more Franklin complained of her lack of the right sort of affection, the more Edith came to resent their union, and, if she were honest, the entire institution of marriage.

Though she had long carried her suspicions of the practice. Once, as an independent-minded twelve-year-old, she had declared to her father that she would never marry. She would be like the hawk that circled the field. Hawks didn't have husbands. They didn't need them.

And her father had replied in his diplomatic way, "Most of those hawks have husbands, Edith. They just lead separate lives. They circle different fields. You don't have to be in love to share a nest."

But her marriage to Franklin had dispelled that pretty fairy tale. Two hawks who could barely stand each other couldn't share a four-bedroom house, much less a nest.

The experience had left her jaded. If love existed, she had not felt its effect.

Then she had been caged with a priggish country headmaster, and it proved to be, to her great annoyance, the most intimate experience of her life.

Though she had not loved him then. That foreign feeling only declared itself after their reunion, when he saw her arm, experienced her changed demeanor, and liked her still. Perhaps liked her more. It seemed a miracle. An inconvenient miracle. He had come to her bedroom in a moment of weakness or of pity, and she had taken advantage of it. What a desperate, foolish thing. Perhaps it was for the best that he had left.

When the Sphinx's moon-faced locomotive turned and charged at her, she felt almost grateful for the distraction. She'd take a dose of adrenaline over introspection at the moment.

She knew Ferdinand did not intend to run her down, but he did a lot of things he didn't intend to do. She raised her iron arm, bracing for impact, and it was well that she did. Ferdinand skidded into her, ramming his hip against her engine's pauldron. The collision knocked her clear off her feet, and she landed with a bump on the tattered carpets.

Immediately remorseful, Ferdinand opened his chest and changed the drum in the music box of his heart. A mournful tune began to play.

Edith stood and slapped the dust from her clothes. It felt wrong somehow to rebuke a machine whose greatest flaw was a shortage of coordination, a condition with which she could sympathize. The Sphinx's gifts were great but unwieldy. Edith insisted she was fine, swore she was not cross, and asked him what he wanted. Ferdinand waved at her to follow him. As they marched to the dirge of his music box, the corridor began to rise.

When the vast hall concluded its ascent and Ferdinand pointed to one door in the valley of doors, Edith had the strange sense that she had not been there before. The last time she had been summoned to an unfamiliar room, the Sphinx had shown her the dreadful—and very much still alive—Red Hand. She wondered what fresh terror the Sphinx had in store for her.

The door opened upon a chamber that was as large as a ballroom. The air smelled of sulfur, wet pelts, sour milk, and other things she could not identify. The walls, high ceiling, and floor were all doused in black paint that seemed to drink the light of the lamps. A glass cistern, large as one of her father's grain silos, presided over the room. The vat appeared to hold a whirling, cement cloud. All about the immense urn, wheeled carts held racks containing hundreds and hundreds of glass vials. She recognized them at once: They were batteries like the ones she regularly pulled from her arm.

The Sphinx looked like a rearing cobra. His black robes sawed beneath him as he moved in front of the bottled storm. To Edith's surprise, Iren was there, too. The amazon held her thick arms crossed over her chest and her feet spread apart as if she intended to square off with the Sphinx. It seemed quite a dominant pose for someone wearing a fluffy white robe.

Edith greeted Iren and asked if this was to be her new uniform. "It would definitely make an impression in a fight. If anyone charged at me in a bathrobe, I'd run the other way."

"The stag is sewing me a new wardrobe for Pelphia," Iren said glumly. "He'd better give me some trousers, or I'm going to take his."

"That would be entertaining," Edith said.

"All right, enough of that!" Though the Sphinx's expression was hidden by his mask, the shrill note in his crackling voice communicated his impatience. "I didn't bring you two here to natter about clothes." Taking a vial from a rack, the Sphinx opened the copper tap at the base of the urn and filled the tube with the muddy ooze. "Do you recognize this, Edith?"

"I do. I had no idea there was so much of it."

"This? This is just a drop in the bucket! Here, take a whiff." The Sphinx passed the open vial to the amazon.

Iren gave the vial a casual sniff. It seemed to make no impression, and she passed it to Edith, who inhaled deeply. Edith snatched her head away, snorting and coughing. The Sphinx's mechanical laughter sounded like rain on a windowpane. As Edith wiped the tears from her eyes, she asked Iren, "Why didn't you warn me?"

Iren shrugged. "Would you have smelled it if I had?"

"It's like rotten teeth and burning hair. What's in this?"

"Gloamine spores, bull snail mucus, chimney cat dander, the silk of the drove spider, and many, many more of the Tower's bounties. Now observe what happens when I put a spark to it." The Sphinx drew the wand from his inky sleeve and touched its tip to the vial. The cylinder lit up like a candle flame. The red light folded upon itself, writhing like a living thing.

Edith had never thought much about the batteries she put into her arm. It was easier not to, and daily exposure to the miraculous things had made them seem almost mundane. But seeing the way the bland medium gobbled up and transformed the lightning filled her with wonder.

"In my more dramatic youth I called it the Blood of Time." The Sphinx sounded wistful. "But it's more accurate to call it a distillation of history, which doesn't have quite the same ring to it, I admit. The medium can hold an electric charge, but it is capable of bearing much, much more. It can suspend a moment, trap a memory, or even slow the advance of time."

A sudden revelation shattered Edith's awe. "The Red Hand," she said. "Why in the world did you put this in his veins?"

"To save his life," the Sphinx said without pause. "He was found floating and blue-faced in the reservoir of the Baths, a nameless tourist in a bathing suit. The local doctors were able to restart his heart and get him breathing again, but he was left a mindless husk, a mute shell of a man. One of the captains who used to recruit Wakemen for me brought him in. I tried everything I could to revive his mind, but all my efforts failed. As a last resort, I decided to try something radical. I put the charged medium into his bloodstream. To my surprise, he woke up.

"He lived, but his former life and understanding were all gone. Since he could not recall his name, I named him Reddleman because the medium turned his fingers red as reddle dye." The Sphinx seemed to shrink as he set the vial he'd lit back into its cradle. There, it glowed dimly like a dying coal.

"He had the mind of a child, and a child's curiosity, too. He had an insatiable appetite for facts and information. So I loaded him with primers and encyclopedias, and sent him back to the Baths to live and work as a Wakeman. I thought it would be a quiet place for him to convalesce and continue his education. I nearly convinced myself that repairing a mind was not so different from refitting an appendage. I did not realize how susceptible his state of mind made him. Reddleman was quick to understand how the world worked, but none of it rekindled his conscience. He was intelligent but without a single scruple. Commissioner Pound filled that ethical void with his own poisonous ideas."

"I saw him tear half a dozen men limb from limb," Iren said darkly. "He nearly killed me, too. If you knew he was so dangerous, why didn't you do anything to stop him?"

The Sphinx sighed and pressed another stopper into a freshly filled vial. "Optimism, I suppose. Denial, perhaps? I'm not sure. But I could just as well ask you why you spent so many years serving a man who made a fortune off of desperate women being turned into novelty acts and unwilling brides. Yes, I know all about your time in New Babel."

Edith watched Iren's brow curdle with pain and rushed to her friend's defense. "The difference is Iren didn't have the resources and alternatives that you do."

"No, the difference is my choice served a purpose. A war is coming, and like it or not, we'll need the Red Hand to win."

"Well, just keep him away from me and Voleta, and we won't have a problem," Iren said.

The Sphinx laughed. "I want you to unknot your thoughts. Picture some pleasant place." Slipping the full battery into an empty cradle, the Sphinx snaked off through the carts full of glassware to a black door they hadn't noticed before. "Are you at ease?"

"Hardly ever," Iren said.

"Well, please try to pretend." The Sphinx turned the handle.

The silhouette of a short man with a potbelly and willowy limbs filled the doorway. Against the gloom, his skin shone with a faint ruby light.

Iren picked up the nearest cart and raised it over her head, sending a shower of empty vials crashing to the floor like hailstones. Edith shouted at her, but not quickly enough. The amazon hurled the cart at the head of the Red Hand.

If the Red Hand flinched, Edith did not detect it. In fact, she hardly perceived the movement of his arms when he snatched the cart from the air. He set it down on the black floor and looked confusedly at the Sphinx. "You didn't say she'd throw furniture at me."

"I didn't know she would," the Sphinx said.

Overcoming her surprise at the Red Hand's quick reflexes, Iren gripped a second cart, but Edith cuffed her arm before she could raise it. "Wait."

"He tried to kill us!" Iren said hotly. "What'll stop him from trying again? What about Voleta?"

"Hold on. Hold. That's an order," Edith said more firmly. "Let go of the cart." Iren reluctantly did, and once Edith was convinced a second assault wasn't imminent, she turned to the Sphinx. "I thought he was paralyzed."

"I was!" the Red Hand said, large teeth crowding a fulsome smile. "I only regained control of my arms yesterday." He raised his hands, and the laces on the sleeves of his linen shirt caught his attention. He tugged them like a cat for a moment, then shook his head vigorously, as if to dispel the distraction. "Then this morning, I got my legs back. I've been having a lovely walk."

"I wasn't talking to you!" Edith was pointing at the Red Hand but glaring at the Sphinx.

"Are you the one who killed me?" The Red Hand's tone was not angry or accusatory. His voice, which was high and a little hoarse, sounded inquisitive, almost amused, but not angry, a fact that confused Edith.

"She is. But in her defense, you were behaving very poorly at the time."

"I was? I'm sorry," the Red Hand said, surveying Edith from fluffy collar to slippered feet and back again. "She looks quite strong. And angry. I think she wants to kill me."

"Very perceptive, Reddleman. Your observational skills are coming along nicely. And I think the answer is probably yes," the Sphinx said.

"Because of who I was?" The Red Hand was approaching Edith and Iren now. He was barefoot and walked with a staggering, wandering gait. When the broken vials began to crunch under his heels, he did not seem to feel any pain. Iren puffed out her chest and stood on her toes and did her best to look daunting. The Red Hand smiled up at her, gaping like a tourist before a monument. "Remarkable," he murmured, and reached up toward her face. Red light glazed his fingertips. "You'd never suspect we were the same species, would you? You're like a mountain. I'm a foothill."

Iren growled at him, and he withdrew his hand. He veered toward Edith, the movement as ungainly as a foal. She made a conscious effort to stand her ground, lest she give him the impression that she was afraid of him—which of course she was. But he seemed too preoccupied with the conspicuous machine hanging at her side to notice her stalwart pose.

"It's such a formidble instrument!" Reddleman said, pinching his chin in thought. As he studied its graceless plates and brutal angles, Edith flexed the engine to show its strength and put him off, though her display did not have the intended effect. He applauded in delight, saying, "It's so nice to see you back in play, master arm!"

"Never mind that, Reddleman." The Sphinx turned to Edith. "You see! He's entirely changed. He's a doe-eyed naïf."

Edith scoffed. "Surely, you can't expect us to believe he's harmless. He just snatched a hundred-pound cart from the air as if it were a pillow!"

"He's naive, Edith, not weak." The Sphinx's robe slithered along under him as he circled the group. "It's important that you get along. Reddleman is going to be your pilot."

"Reporting for duty, Captain!" the Red Hand said, saluting Edith with a lipless, frog-like smile.

"You really expect me to take him on as crew?"

"I do. Perhaps if you hadn't helped your last pilot escape, we wouldn't be in this position," the Sphinx said, and Edith felt a pang of guilt at the thought of Adam. She wondered how he was faring among the sparking men.

"A captain has to trust her crew. How in the world do you expect me to trust him?"

"Would you please turn around, Reddleman?" The Sphinx twirled the air with a black velvet finger. "That's it. Thank you. Now please unbutton your shirt."

Edith and Iren made no effort to conceal their discomfort at the Sphinx's direction, though their revulsion turned to a morbid sort of fascination when they saw the Red Hand's bared back. His spine was shielded in a brass shell, which ran from the nape of his neck nearly down to his waist. The case mirrored the ridges of his backbone, but between the polished vertebrae shined the red light of the Sphinx's powerful medium. "You'll notice he no longer has his cuff," the Sphinx said, tapping his own blank wrist as if asking for the time. "That cuff allowed him to change his own batteries, but that's not the case anymore. No, now he requires some assistance." The Sphinx pinched the third vertebra from the top of the Red Hand's spine, and four chambers along the backbone opened, revealing the tops of four vials. "These will need to be changed every forty-eight hours at least."

"That's quite often," Edith said. Her new arm could run for more than a week on a single battery.

"It is, but then the medium has essentially replaced the energy his body would otherwise produce. He doesn't have the capacity to draw any strength from food or sleep anymore. Since he can't replace the batteries himself, he must rely on you to keep him alive. If he were ever to turn on you, he would only be turning on himself."

"So I just have to trust he has a sense of self-preservation?" Edith asked.

"I certainly do," Reddleman said, buttoning up his shirt again. He turned to face them, wearing an amiable expression. "Death is an interesting drama, but I've seen it once already. I'm not sure I'm prepared to sit through an encore quite yet."

"See!" the Sphinx said happily. "You need Reddleman to fly your ship, and he needs you to change his batteries. Mutual need is better than trust."

"Still, it's a lot of ship," Edith said. "What about the rest of my crew?"

"This is the rest of your crew," the Sphinx said and then laughed at Edith's exasperated expression. "Don't worry. The *State of Art* all but flies itself!"

Chapter Two

An unexpected knock on my apartment door is as welcome as the drums of an invading army.

—Oren Robinson of the *Daily Reverie*

Inside the bridge of the *State of Art*, the alarm sounded: a single xylophonic note that seemed to come from nowhere and everywhere at once.

"Shut up, shut up, shut up!" Iren said with mounting annoyance through clenched teeth.

The alarm had rung once a minute, every minute, for the past six days. In that time, it had gone from an amusement, to a nuisance, to an absolute torment.

The bridge, which was itself larger than the entire main deck of the *Stone Cloud*, looked to have been designed by a jeweler: everything was gold, or silver, or some other precious alloy. The ship's control panels, which consumed three of the bridge's four walls, were filled with buttons and knobs, each as ornate as a signet ring. A hundred faceted bulbs flashed amid the controls. Their red, white, and green lights were bright enough to make the room sparkle. A bank of crystal-faced dials relayed the wind speed and barometric pressure as well as the ship's altitude, air speed, envelope density, coil temperature, oil level, and a dozen other essential measurements, only some of which were familiar to the crew.

In truth, Captain Winters and her bridge crew of two still found most of the ship's functions mysterious. And in the first moments after their launch at the start of the week, they had learned an important lesson about fiddling with controls they did not understand. The ship had hardly cleared the Sphinx's hangar when Iren flipped a toggle that she thought would turn off the ship's running lights—and in her defense the switch was located near the corridor light switch—but which in fact fired several flares from the aft of the ship. The resulting sparking rockets narrowly avoided bouncing through the hangar doors and into the Sphinx's lair. The Sphinx was quick to dispatch one of his winged messengers, which Byron played for the crew after dinner over a somber pudding. Byron's crème brûlée was burnt, but worse the Sphinx was obviously irate: "You can't go about twisting this and mashing that! You'll blow yourselves up! Read the manuals. That's why I gave them to you!"

Inside the bridge, the alarm rang once more.

"Reddleman, please tell me we're making progress on that," Edith said, rubbing her jaw to ease some of the tension that had settled there. She sat in the captain's chair between the gunner's station, presently attended by Iren, and the pilot's console, where Reddleman sat with a fat manual open on his lap.

"Elimination is its own sort of progress, Captain. Knowing what a thing isn't brings us one step closer to knowing what it is!" Reddleman said happily, reading along with the track of his finger. He sat in front of the ship's wheel, which actually didn't look like a wheel at all. The ship's primary steering yoke resembled the horns of a bull, capped on either tip by a gold ball.

Edith frowned at the back of his head. When she had dropped the Red Hand from the Port of Goll, it had never occurred to her that she would one day have to command his revived corpse. The Sphinx considered him both essential and harmless, though Edith was not at all convinced he was either. She certainly doubted he was as civil as he pretended to be. To his credit, since their awkward reunion, Reddleman had made no reference to his murder nor had he shown any sign that he held a grudge.

Which was well enough because she had no intention of apologizing.

Still, there was something unnerving about his demeanor. He was a little *too* cheery. He had the presence of someone who had just surrendered his plate after a wonderful, leisurely meal, or of someone who had only just caught his breath after laughing long and hard at an uproarious joke. As far as she could tell, he had no other emotions: He was never angry, nor sad, nor worried, nor afraid. He had not offered one word of complaint that she had essentially confined him to the bridge, nor did he seem at all annoyed by the incessant alarm. He was just cheerful, and perfectly so, all of the time.

"How would you describe the alarm, Captain?" Reddleman asked. Yellow-white bristles stood out from his pink scalp like the hairs of a pig. Edith marked the bulge of his mechanical spine through his green uniform jacket. That reminder of his dependency was reassuring.

"It sounds like a spike being slowly driven into my ear," Iren said, and as if on cue, the alarm rang again.

The manual Reddleman hunched over was at least three inches thick, and it was only the second of three similarly sized volumes. The manuals were so cumbersome because they not only had to explain the ship's functions and the means to repair them, but also the underlying principles that governed the system. It was, as he described it, "An engineering textbook wrapped in a physics degree, with an encyclopedia for an appendix."

"Would you say that sounds more like a finger cymbal, a wind chime, or . . . water dripping in a teacup?" Reddleman read from one of the manual's many tables.

"What difference does it make?" the amazon asked.

"Well, the alarm that sounds like a cymbal means the heating coil has suffered a catastrophic failure and the ship is going to explode."

"I think we would've noticed that."

"Excellent point, Captain! And the wind chime means that there's been an explosion in the boiler room, which again, would probably have drawn our attention. And the dripping sound . . . let me see . . . is a collision alarm."

"An alarm to tell us when we've run into something? Isn't that like putting a cowbell on a cannonball? What's the point? Keep looking,"

Edith said, and turned her attention again to the array of gold frames that ringed the bridge above the consoles.

Together, the frames formed what the manual called the *magnovisor*. It was, in effect, a window in a windowless room. Each frame of the magnovisor showed a different slice of the landscape outside—the desert valley, the encircling mountains, the sky, and the ships that occupied it. The facade of the Tower filled the starboard panels entirely, though not exactly in order. The world as it appeared inside the gold frames of the magnovisor was all in shades of gray, from pale ash to dark cinder. The shapes shifted and emerged slowly. The effect reminded Edith of drawing on a hot stone with water, though Reddleman said the technology involved iron shavings and millions of minute magnetic pins.

Edith would've preferred the simplicity of a spyglass or the unparalleled view of a bowsprit, but the magnovisor's existence was what allowed the *State of Art* to be so secure. There were even two frames that showed the view beneath the ship, which was a wonderful improvement over having to send a lookout crawling through the under rigging to check for unwanted shadows. It had taken a day for Edith and her crew to orientate to the various angles of the magnovisor, and it took another day for their eyes to adjust to the monochromatic, flattened representation of the world. But they were now more or less acclimated to it.

The magnovisor was just one of the ship's many technological miracles. Unlike the *Stone Cloud*, which had flown at the whims of the wind, the *State of Art* was equipped with a pair of propulsive vents at the stern. According to Reddleman, the vents concealed two powerful steam-fired turbines and, combined with the flaps on the ship's two short fins, provided them a maneuverability that passive airships could not compete with. The *State of Art* did not have to wait for the right current to arise to carry her where she wished to go: She made her own wind.

A new alarm broke the regularity of the familiar chime, and they all looked up as one.

"No, no, I can't do two at once. That's not fair!" Iren moaned. The alarm, which was higher and lighter, came closer together. It sounded like *plink-plink*. "What is that?"

"Aha! I believe *that* is the collision alarm," Reddleman said, shuffling between pages of the manual.

"Did we hit something?" Edith asked.

Reading quickly, Reddleman jabbed the page excitedly. "Wait! It doesn't only sound for violent collisions. It rings whenever physical contact has been made with the ship."

Edith rolled her hand in the air. "Meaning?"

"Meaning, I think someone is trying to board us."

The magnovisor, though miraculous, had the same blind spot that had bedeviled crews ever since a basket had first been lashed to a balloon. It could not peer around the ship's envelope, and so could not see the threats that came from above. Such a view still required a particularly daring and acrobatic lookout, and Edith was not about to bring Voleta into this mess.

They heard the muffled, but unmistakable, sound of footsteps overhead.

"They must've come in from above, repelled around the envelope, and swung onto the deck," Reddleman said, finding the switch to deactivate the plinking alarm. "Shall we shake them off? We could make a steep dive, perhaps?"

"Or I could just have a look," Iren suggested. "It doesn't sound like an army marching around up there, and I still haven't seen the crow's nest." She jerked a thumb at the ladder rungs that scaled the wall at the front of the bridge. The round hatch in the ceiling was closed and secured by a heavy wheel lock. That ladder, which led outside, was a large part of the reason why Voleta was not allowed on the bridge. Edith knew it was too great a temptation for Voleta to resist.

"I'm not sending you up there blind, Iren. There could be one or one dozen armed men waiting for you up there."

"We could check the periscope," Reddleman said.

"The what?" Edith said.

"Hold on, I was just reading about this..." Reddleman flipped to the back of the manual, counted down a row of stoppers in the control panel in front of him, and grasped one near the end. When he pulled the stopper out, the small chandelier that hung above the captain's chair began to descend. The fixture concealed a column that telescoped downward, halting at eye level. Edith pulled down the handles on either side of the pole and put her eyes to the gold-rimmed viewfinder. She found the world outside transcribed there in miniature. She saw woolly clouds pulled into threads by the mountain peaks, and airships, small as ground pepper, rendered motionless by the distance.

The esoteric spyglass, which would've seemed a marvel in its own right aboard another ship, struck her here as almost commonplace. She was learning a curious truth about miracles: when piled together, they became ordinary.

Edith turned the bars of the periscope, exploring the view, then after half a circuit, reared back in surprise, her mouth curled in a funny expression.

"What do you see?" Iren asked.

"A boot," she said, then looked again. She saw six boots, in fact. The men were shuffling about the leveled top of the sleek hull with ropes about their waists and swords in their hands. Their tethers ran upward out of sight. Their legs were tied up with rags to warm them, and their furs were matted and balding. "They're not soldiers," she said. "Pirates probably. Three of them. Lightly armed. They're looking for a way in, I think. Oh. They've noticed the periscope. Hello! Yes, I see you. Get off my ship!" Edith said, knowing they could not hear her. "Why don't we let them know we're not interested in receiving any visitors at the moment. Iren, fire a salvo."

"What am I aiming at?" Iren asked, bending down to press her face against the rubber cradle of the gunner's viewfinder, which, like the periscope, was a peephole into the outside world. "I see . . . Tower, more Tower, clouds, desert, foothills, a barge, another barge, a flock of birds, one more barge—"

"No, no, don't kill anything," Edith cut in. "Just aim for the mountains. We want to rattle teeth, not start a war."

Iren twiddled the adjacent controls, which she had earlier described as *a stupid bunch of thimbles*. Strange as the knobs appeared, she had learned quickly enough how efficient they were at focusing the ship's artillery.

A moment later, the port cannons thundered in unison, and the steel hull of the ship chimed.

Still squinting into the gunner's mask, Iren said, "Oof! I hit the boulder I was aiming at. It's completely gone. Wiped it off the face of the earth. This is fun! We should do more salvos!"

Peering again into her periscope, Edith was disappointed to see the interlopers still bandying about the deck of her ship. They seemed perhaps a little unnerved by the cannon fire, but not at all dissuaded. "They're still there," she said.

"Three is nothing," Iren said, pulling away from her station. She pressed her knuckles into the small of her back, striking an almost musical phrase of pops and cracks from her spine. "I could handle three in my sleep."

Edith puffed her cheeks and said, "Well, if you want the exercise." She swept out her arm in invitation. "Help yourself."

Iren was out of her seat and at the gun locker in two steps. As she opened the glass cabinet door, she started to whistle an aimless, happy tune. Edith had never heard her whistle before and had not known she could. Iren drew out a saber and flintlock pistol, buckling both around her waist before pulling the strap of a rifle onto her shoulder. When she turned around again, she pumped her arms and shuffled her feet to accompany her whistling.

"Are you dancing?" Edith asked.

"No, no. I don't dance. I'm just loosening up," Iren said. "It's been a while."

"Don't forget your tether line." Edith watched the amazon climb the ladder and unscrew the hatch before turning her attention back to the periscope's mask.

"She's a lot of fun, isn't she?" Reddleman said, watching Iren disappear into the shaft that led above deck.

"I wouldn't call her *fun* to her face if I were you," Edith said, then seemed to reconsider. "Never mind. Try it. Tell her she's fun."

"I wish I didn't make her so uncomfortable." He sighed, apparently unaware of the sardonic edge to Edith's remarks. The creak of the second hatch opening was followed quickly by a change to the air pressure and temperature of the room.

"Well, maybe you shouldn't have tried to kill her the first time you met."

"I didn't throw the cart back at her...Oh, you mean on that port. But that was before I died."

"I don't see why that should matter to her." Though Edith continued speaking to him, her attention was on the periscope's view. "You say you're different. Maybe you even feel different, but we don't feel differently about you."

Edith observed the moment the three pirates realized they were no longer alone on the deck of the ship. She turned the periscope in time to see Iren emerge from behind the open hatch. The amazon had her cheek snugged against the stock of her rifle. She fired, and the report rang down the ladder shaft, making the glass of the gun cabinet chatter. Edith watched Iren duck ahead of the returned fire. A lead ball ricocheted off the open hatch, ringing it like an anvil.

"I think she got one of them," Reddleman said. Edith looked away from the viewfinder to see him pointing at the starboard frames of the magnovisor. Their view of the Tower was now obscured by the body of a man, swinging at the end of a rope. His arms and legs jerked a moment, then went limp. His lifeless expression twisted into view as he floated between frames on the wall.

Edith looked back into the periscope just in time to see Iren grab another pirate by his harness and hurl him directly at her. The periscope handles rattled from the impact. The pirate slumped against the periscope's lens, obscuring her view. "No, don't thrash him there, Iren! Move him! Move him out of the way!"

"Captain!" Reddleman shouted.

Edith looked past the periscope's mask to discover the third pirate clinging to the top of the ladder like a spider on the wall. Her hand flew to her sidearm.

"Don't you do it!" the pirate yelled, his pistol already leveled at her. "Stay where you are."

Before she could say anything, Reddleman said, "Hold on, Captain."

The deck tilted sharply beneath her, and in the same instant, a gunshot nearly burst her eardrums. She fell backward, unsure even if she'd been shot, and landed in her captain's chair so forcefully she nearly tumbled over its back. The invader lost his foothold on the rungs as the ship's angle pulled him from the wall. His grip slipped, and he plummeted toward Edith. He would've landed on top of her if the periscope hadn't been in the way. He clipped the column with his hip, spun once in the air, and landed in a sprawling heap. He slid to a halt against Edith's heels.

The pirate looked up, his eyes wide with surprise. She kicked him in the mouth.

"Level us out, pilot." She gave the order without taking her eyes off the dazed intruder. Reddleman pulled back on the golden yoke, and the ship began to right.

Edith stood and drew her pistol. The pirate had a weedy beard and bloodshot eyes and now fewer teeth in his prominent mouth. Edith was not accustomed to people ignoring the barrel of her gun, and yet the pirate did so now. He was looking past her. His lips trembled so dramatically he seemed to nurse at the air.

Edith glanced at Reddleman, standing at her side. The hole in his chest leaked a stream of red light. Reddleman touched the wound, regarding the bright stain on his pale fingers with a warm smile. "Oh, you got me good, sir! Well done!"

The gold frames on the portside flashed, attracting their attention. The hanging body of the second pirate fell into view on the magnovisor, his throat bloody, his arms stretched out as if to embrace his end. On the opposite wall, the first dead pirate still swung back and forth like the pendulum of a clock.

The door to the bridge creaked and Byron stepped inside, complaining as he came, "What on earth is going on in here? Was that a gunshot? Oh my god! Who is that?"

The pirate screamed, "Monsters!"

Byron touched his brocaded vest and sounded a little hurt when he said, "Who, me?"

Iren descended the ladder, her swords and rifle clattering as she came. "Sorry, Captain. I let one get past me."

"We noticed," Edith said.

The amazon skipped the last few rungs and let her boots rattle the floor beneath the traumatized pirate. He turned his gaze from the enlarged, deadened faces of his crewmates, moving like shadows upon the wall, to the horned beast in a tuxedo jacket, to the grinning man bleeding light from a bullet wound, and finally to the woman with an iron arm, who now picked him up by the front of his weathered furs.

"I'll give you a choice," she said. "I can give you over to my crew. They are numerous, and I admit, they are a little bored. Or I can let you go."

"Let me go?" the pirate said, his hope half-drowned by the blood in his mouth.

"Yes, but only if you promise to spread a word for me. I want you to go to the Windsock. I want you to go to Harlot's Cove, and to Port Marrow, and to the Red Cleft, and any other pirate den you can worm your way into. I want you to tell them exactly what you have seen here. We do not hide when you board us. We do not die when you shoot us. We do not forget when you cross us."

Edith shook him until he whimpered then pulled him very close. "Tell them the Sphinx has opened up his infernal zoo and let all his monsters out."

Chapter Three

The rich "learn lessons." The poor commit crimes. "Mistakes" are generally considered a mark of the middle class.

—Oren Robinson of the *Daily Reverie*

Byron dragged a mop through the puddle of urine the pirate had left on the floor of the bridge. "It's just, I thought perhaps we could try to appeal to people's better nature."

"Pirates don't have a better nature, Byron," Edith said. She pressed the linen bandage against the oozing hole in her pilot's chest. Reddleman held his unbuttoned shirt pulled out for her. He smiled into the distance as if he'd just detected a pleasing waft of budding roses.

Edith was still trying to decide what she thought of his apparently selfless attempt to draw the pirate's attention and gunfire. She lifted one of Reddleman's hands and pressed it against the bandage. His skin felt like warm rubber. "Here, hold this."

"But weren't you pirates?" Byron asked.

"Only half pirates," Iren said, as she descended from the crow's nest amid a welcome blast of fresh air. She'd just finished cutting the dead pirates free. To everyone's relief, their view of the ink-wash sky was now free of swinging corpses.

"We wanted to scare him, Byron. A frightening reputation is good armor," Edith said, wrapping a length of gauze about Reddleman's chest. She couldn't quite look her pilot in the face when she asked, "You sure you're all right?"

Reddleman turned his dreamy smile toward her. "Yes, thank you, Captain. I just need you to change my vials, and I'll be fine."

"You did well back there, pilot. Good work," Edith said.

"Oh, thank you, sir," Reddleman said.

"But surely we don't have to go around telling people we're *monsters*." Byron plunged his mop into the pail a final time and brushed the perspiration from his whiskers. "Especially when some of us are so handsome."

Edith turned away so Byron would not see her shudder at the memory of what the Sphinx had hidden away inside his secret attic.

Edith wished the Sphinx had never taken her into his confidence, yet she had no one to blame but herself.

Shortly before their launch, the Sphinx had called them all to his cavernous port, to stand before the prow of the *State of Art* and bear witness as he rechristened the ship. Byron stood at the wharf's edge, holding a bottle of champagne like a club at his shoulder. The stag wore his most grandiose uniform, complete with gold braids and tasseled epaulets. He patiently waited for the Sphinx's signal to swing the bottle and douse the gleaming hull in wine.

Edith stood in a line with Iren, Voleta, and Reddleman while the Sphinx delivered a rambling speech, which swung from historical review to pointed instruction in a manner Edith found confusing. After some minutes of boasting about the contents of the ship's guest registry and her spotless battle record, the Sphinx began to adjure Edith's new crew in a quavering voice. "You will parade her before every ambitious ringdom, king, navy, and pirate. You will dare them to raise arms against you and make them rue the day that they do. You will stir the sky like a summer gale and thunder out my name!" Swept up in the emotion of the moment, the Sphinx spread his thin black arms in benediction. "You will show the Tower that the Sphinx has returned! And the ringdoms shall give unto you those consecrated works of art, the Brick Layer's tokens, to serve as tribute to my many gifts and—"

"Surely Marat is the more pressing concern," Edith said.

The Sphinx dropped his arms. "What?"

"If there is, as you say, a war coming, is this really the time to worry about a bunch of dusty artwork? I'm sure they have sentimental value, but—"

The Sphinx interrupted her in return: "What about this ceremony made you think we were having a conversation?"

"It just seems that showboating might not be the most effective way of disrupting a hod uprising. No offense, sir."

"Why would I be offended? Despite not knowing the details of what's happening, or how it's happened, or why, you still feel informed enough to interrupt me with a critique of my plan. How could that be offensive?"

"If I'm uninformed, it's not by choice."

"Ah. Well, why don't we go for a walk, so I can give you my full and furious attention?"

As the Sphinx and Edith proceeded to the heavy medallion door to the Sphinx's home, Byron held up the bottle of champagne, craning his long neck as he called after them, "Excuse me, are we still going to...? Should I...?" He received no reply.

Following after the Sphinx like a chastised dog, Edith resisted the impulse to apologize, an urge that only grew stronger when they arrived at their destination.

As she parted the flock of ticking butterflies that flapped about the Sphinx's workshop, Edith clutched the cool, humming elbow of her engine. The ache of the surgery had just begun to ebb. The arm still moved as clumsily as a limb in a dream, but already it felt like her own. She did not want to give it back. She wondered, should the Sphinx decide to take it, if he would give her an even cruder device, something club-like. A table leg, perhaps? Her gaze fell upon a mechanical hand on a workbench, curled up like a dead spider. She recognized the detached appendage at once. She had used it to lift a spoon, to hold a hairbrush, to tie a knot, to pull a trigger. She suppressed a shudder.

But amid that surge of existential dread, Edith had an abrupt revelation standing there amid so much half-assembled wonder. She realized something obvious, something that should've occurred to her much sooner.

She stopped and said, "You're desperate, aren't you? That's why you've given me command of your flagship and brought the Red Hand back from the dead and sent someone as inexperienced as Tom off to spy on your behalf. You're desperate. I've been so afraid of you, so overwhelmed by your gifts and your contracts, that I couldn't see it. But you're backed into a corner. You're playing your last cards." Edith laughed dryly. "And they don't seem to be particularly good ones."

The Sphinx surprised Edith by laughing, too, though more generously. "We *all* have our backs in a corner, my dear. Just not all of us realize it yet. I admire how loyal you are to your friends, but I fear that loyalty has blinded you to your greater obligations."

Edith bristled at the implication. "I follow orders. I keep my word. What other obligations do I have?"

"You have a duty to the Tower. To your fellow man. Where is your sense of responsibility?"

"How can you expect me to be responsible for things you keep from me? Why are you obsessed with those paintings? If everything is so bleak, and war looms so large, and the Tower is a powder keg, why waste time gathering up a bunch of old canvases?"

"Why are the young so impatient when they have the most time!" the Sphinx asked the empty room, tilting his mask back in wonderment. "You'll have your answer soon enough, Edith. Come on. I hope you slept well last night, because it's the last good night's sleep you'll get for a very long time."

At the back of the cluttered workroom stood a rack full of mismatched pipes and rods. The jumble appeared to have not been disturbed in a decade at least. The Sphinx turned to make sure Edith was observing, then gripped the end of a rusted length of rebar and pulled. The bar clicked, and the entire cabinet slid smoothly to one side, revealing an open doorway in the workshop wall.

The spiraling stairs beyond seemed to go on forever, an impression that only grew stronger once they began to climb. The ascent didn't appear to tire the Sphinx in the least, but after chasing the black tail of his cloak for some moments, Edith was ready to beg for a rest when the stairs came to an abrupt end, and she found herself standing, wobbly kneed, on a landing.

The Sphinx hesitated before the only door—an iron-banded oak slab that looked nearly as old as the Tower itself. "I don't show my attic to many people. I'd appreciate if you'd not share what you see with anyone. That includes Byron."

Edith was surprised to learn there were places in the Sphinx's home that Byron had not seen, but she quickly gave her word.

When Edith thought of an attic, she pictured exposed rafters, curtains of cobwebs, and old furniture shrouded under bedsheets. Attics were for the unwanted artifacts of youth and the tedious evidence of past generations; they were for outgrown ice skates, toy chests, wedding dresses, and some great-aunt's china that no one loved well enough to live with, nor hated enough to throw away.

But what lay behind that creaking door better resembled a wing of a museum than an attic. The airy, wide gallery ran on for some distance. Electric spotlights threw islands of light, which tempered but did not banish the gloom. Formal exhibits, like something from a natural history museum, lined either wall. The displays were set upon shallow stages behind red velvet ropes. At first glance, Edith mistook the subjects of those exhibits for the assembled bones of extinct beasts, interspersed with suits of fanciful armor. But as they drew nearer, she saw they were in fact machines like Ferdinand or the wall-walker, though stranger and more primitive.

The first cordoned-off engine reminded her of a scarecrow. Its limbs were long and lithe; its head round, its features painted on and crude. The materials that made up its arms and legs were irregular, a patchwork of mismatched parts. The engine stood some seven feet tall and was posed like a slouching butler. When the Sphinx passed it, he declared, "Ah, Mr. Ekes! He was my first! So slow and clumsy— always falling over. But, oh, how I loved him!"

Confused by this sudden effusiveness and not knowing what to say, Edith said, "You made him?" By impulse, she reached out and set the palm of her engine upon the shoulder of the gawkish machine. The iron bones seemed to rise to meet her touch like a cat asking to be pet. She almost recoiled in surprise but willed herself to hesitate. She held the contact and focused upon it.

It was absurd, of course, but she felt an inkling of a connection to the cold, dead engine. No, not a connection—it was more like a slow echo, an internal mumbled dialogue...

The curious sensation was chased away by the Sphinx's chatter, and Edith withdrew her hand.

"I was sixteen years old, I think, when I built him." The Sphinx sighed, the noise like a leak in a bicycle tire. "I made every one of these machines. I brought them to life, taught them to serve, and mourned them when they died." The Sphinx continued down the hall, pointing and remarking upon the bizarre pieces of his collection as he went. There was Horace, whose bottom half resembled the wheel of a riverboat, but was cleated with iron spikes. Horace had the chest and arms of a man and the head of an ox. He had been built to till the fields of the garden ringdoms. Then there was Zoë, who looked like a sofa-sized tortoise, and who rather than a head possessed a single lidless eye at the end of a cabled neck. Zoë was created to be a sewer inspector, though she proved to have a knack for getting herself lodged in unsavory places.

The Sphinx paused before the biggest engine in his maudlin collection. Of all the machines, this one unsettled Edith the most. It seemed a mixture of praying mantis and steam shovel. Its forearms curved into scimitar-like blades. Most unnerving, the engine had a woman's head, statuesque and pale as marble, set on the end of a long, barbed spine. "I had to remove Penelope's batteries after she killed several dignitaries. An accident, of course. But it was quite an unpleasant scene." The Sphinx reached up and patted one of the engine's armor-plated knees.

"What was she built for?"

"Shepherding spider-eaters." The Sphinx moved on, his black robe slithering across the pine-green carpet. "Have you ever heard the parable of the plagued farmer?"

"No," Edith said, the question catching her off guard.

"There once was a farmer who was plagued by black flies. They were vicious things that chewed the leaves of his crops and bit him when he slept. So the farmer bought a pair of frogs to eat the flies and reproduce, which they did—but too well. Soon, he was finding frogs in his sugar bowl and frogs in his bedpan and frogs in his boots in the morning. So the farmer bought a pair of herons to eat the frogs and reproduce, which they did, but they also scratched up his seeds and trampled his seedlings. So the farmer bought a pair of cats to chase off the herons and reproduce, which they did, but they also killed his chickens and ate all the songbirds and pounced on him like little tigers wherever he went. So he bought a pair of dogs, and when that went wrong, he bought a pair of bears, and then a pair of elephants, and then after the elephants had flattened his house and his barn and everything he owned, he bought a pair of black flies. They were vicious, biting things, and they drove the elephants off."

"It's the curse of unintended consequences," Edith said.

"It's the curse of giving a damn!" the Sphinx said sharply, rising to his full height. "The Brick Layer tried to meet the Tower's needs with domesticated beasts, but they were unpredictable and dangerous. They consumed too many resources, contracted too many diseases. It was unsustainable. So I built mechanical alternatives to serve the Tower. But the engines were mindless, dangerous, and susceptible to sabotage. So I founded the Wakemen, hoping that strength with a conscience would bring some balance and sanity to the Tower, but instead I blighted the ringdoms with Luc Marat and the Red Hand. At every step, I meant to sow the seeds of freedom, equality, and ease, but I only scattered plagues." The Sphinx shrank again as if exhausted by the outburst. "So rather than persist in my failure, rather than compound my errors, I withdrew."

"*Errors.*" Edith repeated the word under her breath.

They were drawing to the end of the grand hall. The last exhibits in the Sphinx's so-called attic were unlike the others, and Edith could not help but stop and stare. The three machines were all more or less human in dimension. They had arms and legs, hands and feet. Two were dressed in fitted suits; the third wore a blouse and riding breeches. Edith might've mistaken them for mannequins in a shop-window had it not been for their heads. One seemed to have belonged to a ram, another to a lion, and the last to a wolf. Their bleached, bare skulls jutted ghoulishly from the starched collars of their clothes.

She thought of Byron and how shocked he would be to see his predecessors displayed like trophies. No wonder the Sphinx wanted to keep this from him.

Edith noted the empty space beside the final exhibit. The area was roped off and spotlighted and seemed to yawn for a subject. "Still room for me, I see," she said, meaning to be cavalier, though her voice sounded flat and morose.

"No, that spot is mine," the Sphinx said. "One day, I will climb those stairs, lock the door behind me, and complete the collection. Oh, don't look at me like that, young woman. That day is not today. And this is not what I wanted to show you."

Around the corner from the great hall was an antechamber, which seemed entirely out of place. It resembled the changing room at a spa: tile on the floor, a well-worn wooden bench down the center, a dozen lockers set into either wall. Edith opened the nearest one and stared at the dark rubber suit hanging inside. A bullet-shaped helmet gleamed upon the shelf. It was the same armor the sparking men had worn when they had accosted her and Adam on the Tower's peak.

"Find one that fits," the Sphinx said. "I have to put on something a bit more dramatic, I'm afraid."

The process of selecting, comprehending, and squeezing into the rubber armor took Edith some minutes to accomplish. She had to choose a suit large enough to fit over her engine, which resulted in every other seam being too loose. The rubber squeaked horribly the entire time she struggled to fasten the gold cuffs and collar.

She had just begun to examine the inside of one of the smirking helmets when she heard an approaching clicking sound. The noise was sharp and rapid as the clack of a typewriter. She turned to see a glass orb walking across the tile on eight golden legs. The Sphinx's black shroud hung inside the crystal carriage like a flaw in a polished opal. The coach was nearly twice as tall as Edith.

Inside the sphere, the Sphinx mimed putting on a helmet, and after a moment's confusion, Edith did just that. The interior of the gold helmet was snug with padding. The visor slit appeared to have been sealed with smoked glass. Edith was still getting used to the weight and the narrowed view when the Sphinx's voice spoke directly into her ear. She flinched and ducked, ramming against the locker, even as the Sphinx said, "Don't be alarmed! You're perfectly fine. Please don't thrash about."

Edith gripped the sides of her helmet. "Can you hear me?"

"Don't shout, woman! My god, we'll both go deaf. Yes, I can hear you."

"How?"

"I don't have time to explain all my miracles to you. Now, come on, quick as you can."

Edith found walking in the heavy suit difficult. Her feet didn't quite sit right in the rubber boots and her gait was lumbering as a result. But she followed the Sphinx as best she could as he ticked along in his spider-legged soap bubble. Beyond the changing room were the broad doors of a service elevator. The control panel inside the spacious lift contained just two buttons, one labeled ATTIC; the other, ROOF. The Sphinx asked Edith to do the honors. As the car rose, she asked if they were going to see the sparking men and whether Adam would be there.

"Having regrets about helping him escape already, are you?" the Sphinx asked.

"Not at all." It was odd to feel her breath bounce back against her lips as she spoke.

"Ah! There's still time. The wonderful thing about regrets is that it's never too late to have them. But to answer your question: No, we're not going to see Adam. We're going to *my* roof, not to the roof of the Tower."

"Why?" Edith asked. She tried to guess how quickly they were rising and how far the elevator had already traveled.

"As you probably already know, the Tower is essentially a mill, but rather than milling grain, gravel, or silk, it mills lightning. That energy not only powers our batteries, it supplies many of the upper ringdoms with light, water, industry, and even fresh air. If the Tower were to go dark, tens of thousands would perish in the span of an hour, and hundreds of thousands more in the course of a day. We cannot allow the spark to go out."

Though her rubber armor muted her sensation, Edith became aware that the passage of the car was growing more unsteady the higher they climbed. The electric lamps in the ceiling flickered out briefly, then flared back to life.

"But lightning is not an easy thing to manage, and short of some act of violent sabotage, which would turn a third of the Tower into a tomb, I can't slow the pace of production. I believe those controls are kept behind a sealed door, and the means for opening that door is encoded within those paintings."

The floor of the car shuddered violently. Edith reached out to steady herself. The wall jumped and shook like the handle of a plow.

"For decades, I've been catching the excess lightning and storing it in a reservoir. But I'm running out of room, and the medium can only hold so much energy before it undergoes a catastrophic degradation."

"A catastrophic what?"

"An explosion, Edith—an eruption of volcanic proportions."

Even through the dampening helmet and with the Sphinx's disembodied voice filling her ear, Edith still heard the mounting roar that had begun to fill the car. It sounded like breathless thunder. A primeval sort of terror stirred in the pit of her stomach. It seemed to climb her throat like a rope, squeezing off the flow of blood and air as it rose.

"Here, take this," the Sphinx said. A drawer in the gold cradle beneath his bubble opened, revealing a strange instrument inside. Dazedly, Edith removed the tool. It looked like a compass, but with horns on one end and a handle on the other. "It's an ammeter."

Edith was formulating a question when their ascent came to a clanging halt. The car continued to rattle and quail like a cabin in a hurricane. The Sphinx said, "Walk to the handrail. Hold the ammeter out. Squeeze the grip for ten seconds to take a reading. Then come back to the elevator. And don't dally."

The doors opened, and a hellish glare poured in.

Outside, a blood-red sea boiled.

Waves rose and clapped together, their froth flaring bright as guncotton. There seemed to be no wind, and yet the intensity of the spray made the air roil and shimmer. The sea glowed bright enough to illuminate the cavern it filled. In the distance, Edith saw the surf break upon a rocky bluff that rose and curved in toward the peak of the dome.

She stood atop a silvery needle—a lighthouse stationed in the middle of a furious sea. A gold guardrail banded the narrow observatory deck. Other than the elevator housing behind her, the platform was empty.

Through the rubber armor, she felt something like the pelting of frozen rain on her skin, though it came from every direction, and the feeling seemed to burrow into her until it pecked at her bones. It took all her concentration to shuffle forward. Even shielded by the smoked glass and the visor, her eyes teared and seemed to fizz in their sockets. She reached for the railing, still two steps away, and saw that her gloved hand was covered in round, rolling flames. The queer fire wavered and dispersed like blood spilled into a stream.

Grasping the guardrail with her engine, she held the ammeter out into the sparkling air. She realized that the surface of the sea was closer than it had appeared from inside the elevator. The caps of the tallest waves leapt high enough to lap the underside of the decking. She felt the slapping impact through her boot soles. The tines of the ammeter were haloed in electric pink light. She tried to focus on the instrument's dial, but her gaze went past it, down to the raging sea.

Lightning sparked up from the dim red depths, igniting the abyss with jagged lances as it broke toward the surface. While still submerged, the electricity forked and turned at a dreamy pace, progressing like a crack through oceanic ice. But when the lightning broke the surface, it shattered into seething white static that leapt between the tops of waves.

Edith's transfixion was broken by the Sphinx's voice in her ear. "I said, don't dally!"

Spurred by a large bolt from the deep, a wave leapt higher than the rest. When it struck the plate Edith was standing on, it threw her into the air. Her deathly grip on the guardrail carried her forward, and she swung clear over the railing with a shout. The ammeter flew from her grip as she crashed bodily against the side of the rail and decking, bounced outward, and crashed back again. The rubber padding absorbed the brunt of the shock, but the pain was still enough to make her gasp. She looked down in time to see the ammeter hit the surface of the reservoir and incinerate with a flash of light.

Sped by fear, she pulled herself up. The plate that had thrown her had landed out of alignment, and she stepped over the gap it left behind. She staggered back to the waiting elevator, finding the interior dressed in the same eerie fire that had clung to her outside. The pink plasma licked along the crystal face of the Sphinx's carriage. Edith slapped the button to return to the attic. The doors closed, and as the car sank again, the roar began to diminish. As she knelt on one knee, panting to catch her breath, the electric sprites sputtered out in little pops of light.

"You owe me an ammeter," the Sphinx said.

"What was that hell? What are we going to do?" Edith's voice shook with dread and adrenaline.

"Ah, it worked!"

"What do you mean, it worked?" Edith glared up at the Sphinx, dark and slender as the pupil of a cat.

"The passing of the curse, of course," said the Sphinx.

Chapter Four

I distrust sweet cocktails and cheerful men for the
same reason: It's hard to tell how dangerous they are
until they've knocked you on your ear.

—Oren Robinson of the *Daily Reverie*

I n the days since she'd dangled above the lightning sea, Edith had
spent many hours contemplating the Sphinx's curse. The Sphinx
had gone to some pains to elaborate upon the exact proportion of
their despair, assuring Edith that should the medium in the reservoir
degrade, the resulting explosion would be enough to fill the entire valley with a fireball so intense it would liquefy the ground down to the
bedrock. The Tower would simply cease to be, along with every man,
woman, and child inside it. The sky would go black. An impenetrable
winter would settle upon the land. The nation of Ur would be ravaged
by famine. And in the span of a generation, the epilogue of human history would be written on the wall of a cave.

But this grim knowledge was only one aspect of the curse. Another
was the need for absolute secrecy. If word of the looming catastrophe
were to get out, there would be panic, and hoarding, pillaging, and
war. And that was assuming everyone believed her. Surely, some ringdoms would decry the warnings as a ruse to disrupt their prosperity,
and rather than evacuate, they would sequester themselves. And any
loss of population in the Tower would doubtlessly be replaced by the

destitute and despairing hordes of the Market. As the Sphinx put it: "A drowning man will still scramble aboard a sinking ship."

No, this curse was not a burden that sharing would make any lighter.

But perhaps the worst part of the curse was the feeling of futility that accompanied it. Edith had been right to call the Sphinx desperate, but now that she had been infected by that frantic feeling, she was eager for him to offer some qualification, to tell her that there was time enough to throttle back the lightning, and enough reasonable men and women left in the Tower to make such a thing possible. Rather than encouragement, the Sphinx had offered her a contingency: "I'll monitor the reservoir. If I think it's at a tipping point, then I'll have you sabotage the lightning mill. I think we'd both rather the Tower become a mausoleum than a crater. Certainly, it's preferable to murder a few hundred thousand than to preside over the end of the species."

Edith had not been much consoled by the Sphinx's fallback plan.

She sat brooding in her captain's chair aboard the *State of Art*. It had been mere hours since the excitement of the failed boarding party, but already she longed for another distraction. She had already toured every inch of her spectacular ship, exploring everything from the sheet music in the harpsichord bench in the conservatory to the crawl space beneath the gun deck, where rails full of cannonballs snaked to the base of each gun, and down to the uncomfortably cramped orlop where the water tanks sloshed and the ship's reservoir of the Sphinx's medium, stored in a long crystalline vat, bathed everything in vermillion light. She had inspected all but the engine room, which Byron said was locked to discourage meddling. He described the mechanisms inside the vault as being so finely tuned that even an errant hair might snarl them and cripple the ship.

And yet upon passing the sealed hatch soon after, an inexpressible instinct had brought Edith to a halt before the imposing door. She placed her iron palm upon the plaque, bolted like a grave plate to the steel, and instantly she felt a thrumming so profound it reverberated inside her skull. That trembling made her thoughts seem first to quiver, then peal like a ringing bell, echoing outward, stretching beyond the boundary of her skin.

The experience had been uncomfortable enough to convince her that not all of the Sphinx's veils needed pulling back.

Now she stared at a dark spot on the white cuff of her blouse. The Red Hand's blood, splashed there by the pirate's bullet, had glowed like a lamp wick at first. Now it was dull and gray as ash. She wondered why in the world the Sphinx had made so much of the stuff, enough to fill a sea, enough to burn the earth down to the bone.

Byron appeared in the open door to the main passageway, and said, "Captain, could I speak to you in the hall for a moment?"

Leaving the ship under Iren's command, Edith followed the stag out. Something about the ship's decor in its passages, cabins, and great rooms reminded her of a bank lobby. The fixtures on the bulkheads were stately, well polished, and absolutely devoid of human charm. She wondered if she would ever get accustomed to it, or if she would just go on growing more and more nostalgic for the *Stone Cloud*, that flying splinter factory presently moldering in a corner of the Sphinx's shipyard. He had promised to repair it. Edith wondered if he ever would.

Byron handed her the wingless body of one of the Sphinx's messengers. It wasn't unusual to receive her orders in such a fashion. She was growing accustomed to receiving two, sometimes three missives from her employer a day. The Sphinx had ideas about which ringdoms he wished her to prowl past and which skyports she should test her cannons outside of. Edith dreaded each message, fearing it would be the one when the Sphinx declared the lightning sea too unstable. And what had he meant when he said she might have to "sabotage the lightning mill" one day? Did that mean the destruction of the Lightning Nest in New Babel? Could she even do such a thing without setting off all those stores of hydrogen?

"It's from our vagabond friend," Byron said.

"From Senlin?" she said, her heart suddenly squeezing into a fist. It had been about a week since they'd said their goodbyes in the

Sphinx's stables. The Sphinx had given Byron express orders not to play Senlin's reports for anyone aboard the *State of Art*, including its captain, and yet the stag had found a way to keep Edith apprised of Senlin's status, mostly in the passageways, when he paused in her vicinity to muse aloud about a "vagabond friend" suffering through another uneventful day. The last such casual observation had occurred the day before when Byron had said, "Our vagabond friend seems to be getting a little bored, I think. He's taken to tattling on newsboys and magpies. Though bored is better than endangered, I should think."

Byron had seemed to find the playful subterfuge comforting. Now that they were speaking directly, he seemed less at ease. "Of course, if you-know-who found out about this, he would be . . . *unhappy*. But I did promise our vagabond . . . I did promise Tom."

"When? Promised him what?"

"We shared a moment," Byron said, smiling with ironic wistfulness. "I was in the process of abandoning him on a godforsaken outpost when he asked if I would forward one message to you on one occasion, and I agreed. So I am breaking the rules, defying my master, and likely cementing my legacy as a cad and a turncoat, but after all, it's just this once, and Senlin was very, very pitiful. I thought he might cry."

Knowing that Byron was being droll to cover his discomfort, Edith gripped his mechanical hand with her likewise hand and said, "Thank you, Byron."

If he could've blushed, he probably would've then. Instead, he blinked and snuffled and twitched as if he'd inhaled a little pepper. When he'd recovered his poise, he said solemnly, "Of course, I didn't listen to it."

"I'm sure it's nothing very interesting." Edith tried to sound more at ease than she felt.

"Well, if you'll excuse me, Captain, I have an engagement in the parlor. I'm teaching a jackrabbit how to waltz, and the rabbit does not care for it." He turned on his heel and marched down the corridor with a slight but unmistakable bounce in his step.

* * *

Edith retreated to her quarters on the middeck to listen to Senlin's message in private.

She did not care for her lodgings. The captain's quarters were over-large and overdecorated with portraits of past commanders. Glass cabinets swamped the room, filled with medals and braids and dozens of prominently displayed and seemingly random objects, including a marionette dressed like an admiral, a fan made out of black lace, a model of a sailboat, and a brass bed warmer with a country scene stamped on its bottom. When on the first evening of their voyage she had informed Byron that she would prefer a smaller cabin, he had expressed some puzzlement as to why. She had explained, "Because I can't stand all these knickknacks. I feel like I've wandered into a pawnshop."

"*Knickknacks?*" Byron had whickered in horror. "These *knickknacks* were presented by the Tower's greatest nobility to all the venerable commanders of the *State of Art*. These are invaluable symbols of historic reverence. This isn't a pawnshop. It's a museum!"

"But that's just it: I don't want to sleep in a museum."

"And yet this is where the captain sleeps. It's tradition," Byron had said, and in so saying, he unintentionally summoned the memory of what she had told Senlin when he had balked at the thought of sleeping in Captain Billy Lee's quarters: *A crew needs a little room to cavort and plot their mutinies. It's good for morale.* Funny how different it felt to be on the receiving end of that argument.

Like it or not, this was her cabin, and she had little choice but to accept it.

She shut her door and took up the bottle of rum from the comfortable jumble of books, maps, dishes, and models she had left on the table, as if to stake her own mess amid the curated clutter. She pulled the stopper out with her teeth and poured a dram into an almost-clean pewter mug. She sipped, slipped off her greatcoat, and sat down to study the brass body of the messenger.

"So, Tom, let's see what you have to say for yourself." She twisted the moth's head, and the machine began to hiss softly with the sounds of a distant and foreign room.

"All right, Byron. I hope you remember my request," Senlin said. Though his voice was a little faint, she was so surprised to hear it she stood up, rattling the table as she rose. The Sphinx's miracles were so often unsettling. "I promise this is the one and only time I will impose upon your discretion, but please, please: I'd like to say a few words to Edith...alone. Thank you, Byron. You are a good friend."

There was a pause in the recording. Edith began to pace.

"Dear Edith," Senlin said, and then laughed. "That's a funny way to start. This isn't exactly a letter, is it? Though it isn't a conversation either. I'm afraid it will have to be another lecture! I hope you can forgive me," he said, and she could hear the smile in his voice.

"I've had a rather strange evening. Actually, it's been a strange week. I saved a hod from being beaten, only to have him murder two men in front of me. I escaped suspicion for that crime, but at the cost of seeing eleven innocent men, women, and children executed. I watched an old friend fight for my entertainment. I tried to ingratiate myself to the man who married my wife. And then tonight...I saw her. At last. I saw her. And she was...It was like meeting a rumor, if that makes sense. She was familiar and yet very different. I was wearing a mask, and she was with her duke, and then we rode in a coal car together, and..." Here, Edith heard him struggle and stammer, and though he said nothing coherent, the attempt seemed to speak volumes.

He cleared his throat and carried on. "The upshot is, she made it clear that she prefers her life in Pelphia. I don't blame her. I don't begrudge her her happiness. She seems to have a spectacular life. Part of the dread I've carried around this past year was the thought that once she'd seen a little more of the world, she would think a little less of me. I went to a play where I was a character and...well, it doesn't matter. This isn't a play. I'm not an actor.

"I think you were right, Edith. We aren't what we hope for; we are only what we do. For better or worse, for well or ill, we are what we do. I've spent the better part of a year in denial about what I am, what I have become, insisting that I am somehow above my crimes, my choices, my...feelings. The only thing my denial has done is make me miserable, and I think neurotic. Well, I'm finished with that. I just feel grateful that there is someone in this madhouse who I know and can trust. Someone who is an endless source of encouragement and strength. I can hardly say how much I love your company, your character, your ... But I'll waste no more words. These are sentiments that are better shown than said. I hope to see you soon, and I hope to give you what I could not give her: a man deserving of your affection."

Edith only realized she had begun to pace very quickly when the message ended. She stopped midlap and felt her heart jog on a moment longer.

Sliding back into her chair, she experienced the arrival of her feelings like an approaching rain shower, beginning with a few tentative thrilling drops, then a dozen or so pattering thoughts, then the sudden cloudburst of all the implications and worries and wonders that came along with the possibility of love, all falling more quickly than she could catch.

Then as swiftly as the storm had blown in, it began to recede. Her thoughts thinned into a gauzy, almost sultry sense of longing. She wished she had the time to enjoy the feeling more ...

But her obligations would not wait. The vision of the boiling red sea was never far away. And there was a practical aspect to Senlin's declaration, namely how it affected Voleta's purpose in Pelphia.

Edith went to the communication horn by her cabin door and spoke at a near shout into the small brass trumpet that connected to the bridge. She hailed Iren, and when the amazon answered, she said, "Would you please locate Voleta and Byron and send them to my quarters? Then find yourself some dinner and get some rest. You've more than earned it. I'll take the third shift."

"That'll leave Reddleman here on his own," Iren said, and though her voice was thinned by the plumbing that carried it, Edith still heard her apprehension. They'd made a point of not leaving the Red Hand alone at the helm. But that was before he had distinguished himself by catching the bullet that very well could've ended her life.

"Reddleman, you have the wheel. Keep us circling between the thirty-first and twenty-ninth ringdoms. Let me know if there are any new alarms."

She listened to his "aye, sir," and returned to her table to await Voleta's arrival.

When Senlin's message began to play again, it was by accident, at least at first. Edith had only picked the recorder up to stow it somewhere safe and out of sight and had inadvertently restarted the message in the process. But rather than stop it, she found herself listening to it again. And when it finished playing, she restarted it a third time, though she wasn't entirely sure why. Was it just the sound of his voice she enjoyed, or was there something else, some coded silence between words, which kept her listening ever more closely?

Then Voleta burst into her cabin, and she fumbled the recorder and had to go chasing after it under the table.

As she scrambled to shut the recording off, and Voleta overheard Senlin's bare and honest words bleed into the room like a wound, Edith felt a shock of embarrassment that she had not thought herself capable of. The pang of guilt seemed to be sharpened by the pleasure she had felt just a moment before. It was like walking from a sauna out into a snowy day. The swing between extremes was numbing and painful and yet weirdly invigorating.

She felt entirely flustered, and as a result, she allowed Voleta to direct the discussion more than she usually would've. When the talk turned into a negotiation, as it always did with Voleta, Edith found her ability to rationally deliberate hampered by her guilt. How could she tell Voleta she could not pursue Marya while concealing an intimate communication from Tom in her hand? It was impossible! Yes, Voleta's argument seemed reasonable enough on the face of it, and Edith would've taken any reasonable measure to ensure the safety of Senlin's wife. But she knew her judgment was impaired, and still she conceded: Voleta would infiltrate the Pelphian court and extend an offer of help to Marya for a second time.

Even as Edith made the decision, she knew it would haunt her.

Byron lingered after Voleta's festive departure. Edith could tell by his expression that he was working up to saying something, and rather than watch him squirm his way up to it, she said, "What is it, Byron? You look miserable."

"I don't want to pry, but . . . did he mention anything that made you think that perhaps he might . . . wander off for a while?"

"What do you mean?"

"Senlin, I mean, did he say anything like, um . . . 'Oh, don't tell anyone, but I'm going off on a little romp. Maybe I'll drink too much wine and lose track of the hours and fall asleep in an alley, and not send in my daily report like I'm supposed to.' Anything like that?"

"I don't understand. You just gave me his report, didn't you? Or part of it?"

"Well, that's not exactly wet paint."

"What do you mean? When did this arrive?"

"Two days ago," Byron said. "And before you say anything, yes, I sat on the message because I was having a hard, long think about whether I should give it to you. I don't disobey orders lightly, Captain. And I admit, I very nearly sent it on to the Sphinx, despite my promise to Senlin, but I didn't. I'm glad I didn't."

"And you haven't heard anything from him since?"

"No."

"And that's unusual?"

"It is," he said and watched Edith's warm complexion turn ashen. He hurried to add, "But there are a dozen explanations I can think of for why his reports might have been delayed. He might've accidentally spilled something on his box of messengers, or the messengers might've been damaged in flight. After all, part of the reason the Sphinx sent him to Pelphia was to discover who was destroying his spies."

"But you're worried?"

Byron gave an equivocating grumble. "I'm not worried. Just concerned. I was hoping he might've said something to you that would set both of our minds at ease."

"No. Unfortunately, he didn't. He didn't say anything about the Sphinx's mission or his investigation or any of that."

"Yes, I'm sure. But could I listen for myself, perhaps?"

"I don't know what difference that would make," Edith said a little coolly.

"Well, I've heard all his other reports, and so I'm very familiar with everything that he's gotten up to. I thought perhaps I might hear something interesting that just sounded innocuous to you, but which might—"

"It's private, Byron. It's just . . . a personal message."

"Oh," the stag said and rolled his tasseled shoulders in a tactful shrug. "Yes, of course. I don't mean to pry. Perhaps the thing to do is just wait another day. I'm sure we'll hear something tomorrow."

"All right," Edith said, and though neither of them seemed to find the word particularly hopeful, she repeated it anyway: "Tomorrow."

Edith spent the night drifting between anxious speculation and worried dreams until the two merged into a vision so grim and disastrous it seemed almost a farce: Senlin perished, the boiling sea on the Sphinx's roof melted the Tower like a candle, and she was left with a dying arm on her shoulder and no safe place to alight. Then the sun fell behind the sill of the earth and never rose again.

Chapter Five

A stain is only a stain if anyone notices it. Slosh wine onto the carpet? Scoot a sofa over the spot. Spill gravy on your shirt? Fan your ascot to cover it. Spoil your political reputation with a grievous indiscretion? Start a domestic purge or a foreign war.

—Oren Robinson of the *Daily Reverie*

When Byron arrived at Edith's door at the stroke of seven the next morning, she was already washed, dressed, and finished with breakfast. She had risen early more out of eagerness to be finished with the night than enthusiasm for the day.

Byron delivered the Sphinx's morning dispatch. Since their launch, the Sphinx's commands had been largely concerned with choreographing their promenade. He prescribed which ringdoms to showboat for and at what hours of the day, and which ports to salute and with how many guns. Edith made a point of not asking any questions, which was well enough because the Sphinx supplied no explanations, though Byron had been able to provide some context for some of the orders. When the Sphinx directed Edith to fly the ship in reverse past the ringdom of Zweibel—which even with propulsive vents was something of a challenge—Byron had explained it was to demonstrate the Sphinx's utmost respect for the thirty-eighth ringdom. The Zweibelian people preferred to back their way into rooms, believing it a sign of humility, so the Sphinx wished to pay them the compliment of reversing past their port.

The Sphinx's orders were not always so pacifying. He had directed Edith to prowl past the citadel of Dugaray with cannons blazing, a sign of strength to a people that interpreted courtesy as weakness. Famously, the Dugara eschewed the handshake in favor of a salutatory head butt. Byron described the Dugara as "basically bighorn sheep in frock coats."

It had become tradition that they listen to the orders together, and so, with her cabin door closed, she twisted the head on the dewinged moth. The Sphinx's crackling voice broke their attentive silence.

"I see you've attracted an entourage of curious captains. Well, good. We want the Tower to gawk. Today, you're going to demonstrate the *Art*'s capacity for destruction. You will sidle up to the Silk Gardens' derelict port and lay a little waste with a volley or two of the guns. This will, of course, serve another purpose as well. I know for a fact Marat decamped from the Golden Zoo days ago, but I don't wish to let on that I know. I suspect he's left behind a scout or two, and so the show of force will be for their benefit as well.

"On another note, Byron may have informed you of an interruption to Senlin's regular communications. I assure you, it's not a concern that requires your intervention. Either Senlin is following orders and suffering some technical or environmental difficulty, which I will address, or he has defied me and gone off on his own. Whichever the case may be, you have no role in it, Captain Winters. I emphasize this point because tomorrow you will alight in Pelphia, and there, you will faithfully pursue your own orders, and quickly. Recover my painting, let Voleta do her charming, and be prepared to take off in three days." The recorder hissed a moment more, then clicked into silence.

"Well, he doesn't sound overly concerned about Tom," Edith said, flaring her eyelids. "I don't know what I expected."

Byron was quick to console her. "The Sphinx took him into his confidence; he doesn't do that with just anyone. He may sound unfeeling, but the Sphinx takes care of his interests, and he's made it clear he needs Tom."

"I suppose that'll have to be hope enough for the moment," Edith said, trying to suppress the ready litany of disasters Senlin could have encountered—discovery, arrest, illness, assassination...She hadn't time to dwell on it now. "What sort of reception can we expect in Pelphia?"

"Probably an elaborate fuss. As one of the lowest of the Lower Ringdoms, the Pelphians should be eager to make the most of the honor the Sphinx is paying them. I expect our welcome will be quite warm. Generally, the Pelphians are more interested in parties than politics. I don't expect that King Leonid will argue much about handing over his copy of *The Brick Layer's Granddaughter.*"

"Does the ringdom have a Wakeman?"

"It does. Her name is Georgine Haste, if memory serves. She's been at her post for twenty years, I believe. I don't really recall much about her other than a general impression of a large personality and a pleasant smile. I'm hopeful she might prove to be a willing ally."

"Wouldn't that be nice," Edith said, savoring the prospect of a friendly face.

Byron stopped in the open door to the passageway, turned, and said, "Don't forget. I'm stealing Iren away for a dress rehearsal later this morning."

"You're sure you want to do that on the gun deck? It's going to be noisy down there."

"That is the idea, Captain."

While Byron, Voleta, and Iren practiced tea service on the gun deck, Edith was left alone with Reddleman on the bridge. She unwrapped his bandage as he reported on the nightly traffic and the strength of the morning currents, neither of which was remarkable.

The bullet hole had closed overnight, turning as hard and dark as a knot in a plank. She replaced the bandage more to console herself than out of necessity. For the moment, she didn't wish to ruminate on the fact that Reddleman seemed more or less impervious to bullets. If she ever was forced to dispatch him, she would have to be very thorough in her efforts.

Under her direction, Reddleman steered the ship into the Northern Steady, its currents hastened by the warming sun, and made for the Silk Reef at a quick clip.

When she saw the cannon-chewed portal swell within the frames of the magnovisor, Edith felt a chill at the memory of the swarming spiders, the zealot camp, and Luc Marat's voice, as reasonable as it was cruel. She could still hear the grating creak of his wheelchair echo through the glowing forest.

The mysterious alarm rang again, and her thoughts returned to the bridge.

"We've drawn quite an audience," Reddleman said, swiveling in his pilot's chair to point at the port frames of the magnovisor. Edith regarded the airships that milled about beyond the range of her cannons. The backing light of the morning sun turned them all black as flies.

Edith shifted from her captain's chair to the gunner's station. That panel beamed with rows of green lights, each indicating a loaded and ready cannon. She pressed her face to the gunners' viewfinder. The golden crosshairs floated into view above a black-and-white sketch of the world. Adjusting the knobs on either side of the hood, she brought the ruins of the Silk Reef into focus. "They want a show?" She selected all the bays she wished to fire, flipping the toggles up in batches of three and four. "Let's oblige them." She depressed a ruby-colored button.

The ship's hull rumbled with the firing of the thirty-two starboard guns. Within the golden picture frames, a ghostly rendering of the Silk Reef's port bloomed with flowers of masonry and dust, a violent bouquet that lingered a moment before being de-formed and swept away by the wind.

Reddleman brought the ship about for a second run. The port cannons cracked the sky, and the last erect pillar in the port fell as readily as dead timber.

Edith wondered what Marat's scouts had made of the display, assuming they were indeed lurking inside. She wasn't sure whether it was really such a great show of force to peck at an old port. Perhaps it only made the Tower seem more impervious. The gun hadn't been built yet that could breach those walls. But perhaps that was the Sphinx's intent—to allow a futile display to make the zealots feel safer in their burrows. It certainly wouldn't drive them out into the light.

"They really are magnificent, aren't they?" Reddleman said.

It took Edith a moment to realize he was referring to the airships watching them as if from the gallery of a theater. He pointed at each in turn as he rattled off the ship's name, her commander, and what ringdom she hailed from, information that he'd gleaned from the ship's copy of the *Aircraft Registry*. All the names began to run together, and it was a moment before the list seemed to be coming to an end. "...and there's the *Mane and Fletch* under the command of Captain Jessup from the ringdom of Ludden, and that's the *Red Lawrence* under Captain Dewildt of Nineveh. All formidable ships, all weighted with cannons and crewed with brave men, and all of it lashed to bags of combustible gas. It's a funny agreement, isn't it? To not fire on an enemy's silks?"

"I wouldn't really call it funny, pilot. It's a war crime. If we start shooting envelopes, it would mean the end of the airship entirely."

"But 'lawful war' sounds like a bit of an oxymoron, doesn't it?"

"Perhaps, but it's better than total war. Better than armies attacking civilians, and poisoning wells, and desecrating the dead. And I'm telling you, no matter how big and intimidating we might be, if we fired on any one of those ships' balloons, the rest of them would turn on us like wild dogs. It wouldn't make for a very good death."

"The only people who talk about good and bad deaths are the living. There's really no such distinction among the dead."

"What's it like then?" Edith asked, her frankness surprising them both.

"What's death like? Well. It's like..." He crossed his slight arms on top of his potbelly and closed his eyes. "Death is like what happens to a puddle when the sun comes out. It stops being a puddle and becomes a wisp of a cloud, or a drop of dew in the valley, or foam on an ocean wave."

"All very poetic, but what does it look like? What does it feel like?"

"Oh, there's no more looking or feeling, Captain. You're still thinking like a puddle."

"Can you say if you enjoyed it, at least?"

Reddleman's smile showed a row of teeth that were as big as fingernails. "I was present at the beginning of time. I was there when the first coals of the universe turned red and burned for an age. I was dust floating in dead black nothing for half an eternity. I was a star when it formed. I was a star when it died. I was a ray of light bolting across a galaxy for ten thousand years, only to be caught and devoured by an oak leaf."

"And?"

Reddleman pulled back on the horns of the helm and smiled as the bow of the ship rose. "This is more fun."

Byron was enjoying a moment of peace inside his Communications Closet, which was aptly named and comfortably snug.

He had spent the afternoon arguing with Voleta over tea and having his bolts rattled by cannon fire. The dress rehearsal hadn't gone particularly well. Though a great shot with a pistol, Iren's aim with a teapot left a lot to be desired. Voleta, meanwhile, seemed to believe that she could argue with convention and years of tradition using him as a proxy. One might as well try to dicker with the seasons! *Why can't winter be warmer? Oh, yes, spring is nice, but couldn't we do with fewer showers? And surely the summer doesn't need quite so many flies?* If Byron could convince the young lady of only one thing it would be that she wasn't the first to notice that polite society was irksome, and she wouldn't be the last.

The Communications Closet was located on the bottom deck of the ship along with the crew berths and passenger cabins. Byron possessed the only key to the steel-bound door, and he was under strict orders from the Sphinx to keep it locked at all times and to admit no one under any circumstances. The Sphinx didn't like to share her information, especially not the raw version of it. As much as the Sphinx now had to rely upon Edith and her crew to represent her to the Tower and gather the cells of her zoetrope, she did not fully trust their intelligence or intentions. Though trust had never been very important to the Sphinx.

She would never admit it, but Byron knew her contracts were just a means for figuring out the details of a man's character and motivations. Once she knew those, she could predict what he would do, even if it went against the contractual agreement. She didn't believe in the magical power of a signature on a piece of paper. But trust wasn't required where doubt did not exist. A predictable man was as good as an honest one to the Sphinx.

Byron did not pretend to understand all the ins and outs of his master's plots, but he didn't need to understand to do his duty. He only had to preserve her secrets, which was admittedly sometimes difficult given her predilection for keeping different secrets from different people. Why had she chosen to show her face to Voleta and Senlin, but not to Edith and Iren? The Sphinx hadn't offered him any explanation. He suspected it was because she wished to play to Voleta's and Senlin's sympathy, to appear vulnerable so that they would feel obliged to help her. Edith and Iren, meanwhile, seemed to respond better to the authority and power that the Sphinx's cowl and mask projected. Byron also wondered why she had decided to send Senlin on ahead of the rest of his friends. He sensed that the Sphinx was not surprised by Senlin's silence, which could only mean that it was part of the plan. Byron would sooner pluck out his eyeball than share that suspicion with Edith.

But these were all questions and conjectures for another time and perhaps another mind. At the moment, he was enjoying the peace and quiet, the scent of linseed oil, and the glint of paint on the tip of his brush.

The Sphinx's winged spies came to him through a hole in the hull that was as subtle as the nostril of a shark. The moths and butterflies emerged from the trumpeted mouth of the pipe into a wire cage that was mounted upon the wall. He retrieved them from the corral as his duties allowed and documented their arrival like a hotelier checks in his guests. He noted any damage and repaired them if necessary. He then previewed their recordings, created a duplicate if they seemed important enough to require one, and then released the original via the same vent they'd come through.

The back wall of the closet was covered in corkboard that was so full of the pinned wings it looked like an elaborate quilt. Some wings were blank; others were painted with various domestic camouflage: fabrics, wood grains, and china patterns. His work desk was littered with tools, brushes, paint pots, and mechanical parts. Dozens of cubby holes containing the stowed bodies of erased and copied spies filled the wall above his workspace.

Byron was putting the finishing touches on a marble pattern with the aid of a magnifying glass when the knock came on his door. He yelled for Voleta to go away and leave him alone, but was surprised to hear Edith's voice reply, "It's me, Byron."

He opened the door a few inches, shoved his damp, black nose through the crack, and greeted the captain. He apologized for having mistaken her for Voleta and asked, "Shall I come to your quarters?"

"I'd like to come inside, if I may," Edith replied, and then held up the brass thorax of the moth he'd delivered to her the night before. "I came to propose a trade." He hesitated, and Edith added, "I'm not here as your captain. You can absolutely say no. I'm here as a friend to ask for your help."

It was no small concession that he let her in. Not only was it forbidden, it was inconvenient, too. There wasn't much room to stand and only one stool. But he liked how it felt to be asked for help.

So he offered her the stool and knelt on one knee, grateful that his legs never grew tired or sore. It was only after they were sitting so intimately that he thought how strange the room must appear to her. All the bodiless wings pinned to the wall, the scattering of mechanical legs and moth heads on the workbench. It must look a little macabre. He watched her take in the room and was pleased when she announced, "It's snug. I like it. Must be a nice retreat." He said that he thought so, of course, but it was nice to hear someone else say it. "I suppose you still haven't heard from Tom," she said, peering through the magnifying glass at the canvas of a wing. "Very pretty."

"Thank you," he said. Feeling self-conscious, he began clearing his work away. "I would've told you if I'd heard anything."

"I know. So I thought we should probably come up with some sort of plan for what we'll do when we get to Pelphia."

Byron smiled and laughed. "I think the Sphinx has planned enough for all of us, hasn't he? I think he was pretty clear."

"No, what *we'll* do, Byron. Me and you. About Tom."

"I see," Byron said, his quick stowing of painting supplies slowing to a crawl.

"The Sphinx doesn't care about him. We both know that. Having a use for someone isn't the same as caring. But I care, and I think that you might as well."

"What are you suggesting?"

"I know you've been intercepting Tom's daily reports. Do you still have them?"

"I have copies," Byron said a little proudly. "I made duplicates in case the moths were damaged or waylaid on their journey home."

"Very sensible. I would like to listen to them if I could. And then afterward, I will play for you the message he sent me."

Byron opened his mouth wide. He was going to say something clever, something unkind, which was what he usually did when he felt uncomfortable. But he stopped himself and said instead, "Captain... Edith, I can't. I have my orders to consider here."

"I understand." Edith tapped the tail of Senlin's messenger moth lightly on the worktable. "And I wouldn't want to scandalize you, anyway."

"Oh, do you really think I'm so nosy?"

"No, not at all. Not at all. I'm just saying it might make you blush, and I wouldn't want to embarrass you."

"What do you mean? Why would it make me blush? What did he say?"

Edith sucked in a breath through her teeth and rocked her head from side to side. Byron watched her for a moment before realizing she wouldn't answer. He shook his antlers. "All right, all right! But only in the name of idle curiosity! We're not going to tell anyone else or betray any of our obligations to the..." Edith had been smiling a moment before, but her expression changed so abruptly it halted Byron's speech. "What is it?"

"I was doing it again."

"Doing what?"

"Manipulating you. Going the roundabout way to get what I want." She closed her eyes. "I don't want to treat my friends like obstacles. I don't want to do that. I'm not like him."

"Like the Sphinx, you mean?"

When she opened her eyes, she was staring at him in a forthright way. "It's been three days since we've heard from Tom, and I think that's a bad sign. I'm worried. I know how quickly the worst can happen. One day you have a burn on your arm, the next day you have a fever, and the next day your arm is gone. We can't waste time. I think you may have been right last night. You might be able to hear something I missed in his message. He hinted at things that I don't know the context for. If he's in trouble, I want to know how and where and what I can do to pull him out of it. So will you please listen to this and tell me what you hear? No strings attached."

"Well," Byron said, swinging from offense to forgiveness quickly enough. "Let's hear what Senlin has to say for himself."

When the recording finished playing, it was Edith who was blushing. Tucking dark strands of hair behind crimson-colored ears, she said, "Obviously, the things he said toward the end were just a few personal expressions of friendly affection, but—"

"I saw the kiss, Edith."

"You what?"

Byron spoke as if he wished to get through the confession as quickly as possible. "One of the Sphinx's butterflies recorded you and Thomas kissing in the doorway of your bedroom, and I saw it. I didn't want to, but I did, and also, I put the butterfly in your room, so the invasion of your privacy is entirely my fault." The stag looked down at his workspace and shuffled some of his things about needlessly, glancing at her as he did.

Edith felt a volcanic bubble of anger rise inside of her. But what might've turned into an eruption was cooled by the memory of her own recent apology and by a sense of relief that she would not have to explain nor hide the complexities of her feelings for Senlin. "I suppose I should've guessed there were no secrets in the Sphinx's house."

"It was the first time I was ever ashamed of my work. I am very sorry, Edith. I would not do it again," Byron said. He stood and began selecting the cylindrical recordings from cubbies. "All right, we should probably start from the beginning. I hope your stool is comfortable. Senlin is many things, but succinct is not one of them."

Once they'd listened through all of Senlin's spoken reports, Byron asked if Edith would also like to see the visual records he had of Senlin's movements through the ringdom.

"Did he know he was being watched?" she asked.

"He did figure it out," Byron said, setting up a small projector and screen on his workbench. The projector was little more than a clamp for holding the butterflies steady while they beamed their light onto the white silk screen. The first recording he played for her was of Senlin checking in to the Bon Royal Hotel. She couldn't help but smile at how he bickered pleasantly with the porter, insisting that he could manage his own luggage, and finally tipping the young man to allow him to carry his own bags. In another scene, she watched him brushing his coat through the window of his hotel room, then watched him pace and read a book, watched as he opened his balcony window to release a moth into the night. And there were scenes of him walking through the congested city streets. She was shocked by these glimpses of Pelphia. She couldn't recall having ever seen so many well-dressed people in one place before. There was a frenzied spirit to the town. Senlin seemed to bob through the crowds of the central plaza like a cork in a storm gutter.

Byron changed records and identified the landmarks as they appeared: the Colosseum, the Vivant, the Circuit of Court, and the Gasper Theater. They watched from an inconvenient distance and through the static of rain as Senlin intervened in the alley where two men abused a short and malnourished hod. Splashes of whitewash haloed the scene. Edith was proud of how he fought, and then shocked when the hod took the opportunity of his defense to kill the two men before running off to leave Tom standing in the rain, baffled and alone.

"Remind me, what did Tom say that hod yelled just before he ran off?" Edith asked.

"'Come the Hod King,'" Byron said. "And no, I don't know what it means, but it has been cropping up more and more in the recording. There's been a spate of graffiti, too."

The next scene Byron played was of Senlin in his hotel room being surprised by the arrival of a tall man with a three-foot-long pistol and a woman who was obviously a Wakeman. She asked Byron who the tall man was, and he introduced her to General Eigengrau.

"And what do we think of him?"

"Eigengrau is a militant traditionalist, I would say. He's certainly not an idiot, but I wouldn't consider him the most forward-thinking man either. He's one of those who seems to think the ringdoms exist outside the Tower. As if the one can be preserved while the other rots. That is to say, he's generally in the majority."

"And that's Wakeman Georgine Haste, I presume. Can you tell me anything else about her?"

"I don't know. I mean, she is a functioning Wakeman."

"What do you mean *functioning*?"

"The Sphinx has not been making much of an effort to manage or oversee the Wakemen in recent years, in some cases decades. That's led to some of the Wakemen being less than...reliable, shall we say? Actually, I don't know why I'm being coy about it. Half of the Tower's Wakemen are drunk, delinquent, or dead. They're a dying breed. Before you, it had been a dozen years, I believe, since the Sphinx ordained his last Wakeman. What I mean by *functioning* is Haste is still doing the work. She's keeping the peace. She's not in the general's pocket, though he seems to respect her. As far as Wakemen go, she's one of the good ones."

"Well, that's something," Edith said.

There was no record of Senlin's evening in the Circuit of Court, nor the reunion with Marya that he alluded to in his private message to

Edith. There was a long view of Senlin in the plaza the following day as he interrupted an execution being overseen by General Eigengrau. Edith watched as Senlin waved his arms, nearly throwing himself in front of the firing line. Then came the muzzle flash and the silent, almost serene collapse of the condemned.

"And the Sphinx wonders why there's a revolution brewing," Edith murmured, her expression warped by disgust.

"He really doesn't," Byron replied.

The last glimpse of Senlin was taken by a butterfly in flight. It followed Senlin as he climbed the steps of the Colosseum. The shadow of the interior turned him into a silhouette, and then he was gone.

"There's nothing after this?"

"Nothing," Byron said, switching off the glowing beam of the final recording.

"Are we of the opinion that the Hod King is Marat?"

"I mean, it stands to reason. The Sphinx is sure Marat intends to either rule the Tower or preside over its rubble. It doesn't seem out of character for him to take on the title of *king*."

Edith mulled this over, unhappy at the prospect of Senlin facing Marat without her. "Is it fair to suppose Tom is being held somewhere inside the Colosseum?"

"Not necessarily. He may've changed clothes and left when no one was looking. He must've done something of the sort when he went to meet Marya. He knew the Sphinx couldn't see him inside the Colosseum and used it to his advantage. The clever fool."

"He could be anywhere, then." The revelation made her feel as if a belt had been tightened around her chest. Her breathing ached.

"Frankly, I was hoping that he had run off with Marya. But I don't think that's the case. None of the Mermaid's appearances have been cancelled. She has a show at the Vivant in a few days."

"So, here are the options as I see them." Edith rested the elbow of her engine on the workbench. The hardwood creaked under the weight. She raised a thick, gunmetal finger. "One, he ran afoul of the law. If he was being investigated for the murder, they may have discovered he was in the ringdom illegally. He could be sitting in a prison cell somewhere." She raised a second finger. "Two, he might've discovered exactly the sort of plot the Sphinx expected him to find and, in so doing, exposed himself to the hods. They may have either whisked him off to the Old Vein or killed him and stuffed him in an alley." She didn't linger on that grim specter, raising instead a final finger. "Three, the duke figured out who Senlin really was. The fact that he survived his reunion with Marya unscathed makes that seem unlikely, I think. If she was going to reveal him, or if he was going to accidentally out himself, that would've been the moment for it."

"What are you going to do?" Byron asked nervously.

"Well, I'm going to find him."

"But how are you going to do it? If people see you investigating the disappearance of a tourist from Boskopeia, how long before they start asking questions about his connection to the Sphinx? I don't think that will do your cause any favors."

"What do you mean?"

"Well, imagine if you were the nobility of a ringdom, and we showed up in a ship like this demanding some fusty, forgotten master-piece be returned, only to have it come out that we are involved with a man who has robbed other ringdoms of that very same painting. No one would trust us, and understandably not. You have to remember, this is just our first port of call. We have dozens of other ringdoms to visit and charm."

"Then I'll just have to be discreet."

"Discretion was never your strong suit."

"What do you mean? I can be subtle," Edith said, sounding a little affronted.

"No offense, Captain, but you're about as subtle as a firecracker in a soufflé."

Chapter Six

I love a good scandal. There's nothing more comforting than tut-tutting the public sins of another from the privacy of your own squalor.

—Oren Robinson of the *Daily Reverie*

The next morning, when Edith docked the *State of Art* in Port Virtue and disembarked along with her crew into a mob of fevered Pelphians, she was reminded of the first time she had ever mounted a horse.

She had been ten years old at the time and still timid around large animals. Her father held the gentle old draft horse beside a fence, the crossbars of which served as a ladder to help her up. The saddle seemed an impossibly high and precarious perch. No sooner was she in it than she hunched forward and pressed her cheek against the horse's neck. Her father was quick to chide her, though not ungently. "Sit back, Edith. Come on, come on, you can do it. That's it. The stirrups are here. Perfect. Now, shoulders back...back a little more. Right there. See how that feels? It feels different, doesn't it? Your control, your balance, your security—all of it depends upon good posture and a firm grip." Her father patted and stroked the docile beast. "And that's true of more than just riding a horse."

Of course, she had good reason to be on edge today: Port Virtue was full of armed guards and the same lead soldiers that had once nearly blown the *Stone Cloud* from the sky. Her eye was drawn again and again to those grim turret guns peeking between the tops of potted palm trees. Their blunted shape reminded her of a nesting doll, though she'd never seen a doll that had cannons for arms. She was very conscious of the fact that she wasn't carrying a sidearm of any kind and had only an empty warship to support her. She could only hope that her father was right about the broad value of a straight back and a firm grip, because she hadn't much else to rely on at the moment.

Ever since Byron had called Georgine Haste "one of the good ones," Edith had looked forward to meeting her. Even so, she was pleasantly surprised by how much she liked the gold-chested Wakeman. Haste was charmingly frank, and she shared Edith's dislike of pageantry. When Haste advised Voleta to try to make an impression upon the court and King Leonid, Edith took it as a sign that the Wakeman's allegiance did not lie with the ringdom, at least not solely. She was willing to help them navigate the culture. Perhaps she would turn out to be a friend, but at the very least she was a helpful guide.

The moment after Voleta and Iren were whisked away by their golden-haired host, King Leonid declared that they must parade around the pyramid, because it was a wonder of the Tower and something his honored guests absolutely must see. Edith agreed to the walk but declined the king's invitation to join him on one of the mounts in the mechanical caravan. As the regent mounted a beakless eagle, Edith remarked upon the emblazoned words over the pyramid's entrance, asking what "The Unfinished Birth" referred to.

Leonid replied, "That, you'll have to ask the baby when he's born!"

While the wild-haired king rode upon his carousel, pouring champagne out for the lords and ladies that trotted along beside him, Edith found herself the target of the king's advisers, each of whom elbowed a little space to walk at her side and make the introductions that the king had either forgotten or not cared to make.

General Andreas Eigengrau—commander of the king's navies and keeper of the domestic peace—introduced himself with a sort of weary charm. He seemed a man in need of a nap, but also a man who was resigned to never getting what he needed. Edith recognized him from the butterfly's recording of Senlin's hotel suite when the local constabulary had come to question him about the murders. He seemed even taller in person than he had appeared in that recording.

Eigengrau congratulated her on her command, calling the *State of Art* easily the most stunning ship he'd ever laid eyes on. He assured her that she was in good hands with Wakeman Haste. Before relinquishing his spot at her side, he said, "I hope that you will share with the Sphinx what a lawful and orderly ringdom we are. Our excellence is evidence of our righteousness. If there is anyone deserving of the Sphinx's faith and gifts, it is we Pelphians." As she met his eyes in parting, she discovered that his gaze was not so sleepy as it first seemed. He was a keen and clever man.

The royal treasurer, Crown Prince Pepin Le Mesurier, was the next to introduce himself. He was the king's brother, though Edith couldn't see any resemblance. His face was full, his hair was rusty, and his limbs were thick, though probably more from excess than exercise. He wore a girdle around his middle that raised his chest unnaturally, shaping him like a seal. The leisurely walk around the pyramid appeared to be the most exercise he'd had in weeks. He panted and spoke to Edith as if she were the last sane person in a world of fools. Edith had no doubt this treatment had nothing to do with her and everything to do with his own agenda. He said, "Those upper houses think we must be poor because we're so low on the pole, but they never tire of buying our clothes, do they? Never tire of filling our coffers with gold. Of course, you know that. You're here, after all! You know where the opportunities are. My trouble, as treasurer, is finding investment opportunities as great as our capital. I see in the Sphinx a worthy business partner. I'm sure that's no surprise to you, clever woman like yourself. Personally, I think the day he decides to stop giving away those marvels of his, and starts selling them instead, is the day he becomes the wealthiest man in Ur. The schematics for that ax-head of a warship would be worth ten thousand mina. Twenty thousand, perhaps. You know, if you'd like to leave the blueprints with me, I could provide you with a more concrete estimate." Edith declined the offer. Le Mesurier never once looked her in the eye as he snorted and blathered at her elbow. The crown prince might've tried to grease her further, but the exercise appeared to be too much for him, and he had to quit the undertaking midlap.

The last adviser in the king's inner circle was a little stick of a man who introduced himself as Grand Duke Horace Gardon, the city manager. He had thick-lensed spectacles, an ill-advised, weedy mustache, and the look of someone who'd just been informed that his basement had flooded. He was the youngest of the king's advisers by twenty years, perhaps, but the work had aged him, stealing first the majority of his hair, then the color from his cheeks, and finally the starch from his spine. Gardon was eager to hear what she thought of the parade route and the reception she'd received. Edith assured him that everything had been very fine, but this proved to be an insufficient compliment. Gardon was the sort of person who liked to farm praise by self-criticism. He bemoaned the absence of his usual master of ceremonies, who'd been felled by a head cold, and apologized for the street sweepers who'd let the confetti pile too thickly on the road, and he scolded himself for not having organized more banners to mark this historic occasion. Edith patiently complimented Gardon on each point, which seemed to satisfy him well enough. As their circuit about the pyramid approached its conclusion, Gardon said that King Leonid would very much appreciate a private consultation at his royal palace.

Edith of course agreed, though she was disappointed to learn that Georgine would not be coming along. Haste explained, "I'm a better constable than a counselor. I never have much to contribute to important conversations. Not that they've ever asked. When you're finished, we can meet for a drink if you like." Haste pointed up at a dim constellation of blue-white pilot lights. "See the boot? The toe of it hangs over a rooftop pub called the Hope and Pride. It's a nice, quiet spot. Not too showy. I'm usually there around four. And a word of advice: Avoid committing to any royal dinners if you can help it, or you'll spend the evening being trotted about like a show hound."

Edith, the king, and his advisers hadn't far to go. The palace overlooked the plaza. As they crossed the milk-white mall, King Leonid threw out handfuls of hard candy to the children who flocked after them. The children squealed in delight, and the king tilted his head back and crowed. Edith thought, if he wasn't mad, he certainly was odd. And his home was no less so.

The word that leapt to mind when she gazed upon the palace was *ramshackle*. The structure reminded her of an old country manor that had begun as a cottage, and then been added to by successive generations, until the original home was swallowed up by the additions. Edith would learn that something similar had actually occurred with the Palace of the Pells. Going back many, many years, each member of the ringdom's monarchy had endeavored to make a mark on the royal home. The result was a jumble of styles and ideas. The facade featured two arches of inconsistent size, one round and the other pointed. The portico had an odd number of pillars, all with unique capitals. There were scores of windows, but not one on a common line. Each of the palace's five corners boasted a turret, and some of those had sprouted secondary turrets like limbs branching from the trunk of a tree. Two domes topped the palace, to something of a rude effect, though one had a cupola and the other was leafed in gold, an addition that King Leonid had personally overseen. "Something about the one dome seemed to cry out for the second," the king told Edith proudly, then popped a piece of rock candy into his mouth.

Edith was accustomed to sizing a person up quickly. Haggling with pirates had taught her to trust first impressions and her instincts. Admittedly, she was not a perfect judge of character—her first impression of Senlin, after all, had been that he was a useless sop—but she felt certain that her ability to distinguish harmless oddballs from violent maniacs had saved her life more than once.

And yet she struggled to get any real sense of the king's character.

The royal address consumed a city block and towered above its neighbors. As they mounted the palace steps, the last tagalong lords and ladies peeled away. The children ran off with cheeks full of candy, and the reporters were dispatched with a parting raspberry, which Leonid said they could quote him on.

Edith followed the king and his three advisers through the gold-hinged palace doors. The interior of the king's home was just as grand

and confused as the exterior. Every stick of furniture seemed a work of art, and all the fixtures were as fine as jewelry. But since none of it matched, the result was something like an extravagant curiosity shop.

Edith marked the change that came over the king the moment they were indoors. He shooed away his servants, who vanished like mice at the striking of a light, and began stripping off the pieces of his clockmaker's costume—hat, coat, vest, and tie—as he walked, casting them onto the museum pieces of his home without breaking stride. He seemed younger, his actions more staid. Leonid's voice lost the theatrical lilt it had possessed in the court. He spoke to Edith almost casually. "I'm old enough to remember when the Sphinx's name didn't sound so mythical. My great-grandfather saw the *State of Art* the last time it flew— When was that, General, a hundred years ago?" Leonid paused long enough to let Eigengrau nod. "The Sphinx certainly has mastered the long encore."

"And he thought Pelphia would be the perfect stage for it," Edith said.

"That's very flattering. I hope you don't mind if I dispense with the royal tour. It's a big house, and I'm sure we both have better things to do with our time than pretend to appreciate all the hearths and tapestries," Leonid said in a guileless way. Edith agreed at once, grateful to be spared the boring perusal. "Anyway, I prefer the roof. I like the air."

The terrace jutted from the palace with all the subtly of a codpiece. The extravagant expanse was shaded by rows of palm trees in massive glazed pots. Leonid explained that every morning, wilting trees were carted out to revive in the port sunshine while fresh ones were rolled in to languish in the gaslight. He said, "It's a terrible indulgence, I admit. Being king does have its perks. And I can't think of anything more serene than tree shade. Honestly, I'd rather have greenery than gold."

It was a sentiment Edith could relate to. She was beginning to like the regent. Leonid stood at the rail, overlooking a city that seethed with life. Now wearing nothing but his suit trousers and a white shirt, undone at the collar, the king looked common, unremarkable, except for the spread white wings of his hair. "When I was a boy, I'd pull feathers out of my pillow and then bring them up here to see how far I could sail them over the rooftops. I made a whole game of it. There were points and penalties and...I frittered a hundred afternoons, launching feathers, tallying scores." He fluttered his fingers in the air. "When my mother caught me at it, she gave me a horrible telling off. I had ruined her pillows! Destroyed her duvets! I was a vandal and a wastrel!" He chuckled. "Funny, now I can't remember a single rule of my feather game, but I can recall with perfect clarity every word of that scolding." Leonid looked Edith in the eye with an appealing amount of honesty. "I hope I'm not due for another one now."

Edith realized with a flicker of surprise that Leonid anticipated some sort of censure. The revelation came as a relief because it meant the Sphinx still commanded a little respect here. "Not at all, Your Majesty. The Sphinx sends his warmest regards. He wishes he could've come himself. He has nothing but fond memories of your ringdom and your lineage."

"I run hot and cold on them myself. I'm not one of those who thinks every dead relative is a saint. So, to what do we owe this honor, Wakeman Winters? What really brings you here?"

"It's come to the Sphinx's attention there has been some turmoil in the Baths," Edith said.

"You mean the loss of the Red Hand," the king said solemnly.

"*Pound* lost him," Le Mesurier interjected with a disgusted pucker of his lips. The king's rotund brother had somewhere during their walk procured a tumbler of ice and gin, which he slurped at before going on. "Hardly surprising. Pound goes through money like my boy goes through girls. We gave him a resource like the Red Hand, and he squandered it. The man's too busy collecting doodles to run a ringdom."

"There were mitigating circumstances, Your Highness," Eigengrau said. "Pound was surprised by a trap in an unfriendly port."

"Itself an embarrassment!" Le Mesurier barked back.

"I do not disagree. I'm merely stating the defense that Pound himself will mount," the general said.

"Gentlemen," Leonid said, raising his hands. "Do these excuses matter to the Sphinx? The fact remains that it was our man who contributed to the death of a Wakeman. I'm sure the Sphinx won't care which one of our hands we decide to slap."

"The Sphinx has sent me to offer Your Majesty some compensation for the loss."

"Compensation? For our blunder?" Leonid said. "I thought he'd be furious."

"I would not pretend to know what the Sphinx feels," Edith said with a diplomatic shrug.

"Still, that seems exceedingly generous," the king said.

"*Exceedingly*," the crown prince echoed, sucking on the rocks of his drink.

"In exchange, all the Sphinx asks for is your copy of *The Brick Layer's Granddaughter*."

"You mean the painting that Pound lost?" Eigengrau asked, shifting aside his cape so he could better fold his arms. It was an imposing stance that did little to impress Edith. "I assure you, Captain Winters, we have made every effort to get it back. Some muddy pirate absconded with it. But there's a reward out for him and the search goes on."

Edith continued to address the king, "Actually, Your Majesty, I mean your copy of it."

Confusion wrinkled the king's brow. "My copy. But why? We still have our Wakeman. You met her. Georgine. We get along fine."

"I really couldn't say why the Sphinx wants your copy, Your Majesty. Only that he does. I can tell you that you're not the last ringdom I will visit with this request. And none of them, to the best of my knowledge, have lost Wakemen."

"So this isn't about the Red Hand," the king concluded. "And you say I am the first?"

"Yes, Your Majesty."

"If it is because he worries his painting is not safe here, I can assure you our copy is perfectly secure," King Leonid said.

"Pound should never have had the Baths' copy on display," Eigengrau added. "It wasn't his to show. It belonged to the ringdom."

"The man is obsessed with frames," Le Mesurier said. "If you put a frame on a toenail, he'd hang it on his wall!"

"Brother." The king's tone of voice did not require any further rebuke. The crown prince chewed an ice cube noisily but said no more. "Just as I can recall the stories of the *State of Art*, I have not forgotten the value of the Sphinx's tokens. Does this mean the Sphinx is withdrawing his favor from the House of Pell?"

"Not at all, Your Majesty."

"Is he changing the agreement?"

"No, Your Majesty."

"Here is my concern, Wakeman Winters: I have spent my tenure on the throne pursuing and maintaining peace with the Algezians. It is not an absolute peace. We've seen those before, and how wildly they swing to bloody war. No, the truce I have built is tenuous and tepid. Because it is lukewarm, our defenses are stout and our navy is ready. But because there is peace, our ports are full, our markets are healthy, and our culture is thriving. I am concerned that your presence, that the Sphinx's reemergence, could turn my tepid peace into fiery war."

While the king spoke, Eigengrau nodded along. The general agreed with the policy, though based on how the crown prince had buttoned his top lip into his lower, Edith didn't think he shared the political strategy. "Your Majesty, the Sphinx and his Wakemen wish to keep the balance between ringdoms. We exist to preserve the peace. You've experienced this, I'm sure, by Haste's service. The painting is merely a treaty, a sign of good faith."

Leonid smiled, though there was no pleasure behind the expression. "Do you know what a treaty is, Captain Winters? It is a document that tells us what the next war will be over."

"You mentioned *compensation*," Le Mesurier said. "I'm not clear: Are you offering us another Wakeman?"

"No," Edith said. The Sphinx had prompted her what to say next, and still she made the king and his advisers hold their breath a moment before continuing. "The Sphinx will provide every ringdom that turns over its copy of *The Brick Layer's Granddaughter* with access to a new technology."

A flight of surprised expressions followed as the men processed this unanticipated but welcome news. "What is it? A weapon? A power source? Is he going to share the lightning with the rest of us?" The crown prince's eagerness and his girdle left him short of breath.

"I don't know," Edith said.

"Well, that all seems very vague," Le Mesurier said, his excitement souring.

"Be quiet, Pepin," Leonid said, not sharply, but with the authority of an older brother. "You're going to grouse us out of a gift. The Sphinx is paying us an immense honor. He has brought the announcement of this endowment to us first. This is a proud moment for all Pelphians. Captain Winters, please tell the Sphinx we accept his generous offer. We will have his painting ready and waiting for you in the morning."

Chapter Seven

I don't understand the appeal of those hateful screw-
booths. I've heard some claim to have seen visions of
lost loved ones, and others say they saw their true
and shining selves buried beneath age or ugliness,
but I've only ever been lampooned by the Will-o'-the-
Wisps. All they've ever taught me is that my inner
nemesis is a crueler critic than my gravest enemy. So
what? I still have to sleep with the fellow!

—Oren Robinson of the *Daily Reverie*

When Edith emerged from the palace, she found the ringdom's attention had turned elsewhere. An hour earlier
she'd nearly been crushed by a parade thrown in her honor.
Now she hardly merited a glance. Not that she was complaining.

Following Wakeman Haste's advice, Edith had ducked King Leonid's invitation to a soiree that evening, insisting that she had matters
to attend to on her ship. "With such a large crew, I find I have very
few hours for leisure," she had told the king.

"Well, you should give them some time ashore. We'd be sure to
show them a grand time!" the king had said.

Thinking quickly, Edith replied, "Thank you, Your Majesty, but if
I've learned one thing as a captain it's that shore leave is best used as
a reward at the end of a voyage rather than the start of one. My men
have to earn their ease." The excuse had seemed to satisfy the regent.

She found herself with a few hours to spare before she'd meet Georgine for a drink. She knew just how she meant to spend them.

The Bon Royal was a short walk from the palace. The lobby of the hotel was such a spectacle Edith had to pause to take it in. Porters carried valises, trunks, and hatboxes up a grand staircase like ants swarming an anthill. A hundred guests at least lounged in the seating area on leather couches while white-gloved waiters lavished them with drinks and hors d'oeuvres. The check-in desk was as made up as a wedding altar in lilies, green garlands, and potpourri. Crystal chandeliers varnished everything in a shattered yellow light.

Edith tried to picture Senlin blending into such a scene and felt a flutter of amusement.

She was glad to see the awe in the concierge's eyes when she approached his podium. She was prepared to be intimidating, but it seemed her uniform and engine did enough to soften him before she'd even uttered a word. An impeccably groomed middle-aged man with penciled-in eyebrows and a scant mustache, the concierge introduced himself as Mr. Stull. "What can I do to assist you this afternoon, Madam...Wakeman...Captain?" he said, cycling through the honorifics.

"I'm here to assist in the investigation of one of your guests. He's a person of interest in a murder inquiry."

"Yes, I know to whom you are referring. Mr. Pinfield. He has been something of a...*trial* for myself and my staff." Stull leaned nearer as he spoke. "We're actually curious to know where he is ourselves. He's not been in for several days now, and we're not sure what's to be done with his things."

Edith was not surprised to hear the news, but she had been holding out some hope that perhaps Senlin had only been lying low. "Has his room been disturbed?"

"No, not at all. Not even the maids have been in because when there's no guest, there's no mess. The room is paid for through the week. We were going to wait until the weekend to remove and store his things. Assuming, of course, he hasn't returned in the meantime."

"I'd like to see his room," Edith said, and Mr. Stull quickly conceded. He called another porter to watch over his station and led Edith up the broad stairs to the second floor. As they traversed the long corridor to his suite, Stull complimented Edith on her ship, which of course he had not seen for himself yet, but which he had heard was very impressive.

When they arrived at the room and Stull unlocked the door with his master key, Edith thanked him in such a way as to make it clear that she would prefer to go in alone. Ever sensitive to subtle cues, Mr. Stull bowed and left with an offer of further assistance should the Wakeman require it. Before departing, he said, "If you do find Mr. Pinfield, could you please remind him that we still need to settle his room service tab. Most of it is for toast, but even toast adds up."

She closed the long curtains over the balcony door, remembering the direction from which the Sphinx's spies had recorded him. She didn't wish to be watched. Though it was probably unavoidable. Still, the Sphinx should've known she would have to look for Senlin herself. She anticipated a scolding for what she was doing, but she didn't care.

Senlin's presence lingered in the order of things, in the hung coats, the neat row of shoes beneath, and the squared objects on the bureau. Taking up the ripped sleeve of the first coat, she held it as if it were his hand, then a moment later felt silly and let it drop. She wasn't here to reminisce.

The coats seemed a sort of chronicle of misfortune: The first was torn, the second spattered in whitewash, and the last pitted with burns. Rummaging through the pockets, she came upon a program for *The Mermaid's Tale*. The subtitle described the play as the authorized account of Marya Pell's origins and the duke's courtship of her. Edith wondered why Senlin had subjected himself to it. He had to know by now that all the Tower's plays, authorized or not, were farcical. Morbid curiosity, perhaps. If her life were turned into a play, she supposed she would want to see it, too, if for no other reason than to boo.

In the pocket of the singed coat, she found a folded letter from Duke Wilhelm Pell in which he agreed to meet with Mr. Pinfield to entertain his business proposal. The discovery made Edith reconsider her assumption that Senlin had managed to encounter Marya without involving his rival. No, it seemed Senlin had sought the duke out and had contrived an excuse to get to know that man. Why? It could only have been to see whether the duke was worthy of his wife. Edith wasn't surprised that Senlin had taken the matter into his own hands. Though it made her reconsider the duke's involvement in Senlin's disappearance. If Senlin had weaseled his way into the duke's company, it was possible that the duke had investigated him in return. She wondered how well Senlin's forged credentials had held up to scrutiny.

The purple-and-orange grotesque mask on the dresser drew her eye. She snorted when she read the label on the reverse side: MASK OF THE SPHINX. It must've been what he'd worn to conceal his reunion with Marya from the Sphinx's spies. Edith wished she could've been there to advise against such an ugly thing. Surely there were more handsome disguises. Smart as he could be at times, Senlin had a talent for undermining his own causes.

Unless that had been his intention.

She didn't flatter herself by lingering on the question any further.

In a private moment before she'd left the ship that morning, she'd asked Byron what she should search for if she were to go have a peek at Senlin's room. The stag had told her that she should absolutely not do that, but if she decided to defy the Sphinx and common sense, then she might as well look for a box of cigars. Senlin's stock of messengers would be hidden there, wrapped in tobacco leaves. "And if you're so fool as to find them, I don't think there's any point to leaving them lying around," Byron had said.

Spotting the cigar box on a corner of the bureau, she flipped open the lid. Other than a few crumbs of tobacco, it was empty. She wasn't sure what that meant, but it made her uneasy. Had he removed the messengers, or had someone else?

She spent nearly an hour searching the room. She pried off the vent covers and peered into the ducts. She pulled down the paintings and inspected their papered backs. She stripped off the bedding, shook out the duvet, and all but disassembled the bed frame. She turned out each drawer and carefully checked every underside. The only other discovery was an old book, stowed under a stack of folded vests, entitled: *Trilobites and Other Ancient Arthropods*. She recognized it from the reports Byron had played for her as the book the murderous hod had dropped. She leafed through it, saw some numbers scribbled in the gutters, a few pretty diagrams of ugly shellfish, and many dense paragraphs that ran on for pages and pages. Nothing remarkable leapt out at her. Still, if Senlin had stowed it out of sight, it deserved a more thorough perusal. She was pleased to find the volume just fit into the outer pocket of her greatcoat.

She was disappointed that her search turned up nothing more. The tidy state of the room suggested to her that Senlin had been taken by surprise, and it had happened elsewhere. But whether the constabulary, the hods, or the duke were behind his disappearance, she was no nearer to knowing.

She returned to the lobby to find Mr. Stull at his station.

"Did you find what you were looking for?" the concierge asked with professional concern.

"Not yet." Edith laid a ten-mina note on the podium. Mr. Stull's eyes widened with pleasure at the sight of the bill. "You're certain no one's been in his room since his disappearance?"

"Captain, the only thing I can be certain of is what I myself have observed. But there are many hands, many keys, and many crisp mina notes in the Bon Royal."

She laid down a second note. "If Mr. Pinfield returns, tell him I would like to have a word with him."

In one of his morning dispatches to the captain of the *State of Art*, the Sphinx had explained an essential function of the Pelphian ringdom. Pelphia acted as the Tower's fuse box. The purpose of the fuses, which the locals sometimes called candles because of the pleasing glow they emitted, was to protect the electrical systems that were spread throughout the Tower from surges in the main current. Most basically, the fuses kept the light bulbs from popping every time the lightning ran a little fierce.

But rather than create another unenjoyable labor that would doubtlessly be foisted upon some unfortunate hod, the Sphinx had contrived to make the regular and speedy replacement of fuses a source of merriment for the locals. In his recording to Edith, the Sphinx had described an amusement ride that trundled passengers in a railcar along a decorated track through some pleasing twists and turns, and ultimately to their purpose: a great spire of cradled fuses, some of which needed replacement. The other system was a series of booths called Will-o'-the-Wisps, which the Sphinx described as a sort of "cathartic shadow box" that provided a moment's entertainment after the user reset the tripped breaker.

The Sphinx admitted that the egalitarian nature of the fuses' maintenance left them vulnerable to mishandling. The Pelphians weren't even fully aware of the vital service they were providing the Tower. They knew only that they liked the pretty spots of light in the streets and enjoyed the entertainment related to their replacement. Both the local Wakemen and the constabulary had orders to guard the system, and yet the Sphinx was under no illusion that the fuses could be a target for sabotage. Interrupting the work of the fuses would not only disrupt the distribution of energy, it would also intensify the torrent of lightning coursing up the Tower's spine.

After parading through the city, meeting with the king, and investigating the Bon Royal for signs of Senlin, Edith had all but forgotten about the Sphinx's surreptitious fuse box. But as she made her way across the blanched plaza, chasing the constellation of a boot and the promise of a quiet drink with Georgine Haste, she was surprised by the sudden unscrewing of a glass manhole cover in the ringdom floor. As the column rose on oiled gears, she observed the plaque above a curved door that read WILL-O'-THE-WISP: GIFT OF THE SPHINX.

The rising pillar quickly drew a crowd. When the mechanism completed its assent and a door in the threaded column cracked open, a man in a tangerine waistcoat attempted to leap in front of Edith and dive into the revealed chamber. Edith caught him by the waistband and hauled him back out again. She turned and shouted at the crowd,

"I'm on official business from the Sphinx!" which seemed to quell them a little, enough at least that she had a chance to peer into the gloom. She could make out a round seat and little else. The crowd, sensing her hesitation, seemed ready to surge again, but she didn't give them a chance to.

The clamshell door closed behind her on its own accord, and she found herself sitting inside a closet that, at first and second blink, appeared as dark as a crypt. But then faint words on the wall before her came into relief. The letters glowed with a ghostly light, which she recognized from the porcelmore forest of the Silk Reef. The message read:

> DO NOT FEAR THE SHADOWS CAST BY MY LIGHT.
> THOUGH THEY MAY HOLD THE SHAPE OF TRUTH,
> THESE VISIONS ARE NOT REAL.
> PULL THE LEVER TO CONJURE.

On the wall to her left, the bar of a sturdy pull lever cast the same peculiar light. She pulled it, and the closet began to turn and descend in the same moment an electric bulb switched on behind her. She jumped when she saw the haloed woman sitting before her, then laughed nervously when she realized she was facing a mirror. Though it was a curious looking glass. It seemed deeper than a regular mirror, as if it were a reflection inside a reflection, or still water at the bottom of a well.

Perhaps it was just a trick of the sallow light above her head and the sensation of drilling down into the earth, but as she looked at her image, it seemed to grow uncertain. She tried to focus on her unsleeved engine, hulking at her side. The ugly thing made her look so unbalanced, like a crab with one dominant claw. Her flesh-and-blood hand resting upon her knee looked so small. She noticed it had taken on a curious bronzy cast. In the mirror, the skin of her knuckles looked like the heads of rivets. She raised her living hand and splayed her fingers. Steam rose from between the joints. Then she saw her neck above her shirt collar had turned into an iron spring, like something from

410

the undercarriage of a railcar. She looked into her own eyes and saw a red glimmer flickering behind the black. The ruby light grew brighter as she stared.

She yelped when the booth's downward spiral came to a stop with a hard jolt. The door opened of its own accord, and brighter light streamed in, erasing the ghastly vision from the mirror. When she regarded her reflection again, the only thing unusual about it was the wild look in her eyes.

Climbing out, she found herself standing in a corridor with rough-cut stone walls and gas lamps bolted to the ceiling. Her knees quaked beneath her. She put a hand out to steady herself. The cold masonry felt reassuring under her fingers.

"Rough trip, Captain?" an age-worn voice said. Edith turned to find a small man in a blue dress coat and a gold kepi standing in the intersection of another passage.

"Just a little dizzy," she said, straightening. To hide her embarrassment, she busied herself composing the lapels of her coat and shirt.

"Of course," he said. He pulled up his broad black gun belt. He seemed to have trouble keeping it on his narrow hips. The holster sagged again as soon as he let go. "May I show you the exit?"

"Please," Edith said.

She followed him through passageways that seemed almost indistinguishable, noting when they passed the threaded doors of other Will-o'-the-Wisp booths. Edith took very little of it in. She was too busy trying to figure out what had brought on the vision and why it had unnerved her so. It'd been a year since the Sphinx had replaced her lost arm with one of his own, and in that time, she'd had troubled thoughts, she had felt ugly and obvious and awkward at times, but she'd not really feared that she was losing herself or turning into some sort of clockwork nightmare. That wasn't the case now. What had changed?

Her arm, of course. That had changed. When she saw the hand of her former engine lying detached on the Sphinx's workbench, something had turned inside her like a tumbler in a lock. And then she had seen the dead mechanical marvels in the Sphinx's attic, and . . .

"May I just say what an honor it is to meet you," her elderly guide said.

"I don't think we've actually met, though," Edith said.

"Well, I certainly know who you are, Captain Winters. And many congratulations on your incredible vessel. Deputy-Wakeman Luis Osmore, at your service."

"Deputy-Wakeman?"

"Yes, indeed. I've been watching over the Circuit for fifty-two years now," he said proudly.

"That's quite an achievement."

"Well, my father was a cobbler, so I think I did well enough. Though I was starting to worry I was serving a dead master. It's good to know he's back." He sounded so cheerful, Edith couldn't help but smile. The deputy told her to watch her step on the stairs, and as they climbed upward from the maze of hallways, he said, "I hope it'll make it easier to attract some new recruits. Young men these days don't want to spend their time serving a myth. They don't see the point in it." He opened the door at the top of the stairs for her, and Edith was a little surprised to find herself staring at an earless llama, one of the beasts in the Circuit of Court's carousel. She realized she was standing in the doorway of the white pyramid.

"What is the point?" Edith asked, sensing that he wished her to.

Deputy-Wakeman Luis Osmore yanked up his belt, and as gravity tugged it right back down, he said, "To finish what was started, of course."

Chapter Eight

Whenever I stand on a rooftop and look down at the people in the streets, the world makes perfect sense.
—Oren Robinson of the *Daily Reverie*

The Hope and Pride was a modest pub with a boastful view. Below, the streets of Pelphia roared, but from the roofline, the noise dimmed to a murmur.

Edith found Haste already hunched at the counter with an inch of beer left in her glass. The bar was made of long planks that looked to have spent a previous life as the decking of an airship. The boards were mottled with pitch stains and speckled with nail heads, but all was kept clean by a vigilant, ancient bartender. There were only a few empty seats left. Most were filled with porters in unbuttoned coats and cooks with aprons draped on their shoulders. A pair of uniformed maids held their own at the crook of the bar, drinking tawny port and laughing.

Haste greeted Edith enthusiastically. She slapped the stool beside her, and said with a little mischief in her voice, "I wasn't sure you were going to come. Thought the stairs might've scared you off."

To reach the rooftop pub, Edith first had to climb through what appeared to be a workhouse. Drying laundry hung from the handrails, moistening and perfuming the air. Most of the apartment doors stood open, showing rooms full of women mending, washing, and ironing linens. Younger children played on the steps, while older children folded laundry on the landings.

413

"You thought I'd be too prissy to walk up an old spike?" Edith looked at what Haste had in her glass, supposed it was probably stout, and held up her finger to signal that she would have the same.

"Not at all, not at all. I liked you the moment I saw you," Haste said with a smile that made the red in her cheeks more pronounced. Edith guessed she wasn't finishing her first drink. "So come on. Let's get the how-do-you-dos out of the way. How's your crew? How's the Sphinx?"

"My crew's fine. And the Sphinx is the Sphinx."

"Appropriately vague! He does not like to tip his hand. A man of mysteries and smoke and mirrors," Haste said, fluttering her fingers like a stage magician.

"He's a manipulative ass, who also happens to have saved my life," Edith said and thanked the bartender for the beer he set in front of her.

"You're honest when you're sober. And here I was looking forward to getting you drunk!" Haste held up her glass, and they clanked them together. "Honestly, I hadn't heard from the Sphinx in so long, I was starting to wonder if I'd imagined him." She leaned back and stuck out her golden chest. "But then I remember this! What do they call me, Harold?" she called to the bartender. "Tell her what they call me!"

The bartender smiled. "The Gold Watch."

"The Gold Watch!" Haste raised a declarative finger. "Get it? Because I'm the Sphinx's watchman and I'm made out of gold." She let her hand drop and it clanged against the counter. "I never said they were very creative. But it's probably the best out of the names they've floated over the years. They've called me the Brass Bushel, the Lady Kettledrums, the Angry Urn." Edith winced at the list of unflattering names, though they didn't seem to bother Georgine. "But it's not such a bad life, all things considered. They tolerate me, even appreciate my help at times. Best of all, they don't expect me to come to their parties anymore. Ouf! I've beaten that out of them, thank god. What we have now is like the later years of a marriage: a cool affection that benefits from separate bedrooms. I certainly don't want to shake the basket, as the airmen say. Though sometimes I . . ." She paused to choose her words. "I wonder if I'm still employed, or if I've just become a sort of curious remnant of a vanished age. Sometimes I wonder if the Sphinx is even up there anymore."

"Of course he's up there. He's still sending your vials, obviously. Your engine hasn't run down."

"That's true," Haste said, sticking out her bottom lip. "A crate comes every month. Thirty ampules of the red stuff that keeps my gears whirring."

"It's a beautiful engine," Edith said.

Georgine straightened so she could affect a little bow. "Thank you. That actually means something coming from a fellow Wakeman. When the natives here say it, I know they think of it like jewelry—like something I put on in the morning and take off at night."

"I wish I could take it off at night!" Edith said.

"Before this, I slept on my stomach. Ever since I was a baby—always on my stomach. If I tried that now, I'd smother."

"I used to sleep on my side. Though I guess I still could. I can remove my arm with a spanner and a little help. The Sphinx showed me that much . . ."

"There's a story there," Haste said, pointing with one finger while still holding her glass with the others.

"There is," Edith said. She was amazed how lithe Georgine's digits were. She only held glassware in her human hand anymore.

"See, if I could peel this shell off for a night, I'd take a bath. Oh, what I'd give for a real bath! Just a long, uncomplicated soak. But the days of baths are gone, gone."

"It's like that with a lot of little things, isn't it? Losing my arm and getting this engine is like this . . . meridian running through my life. There's everything that came before, and that was one life, and then everything that came after, and that's this life."

"How did you lose it?"

"Infection. How about you?"

"Boiler explosion. My father was an engineer on a cargo airship. I spent half my youth in an engine room. Used to love engines, funnily enough. Now I've kind of had my fill of them." She smiled good-naturedly and drank.

"Were you born in the Tower?"

"No, I'm one hundred percent unadulterated mudbug. From the west originally, though I hardly remember it now. That was before—what did you call it?—my meridian. How about you? Are you a citizen of the spire?" she said, affecting a posh accent.

"From the muddy south. I come from a family of farmers." Edith realized she was enjoying herself—which was the absolute last thing she had expected of her day. It hadn't occurred to her that she might find her counterpart easy to talk to or feel the urge to talk about herself, as she seldom did. And yet here she was, feeling—for the first time in many, many months—very nearly *normal*.

Then the sun went out.

She could still see it when she looked up. The streetlights and the other stars cast enough light to illuminate the sun, but the great bronze platter was frozen in place, its jets of flame extinguished. "What's happened?" she asked.

"Sun's stuck. It's been stuck for a half hour or so, I think," the bartender said.

Haste scowled. "Why didn't you say something?"

"I thought you'd noticed," the bartender said with a shrug.

"The sun goes out when it gets stuck?" Edith asked.

"No, they shut off the gas so they can poke it with a stick to get it going again," Harold said.

"Poke it with a stick? How do they poke it with a stick?" Edith asked, realizing that Haste had stopped speaking because she was charging through the rest of her pint.

Beneath the sun and half a city away, a red balloon was beginning to plump up on a rooftop.

Haste finished her beer with a gasp, slapped several shekels on the bar, and said, "Come on. Duty calls."

Haste descended the stairs with all the subtlety of a cannonball. She bellowed as she bounded from landing to landing for the children to get out of her way. And they did. They dove into doorways and pressed into corners. Edith managed to keep up, but only just.

They burst upon the street, nearly knocking a nobleman off his sedan chair as they did. His footmen had to swing and pitch about to keep him on his chair. Haste didn't stop to apologize. She charged down the street in the direction of the stymied sun and the red balloon rising to it. Haste clanged as she ran, her engine shell ringing like a fire brigade.

Edith found the immediacy of their sprint, the unsubtlety of it and the clear sense of purpose, exhilarating. Though she still didn't understand exactly why they were running. Haste gasped out a few words about a warped track and rusted spots that caught the sun's gears, which, while odd, didn't quite seem a disaster. It wasn't until the balloon's cargo rose above the roofline that Edith understood the urgency, and all sense of delight evaporated.

A person dangled from a harness under the balloon. The unlucky soul clutched a long, bowing pole, like something a tightrope walker might use to keep their balance. The dangler seemed to struggle with the awkward weight of the thing. It certainly wasn't a very big person who'd been sent up to nudge the sun.

Then Edith realized it was a child.

Haste ran faster as the balloon swam nearer the gloomy sun, the rays of which stood out like scimitars. When they arrived at the apartment building that the balloon had launched from, they bolted past an ineffectual doorman and sprang up the stairs, which were much nicer than the ones they had recently descended. They broke onto the roof, startling the two soldiers who occupied it. The young man holding the tether nearly let go of the line from surprise.

Both wore the black-and-gold uniforms of the ringdom's guard. The man in charge of this inhuman exercise, as far as Edith could tell, was the one with a slightly taller cap, a sergeant perhaps. Haste began shouting at him at once.

"I told you never again, Larson!"

"Do you think I like this?" Larson said, his voice squeaking with indignation. He held a short spyglass, which he began to wag at her like a finger. "You think this is the day I had in mind for myself? The sun stalled, and the city manager ordered me to send someone up. I don't have the authority to disagree." The sergeant had several chins, none of them particularly strong.

Haste took another step toward him, raising a hand. "It's not authority you need. It's a beating!"

The floor of the rooftop showed the evidence of a recent party. Several cane chairs lay on their sides among empty bottles and unsavory puddles. A wadded orange dress had been abandoned in a corner of the parapet. To this mess, the soldiers had apparently added a pair of black knapsacks, a wooden toolbox, and a small steel keg.

A thin whimper drifted down from above. The four of them looked up as one at the bare feet of the hanging boy. The crown of his balloon had nearly reached the limit of the ringdom. Edith took the spyglass from the sergeant, ignoring his blustering protest, and trained it on the boy. He looked eleven, perhaps twelve years old, or at least part of his face still had its youth. The other half was marred by a long scar that pointed toward an absent ear.

The private holding the tether, which was connected to the boy's harness as well as the balloon, suddenly strained at the line, his feet slipping on the champagne-slickened marble floor. "There's a draft," the private said, trying to walk back against the current.

"Of course there's a draft. There's always a draft in the afternoon! Reel him in, you idiot, before he drifts into a star!" Haste shouted, marching at the young man.

Before she could reach him, the private suddenly rushed across the roof, scattering a pair of chairs as he went. He slid on his heels, dragged by the balloon that had been caught by a gust. Before Haste could catch him or the line, the balloon crashed into the sun.

The metal rays gashed the silk, and the gas inside rushed out in a single hard breath. The boy screamed, the sound cupped and amplified by the bowl of blue sky. Edith waited for him to fall, waited for the flash of limbs as he plunged by, and the sickening sound of his body striking the street below...

But to her surprise, the boy did not fall. The deflated envelope had snagged upon the same rays that had torn it. The boy hung from the tatters, some fifty feet above the rooftop.

"Don't! Don't pull!" Haste shouted at the private who was still holding the tether, though it was now slack. "You'll drag him off."

"What do we do?" The private's voice shook.

"Do you have another balloon?" Edith asked, and the private dumbly nodded. "And enough gas to fill it?" Again, he nodded. He looked hardly older than a boy himself. "How much can it lift?"

"A hundred and thirty, a hundred and thirty-five pounds, maybe," the private said. Edith told him to get it filled as quick as he could. The private opened one of the rucksacks and began pulling out the silks of a second balloon.

"We'll need another boy," the sergeant said.

"My eye!" Haste barked. "I'll cut off your arms and legs and send your useless stump up there first!" Haste was staring up at the boy as if she might hold him there with her gaze. "Don't move! We're going to get you down! Stay calm!" she shouted through cupped hands.

"Where are your tools?" Edith asked the private, who was busily connecting the balloon's collar to the valve of the gas keg. He nodded to a lump under the spread silks, and Edith excavated the toolbox. She rummaged through until she found a large spanner. "Georgine, come here. I need your help." Edith pressed the tool into Haste's hand. Then she stood up a chair and sat down on it. "There are four bolts in the shoulder, I think. They're under this plate here." She tapped a panel in her shoulder that was held in place by several heavy twist locks.

Haste stared at the spanner in her hand. "What are you talking about? You want me to take your arm off?"

"I'll be light enough without it."

"But . . . are you sure you want to do this?"

Edith smiled up at Haste thinly. "Maybe I just want to sleep on my side for a night." She looked straight ahead. "Now, get the plate off. Look for the bolts."

Haste unlocked and then unhinged the plate that covered Edith's shoulder. Four large hexagonal bolts stood out from the intricate machinery. The glow of the Sphinx's battery painted the coils and rods in a bloody light. "I see them," Haste said at last.

"Then do it. Come on!"

Haste clamped the first bolt and began to turn.

The sergeant seemed to realize that he was the last man under his own command. So he took it upon himself to encourage the stranded youth. He called up, "Stay calm, young man! We're sending someone right up to get you. Everything will be fine so long as you don't struggle. Just pretend you're an apple hanging from a branch!"

The youth, silent a moment before, shouted something unkind about Sergeant Larson's parentage, then threw the pole down at him. The pole waggled in the air like a javelin, missed the roof entirely, and broke upon an empty terrace below.

Edith felt the friction and pressure of Haste's wrenching in her bones. It was like the deep, rattling sensation of striking an anvil with a hammer. It seemed to her that everything was happening very slowly: the turning of the bolts, the filling of the balloon. "Where's the boy's mother?" Edith asked the sergeant, trying not to watch Haste's progress on her screws.

"He's a hod. I haven't the faintest idea where his mother is," the sergeant said. "Whoever the woman is, she might've taught him not to throw sticks at people who are only doing their job."

Edith saw why Georgine loathed the man, but she was also glad the Gold Watch was concentrating too hard at the moment to snap at him.

Then all at once the second balloon was plump enough to show its seams. The private had anchored it to the steel keg, and the balloon had enough lift now to hold the barrel suspended on one edge. "That's all it can hold."

Edith felt a sudden lightness in her arm, as if the engine had been tied to the balloon.

Edith turned to see Haste holding her arm away from her side. The sight made her head swim. "There are cords running between the arm and your body. Can you see them?" Taking a deep breath, Edith pressed her chin into the iron collar that capped her empty shoulder. When she strained, she could just see the cables, wound in cloth, that crossed the gulf between her body and the limb. She could still feel her arm, could still make the fingers curl. She knew this was madness. They could wait for someone to fetch another balloon, another keg, another person to do the job. If the boy fell, it would not be her fault, not entirely, not only. There would be so much blame and guilt to go around that she might not feel it at all.

She knew that was a lie.

She grasped the cables and pulled like a child yanking out a loose tooth.

Her engine arm seemed to vanish. It just disappeared from her sense of the world. Though of course she could still see it, hanging motionless in Haste's hands. She watched Georgine turn and set the silent engine on the ground.

"Help me with the harness," Edith asked in a voice not quite as commanding as it had been a moment before. Haste helped her into the harness. The leather belts ran about her waist, around either leg, up her back, and between her shoulders.

As Haste buckled her in, Edith told her and the private what she intended to do. She would follow the boy's tether up and get as close as she safely could to the sun. Then she would yank his line, and when he came free, she would hold him by the reins while they descended.

"That's insane," the sergeant said.

"No, it's not," Haste said to him, and then to Edith, "Here, take his glove. You'll have a better grip."

Edith took the private's glove when he offered it and pulled it on with her teeth. "Haste, you'll be my brakeman," she said while the private lashed her to the fresh balloon.

"Of course." Haste attached a second tether to Edith's harness, the effort bringing her head close to Edith's ear, so she could say without the soldiers overhearing, "First honesty, now bravery. You're going to make me look bad."

"Must be the mud in me. Always something to prove. Keep an eye on my arm for me. I'm going to want it back."

"Who's your second-in-command?" the sergeant asked. "In case something happens to you."

"Larson, you're a coward and an idiot," Haste said sharply. She patted Edith on the chest. "This is going to work," she said, then let the line out.

Edith felt the sudden pressure of the harness as it hiked her from her feet. The city grew a little smaller and wider beneath her.

The stars in the ceiling lost their splendor the nearer she drew to them. They looked like little more than naked streetlights, the tile about them stained with soot. She had a funny thought that perhaps that was all the black sky at night was: centuries and centuries of soot thrown off by the stars.

The clamor of metal on metal reverberated through the ringdom. The sun had come unstuck and lurched back to life. The boy's tether went slack in her hand.

Haste began to shout something. Edith tightened her grip on the line as the boy fell past her in a blur.

In the street below, the afternoon mob finally felt obliged to look up. The boy's scream was so pure and authentic, so full of awe that for one second, it stole all the attention from the world. A moment before, they had all been studiously ignoring the afternoon eclipse, which really wasn't *that* rare. Even after the boy had begun to dangle and yelp, they were not impressed. Why should they let a hod on a string steal their spotlights?

But then the boy screamed, and it really was sublime.

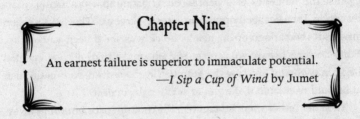

Chapter Nine

An earnest failure is superior to immaculate potential.
—*I Sip a Cup of Wind* by Jumet

When the boy reached the end of his tether, the sudden jerk nearly pulled Edith's arm from its socket. But her grip held. Unfortunately, the balloon's grip on the air did not. The addition of the boy's weight was too much, and before the balloon had reached its zenith, it began to sink, and quickly.

All of her reflexes seemed unconvinced that she had only one arm to work with. The urge to shore up her grip with her absent engine was as powerful as it was useless. All she could do was grit her teeth and hang on, even as they fell.

She hoped to shorten their plummet by landing on a rooftop, if not the one she had launched from, then an adjacent one, but the draft that had caught the boy's balloon now caught hers. They drifted from the rooftop and dropped into the canyon between city blocks. A class of dancers in leotards and tutus reached out from the studio balcony trying to grab the boy who was thrashing like a trout at the end of a line. But he plunged through their arms.

Their descent was not quite as quick as a free fall, but it was rapid enough that when the boy struck the canvas canopy over a street café, he tore through the fabric at once and crashed into the tables beneath to a chorus of shattering glasses and startled screams.

The same moment the boy landed, Edith's grip gave out. She dropped his tether, and with it the anchor that had overwhelmed her buoyancy. She bounced inside her harness and began to rise again. In the narrow space between buildings, the gas envelope bunched against the windows of a penthouse, frightening a practicing quartet inside, then snagged upon a prominent gargoyle. The beast's sharp snout slit the balloon open. Just as quickly as she'd been yanked up, Edith now felt her weight return. She fell amid a snarl of rope, tangled like a marionette. She saw the granite tile of a second-floor patio rush at her and wondered if she would survive the impact.

Then her tether snapped taut. On the rooftop three buildings away, Haste had gotten a firm grip on the brake line. Edith landed on the patio in an ungraceful but living sprawl.

She floundered about in the piles of silk that fell over her and emerged to discover she had landed in the middle of a whist tournament. An upturned table and chairs lay amid a spray of playing cards. The players stood in frozen shock, many still holding fans of cards clutched to their chest.

A woman, who was wearing a hat like a layer cake, cried out, "You all saw it! It was a trump card! I played a trump! I win the round!"

Out on Port Virtue's long pier, the late-afternoon sun had cracked upon the mountains and spilled its orange yolk.

Georgine Haste presented Edith's arm to her as if it were a bunch of roses and she had just won a race.

Edith thanked her for having carried it and slung the heavy engine over her empty shoulder.

The big port was much more serene without all the fanfare and crowds. Half of the slips were empty, and the docked ships were still except for a flat-bottomed barge being unloaded by a gang of stevedores. The workers shifted colorful bolts of cloth down a bouncing gangplank and stacked them upon a dray. One spool of silk escaped the rest and rolled across the pier, leaving a train of blue behind it. Before anyone could catch it, the bolt rolled off the edge and vanished with a snap of its tail. The port guards laughed at the loss.

"You'll make sure he's looked after?" Edith asked. The young hod had survived his fall, but not without injury. In addition to some nasty bruises, he'd broken his wrist.

"I will. There's a mission that takes in injured hods. It's run by ladies of the court who admittedly like dressing up as nurses more than they like doing the work, but they'll give him a bed and meals till he's recovered," Haste said. The Wakeman was smirking as she said it, but now she began to shake her head in wonder. She seemed to deliberate a moment before speaking her mind. "You know, I can't tell whether you're insane or just burdened by an overlarge conscience. I'm sure half the people of Pelphia wouldn't have done what you did to save their own child, much less a hod. I would've thought the Sphinx's priorities were different."

"If I ever get to the point where I can stand idly by while a child falls to his death, I don't think I can claim to have priorities of any kind anymore."

"A refreshing perspective." Haste's gaze roved over Edith's head, up the hull of the *State of Art*, bright as mercury, and farther upward to the immense envelope and the Brick Layer's green crest that decorated it. "She is quite a sight! Almost seems a different species, like a condor flying among pigeons. I'd love to see what she's like inside. How about a tour?"

Edith's lips puckered. As much as she liked Georgine, she wasn't ready to invite her aboard. Not just yet. It seemed a silly reservation given the fact that Edith had let Haste remove her arm. And perhaps Haste's fidelity really hadn't shifted to the ringdom that had adopted her. She certainly didn't seem to care for many of the locals. But revealing the ship's hollow state seemed an unnecessary test of Haste's loyalties, and there really was no benefit to it other than to satisfy her curiosity.

"This isn't a good time," Edith said as diplomatically as she could.

Georgine smiled, perhaps to conceal her disappointment. "Some other time."

"Yes, perha—" The thought was suddenly overshadowed by the ascent of three black globes above the port's horizon. The appearance of the massive balloons was enough to divert the course of the wind. Edith's greatcoat flapped, her hair streamed, as she watched the *Ararat* rise into view. Despite her changed circumstance, the abrupt return of the flying fortress filled her with horror.

She had grown accustomed to looking at it through a spyglass, which carved the terror up enough to make it bearable. But hanging a hundred yards away, the *Ararat* was an overwhelming presence. She could see far too many of her seventy-eight guns, could see the iron bands of her drawbridge, heavy enough to crush a man. Her hull gleamed like wet ink with a fresh coat of tar. The crew of the *Ararat* cast lines to the longshoremen from the battlements, and as they pulled the black warship in, Georgine Haste remarked, "Come home to roost at last."

"What?" Edith said, rousing from her astonishment.

"Commissioner Pound has been recalled. Seems Leonid finally tired of his excuses. It's a reckoning that's been a long, long time coming."

"A reckoning? You mean, they'll remove him from his station?"

"I mean they'll probably remove him from this life."

When Edith walked onto the bridge of the *State of Art*, Byron had all but whipped himself into a panic. He and Reddleman had watched her approach with the native Wakeman on the magnovisor and had observed that their captain had been quite literally disarmed. The stag's fright had only been compounded by the abrupt appearance of the *Ararat*, whose approach had escaped the pilot's attention because he was too busy nosing a manual! Edith tried to calm the stag with logic and an explanation that he did not allow her to finish because he was not ready to be soothed. He said, "Yes, I'll grant you, the ringdom's flagship probably isn't going to start a firefight while docked in its own port, but why in heaven's name did you remove your arm?"

Falling heavily into her captain's chair, Edith said, "Byron, I can't tell you what you want to hear and listen to what you have to say both at once. Soon as you're ready for an answer, let me know."

"Oh, I'm ready, Captain!" he said, crossing his arms.

First, she explained what interested him least: Namely, what had brought the *Ararat* to port. Though she thought it probably unnecessary and perhaps antagonistic, she still directed Reddleman to aim the aft cannons and six of the port guns at the timber warship. Then she explained that it had been her idea, her own choice, to remove her engine, and that Georgine Haste had not taken advantage of the occasion, though she might well have if she'd wished to. Admittedly, removing her arm had been an extreme step, but she'd done it to save a boy's life.

Byron was at such a loss for words, he spent some moments pawing at the steel floor with the toe of his boot. While he stamped out his anxiety, Edith asked Reddleman to collect the tools Byron would need to refasten her arm.

"But I've never attached an engine before," the stag complained.

"Byron, if we're going to stand here and list all the things we haven't done before that we have been called upon to do, we're going to be here all night." She was interrupted by the chiming of the mysterious alarm, the source of which Reddleman had still not discerned. "Here, take the pliers, and let's see if we can't get these cables sorted."

Byron continued to object even as he worked on matching the dangling cords with the proper plugs. To calm him, Edith recounted that morning's parade, the unnecessary train ride, the king's bizarre tableau, and Voleta's performance in the Circuit of Court. The details of the day made Byron alternately chuckle with delight and cluck his tongue in disapproval, but Edith was relieved that at least it stopped his scolding.

"I'm glad to hear they liked Voleta," Byron said. "But I can't understand why she couldn't just let them cage the squirrel. Not every inconvenience needs to be turned into a matter of state!" With that, the stag rejoined the last cable, and Edith felt the presence of her arm return. It prickled and tingled as if she'd slept on it wrong for hours and hours and been awoken by the throbbing numbness.

Byron began tightening the arm's bolts while Edith shared what she'd encountered in her investigation of Senlin's hotel room: the concierge, his coats, the play program, and the duke's letter.

"And the moths?" Byron asked, apparently unsurprised that Edith had gone in search of Senlin. Perhaps the stag had just run out of outrage.

"All gone," Edith said, her reply eliciting a concerned frown from Byron. "I don't know if Tom took them or someone else."

"But nothing else?" Byron asked.

"Actually," Edith said, recalling the curious book she'd found under Senlin's undershirts, "Reddleman, look in my coat pocket. I want you to read that and tell me what sort of use it could be to anyone. There are some numbers in the margins. They may be important. See what you think."

Reddleman eagerly retrieved the book, then returned to his pilot's chair where he sat with his legs crossed and the open book propped on the dash of the controls. "Captain, where's Ostraka University?" he asked, pointing to the bookplate that was tucked into the front of the volume.

Edith recalled what Senlin had revealed in one of his later reports. "Ostraka University isn't anywhere anymore. It was shut down years ago. The Coterie bought the building and used it to open the Colosseum."

While Reddleman studied, Byron worked to fit the wires around the engine's mechanisms.

"Have you ever heard of the Sphinx's Will-o'-the-Wisps?"

"I have."

"What sort of magic is that?"

"I don't believe it's any sort. It's just a trick of the mirror, the light, and the imagination. Don't tell me you took a turn in one?"

"I wish I hadn't."

Byron asked what the Wisp had shown her. Edith glanced at Reddleman to see if he was listening, but he appeared absorbed by his study. So Edith described the vision, and did so honestly, but without inflection. When she finished, Byron asked her what she thought the vision meant, and she said, "I suppose I'm worried how many pieces I can lose, how many parts can be replaced before I lose myself."

"Well, I think I understand a little better now why you were so quick to pull off your arm," Byron said, and Edith immediately rose to her own defense, citing the boy, the urgency, the lack of alternative.

"Of course, all of that is true, but still, you thought to do it, and it occurred to you quickly. The question is why?"

"I don't know. Maybe I wanted to know how it would feel to have it gone."

"And how did it feel?"

"Awful. But I don't like that either. It's not my arm, but now it feels like a part of me, and what happened to that other part of myself?"

"I've pondered that question: Am I the sum of my parts or am I something else?"

"And what do you think?"

"My sense of being, my identity, whatever you want to call it, it doesn't reside in my parts. It lives in my past, and in the continuity of my present thoughts, and in my hopes for the future. I'm more afraid of losing a memory than a limb." Edith regarded Reddleman, rocking and snickering in his chair. "Though I am fond of these hands," Byron said brightly. He patted the sealed plate in Edith's shoulder. "There. Finished. How do you feel?"

Edith flexed the wrist of her engine, curling and straightening her fingers. "All there."

"Aha!" Reddleman exclaimed, and Edith and Byron turned in time to see the pilot swivel around in his chair. "This is an equation of a curve."

"What's it doing there?" Edith asked.

"I think it's describing the trilobite's anatomy," Reddleman said. When Bryon expressed his perfect ignorance of the creature, the pilot explained, "It's a type of ancient arthropod, like a crab or a scorpion. It has plated armor and many legs and some of them have a fork-like protuberance at the front. Once upon a time, trilobites ruled the earth. Then they all perished when..." He stopped and waved the detail away. "Well, that doesn't matter. All that remains of them now are their shells. Maybe one day, it will be the same with us! Our whole race reduced to a picture in the book of some foreign species." The occasion seemed to strike him as a happy one.

Ignoring the digression, Edith asked, "The measurements don't appear in the text?"

"No, the text is more of a biological overview with pictures. I think some clever soul used these diagrams as the basis for some very novel calculations."

"For what purpose?"

"I haven't the foggiest idea!" Reddleman said cheerfully. "I suppose they could be useful for identifying a new species or subspecies of trilobite, or for building a model."

"I don't see how a model of an extinct crab could be of much use to anyone, and certainly not worth all the effort they took to try to smuggle the book out of the ringdom."

"Maybe the notes aren't relevant. For all we know, they were written by a student fifty years ago." Reddleman shut the book so he could inspect the catalog numbers painted on the spine. "You know, Captain, I might be of more help to you if I had an active role in the investigation. I could come ashore with you. Perhaps I'd see something that you overlooked," Reddleman said, though Edith had already begun shaking her head.

"Out of the question."

"But surely just sitting here is a squandering of my talents. I could—"

"I wasn't opening the floor to debate, pilot. You're supposed to be dead. So you'll stay here on the bridge—" The mysterious alarm pinged again. "And you'll figure out once and for all what's making that blasted racket."

Reddleman beamed like an imbecile. "Aye aye, Captain!"

His merry response made Edith uneasy. He was like a cannon whose fuse had burned down but failed to ignite. She couldn't decide whether he was a harmless misfire or a smoldering bomb, but she had a sinking feeling they'd find out which it was soon enough.

When Edith opened the ship's hatch the next morning, she was met with a very different sort of welcome. Port Master Cullins loitered at the end of the gangplank, a troop of armed men at his back. A heavy mist fell, an unusual gift from the clouds that collared the Tower's peak. The port master's usually impeccable mustache drooped in the rain. He craned his neck and tried to peer past her into the ship while the hatch was still open, but she blocked his view as she shut the door.

"Good morning, Captain Winters!" Despite his wilted mustache, the port master seemed much more composed than he had the previous day. "I trust you slept well?"

"Just fine, thank you." Edith shifted to step past him onto the sturdy, square beams of the port, but he moved to block her way.

Cullins said, "Of course, it's a formality that we typically address on the day of arrival, but yesterday was such a delightfully busy day, we never had the opportunity to."

"I don't know what you're talking about," Edith said.

"The inspection, of course." Cullins held up a large magnifying glass as if it were some inarguable credential or perhaps a magic wand. "As part of my charter as port master, I must inspect each ship that docks here. I assure you, it won't take a mo—"

"No," Edith said.

"I beg your pardon?"

"No, you can't inspect my ship."

The port master's confidence cracked. "But . . . but it's the law."

"Let me be very clear," Edith said, relishing the moment of revenge upon this man who'd once shot at her as if she were a feral dog. She plucked the magnifying glass from his grip. Holding the thick lens in the palm of her engine, she closed the pistons of her fingers until the glass popped with a glittering spray. "If anyone attempts to board my ship, I will blast this port and every man in it from the face of the Tower." She handed the deformed instrument back to him.

The port master's mustache dribbled as he numbly examined his ruined glass.

He did not resist when she brushed past him and parted his men with her gaze.

When she arrived at the patchwork palace, the doorman invited her to wait in the Queen's Foyer while he announced her and discovered the king's wishes.

The Queen's Foyer was walled in quartz as translucent as pig fat.

The floor was swamped with decorative poufs and floor pillows. Not wishing to squat, Edith sat upon the only available bench, a high-backed, unpadded affair, with her tricorne in her lap. She was forced to fend off repeated attempts by maids and butlers to bring her refreshment or diversion. She refused tea, a copy of the morning post, a full breakfast, hot chocolate, a selection of pastries, a book of amusing limericks, a second breakfast, and a bottle of champagne. With each successive offer, Edith's answer grew more and more curt until at last she stopped speaking altogether and just glared at the unfortunate hallboy who offered her a massage.

After an hour's delay, the doorman invited her to return that afternoon when King Leonid would no longer be indisposed.

Through gritted teeth, Edith said, "Please tell His Majesty I'm happy to wait for as long as it takes for him to keep his word."

Five minutes later, the doorman returned to announce that King Leonid was ready to receive her.

Edith followed the doorman through the palace's overfilled chambers. Frequently and without prompting, her guide would pause to point out some object of interest, which of course required exposition to fully appreciate: "That harp was a gift of the King of Nuxor, repaired by the royal harp maker, Blankenburg, after it was damaged in a fire. The stones of that hearth were donated by the Earl of Kowert from his land on the shores of the Ferrian Sea, and had been laid by the peerless master mason, Filipe Tucker."

After enduring several of these asides, Edith finally interrupted the doorman and said, "Look, I understand that you've been told to delay me for as long as possible. But I have already waited half the morning. Can we please dispense with the charade?"

"Yes, indeed," Leonid said from the doorway of an adjoining sitting room. The king wore a black waistcoat, rolled shirtsleeves, and striped trousers. The wild fringes of his hair were brushed down. He looked more like a bank clerk on his lunchbreak than a regent. "I'm sorry to have kept you waiting, Captain Winters. Would you please join me on the gallery?"

The second-floor gallery overlooked Cooke Street and Cooke's

Arcade, where ring tosses, cakewalks, shuffleboards, and tetherballs entertained a crowd of well-dressed children.

"I'm so sorry, Captain. Today is Airman's Day. If you could permit me a few moments more," Leonid said.

With the assistance of a footman, King Leonid donned a bright white smock and a stocking cap, sewn to resemble an orange candle flame. Then he approached the railing of the gallery, raised his arms, threw back his head, and crowed.

The children in the arcade below roared back at him. With the help of his staff, the king lit votive candles inside paper lanterns, making them puff up and float. Into a paper gondola beneath each lantern, the king placed a single shining penny. He released these gifts, one after another, to the screeched approval of the children. Edith saw that many of the children had come prepared with peashooters and sling-shots. Some of them targeted the balloons themselves, others shot at the children who raced to catch the falling coins. One of the tea lights shifted midair, igniting the envelope that carried it. Half a dozen children ran toward rather than away from the fiery mess when the lantern plopped upon the cobblestones. The adults in the surrounding cafés marked the commotion with vague amusement.

Observing the general chaos that the lanterns caused, Edith wondered why anyone would encourage such bedlam among the young. King Leonid noticed her consternation and explained, "It's called a Penny War. And I thought the same thing when I was a younger man: *What on earth are we teaching our children with such a thing?* But you know what's interesting: The children who do the shooting rarely get to collect the prize. Often the pennies just go rolling off, so even the first to arrive when the lantern comes down aren't always the one to walk away with the gold. Perhaps those children will spend the rest of the day complaining about the unfairness of it all. Which of course *is* the lesson. Nothing is fair. I believe in love and chance and beauty. But I think it is unkind to pretend that fairness exists in the world."

Edith had a different interpretation. She thought the so-called Penny War was a patronizing sham. The king had created a dishonest circumstance, incentivized bad behavior, and then interpreted the predictably desperate result as having some instructive merit. It was hard to listen to an old man opine about fairness while he stood there throwing crumbs at children like they were pigeons in a park.

Edith was just about to voice her opinion when King Leonid's brother arrived. The girdled crown prince, red-faced from the walk, seemed surprised and unhappy to see Edith there.

"Well, this puts me in a very bad light, doesn't it, Leo? Or maybe that was exactly the point."

"Really, Pepin," the king said, shooing off the servants who'd helped him launch his penny flotilla. "How is your blunder possibly my fault?"

"It is not my blunder!" the treasurer snapped, hooking his thumbs behind the lapels of his overstretched sienna jacket. "I told you last night, the error lies with the archivist."

"I'm sorry you had to witness this, Captain Winters. I was hoping to spare you the scene." King Leonid pulled the candle-flame stocking from his head.

"I don't understand," Edith said.

"It seems my brother has lost track of the Sphinx's painting."

"I told you, I know right where it is!" Le Mesurier tugged a small notepad from the pocket of his waistcoat. He opened it and riffled to a page. "See here—*The Brick Layer's Granddaughter* is in the one hundred and second locker on the third shelf beneath Grandfather's collection of pewter tinder boxes and above Princess Hannah's tiara, seized during the Battle of Port Eccles." The swallow-breasted treasurer tapped at his pad vigorously. "It's right there!"

"You've lost it?" Edith said.

"It's not lost!" Le Mesurier patted the red fringe of his hair. "It's just not where it's supposed to be. The matter is already under audit. I have never failed an audit. Never! I am confident that I will have the object in hand soon."

"I'm sorry, Captain. This is inexcusable," the king said, looking ashamed for his brother. "The Royal Vaults are embarrassingly immense and, unfortunately, not as well organized as we would like. We sometimes mislay one treasure amid the trove. But all my vaults are absolutely secure, and it is only a matter of hours until we find and can deliver *The Brick Layer's Granddaughter* to you. In the meantime, I ask for your patience."

Edith had removed her tricorne when she had entered the palace. She had spent the interim with it in hand or under arm, but she reseated it on her head now, and said, "I understand. I shall return in the morning, Your Majesty. I hope that will give you sufficient time to sift through your fortune and find me my painting."

Chapter Ten

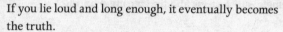

I don't know why you came if you aren't going to eat anything," Haste said, taking an immense bite of her chocolate éclair.

"I've already had a tart, a turnover, and a cupcake. If I eat another sweet, it's just going to come right back up," Edith replied, grateful to be leaving the latest bakery in their spree. It was a wonder between the pressing crowd and all those fragile displays and tenuously tiered cakes that she'd not put her elbow through anything. Or anyone.

Haste had spent the past ten minutes eating cream puffs and listening with undisguised amusement as Edith complained about her morning, but now she seemed ready to move the conversation along. "So the upshot is, the Sphinx wants his old painting back. They've lost it. Now what?"

"I guess I go back in the morning," Edith said.

"And I'll show you how to do it right this time," Haste said, eyeing the éclairs displayed behind the shopwindow of the bakery next door. Edith couldn't see any obvious difference between that confectionary and the one in Haste's hand, but Edith had learned that the only truly unpopular opinion one could hold when it came to the question of

436

which bakery reigned supreme was the opinion they were all more or less the same.

Detecting a discordant clank, Edith snapped her head back. The grinning sun chugged a little, then rattled on.

While she had been waiting for Haste outside the first bakery, Edith had bought the early edition of the *Daily Reverie* off a news-boy. She'd scanned the headlines for mention of the stalled sun, the dangling youth, and their crash landing, curious to know what the repercussions would be and when the track repairs would commence. But apparently the incident didn't merit a single mention. Edith was doubly annoyed to see that the editors had found plenty of room to opine upon Voleta and her defense of a parrot.

Edith had made the further error of reading some of the account of her own arrival to the ringdom and discovered that she was described as "an earnest woman with a drainpipe arm and a tatty cocked hat." She took exception to her tricorne being called *tatty*. It wasn't shabby; it was experienced.

"Have you heard of the Mermaid?" Edith asked.

"Of course! She's the latest object of our public affection, though I think her fame is probably about to wane."

"Why do you say that?" The two women paused and lifted their arms to allow a school of small children to rush around them.

"Well, it's just the way things go here." Haste peeled the paper cup from her éclair and threw the sticky wrapper in a public waste bin, which, judging from the trash in the street, was treated as largely deco-rative. "Women are treated like cut flowers: They're plucked from their roots, stuffed into some fancy staging, set out on display where they become the object of praise and critique for, oh, a week or two. Then when the blooms begin to droop or fade or just look a little too familiar, they're put out with the rubbish."

"That's a hateful cycle," Edith said, scowling. She wondered if such a thing might've happened to her if she had not been disfigured by a Parlor brand. She liked to think she would've evaded such a fate by dint of willpower and self-possession. But then, hadn't Marya been independent and clever when she arrived at the Tower? Hadn't she been resourceful and determined? Acknowledging that Marya had been a victim of the Tower required Edith to admit she might've been one, too. Edith wondered whether Marya was a beneficiary of her fame or the victim of it. Did she have the ringdom wrapped around her finger, or was she, as Haste suggested, nothing but a spoiling bouquet?

Haste licked cream from her gold fingers. "I don't think it's hateful so much as fearful."

"What do you mean?"

"Well, I can't speak for the rest of the Tower, but I think most Pelphian men are just leery of women. I really do. They'll say, 'No, no, no, women are weak. They're foolish. They need looking after and direction.' But I think deep down they can't forget that they came out of a woman, were nursed by a woman, and had their little minds sculpted by one as well. When they grow up, just the thought of it makes them uneasy. But rather than face their fear, they look for ways to dominate and possess us, to create proof that we are weak, and they are strong. I'll tell you this: The harder a man brags about his thunderous escapades in the lady's boudoir, the more frightened he is. I'm sure you've noticed how much they love giving us diminutive nicknames. The Mermaid, the Leaping Lady..."

"The Gold Watch?"

"Exactly, because we shake them to their infant bones."

"Cowards."

"Ah, but there is nothing so dangerous as a coward!" Haste said, then crammed the rest of her éclair into one cheek, chewed a little, then spoke around it: "I'm curious, what do you make of Leonid?"

"He's a fine actor," Edith said.

"Doesn't mean he's not dangerous, though," Haste said as soon as she had swallowed.

"I came in through the Parlor. Believe me, I know how dangerous actors can be."

"What about the Sphinx? You can't say he's not theatrical."

"Well, he's not throwing pennies at children, but yes, he's theatrical." When they passed the open door of a cake maker's shop, a young woman in a white apron burst out holding a round, white cake piled with flowers of orange icing. She forced the cake on Edith, deflecting her firm refusal with a firmer insistence, until Edith would've either had to let the cake fall on the street or take it in hand.

She carried the cake until they were out of sight of the bakery, then she found a newsboy who was quite delighted to receive an entire cake.

Haste watched the whole exchange with amusement and, once the cake had been disposed of, said, "I do wonder sometimes if all of this was really necessary." She waved a hand over her golden chest. "I wonder if I could've survived with something a little less showy."

"Can I ask, is it mostly a shell, or...?" Edith let the question hang, unsure how sensitive the subject would be.

But Haste seemed unperturbed. "No. I lost half my ribs, one lung, my stomach, and most of my bowels to the explosion. The heart's still mine, but the rest is the Sphinx's plumbing."

"Incredible," Edith said, thinking how simple her arm was in comparison.

"I imagine. I haven't seen it. Though I suppose most people haven't had a look at their guts. Not the lucky ones, anyway." With the bakers' alley now behind them, Haste craned about, looking for open seats in the nearest public house. "I'm thirsty. What say we find ourselves a drink?"

But Edith had something else in mind. That morning's dispatch from the Sphinx had included no mention of either Senlin or her investigation of his hotel room. She took this as license to continue her search because either the Sphinx was aware of her efforts, and looking the other way, or he was not so omniscient as he liked to pretend, in which case, he could use the help.

"Does Pelphia have a jail?" Edith asked.

"It does, of course. Why?"

Not wanting to reveal the true nature of her interest, Edith fabricated an excuse. She said that the Sphinx wished to make certain that the prisons of the Tower were humane and decent places, concluding, "You can learn a lot about a society by examining how it treats its prisoners."

"All right," Haste said, smiling at a joke Edith had not detected. "Let's go to jail."

The jail sat between two ornate playhouses in the crowded theater district. From a distance, the prison looked like an old maid squeezed between a pair of fashionable ladies. The playhouses were arrayed in lights and alabaster shades, with pearlescent fixtures and colorful bills. Their marquees were as crowded as a princess's dance card. The jail looked comparatively drab. And yet, it seemed to attract a larger crowd than either theater.

The face of the prison was composed of a collection of cages, stacked four high, one upon the next like blocks from a toy chest. The inhabitants of these cages ranged in appearance from half-naked wretches to overdressed lords. Many of the inmates reached through the bars, calling the crowd to harken to their tales of misfortune and misdeed. The audience, who loitered about the curb, ate tea cakes and snap bread, popcorn and bonbons, and between bites heckled or encouraged the prisoners to continue their dramatic efforts.

The bars of the cages, Edith soon realized, were set far enough apart that the prisoners could slip in and out at will. Indeed, even as she watched, a young man squeezed between the bars of his street-level cell to retrieve a flower that an admirer had thrown short. The moment the young man had the flower in hand, he returned to his cell by the same manner he'd escaped and resumed his loud lamentation about how he had been driven to slay his romantic rival in an unsanctioned duel. In the cage immediately above his, a lady in a fashionably ripped frock flung herself against the bars and cried for the king's mercy. A group of top-hatted fops in the street applauded and whistled, suggesting what sort of mercy they'd show her if she would come down to join them for drinks.

The higher cages were accessible via a ladder that was attended by a constable in a pickelhelm. The constable was responsible for helping prisoners in and out of cages rather than keeping them there. A coin dispenser gleamed from his belt. He punched out change for a middle-aged man who arrived in a white suit splattered with red, which looked more like merlot than blood. This new prisoner claimed to have stabbed his father with a carving fork, to the constable's obvious indifference.

"It costs a shekel for five minutes," Haste said, and stopped a young girl who was carrying a tray full of sweets. Georgine bought a bag of candied roses and began to pop the crystalized petals into her mouth as she spoke. "For three minas, you can stay overnight."

"Why in the world would anyone want to do that?" Edith asked.

Haste smirked and rummaged through her bag of candy. "Entertainment. Boredom. Latent guilt. Who knows? You see that man up there in the top right cage, the one wearing dishrags and an eye patch? He's an earl. He's been up there for three years. I don't know how he affords it. I don't think he ever leaves." And as they watched, the shabby earl stuck his pale bony legs between the bars and began kicking them merrily.

"Doesn't he have a family or a business or a wife?"

"None that he cares for, apparently."

"Is the whole prison a sham?" Edith shoved aside a young man who'd backed into her while trying to catch a garter slung through the bars by a pretty inmate.

"Most of it, but not all. There's a pen in the back where they sober up the violent drunks and stow the rabble-rousers. And there are maybe a dozen cells for legitimate prisoners. The most common crimes are financial in nature and committed by influential men. So the cells are well furnished and usually not occupied for very long. Honestly, half the time it's impossible to tell the prisoners from the visitors. Here, I'll show you."

Despite having little hope that she'd find Senlin confined there, Edith followed Georgine on a tour of the jail. It was the jolliest prison she'd ever seen. There were guards present, but most of them sat inside the cages with the formal prisoners, playing Beggar-My-Neighbor. A female prisoner (or perhaps she was a visitor) had convinced a guard to allow her to apply some of her makeup to his rather weathered face. The guard sat with her in his lap and his eyes shut as she tried to apply a deep blue shadow without blinding him. The prison floor was strewn with streamers and smashed flowers. Empty bottles and glasses seemed to fill every surface. If it had not been for the abundance of iron bars, Edith would've thought she'd stumbled upon the drunken conclusion of a week-long wedding.

When she saw no sign of Senlin, she was almost relieved. He would've found all of the carousing insufferable. "So this is where the condemned hods were kept before the execution?" she asked.

"You heard about that, did you?"

"I try to keep informed," Edith said vaguely. Of course, she couldn't add that she had learned of the injustice from Senlin's reports rather than the Sphinx, who'd stayed mum on the whole ordeal.

"No, they weren't kept here," Haste said, her expression clouding. "Hods are held in the gatehouse between the ringdom sewers and the black trail . . . or the Old Vein, or whatever you like to call it."

Someone nearby retched violently. The unpleasant splash was followed by a round of cheers.

"Could you show me the gatehouse?" Edith asked.

"Why?"

"Why not?"

Haste crumpled up the empty candy bag and put her fists on her hips, the same pose she'd struck when she'd first met Edith, though it seemed less welcoming now. "Look, if the Sphinx sent you to investigate me or how I've dispatched my duties, I wish you would just come out and say it. I thought we were going to be honest with each other."

Edith raised her human hand in a gesture of peace. "I'm not here to check up on you, Georgine. I'm really not. I'm completely convinced that you are a conscientious defender of the peace, and I have nothing but admiration for the work that you do. But you're just one person, and you yourself have said that you don't have much access or influence over the political activities of the ringdom." Edith lowered her voice before she said, "The Sphinx is worried about the possibility of a coming conflict between the ringdoms and the hods. I'm just trying to figure out if the Pelphians are banking the fires of war or defending the rule of law. As an outsider, none of this makes much sense to me." She paused to wave at their surroundings. A drunken fop in a crumpled jacket waved back at her, believing that he had been summoned. He took a few steps toward her, and she pointed an iron finger at him. "No!" she barked. He turned on his heel and staggered into an open cell to flop upon an empty cot. Edith resumed her speech. "But I'm at least wise enough to know that the *Daily Reverie* is probably not an immaculate record of the truth. I just want to see the facts for myself."

Every word of what Edith had said was true, even if it wasn't the whole truth. She might also have added that she was fed up with the Sphinx controlling what everyone knew. If she was going to be an effective enforcer of the Sphinx's will, there were certain things she needed to know, even if he didn't agree.

Haste hesitated a moment longer, deliberating amid the happy chaos of the jail. Then she patted her infallible abdomen and said, "Oof! Well, now I wish I hadn't eaten all those sweets. I hope your stomach is as staunch as your arm, Edie."

Passing from the pearly streets of Pelphia into the sewers was a little like waking from a pleasant dream to a dark room and soaked bedsheets. Water stood on the chiseled floor and sweated from the walls. Here and there, sturdy timber doors interrupted the monotony of bricks. Edith was surprised to discover that each tunnel intersection, of which there were many, was marked with a street sign that corresponded with the street above. At first, she supposed the signs had been installed for the benefit of the municipal workers. Then they encountered a well-dressed man with a cane in one hand and a candle in the other, hurrying through the sewers with his hat still on his head.

"Many of the lords and ladies use the underground to escape awkward moments or unwanted encounters," Haste explained. "Half of the manors have basements with access to the sewers."

"I'm surprised anyone would want to try to hide a scandal here. I assumed everyone would want the scrutiny." Edith held up the heavy lantern Georgine had given her to drive off the gloom.

"Well, just because we're all a bunch of spotlight-seeking hedonists doesn't mean we don't have our secrets, too," Haste said.

"Does this system connect with the Circuit of Court?"

"No, that's separate, thank goodness. Those Deputy-Wakemen have always driven me mad. They're so sincere."

"Why do you say that?" Edith said, squinting as she considered her own impressions of Deputy-Wakeman Luis Osmore. She'd rather liked the man.

"Every time I've brought them a willing cadet who's interested in joining the order, they've found some reason to reject him. They're just fanatical."

"Passing the torch to the next generation is never easy, I suppose."

After a few moments of turning through the tunnels, they came to what seemed a formal outpost. Two sentries with rifles and sabers guarded an iron-banded door set back from the passageway. As Georgine shook the hands of the guards, Edith caught a trace of stale, putrid air. Discreetly, she shielded her nose with the side of her hand as one of the sentinels unlocked and opened the door.

She nearly gagged when the warm gust of effluvium and decay struck her. She sucked in a breath, held it, and marched through with as much composure as she could muster.

As soon as the guard closed the door behind them, Edith ran to the nearest corner, braced herself against the wall, and retched onto the floor.

"Don't feel bad," Georgine said, taking several paces deeper into the tunnel to allow her a moment to recover. "I did the same thing the first time I came down here. And the second. Unfortunately, the stink sticks to you. No one ever has to ask if you've recently visited the Old Vein."

Edith wiped her mouth on her coat sleeve and bent her lapel over her nose. It was too warm to be wearing wool, and yet she had no desire to take her jacket off. At least it provided some buffer between her skin and the noisome air.

"The guardhouse isn't far. Come on. The sooner we get there, the sooner we can get back," Haste said.

The passage to the gatehouse seemed a worse version of the sewers.

The brickwork was cruder, the stones misaligned like kernels in an ear of wild corn. She felt the weight of the Tower press upon her in a way it did not in the ringdom. She could feel the Tower's thick pulse here, roiling like molten rock under the earth's crust. She wanted fresh air, wanted the open sky, wanted to shut her eyes and picture furrows in freshly tilled soil. She wanted anything but this wormhole, this oily dark, and this infernal stench.

They did not speak as they walked. She had no desire to open her mouth. When the tunnel expanded and the gatehouse appeared before them, cheered by the presence of torchlight, she felt a little rush of relief.

The gatehouse's guards were all admirably stalwart considering their difficult assignment. They generally struck Edith as being either too young to have made a name for themselves or too old to have had time to redeem whatever reputation they'd earned. The gatehouse completely plugged the end of the tunnel, with enough room on one side for a slender barrack building, and opposite it, a mess hall. Both had lit windows and a fresh coat of paint. The gatehouse, meanwhile, was much sturdier in appearance. The beams of the portcullis were as thick as a railway sleeper.

None of the guards seemed particularly surprised to see Haste. The sergeant in command, a jowly man in a strangling collar, who she called Horace, greeted her warmly.

"It's been a quiet couple of days," he reported. "The usual traffic, a few sob stories, but nothing remarkable. I'm looking forward to some liberty this weekend. I don't think I've pulled my socks off in a fortnight."

"I'll warn your wife," Haste said, and the sergeant laughed. "Are there any hods in the holding cell?"

"Not at the moment. Like I said—quiet. And you know Eigengrau cleaned us out a few days ago for his *recompense*." The sergeant accented the word as if it were exotic. "Anyway, we've spent the morning playing cards. Beaumont there owes me a week's pay." He showed a top shelf of yellow teeth.

"I'm glad you're staying entertained," Haste said.

She introduced Edith then, who shook the sergeant's hand, offering the sort of forthright gaze that she knew most military men appreciated. She fielded a few comments about her arm and a question about her glorious warship, which they were all eager to see. Edith did her best to ingratiate herself to the sergeant in preparation of the one question she'd come to ask.

When she finished laughing at one of the sergeant's unremarkable jokes, she asked, "I don't suppose you've had any interesting characters come through lately, have you?"

"Interesting characters? You mean like you?" Sergeant Horace said, a smile lifting the empty bags of his cheeks.

"Just anyone who stood out," she said.

"No, not really. I mean, a hod's a hod. Duke Pell did come down a few days ago to drop off a couple of brawlers from the Colosseum who were giving him trouble. You know how it is when a big title like that comes through. You have to click your heels and hide your cards and pretend like you came out of your mother saluting. Heaven save us from our superiors, eh?"

Edith felt the hairs prickle at the nape of her neck at the mention of Duke Pell. "What did the hods look like, the ones the duke dragged down with him?"

"I didn't really study them. I mean, there was a big one with a beard. And a thinner one who had a blinder on."

"What's a blinder?" Edith asked.

"It's like a bucket they weld onto your head," Sergeant Horace said, drawing a ring around his head with his finger. "They put blinders on the really nasty ones, you know. To keep them docile, or at least to keep them from spitting and biting. Anyway, Pell must've really had it in for him because he didn't remove the blinder before we put him through. We shut the gate, we drove the hordes back, and I think then we played a round of Beggar-My-Neighbor. I can't really remember anything else in particular. I mean, a hod's a hod."

"So you've said." Edith's smile tightened. "Could I have a look through the gate? I've never seen the black trail before."

"Oh, that's what the hods call it. They're so dramatic. Still, if you want to see the Old Vein, the portcullis is down. It's perfectly safe at the moment. But I wouldn't get too close. They do like to spit."

Edith approached the grille of the portcullis. She raised her lantern to give a little more definition to the dim tunnel beyond. She could see only as much of the black trail as the aperture of the gatehouse showed, but that was enough to make out the shuffling traffic of bodies and the familiar blue light of gloamine. She watched the passing strangers attentively for a moment before recognizing what a foolish urge it was. If Senlin had been cast onto the black trail, she would never find him by looking through a peephole.

She watched an elderly woman with a spine as curved as a crozier stumble near the mouth of the gatehouse. Instinctively, Edith reached out to catch her. But there were many feet and two gates between them. As Edith watched, the old woman pulled a battered almanac from her pack. She opened it and, using a fragment of coal, began scratching at the text. She seemed short of breath. She panted as she rubbed. Her scribbling slowed, and her chin sagged to her chest. She seemed to have fallen asleep, though Edith wasn't sure.

"That's the hods for you," the sergeant said, standing behind her shoulder.

"What do you mean?" Edith asked.

"Oh, you know—sitting around, hoping for a handout. Meanwhile, the rest of us slave for our supper. Honestly, once you get past the smell, I imagine the life of a hod isn't all that bad."

Back aboard the *State of Art*, Edith arrived on the bridge with her hair still wet from a scalding bath. Since her return, Byron had not stopped complaining about how awful she smelled. He'd already threatened to stuff all of the offending articles of clothing into the ship's furnace with an extra shovel of coal for good measure. Edith agreed that it could all go, if need be, except for her tricorne.

"Soak it in lemon juice if you have to," she said. "But don't you dare burn my hat."

Seated in her captain's chair, Edith listened to Reddleman's report of the day, which the former Red Hand delivered with chirpy brevity. There had been some commotion aboard the *Ararat* around midmorning when a squad of port guards approached the barrel-shaped warship to arrest Commissioner Pound. Reddleman described a brief standoff between the crew of the *Ararat*, some of whom still felt quite loyal to the commissioner, and a tall man in a cape with hair done up in a shark fin. Edith said that had to have been General Eigengrau. Eventually, Commissioner Pound had elected to go with the general, though without the insult of shackles.

Edith recounted her own discoveries of the day, from the moment she'd met with the empty-handed king to the moment that Georgine Haste had escorted her back through the underground street, out to the fresh-aired port.

At the end of her account, Edith asked the stag what he made of the day's events. Byron balked. "I've never claimed to be a strategist! I do tea cakes, not tactics, Captain."

Edith knew that wasn't at all true but thought the stag was probably deflecting because he was unsure. She turned in her chair and leveled Reddleman with a gaze. The pilot sat tugging on his lower lip and staring at a cloud of birds writhing against the evening sky. On the magnovisor, the flock looked like a single entity, an undulating life-form. "All right, Reddleman," she said. "I want you to be frank with me. All that talk about the universe and planets and stars... You made it sound like you think you were there."

"No, no, sir, I wasn't there. No, I wasn't anywhere for a very long time, and I'll not be anywhere again very soon. But I have the *memory* of being there, of seeing it all transpire. Honestly, I believe we all have that memory. We just have to know how and where to reach for it."

"I really don't care to," Edith said. "All I want to know is, if you're able to remember the ancient past, are you also able to see the future? Do you know what's going to happen to us?"

"No, sir. No, that's not how time works. The present, you have to understand, is like the mouth of a river. Behind us, everything is a singular current; that's the past. But ahead of us, the river breaks into a nearly infinite delta. I can't see the future because we haven't chosen which estuary to paddle down."

Edith scowled at the explanation, which she could envision but not quite understand. "All right—so no prophecies. What do you *think* is going to happen?"

Reddleman folded his thin arms and flapped his hands against them. He was wearing a dark green jacket, part of the pilot's uniform. Reddleman was forever finding excuses to take it off and walk around in his undershirt, and Byron was constantly pestering him to put his clothes back on and comport himself like an officer of the Sphinx. "I think they're going to try to board us."

"For an inspection?" Edith asked.

Reddleman shook his head. "To take the ship. That's what I would do."

"That's what I would do, too." Edith rocked back and rubbed her face.

"It's not a good sign that they aren't turning over the painting," Reddleman said.

"No, it's not," she agreed. She thought of Voleta and Iren and how exposed they were. Her first impulse was to recall them. But then, if she did, if the port guard saw them falling back, it might goad them into attacking, assuming that was their intention. And while it seemed a strong possibility that Duke Pell had caught Senlin, put a blinder on his head, and thrown him onto the black trail, there was still a chance that he was locked up in the Colosseum. She was determined to have a look before shoving off. "Byron, I want you to get word to Iren that she needs to start looking for a point of exit. Sooner rather than later, but not so suddenly as to seem like a retreat."

"Tomorrow night they're going to see the Mermaid—*Marya*—perform at the Vivant."

"Good. That seems like a natural finale. Tell them we'll expect them the morning after." Edith stood and crossed the riveted floor to the arms locker. "In the meantime, everyone wears a sidearm." She didn't relish the idea of arming Reddleman, but then, he didn't really need a weapon to be deadly, and she didn't have enough of a crew to be picky.

Byron clasped his hands behind his back nervously. "Captain, you do realize I've never fired a gun before?"

Edith twisted the key in the door of the arm's cabinet, revealing the racks of sabers, pistols, and rifles stowed within. "Not to worry," she said. "The only thing simpler than firing a gun is getting shot by one."

Chapter Eleven

The mob does two things well: nothing and revolution.
—*I Sip a Cup of Wind* by Jumet

Edith had never much cared for presents. That fact might've been owed to her father's dislike of gifts, though he was not heartless about it. He did not neglect her birthday, and she always had what she needed. But her father had preferred to give her rewards for good work, usually in the form of small sums of money, which she could spend as she liked, rather than presents. Edith was well aware that many of her peers were showered with gifts, often by fathers who seemed both besotted with their daughters and insecure in the mutuality of these affections. And the girls who were not spoiled to their satisfaction were unsubtle in their campaigns for more and grander things.

Then Mr. Franklin Winters had come along and demonstrated early on in their misbegotten courtship that he was a gift-giver. It was a flaw that Edith had tolerated. But she didn't care for his gifts, which were usually some bauble or article of clothing that didn't suit her taste or activity, and she absolutely loathed the expectations that always came along with them. Franklin would give her a lacy handkerchief with her initials embroidered upon it or a box of ribbon candy, then say, "Now you have to be nice to me for the rest of the afternoon."

To be sure, Edith appreciated very little about the Tower, but since she'd arrived, she'd been spared the burden of gifts and had been happier for it.

Yet, when she had returned to her room in the Sphinx's home the prior week and discovered a parcel waiting on her bed, she had, perhaps for the first time in her life, been delighted by the appearance of a gift. The card that accompanied the present was half the pleasure. She recognized Senlin's prim cursive at once. The note read:

Dear Edith,

Congratulations once again on your new command. I can think of no one more deserving and capable than you. I know you will bear the weight of the station with selflessness and grace, and I only regret that I will not be there to share in your inaugural triumph.

Love,
Tom

P.S. I asked Byron to clean it for you, but it won't hurt my feelings if you prefer a new one.

When she unwrapped the familiar black cocked hat and tried it on in the mirror, she felt a wave of serenity wash over her. She liked how it looked, liked how it fit over her unbrushed hair and how it made her feel.

The first time she wore the tricorne aboard the *State of Art*, Voleta and Iren had recognized it at once. Both agreed it suited her, and it wasn't long before they seemed to forget she'd ever been without it. Though Edith never forgot who'd worn it first.

Byron presented her with the deodorized hat the next morning as she prepared to disembark. She sniffed it and, detecting nothing, put it lightly on. For a moment, she stood there as if she were balancing a book on her head, then relaxed and said, "How'd you do it?"

"If I revealed all my secrets, I'd be out of a job," he said, with a swat of his hand. He helped her into a new greatcoat that was the earthy color of a forest shadow.

"May I make a suggestion, Captain?" he asked, grooming her lapels with a brush.

"What's on your mind?"

"If things really are so dire, perhaps it's worth bringing Wakeman Haste back into the fold. I'm sure that I can rebuff an entire boarding party of armed men on my own," he said, nervously patting the butt of the pistol he wore strapped at his hip. "But it wouldn't hurt to have a few more hands supporting the cause." Edith had picked the two-barreled cartridge pistol for him because it was easy to fire and simple to reload. "Presuming, of course, that you still trust her."

"I do," she said, straightening her collar by the reflection of the ship's porthole. "And you make a fair point. I'll certainly consider it."

"I could make the two of you dinner—a proper sit-down dinner, not one of your crumb-sowing sessions. I could make a flan."

Edith laughed and said, "Let's see how the day goes. Oh, and did you forget to bring the Sphinx's morning dispatch?"

"No, I didn't forget. None came."

"Oh," Edith said, scowling briefly before rallying a smile for Byron's benefit. "Well, we have our orders. Nothing's changed. I'm sure he just has other things on his mind."

"Yes, I'm sure that's it," the stag said stalwartly enough, but then she saw the fine thimbles of his fingertips tremble. She hadn't known that they could.

"I'm sure he's all right, Byron. He'll outlive us by a thousand years."

He'd been ducking her a moment before, but now he met her gaze. His large black eyes glistened with emotion. "It's not just that. It's that and everything else! Reddleman frightens me, but I'll need him if we're boarded. I'm worried about Voleta and Iren and all the scrutiny they're under. I'm worried about you, out there unscrewing your arm and toeing the Old Vein." He finished the litany with a shudder that ran to the tips of his antlers. "You know there was a point, and not so long ago, when I *wanted* to see the world. At least a few of the nice bits. The mountains. A forest, maybe. But now I just want to be back home and . . . Well, it doesn't matter what I want. That's the thing about life, isn't it? You don't get to say when you've had enough."

Edith thought of Adam disappearing into the fog with the men who threw lightning, and of the red sea boiling in the head of the Tower, and of Senlin stumbling blindly down the black trail with a can on his head. She swallowed and said, "No, we don't."

"Well, we've had enough moping for one morning at least," he said, with a steady-handed and final swat of his coat brush. "Please come back as quick as you can, Captain. Bring a friend. I'll make the flan, just in case."

It was with some relief that Edith discovered the *State of Art* was not the center of attention that morning. Rather, it was the *Ararat* that had drawn a crowd. Even across the two piers and many berths that separated her from the Pelphian warship, Edith had no trouble spotting General Eigengrau, who stood well above the heads of other officials, and Georgine, whose golden engine scattered the morning light.

Edith wasn't sure whether it was curiosity or some vague premonition that drew her to the edge of the gathering, though she knew her approach was not without risk. One of the *Ararat*'s airmen might see through her changed wardrobe, see past her new arm and the camouflage of her command, and recognize her as one of the fugitives he'd spent months pursuing.

But the fact that she hadn't been recognized so far made her a little fearless and, she would grudgingly admit, perhaps a little foolish, too.

The noblemen at the mob's periphery were doing their best to appear unimpressed by the spectacle that had summoned them, the nature of which was still unclear to her. They pinched snuff, dashed handkerchiefs at nagging flies, and traded quips with other bystanders. Some smelled of their morning showers; others reeked of their evening's pleasures.

A man in a fez with a spud for a nose said, "A shekel says he won't be able to keep his chin up."

A dandy in a rumpled suit smoking a long ivory pipe replied, "I want to see snot all over his face. I really do. I want to see the man weep."

"He's too committed to the role for that," a third lord said, polishing the lenses of his spectacles. "He is a consummate actor. A man only gets one exit."

"Ah, he'll beg for mercy! My carbuncle has more character than that washed-up toll collector. I have a mina here says he sucks his thumb," the man in the fez declared.

"Preposterous!" The bespectacled lord's voice rumbled with a dramatic timbre. "Mark my words, he will take a bow. He'll recite a few appropriate lines from the airman's oath, then salute his men as he delivers his body to the wind!"

"Excuse me, what are you all talking about?" Edith asked. "What's happening here?"

"The execution of Commissioner Emmanuel Pound," the pipe-smoking dandy said.

"Commissioner no longer," the fez corrected. "It's *Mister* Pound, now. King Leonid hasn't announced his replacement yet, but my money is on one of the dukes. I wouldn't be surprised if it weren't Wilhelm Pell that took the station next!"

"If they can ever peel him off his wife," the dandy said.

"Was there a trial?" Edith asked.

The noble in a fez snorted so enthusiastically he wetted his upper lip. "Trial! There was no need. The man confessed yesterday evening to having been derelict in his duty. He let the Crown be robbed, let his Wakeman and dozens of airmen perish, and failed in every effort to catch the perpetrators. We gave him our best warship, and he couldn't catch a pirate in a scow that was crewed by a bunch of trollops!"

"How embarrassing," Edith said dryly.

The bespectacled lord, who seemed the only one to have any sympathy for Pound, said, "And did you hear about his daughter? She plunged from a rooftop last night and died."

"A shame-inspired suicide, I imagine." The dandy drew on his pipe, appearing suddenly wistful. "Even though she was a little chicken-breasted, she had such a pretty face."

Edith hardly heard the idiotic remark. She was too busy craning about to get a glimpse of Pound. She asked if anyone else could see him, only to learn that he had not yet arrived. He was, according to the man in the fez, being collected by Port Master Cullins and his guard. Hardly a moment later, the group in question emerged from the city gates. The port master led the eight-man squad, each of whom held a ceremonial rifle cocked on his shoulder. The condemned man's hands were bound in iron shackles that jangled more loudly as the observers fell silent.

Edith and the other men made room, backing against the roped stanchions that guarded the pier's edge. She caught a glimpse of Pound, slouched between the ranks of guards. He was unshaven and wearing a nightshirt that had been hastily tucked into his uniform trousers. His hair stood out in wisps of ashy gray. His eyes were red and raw. There was no hint of the vanity or condescension for which he had been so well known. He no longer had his gas mask, wealth, or uniform to shroud his humanity. If he had passed Edith on the street at that moment, she would not have known him.

The languid-eyed Eigengrau awaited Pound at the foot of a plank. The board extended a short distance from the pier, its purpose apparent to all. The general had his chin down, showing he took no pleasure in this duty. The armed regiment that had accompanied Pound peeled away. The general signaled for the shackles to be removed, and once they were, Pound began kneading his hands as if he didn't know what to do with them. Edith thought he looked like a man who had missed his train—worried, distracted, searching.

Eigengrau spoke over Pound's head to the crowd of lords, officers, and onlookers. His cape lifted in the wind, flashing its crimson lining. "It is never a pleasure to deliver a man to this recompense, nor to act as the arbiter of his failures. But our excellence is evidence of our righteousness, and where our excellence wanes, so does our virtue. Think of the hod, who debased himself with indolence and indulgence, and then cursed the Tower for accommodating his depravity. Think of the drunk who blames the bottle. Think of the debtor who blames his purse. We cannot raise a man up by lowering ourselves, no more than we can save a sunken ship by draining away the sea. There is no greater insult to a man, nor the institutions he has served, than the gross affront of mercy." His voice, which had grown more booming, now shrank a little. "And yet, I do not relish my role as the king's right hand in matters such as these. It is a solemn duty for which I am—"

Pound interrupted the general by stepping forward, a move that inspired the drawing of many swords. Eigengrau held up his hand, deferring the violence.

"My daughter is dead, Andreas," Pound said, and reached up to pat the general on his proud chest. "My daughter is dead."

Edith felt a flicker of sympathy for the man who'd spent months terrorizing them. It was a strange, unwanted feeling.

Emmanuel Pound did not glance at the *Ararat* or the airmen who watched him from her deck. He dug his hands into his pockets as if he'd felt a chill, then strode onto the plank and out into the open air.

Georgine found Edith when the crowd dispersed. The two Wakemen walked the length of the train station together. The tiled tunnel echoed with the chug of the warming engine. They arrived in the city while the locomotive was still gathering steam for its short trip. Pound's hurried execution had put them both in a contemplative mood. Haste offered to go with Edith to the palace to collect the Sphinx's painting, and Edith was glad for the company. As they walked the hysterical streets of the city, doing their best to ignore the café frenzies and balcony melodramas, Edith felt her gaze drawn again and again to the ridiculous constellations and the smarmy sun. She would rather spend the rest of her life under an overcast sky than endure one more day beneath that counterfeit.

When they arrived on the steps of the palace, Haste said, "Leonid always keeps you waiting, but I've learned how to make the most of it. Here, I'll show you." As soon as the doorman invited them in, Haste began directing the king's staff. "We'll need a pitcher of gin punch, two cigars, and two of whatever His Majesty had for breakfast. And we're not sitting on these ottomans, either. You have a hundred rooms. Find us one with some proper furniture."

The butler and his footmen seemed unperturbed by Haste's manner, and all of her wishes were granted in short order. Soon, Edith found herself sitting in a plush chair before a freshly built fire with a cut crystal goblet full of rosy punch in her hand. She had refused the cigar, which Haste didn't mind as it left her with a spare, but when the breakfast cart arrived with chafing dishes full of sausages, scrambled eggs, porridge, and bread pudding, Edith served herself a small mountain of food and ate with the plate balanced on her lap.

"I learned long ago, if they're going to make you wait, best make them pay for it," Georgine said in answer to Edith's enthusiastic review of her breakfast.

Edith hardly spoke another word until she'd cleaned her plate. Then she wiped her mouth on a napkin and said with a satisfied sigh, "I suppose I've kept you waiting, too. You've been asking for a tour of the ship."

"Oh, and my patience accrues interest," Haste said, smiling through the smoke of her cigar. "Just you wait till the bill comes due!"

"Do you remember Byron?" Edith asked. Haste crossed her legs, slouching down into her chair. She puffed happily at her cigar for a moment before announcing that she did not. "He's the Sphinx's footman. I think you'd remember him if you'd met him."

"Wait," Haste said, squinting at the memory. "He's the one with the buck's head and the clockwork body."

"That's him. He's offered to make us dinner this evening, if you'd care to be our guest."

"That sounds delightful."

"I would've been surprised if you'd entirely forgotten him."

Haste shrugged, the skin of her neck wrinkling against her perfect shoulders. "All my memories of the Sphinx are vague. Just snatches of ether-drenched dreams, really. As soon as the Sphinx had finished tinkering with me, I was out the door. He does not like hangers-on."

Edith would've liked to have pursued the conversation further, but at that moment King Leonid appeared in a starched chef's hat and a white apron. They stood and bowed, greeting the regent, who seemed in a great hurry. "I'm so sorry to keep you waiting, Captain Winters, Wakeman Haste, but I am running late for the recommissioning of our Royal Bakery. I'm making the toast." He cocked his head and chuckled.

"I'm toasting the men who toast our bread! That's pretty good. I might use that." He absentmindedly patted his pockets for something, a pencil perhaps.

"Very good, Your Majesty," Edith said. "And if you'll just return the Sphinx's painting, we can be on our way."

"Ah!" King Leonid said with a shake of his finger. "*The Brick Layer's Granddaughter*. My brother has all but located it. The treasurer and his pages worked half the night, and they expect to have it any moment now. They think the trouble is that it was mislabeled under *T* for *The* instead of *B* for—"

"Your Majesty, I completely understand," Edith said, interrupting the regent in a manner he was obviously not accustomed to. Her morning with Haste had convinced her that perhaps politeness was not the best tactic here. "I'll trouble you once more tomorrow morning, and then not again. I trust you understand: I have a long list of ringdoms to visit, and I won't be able to delay my commitments any longer. The other ringdoms are eager for us to visit."

"Of course," the king said, his former enthusiasm muted by his surprise at this ultimatum. "And I assure you, Captain Winters, no one will sleep until I have the Sphinx's painting safely in my hands so that I may place it in yours."

"Bravo, Edith!" Haste said, applauding on the steps of the palace. Her hands clanged together like pans. "Bravo! Now that's how you handle a king: like a tenant who's late with the rent."

Edith waved at her to quit making a fuss. "No, I just recalled what my father used to say: 'Asking nicely once is polite. Asking nicely twice is just begging.'"

"Wise man! My father used to say things like 'If it hasn't exploded so far, it probably never will!'" She laughed hard enough to attract the attention of a lady cruising past on a sedan chair. The lady gave Haste a withering look, and Georgine thumbed her nose at her. "Anyway, now we have the whole day to play with. It doesn't all have to be inspections and daring rescues. We could take in some amusement. You know, pose as Pelphians for an afternoon. There's usually a raunchy singalong at the Gog and Fardel after lunch. You'll never guess how many words rhyme with *bum*."

"Actually, I'd like to have a look at the Colosseum," Edith said. She smiled at a young girl in ballet slippers who'd stopped to stare at her. The girl's governess soon pulled her away by the arm.

Haste chewed on her cigar. It had gone out some minutes ago, and she'd made no effort to relight it. "Really? The Colosseum? I don't understand the appeal. The fights are sad, and the beer is stale. Why do you want to go there?"

Edith couldn't very well say that she wanted to search the Colosseum because it seemed her last, best hope for finding a friend. She could not confess that the thought of finding Tom bound up somewhere inside a blood-sport arena was a happier prospect than believing he'd been banished to the black trail in a blinder. Since she could not admit the truth, she said something that was at least true: "It seems like the hods have had a hard go of it here. They're hung from the sun and shot in the square and have buckets clamped on their heads. I don't care about the fights. I just want to know how the hods are being treated. Are they all surviving on scraps and sleeping on rags, or are they looked after?"

Haste crossed her golden arms and smirked around the wet stump of her cigar. She said, "You're turning out to be quite the humanitarian."

The fact that at the moment Edith felt more concern for one man than an entire caste was a source of shame. She smiled to cover her guilt and said, "Afterward, we can go sing songs about bums, if you like."

Georgine's expression brightened. "Good, because they don't sing themselves."

The closer they drew to the Colosseum, the stranger it looked to Edith. Other than its expansive size and noble shape, there wasn't much left of the former university's glory. The high bricked windows and barred portico had made shabby a structure that would otherwise have been majestic. The guards at the entrance made no effort to stop a gang of boys who were vandalizing the base of one massive pillar with penknives. Edith and Georgine reached the base of the wide steps at the same moment that a semiconscious drunk was forcibly removed from the arena. Two guards dragged the man out by his armpits and gave him the old heave-ho from the top of the stairs. If Edith had been any slower stepping aside, she would've been thrown to the cobblestones with him.

"Technically, women aren't allowed in the Colosseum," Haste said as she saluted her way past the doormen. "They make an exception for me, though."

"And why is that?" Edith asked.

"Because I insist."

The lobby of the Colosseum would've been large enough to raise a barn inside, Edith thought. It echoed with birdsong and the cheers that trumpeted from the arena. There was enough rubbish and beer slop on the floor to make a sort of marsh. It was a detestable place, and Edith wondered if the Sphinx's dreaded blind spot wasn't the result of chaos rather than conspiracy.

"Can I borrow a button?" Haste asked, pointing at the brass row on the cuff of her greatcoat. When Edith looked a bit confounded by the request, Haste added, "I just want to show you something. You'll get it back." Edith snapped a button from its thread, already anticipating what Byron would say when he discovered the loss, and handed it to Haste. "A while ago now, the local boys invented a game called Bump and Basket." At the center of the lobby, Haste looked up at the pillar capitals where doves and magpies sat on tangled nests. "There are a few rules, but never mind them. This is the fun bit. Watch." Haste flicked the button high into the air. A flash of black and white shot down from one of the pillars, intercepting the glittering disk at its peak. The magpie caught the button in its beak and carried it back to its nest while Edith watched in amazement.

"It's an impressive trick. Very impressive. But how do you get the button back?"

"Well, first you need to hire a fifty-foot ladder, and then you—" Haste began, and Edith stopped her with a good-natured shove of her shoulder. "So this is the Colosseum. You seen enough?"

"We haven't seen anything yet! What about the living quarters?"

"You want to see the dormitory?"

"Well, only if you can manage it. I mean, it's pretty impressive that they let you in the lobby to play with the birds."

Georgine rolled her eyes. "Oh, you're good at getting your way, aren't you? All right. Let's go."

The dormitory entrance lay at the end of a short but crowded hall. Edith counted a dozen soldiers in dark uniforms and short-brimmed caps, each armed with a pistol and saber. They guarded a set of enormous doors, decorated with iron braces and panels of darkly tanned leather, stamped with the noble profiles of men and women who Edith took for scholars and philosophers. Their ascetic faces were marred by the drawn additions of mustaches, eye patches, and harlequin makeup. Above the doors, the marble lintel bore an epigraph. Some of the letters had been chiseled into oblivion. What remained read: _ _ C _URE _ALL.

Haste greeted each of the guards in the corridor. She asked after their wives and children, often by name, and remarked on the men's pastimes, distinctions, and celebrations. Then she made a joke about how fat she was getting, ringing her perfect golden stomach like a cymbal. All the men laughed. They obviously adored her. When Haste introduced Captain Winters, that adoration seemed to be to her credit as well. No one remarked upon her being a woman, though there were several questions about her ship. How did she move so fast? What was her top speed? How big was her crew? Edith answered all their questions gamely enough, some with impressive truths, others with intimidating fictions.

Then a sergeant with a fatherly face and a fitting paunch, who Haste had called Burton, remarked, "Oh, and we found the tunnel."

"You found the tunnel?" Haste repeated, her expression flattened by confusion.

"Yes. We're plugging it up this afternoon, in fact," Sergeant Burton said. "You remember how we had a problem with those Coattail boys? Remember how every so often, we'd find one of them wandering around inside the dorm?"

"I thought that only happened the once," Haste said.

"No," Burton said, his voice trembling with rueful laughter. "No, much more than once. We couldn't figure out how they were doing it. At first, we just assumed one of us was taking a bribe. But nobody was. None of us would be stupid enough to do it a second time after the general's interrogations, and it happened six times. Six times! And that's just counting the occasions we caught them. Anyway, it turns out the Coattails were using a tunnel from the outside to get into the dorm."

"How many hods escaped?" Edith asked.

"None."

"There's a tunnel to the outside, and none of them escaped?" She was incredulous.

"Well, it's not a very big tunnel." Burton approximated the size with his hands. "It goes through the soft mortar between large blocks. You'd have to be pretty small to fit through, and most of the brawlers are quite big. That's sort of their distinguishing characteristic, you might say." When he smiled, a gap between his front teeth showed.

"So the hods went to the trouble of digging a tunnel they couldn't use to escape?" Edith shook her head. "That doesn't make any sense."

"Well, where would they go?" Sergeant Burton asked. "There's a constable on every corner and a port full of soldiers. They're slaves, not prisoners, Captain Winters."

"Was this your idea?" Georgine asked. "Looking for a tunnel—you thought of that?"

"No, it was General Eigengrau's idea. After he questioned every last one of us, and we convinced him we weren't responsible for letting the Coattails in, he went looking for an alternative."

"Well, let's have a look at this tunnel, then," Haste said, reaching for the door pull.

"You can, of course, but I can't let Captain Winters in. No offense, but General Eigengrau said absolutely no unauthorized personnel, and begging your pardon, Madam Wakeman, you are a foreign agent."

"It's all right, Sergeant," a deep voice said from behind them. They turned to find Eigengrau. The tall general was wearing his long hip cannon but not his cape. He was down to his black waistcoat and had the sleeves of his shirt rolled to his elbows. There was dirt on his face, and the peak of his oiled hair was a little frayed. "Captain Winters is with me, soldier. I wouldn't mind hearing her opinion on this. What do you say, Haste?"

"I'm surprised to see you taking such an interest in a bunch of penned-up hods," Haste said.

"Well, you know, recently enough, an odd little tourist said something to me that I've been thinking about ever since." Eigengrau wiped his hands on a handkerchief as he spoke. It seemed a methodical sort of ablution. "He said, 'Underestimating your inferiors is how every revolution starts.' It's all too easy to confuse subordination with obedience. It's a mistake many a king has come to regret."

"So you know why the tunnel is there?" Edith asked.

"I do not," the general said.

"What are you going to do now?" Haste asked.

"Interrogate the brawlers, of course." Eigengrau stuffed the handkerchief back into his pocket and turned to face the guards behind him. "All right, gentlemen. Mind yourself. Watch each other's backs. And if a fight breaks out, shoot the biggest ones first, then work your way down."

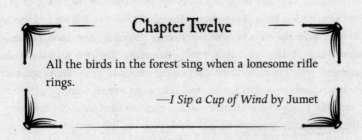

Chapter Twelve

All the birds in the forest sing when a lonesome rifle
rings.

—*I Sip a Cup of Wind* by Jumet

The dormitory's ceiling was high and curved and painted a flaking crimson. Thick bands of white plaster ribbed the ceiling, making Edith feel as if she were standing inside the carcass of some immense beast. Exterior windows filled one wall, and opposite those bricked-in frames stretched a platform. A thick tumbling mat lay center stage, and upon this pad, two hods were caught in a dramatic grapple, their heads pressed ear-to-ear.

The chamber was a maze of cots and trunks, tables and chairs, but despite this crowding, the beds were all made and the floor clean-swept. Still, it seemed more a bivouac than a dormitory. At a glance, Edith estimated there were forty or forty-five hods in all. They looked strong and well fed. She didn't see Senlin among them. She was sure he would've stood out among so many formidable physiques.

Speaking near Edith's ear, Sergeant Burton said, "This used to be a lecture hall. Those doors on the far side don't go anywhere anymore. They bricked them up years and years ago. Makes it easier to keep an eye on the brawlers. Keep them all in one place."

The moment General Eigengrau and his company of armed men appeared, the hods fell silent and still. A second before, they had been eating lunch, lounging on their cots, conversing boisterously as they watched the two men wrestle upon the stage. But the hods saw at once that this was not a usual visit, and they all stood and turned to face the armed men who'd come into their sanctum.

Eigengrau strode with his pistol drawn. The barrel of his hip cannon was as long and thick as a table leg. He passed between the empty cots, marching toward the stage. He did not have to ask for anyone to move out of his way. Half of his guards stayed by the door, half followed him up the steps, their heels drumming. The two sparring hods stepped apart, panting from their recent exertion. They didn't seem to know where to go. Edith, who had followed Georgine up the platform stair, felt conspicuous standing above the crowd of bare-chested men. Many bore the scars of whips, black powder, fire, and steel, injuries they'd suffered outside the arena. It was strange to think these men's lives as brawlers could be safer and gentler than the lives they'd led before. She stood away from the front edge and tried not to look as exposed and disconcerted as she felt.

There was something about General Eigengrau that made her uneasy. He reminded her of a smug uncle, the sort of man who complained about the incompetency of entire generations or the ubiquity of fools in the world. He seemed the type to confuse ambition with duty and good fortune with merit. When they had first met, he had valorized Pelphia by saying, "Our excellence is evidence of our righteousness," but she was certain he had mostly been referring to himself. She thought him wrong on both counts.

Eigengrau turned toward the floor of the former lecture hall and said, "I am here for the truth. Unfortunately for all of us, honesty is easily forged. The only reliable means I have found for discerning the truth is through consensus and confirmation. Consensus. Confirmation. These are the legs on which truth stands."

The general turned to the two hods on the stage with him. One was young, hairless, and handsome. His skin was thin and pale, and his wide eyes were ocean blue. Eigengrau asked his name, and the youth gave his performing name: The Ritzy Pup. Eigengrau pressed him for his real name, the name his mother had given him. The muscular youth said his name was Paul. The other brawler was older, his muscles larger, his skin leathery. His eyes didn't quite line up, and he was missing several teeth, but there was a cool dignity to how he held his shoulders. When Eigengrau asked, the hod said his name was Harlan.

Eigengrau stood between the men. Even without his cape, he looked suited to the stage. Resting the barrel of his pistol on his shoulder he said, "We have discovered your tunnel." The general lifted his chin at one of the uniformed men standing near the entrance to the hall. "Private, if you would unveil it for us."

The guard saluted, walked to the edge of the nearest window, and began to pace along the wall, counting his steps as he went. After a short distance, he stopped and faced the block masonry where several unused cots lay in a flattened stack. He shifted these to the side, revealing a gap at the base of the wall. From the stage, it looked like little more than a mouse hole to Edith, though it was large enough to accommodate a boy.

None of the hods looked at all surprised.

"Now, I'm going to ask you a question, Harlan," Eigengrau said. "And I want you to whisper the answer to me. If anyone overhears you, regretfully, I'll have to shoot you and start over again with someone else. And no one wants that, so please be discreet." The older hod flinched, though it seemed more an attempt to swallow his bile than to bottle his fear. "What I want to know is this: Why is that tunnel there?"

Everyone in the hall watched the tall general lean toward Harlan, who was ashen with anger. After a moment's hesitation, the elder hod spoke a few furtive words into Eigengrau's ear. The general straightened, his languid expression unchanged, his eyes still half-open.

"Thank you, Harlan. Now. Of course, the problem here is that I believe this was an act of collusion. I do not believe that some of you were aware of this tunnel and others were not. Which means that you have probably discussed the possibility of the tunnel being discovered. And if you've discussed the possibility, then you've probably agreed upon a lie to tell as an excuse for its existence. So now, Paul, I want you to confirm for me the agreed-upon lie that Harlan just told me. If your answers match, then we may continue with our chat. But if your answers do not match, then I'm afraid we'll have to dispense with you both and start again with two of your friends. So, quiet as you can, tell me the lie." Eigengrau pointed to his ear and leaned in.

The handsome young man looked feverish with fear. His chin trembled. Red rimmed his blue eyes. Paul cupped his hand to his mouth and whispered into the general's ear.

Edith didn't think Eigengrau was bluffing. He had no trouble shooting innocent hods, and if he believed these men were guilty, he'd kill them all.

Eigengrau straightened, and said, "Wonderful. We have a leg of truth. Consensus. The agreed-upon lie was that the tunnel was dug to allow the import of the narcotic Crumb. A very convincing falsehood. Now I will ask you the same question again: Why is that tunnel there? This time, you shall tell me the truth. How will I know if you're telling the truth? Because the truth is the only answer that both of you know."

Eigengrau signaled his men to level their guns. "Now, Harlan, from your lips to my ear. Tell me the truth."

Edith felt the hairs on the back of her neck rise. She glanced at Haste, who was as red-faced as a hanged man; her golden fingers curled into fists. And yet Edith felt sure she would not object. The general never would have invited her if he had thought she would undermine his authority. For all her bluster, Haste had proven, time and time again, that she knew her place. She cursed and complained, but she did not intervene. She had not intervened when the hods were shot against the Wall of Recompense; had not stepped in to stop the local noblemen from using the Baths and the ringdom's ports as their personal hunting grounds for vulnerable women, or from using the black trail as a final solution for irksome persons. Haste had blustered mightily when the young hod was sent up to prod the sun, but even then, alluded to the fact that this wasn't the first time a child had been used for such a purpose. And what had she done to stop it from happening again?

Perhaps Haste could not interfere. She was a guest of the ringdom, after all, and with only the vestiges of the Sphinx's influence to back her. Perhaps that was the watchman's curse: Witness without influence. Of course, Edith had something Haste did not. She had a warship.

Edith looked down at the stage floor, searching for what she would do. Could she really stand by and watch the general shoot these unarmed men, one after another, until he got his answers? Of course not. The real question was when she interfered, whether Eigengrau would listen to reason, arrest her, or start a brawl. She wasn't sure which was more likely given the general's troubling sense of righteousness. And would Haste be on her side or the general's side if events spiraled out of control?

This internal debate was interrupted by the realization that she was staring at a dusty, bare footprint on the otherwise tidy floor. It seemed out of place. It was not an entire footprint either; just the toes and the ball of a foot peeked out from beneath the tumbling pad. She looked around for other prints but saw none. Using the edge of her boot, she lifted the mat, and saw the heel of the pale print, hidden along with many others.

Edith looked up to discover Georgine was watching her with an expression that seemed to say, *Why are you staring at your feet at a time like this?*

The general, who had just received Paul's whispered answer, said, "Oh, that is unfortunate." He raised his great pistol. The barrel was braided in silverwork, fine as a scribe's signature. "I'm sorry, Paul. We do not have a consensus."

"Excuse me, General," Edith said. Eigengrau lifted one eyebrow at her, obviously displeased by the interruption. He did not lower his weapon. She squatted down and lifted up the edge of the pad, revealing a trail of pallid footprints on the floor. "I think I've found something."

Four guards lifted the heavy mat away, revealing an array of foot- prints, all of them small. At a glance, Edith counted several distinct sets. The prints radiated out from a trapdoor in the stage, which looked to have been part of the original construction.

Ever-cautious, Eigengrau decided not to explore any further until they had removed the hods from the dorm. He ordered the rest of the day's fights cancelled and had his men escort all the brawlers to the holding cells at the gatehouse to the Old Vein. He announced that he would decide what to do with them later.

Once the hall was emptied, the general asked Edith to open the trapdoor while he and Haste stood ready to act should some hidden villain spring out. When none did, they peered warily into the gloom.

In the hollow under the stage they saw the evidence of dusty, long-forgotten props: rolled backdrops, ceremonial vestments, coiled ropes, and sandbags. A little light beamed in through gaps in the stage, and faint as it was, it was enough to illuminate the considerable hole at the center of an eruption of tile and masonry.

Climbing down to investigate, they had to stoop to keep from knocking their heads on the beams of the stage. Once their eyes adjusted, they saw the unlit miners' lamps hanging from struts near the hole in the floor. A tied-off rope descended into the abysmal dark.

Eigengrau put a match to the oil wick of a lamp and tilted the mirrored shade, focusing the beam into the hole. But the light did not reach the bottom. The fact seemed to make him nervous. He said he would summon a few men to go down first, but Edith pointed out that the delay might allow for whoever was down there to escape. She volunteered to climb down first, not because she was particularly enthusiastic about exploring an eerie pit, but because there was a chance, albeit slim, that Senlin was down there. She could hardly imagine the sequence of events that would have led to him being smuggled into the dormitory, then stuffed into a hole in the floor, but even this scant, unhappy hope seemed preferable to the alternative of the black trail. If he was down there, she didn't want one of the general's men shooting him on sight.

The general agreed to let her go. She hooked the lantern onto her belt, took the rope in hand, and tested its hold. Satisfied that it wouldn't drop her, she eased over the ragged edge, and, with the line wrapped about her thigh and her boots acting as a brake, descended into the unknown.

Only a few feet down she looked back up at the hole to find she had passed through a painted ceiling. The hole interrupted the edge of a broad medallion that was immediately familiar. Sliding a little farther, the full design came into relief: It was the Brick Layer's seal, the same green ring of figures marching in a circle that decorated the Sphinx's front door and the *State of Art*.

A maze of curved partitions emerged from the motionless dark beneath her. No, not partitions—they were the tops of shelves. Hundreds of them, set narrowly as the ridges of a fingerprint, retreated farther than the light of her lamp could reach.

She was rappelling into an enormous library.

When her heels hit the ground, she called that she was safely down. As she waited for the general and Georgine to descend, she examined her surroundings. A layer of dust as thick as flour coated the floor, the long reading tables, the sturdy high-backed chairs, and the library carts, abandoned with books still on them. And yet for all the evidence of long disuse, there were signs of recent activity. The floor had been scuffed clean around the end of one long table, and the chairs moved. Edith ducked to inspect the underside and found a store of bedrolls, water jugs, and crates of provisions. She pulled the cloth back from one box to find several stale loaves of bread, and under those, a white paper box full of moldering éclairs.

She was still rummaging through the cache when Eigengrau came up behind her, startling her. As she caught her breath, she told him what she'd found. "I think someone was living down here. By the look of it, several someones."

"So that's what the Coattails were up to: They were bringing someone food and water. I wonder who?" The general raised his lantern. The light glinted off of a battery of brass plaques set into a cabinet that was as long as a garden wall. They could see where the card catalog's drawers had been swept clean by searching hands. "They sealed this area up decades ago, even before the university closed." When Edith asked why a university would shutter its library, Eigengrau shrugged. "Why is anything abandoned? A lack of use, I suppose."

The general had just begun to study the trails of footprints on the floor when Haste landed with a heavy clomp behind him. Georgine glanced at Edith's discovered provisions, then addressed Eigengrau. "Probably just some bored brawlers stretching their legs. I mean, where would they go from here?"

"That is the question. Let's see where the trail leads, shall we?" Eigengrau said, nodding at the floor. The footprints seemed to funnel and converge upon a single aisle between shelves, which curled into the subterranean dark.

It was strange that a library should call to mind the depths of a forest, but that was precisely what Edith thought of. The darkness, the smell of pulp and decay, the meandering trail, the vaulted shelves, which had a way of making her feel as if she were shrinking the deeper they went, it all brought to mind the wildwood outside her father's land—a place that seemed at once empty and also full of watching eyes.

After a few minutes of tracking the prints and wending between rows, they came upon another open area, larger than the last. It seemed a space made for symposiums. Long tables and benches stood in rows, eight or nine deep, facing a blackboard that was tall enough to require a ladder to reach the top of, and twice as long.

They turned the lamp beams upon it. From edge to edge, top to bottom, the blackboard was filled with numbers, symbols, and letters, all laid as compactly as one of the Sphinx's contracts and drawn in skeletal white. The work showed evidence of many hands, many erasures. For a moment, there seemed to be nothing else in the library but this dense and monolithic code.

Then Haste shouted, "Look out!" and a shadowy lump that had been lying on one of the benches sat up with a startled cry.

Shrouded in a blanket, the hod looked to have been roused from his slumber, though his grogginess was quickly cured by the sight of Eigengrau's pistol. The hod rolled from the bench a moment before the general fired his cannon. The muzzle flash was bright as a meteor cracking open upon the sky. The shot cleaved the table in half and made splinters of the bench behind it.

Through the cloud of kicked-up dust and smoke, the hod appeared again several paces away. He was fumbling with something as he ran, something small and delicate, something that seemed to break, then break again. The general cracked his pistol open to pull out the cinder-hot shell. Edith clambered onto the nearest tabletop, leaping to be next in pursuit of the hod, who'd dropped his blanket and was now naked to the waist. When he reached the main aisle between tables, he stopped, crouched, and finally struck the shortened match he'd whittled nearly to the head with his attempts to strike it. He glanced back at Edith, bounding onto the table nearest him, and dropped the flame into a furrow of gunpowder on the floor.

The sparking powder ran away from him, quick as a mouse, searing a route toward the blackboard.

Edith didn't know where the line of gunpowder led, only that nothing good waited at the end of a fuse. She leapt over the hod's head, staggering as she landed, but she kept herself from going down and raced after the seething spark on the floor, which dawdled one moment only to surge the next. The aisle ended, and the flame was near enough then to light up its destination: a wooden keg tucked under the chalkboard's lip.

With little room left to run and no time to deliberate, Edith dove forward, reaching with her engine for the spark. It flashed at the edge of the keg.

Her palm clapped down upon the light, dousing it so violently, the stone beneath it cracked.

"Stop him! Stop him!" Eigengrau yelled from behind her. Edith rolled onto her back and watched as Georgine and the general reached after the hod. The hod drank greedily from a small glass vial. Haste grasped his wrist and shook the tube loose. It shattered, already empty, upon the flagstone floor. Eigengrau grasped the hod under the arms and threw him onto the top of a table.

Returning to her feet, Edith rushed back to where the general pinned the writhing hod.

He was a diminutive person—certainly small enough to navigate the tunnel through the Colosseum wall. Though his bones were hardly larger than a child's, they were wrapped in an older man's sinews. The thick lenses of his spectacles were shattered, apparently in the scuffle.

The remaining wedges of glass exaggerated his small, deep-set eyes. The evidence of the poison he'd drank already showed on his face. His lips were blue and the blood vessels in his cheeks budded and burst.

"Are there others?" Eigengrau demanded, his voice full of energy though his expression was not.

"All gone," the hod said, smiling at the thought, though he just as quickly grimaced and coughed. "I can't believe I fell asleep. Days and days of vigilance, all for nothing."

"What is all this?" the general asked, shaking the man to gather his dwindling attention. "Why are you here?"

"If you wish to ax a tree, you must use a little wood for the haft," the hod said, his voice growing rougher as he spoke.

"What are you talking about? What are you planning?"

"To see heaven's collar pulled into a noose. To see the Hod King pluck the black worm out of his hole. To see the kings erased, and the men who remember them forgotten. To see the rubble of the Tower spread across the earth. To swallow our tongues and grow new ones." The hod's vein-shattered gaze seemed to stare through those who leaned over him. He spoke words they did not understand, his voice thinning and weakening into a hoarse whisper as he babbled. Then he said with abrupt clarity, "Come the Hod King!"

His last breath came out in a hiss.

While the hod cooled on the table, the general sat on the bench nearest the blackboard and looked up at the unintelligible code with his hands on his knees.

"Maybe it means nothing," Haste said. "They babble with letters; perhaps they babble with numbers, too."

"Perhaps," the general said. "I know a few men around town who studied maths in their youth. They might be able to make some sense of it—at least enough to say whether it's intelligible."

"And here I thought the zealots were a bunch of illiterate Luddites," Edith said, squinting at the formula. "Marat is full of surprises."

"Luc Marat?" Eigengrau said. Edith asked how the general knew the name. "He has a small gang of zealots who pop up now and again to make a nuisance of themselves. They even took a run at the gatehouse a few years back. We repelled them easily enough, but I was impressed by their determination, if not their stratagem."

"It's more than 'a small gang,' General," Edith said with a tilt of her head. "Marat has grand plans, I think—ambitions that would affect every house and ringdom in the Tower. The Sphinx thought Marat was hiding something here; though he didn't know what it was. This must be it. Whatever *this* is."

"The zealots liked to ruin books, not read them," Haste said.

"War is for defending ideals, not exercising them." Unrolling his sleeves, Eigengrau stood. "If Marat thought he could gain an advantage from these shelves, I have no doubt he would pursue it."

Edith's lamplight flared upon something under the bottom lip of the blackboard. "Wait a minute," she said, and pulled up on the edge of the board. The blackboard rose with a groan, climbing on rails, aided by weighted pulleys. The metal chalk rail of a second board peeked out from beneath the first. With a firm shove, she sent the outer blackboard sailing upward.

An immense and detailed diagram crowded the revealed board. Edith had to step back to take it all in. The schematic appeared to include several perspectives of a single machine—a side view, a top view, and a cross section. At a glance, it roughly resembled one of the Sphinx's wall-walkers, but this engine had dozens of jointed legs. Some of its parts called to mind a millipede. Curved armored plates covered the length of its back. On second thought, Edith decided it called something else to mind. It looked like one of the fossils in the book she'd removed from Senlin's room, the book that bore the plate of this very library. The engine looked like a trilobite, but with cannons and pikes jutting out from under its shell. The side view, which showed the inside of the engine, contained seated and standing figures, dozens of them all drawn for scale. At a glance, she imagined those chambers might transport a hundred men.

"What is it?" Eigengrau asked, his voice hushed with awe.

"I think . . . I think it's some sort of siege engine," Edith said, her eyes drifting over the spines on its back that spewed flames, the carefully placed slits to accommodate riflemen, and the trident anchors that hung from its belly. At the machine's fore, a great prong like a serrated tuning fork jutted out, some sort of battering ram, perhaps?

"My god! It would have to be immense," the general said. "They can't actually hope to build such a thing, can they?"

"Something tells me they do," Edith said, pointing to the bottom corner of the board. "Look."

There, in block letters better suited to a gravestone, were the words: THE HOD KING.

Chapter Thirteen

A man may rot like an egg: His shell does not show it, but all that is within him has gone foul.

—*I Sip a Cup of Wind* by Jumet

By the end of the afternoon, the once crypt-like library was bustling with life and light. Dozens of soldiers combed every aisle, shelf, and cubby, hunting for further revelation. Munition experts searched for booby traps and removed the rudimentary bomb the hods had left to destroy the evidence of their work. Dusty gas sconces were cleaned and relit, the *Reverie*'s photographer and his precious equipment were lowered down amid much nervous squawking, and the ringdom's brightest minds were summoned to study the two boards.

Constables inspected the secret camp for clues, and after some hours, announced that six hods had been living and working in the library for a year, perhaps longer. Based on the evidence of their footprints and remaining garments, none of the hods had been more than five feet tall. While the identities of the hods were still uncertain, there were hints regarding their individual expertise. The placement of their bedrolls corresponded with stacks of books dedicated to particular topics. Based on this, the constables believed that two of the hods had been mechanical engineers, two physicists, one a biologist, and one a chemist. Several former Coattail boys were brought down and quizzed by the general. The lads quickly admitted to smuggling in provisions in exchange for erotic books and anatomical studies, which had formerly resided on the shelves of the library. The Coattails had learned of the salacious opportunity via rumor, the exact source of which they could not recall.

Edith and Georgine helped as Eigengrau would permit. The similarities between the schematic and the Sphinx's roving engines that repaired the Tower were not lost upon the general, and he seemed unsure of whether the discovery suggested a conspiracy between the hods and the Sphinx or an uprising against the enigmatic inventor. Edith reminded the general that she had been the one to uncover the footprint that led to the library. If she were a conspirator, she must also be an idiot and a saboteur. She eventually convinced Eigengrau to provide her with a photograph of the schematics so that she could share them with the Sphinx. Eigengrau agreed to deliver the images in the morning.

By the time she and Haste climbed back out of the hole, evening had come. Realizing they were both famished, the two Wakemen left the empty Colosseum amid a chorus of birdcalls befitting an orchard in springtime. The plaza was clogged with rocking sedan chairs and children on stilts selling papers, bouquets, and little flasks of blackberry brandy. They made their way back to the port, where the guns of the lead soldiers had been lowered, and all the harbor flags flew at half-mast in honor of the late Commissioner Pound. The tribute struck Edith as insincere, but it seemed already the dead man was enjoying a resurgence in popularity. The headlines of the evening post, which they'd heard shouted through the streets, had called Pound *tragic* and *unlucky*, and made allusion to a complex legacy. Haste attributed the swing in public sentiment to the untimely death of his daughter. "The only thing the Pells love more than a scapegoat is a pretty corpse," she said.

The *Ararat* was now under the temporary command of Crown Prince Pepin Le Mesurier, who in the dwindling daylight was overseeing the replenishment of the ship's stores. The gourd-shaped prince saluted them over the gulf of open air. As Haste waved back, she said, "I see Pepin is preening the nest. He wants the commissionership for his son, Francis. I think the king will probably give it to Duke Wilhelm Pell, but we'll see."

"Who would you prefer?" Edith asked.

"I'd sooner give an ape a loaded pistol than a popgun to either one of them."

They crossed the gangplank and Edith lifted the heavy handle on the steel door. Before she pushed the hatch of her ship open, she looked at Haste over her shoulder and said, "Byron is a bit sensitive about his appearance. I know it's been a while since you've seen him, but I'd appreciate it if you didn't gawk." Haste assured her that she wouldn't make a scene, and Edith welcomed her aboard.

Byron met them in the corridor. He wore a red suit that seemed to fall somewhere between a military uniform and a butler's waistcoat. His recent exertions had left him a little breathless, but he looked happy enough. On one outstretched palm, he held a silver tray with two flutes of bubbling champagne. Edith was pleased to see he still wore his sidearm under his coat.

"Wakeman Haste, it is a pleasure to see you," he said, bowing his head.

With a winsome smile, Haste bowed back, accepted the proffered glass, and said, "Byron, it's good to see you, too. I don't quite remember the last time we met, but I blame that on the blood loss rather than a weak impression." She sipped her wine and glanced about the hallway that beamed with light, glass, and polish. Edith wondered what she was making of it all: the funny friction between the steel hull outside, and the frosted glass panes of the cabins inside. "You keep a tidy ship," Haste said.

"He follows me around with a dustpan," Edith said, smiling as she took her glass and dashed it off in one swallow.

"That's how I keep the ship so clean," Byron said, then seeing the general rumpled state of his captain, added with a fleeting frown, "Long day, sir?"

"And eventful. I'm glad to be home." She pulled off her greatcoat.

"Where's the rest of your crew?" Haste asked, craning her head about.

"Come on. I'll introduce you to them," Edith said.

Byron excused himself to conclude the dinner preparations, and Edith led Georgine up the forward stairwell to the gun deck. When they passed the overlarge door in the vestibule that bore the label ENGINE ROOM, Haste stopped and said, "I'd love to see what sort of boiler you have in there."

"It's more of a storage closet, really," Edith said with a dismissive swat of her hand. "And I think you'd rather see this first anyway."

When they came to the edge of the long, wide gun deck, Edith shouted, "Attention! Wakeman on deck!"

Haste gasped at the gleaming rows of ornate cannons. The horses, goats, elephants, and tigers represented in the shape of the cannon barrels seemed to present themselves for inspection. She reached out and petted the silver mane of a lion, then the horns of a bull and the snout of a boar. She brushed off the shoulders of a mechanical cannoneer. Its round head held a painted expression of perfect, if somewhat weathered, calm.

"It's all automatic?"

"It is," Edith said.

"Incredible. A warship without a crew." Georgine shook her head in awe.

Edith thought of Reddleman, and quickly decided not to mention the pilot, saying, "Obviously, it's not something I advertise. And I wouldn't mind one or two more hands if I'm honest."

"Oh, is that what this is—an interview?" A smile hooked the corner of Georgine's mouth as she ran a golden hand along a cannon barrel, eliciting a rasp like a blade on a honing steel.

"More of an open question, I guess." Edith folded her coat on her arm. She hadn't had a chance to think through what she hoped would come of the evening. Byron was right to say they could use the help, but she hadn't considered what shape that help might take. The thought of facing the next ringdom, the next evasive king or difficult general, with Haste at her side filled Edith with a buoyant hope. She wondered what the Sphinx would think of the addition. Though how could he object? He'd chosen Georgine, after all. And what use was she to anyone in Pelphia? She was tolerated and overlooked, but never appreciated. Edith admired her good humor and candor, prized her intolerance of fools and her willing spirit. And if circumstance required them to scour the black trail for signs of Senlin, at least Edith knew Georgine could stomach the stench. She would need a friend where she was going.

"And now to the bridge?" Haste asked.

"Dinner first, then we'll finish the tour."

Opening the door to her chambers, Edith discovered that Byron had been busy in her absence. He had made the bed, hung her clothes, cleared off the table, covered it with a cloth, set it with bone china, and lit a blazing candelabra. His efforts, while surely well intentioned, ruined her attempts to introduce a little humanity to the shrine that was her current bedroom. The stag's careful staging somehow made all the curio cubbies, shadow boxes, and display cases seem more pompous, their treasures more insufferable. Her embarrassment pinched some color into her cheeks.

Drawn by the historic baubles, Haste approached a cabinet. She tucked her silvering red hair behind her ears and leaned in. Her laughter was almost immediate. "A jade bedpan? You have a jade bedpan... *on display*? Or is this your backup bedpan, you know, for when the diamond one is dirty?"

Seeing no reason to fan her embarrassment with excuses, Edith decided to embrace the absurdity. "Actually, that is one of my favorite pieces. It belonged to the *State of Art*'s original commander, Captain Pondersquat."

Haste straightened. "Pondersquat? Are you serious?"

Edith snorted. "No, of course not."

Haste pointed to the four-post canopy bed, draped in white tulle, her face lighting with mischief. "And that? You actually sleep on that frilly thing?"

"Yes, but only in full dress uniform."

Haste laughed as she turned to the bank of painted portraits of red-eyed old men with white whiskers and medaled breasts. Her smile dwindled as she stared.

"What?" Edith asked, sensing the change in her humor.

"It's just strange to think how long all of this has been going on."

"How long what's been going on?" Edith opened a pretty lidded pot on the table and peered in at the black currant jelly.

Haste turned to face Edith. Her smile reappeared, but the moment of giddiness was obviously over. "All this passing of the torch, I suppose. The Sphinx has persisted for a long, long time."

"And he owes it all to clean living and my cooking!" Byron said from the doorway. He pushed a dining cart ahead of him. The silver dish covers rattled as the carpet swamped the old casters. The stag manhandled the cart a little farther before giving up the effort with a sigh of exhaustion. "Now, if you would just find your seats, dinner is ready to be served."

With the Wakemen seated and napkins dressing their laps, Byron presented the first course of morel soufflé with a chestnut gravy. The women's conversation was momentarily diverted by a round of compliments for the dish, but Haste soon returned to the topic of the Sphinx.

"It's been the same for years," she said, cutting into the soufflé with her salad fork. "I send up my monthly accounts, and a crate of thirty vials arrives in port with my name on it."

"No correspondence the other way? No directives or orders?" Edith asked.

"Oh, well, there's always a letter. Every crate comes with a single typed sheet that says more or less the same thing: Keep the peace. Be on the lookout for structural malfunctions. Stay neutral in politics. Enforce the rule of law."

"That sounds fairly instructive to me," Byron said, setting down a boat of chestnut gravy.

"Hardly! Keep whose peace? Enforce which laws? The ones the Pelphians wrote for the hods, or the ones they sometimes apply to themselves, usually on a sliding scale of wealth and influence?" Haste jabbed the air with her fork. "The only thing the Sphinx has ever showed any interest in is whether the candles of the Merry Loop are receiving regular attention. In the past fifteen years, he has never answered one of my questions, nor given a word of useful guidance."

"Perhaps that's because the Sphinx trusts your judgment," Byron said, scraping crumbs from the tablecloth into his palm. "Captain, you may recall, the Merry Loop is what the locals call the maintenance track that accesses the Tower's main battery of fuses. They're part of the system that includes the electrical dynamo housed in New Babel."

Haste nodded along with the explanation, then said, "You ever notice how the Sphinx likes to hide his chores with amusements? The beer-me-go-rounds inebriate the masses as they happily pump water from the well. The fires in the Parlor are stoked by amateur actors on holiday. The fuses are changed by joyriders in a mine cart."

"Yes, how wicked of him," Byron said with a dry smile.

"Well, it's not without cost, is it?" Haste said, sloshing her wine-glass side to side in a manner that appeared to make Byron a little nervous. "Livers are ruined; eyes are gouged. The maintenance takes its toll."

"But it's not all so sinister," Edith said, sopping up some gravy with a dinner roll. "Take the hods in the Colosseum. Those brawl-ers. They're not really fighting, are they?" The point had been first suggested by Senlin in one of his daily dispatches to the Sphinx, but when Edith saw the hods practicing a grappling hold on the stage of their dorm, she'd suspected it was true. "They're just miming the vio-lence while the lords throw money at the charade."

Haste smiled. "It's funny: That's an open secret that no one seems to believe. But the brawlers figured out long ago that what the general population really wanted was a show, which they've learned to put on without killing one another."

"I admire that," Edith said, swabbing gravy from her chin with a napkin.

"I taught them a form or two," Haste said, a little proudly. "I have to stay in shape somehow, and all Eigengrau's men are too delicate. The brawlers were happy enough to have a new sparring partner."

"Really?" Edith said, letting her amusement draw the word out. "You showed them how to pantomime a fight?"

"Oh, just a stance or two." Haste doused her nearly finished souf-flé in more gravy. Byron winced as if personally critiqued by the addition. "You do realize General Eigengrau is going to kill them, don't you?" Haste's abrupt change in tone changed the mood of the room. "He's going to kill every last one of those hods."

It dawned upon Edith that Byron would relay everything Haste was saying directly to the Sphinx, and probably in short order. In the process of venting her irritation with an unjust ringdom and a distant employer, Georgine could talk her way out of the Sphinx's good graces and so spoil any chance of escaping her tiresome post. And, Edith reflected, if it was fair and wise to give a crew time to talk without their captain present, was it not also reasonable that a couple of Wakemen have the opportunity to speak frankly about their frustrations beyond the Sphinx's hearing?

Edith held up a finger to pause the conversation and turned to address Byron, who had just finished serving the main course of duck, rice salad, and whipped peas. "Everything looks delicious, Byron. Thank you so much. Could you perhaps give us a little time to talk?"

She thought the request might disappoint him, but the stag seemed almost relieved. Perhaps he was just pleased to see her enjoying a normal dinner with a guest, or perhaps he was grateful to be spared the burden of bearing witness to a difficult conversation. Either way, Byron refilled their glasses, gave a brisk bow, and shut the door behind him without a word of argument.

Haste immediately resumed her point. "Once the general has had a chance to question them and twist their thumbs or rack their bones, he's going to stand them up against the Wall of Recompense and shoot them dead."

"I'm not going to let that happen," Edith said, sawing at the thick slab of duck breast on her plate. "Maybe they're all conspirators; I think probably a number of them were just caught up in the plot. Either way, there'll have to be a trial, several trials, probably."

"Trials! What a novel idea!" Haste said. "Come now, do you really think that you can sway Eigengrau one way or another? The man's a lot of things, but open to critique is not one of them."

"Leonid cares what I think, even if Eigengrau doesn't. I can convince the king there are better ways to spend his goodwill than the wholesale slaughter of forty hods."

Georgine stopped shaking her head only to take a sip of wine. "I don't see how it's possible to support both sides in matters like this. You can't half execute a man or save half his life."

"Do you really think my support of the hods is so insincere? You saw what I did. I wrenched off my arm and risked my neck to save a boy! I stopped Eigengrau from shooting a room full of hods!" Edith's knife squealed upon her plate, and she shuddered in revulsion.

"And yet you represent the Tower as well. Let's be honest: The Tower is a system that depends upon the existence of the hods. The hods ferry most of the goods and hold most of the debts. And they impose the least upon the Tower's many bounties. The hods are the blood of the Tower, yet they are treated like a cancer." Haste assembled a bite on her fork, using her knife to build and shape the morsel before dousing it all in gravy.

"Oh, do you want me to complain about the ringdoms, to complain about Leonid and the Pells? Do I like them? No, not especially. I think their shirts are overstuffed and their thoughts are undercooked. Though some of them are all right, obviously."

"As an exception, I thank you and still press the point: The nobles are uniformly awful. Really. They're robbers and rapists and sadists and imbeciles. Leonid is—"

"The king isn't so bad," Edith interjected, causing Haste to put down her utensils in frustrated protest. "Yes, he's flawed and short-sighted and probably an imminent danger to me and this ship, but he's not some salivating villain." Haste began to protest, but Edith held up a hand to stop her. "I admit, he seems to employ a few. But if I refused to engage anyone who I found the least bit detestable, corrupt, or stupid, I'd never work with anyone. Nothing would get done. The inability to compromise isn't a sign of *moral rectitude*"—she spoke the phrase with haughty emphasis—"it's a sign of immaturity. You know who can't be bargained with? Little children and madmen."

"How do you compromise with a man who thinks the worth of a

soul can be calculated down to the penny? He hides behind the general, but make no mistake, Eigengrau enacts the king's will."

"I'd like to see his will changed. And the way you change a man's will is by parlay and negotiation."

"Or exclusion. Or execution. There are many ways to change a man's mind. All I'm advocating for here is that we admit there are two sides to this contest."

"Luc Marat and the Sphinx, you mean?"

"The hods and the Tower," Haste corrected. "The one is a slave to the other. To me and you, the Tower is a home; to the hod, it is a prison. To us, it is a life; to them, it is a life sentence."

"I agree," Edith said, sitting back and folding her arms. "And it's deplorable."

"But how can you say that and still serve him? Still defend his interests? Still carry his vision of the Tower as some lofty ideal rather than the meat grinder it truly is?" Georgine said, holding out her arms and panting with unhappy laughter.

Edith balled up her napkin and dropped it onto her plate. "Because unlike Marat, the Sphinx is not trying to bring the Tower down, nor is he trying to gin up a war. He's putting out fires. He's posting watchmen. Yes, the Tower is rotten. You don't have to tell me that. It took my arm!" Edith raised and shook her bulky engine in evidence. "But I would rather see the hods brought in or let go and the Old Vein bricked up than see tens of thousands perish in some violent coup. Which is what Marat wants." She tapped the words out on the table as she spoke them: "He wants to overthrow so that he can reign. He doesn't care if he presides over the Tower or its rubble. He just wants to rule. I met the man. I heard his patter. He's a silver-tongued scoundrel who would kill you, me, and everyone in this ringdom to get what he wants."

"Which is what, specifically?" Haste said, resting her arms on the table, the planks of which complained of the added weight.

"All those blasted paintings!" Edith continued her list with passionate swings of her hand. "The secrets of the Tower! The Sphinx's head on a stick! A throne made out of gold! A bed full of waifs!" She brought her fist down, making all their silverware leap and ring. "Who cares what he wants? It doesn't matter to me, because no one matters to him. The worst I can say about the Sphinx is that he's irrelevant and cursed by unintended consequences. He's sat on his hands for far too long, and now you're fed up waiting for him. Fair enough! Me too. I've joined an exhausted army! I have no illusions about what I've signed on for here. I'm not optimistic! I've seen things, Georgine. Hopeless things. We are sitting beneath a boiling sea! But you saw that drawing in the library today. You can guess what Marat means to do with it. He'll fill that engine up with hods and send them forth to kill and be killed. Many, many people will die."

"Many people are already dying!" Haste said, her eyes shining with rage. "How can you be so naive? The Sphinx just wants to save this whole free-standing hell because it's all that keeps him alive. If the Tower has a tyrant, he lives in the clouds!"

Edith's shoulders dropped. The tension drained from her face. "Oh my god. You're one of them, aren't you? Of course you are. Why didn't I see it?" she asked, though she knew the answer. She had not seen the truth because she liked Georgine and because she wanted a friend, a confidante, especially one who understood the solitary nature of the station, who understood all that had been surrendered with the acceptance of the Sphinx's gifts. Edith's fantasy of facing the kings of the Tower with a companionable peer seemed so desperate and foolish now. "You knew about the tunnel and the hods squatting in the library?"

"Yes, I did," Haste said, swirling the wine in her glass. She seemed almost relieved to have finally arrived at the truth. "Marat calls them the *Ingeniare*. They're six brilliant men and women who, despite their many talents, were ruined by the Tower. Marat found them, saw their potential, and gave them a purpose: To build an engine that could challenge the Sphinx."

The weight of her mistake settled in her stomach like a stone in a sling. She had given Georgine exactly what she wanted, what she had wanted from the very beginning: an invitation onto the *State of Art*. Edith risked a glance over Haste's shoulder to where her sword belt and holstered pistol hung upon the wall, much too far away.

Haste seemed to grow more relaxed. The argumentative edge had left her voice. She spoke breezily, as if recounting a recent dinner. "When Marat realized the Ingeniare needed access to a library, a good one, he thought of the once-famous Ostraka University that had been transformed into an arena. He sent some of his biggest men to the Pelphian trading station, and it wasn't long before they were taken on as brawlers. They didn't have much trouble opening the hole to the library. At first, the Ingeniare would send word of which book they needed, and one of our brawlers would descend into the library and retrieve it. I helped smuggle the books out. But it didn't take Marat long to realize how inefficient the whole process was: The Ingeniare's requests were more or less constant, and the men of the arena were not exactly librarians. It took them days and weeks to find some of the books." Haste pulled a bent cigar from her pocket, tut-tutted its misshapen state, and lit it anyway. "Some valuable books were lost in the process of delivering them. Since we could not effectively bring the library to them, we brought the Ingeniare to the library. The tunnel came first. The Coattails, before they were even called that, dug it under my direction. They set up a newsstand against the wall and sold papers from the front while excavating out the back. I plied them with brandy and pocket change, and told them they were working for the Sphinx, and that one day, if they kept their mouths shut, they would be rewarded with an engine of their own."

Edith laid her hand over her steak knife as discreetly as she could, though the move was not lost on Georgine. The other Wakeman took up her own knife and began twisting it on its point upon the tablecloth.

"And those Coattails helped solve another problem: the Sphinx's Peeping Toms. There was no way I could keep all of those butterflies out on my own, so I taught the boys to train the magpies to do the job for me. Then, with the Sphinx blinded, I smuggled the Ingeniare in through the gatehouse. Getting them to the arena was simple enough. Everyone is always so eager to overlook a hod."

"The hod we found down in the library this afternoon: When you shouted, 'look out,' you weren't warning us. You were warning him so he could destroy the evidence."

"Oh, Banu! He was a genius, but also the unluckiest man I ever met. It broke my heart to see him suffer through that poison. He shouldn't have taken it. I was there. I would've snapped his neck for him. But at least he didn't suffer in vain. He died protecting his life's work."

"It's sort of ironic to call a death machine a life's work, isn't it?"

Haste smiled vaguely as she twisted her cigar, crooked as a finger. "It took the Ingeniare fifteen months to complete the plans for the Hod King. They finished the main work just a few weeks ago. The rest of them are already at the work site."

"I'm guessing that's not in the Silk Reef. Somewhere on the black trail, probably," Edith said, probing since Haste seemed in a divulging mood.

"It hardly matters now. It won't be long until the Hod King has his coronation."

"Well," Edith said, setting down the knife and scooting back from the table. Hoping to bring the evening to a peaceable end, she said, "So, thank you for coming to dinner. It's been an . . . *illuminating* evening."

"He's not a silver-tongued scoundrel, Edith," Haste said, setting her knife down, too. "The Sphinx saved my life, but Marat gave it meaning. He's a good man. He surrendered his legs because he's willing to sacrifice—a sacrifice the Sphinx is not willing to make—for what he believes to be true."

"Which is what?" Edith asked.

"That we're all prisoners here." She snuffed her cigar out on her dirty plate, the ember squeaking in complaint as it died. "Hod, commoner, lord, lady—all of us. The bars of this prison have caged every aspect of our lives. They trap our speech, corral our habits, and divide our days from our dreams. It is an insidious jail. Some of us have windows with better views, some of us live longer lives, but we're all inmates here. I think you know that. But you're just another prisoner working for the warden, you and that other spy—"

Edith leapt at the mention of another spy. "The other spy? Pinfield, you mean? You met him?"

"So you knew that lanky fellow? Seemed nice enough, but not a very good infiltrator. I found his cigar box full of the moths. He didn't think I knew, but of course I did. I know what a cigar smells like, and it doesn't smell like clock oil."

"What did you do to him?"

It was Haste's turn to look surprised. "Wait, is that who you've been hunting for all this time? The jail, the gatehouse, the Colosseum . . . It wasn't about the library or the Hod King. You were looking for him. Well, he must be very important to the Sphinx."

"He's important to me," Edith said, squaring her jaw.

"Yes, I can see that. I am sorry, Edith. This place is not kind to lovers. I do understand."

But Edith would not be baited by Haste's sympathy. "Where is he?"

"I saw him palling around with Duke Wilhelm before he disappeared. If I had to guess, I'd say he irked the duke, and was either dropped off the end of a port or tossed onto the black trail. Honestly, I thought I would have to be the one to kill him, but he kept confusing me by intervening on behalf of the hods. Just like you. That's what I can't figure out: Why are you both so determined to undermine the Sphinx while insisting that you act at his behest?"

"Because the Sphinx does not stand against the hod!" Edith shouted. "That's the poison Marat has poured into your ear to convince you that he is the simple solution to a complex problem. I'm not being duplicitous; I'm trying to act with a conscience, you brainwashed fool!"

Haste leaned back, but it did not seem a retreat. Her expression was one of absolute serenity. "I thought I could save you. I really did. I thought if I could just show you the prison you are living in, you would . . . But you do see it, don't you? You see it perfectly. You see the bars. You know the jailers. You realize what must be done to escape. You've just decided to stay in your cell. Well, I can't. I can't do that. I did try to save you, though."

Haste flipped the dining table aside. And as the china hung suspended within a cascade of gravy, candle wax, and wine, she lunged at Edith's throat with uncurled golden claws.

Chapter Fourteen

Sometimes a wheel squeaks not because it is faulty
but because it bears the most weight.

—*I Sip a Cup of Wind* by Jumet

After many hours of enjoyable distraction, Reddleman had finally forced himself to return to the third volume of the ship's operations manual, setting aside the enthralling book on trilobites. He had delighted in the illustrations of those vanished creatures, most of which were accurately drawn, and had giggled at the author's theorizing as to their behaviors, diets, and reproductive processes, most of which were wrong. If he concentrated, Reddleman could still remember what the trilobites had looked like in their original habitat, how they had swum through the water like shrimp, how they had battled on the ancient ocean floor with all manner of chitinous lances, and how they had coupled like two ships exchanging cannon fire at night.

But the captain wanted the nagging alarm muffled, and he'd still not found the cause. So back to the manuals he went.

The ship was incredibly complex. There were systems for scrubbing and storing fresh air, systems for sealing off decks, for venting excess heat and cold, and for directing the energy that the ship's vast batteries produced. The primary power reserve was housed under the floor of the birth deck. The related circuitry, which veined the walls and ceilings, required a hundred pages to diagram and explain. Reddleman had learned how to open the main hatch remotely and that the ship had a fog horn. He had discovered that the reinforced bow could be used as a cleaver to split a wooden hull in two, and he had read how many gallons the septic tank could hold before the ship would either have to return to home port or drop a fertile shower upon the valley. And still he had not deduced which of the thousand switches turned off the pinging alarm, nor why it pinged in the first place. He was beginning to wonder if he ever would.

And just when his eyes began to cross from reading about the appropriate solvents for cleaning the carpets, Reddleman began a new chapter in the manual and realized at once his search was at an end.

He cackled at the discovery and stabbed at the page of the unhandsome tome with a softly glowing finger. He stood and roved away from his station, moving along the wall of controls, hunting up and down the banks of blinking green and amber eyes until he found it: a small throttle with a brass knob shaped like a bumblebee. The throttle's cradle had three marked positions: SAFE, CHARGE, and BURN. Above it was a gauge that contained a spectral stripe that ranged from red to green. The needle quivered deep in the red. He shifted the control from CHARGE to BURN, then listened. He stood there with his head cocked for more than a minute, long enough to be sure that he had solved the mystery of the maddening alarm.

Then he gave a celebratory whoop and, to reward himself, opened up the military jacket the stag insisted he wear. It strangled him terribly. He unbuttoned the shirt beneath it and scratched happily at the thin vest that stretched over his round belly. He was about to return to the manual to continue reading the new and fascinating section when something on one of the magnovisor frames caught his eye.

The port had grown increasingly quiet over the course of the afternoon. Other than a couple of common barges bobbing in the inner slips, the only other moored vessel was the *Ararat*, and it was dark except for a few running lamps on the bulwark. The magnovisor's image of the port had lost some of its detail with the arrival of night. Reddleman could see little more than charcoal shapes, pierced here and there by the light of the lampposts that lined the piers. At a glance, all seemed tranquil and still. He wasn't sure what had drawn his attention.

Then one of the lampposts at the foot of the city steps winked and went out.

Reddleman squinted at the screen. The edges of the shadows fluttered with movement. He watched the pooled light of the next lamp to see what would emerge there, but then that light flickered and failed, too. The spreading darkness appeared to seethe with activity. When the next lamp failed, he realized the trail of shadows was not snaking idly about the port. No, it was drawing a straight line from the city gates to the gangplank of their ship.

Someone was trying to conceal their approach.

He crossed the bridge, trying to recall which frame showed the view out from the main hatch. Even after the last nearby port lamp blew out, the ambient light of the twilit sky was sufficient to show the silhouettes of the men gathering outside the ship. He could see the wagging tails of sheathed swords and the horns of rifle barrels. They were soldiers. Two score at least, probably more. They encircled the lip of the gangplank. A tall man in a short cape, who seemed to be the party's leader, pointed at the ship's steel hatch. Two of his men carried a small keg across the gulf and set it against the ship's hull. The flash of a match flickered in the gloom.

Realizing what they were about to do, Reddleman murmured, "No, no need for that." He reached out and flicked one switch in a row of fifty.

The lock on the main hatch clanged, and the door swung open. The light from inside the ship lit the faces of the startled boarding party inside the magnovisor's frame. None of them seem to know what to do with the unexpected invitation, nor with the keg of powder they'd brought to blow the hatch in.

Then their imposing commander stirred them from their stupor. The bomb was withdrawn, and the soldiers began to file cautiously across the gulf of air and into the ship.

Reddleman laughed and pulled off first his open jacket and then his dress blouse, stripping down to his thin vest. He scratched his belly happily, pulled off his boots, and walked with arms swinging and bare feet slapping over to the weapons locker. He shunned the flintlock carbines and cartridge pistols. Such barking, overbearing instruments! He dug past the curved sabers and pointed rapiers, which were elegant but gratuitous. He rooted his way down to the toolbox at the foot of the locker. There, he found what he was looking for: a bodkin needle.

He held the leather-working tool up to his eye, admiring the dullish point and the rust-speckled shaft.

"Ah, how humble is the key that unlocks the infinite mind!"

Despite Wakeman Haste's jabs at the Sphinx, Byron was generally pleased with how well Edith and her guest were getting on. Their good mood seemed to have sharpened their appetites—though perhaps a little *too* well. The women had dispatched his morel soufflé, which had taken him several hours to prepare, with all the relish of starved dogs.

He would admit he'd been a little ambitious in his menu selections. Most of the meal had come out well enough, though the duck was undeniably oversalted, and the flan that he'd promised the captain had turned out to be a flop. The gooey lagoon had refused to set, and he'd had to abandon the effort in favor of a simpler egg custard with lavender-honey drizzle. In his opinion, drizzles, gravies, and icing were just savory apologies for incompetent dishes. He hated that he had to rely on such a culinary crutch, and he half hoped they'd be too full to eat dessert, thereby sparing him the embarrassment of having to serve it.

While Edith and Georgine gulped their main courses, he went to retrieve the custard from a warm oven. He found the galley, which was perhaps his favorite room in the ship, had filled with smoke in his absence. The beaming steel surfaces and the hanging copper pots were all but obscured by a rank, gray cloud that fumed from the oven door. Dashing the smoke away with a towel, Byron turned on the hood vent and opened the oven to extract two smoldering ramekins. He dropped the cups into the sink and doused them with the tap. The ceramic dishes cracked from the shock.

As he stared down at the blackened coals of his second failure of the night, he suffered a brief but furious urge to weep. But he composed himself with a little slapping of his cheeks and snatched a bottle of sweet port from the wine rack. He marched from the kitchen with as much dignity as he could muster under the circumstances. The captain and her guest would just have to drink their dessert.

Before he returned to the captain's quarters, he thought to stop by the Communications Closet on the lower deck just to see if any new messenger moths had arrived. He made the decision casually, as if this were not the umpteenth time he'd visited the closet that day. The fact that he'd heard nothing from the Sphinx in twenty-four hours could reasonably be chalked up to some unforeseen interference. The master's communiqué might've run afoul of a bird or a bat or an errant gust of wind. Those were the most likely scenarios, and certainly more likely than the Sphinx's batteries running out, leaving her stranded in some corner of the house.

Before their departure Byron had asked how she expected to survive without him and who exactly would change her vials. The Sphinx had replied, "Do you really think I'm so frail? I have my ways!"

It was a sentiment that he had found somewhat cheering, right up to the point that her messages stopped arriving.

She was dead. He knew it. She had died on her levitator trying to coax the librarian into changing her batteries. The cat had wandered off, and now Byron's master was dead, dead, dead.

He quelled the rising panic with a sharp shake of his antlers. No. He was being dramatic. What had Edith said: "He'll outlive us by a thousand years!" Surely she was right.

Unlocking the thick door of his communications booth, Byron was delighted to see a fluttering messenger in the incoming cage. But his relief was short-lived as he recognized the wings as belonging to a spying butterfly rather than a messenger moth. He removed its wings, set up the screen, and activated its projector. A ghostly peephole of light flashed to life on the silken square.

Byron had no trouble identifying the four men in the field of view. He'd seen their captured profiles many times before. King Leonid, his brother Crown Prince Pepin, the city manager—whose name was Garden or Garcon, or something like that—and General Eigengrau, who looked like a shark in a cape. They stood on one of the palace's patios, drinking wine and arguing. The fronds of a palm tree framed the scene, hinting at the butterfly's hiding spot.

"Not this Hod King stuff again!" Crown Prince Pepin said, his angry bark tempered by the projector's small voice box.

"I'm afraid so," Eigengrau said.

"So they weren't idle threats, then?" the king said. He was wearing a long morning coat, and his white hair seemed to be attempting to fly off with his head. "The letters, the graffiti, the parroted cheers . . ." His voice sounded thin and tired. "The Hod King is real."

"Meanwhile, the Sphinx's warship rests upon our port like a fist!" Pepin's girdle-sculpted chest caught the wine that missed his lips. He was in a near frenzy. "I think it's pretty obvious now that we're about to be caught in the middle of a war, brother. And it won't matter whether the hods or the Sphinx emerge victorious: The battlefield is always destroyed!"

"I believe the Sphinx is sincere in his offer of a renewed partnership and a new technology. If you want Captain Winters to move her warship, why don't you just give her what she came for?" the king said, retying the cord of his robe about his emaciated waist.

"We can't return what we don't have, Your Majesty," the city manager said.

"You're certain the painting has been stolen? Not lost. Stolen?" the king asked.

"Yes! For the last time, yes!" the prince barked. "We've scoured every inch of the vault. The painting is gone! And since I haven't given it a second thought in decades, I haven't any idea *when* it was removed. It might've been snatched last week, or it could've walked off years ago. I presume it was the hods but—"

Eigengrau interrupted the prince. "I can handle the hods."

"Apparently not!" Prince Pepin said, his ruddy jowls quivering with anger. "For all you know, they could be building that bloody siege engine right under our feet!"

"Or it could be nothing more than a dream scrawled on a board," Eigengrau said, seeming to grow calmer the more the prince raged.

The prince was not at all soothed by the general's confidence. "We have to take the ship. We have to take it now while it's vulnerable and within our reach. If the hods' war engine *is* real, how can you possibly defend our ports against it? Eighty-six cannons, three-inch-steel-plated armor, and carrier space for a hundred and twenty men! Are you going to tell me, General, that we would not be better off with the *State of Art* leading our armada?" The prince picked up a wine bottle and filled his glass until it overflowed.

"Your Majesty, I think it is a mistake to try to take that ship," the city manager said, bracing himself for the prince's attack, which came quickly enough.

"Who asked you, Gardon? I've never met a man more eager to put a spade to his own grave. Have some courage, man!" Prince Pepin spat.

Despite the verbal thrashing, the city manager persisted. "Your Majesty, I don't think the Sphinx is our enemy, at least not yet. But he definitely *will be* if we do this."

Leonid reached up and groomed the fronds of a palm. The act belied the tension of the moment. He suddenly looked like an old man being kept from his gardening. "And what do you think, General? Do we attack our guests? Do we forsake our reputation as the hosts and hedonists of the Tower? Do we spoil an alliance that has endured for more than a century?"

"We are in an untenable position, Your Majesty," Eigengrau said, clasping his hands behind his back. "We can't return the Sphinx's painting, which means we will not benefit from the new technology he has promised. Our enemies, however, very likely will. I feel certain that I can hold back the hods, whatever they wish to throw at us, but I can't fight a war on two fronts, especially not at such a disadvantage. What if the Sphinx gives the Algezians fleeter airships or longer guns?"

"All right, all right," Leonid said wearily, scowling at the decision even as he made it. "Take the ship. Tonight." The words made Byron's ears drop. The king quickly added, "Don't kill the crew if you can avoid it."

"I'm sorry, Your Majesty, that's probably not going to be possible," Eigengrau said.

"Not only is that impossible, brother," the prince interjected hotly, "but if we bungle the attempt, if they rebuff us, then we'll have to shoot her down. We can't afford to wound that raptor and let her escape. If we can't have her, then no one—"

Byron did not hear the recording's end. He was already out in the corridor, his heart in his throat. He had to warn the captain. He had to get to the—

When the draft struck the whiskers at the end of his snout, the shiver seemed to drill straight down to his skull. He smelled the fresh air first and the nervous men second. When the soldier in black rounded the corner of the ship's entryway with his pistol raised and his eyes wide as globes, Byron felt the familiar grip of his instinctual paralysis. Even as his limbs froze, even as his throat constricted and his neck hardened, he fought to resist the reflex. He could not afford this crippling panic—not now! He had to draw his weapon. He had to fire. He had to warn Edith!

Then the soldier saw him, saw his rack, saw the brass scales of his knuckles and the black balls of his eyes. The soldier shrieked, "Monster!"

That word released Byron from his trance. He was emphatically *not* a monster. Monsters didn't have feelings, or friends, or fashionable sensibilities, or wit. Monsters could not hold a brush, or organize a tea, or even burn a pudding. No, if there was a monster in the hall, it certainly was not him.

He raised his pistol and fired in one fluid stroke.

A crystal sconce at the far end of the hall exploded from his errant shot.

The bad miss seemed to give the soldier courage. He straightened his arm and blasted away at Byron's head.

It felt as if he'd bitten down on a quivering tuning fork. The vibration shook his jaw and ran down his spine. He thought for a moment the shot had found its mark, that he had been killed, but when he reached up to feel for the ooze of blood, he found his skull intact and his right antler missing.

Then another soldier and a third blundered in behind the first. The new arrivals gaped at the one-horned stag while the first scout shouted at them to quit gawping and shoot "the devil."

Byron would've liked to stay, reload, and correct the soldier's choice of words, but even counting his ego, he was outnumbered. Self-preservation prevailed. He turned and ran.

He could not recall the last time he'd run. In fact, he wasn't entirely sure he'd galloped with these legs before. They were much swifter than he would've supposed, and half as noisy as they had any right to be. It was exhilarating, making his own breeze, seeing the doors of the cabin blur past! If he survived the night, perhaps he would have to take up running. Somewhere placid. A forest perhaps.

When his scout called back that the entrance was secured, Eigengrau led the rest of the boarding party, who numbered forty-eight in all, across the gangplank and onto the ship.

He was surprised to find the lower corridor deserted. When the hatch had swung open of its own accord, he had assumed they were stepping into a trap. Which was why he'd sent a few of his most disposable men on ahead to spring it. After surveying the brightly lit, carpeted hallway, and the many cabin doors, nearly all of which his men had already opened and checked for occupants, he began to wonder if perhaps the open hatch had heralded a surrender rather than a snare.

Still, it made him uneasy.

He might've felt more confident if it hadn't been for the scout's insistence that he had seen some sort of monster. In evidence of this, the scout had produced the broken antler of some woodland animal—proof, he insisted, that he had wounded the beast.

"And where is this monster now, Private?" Eigengrau asked.

"He ran that way." The private pointed to the foot of a stairwell at the end of the hall.

"And you didn't pursue him?" Eigengrau's tone was one of paternal disappointment.

"Yes, sir, I did. He ran to the second floor. He locked himself inside the engine room. I thought I should wait to pursue him."

"Fool! He could be sabotaging the ship! Sergeant," Eigengrau said, turning to address a man with grand muttonchops and a mouth like a coin slot. "Get inside that engine room. Shoot whoever's in there, including the private's monster. Then work your way down the gun deck to the aft of the ship. Kill whoever you encounter. I'll take the other half of the men to the aft stairs and proceed to the top deck. We're not taking any prisoners today, but try not to ruin the ship. You may find yourself part of its crew in the morning."

The sergeant turned to organize his men, but Eigengrau called him back for a final word. "And if I catch a single one of you retreating, I will hang you from the port and let the vultures peck you free!"

Chapter Fifteen

A man who is not suspicious of a philosophy that appeals to his nature is like the bull comforted by the rutted path that leads to the slaughterhouse.

—*I Sip a Cup of Wind* by Jumet

Edith tipped back in her chair ahead of Haste's attack. As she fell, she saw Georgine's flame-bright hair flare out like a corona. Her expression was one of perfect determination, but there was no hate nor loathing reflected there. They had been friends, had shared a few sincere and vulnerable moments, but friendship in the Tower could only be a luxury, a holiday that everyone wished would not end, but must, and always did.

As her chairback hit the floor, Edith raised her heels, catching Georgine's sculpted breastplate above the navel. Edith rolled backward and kicked as she did, sending the golden Wakeman flying. The effort took all her strength. Georgine's engine was as heavy as an anchor. Edith felt the steel bulkhead tremble when Haste landed flat on her back some feet away.

Edith sat bolt upright. Her scabbard and holster dangled like a lure on the wall. She lurched to her feet and made a dash for it, stumbling around the table and through the spilled remnants of their dinner. Perhaps if she shot her in the leg, it would be enough to subdue Georgine, enough to get her off the ship, but not so much as to kill her. Edith reached for the steel pommel of her pistol.

The next thing she knew, she was hurtling sideways. It felt and sounded as if she'd been struck with a shovel. Her engine absorbed the brunt of the attack, but the force was still sufficient to throw her into a display case. Pain shot down her arm as she crashed through the cabinet. An explosion of glass and trinkets followed her to the floor.

She landed awkwardly on all fours amid the scattered knickknacks. Looking over her shoulder, she found Georgine rubbing the ham of one golden hand as if the strike had bruised it.

"You're faster than you look," Edith said.

Georgine unholstered Edith's pistol. She took a moment to appreciate the craftsmanship of the etched grip and the line of the barrel, then she cracked the weapon in half and let the pieces bounce in front of Edith. Georgine broke off the saber's cup guard while the sword was still sheathed, then slid the naked steel out into her hand. Casually, she whittled it down several inches at a time, breaking it as if she were snapping long beans. "Come now, Edith. Look at us! We don't need pistols and swords, do we?"

"I liked that sword." Edith raised herself to one knee, leaving a bloody handprint on the rug amid the shards of glass.

"You won't need it again," Haste said, dropping the last pieces of the ruined blade. She balled up her fists and stepped toward Edith, still kneeling on the floor.

Edith snatched the jade bedpan from among the clutter and slung it at Haste, who ducked, but not quickly enough. The bottom of the pan glanced off the top of her skull. She grasped her head, hissing in pain. Edith took the chance to regain her feet.

Haste dropped her hands, one eye still clenched shut. "That wasn't very sporting."

"Maybe you're not so fast after all," Edith said.

"Ah, the Gold Watch never runs slow!" Haste swung for Edith's jaw.

Edith deflected the first strike with her engine but missed the second. The jab was too short to catch, and the most she could do was try to bend away from it. Still, it caught her cleanly on the ribs. She doubled over, then, since she was already low, plowed forward into Haste. Her momentum was enough to tip Georgine off balance, and the two fell heavily to the rug among the strewn saucers and cutlery. Haste raised her arms to shield her head even as Edith lifted an iron fist over her. She struck at Haste's collarbone, ringing her chest like a cowbell and leaving a dent in the beautiful carapace. Grunting, Georgine rolled onto her side, shaking Edith off, and scrambled back to her feet again.

Edith popped up, clutching a candelabra in her bloody hand. Haste shook the hair from her eyes and swung almost tentatively at Edith, who parried with the candleholder.

"Not used to fighting with your hands, eh?" Haste asked.

"I wouldn't call those hands, George. They're more like clubs with thumbs, aren't they?"

"Says the woman with the iron mitt!"

Georgine came at her with a flurry of punches—hooks, jabs, and uppercuts. In doing so, she showed Edith the evidence of her hours sparring with the brawlers of the Colosseum. She advanced so skillfully and with so much force, Edith could do little more than retreat and let her engine take the brunt of the attack. But her cabin wasn't large enough for her to lead Georgine on a merry chase. The candelabra was already bent and missing two of its stems. She wondered how long she'd be able to defend herself with one arm against two. Even a glancing blow to her head would be enough to end things, and she was sure now Georgine would kill her. She would feel bad about it, most likely. She'd get drunk and reminisce a little about the time they'd spent a morning together eating and drinking the king out of house and home. She might shed a tear. But she would kill her.

Georgine threw a cross that missed Edith's chin by an inch. When she recoiled, one of her calves bumped against the edge of her mattress. And that was that. She was out of room.

Meaning to finish her, Haste lunged with one arm raised to fend off Edith's engine, and the fingers of her other hand pointed, plunging for her heart.

Edith dove to one side, shattering a bedpost with a swat of her arm. The canopy dropped upon Haste like a net, even as Edith sprang clear of it.

For a moment, the golden Wakeman thrashed under the bed's sail, tangling in its threads.

Edith dropped the warped candelabra, panting with exhaustion. As hopeless as it might be, she felt she had to make one more plea, if not for Haste, then for her own conscience. "Let it go, Georgine! We don't have to do this if we don't want to. There's no reason one of us has to—"

The muffled ring of a gunshot stopped Edith short. She cocked her head, trying to decide whether the sound had come from inside the ship. The knelling of the second shot convinced her that it had. "You brought friends?" she asked.

Haste tore the canopy with one great stretch of her arms. Rising from the mattress, she snapped off another bedpost, gripping it by the finished end. "I'm not sharing this ship with anyone," she said, and swung the club like a maul at a railroad spike.

When Byron fled from the soldiers, bounded up the stairs, and locked himself in the engine room, it hadn't occurred to him that he didn't have a lamp and didn't know where the switch for the electric light was.

The dark was crowded and unfamiliar. It smelled like oil and stale water, aromas that he was particularly sensitive to. He took great pains in his daily toilet to diminish his own mechanical odors with an application of myrrh gum powder to his fur, what there was of it, and rose water to his reservoirs. The Sphinx had chided him for years for polluting his boiler with scented water. "It leaves a film!" she said. "It clogs up your plumbing!" But Byron continued the minor rebellion because he would rather have a little plaque in his pipes than smell like an old bog.

His remaining antler bumped and scratched upon the machinery that consumed most of the open space. The tails of his coat caught on the corner of something sharp, and he had to tear it to tug it free.

As he squeezed his way around the engine, he nearly tripped over the taut cables that tethered the mechanical bulk to the ship's hull. He unfastened the lines as he found them and whispered hoarsely as he worked: "All right, wake up. Rise and shine. I need you to wake up, but softly, softly. Don't shift around. You'll squish me into jelly if you do. Shh! That's right. Softly, now."

The wide disc of the locomotive's face began to glow with a pale lunar light. The heavy joints of the Sphinx's doorman breathed with warming steam.

Something scraped upon the hatch of the engine room, the sound so grating it made Byron's ears flatten to his head. The invaders were trying to force a pry bar between the door and the jamb. He wasn't sure they could prize it open, but he didn't wish to wait to find out.

"I don't know if you can really comprehend the gravity of our situation, but please, *please* try to understand. I want you to go out there and play very roughly with our guests. You can toss them around like balls if you like, but, *but* be very gentle with the ship. There aren't any carpets here. If you kick a hole in the bulkhead, I will be very, very cross with you."

A bar of light split the darkness further. The soldiers were making progress on the door. He hadn't much time now.

"You know that jaunty tune you like to play when you think I'm not around to hear it? I want you to play that song now. That's right. Change the drum. And please don't step on me. I don't want to die on your shoe."

The door hinges failed with a shriek of rending metal and the hatch fell away with a bang.

The waiting soldiers stood in an organized bank, swordsmen behind kneeling riflemen. And still, they seemed unprepared.

The music box began to play, slowly at first, but with a quickening intensity, a song that was perfect for romping and stomping and running down corridors.

That was exactly what Byron hoped Ferdinand would do.

Eigengrau led his squad up the stairwell at a measured pace. He let the barrel of his pistol lead, determined to shoot whoever appeared over the horizon of the steps above him. There'd be no questions, just the answer of his thunder. The custom-made weapon could pierce plate armor, and since it used specially made shells rather than the usual ball and powder, it could be quickly reloaded. It was to the general a very comforting totem.

But the farther they climbed without seeing evidence of a crew, the more disconcerted he felt. A ship of this size would require many hands to fly. The act of reloading the cannons alone would take fifty able men. If they meant to surrender, they certainly were going about it in a manner that was likely to get them killed. No, either they had fallen back into a defensive position, probably on the bridge or the engine room, or they were hiding in the closets and the crawl spaces, waiting for the right moment to spring an attack.

At the middeck landing, he stopped long enough to quickly survey the gun deck, which was wide enough to exercise an elephant inside, though it stood empty except for the cannons and ranks of brass dummies that stood at lifeless attention. At the far end of the steel floor, the other half of his men gathered about a broad hatch, which he took for the entrance to the engine room.

By the time he reached the top landing of the stairs, he was convinced a trap lay just ahead. The corridor there was narrow, paneled in dark wood, and lit by crystal globes that seemed to cataract the light inside them. The first hatch on the left stood open, and a brighter yellow light spilled out from it.

The general approached with his back pressed to the wall. He drew from his belt a small, collapsible periscope, an instrument he sometimes had cause to use to peer over the plaza crowds when the sedans gathered too thickly. With the steady hands of a jeweler, he extended the periscope's barrel and stretched the hooded prism past the lip of the door. He peered into the eyepiece at the room beyond.

An ugly man in his undershirt sat cross-legged in the middle of the floor. Behind him, all around him really, stood great banks of switches, throttles, and knobs, the likes of which Eigengrau had never seen. The controls were packed as densely as the keys of a typewriter and were lit by a bevy of tiny lights. Incredible as the interface was, the gold frames that hung above those cabinets were more fantastic still. The paintings were colorless but living, moving images. By some magic he could not fathom, they contained glimpses of the port outside. The moon rose inside one frame. In another, the trio of the *Ararat*'s envelopes blotted out the stars. In a third, he saw the clouds wrapped about the necks of the distant mountains like scarves.

The fantastic bridge of the ship seemed entirely empty except for the thin-haired cretin who sat smiling on the floor. When Eigengrau looked at him again, he realized the wretched little man was staring at him. Not staring at the periscope's hood but staring through its lens and around the corner at him. Eigengrau shivered under this gaze. Steam seemed to rise from the stranger's eyes. His ears and nose and mouth glowed red like a raw egg held before a candle.

Then the general recognized who it was. He pulled away from the eyepiece with a start.

It was impossible. The Red Hand was dead.

Eigengrau turned to find the private who he'd originally sent in to scout the ship. He grabbed the man by the back of the neck and pulled him close to his face and said, "I want you to go in there and say hello. Whatever happens, do not fire your weapon. If you shoot any part of that machinery, I will skin you and pack you in salt. Is that clear, Private?"

The private nodded until his cap rattled on his head. He was still nodding when Eigengrau pushed him in front of the open hatch. The frightened soldier stumbled as he struggled to draw his saber. Once he had his sword drawn, he glanced at the general, who thrust out his chin, directing the man onward. The soldier slid one foot forward, then the other, his knees trembling as he advanced. He disappeared into the room.

Eigengrau turned to the rest of his men who clogged the passageway and spoke in a near whisper: "No one discharges their sidearm in that room. Is that clear?"

"Hello?" the private called from inside the bridge. "Hello, you there...on the floor...stand up! Put your hands in the air."

The general lifted the periscope again to watch what would occur, but he hadn't gotten the piece to his eye before he was stopped short by a sharp, brief shriek. He heard the squeak of bootheels, a rustle of cloth, then abrupt quiet.

He felt his men shrink behind him. They were all too young to be such cowards. Eigengrau was about to enliven their bravery with some well-constructed bodily threats when the private reemerged from the bridge. He dragged the tip of his saber upon the floor. His mouth hung open, spilling out a thread of drool. He walked straight out, bumped against the opposite bulkhead, then turned listlessly to face the general and his men.

He appeared uninjured except for a single, thick tear of blood, which streamed from the inside corner of one eye. His gaze was vacant, his shoulders round. He did not seem to recognize them, nor indeed anything. With one strike, the Red Hand had reduced the man to a mindless husk.

"Draw your swords," Eigengrau said. "One hundred mina for whoever kills the fiend. A noose for any man who tries to leave before he's dead!"

The bedpost cracked against Edith's engine. The ragged end broke loose and bounced against the top of her head.

Taking advantage of Edith's momentary confusion, Haste bullrushed her, grabbed her by the shirtfront, and drove her into the wall, shattering a pair of picture frames.

Edith felt like a house had fallen on her. The breath flew from her lungs, and a ringing filled her ears. If Haste hadn't been pinning her to the wall, she would've collapsed into a heap.

Edith searched for but could not find Haste's eyes. The Gold Watch had turned her head to one side. Her profile held the expression of one engaged in an unlikable but unavoidable chore. It seemed a very bad sign. Haste's grip on Edith's throat made her head feel like an overfilled balloon.

The strangest thing came to mind the moment Edith realized she would die. She remembered the smell of horses. She recalled the day she had ridden out early before anyone was awake. A heavy fog had settled overnight. It made the world seem at once small and infinite. She didn't ask permission because she knew her father would not grant it. It was dangerous to ride through such a blinding mist. She might charge into a fence or a ditch or a hedgerow. The horse was unfamiliar, and she inexperienced. She couldn't remember why she had done it, but the feeling of thundering through the fog with her heart in her throat and the path appearing ahead of her just in the nick of time had filled her with a consuming sense of joy.

And she had not been afraid, not even when the limb of a branch jousted her from her mount. She broke her wrist in the fall. The fog thinned into a light rain, and she could see the path she had missed, the tree that had unseated her, and her father's house in the distance. The sight filled her with dread because she knew she would have to go home, have to face him, have to endure the inevitable scolding, and all manner of restriction as she waited for her wrist to heal.

And she realized then that she would rather run toward danger and uncertainty than to have an unobstructed view of the unforgiving truth.

That thrilling fog she had once galloped through had begun to fill her cabin aboard the *State of Art*. It ate the furniture, crawled up the walls, and devoured the light of the lamps, until the only thing left in the world was a shaking fringe of red hair and a hand upon her windpipe.

And suddenly Edith knew exactly why the Sphinx had given her such a heavy, ugly engine: because it was stronger than all the others he had ever made.

Edith gripped the arm that pinned her chest and pulled with all her might.

The rending metal howled. The gilt shell buckled. Rivets popped in quickening succession. She wrenched the golden limb from Haste's shoulder, drawing out with it a tail of vital machinery, down to the bone and veins. The arm flew across the cabin, shattering a showcase of compasses and boatswain whistles. It clattered to the carpet, flailed a moment like a fish thrown upon the shore, and was still.

Haste released Edith's throat, and staggered backward, grasping at the absence of her arm. Oil, blood, and the Sphinx's glowing serum gushed from the wound and flowed down her ribs.

Haste struggled to catch her breath as the engine inside her chest faltered. She gaped at Edith with an expression of vulnerable horror, then swung her remaining arm with a childish grunt. The strike was wild and weak. Edith caught Haste's hand, and tried to hold her by it, but Haste fell to her knees, the color draining quickly from her face.

The machine in her chest groaned. Edith knelt down with her.

"I thought that would've gone differently," Georgine said, slumping forward.

Edith caught her and held her up. "Well, it nearly did."

Haste panted but could not seem to draw a breath. "Ah, ah, we would've had a falling out sooner or later. Too much alike. Headstrong. Stubborn. We could never have been friends. Sisters, maybe." She managed a drowsy smile. "I would've liked to have had a sister."

Edith felt Haste's weight shift fully against her, and seeing the retreating light in Georgine's eyes, quickly replied, "Me too."

Chapter Sixteen

The universe breathes in ragged breaths. The body dies. The fungus grows. The loam spreads. The tree roots. The forest burns. The cloud bursts. The flood drowns. The alluvium feeds the fields. In, out. In, out. There is no stasis, no stillness. The source of all misery lies in our insistence that tomorrow be like today. But if it were, if it ever were, it would spell the end of everything.

—*I Sip a Cup of Wind* by Jumet

From the safety of the corridor, Eigengrau watched through his periscope as the Red Hand lobotomized and murdered his men, one after another. The little devil laughed as he dispatched them with an acrobatic grace that belied his ungainly shape. He leapfrogged over the first private who charged him to step onto the shoulders of the next man, who panicked at this unexpected mounting. The Red Hand squatted down upon his head like a potter at the wheel and stabbed him in the eye with his bodkin. The man yelped horribly while the Red Hand stirred his needle around inside him. Then he leapt from the soldier's back, and the man crashed senseless to the floor.

Though the bridge was nearly filled with men with drawn swords, few of them were quick enough to make contact, much less really wound the Red Hand. The mad assassin sidestepped a lunging rapier, went belly to belly with his attacker, and goaded the recruit in the ear with his stylet. The brief, almost imperceptible strike had the immediate effect of ending the man's life.

One handsome petty officer, who had distinguished himself to the ladies of Pelphia as an able swordsman and an aggressive duelist, caught the Red Hand in the back with such a forceful thrust, half of his blade was left protruding from the lunatic's chest. Rather than temper the Red Hand's activity, the wound seemed only to spur him on. The handsome swordsman lost his grip on his hilt when the Red Hand turned to face him, and then lost his life when the assassin embraced him, piercing his heart with the point of his own sword.

Once the remnant of the general's squad saw the frog-bellied man leaping about with a sword through his chest, they began to lose their nerve. Their flagging courage was not at all helped by the Red Hand crying out, "Do not fear the darkness, friends, for it is full of stars!"

Rather than press upon the fiend in any concerted way, Eigengrau's men began to jockey with one another to get away from him. The Red Hand took advantage of their confusion with brutal rapidity: He pierced the throat of one man and the heads of two others at the temple. Forgetting the general's orders, the men who had pistols drew them. But their attempts to shoot the bouncing, chortling target ended in either errant shots that clanged haplessly about the room or in the accidental execution of one of their brothers-in-arms.

Eigengrau had seen enough battles to recognize a rout. The only thing that his lingering could possibly contribute to this fight was another body.

He thought to regroup. He would gather the rest of his men, draw the Red Hand out into the passageway, and fill him with every ball and leaden slug they had between them.

And if that didn't work, he'd call on the crown prince to fire the *Ararat*'s cannons at the ship's silks, and let gravity take her and the devil in its ungentle embrace.

Byron hunkered inside the engine room with his fingers in his ears. The gun deck rang with the sound of gunfire, Ferdinand's heavy steps, and horrid screams. The more fortunate soldiers were killed by ricochets and the wayward shots of their panicked peers. The unlucky ones fell under Ferdinand's colossal feet as he charged up and down the deck, or they found themselves picked up and squeezed to a boneless jelly by his steam-shovel hands.

Byron couldn't bear to watch for long.

He was ashamed of himself—ashamed of the absolute deficit of courage that this emergency had roused within him. He had at times in the past wondered whether, given the opportunity, he would prove to be a hero or a coward. Naturally, he had flattered his ego by imagining that if he ever was called to action, he would find himself suddenly possessed by such a spirit of valor and poise that his foes would quake before him. At the very least, he had imagined he wouldn't run away and hide in a closet at the first sign of trouble. The instinct to flee had proved unconquerable.

But as he cowered with his back wedged in a corner, a new fear began to grow inside him. It grew so large, in fact, it eclipsed even his mortal terror. Because there was one thing worse than dying, and that was living to see a bleak future. Did he really wish to survive if Edith perished? Did he want to be the last man left alive? Did he want to be taken prisoner, interrogated, tortured, or worse—put on display, flogged to the public, treated as a monstrous curiosity for the rest of his life? Was a quick death in defense of his friends not preferable to a long life of suffering and humiliation?

He pulled his fingers from his ears. The snap of gunshots and boom of Ferdinand's pistons shuddered through him. He cracked his pistol open at the breech, pinching the rim of the spent shell, and replaced it with a fresh shot drawn from his vest pocket. He stood, held the gun far out to one side as if it were a viper he'd caught by the tail, and counted to three.

When he stepped out into the open doorway of the engine room, pistol and life ready to be spent, he was met by an abrupt stillness.

The Sphinx's clock-faced doorman stood near the center of the deck amid the strewn corpses of nearly two dozen men. Some of the dead lay draped over the ornate cannons where Ferdinand had cast them. Dark blood streaked the ceiling and spattered the walls and pooled underfoot. The carnage was absolute; the stink of gore, bowels, and smoke, nauseating.

The hulking Ferdinand was, at present, trying to stand a soldier back on his feet. The man's neck was obviously broken, but the black iron locomotive tried to pose him upright anyway. The corpse's ankles rolled, and the soldier fell into a heap the moment Ferdinand released him. The simple-minded doorman seemed to regret what he had done, or more precisely, he seemed to not fully comprehend it. Byron wondered how he could possibly explain death to something with the soul of a music box.

The pale light of Ferdinand's clocklike face dimmed as he opened a drawer in his chest and plucked the musical cylinder from its cradle. He returned it to another drawer and replaced it with a new drum of music. The plaintive song that began to rumble from his chest sounded, Byron thought, reminiscent of a funereal bugle call.

Both Byron and Ferdinand seemed to hear the stamp of bootheels at the same time. The mourning engine turned, his blank face flaring bright.

From the other end of the middeck, General Eigengrau marched at him with hip cannon leveled, his cape fanned out by his pace. The gun's report was so intense Bryon felt it rattle the gears of his heart.

Ferdinand twisted back around, showing Byron the black hole that stood amid his shattered face. The music stopped. The giant reached to touch the wound, and the rest of the frosted glass fell away in a ringing shower. Inside the dark plumbing of the machine, Byron saw the head and shoulders of a hound suspended in a matrix of black pipes and rubber cabling. Blood poured from the hound's gray muzzle. The lids of his dark eyes fluttered with mortal exhaustion. Ferdinand fell forward and crashed upon the deck so heavily the quake nearly threw Byron from his feet.

But he did not fall. His mind reeled at what he had just seen, but his emotions seized upon a purpose more quickly than his thoughts.

Byron ran at the general, bleating with fury. He leveled his pistol and fired. And this time he did not miss.

* * *

When Eigengrau retreated to the gun deck to gather his forces only to find them lying at the feet of what appeared to be a train engine that had sprouted arms and legs, he felt he'd had about enough of this vicious ship and its monstrous crew.

So he shot the brute right in the middle of its dinner-plate face. He'd half expected the wound to have no effect, but as he watched the locomotive fall, he felt a surge of optimism: The Sphinx's monsters could be killed after all. He thought it a hopeful sign that there didn't seem to be very many of them. Yet, even as he began to calculate how large a reinforcement he would need to fell the Red Hand, the one-horned beast who'd been concealed behind the clockwork Goliath charged at him with a gun in its hand, screaming like a goat.

Before Eigengrau could think to defend himself, he heard the shot and felt the slug pass through his shoulder and erupt from his back. The impact spun him about. His pistol flew from his hand and skittered across the floor. He reeled against the chest of a faceless cannoneer who made no effort to catch him. Having never been shot before, Eigengrau was surprised to discover just how widely it hurt. It wasn't like a cinder burn or a cut on a finger; it was not localized to one place. He felt the ache in every limb; he felt it in his toes and earlobes. He wanted to squirm away from the pain but could not because it writhed right along with him. In fact, the more he shifted about, the deeper the agony twisted inside of him. But he had to move. He had to get out.

The general groped along the line of guns, leaning on them to hold himself erect as he staggered back the way he had come. Hazarding a backward glance, he saw the horned abomination dashing after him. Eigengrau feared it meant to gore him with its horn and finish what it had begun.

His terror made him swift despite the mounting loss of blood. He was down the stairs and loping past the cabins of the bottom deck in a matter of heartbeats, which seemed to be coming too quick now. He expected at any moment for some fresh ogre to leap out at him. But none did. Then he smelled the fresh air, sweeter than any perfume, and he knew he would escape.

He gripped the sides of the open hatch and leaned into the night. A chilled wind slapped his cheeks, and he savored the rush of euphoria.

And yet, he did not trust his unsteady legs to carry him across the open air. He dropped to his hands and knees and crawled the length of the quivering gangplank with his cape tangled about his ears. The moment he was safely back upon the hardy Pelphian pier, he stood and waved his arms high above his head. Ignoring the sharp throb in his chest, he delivered the signal to Pepin aboard the *Ararat* to open fire.

He jogged toward the palm trees and lead soldiers that banked the city gates. His toes dragged, his breath rattled, but the thought of the coming barrage kept him moving forward. He shouted at the guardhouse at the end of the pier before he reached it, summoning out two sleepy-eyed watchmen. "You two! Man the lead soldiers! Sound the ala—"

His words were blotted out by the boom of cannon fire. He turned to watch the arc of three flaming lances as they leapt from the ramparts of the *Ararat*, sailed above half the port, and speared the *State of Art*'s envelope.

The ensuing fireball turned the shadows of the three men into long, black tails. They winced at the heat as the combusting gas turned the silks to ash. The steel ship, sharp and sleek as the rail of a sleigh, plunged from the port, sucking the smoke and flames down with it.

The quiet that followed was surreal, like the muted ambiance of a scorched forest.

It took Eigengrau scarcely a moment to regain his dispassionate poise. He found the strength to straighten his spine and cleared his throat into the ball of one fist. He pulled the corner of his cape away from his wound, and said without much urgency to the night watchmen, "All right, one of you fetch me a doctor, and the other, fetch me a drink. It's been a long night, and my throat is awfully dry."

When Edith strode from her destroyed stateroom where Haste lay uncovered and uncomposed, she nearly collided with Byron. He had a wild look in his eyes. Seeing the shattered stump of his antler, she wondered what trauma he'd suffered. He told her that Ferdinand was dead, along with most of a boarding party, and that he had shot Eigengrau, who had run away, though maybe she could still catch the general if she hurried. The words spilled from him. He seemed in shock. Edith gripped him by the shoulders and said, "Forget Eigengrau, Byron. We have to make sure we haven't lost the bridge. Come on!"

She led him in a drumming ascent up the aft stairwell. As soon as they crested the last step, they saw the first sign of the battle that had occurred. One of the general's men knelt, with his cheek pressed against the wainscoting. Blood trickled from the corner of his eye, but he seemed otherwise uninjured. He moaned softly. He seemed not quite living and not yet dead. She wondered how Reddleman could've done such obvious damage with so little evidence of violence. Though perhaps she should be grateful. Surely this was better than the decapitations he'd once been known to dole out by hand.

Then she saw the bridge.

There were bodies everywhere. Most were clearly dead, their uniforms like black islands in lakes of blood. But some seemed to have suffered the same fate as the recruit in the passageway. They were senseless as miserable drunks and shedding crimson tears.

The Red Hand stood amid them, in a gory undershirt with a sword through his chest. He turned around and around, reaching for the hilt that protruded from his back. Amid his spinning, he noticed them in the doorway and smiled. "Hello, Captain! I feel like a dog trying to catch his own tail!" He laughed as if it were some sort of parlor game.

"Stand still," Edith said sharply. Reddleman complied, and she gripped the handguard and pulled the blade straight out.

He stumbled forward a little, giggling with relief and scratching himself. "Oh, that's so much better. I couldn't sit down!"

He went to his post and settled into the pilot's chair with a contented little sigh. He seemed unaware or at least indifferent to the death that surrounded him. "I have good news. I found the culprit behind our nagging alarm. The ship's levitators were fully charged."

"Our what?" Edith said.

But before he could answer, Byron shouted, "Edith!"

She looked round to find him pointing at one of the magnovisor's gilded frames. The flaming missiles had already left the *Ararat* and were hurtling toward them.

They all knew what it meant, knew there wasn't time to do anything to stop it, or to save themselves.

The flaming lances passed from their field of view. They heard the *whump* when their silk envelope exploded and felt the warmth of the flames even through the ship's steel shielding. Then the bodies surrounding them began to float. For one sickening moment, Edith thought that they were all ascending while she alone was plummeting down. The frames of the magnovisor flashed with a confusion of unidentifiable shapes. She felt the descent in the pit of her stomach, but without a clear view of the horizon or the ground to orient herself by, the falling feeling quickly turned into a sense of weightlessness. It was a strange sensation, not exactly like swimming, not exactly like flying. It was like floating in honey. She might've found it serene had it not been for all the hovering corpses and the certainty that she was about to join them.

She looked about for Byron and saw him twisting in the air several feet off the floor. He flailed his legs, trying to propel himself toward the lowered periscope column, but made little headway. Though what would it matter if he did? Having something to hold on to would not change the end of this ride. Reddleman was still in his seat. He had his feet hooked about the fixed base of his chair. His hands ran over the controls, making fine adjustments to many dials. A dead soldier bumped into her. She shoved him away in revulsion, a motion that had the unintended effect of making her drift toward the ladder; she grasped a rung as soon as it was near enough. No, clinging to something wouldn't make any difference in the end, but it felt good to do it.

"Hang on, Captain. I'm going to try something," Reddleman said, grasping a twin-bladed throttle and pushing it gently forward.

Edith felt her weight return, and she tightened her grip on the rung. The floating dead men smacked upon the floor again like wet rags.

Byron yelped as he tried to get a grip on the periscope column, only to slide quickly down its length. He landed under it on his rear with a thump.

It took Edith a moment to believe they were not all dead. Though the drop seemed to have gone on forever, it had lasted scarcely eight seconds. She was certain just a moment or two more, and Byron would've landed with much worse than a bump. They all would've.

Leaping from the ladder, she asked her pilot what he had done to save them.

Gripping the horns of the ship's controls and studying the sudden activity of all the gauges before him, Reddleman said, "Ah! Well, I activated the levitator."

"You keep saying that like I know what it is. What is a levitator?" Edith stepped over bodies, picking a path to the pilot's console.

"A means for repelling gravity!" he said merrily. "It's sort of a balloon in a bottle, or a cloud in a fist."

"Are you telling me this ship can fly without an envelope? Without hydrogen?"

"Indeed it can, Captain. And I'm happy to explain the technology to you in as much detail as you like. *Or...*"

Edith leaned over his shoulder, her mouth hanging open as her gaze swept over the bank of watch-faced dials and all the quivering needles and winking lights. "Or what?"

"Or I could take us back to port and give you a chance to return fire."

Byron clambered to his feet and said, "They were all in on the decision, Captain. Eigengrau, Pepin, Leonid. I heard them planning it. This was a premeditated act of war."

"It's a war crime, in fact, isn't it, Captain? Lancing a ship's silks like that?" Reddleman said.

The frame in front of her showed a view of the Tower's facade. Even by dim moonlight, she still recognized the charmless blocks of stone, the crumbling mortar, and bolted-on coops. The ship had fallen as low as the Parlor. They were close enough for her to discern that not all of the cages were empty. She thought of Senlin, how they'd sat on her skirts like picnickers sharing a blanket and talked about their lives as if they understood them.

She couldn't tell whether the wire pens held corpses or the detained living, still waiting to be told by some dupe, some actor, whether they would be maimed or released.

She looked forward to playing the arbiter for a change. "All right, gentlemen, let's show these Pells what sixty-four guns and no mercy can do to a port."

Eigengrau knew the moment he saw the corpulent prince lumbering down the gangplank of the *Ararat* that Pepin was coming to gloat. The general had insisted once or twice during the preparations for his boarding of the Sphinx's flagship that they wouldn't have to scuttle the ship. There'd be no need to put such a black mark on the port's record. It wouldn't come to that. With a squad of able men and the benefit of surprise, he would have no trouble prying that oyster from its shell.

Of course, when he'd said that, he'd expected to be confronted by human troops or Wakemen at the worst, not immortal devils and an iron hulk. He hadn't even seen a glimpse of Captain Winters. Perhaps she'd been sitting in her stateroom sipping brandy the entire time. If that was the case, then she got what she deserved.

Pepin was out of breath by the time he had jogged down the pier, around the main dock, and over to the guardhouse where Eigengrau waited. As soon as he saw the general was drinking something short and strong out of a tumbler, the crown prince demanded a draught of his own. The watchmen didn't have another glass to offer the royal, and so he had to make do with drinking directly from their dented flask. He smirked at the general even as he sucked away like a hungry calf. When he stopped for breath, the flask was nearly empty, and his chin was wet.

"'We won't need you,' says he. 'I have it all in hand,' says he." A smile broadened the crown prince's already wide face. "Good thing I don't listen to you, Eigengrau."

"Obviously, Your Highness, I am now and will eternally be grateful for your timely intervention," the general replied drolly. He managed a short bow, despite his wound. The physician still hadn't arrived, but the brandy was playing a fair nurse in the meantime. "It's only a pity I couldn't save her."

"Yes. I look forward to rubbing your nose in that for years and years to come. You know the old Gold Watch was on board," Pepin said, shaking the flask to listen to the rattle of the last sip.

"Was she?" Eigengrau crooked an eyebrow.

"My lookout saw her arrive with that Winters woman a couple hours ago. It's for the best, really. Can't declare war on the master and keep peace with his dog." The prince drained the last from the watchman's flask. "Never liked her anyway. Too high on herself. You know, she once nearly broke my hand for stroking that breastplate of hers. As if she could feel anything. I hear she wasn't golden to her toes though, if you know what I mean." The prince winked at the general, who looked unamused. "I would've liked to have seen th—"

The *State of Art* rose over the horizon of the port, robbing the crown prince of his revelry. The ship seemed to float on a bed of red light. The air beneath the hull churned and flashed like a sunset on a rough sea. It made a hum that the men of the port felt in the pits of their stomachs.

Without need for silk or the assistance of wind, the Sphinx's ax-headed warship seemed to slide through the air. It was a bird without wings, a spear without weight. The ship positioned itself over the second pier between the port guns and the black cake of the *Ararat* and before either could rouse their gunners, fired its first barrage.

The sixty-four cannons cracked as one, the barrel flash brightened by the night. The crenelated ramparts of the *Ararat* shattered, the broken teeth of the ship's defenses shredding the men who took shelter behind them. The main hatch, stout as a city gate, cracked in half. The force of the blows swung the *Ararat* on its tethers. Though not one shot struck its envelopes, the rigging to one of its three immense balloons began to lose its anchoring as iron cleats vanished with the passage of a cannonball. The mighty warship began to list. The hull swung out from the end of the pier, then back again, cracking upon the stout beams of the dock like a wrecking ball.

Then the *State of Art* fired a second volley. The cabins inside the *Ararat* were blown open and exposed to the wind. The ship tilted like a pitcher, and poured its contents out: cots, kegs, boots, rifles, charts, and men. The deep-seated furnace broke from its moorings, spilling its coals, which tumbled down among the barrels of black powder in the orlop below. The explosion roared like a rockslide as the once formidable beams and stringers of the *Ararat* turned to slag. Above, the titanic envelopes became a trinity of flame. The fireball licked the fins of the *State of Art*, which glowed with the light like a blade in a forge. The unlucky barges that were tied in port did not escape the rain of flaming debris. Their silks went up like guncotton, and their hulls fell like stones.

When the smoke drifted clear, a full third of the port was gone. And though it would be reported differently in days to come, the *Ararat* had never fired a shot.

While the *State of Art*'s starboard guns turned the *Ararat* into a cloud, the port guns attacked the lead soldiers. The turrets stood no chance, though one or two of them got a shot off. Their twenty-pound balls rang the steel hull of the warship, but did not break it. The guns of the *State of Art* had more luck. They beat the armored turrets onto their backs. The guardhouses fell as readily as tented napkins. The palms shattered into splinters and fronds, leaving behind bare bowls of earth. The sweeping, regal steps to the ringdom were marred by craters and falling wreckage. What wasn't on fire was buried in ash.

The second Eigengrau saw the *State of Art* reappear, he began to run. The crown prince was too slow to recognize a devil ship when he saw one. But he hadn't been aboard the cursed thing, hadn't seen her diabolical miracles. Eigengrau had. And so, when the *State of Art* popped up again like a submerged cork, he did not stand and gape and wait to understand. He fled.

Out of the corner of his eye, Eigengrau saw the crown prince trip and fall at his first retreating step. The pier where the royal flopped was a second later chopped up by mortar fire, leaving little doubt about the man's fate. *Good riddance*, Eigengrau thought. He reached the city steps even as they began to explode about him. Chips of marble pelted his cheeks and neck as he climbed. He dashed through the wrought iron gates, chiming with their destruction, and into the train tunnel.

He was going deaf for sure. The blast of the guns behind him popped as gaily as bottles of champagne. The air was clearer in the tunnel, and yet he realized he still struggled to catch his breath. The loss of blood was catching up with him. His head swam; his feet began to cross and tangle beneath him. He wondered if perhaps the brandy hadn't been a mistake.

The concourse beside the vacant tracks was deserted except for a pacing governess who seemed to be clutching a child in her arms. His eyesight had begun to falter too because the woman looked stretched out and overlarge. Eigengrau shouted as he approached that it was not safe to be there, that the city was under attack. Even in his own ears, his voice sounded like the last volley of an echo. It wasn't until he came a little nearer that he realized she really was immense.

Then he recognized her. She had come aboard the *State of Art*.

Rethinking his decision to engage, he swerved his path, intending to step down to the level of the tracks. He didn't expect to be kicked from behind. The boot struck him at the base of his spine. The force of the blow surprised him. He fell awkwardly to his knees, the wound in his shoulder stinging more sharply. Before he could rise, he saw that she had leapt down after him, still clutching the child to her chest. Her face reminded him of a gargoyle: an expression of rage and madness. He hadn't long to study it before she kicked him under the chin. The blow lifted him into the air and threw him onto his back. A new pain flared as he realized he had landed with his neck on one of the cold iron rails.

The image of the lady's bootheel careening down at him was dimmed a little by his blurry vision and the denial in his heart. Surely a man of his record and station deserved a less ignominious end. Even a filthy hod was paid the respect of a public execution! To be stomped to death by a nanny was an insult to his very humanity!

It was, at least, the last insult the general ever endured.

On the blood-splashed bridge of the *State of Art*, Edith and her crew watched as the few surviving port guards dashed and crawled up the ringdom steps. Their retreat was illuminated by the small fires that had broken out across the formerly immaculate wharf. Edith was deliberating on whether to finish demolishing what remained of Port Virtue—her preference was to scrape it from the face of the Tower so completely there was not a pimple of it left—when Byron spotted someone bucking the retreating traffic. He recognized her at once and shouted to cease fire.

Iren hurried down the steps. She cradled a bundle in her arms. The sight of her swaddled cargo filled Edith with dread. Leaving Reddleman to pilot the ship low enough to reach the shattered remnant of the dock, she and Byron rushed to the main hatch. They hardly had it open before Iren leapt aboard. Edith had never seen Iren look frightened before, and they had witnessed some fearful things together. Her expression seemed to confirm her worst fears.

Iren carried Voleta to the nearest stateroom and laid her gently on the bed. The cloak she had carried her in was stained with a halo of blood. Byron sobbed when he saw her, saw the wound under her chin, the purple tinge of her lips, the tallow-like aspect of her skin. Edith was sure she was dead.

And yet Iren insisted she was not, because she was still breathing. Or she had been breathing until very recently. She was not dead, but someone had to do something, and do it now!

"I'll fetch a doctor. At gunpoint if I have to," Edith said. She was about to march through the cabin door when she found Reddleman filling it.

He had a leather case in his hand and a smile on his face. "May I have a look at her?"

"What are you doing off the bridge?" Edith asked.

"I brought the medical kit. I had the opportunity to learn a thing or two about human physiology while I was coalescing in the Sphinx's crystal chamber. I know we both can fire the cannons, Captain, but how are you with taking vitals?"

Edith glared at him. He looked like a ghoul in his gory vest. He wasn't wrong, but she also didn't believe he had a single empathetic bone in his body. His sudden interest in Voleta was unnerving.

But he was not wrong. There was nothing she could do here, and the bridge could not stand unattended. Edith looked to Iren, and the sight of the amazon gave her some comfort. There could be no safer hands to leave Voleta in than hers. If Reddleman meant to do the cub harm, he'd have to get past the mother bear first. Edith had no doubt Iren would defend her to the end.

Still, she hated the decision even as she made it. Standing in the doorway, Edith said, "Save her if you can, pilot. That's an order."

"Aye, sir!" Reddleman cried and gave a merry salute.

Iren felt as if she had expended just a spark of her anger upon the big man's head. A much greater fire blazed inside of her. That moment of viciousness on the train tracks hadn't so much assuaged her rage as it had confirmed a fact: If Voleta died, Iren would grieve through violence, the likes of which the Tower had never seen.

But of course, Voleta would not die. She could not. She had to live.

Dropping his case into a chair beside the bed, Reddleman opened and extracted a stethoscope. He plugged the tips into his ears, blew on the diaphragm to test it, then set it upon Voleta's narrow chest. Iren did not breathe as he listened. He picked up Voleta's wrist and held it delicately. He felt her neck, then peeled back her eyelids to examine her eyes.

As he wrapped up the stethoscope, the pilot said, "I'd say she died about ten minutes ago. Maybe fifteen."

Iren grabbed Reddleman by his arms and lifted him from his feet. She held him close to her face and tried to stare past his stupid, merry gaze down to whatever idiotic, addled mind he had left. She said, "You were dead. The Sphinx saved you. You can do something. I know you can. Do it, do it now, or I will tear you into so many pieces not even the Sphinx will be able to put you back together." She shook him hard to punctuate her point.

"Wait, all right, hold on!" Reddleman's eyes rolled in his head from the shaking, but his smile beamed on just the same. With his nose pressed against Iren's nose, he said, "I can save her. If you could just put me down."

The moment Iren released him, he returned to his satchel and extracted a fat syringe and one of the Sphinx's scarlet vials.

"Why did you have that in there?" Byron asked.

"Call it a treatment of last resort," Reddleman said. Jabbing the needle through the cap and into the glowing fluid, he drew the medium up into the syringe.

"I'm getting the captain," Byron said.

"No!" Iren shouted. One foot in the passageway, Byron stopped and looked back at her, his eyes wide. She scowled at the floor, searching the ancient maze of the carpet for an answer it did not possess. She thought of the curse Edith had once mentioned in the presence of the Sphinx: the curse of unintended consequences. Then she thought of the head of the tall man crumpling under her boot, how good it felt, and how full the Tower was of heads.

"Iren, think about what you're doing," the stag said.

Holding the full syringe upright, Reddleman emptied out the air, clicking the tube with his fingernail. "You know, if I wanted to kill her, I'm running a little late."

They watched Reddleman administer the shot. Iren winced as the needle pierced Voleta's neck, and then stood in a state of dwindling hope as nothing seemed to happen.

Iren asked the Red Hand if he had any more of the infernal vials. He said he did, of course. He prepared and gave a second shot to Voleta, who lay like a ghost on top of the dark bedspread.

"How many are you going to give her?" Byron asked, kneading his hands.

"As many as he has. As many as it takes," Iren said.

After the fifth shot, they began to observe a change in Voleta's complexion. The lobes of her ears began to show a little pink, and the purple around her mouth lightened. The sockets of her eyes, which seemed to have receded into pits, began to plump again.

Then she drew a breath. Her back bowed and her chest swelled with the resurgence of her life. Iren pushed Reddleman out of her way. She cupped Voleta's face in her hands and called down to the young woman to wake up. To open her eyes. To come back to her.

Though Voleta continued to breathe and blush with life, she did not wake. She did not stir a second time.

And so, Iren's vigil began.

Chapter Seventeen

Some men spend their days pretending to be distinct,
assured, or enigmatic. But in death, they are all as
guileless as infants. In death, we are ourselves at last.

—*I Sip a Cup of Wind* by Jumet

No one slept that night. As the fires of the port burned themselves out, the crew of the *State of Art* lined the bodies of the fallen soldiers before the ringdom steps. They handled them with as much care as they could, using bedsheets to cover their pale faces.

Edith was at a loss for what to do with Georgine. She kept recalling her words about the ringdom's fondness for pretty corpses. She had no intention of exposing Haste as a zealot—there was nothing to be gained from tarnishing her name now—but even so, she scarcely believed she could trust the ringdom to pay their Wakeman the respect she deserved. Though how could she bury or cremate Georgine without inadvertently turning her into treasure? The thought of grave robbers digging Haste up to shake her bones from her breastplate or panning through her ashes for gold filled Edith with rage. The problem of Haste's final resting place occupied her thoughts through the night.

Three of the men whose brains Reddleman had needled had not yet perished, though they were capable only of moaning and drooling and very little else. Reddleman wished to keep them for what he called "harmless experimentation," but Edith would not hear of it. Since the mindless men could still walk on their own, albeit in a loose, wandering gait, Edith released them into the train tunnel. She did not stay to observe them shuffle numbly back to their city. She did not want to see the expressions on the faces of their families when they reunited with the ambling ghosts of their sons, brothers, husbands.

If the Sphinx hoped to reform his reputation for being a boogeyman, Reddleman seemed determined to claim the label for himself.

Edith detested her pilot almost as much as she needed him.

Byron attacked the gore on the floors, walls, and ceiling of the bridge with a mop, bucket, and a string of oaths, all of them directed at Reddleman, who surely could've conducted a tidier slaughter. Any gratitude the stag felt toward the pilot for saving the ship and all aboard was depleted by the time he had to change the mop water for the tenth rinse.

The first thing Byron did after Reddleman injected the medium into Voleta was to send a message to the Sphinx. He reported the attack, Haste's betrayal, and Voleta's terrible ordeal. This, in spite of not hearing anything from his master in nearly thirty-six hours. Something was definitely wrong. But then, many things were wrong. It had been a mistake, surely, to send the Red Hand with them, a mistake to leave the homestead so empty, a mistake to visit such a hateful port under the rule of such an anemic king.

At the moment, the only thing holding back the tide of panic inside Byron was the near infinite mess and his determination to make things sparkle again.

When Byron saw the utter devastation of the captain's stateroom— the shattered glass, gouged paintings, and spurts of oil and blood on the carpet—he threw down his mop in protest and briefly considered locking himself in his room. But there was too much work to be done, and no time to pout about it.

In the wee hours of the morning, Byron called everyone to the gun deck to help him shift the fallen Ferdinand. Iren took a break from her watch at Voleta's bedside long enough to help sit the automaton upright. The revelation that the Sphinx's doorman was piloted by an old hound disturbed and saddened them all—everyone except Reddleman. The maudlin pilot found the manner in which the dog had been tethered to the engine a point of fascination and said that he wished he could've performed a vivisection on the augmented beast. Byron told the pilot he would happily trade ten of him for one Ferdinand.

And yet, Byron could not give Ferdinand the respect he deserved without the pilot's help. As Reddleman assisted, Byron uncoupled the hound from the engine, separating tendon from cable, bone from piston. After an hour's work, they at last laid the gray-muzzled hound upon a quilt on the gun deck floor. Even with the blood on his jowls and mechanical mounts bulging from his fur, Ferdinand looked almost serene, almost ordinary. Somehow, that made the loss all the more unbearable.

Knowing he had to say something, and that he of anyone there was in the best position to articulate Ferdinand's life, Byron gave a brief but sincere eulogy in which he described the hound's love of frolicking, his loathing of carpets, and his absolute courage in the face of much uglier monsters.

Bryon and Edith carried him out to the port in their joined arms. Using split decking for fuel, they built a small pyre in one of the treeless planters. As the birds began to pipe their bright morning song, a tune Byron thought Ferdinand would've enjoyed, they committed his body to the flames.

It was fair to say that Edith was alarmed by what had been done to Voleta in an effort to revive her. It hadn't been two weeks since Edith had aided in Adam's escape in an effort to save him from her master's gifts. With Voleta away from the Sphinx's side, Edith had thought the young woman finally safe from his influence. How wrong she'd been.

If Edith had been present when the decision was made, she doubted she would've allowed Reddleman to inject Voleta with the Sphinx's medium, and certainly not as many vials as he did. Considering how violent small intravenous doses had made the Red Hand while he served as the Baths' Wakeman, and how aloof and strange Reddleman had become since his spine was suffused with the stuff, Edith wasn't at all certain that, even if the treatment were successful, it would be Voleta who returned to them. The Blood of Time warped conscience and personality in unpredictable ways.

When Edith stared down at the young woman tucked like a doll in her bed, her lips and eyelids glowing with a ruby light, she wondered if it might not be for the best if she never woke again.

Edith was certain of one thing: Iren would never have let her stop Reddleman from giving her the injections. No, the amazon would've snatched the moon out of the sky, chewed it up, and made a poultice of it if she'd thought it might bring Voleta back. As abhorrent as the result might ultimately be, Edith's opinion on it was moot, and she was privately grateful that she had not been there to make an impossible decision more difficult.

Edith could've used the amazon's help but knew better than to ask. Voleta's coma effectively chained Iren to her side. That left Edith with little choice but to put Byron in charge of the bridge and take Reddleman on a brief but necessary excursion into the city. The plan made Byron unhappy, but Edith didn't think they had anything more to fear from the Pelphians. The *State of Art* had decimated the ringdom's greatest warship and proved herself superior to the city's defenses, and her crew had demonstrated the limit of their patience. Attacking her captain now would be tantamount to suicide.

Edith donned a formal coat, her beloved weathered tricorne, and a new saber and sidearm. Reddleman protested when Byron presented him with a fresh uniform, complaining of the fit, which he insisted did not accommodate his figure. Byron said the pilot couldn't walk around naked as an apple core, and Reddleman asked if perhaps a bathrobe might not suffice. Then Edith, who was not in a compromising mood, said that he would wear the uniform and a gag along with it if he uttered one more word of complaint.

They disembarked and were nearly through the tunnel to the ringdom when they happened upon one of Reddleman's mindless victims. The imbecilic soldier sat cross-legged on the tracks. He stared up at the tiled ceiling with his mouth hanging open.

"Why did you do that to them?" Edith asked without breaking stride.

"I was trying to be helpful, Captain. I thought you could do with a crew of four or five more like me. I wish you hadn't released them. I could've brought them back around."

Reddleman made the confession breezily enough, though it filled Edith with dread. "Is that what you did to Voleta? Try to bring her around? Make her like you?"

"*I* didn't shoot the girl. I only did what your first mate told me to do. And if you wish to undo it, I'm sure you know how," Reddleman said.

Edith was about to tell him how repugnant he was, how if Voleta recovered, he would never be allowed to poison her spirit or twist her thoughts. Edith wished to tell him that she looked forward to the day when she could be rid of him forever, preferably by dropping him into an active volcano. Then they emerged from the tunnel upon a vacant city, and the rebuke died on her lips.

The streets were utterly deserted. The music halls and theaters were silent, their lamps turned as low as embers. The burlesque barkers had taken in their footstools and barred their doors. The roofs were all as bare as mountaintops. Edith had not known the city had so many curtains, blinds, and shutters until that moment. Above them, the gas jets of the sun guttered amid the quiet—a shushing librarian in an empty archive.

"Do you think it's a trap?" Reddleman asked.

"No, I think it's a surrender."

When they came upon the first Will-o'-the-Wisp, unlit and jutting from the cobblestones of a lane, Edith thought it only a by-product of the empty streets: No one had been out to ride the screw down into the underground. Then they turned onto a wide street that ran like a spoke to the plaza, and she realized it wasn't just one Will-o'-the-Wisp that had popped up. It appeared to be all of them. As far as the eye could see, the bronzy columns stood out from the ground like prairie dogs.

She thought it unlikely that all of those Will-o'-the-Wisps would have been tripped overnight. She ducked into one of the open booths and sat down. The door did not close behind her. She plunged the switch to reset the circuit and start the downward spiral, but nothing happened. She repeated the process twice. The column remained unlit and motionless. Even the mirror inside seemed dead and ordinary.

"Do you smell smoke?" Reddleman asked. Edith said the fumes of the port fires had probably just wafted inside, but the pilot appeared unconvinced.

The plaza was no less desolate. Here and there, sedan chairs lay abandoned on their sides. Dropped gloves and lost slippers lay amid a muddle of broken glass and cigar ends. The scores of Will-o'-the-Wisps were all exposed here, too, their capitals acting as perches for birds. Indeed, it seemed a colorful flock had alighted on the plaza, taking advantage of the stillness. A big yellow-breasted parrot dominated the stack nearest them. When they passed under it, the bird threw out its turquoise wings and cried, "Come the Hod King! Come the Hod King!" The phrase reverberated across the plaza, increased by the throats of a hundred other macaws all shouting at the uninhabited streets. Though it seemed a petty sort of terrorism, the furor still made Edith's skin crawl.

"Look!" Reddleman said, pointing to a tendril of smoke rising over the green silk hedge of the Circuit of Court. They found the whorled iron gates hanging open. Inside, the animals of the desert carousel hung frozen in midleap, their parade around the white pyramid at an end. The smoke came from the monument's darkened door. The gold letters above its lintel were now coated with soot. Reddleman asked, "What does that mean: 'The Unfinished Birth'?"

Edith didn't answer, her attention absorbed by the bodies that were gathered about the pyramid's entrance. There were four of them, gray haired and bald from age, their bodies tangled together in evidence of their attempts to save one another. She recognized Luis Osmore's narrow frame among them. The Deputy-Wakeman had died clutching his blue kepi over his mouth. The cap was stained black from smoke.

"Some sort of skirmish, I suppose," Reddleman said, but Edith shook her head and pointed at the holstered sidearms of the dead men. Not a one had drawn his gun.

"No, this was something else," she said, looking around at the eerie empty court—the lifeless fountains and the false greenery. "This looks like sabotage."

They were still climbing the two-toned steps of the piebald palace when the massive doors creaked open. King Leonid squeezed through the crack, holding the door open behind him with one hand. With the other, he clutched the front of his housecoat at the neck as if to fend off a chill. He looked like a man who'd been drummed out of bed to deal with an unexpected guest late in the night.

"I don't have the Sphinx's painting!" the king snapped. "You must know by now that I don't! It was lost or stolen, or I don't know what—but it's gone." The king looked past Edith at the Red Hand. Leonid seemed to recognize the former Wakeman of the Baths at once. Reddleman smiled, licking the front edge of his teeth. The king shuddered. "Do you want gold? Is that what all of this has been about? Money? Are we being held hostage?"

"You attacked us, Your Majesty," Edith said coolly.

"And you killed my brother and my general. You scuttled my warship and bombed my court. The city may never recover."

"Don't act like you're the victim of some injustice here, Leonid. You picked a fight and lost. And we had nothing to do with bombing your court."

The king lifted his chin, as if he might drive her off with indignation. "You expect me to believe you weren't working with the zealots?"

"Is that what happened?" Edith asked, refusing the king's bait. She hadn't come to entertain his excuses nor defend her actions. They were past such things now.

"Don't pretend you don't know! There were witnesses who saw the little hod climb into the Will-o'-the-Wisp with a gunnysack, and not ten minutes later, a bomb goes off, and there's a fire underground. Before you came, the Hod King was just whispers. Now the birds are shrieking the name in the street!"

"Obviously, Marat's agents took advantage of your preoccupation with trying to commandeer my ship. But if I was on their side, if I wanted to see an end to your reign, I would finish the job now."

Whatever hubris the king had managed to bring to his door seemed to drain from him. His neck appeared to shrink into his robe. "What do you want?"

Edith had expected him to invite her in to hear her demands, but she was perfectly content to deliver them on his stoop. "I have three requirements. First, I want your word that the brawlers from the Colosseum will not be harmed. You have a jail; use it. You will close the arena and will stop sending up hods to prod your sun. And no more executions, public or otherwise. You are stoking the fires of a war you are not prepared to fight."

The king nodded feebly. "All right."

"Second, you will send a courier to my ship within the hour and deliver every image of the Hod King diagram that your photographer took. Then you will erase the blackboards, seal up the library, and place it under guard."

"But you must promise to defend my ringdom if the hods bring that engine here. I've seen its dimensions. It's enormous. Some of my scholars think it might be capable of chewing through stone." The pleading edge in his voice did not recall any of his prior performances. Edith wondered if she was at last speaking to the man behind the act.

"We will protect every ringdom that deserves our protection," Edith said, which scarcely seemed to placate the king. "And third, I'm entrusting you with the body of Wakeman Georgine Haste. I want her interred in a mausoleum that is guarded around the clock. Put her in your own tomb if you have to. I will return to pay my respects, and if her body or her engine have been interfered with in any way, I will see you buried in an unmarked grave in the desert—preferably while still alive."

"She will be looked after." Leonid struggled to look her in the eye.

When he did at last meet her gaze, she gave him an acknowledging if unfriendly smile. "Good. Oh, and one more thing. I need an address."

*   *   *

The butler who received Edith and Reddleman said they could not see the duke without an appointment, and certainly not before lunch. Edith put her hand on the door and pressed her way in without a word of further debate. The servant hurried away to tell his master of the intrusion, even as Edith and Reddleman wandered through to the parlor of Duke Wilhelm Pell's home.

Unlike many nobles, the duke did not share a ceiling or wall with anyone else. His three-story residence boasted a private courtyard and a fountain and employed a staff of nine. Outside of the king's palace, it was considered one of the most lavish homes in the ringdom.

Edith had always felt that there was a certain point at which the cleanliness and order of a room veered from tidiness into tyranny. Such was the case here. The velvet sofa had been brushed and the cushions plumped; the bookshelves stood devoid of gaps and gewgaws; the end tables were empty of anything so shameful as a saucer or a newspaper. And even so, the immense grandfather clock that loomed upon the wall between bay windows seemed to tut-tut the imperfections of the room: Was that a hair on the ottoman? Was there a cinder smoldering on the fire grate? Was that a scuff on the molding?

Initially, Edith didn't even see the maid who was down on her hands and knees combing the tasseled fringe of a rug. The woman's uniform was immaculately pressed and a cheerful white, but she had the bleak expression of someone accustomed to wartime. The moment the two observed each other, the maid stood, curtsied, and fled.

"What are we doing here, Captain?" Reddleman asked.

"Helping out a friend," Edith said, and then hearing a commotion approaching from an adjoining room, added, "Be ready with your sidearm."

The duke burst into the parlor in a housecoat and slippers. Even in his disheveled morning state, Edith could see he was a handsome man. His hair was as tawny as a gosling, and his eyes were as bright as chips of lapis lazuli. His high cheeks above the perfect line of his beard were blushed with anger. "How dare you! How *dare* you! You can't barge into my home like this. I am a Lord Duke of Pelphia!"

Edith did not react to the mention of his title. "I'm not here for you. I've come to speak with your wife."

The demand appeared to catch Duke Wilhelm off guard, though he was quick enough to cover his surprise with disdain. He tightened the belt of his dark robe and said, "Absolutely not."

A woman with unbrushed auburn hair and fine features peered from behind the door the duke had lately come by. She wore a morning gown, ruffled about the collar, and a headband, both a pale shade of lavender.

When the duke noticed her, he said, "Darling, go back to your room, please. I'm dealing with some trespassers. I've already sent my man to fetch a constable."

"Marya." Edith could not keep the awe from her voice. She recognized Senlin's wife at once; she looked more like the poisoned painting he had carried than Edith would've expected, and yet she was shocked by how different Marya seemed, too. In all of Senlin's stories, she had been full of a sort of contagious vivacity, an impish joy, and boundless confidence. In the painting, she had projected an unabashed self-possession, which was more arresting than her nakedness.

Now, she seemed anything but self-possessed. She looked timid and haunted and ready to bolt. Dark circles underscored her eyes. Her gaze flew again and again to the duke, even though he wasn't facing her. Without looking, he pointed at the door like a man commanding an old dog from the room, and she began to withdraw. Edith called to her, "Marya. Please, wait. I'm not here to hurt you, and I will leave if you ask. But I need to speak to you for one moment first."

This direct address seemed to embolden her a little. Gathering her courage, Marya took two steps into the room, a movement that brought the duke's head around quick enough. The lower half of her arms were bare, and when she reached up to tuck a strand of hair under the crocheted band, Edith saw the dark bracelets of bruised flesh.

Marya said, "You're the girl's friend, aren't you? The one with the cropped hair."

"Yes, I am." Edith pulled her cocked hat from her head.

"What are you talking about, Marya?" The duke spoke at twice her volume, his voice pitching higher with annoyance. "This woman is responsible for destroying our port and murdering a score of young men in their prime. She is a fanatic! She is the reason we're all stuck indoors. And she is leaving! Now, please, go to your room!"

Edith ignored the duke's interruption, saying, "I'm a friend of Tom, too."

"Are you?" Hope and sorrow seemed to fight over Marya's expression.

"Yes. I met him just days after he lost you. He's been looking for you ever since."

"He found me." Marya looked over her shoulder as if she expected someone to be there. For a moment, Edith thought she would leave, but then she came back around and said, "But I fobbed him off. I told him to go away. I was..." She glanced at the duke.

"Perhaps you were afraid," Edith said. "I don't blame you if you were. I'm sure Tom doesn't blame you either. You have every reason to be afraid. Your husband is a dangerous man and your position here is tenuous."

"Now, see here, you ugly doxy—" the duke began.

"If you speak again, my pilot will escort you out of the room," Edith said, pointing at the duke with her engine. The duke glanced at the potbellied officer, and Reddleman waved at him like a schoolboy. Edith continued to address Marya: "I know your husband has fooled a lot of people into thinking he is likeable, or at least decent. He fooled Senlin, too, at least for a time. Tom was always trusting. I have benefitted from his faith in people, but I do not share it." Her thoughts flickered to Georgine, bleeding to death on the floor of her cabin. "Certainly not anymore. Here is what I believe: I believe the duke took advantage of you when you were desperate. He kidnapped you and called it a rescue. He isolated you and removed every option you had until you could not even think of escape, not even when the opportunity presented itself. I think you were trying to protect Tom from the duke. I don't think that makes you weak or him strong. It makes you a casualty of a careless city and an impotent coward."

The duke lunged at an end table, flung the drawer open, and drew out a pistol. As he spun around with it, Reddleman picked him up at the hip and shoulder, hoisted him up like a dumbbell, and flung him through a bay window. The sound of shattering glass, cracking wood, and tearing curtains almost drowned out the duke's undignified yelp. Almost.

Dusting his hands, Reddleman turned to see the startled expressions of the two women in the room. "Should I have used the door?"

"The window's fine," Edith said. "Marya, I know you told Senlin you were happy here. I suspect you told Voleta the same thing. But I want you to tell me. Are you here because you wish to be? Is this the life you want?"

Marya continued to gape a moment longer at the shattered remnant of the window that had swallowed her husband, but soon she stirred from her shock and said in a stronger voice, "No. No, I don't like this life at all. He's an absolute maniac. This place is a prison. But he'll kill us if I cross him, he'll kill—"

"No, he won't," Edith said. "I won't let him. If you want to leave, we'll go this instant. I have a ready ship and plenty of room."

"And Tom?" Marya squeezed her hands till the knuckles whitened.

"We'll worry about Tom next. Let's take care of you first," Edith said.

Marya's chin rose with resolve. "All right. Yes. Yes, please take me with you. I want to go. Just let me get—"

The duke dashed into the room and fired his pistol before he'd cleared the threshold. The shot caught Reddleman in the shoulder and turned him on his heel. Edith drew and returned fire almost as quickly. Her shot hit the duke in the thigh, knocking his leg out from under him. He fell to the floor with a pained shout.

Edith looked to Marya, her hands cupped over her mouth in shock, and said, "As soon as you're ready."

"I'll just be a moment," Marya said, and left the parlor in a rush.

Edith asked her pilot if he was all right. Reddleman laughed and declared the newest hole in his person hardly a nick. Considering how quickly he'd recovered from being skewered by a sword, Edith wasn't concerned. She wouldn't be rid of him that easily.

She strode to the hissing duke, his face contorted with agony, and knelt down beside him. He clutched at his thigh, pressing the skirt of his housecoat against the darkly seeping wound. Edith threw his pistol out into the foyer. "Let's talk about Thomas Senlin," she said in a tone that seemed to suggest they were settling down for a nice chat in the snug of a public house. "I need you to confirm a few things for me. I suspect that you turned Tom into a hod, put a blinder on his head, and set him on the black trail. Is that right?"

"I will see you pinned to the Wall of Recompense, you tin-armed harlot!" the duke spat back at her.

"Will you?" she said, pulling his hand away from where it clutched his wound. Her iron fingers enclosed his hand completely. "Perhaps I should pose it as a question: Did you make Tom a hod and put a blinder on his—"

"Yes!" the duke shouted in her face. "Yes, I put the mudder's head in a can and threw him on the trail! I did it days ago. He's dead already!"

"I see," Edith said.

The sound of snapping bones was quickly drowned out by the duke's screams. He tried to kick and struggle away from her, but the more he fought, the more she squeezed until at last he lay flat on his back pleading with her to stop. She lightened her grip and said, "Give me your other hand." He sniveled and shook his head, so she resumed her pressures.

When she observed the duke's blood running between the black billets of her hand, Edith felt nothing. She thought of Tom lying dead in some unlit tunnel with his head entombed and his body uncovered. Even that awful vision seemed only to expand the numbness inside her.

Not so long ago, Tom had shared his fear that the pirate life was ruining Voleta, was transforming the once callow girl into a ruthless woman. He blamed the change upon friction, the abrasions of hardship, violence, and loss, a friction that toughened tender skin into unfeeling callus.

As Edith watched herself coolly torture the duke, she realized it was too late for her. The callus she'd built up to protect herself had spread too deep. It had touched her heart and turned it as hard as a horn.

The shrieking duke stuck out his unbroken hand.

She took it up and said, "I've lived with the use of only one hand. I can tell you, it is not easy. Some days you will wake up angry, and you will go to bed wanting to weep from frustration." She regarded the quaking tips of his fingers protruding from her iron grasp. "But, I think, even at its worst, living with the use of one hand is better than surviving with none. Wouldn't you agree?" She paused long enough to listen to his bawled affirmations. "I've always preferred to shake hands when I give my word. So here's my promise to you, sir duke: If you ever make a single inquiry or cast so much as a shadow in Marya's direction, I will come back and squeeze the rest of you, one bone at a time. Does that sound fair to you? Are you willing to shake on that?" Edith spoke to him lightly, as if he were a pup. The duke nodded eagerly. She pumped his arm twice and said, "Good."

"I'm ready!" Marya called from the doorway. Edith turned to find her clutching a swaddled infant to her breast.

When Edith stood, it felt as if the room rose with her. It took all her concentration just to cross the open space. The floor pitched like a ship beneath her. "Who do you have there?" she asked.

"This is Olivet," Marya said, swaying the child in her arms. "She's mine. Mine and Tom's."

Marya peeled back the cover to show the infant, squinting with drowsiness and the newness of life.

"She's beautiful," Edith said in a hushed tone. Tears rose to her eyes. As she marveled at the child's face, Edith felt a wash of relief that she was not entirely desensitized to wonder and anguish.

Then she felt a new weight settle inside of her—the weight of errant hope and misplaced affection. The feeling was as heavy as her arm and, she knew, just as permanent.

Aboard the *State of Art*, Byron knocked lightly on the doorway of the great cabin where Iren watched over Voleta. The amazon overwhelmed the chair she sat upon, and yet she looked as small as Byron had ever seen her with her elbows on her knees and her face in her hands. Voleta, still tucked neatly under the covers, looked peaceful, but whether it was the serenity of death or slumber was difficult to say.

Iren looked up when she heard the knock, her eyes red and raw. Byron said, "There's someone outside who wants something. I thought she might go away, but she's been loitering for nearly half an hour. I really don't think I should be the one to answer the door. I'm sorry, but can you go see what she wants?"

Iren patted the bedspread where Voleta's hand was buried and stood with a grunt. "Stay with her. I'll be right back."

She took the holstered pistol off the coatrack by the door and went to see who was pacing in the port.

When she opened the hatch, the morning sun had added its flattering rouge to the devastation. A few braids of smoke were all that remained of the fires. At the bottom of their makeshift gangplank, a petite woman with her back to the ship stood between a suitcase and a covered birdcage.

Ann turned at the sound of the opening hatch and smiled tentatively up at Iren. "Good morning! It appears they've been doing some remodeling since last I was out. A touch extreme, but you know how wildly fashions swing." Ann's light tone nearly concealed the nervous quiver in her voice. "But, my goodness, you have a magic ship! Look at that. It just sort of floats there, doesn't it? Like ... like a needle on water. Very handsome! I'm sure it'll make all the other boats jealous."

Iren said nothing in reply as she strode down the bowing boards onto the charred pier. She stood before Ann, her arms hanging loose at her sides, a stormy expression on her face.

Ann dipped to pick up the sheathed cage and lifted up the hem of the cover to show Squit, curled up on a shawl inside. The squirrel's black eyes were wide with apprehension. "I realized that you and Lady Voleta left in such a hurry there wasn't time to retrieve her pet. So I thought I'd bring her to you."

Still, Iren said nothing. Ann swallowed and set the cage back down. She waved at the small suitcase at her hip. "I've recently found myself looking for new employment. I and the Lady Xenia have parted ways,

I would say *amicably*, but such a word would be both inaccurate and confusing to her, so instead, I'll say that I'm out on my ear and looking for work. I thought to ask whether you had any need of an experienced governess or a novice cabin boy." Ann saw the tears rising to the corners of Iren's eyes and her prattling faded. "Oh, Iren dear, what is it? What's happened?"

Iren fell to one knee and took Ann in an embrace that nearly consumed her. She began to weep, each sob ending in a shuddering gasp. Ann stroked her coarse hair, filled her ear with consoling murmurs, and waited for the long-deferred flood to crest.

Chapter Eighteen

Memory is not like a box of stationery—easy to browse, reorder, and read. No, memories accumulate like leaves upon the forest floor. They are irregular and fragile. They crumble and break upon inspection. They turn to soil the deeper you go.

—*I Sip a Cup of Wind* by Jumet

The darkest hours are behind us. Brighter days lie ahead. Everything will be all right.

Byron had found numerous applications for this mantra in the days since their departure from what remained of the Pelphian port. When he peeked in on his receiving cages in the Communications Closet and found them empty, he said, "The darkest hours are behind us." When he caught Reddleman stripped to his vest and dissecting a songbird on a dining room table in the middle of the night, Byron said, "Brighter days lie ahead." When he found the amazon ringing the bulkhead with her fist so fixedly she left a bloody spot on the steel, he said, "Everything will be all right."

Edith had inadvertently suggested the mantra shortly after they had bid a hasty retreat to home port. It seemed obvious to all that if anyone was capable of healing Voleta, it was the Sphinx. But when the *State of Art* presented herself before the seamless, secret gates near the Tower's summit and delivered a perfunctory flash of her signal lamps, nothing happened. And nothing continued to happen for the rest of the day into the evening.

The captain suggested that perhaps Henry, the Sphinx's walking port crane, was asleep. In response, Byron scoffed to hide his alarm and said, "Henry does not sleep! The motors that operate the gates do not sleep! The Sphinx does not sleep either!"

And yet, the gates remained shut.

Byron might've descended into a panic then if Edith had not been there to talk him down. She said, "All right. I admit, it is worrying. But you need to understand, Byron, this state of anxiety, this is how the rest of us have been living for quite a while. You aren't accustomed to being on this side of things. I am. And I can tell you, sometimes the Sphinx doesn't answer his door. Sometimes messages are slow to be delivered and slow to return. Sometimes his silence seems an answer in itself. But let's be reasonable. Perhaps the Sphinx is indisposed. Perhaps his machines were affected by the bomb in the Circuit of Court, and if that's the case, I'm sure he has his hands full with repairs. We both know he is capable of miracles, and I'm sure a stuck door is not beyond his powers to fix. And short of blasting his gates open, which I doubt we could manage even if we tried, there's nothing to be done but be patient. You'll keep sending your reports—I trust you have much to say—and we shall carry on with the work, because there's plenty to be done. We may not have our daily orders anymore, but we still have our mission. We're going to go ringdom to ringdom, in order and all the way up until we're told to do differently. The Wakemen are peacekeepers, so we will keep the peace. And Reddleman will continue to look after Voleta, and she will improve. We will take care of each other, and we will wait. The darkest hours are behind us. Brighter days lie ahead. Everything will be all right. You'll see."

Byron wasn't sure that he believed her, but he wanted to, and for the time being, that had to suffice.

Fortunately, there was no shortage of work to keep him occupied. The passenger list of the *State of Art* was growing. As far as Byron was concerned, that was a fine thing. He'd rather have a noisy ship to complain about than a lonesome quiet to stew in. He'd had enough of that to last a lifetime.

The first days after their uncelebrated departure from the Pelphian port were spent choosing cabins, touring the ship's amenities, unpacking what they had managed to bring aboard, and finding replacements for what they lacked. Byron showed the newcomers how to operate the oven range, how to talk between decks via the communication horns, and how to operate the electric lights, which the ladies found an astounding feature aboard an airship. Byron learned to dodge certain questions about the ship and the Sphinx, which he either could not or should not answer, at least not yet. And though every allusion to the Sphinx reinvigorated his anxiety, he was too busy to fret for long. There were meals to prepare, dishes to scrub, and an apparently endless procession of diapers to wash.

Byron liked Ann Gaucher at once. She was talkative and bright and eager to contribute to the work that had to be done. She seemed to make peace with his unusual appearance after hardly a pause, declaring him too charming and well dressed to be frightening. She took Reddleman's personality and unusual foibles in stride, and she praised Captain Winters as an obvious leader and a gracious host. Perhaps most incredibly, she raised Iren's spirits when nothing and no one else could. Were it not for Ann, Iren might've perished from exhaustion or malnourishment. It was Ann who brought her meals and made sure she ate them. It was Ann who dressed Iren's battered knuckles and convinced her to bathe. It was Ann who chased her off to bed for a few hours' sleep, and Ann who stayed at Voleta's bedside in her place.

Byron saw in the small governess a kindred spirit. She was a person who seemed content to sublimate her own needs in the service of others. It was a choice he could relate to.

Marya was more tentative in her engagements and more fragile in her moods, though taking into account her recent unwanted, abusive marriage, her abrupt divorce from her life, and her introduction to the queer world of the Sphinx, Byron could hardly fault her for it. To her credit, she was always grateful for his assistance in the care of her child, and she had done a fair job of not gawking at him, though Byron felt her lingering unease. When he caught her staring at him over the dinner table, Byron had suggested that perhaps it was his missing antler that was to blame for her ogling. While Marya blushed and apologized, Ann had hurried to suggest that the result was dashing enough. She said his one horn reminded her of the men who wore their hats at a tilt, an allusion that Byron liked quite well.

Still, underneath the fresh wounds of Marya's ordeal, Byron found every indication that she was a good person. When he informed Marya that the ship's comforts included a small harpsichord, she was so happy that she cast her cautions aside and hugged him. He had found the moment awkward, but not unwelcome.

Living with the Sphinx had not given him many opportunities to interact with infants—if one did not count pirate captains. Byron was finding the experience to be alternately fascinating and infuriating. At points, the child could be entertained with nothing more than a teaspoon, which she gripped and shook with all the gusto of a conductor amid his finale. But at other times, she could not be consoled by all the amusements in the world. Still, when Marya at last knew him well enough to let him hold little Olivet, Byron found the sight of the child's awed expression and probing gaze nothing short of enthralling.

At first, Marya had been vocally perplexed when, shortly after she climbed aboard, the *State of Art* cast off from Pelphia. Were they abandoning Tom so quickly? Hadn't the captain promised to look for him? Weren't they friends? But Edith took pains to explain her reasoning: The Old Vein threaded the walls of the Tower from base to spire and encompassed hundreds, perhaps thousands of miles; it was home to an uncertain number of murderous zealots who were difficult to distinguish from the hordes of innocent hods; and if she hoped to find one man in that maze of tunnels, she would need much, much more than the eagerness to do so. In the Tower, reunions required careful planning, more resources than they presently had at their disposal, a dash of good luck, and a great deal of patience. But Edith assured Marya, and all of them, that the search for Thomas Senlin would begin soon enough. If he could be found, she would find him.

In addition to looking after Iren, Ann seemed to have taken on

Voleta's recovery as something of a personal challenge. She prepared soup that Voleta could not eat, herbal tea she could not drink, applied hot compresses she did not appear to feel, and was not in the least discouraged by any of it. She insisted that the girl be read to or spoken to as often as possible and spent many hours at the young lady's bedside with a book in her hands. "We want to make sure she never feels alone," Ann explained. "Even if she doesn't seem to be listening, she might still hear us."

The idea inspired Byron to bring the ship's music box down from the conservatory, and to play some of the songs that he had tried to teach Voleta to dance by. In the young woman's stateroom, Byron gave a solo demonstration of the steps Voleta had once failed to absorb. He was delighted when Ann offered to join him. She proved to be a willing and capable partner. Iren observed their merriment with what Byron at first mistook for revulsion, though it turned out to be the amazon's version of envy. After a time, Iren asked Ann to show her the steps, and she delightedly obliged. Iren struggled to manage her feet as Ann encouraged her with directions and compliments. Voleta gave no indication that she was aware of them, the music, or their lively commotion, but Ann insisted it was all for the good: They danced for the same reason that Squit ran rings about Voleta's head—to fan the light that would lead her back from the darkness.

Reddleman continued to give Voleta injections of the Sphinx's glowing medium twice a day under much supervision. He took her vitals, too, and declared each time that though she did not appear to be improving, she was at least not getting any worse.

On the fourth evening after their departure from Pelphia, the *State of Art* docked at Port Crestal in the ringdom of Algez. Captain and pilot were welcomed ashore by the Algezian regent, Queen Wilhelmina Cassira. She seemed on the surface to be Leonid's opposite in all regards. Where he had been demonstrative, her demeanor was staid. Where his fashion had been extreme, hers was subdued. He was old, she young. And yet, Edith discerned quickly enough that the two rulers shared more subtle things in common. Both were cautious, both shrewd, and both happy to let their advisers say the difficult things they wished to have aired without the burden of voicing them. Queen Cassira received them at a long, ashen table of bonewood set under a flowering arbor and served them chilled mead made from the honey of the royal hives. She complimented both the Sphinx's ship and the mark it had left on the House of Pell.

But in addition to requesting the return of the Sphinx's painting, Captain Winters made it clear that despite Pelphia's weakened state, this was not the time to resume old conflicts. As she had with King Leonid, Edith alluded to the Sphinx's desire to distribute a new technology to the ringdoms that distinguished themselves as peace-loving and cooperative. The devastated Pelphian warship and the Sphinx's levitating flagship made the prospect of the Sphinx's new gifts virtually irresistible to Queen Cassira. Even while they shared a meal in the noonday light, she sent an envoy to retrieve the Sphinx's token from her private vault.

While the captain and pilot parlayed with Algezian royalty and Byron watched the proceedings from the bridge, Ann sat upon the foot of Voleta's bed reading a book of droning verse to an unresponsive audience. Midstanza, Iren interrupted her to ask, "Did you ever want to have children?"

"Me?" Ann said, closing the book with her finger still in it. "I had children. I had many. Xenia was the last, and I think she finished off my appetite for any more." Her cheeks puffed with an exasperated sigh. "Although that Olivet is the dearest little infant I've ever seen! I have to confess, that will always be my favorite age."

"But those are just the children you looked after. They weren't really your own, were they?"

"Why? Just because I didn't have them? Just because they didn't carry my physical traits or my family name? I've never put much stock in all that, really. Those children were as much mine as they were their mothers', who rarely spoke to them, rarely fed them, and never nursed them when they were ill. I knew their dreams and their fears. I could recognize a change in mood from across the room. I could tell what they were thinking just from a smirk." Ann kicked her legs as she sat, cheered by her memories. "It was a job, of course, but it was also a choice and a privilege and a passion. I adopted them all into my heart. Even Xenia." Ann was about to reopen the book when she stopped and asked, "But what about you, dear? Did you ever want children?"

"I did. It took me a long time to realize that I did—much longer than mattered." She looked down at her calloused palms, seeing the full history there that would always be inscrutable to anyone else. "Sometimes you don't know what you want until you can't have it anymore."

"Oh, don't be so grim! Come on! There's still time for love, dear; there's time for caring. There's time for doting and embracing until the very end."

"I did tell her that I loved her," Iren said, looking down at Voleta. "I'm glad I did."

"And you will have the chance to tell her again. Don't lose faith. Now I'm sure milady would like to hear how this epic poem ends." Ann flipped ahead to see how many pages remained of her book. She rolled her eyes at the number. "Heaven knows I'd like to hear the end of it."

Voleta gave a startled gasp. Her eyes snapped open, and she sat upright in bed as if launched by a spring. Her expression held the alarm of one emerging from a nightmare. Before Iren or Ann could move or say a word, she shouted, "Adam!"

Then Voleta pitched forward and spit a bullet onto the quilt.

The Black Trail

Old Father Hodder
said, "Sons and daughters,
I'm out of mortar.
Make more bones."
—"The Hod on High," traditional, Anonymous

At one point in their miserable scramble up the dark arteries of the Tower, Senlin had entertained the hope that they would be able to sneak up on the zealot camp and assess what sort of madness they were walking into. But by the time they were nearing Mola Ambit—the spot on the map that purportedly marked Luc Marat's present address—Finn Goll had nearly convinced them all that they had wandered off course many hours earlier and were now well and truly lost.

And Goll's dread was not without cause. They had passed through a simple but inscrutable fork in the ductwork. According to the map, there was only one degree of difference between the slopes of the two passages, a distinction that Senlin's cobbled inclinometer was not accurate enough to gauge. They had just begun measuring the slopes for a third time when Tarrou had sniffed the air and announced with reasonable certainty that a chimney cat was nearby. Rather than die in deliberation, Senlin had picked the chute with the freshest breeze. No one had complained. At least, not until later.

Finn Goll's latent gloom was an aspect of his personality that Senlin had not noticed during their time in New Babel. Now Goll reminded Senlin of the Isaugh fishermen who had never in their life caught the *right* amount of fish. Either their catches were too small or too large, both of which heralded disaster. A small catch would spell the ruination of the fisherman's livelihood and the starvation of his family. Conversely, preserving and storing an abundant catch before it rotted was arduous if not impossible. Those gloomy men of the sea appeared to prefer perennial failure to the possibility of disappointment.

Goll was sure that the spring they'd filled their remaining water-skin with was poisoned, and the effects merely delayed. Every time they paused to drink, he'd refer to it as their *hemlock tea* or *arsenic wine*. Later, when John suggested he stop hogging the poison if he hated it so much, Goll began to remark on the insufficiency of their supply. They would all perish from thirst long before the poison had time to do its work. Whenever the bottom of their last gloamine lamp scraped against a rock, Goll would blurt out some dramatic phrase like "That's the end, gents!" or "Now comes the night!" or "I love you, Abby," Abigail being the name of his absent wife. Then, when the lightshade did not burst, plunging them into eternal dark, Goll would insist it was only a temporary reprieve. Disaster lay just around the corner. And unfortunately for Tom's and John's nerves, the ventilation system of the Tower was full of corners.

As much as Tarrou cursed Goll whenever he made his glum remarks, his oaths did not inoculate him against the despair. Goll's pessimism was contagious. Even Senlin, who did his best to put some hopeful twist on Goll's miserable observations, found his confidence in his navigation eroded. Doubt began to creep in.

Then during one of their rests, while the three climbers huddled together under their last blanket in an attempt to get a little sleep, Senlin had dreamed of Marya. In the dream, she was walking away from him up a grassy hill. An infant's round face peeked over her shoulder. He followed after them as quickly as he could, though with every step he slid back a little down the dewy slope. He stumbled over and over until the knees of his pants were soaked through and his joints ached. But every time he fell, he was quick to rise again, heartened by the sound of Marya's soft humming and Olivet's bright gaze.

Then a gust of frigid air brought Senlin back to the wan gloamine light, his sandstone pillow, and Tarrou's elbow in his ribs. He closed his eyes again and tried for hours to find his way back to that tantalizing dream. But it was like he had leapt from a rushing train. He could not board that vision again because it had thundered on without him.

After three days of no food, little water, and uncertain headway, they were all in such an exhausted state that when they blundered upon a troop of six armed hods at a level junction, they could hardly believe it. John embraced the nearest guard, even as the others shook their pistols at him and barked in hoddish. It was a diverse group: men and women, one of whom seemed to be in her sixties. The beard of the youngest man appeared to have only recently come in. The color of their skin was similarly varied, though they all shared the same vigilant, sober expression. As much as he loathed Marat and his practices, Senlin still appreciated the zealot's evident belief in equality.

In those first moments, it wasn't clear to Senlin whether this was in fact Mola Ambit, or merely its doorstep. The guard post was just large enough to include a row of cots, six stools, a low table, and a great brass bell, which the guards rang a second after Senlin and his friends appeared. Though they had raised the alarm, the guards did not seem to believe the giddy, starved climbing party posed much of a threat to their camp. Though probably their confidence had something to do with the presence of their swords and firearms.

The hods appeared to speak only hoddish, and so it fell to Tarrou to engage the guards. During his babbling conversation, John gestured at Senlin several times, finally uttering the phrase "Captain Thomas Mudd Senlin." The response from the armed hods was both immediate and unfavorable. They glared at Senlin with thinly veiled hate.

"Good news, Headmaster," John said after another moment's discussion. "Mola Ambit lies just ahead. They've agreed to take us to Marat. Though you'll have to be bound."

"Splendid," Senlin said, presenting his wrists to the young guard who came at him with a rope and a scowl.

"I'm afraid it goes around the neck, Tom," Tarrou said, wincing as the guard wrapped the line about Senlin's throat.

"Look on the bright side," Goll said through a barely contained smile. "At least this'll give you a chance to break it in. I hear nooses pinch at first."

Mola Ambit was like the main street of a town squeezed into a mineshaft. The main bore was broad and squared at the edges. This was not some dug-out burrow. No, Senlin thought for sure this was part of the original architecture. Perhaps it had once housed the hods who helped to raise the Tower.

The tunnel that held the town elbowed this way and that, so it was difficult to discern from the outset how large it was. There was a post office, a bank, and a general store, though none of those structures were being put to their original use. Laundry hung in the post office, the bank appeared to have been converted to an armory, and the general store was full of bunkbeds, many of which were occupied. The town teemed with hods—hundreds of them, perhaps thousands—of all ages, including many children, all shaved to the scalp, all dressed in simple rags and sarongs, and all with bare necks, though the scars of their broken shackles still lingered on many. Senlin felt conspicuous with his full head of hair and the iron band rattling under his chin.

They turned a corner in the crooked town and found themselves walking past a succession of ancient hoists. The equipment had obviously once been used to raise immense blocks, though now the struts of the rusting cranes were strung with lines and hung with curing meat. Rows of clay kilns, once used to fire the tiles that would come to fill the streets and ceilings of many ringdoms, had been converted to coops for the camp's population of chickens.

But there was another layer of oddness to Mola Ambit. Here and there, Senlin saw pieces of modern machinery. He recognized the style at once, and even knew the origin of some parts. The front grill of a wall-walker had been turned into a drying rack for flannels outside an outhouse, and the spidery legs of a brick nymph had been lashed together to form a pen for goats. Senlin wondered if the Sphinx would be surprised to learn that this was where so many of her machines had disappeared to. Or did she already suspect Marat's role in her shrinking fleet?

Still, there was something almost quaint about it all. It was hard not to see children and the chickens and hanging laundry and not feel a little charmed by the normalcy of the scene.

Then they entered the throne room—though they would only learn it was called that later—and Senlin wondered if anything would ever seem normal again.

They stood with their toes at the edge of a sheer drop. In its depth and breadth, the pit before them called to mind a quarry. The floor of the hollow was almost entirely consumed by the presence of the single largest piece of machinery Senlin had ever seen. Indeed, he wondered if it wasn't the largest that had ever been built by man.

To his surprise, he recognized the curve of the bands that crossed its spine and ran down its broad back, recognized the vicious trident that projected from its forehead and the knife-like fringe that lined its carapace. He'd seen the shape of the engine before in the diagrams of the book Sodiq had dropped in the rainy, bloody alley. It resembled one of those creatures from the deepest valleys of the ancient ocean— a trilobite, one that was as large as a city block.

But Marat had obviously not built some harmless replica of the extinct arthropod. No, it was unmistakably a siege engine. The black snouts of cannons protruded from embrasures between plates of armor. The perimeter of blades that edged the shell were all as sharp as scimitars, and the horns that curved back from the front of the monstrosity were honed as finely as a lance.

The war crab appeared to be made from a grand variety of mechanical parts—some new, some tarnished, some pitted with age. Senlin recognized many of the Sphinx's refined metals mixed in among the rusting I-beams and pig-iron scrap. The machine did not so much resemble an engine as it did an assemblage, a flotilla, a clockwork collage.

Their armed escorts barked at them, indicating the ladder that descended into the pit. For a moment, the astonishment of the three companions rendered them deaf and unresponsive. But quickly, the guards recovered their attention with a few sharp slaps, and the men were goaded down the ladder to the floor of the throne room.

They were led under the siege engine. It hunkered some ten or twelve feet off the ground. The belly of the machine was not braced by iron bands. Rather, the undercarriage was covered in something like scale armor, though the individual scales were quite irregular. It took Senlin a moment of looking up and squinting to discern there were recognizable artifacts amid the makeshift plates. There were shovel heads and sewer covers, skillets and plowshares, bed warmers and pot lids, and a hundred other domestic things, all riveted together to form a protective shield. The machine was silent at the moment, but Senlin could only imagine how much it would roar when its furnaces were lit.

Each leg of the machine tapered to a spearpoint that was sharp enough to pock the stone. The legs were so numerous Senlin felt as if he were walking down an allée of trees, an odd impression that was likely owed to the unexpected presence of sunlight.

He'd not noticed it while they'd been standing awestruck above the pit, but now he saw how the siege engine was illuminated. Ahead of them, a borehole as large as the monstrous engine pierced a hundred feet of Tower stone and broke upon open air. The black trail had stolen all sense of the hour. He was a little surprised to discover that outside it was morning.

As they emerged from the undercarriage, Senlin peered up at the jutting trident. An immense, oily driveshaft connected the tines to the wide head of the machine. The edges of the prongs were lined with square teeth. Only then did he understand: It wasn't only a siege engine. It was an excavator as well, a drilling machine that could bore through rock as readily as a mole through garden soil. The evidence of it lay before him.

Luc Marat had built an engine that could chew through the Tower itself.

The implications were chilling. Could he drive the thing into the heart of a ringdom, circumventing the navies and the port defenses in the process? Could he climb the Tower and crack the Sphinx's lair open and steal her marvels? What would Marat do with a wand that shot lightning or a doorman like Ferdinand? Could he carve through enough of the base of the Tower to threaten its very foundation?

Until that moment, Senlin had remained unconvinced of the Sphinx's assessment of Luc Marat. Yes, the man was an opportunist. Yes, he was a hooligan who had no compunction about pretending to run a charity while building and arming a gang. And certainly, he was a bully who liked to tell people what to think and who used juvenile tactics like scribbling in books to illustrate his idiotic ideals. And while all of that was reprehensible and foolish, Senlin had not been certain that it was as dangerous as the Sphinx believed. Marat seemed a threat to no one but the hods who were unfortunate enough to fall under his spell or get in his way.

Now, Senlin realized Marat was something much, much worse. He was an aspiring tyrant, a man actively creating a new reality in which ignorance was holy and his consolidated knowledge divine. The evidence of it lay in his acts. Marat fetishized the destruction of books and all that they contained, and then stole from libraries when his designs required it. Marat had banged on about how they were all enslaved to the machinery of the Tower, even as he built a monstrous engine of his own. But then, Marat didn't truly wish to return to the romanticized past when small tribes lived upon the simple bounties of the earth, untroubled by the evils of society or the uncertainty that came with study, discovery, and growth. He wished to promote a new sort of barbarism, wished to rob people of their intellectual resources and then present himself as the only reliable, sane, and righteous fount of wisdom. He didn't wish to fell the Tower, he wished to become it!

But Senlin knew that while tyrants had many strengths, their weakness was generally the same. They were gullible. For the tyrant, there were no reigning facts, no universal systems of inquiry, no demonstrable truths. Because they preferred their own rationalization to reason, their dogma to discourse, the main means a tyrant had for testing another man's integrity and loyalty were oaths and intuition. But since the tyrants had no choice but to teach everyone exactly what they wished to hear, they were simple to pander to and easy to fool.

At least, such was Senlin's hope.

Luc Marat sat upright in his wheelchair at the sunny brink of the borehole. An entourage of hods, each of whom was as big as John, stood about looking alert and suspicious of the approaching strangers. Marat faced the morning and did not turn around even after Senlin's chaperone announced their arrival. The leader of the hods seemed reluctant to surrender his contemplation of the sky. When Senlin looked out, he saw in the distance a smoldering airship. The thread of smoke quickly grew into a fat black ribbon as the ship's envelopes caught fire. The vessel began to twist and plunge. From so far away, the descent looked almost leisurely, almost serene. When the aircraft crashed in the desert, it raised the slightest puff of dust.

"I had wondered, was it possible to bring down a military ship with nothing more than a hod and a simple means of sabotage?" Marat said, addressing the barren blue sky. "I had wondered, could something as small as the will of one boy be enough to crack the defenses and discipline and firepower of an old warship? Though, what is more ancient than the instinct to be free? Even the young feel it. Even the unborn."

Only then did Marat turn to face them. His gilded legs were uncovered. The wicker-backed chair with ungreased wheels seemed too humble a throne for such magnificence. His kneecaps shone like stage lights. A small, beatific smile stood on his handsome face, an expression that only brightened when he saw Senlin with a rope about his neck.

"Ah! Captain Mudd!" Marat said, his chair creaking as he rolled a little nearer. "Or should I say, Thomas Senlin? Or perhaps Cyril Pinfield?"

Knowing he would only get one chance to deliver a perfect performance, Senlin did his best to appear humble. "I prefer Hodder Tom."

"*Do you?* And yet all those former lives still stick to you like tar, don't they?" Marat turned his chin but not his eyes and said something in hoddish to the guard who held Senlin's leash. The youth approached an iron eyelet driven into the stone. The ring was already occupied by a rope that ran taut over the edge. The guard hacked at it with his sword until the jute frayed and snapped, and the end ran over the cusp with the urgency of an anchor chain. Clearing the rest of the old rope away, the guard tied the end of Senlin's tether to the stake.

A morbid thought flitted through Senlin's head: *So Goll was right. It will be a hanging after all.*

"And you're the two men who caught the fugitive, yes?" Marat said, glancing between Finn Goll and John Tarrou, both of whom appeared cowed and ashen in the sunlight. "How was the trek up?" The zealot leader's overbearing version of hospitality, which Senlin had observed in the Golden Zoo, was apparently still very much part of his act.

"Fine, fine, thank you," Tarrou said, adding with a dismissive roll of his hand, "We did run into a chimney cat."

"Yes, I see that you did." Marat indicated the welts on Senlin's chest. "Usually I only see those marks on the dead. How did you survive?" Tarrou answered in hoddish, a choice that made Marat's forehead wrinkle with pleasure. "Yes, yes. Just as it should be, Hodder John. Hods die alone but thrive as one. I suppose you'll be ready to collect your reward, then?"

"Oh, I've already received it." John bowed his head. "My reward was given to me by Sodiq in the form of this second chance to prove myself to the cause."

"Truly," Marat said, his expressive brows curling in Goll's direction. "But you, Hodder Finn, surely won't turn down the wages of your labor! After all you've been through, a hundred mina would take the sting out of your suffering, not to mention a bite out of your debts."

Senlin held his breath, unsure what his bitter and unwilling companion would say.

Finn Goll cleared his throat and said, "I'll be honest, the reward I really hoped for was to see Thomas Senlin strangled until his eyes popped out." The weight of the rope about Senlin's neck seemed to double. Goll went on: "A few months ago, I was chased into a zealot camp by angry debtors who blamed their insolvency on my misfortune. Which didn't seem fair, considering that I had always paid my debts before I met this man and he decided to ruin my life." Goll spat on the ground near Senlin's feet. "When I joined your cause, I did my best to forget my past—to erase it, word by word, as Hodder Sodiq taught me. I like to think I was making progress on that front. But then I heard that you were offering a bounty for old Tom, and it put the bellows to my anger. I never wanted the money, I just wanted to see him swing." Finn Goll pointed at Senlin, who looked as if he had something lodged in his throat. "Look at his face, now! He knows it. I told him so. I threatened to kill him myself and save you the trouble. I held the gun in my hands and him in my sights. I felt the trigger's pull upon my finger." Finn Goll punctuated each word with a shake of his fist.

Senlin could see John tensing out of the corner of his eye. He could only hope he wouldn't do anything foolish. There was no reason they both had to die today. Goll regathered Senlin's attention with a yap of laughter. "But then, do you know what this man did? When the chimney cat had me cornered, and it was licking its lips, Tom could've grabbed our pack and gotten away. But old Tom didn't run. No, he stayed and fought." Goll's expression softened. His fists broke open, and he held out his palms, surrendering his resentment. "And I realized then that he was different. He was not the same man who burned my life to the ground, just as I'm not the same man who was scorched. He is Hodder Tom now. And I'm Hodder Finn."

Senlin wondered if John had been wrong about Goll's acting ability or if his tale was heartfelt. Goll sounded sincere enough when he said, "My reward is to be here, to be freed of my anger, and to meet the Hod King in person."

Marat surprised them all by laughing. "Oh, I'm not the Hod King! No, no, I'm Hodder Luc to my friends and Marat to my enemies. No, the Hod King is there." He pointed back down the borehole at the dormant siege engine. Seeming to sense the surprise of his guests, Marat explained, "Or I should say, that will be the Hod King once it's fully crewed."

"I don't understand. Our king is a machine?" Goll said.

"Not quite. Have you ever heard of a rat king?" When the newcomers shook their heads, Marat continued, "Sometimes when rats are forced to live in too small a space, their tails become entangled, and those tangles become knots. The rats who find they have become entwined with their brothers and sisters are presented then with a choice: They can learn to think, coordinate, and work as one, or they can die as one. That is a rat king."

Senlin suppressed a shudder at the picture Marat painted. Senlin was doing his best to project an air of thoughtless devotion, but the delicate, vacuous expression kept slipping off his face. It felt like he was trying to saddle a snake. Mercifully, his host didn't seem aware of his struggle, as he continued on: "Our great engine requires a hundred and eleven hods to operate. Each leg of the machine, each cannon, each hinge of the head must be steered by a separate hod, all working in perfect unison. We will go forth as one, conquer as one. That is the Hod King."

"What are you going to do with it?" Goll asked.

"All in good time, Hodder Finn," Marat said with a showman-like expansion of his arms. "I must admit, I can understand why you would feel a certain degree of hatred for this man." Marat turned his chair to face Senlin. "After you flouted my hospitality and attacked my followers, I felt compelled to look into Captain Mudd a little further. When I learned you had passed through the Windsock, I paid it a visit. It was something of a challenge, as you might imagine, for a man of my condition to join her in her web, but I had the most fascinating conversation with Madame Bhata. You were a teacher once upon a time."

"I was," Senlin said, wishing not for the first time that he had been more discreet in the past.

Marat smiled brightly, his teeth straight and white. Somehow Senlin doubted the man subsisted on a diet of beetles. "Tell me, do you miss it? Teaching?"

"I do not. I know now that my education was just the amassing of trivia and lies, lies that I'm ashamed to say I passed on to children, lies that revealed themselves to me at the worst possible moment." Senlin had been holding Marat's piercing gaze to that point but surrendered it now in a show of humility. "I confess—I sometimes miss that sense of security, false as it was. But I know it was my scholarly arrogance that delivered me here. I feel like the ant lured to the pitcher plant by the scent of nectar. The Tower is a honeyed trap."

"Pitcher plants. Fascinating. You haven't forgotten your education entirely."

Senlin winced. "It's an ongoing effort. It's hard to forget what took half a lifetime to learn."

"That's the truth for us all. But what of your friends, your crew? What happened to those people who you were so ready to slay my followers for?"

"I don't know," Senlin admitted with a small shrug. "I haven't seen them in weeks."

The sky behind Marat seemed to shrink into a backdrop. And perhaps it was the effect of the round mouth of the bore, but Senlin felt increasingly as if his vision was tunneling around the gold-legged zealot. "What were you doing in Pelphia?"

"I was looking for someone."

"Oh, that's right! Madame Bhata mentioned you'd lost a—what was it—a young wife? How did she fare in that polite society?"

"Polite society!" Senlin scoffed. "I've learned the true nature of civility. Civility is critiquing how another man pronounces a word or knots his necktie, and then saying nothing about how a ringdom hangs its poor. Civility is having ardent opinions about plays and actors and made-up stories, and no opinion whatsoever about the real tragedies of the black trail. Civility is a crowded execution."

"Well said, Hodder Tom. It seems you've undergone quite a conversion." Marat leaned his chin upon the pedestal of his fist and squinted. Senlin could sense the tyrant's internal deliberations about whether or not to believe this enemy who came to him now as a friend. Marat still seemed unconvinced, but Senlin could see he was wearing his doubt down. "I'm grateful that you intervened when Hodder Sodiq was in need of it. I heard you tried to stop the firing squad as well."

"Those deaths are on my head," Senlin said wretchedly. "After Hodder Sodiq defended himself against the two brutes in the alley, some constables paid me a visit. I did my best to undermine their investigation, of course, but they still used me as an excuse to murder those innocent hods."

Marat leaned back with a deep sigh, settling his arms upon the humble rests. His face seemed to fall into shadow behind the spangling light of his legs. "Tell me, Hodder Tom, what are your debts?"

"Here," Senlin said, and pulled the bondlet out from under the rope about his neck. "Unseal it. Look for yourself. I have no secrets."

At Marat's signal, one of his guards opened the ring that bound the iron tube to Senlin's throat and presented the small cylinder to his master. "There's no going back after this, Hodder Tom. You're certain of your choice?" He paused a moment to see if Senlin would vacillate, but when he remained steadfast, Marat used his thumbnail to break the wax seal. He unscrewed the bondlet's cap and extracted the rolled-up scrap of paper from inside. He read it, then laughed. "Do you have any idea what this says?"

"No, though I know who wrote it."

"Well, it's the Pelphian address of some duke and a promise of a two-hundred-and-fifty-mina reward for whoever opens this bondlet and returns it along with your severed head. You are alarmingly good at making enemies."

"He married my wife," Senlin said, knowing this would be a revelation for Tarrou as well. He turned away so that his friend would not see his face when he followed up that truth with a lie. "He made her happier than I ever could. She has riches and fame, a husband who is young and handsome. She turned me away, of course, and when the duke found out... Well, you know what he did: He put a blinder on my head and a ransom around my neck."

Marat held up the scrap of paper, pinching it between his fingers. The wind bent and tugged at the little scroll, and after a moment of teasing it in the breeze, Marat let the paper go. The scrap flew into the daylight and was gone. "It seems to me our tails have become entangled. I appreciate your determination, your humility, your courage. I truly do, but..." Marat drummed his long fingers on his thighs, making them chime. "The last time I saw you, you were traveling with a Wakeman. I cannot believe you are not a saboteur and a spy."

Senlin did not flinch. "I hadn't met the Sphinx at that point, though I have since."

"You have?" Marat's perfect composure seemed to waver. Senlin wasn't sure whether it was a sign of anxiety or excitement. "Tell me, what does he look like?"

It was obviously a test, and yet something told Senlin that he should not confess the Sphinx's true face, which she showed to so few, but rather the mask she wore. He described her silver-spoon face and the snaking black robes and her curiously variable height, and when he was finished, Marat eagerly asked if the Sphinx had made him sign a contract.

"Yes, I signed a contract."

Marat looked amused by the baldness of this confession and angry at what it suggested about Senlin's loyalties. Senlin thought Marat seemed very close to making up his mind about him, one way or the other. "Tell me, Hodder Tom, what was the nature of your agreement?"

"The Sphinx got control of my ship and my crew—he was particularly keen to have the able-bodied siblings under his charge. In exchange, I was given transport to Pelphia, some forged credentials, pocket money, and a chance to reunite with my wife. Or so I believed."

"Seems a rather ruthless bargain."

"Especially considering the fact that the Sphinx must've known. He knew my wife was never going to run into my arms or call me husband again. The Sphinx knew all about the fabulous new life she was living, and rather than warn me, rather than be honest about my bleak luck, he took advantage of my hopefulness." Senlin affected the stifling of a sob, then pressed his voice to rise in anger. "Now I have no ship, no crew, no friends, no wife. The last time we met, you told me that the Sphinx turned everyone he met into either an enemy or a machine. Well, I am not a machine!"

Marat smiled with paternal patience. "What would you do if you saw the Sphinx again?"

"I would drag the worm out of his hole and watch him shrivel in the sunlight."

"You would kill the Sphinx?"

"I would. And then I would pound this wretched coffin nail of a Tower into the earth."

"Come the Hod King," Marat said.

"Come the Hod King," Senlin parroted.

Marat looked like a man settling into a warm bath. He sighed and said, "I want to teach you a word. It will be your first word in hoddish. The word is *mhul-ky*."

"Mhul-ky." Senlin appeared to mull the sound over, to savor it. "What does it mean?"

"One who opens the heavens. Mhul-ky: That is what we are, and that is what we shall do. We will tear the cloud from the Tower's top and expose the Sphinx to the world."

Marat held out his palm and uttered an inscrutable command. One of his bare-chested bodyguards slid a long knife from the sheath at his hip and laid the wire-bound handle in his master's hand. "Come here. Let me free you. I'm afraid you'll have to kneel because I cannot stand," Marat said as Senlin went to one knee by the arm of his chair. Senlin offered Marat his throat.

The zealot lord set his blade to Senlin's neck and held it there.

Senlin conjured up the vision of Marya walking up the green mountain with her back to him and the round face of their daughter staring wide-eyed at him, stumbling after them.

Marat jerked the knife, and the noose fell from Senlin's neck. "Your hair is long, Hodder Tom. It's turning gray as well. Here, let me lighten your burden."

Marat turned Senlin's head with the gentle authority of a barber and set the knife to his temple. He began scraping the hair down to the stubble, erasing the evidence of many seasons of Senlin's life. The desert wind stirred and swept his mane away.

Acknowledgments

I redrafted a sizable portion of *The Hod King* while my wife, Sharon, was pregnant with our first child. The constant support she gave me during those months was surpassed only by the patience she provided after the arrival of our daughter, Maddie, when I had to sequester myself for hours and weeks to revise the draft. This book would not exist if it were not for her steadfast insistence that I get back to work, even as our miracle cooed, cried, and grew. I would also like to thank my parents, Barbara and Josiah, and Sharon's parents, Carol and Bob. I owe them thanks for many things, but in particular, I am grateful for their support of Maddie and Sharon. My sister, Jesse, was a wonderful source of perspective and understanding throughout this odyssey. She flew across the country to make us cookies. They were delicious.

I must thank my editors at Orbit Books, Bradley Englert and Emily Byron, for their assistance in the completion of this volume, which would be much worse but for their intervention and guidance. I'd also like to thank my agent, Ian Drury, and all of the exceedingly helpful members of Sheil Land Associates—particularly Lucy Fawcett and Gaia Banks—for their work in helping to expand my audience.

Writing is solitary work, but fortunately I found commiseration and encouragement from a community of personable and talented writers, including Jonathan French, Dyrk Ashton, Baird Wells, Benedict Patrick, Timandra Whitecastle, David Benem, and Phil Tucker, among many, many others. If you are not familiar with their work, I would encourage you to seek them out. They are deserving of your attention and affection. Of course, without Mark Lawrence's enthusiastic endorsement, none of this would've occurred. I am, and will forever be, indebted to him and his magnificent Self-Published Fantasy Blog-Off. He changed the trajectory of my career and life.

Acknowledgments

And many, many thanks to my readers and fans. Your personal notes, your thoughtful comments, and your generous reviews warmed my heart when it had cooled and raised my spirit when it was low. The success of the series is the direct result of your efforts to share your enjoyment of these books with other readers. I am so grateful for your support.

This book is dedicated to William Barber Bancroft, my uncle, who passed away in 2004. Barber was responsible for introducing me to so many of my formative influences, including Fritz Lang, T. S. Eliot, Gertrude Stein, and Jacques Derrida. Barber taught me that good writing requires more than style, theory, and poetry. Good writing, at its core, is an extension of the tradition of storytelling, which is fitting because I never met a more entertaining and spirited storyteller. A formidable writer and a consummate teacher, Barber treated me like a peer when I was not one and behaved as if I were a talent when I hadn't any. He encouraged me to begin and to persist. I would not be the writer I am were it not for him.

extras

extras

about the author

Josiah Bancroft started writing novels when he was twelve, and by the time he finished his first, he was an addict. Eventually, the writing of *Senlin Ascends* began, a fantasy adventure not so unlike the stories that got him addicted to words in the first place. He wanted to do for others what his favorite writers had done for him: namely, to pick them up and to carry them to a wonderful and perilous world that is spinning very fast. If he's done that with this book, then he's happy.

Josiah lives in Philadelphia with his wife, Sharon, their daughter, Maddie, and their two rabbits, Mabel and Chaplin.

Find out more about Josiah Bancroft and other Orbit authors by registering for the free monthly newsletter at www.orbitbooks.net.

if you enjoyed

THE HOD KING

look out for

ONE OF US

by

Craig DiLouie

THEY CALL IT THE PLAGUE
A generation of children born with extreme genetic mutations

THEY CALL IT A HOME
But it's a place of neglect and forced labour

THEY CALL HIM A FREAK
But Dog is just a boy who wants to be treated as normal

THEY CALL THEM DANGEROUS
They might be right

The story of a lost generation, and a boy who just wants to be one of us.

One

On the principal's desk, a copy of *Time*. A fourteen-year-old girl smiled on the cover. Pigtails tied in blue ribbon. Freckles and big white teeth. Rubbery, barbed appendages extending from her eye sockets.

Under that, a single word: WHY?

Why did this happen?

Or, maybe, why did the world allow a child like this to live?

What Dog wanted to know was why she smiled.

Maybe it was just reflex, seeing somebody pointing a camera at her. Maybe she liked the attention, even if it wasn't the nice kind.

Maybe, if only for a few seconds, she felt special.

The Georgia sun glared through filmy barred windows. A steel fan whirred in the corner, barely moving the warm, thick air. Out the window, Dog spied the old rusted pickup sunk in a riot of wildflowers. Somebody loved it once then parked it here and left it to die. If Dog owned it, he would have kept driving and never stopped.

The door opened. The government man came in wearing a black suit, white shirt, and blue-and-yellow tie. His shiny shoes clicked across the grimy floor. He sat in Principal Willard's creaking chair and lit a cigarette. Dropped a file folder on the desk and studied Dog through a blue haze.

"They call you Dog," he said.

"Yes, sir, they do. The other kids, I mean."

Dog growled when he talked but took care to form each word right. The teachers made sure he spoke good and proper. Brain once told him these signs of humanity were the only thing keeping the children alive.

"Your Christian name is Enoch. Enoch Davis Bryant."

"Yes, sir."

Enoch was the name the teachers at the Home used. Brain said it was his slave name. Dog liked hearing it, though. He felt lucky to have one. His mama had loved him enough to at least do that for him. Many parents had named their kids XYZ before abandoning them to the Homes.

"I'm Agent Shackleton," the government man said through another cloud of smoke. "Bureau of Teratological Affairs. You know the drill, don't you, by now?"

Every year, the government sent somebody to ask the kids questions. Trying to find out if they were still human. Did they want to hurt people, ever have carnal thoughts about normal girls and boys, that sort of thing.

"I know the drill," Dog said.

"Not this year," the man told him. "This year is different. I'm here to find out if you're special."

"I don't quite follow, sir."

Agent Shackleton planted his elbows on the desk. "You're a ward of the state. More than a million of you. Living high on the hog for the past fourteen years in the Homes. Some of you are beginning to show certain capabilities."

"Like what kind?"

"I saw a kid once who had gills and could breathe underwater. Another who could hear somebody talking a mile away."

"No kidding," Dog said.

"That's right."

"You mean like a superhero."

"Yeah. Like Spider-Man, if Spider-Man half looked like a real spider."

"I never heard of such a thing," Dog said.

"If you, Enoch, have capabilities, you could prove you're worth the food you eat. This is your opportunity to pay it back. Do you follow me?"

"Sure, I guess."

Satisfied, Shackleton sat back in the chair and planted his feet on the desk. He set the file folder on his thighs, licked his finger, and flipped it open.

"Pretty good grades," the man said. "You got your math and spelling. You stay out of trouble. All right. Tell me what you can do. Better yet, show me something."

"What I can do, sir?"

"You do for me, I can do plenty for you. Take you to a special place."

Dog glanced at the red door at the side of the room before returning his gaze to Shackleton. Even looking at it was bad luck. The red door led downstairs to a basement room called Discipline, where the problem kids went.

He'd never been inside it, but he knew the stories. All the kids knew them. Principal Willard wanted them to know. It was part of their education.

He said, "What kind of place would that be?"

"A place with lots of food and TV. A place nobody can ever bother you."

Brain always said to play along with the normals so you didn't get caught up in their system. They wrote the rules in such a way to trick you into Discipline. More than that, though, Dog wanted to prove himself. He wanted to be special.

"Well, I'm a real fast runner. Ask anybody."

"That's your special talent. You can run fast."

"Real fast. Does that count?"

The agent smiled. "Running fast isn't special. It isn't special at all."

"Ask anybody how fast I run. Ask the——"

"You're not special. You'll never be special, Dog."

"I don't know what you want from me, șir."

Shackleton's smile disappeared along with Dog's file. "I want you to get the hell out of my sight. Send the next monster in on your way out."

Two

Pollution. Infections. Drugs. Radiation. All these things, Mr. Benson said from the chalkboard, can produce mutations in embryos.

A bacterium caused the plague generation. The other kids, the plague kids, who lived in the Homes.

Amy Green shifted in her desk chair. The top of her head was itching again. Mama said she'd worry it bald if she kept scratching at it. She settled on twirling her long, dark hair around her finger and tugging. Savored the needles of pain along her scalp.

"The plague is a sexually transmitted disease," Mr. Benson told the class.

She already knew part of the story from American History and from what Mama told her. The plague started in 1968, two years before she was born, back when love was still free. Then the disease named teratogenesis raced around the world, and the plague children came.

One out of ten thousand babies born in 1968 were monsters, and most died. One in six in 1969, and half of these died. One in three in 1970, the year scientists came up with a test to see if you had it. Most of them lived. After a neonatal nurse got arrested for killing thirty babies in Texas, the survival rate jumped.

More than a million monster babies screaming to be fed. By then, Congress had already funded the Home system.

Fourteen years later, and still no cure. If you caught the germ, the only surefire way to stop spreading it was abstinence, which they taught right here in health class. If you got pregnant with it, abortion was mandatory.

Amy flipped her textbook open and bent to sniff its cheesy new-book smell. Books, sharpened pencils, lined paper; she associated their bitter scents with school. The page showed a drawing of a woman's reproductive system. The baby comes out there. Sitting next to her, her boyfriend Jake glanced at the page and smiled, his face reddening. Like her, fascinated and embarrassed by it all.

In junior high, sex ed was mandatory, no ifs or buts. Amy and her friends were stumbling through puberty. Tampons, budding breasts, aching midnight thoughts, long conversations about what boys liked and what they wanted.

She already had a good idea what they wanted. Girls always complimented her about how pretty she was. Boys stared at her when she walked down the hall. Everybody so nice to her all the time. She didn't trust any of it.

When she stood naked in the mirror, she only saw flaws. Amy spotted a zit last week and stared at it for an hour, hating her ugliness. It took her over an hour every morning to get ready for school. She didn't leave the house until she looked perfect.

She flipped the page again. A monster grinned up at her. She slammed the book shut.

Mr. Benson asked if anybody in the class had actually seen a plague child. Not on TV or in a magazine, but up close and personal.

A few kids raised their hands. Amy kept hers planted on her desk.

"I have two big goals for you kids this year," the teacher said. "The main thing is teach you how to avoid spreading the disease. We'll be talking a lot about safe sex and all the regulations about whether and how you do it. How to get tested and how to access a safe abortion. I also aim to help you become accustomed to the plague children already born and who are now the same age as you."

For Amy's entire life, the plague children had lived in group homes out in the country, away from people. One was located just eight miles from Huntsville, though it might as well have been on the moon. The monsters never came to town. Out of sight meant out of mind, though one could never entirely forget them.

"Let's start with the plague kids," Mr. Benson said. "What do all y'all think about them? Tell the truth."

Rob Rowland raised his hand. "They ain't human. They're just animals."

"Is that right? Would you shoot one and eat it? Mount its head on your wall?"

The kids laughed as they pictured Rob so hungry he would eat a monster. Rob was obese, smart, and sweated a lot, one of the unpopular kids.

Amy shuddered with sudden loathing. "I hate them something awful."

The laughter died. Which was good, because the plague wasn't funny.

The teacher crossed his arms. "Go ahead, Amy. No need to holler, though. Why do you hate them?"

"They're monsters. I hate them because they're monsters."

Mr. Benson turned and hacked at the blackboard with a piece of chalk: MONSTRUM, a VIOLATION OF NATURE. From MONEO, which means TO WARN. In this case, a warning God is angry. Punishment for taboo.

"Teratogenesis is nature out of whack," he said. "It rewrote the body. Changed the rules. Monsters, maybe. But does a monster have to be evil? Is a human being what you look like, or what you do? What makes a man a man?"

Bonnie Fields raised her hand. "I saw one once. I couldn't even tell if it was a boy or girl. I didn't stick around to get to know it."

"But did you see it as evil?"

"I don't know about that, but looking the way some of them do, I can't imagine why the doctors let them all live. It would have been a mercy to let them die."

"Mercy on us," somebody behind Amy muttered.

The kids laughed again.

Sally Albod's hand shot up. "I'm surprised at all y'all being so scared. I see the kids all the time at my daddy's farm. They're weird, but there ain't nothing to them. They work hard and don't make trouble. They're fine."

"That's good, Sally," the teacher said. "I'd like to show all y'all something."

He opened a cabinet and pulled out a big glass jar. He set it on his desk. Inside, a baby floated in yellowish fluid. A tiny penis jutted between its legs. Its little arms grasped at nothing. It had a single slitted eye over a cleft where its nose should be.

The class sucked in its breath as one. Half the kids recoiled as the rest leaned forward for a better look. Fascination and revulsion. Amy alone didn't move. She sat frozen, shot through with the horror of it.

She hated the little thing. Even dead, she hated it.

"This is Tony," Mr. Benson said. "And guess what, he isn't one of the plague kids. Just some poor boy born with a birth defect. About three percent of newborns are born this way every year. It causes one out of five infant deaths."

Tony, some of the kids chuckled. They thought it weird it had a name.

"We used to believe embryos developed in isolation in the uterus," the teacher said. "Then back in the Sixties, a company sold thalidomide to pregnant women in Germany to help them with morning sickness. Ten thousand kids born with deformed limbs. Half died. What did scientists learn from that? Anybody?"

"A medicine a lady takes can hurt her baby even if it don't hurt her," Jake said.

"Bingo," Mr. Benson said. "Medicine, toxins, viruses, we call these things environmental factors. Most times, though, doctors have no idea why a baby like Tony is born. It just happens, like a dice roll. So is Tony a monster? What about a kid who's retarded, or born with legs that don't work? Is a kid in a wheelchair a monster too? A baby born deaf or blind?"

He got no takers. The class sat quiet and thoughtful. Satisfied, Mr. Benson carried the jar back to the cabinet. More gasps as baby Tony bobbed in the fluid, like he was trying to get out.

The teacher frowned as he returned the jar to its shelf. "I'm surprised just this upsets you. If this gets you so worked up, how will you live with the plague children? When they're adults, they'll have the same rights as you. They'll live among you."

Amy stiffened at her desk, neck clenched with tension at the idea. A question formed in her mind. "What if we don't want to live with them?"

Mr. Benson pointed at the jar. "This baby is you. And something not you. If Tony had survived, he would be different, yes. But he would be you."

"I think we have a responsibility to them," Jake said.

"Who's we?" Amy said.

His contradicting her had stung a little, but she knew how Jake had his own mind and liked to argue. He wore leather jackets, black T-shirts advertising obscure bands, ripped jeans. Troy and Michelle, his best friends, were Black.

He was popular because being unpopular didn't scare him. Amy liked him for that, the way he flouted junior high's iron rules. The way he refused to suck up to her like the other boys all did.

"You know who I mean," he said. "The human race. We made them, and that gives us responsibility. It's that simple."

"I didn't make anything. The older generation did. Why are they my problem?"

"Because they have it bad. We all know they do. Imagine being one of them."

"I don't want things to be bad for them," Amy said. "I really don't. I just don't want them around me. Why does that make me a bad person?"

"I never said it makes you a bad person," Jake said.

Archie Gaines raised his hand. "Amy has a good point, Mr. Benson. They're a mess to stomach, looking at them. I mean, I can live with it, I guess. But all this love and understanding is a lot to ask."

"Fair enough," Mr. Benson said.

Archie turned to look back at Amy. She nodded her thanks. His face lit up with a leering smile. He believed he'd rescued her and now she owed him.

She gave him a practiced frown to shut down his hopes. He turned away as if slapped.

"I'm just curious about them," Jake said. "More curious than scared. It's like you said, Mr. Benson. However they look, they're still our brothers. I wouldn't refuse help to a blind man, I guess I wouldn't to a plague kid neither."

The teacher nodded. "Okay. Good. That's enough discussion for today. We're getting somewhere, don't you think? Again, my goal for you kids this year is two things. One is to get used to the plague children. Distinguishing between a book and its cover. The other is to learn how to avoid making more of them."

Jake turned to Amy and winked. Her cheeks burned, all her annoyance with him forgotten.

She hoped there was a lot more sex ed and a lot less monster talk in her future. While Mr. Benson droned on, she glanced through the first few pages of her book. A chapter headline caught her eye: KISSING.

She already knew the law regarding sex. Germ or no germ, the legal age of consent was still fourteen in the State of Georgia. But another law said if you wanted to have sex, you had to get tested for the germ first. If you were under eighteen, your parents had to give written consent for the testing.

Kissing, though, that you could do without any fuss. It said so right here in black and white. You could do it all you wanted. Her scalp tingled at the thought. She tugged at her hair and savored the stabbing needles.

She risked a hungering glance at Jake's handsome profile. Though she hoped one day to go further than that, she could never do more than kissing. She could never know what it'd be like to scratch the real itch.

Nobody but her mama knew Amy was a plague child.